'Well-paced action . . . This wo

...ner

'The surprises keep on coming . . . but quietly and su...
...eaded knock on the door of an apartment in a brutalist concrete
...wer block in the dead of night. [An] excellent debut novel'
David Barnett, *The Independent on Sunday*

...entient water, censored artists, mechanical constructs, old-
...hioned detective work, and the secret police are all woven
...gether in this rich and fascinating tapestry'   *Publishers Weekly*

...ke vintage China Mieville, but with all the violent narrative
...ller drive of Ian Fleming at his edgiest. I fell into *Wolfhound*
...tury and devoured it . . . Peter Higgins is a great discovery,
...gifted writer with a route map to some fascinating new
...k corners of the imagination, and a fine addition to the
...ntemporary fantasy canon'   Richard Morgan

... amazing, fast-paced story in a fantasy world poised
...gerously on the edge of quantum probability, a world where
...els war with reality'   Peter F Hamilton

...solutely loved *Wolfhound Century*. Higgins's world is a truly
...nal creation, Russian cosmism and Slavic mythology filtered
...gh steampunk and le Carre. What really captured me was
...eautiful style and language: his metaphors and associations
...smoothly like the waters of the Mir, and, like Lom without
...gel stone, make you see the world in a new way'
Hannu Rajaniemi

...illiant exploration of the power of fantasy: the tender green
...l of Russian history set free for uncanny battle with its grey,
...unmetal carapace'   Francis Spufford

'*Wolfhound Century* is an extraordinarily accomplished debut from a real master of atmosphere. Peter Higgins has managed to create a completely unique fantasy world with a plot that wouldn't be out of place in a modern day thriller'   Fantasy Faction

'There is much to admire in Higgins's writing, and his fantastical inventions are compelling and enjoyable. It's certainly an intriguing thriller. The plot unfolds swiftly and with an engaging clarity. You turn the pages, eager for clues. Events happen. People you were coming to think of as major players get brutally murdered. Still there is a mystery at the heart of things. The world Higgins creates is immersive and often compelling'
                                                            Strange Horizons

WOLFHOUND
EMPIRE

The complete trilogy

Wolfhound Century
Truth and Fear
Radiant State

PETER HIGGINS

First published in Great Britain in 2016 by Gollancz
an imprint of The Orion Publishing Group Ltd
Carmelite House, 50 Victoria Embankment
London EC4Y 0DZ

An Hachette UK Company

1 3 5 7 9 10 8 6 4 2

A CIP catalogue record for this book is
available from the British Library.

ISBN 978 1 473 21064 6
Printed in Great Britain by Clays Ltd, St Ives plc

MIX
Paper from
responsible sources
FSC® C104740

www.wolfhoundcentury.com
www.orionbooks.co.uk
www.gollancz.co.uk

Contents

WOLFHOUND
CENTURY

The wolfhound century is on my back –
But I am not a wolf.

OSIP MANDELSTAM (1891–1938)

Part One

Part One

1

Investigator Vissarion Lom sat in a window booth in the Café Rikhel. Pulses of rain swept up Ansky Prospect, but inside the café, in the afternoon crush, the air was thick with the smell of coffee, cinnamon bread and damp overcoats.

'Why don't you go home?' said Ziller. 'No one's going to come. I can call you if anything happens. You can be back here in half an hour.'

'Someone will come,' said Lom. 'He's not sitting out there for no reason.'

Across the street, a thin young man waited on a bench under a dripping zinc canopy. He had been there, in front of the Timberworkers' Library and Meeting Hall, for three hours already.

'Maybe he spotted us,' said Ziller. 'Maybe the contact is aborted.'

'He could have lost us straight off the boat,' said Lom. 'He didn't even look round. He's not bothered about us. He thinks he's clean.'

They had picked him up off the morning river-boat from Yislovsk. Briefcase – that was the cryptonym they gave him, they didn't know his name – had hung around the wharves for a while, bought himself an apricot juice at a kiosk, walked slowly up Durnovo-Burliuk Street, and sat down on a bench. That was all he had done. He carried no luggage, apart from the small leather case they'd named him for. After an hour he'd taken some bread out of the case and eaten it. Except for that, he just sat there.

Ziller picked up his glass of tea, looked into it critically, set it down untouched.

'He's an arse-wipe. That's what he is.'

'Maybe,' said Lom. 'But he's waiting for something.'

The truth was, Lom rather liked Briefcase. There was something

7

about him – the way he walked, the way his hair was cut. Briefcase was young. He looked … vulnerable. Something – hatred, idealism, love – had driven him, alone and obviously frightened, all the way across the continent to Podchornok, his ears sticking out pinkly in the rain, to make this crude attempt at contact. The call from Magadlovosk had said only that he was a student, a member of some amateurish break-away faction of the Lezarye separatists. The Young Opposition. The Self-Liberation Will of All Peoples. He was coming to meet someone. To collect something. Magadlovosk had sounded excited, unusually so, but also vague: *The contact, Lom, that's what matters, that's the target. The contact, and whatever it is he's bringing with him.*

'You really should go home,' said Ziller. 'What time did you finish last night?'

'I'm fine,' said Lom.

'Fine? You're over thirty, you do twice the hours the others do, you get no promotions, you're on crappy pay, and you need a shave. When did you last eat something decent? '

Lom thought of his empty apartment. The yellow furniture. The unwashed plates and empty bottles. Home.

'Why don't you come round?' Ziller was saying. 'Come tonight. Lena's got a friend. Her husband was killed when the *Volkova* went down. She's got a kid but … well, we could invite her—'

'Look,' said Lom. 'I had some paperwork last night, that's all.'

Ziller shrugged. He lit a cigarette and let the smokestream drift out of his nose.

'I just thought …' he said. 'Maybe you could use a friend, Vissarion. After the Laurits business you've got few enough.'

'Yeah. Well. Thanks.'

They sat in silence, awkwardly, staring out of the window. Watching Briefcase staring at nothing.

'Shit,' said Ziller, half-rising in his seat and craning to see down the road. 'Shit.'

A line of giants, each leading a four-horse dray team and a double wagon loaded high with resin tanks, was lumbering up the hill from the direction of the river quay. They were almost in front of the Rikhel already – the rumbling of the wagons' iron wheels set the café floor vibrating faintly – and when they reached it, Briefcase would be out of sight. The teams were in no hurry: they would take at least ten minutes to pass.

'You'll have to go outside,' said Lom. 'Keep an eye from the alley till they're gone.'

Ziller sighed and heaved himself reluctantly to his feet, trying to shove the loose end of his shirt back under his belt and button his uniform tunic. He took a long, mournful, consolatory pull on the cigarette and ground the stub into the heaped ashtray, squeezed himself out of the booth and went out into the rain with a show of heavy slowness. Theatrics.

Lom watched the giants through the misted window. They walked patiently under the rain: earth-coloured shirts, leather jerkins, heavy wooden clogs. The rain was heavier now, clattering against the window in fat fistfuls. Only one person was standing out in the street. A soldier, bare-headed and beltless, grey uniform soaked almost to black, left sleeve empty, pinned to his side. He had tipped his face back to look up into the rain and his mouth was wide open. As if he was trying to swallow it down. He had no boots. He was standing in a puddle in torn socks, shifting from foot to foot in a slow, swaying dance.

Two kinds of rain fell on Podchornok. There was steppe rain from the west, sharp and cold, blown a thousand versts across the continental plain in ragged shreds. And the other kind was forest rain. Forest rain came from the east in slow, weighty banks of nimbostratus that settled over the town for days at a time and shed their cargo in warm fat sheets. It fell and fell with dumb insistence, overbrimming the gutters and outflows and swelling the waters of the Yannis until it flowed fat and yellow and heavy with mud. In spring the forest rain was thick with yellow pollen that stuck in your hair and on your face and lips and had a strange taste. In autumn it smelled of resin and earth. This, today, this was forest rain.

Ziller was taking his time. The giants and their drays had gone, and Briefcase was still on his bench. The soldier wandered across to him and started waving his one arm. He seemed to be shouting. He had something in his hand and he was trying to show it to Briefcase. Trying to give it to him. Briefcase looked confused.

Shit. This was *it.* This was the *contact*!

Lom crashed out into the rain and across the road.

'Hey! You! Don't move! Police!'

Where the hell was Ziller?

Briefcase saw Lom coming. His eyes widened in shock and fear. He should have waited. Showed his papers. Said he had no idea who this soldier was, he'd just been sitting there eating his bread and watching the rain. Instead, he ran. He got about ten paces across the road, when Ziller came out of the alleyway by Krishkin's and took him crashing down into the mud.

The soldier hadn't moved. He was staring at Lom's face. His eyes, expressionless, didn't blink. They were completely brown: all iris, no whites at all. He opened his mouth, as if he was going to speak, and Lom smelled the sour, earthy richness of his breath, but he made no sound. His one hand worked the small cloth bag he was holding as if he was crushing the life out of it. Lom snatched it out of his grip.

'Give me that!'

The man's fingers felt cold. Hard. Brittle.

Lom undid the cord and looked inside. There was nothing but a mess of broken twigs and crushed berries and clumps of some sticky, yellowish substance that might have been wax. It had a sweet, heavy, resinous perfume.

'What the fuck – ?' said Lom. 'What the fuck is this?'

The soldier, gazing into him with fathomless brown eyes, said nothing.

2

Five time zones to the west of Podchornok, on the roof of the Grand Hotel Sviatopolk in Mirgorod, Josef Kantor waited. Despite the ragged fingernails of wind scraping at his face, he was immovable: a pillar of patient rock in a dark and fog-soaked coat. The fog had come and gone. Drifting in off the river before dawn, it had enfolded him in blankness and sifted away at the cold rising of the sun, leaving him beaded with dull grey droplets. He had not moved. He was waiting.

Kantor teased the cavity in his tooth with the fatness of his tongue. The hurting was useful. It kept him rooted in the true present, the only now, the now that he was making come to be. He only had to wait in the cold and it would happen. He only had to not be deflected. Not be moved. And it would happen.

Far below him, Levrovskaya Square, transected by tramlines, was monochrome with yesterday's snow under the blank white dawn. Twelve floors beneath his feet the lobby roof projected, taking a small trapezium bite out of the squareness. Pavement tables were set in two neat rows, penned in by a rectangle of potted hedge. Empty. Sellers were setting up next to the tram stop: a woman putting out a stall of old clothes, linen and dressing gowns; another, wearing a sheepskin coat, lighting a stove for potatoes; an old man arranging his trestle with trays of pancakes, bowls of thin purée, cans for kvass. For the first time, Kantor consulted his watch. Exactly nine a.m.. It was time.

The iron car rattled around the corner and into the square, drawn by a pair of horses, stepping carefully, leaning into the weight, heading for the Bank of Foreign Commerce. His people would begin to move now. He looked for the women first, and there they were, Lidia and

Stefania, the edges of their skirts wet with melting snow, crossing to the gendarme in his kiosk on the corner. The women were laughing, and soon the young gendarme was laughing too. He would be smelling their heavy, promising scent. Kantor used the women to ferry explosives, and they soused themselves with perfume to cover the clinging smell of dynamite strapped against their sweating bodies.

Lidia drew the revolver from her skirts and shot the young gendarme twice. His legs gave way and he crumpled into a sitting position, hunched over his burst belly: blood in the slush; crimson in pale grey. He was still alive, moving his body from side to side, pawing weakly at his face. Lidia stepped in close and shot him in the side of his head.

In Levrovskaya Square, no one noticed.

No, that wasn't correct. An old man in the uniform of the postal services was staring across from the opposite pavement. He took his bag from his shoulder and laid it on the ground, gazing at the dead boy. That didn't matter. The strong-car had reached the middle of the square. But where was Vitt? He should have come out of the Teagarden by now.

And there he was, but he was running, his grenade already in his hand. He dropped it hastily into the path of the horses. It didn't explode. It simply lay there in the snow, inert, like a round black fruit. Like the turd of a giant rabbit. Yelling, the driver hauled on the reins. Kantor watched Vitt stand, uselessly, eyes blank and mouth slightly open, gazing in abstraction at his hopeless failure of a bomb.

Vitt turned and ran out of sight down the alley between the Teagarden and Rosenfeld's. The driver was still screaming at the horses. They stood confused, alarmed, doing nothing. The back of the car opened and soldiers climbed out, looking around for something to fire at. Kantor saw Akaki Serov saunter towards them, smiling, saying something jaunty. When he was close enough he lobbed a bomb with casual grace, going for the horses, and another that rolled under the car. The double flash came, and sudden blooms of smoke and flying stuff, and then the sound of the concussions. The force of the double explosion disembowelled the horses and tore legs and arms and heads off the men. Akaki Serov, who was too close, was burst apart also.

Into the silence before the screaming began, the rest of Kantor's people surged forward, the giant Vaso wading among them like an adult among small children. Lakoba Petrov, Petrov the Painter, hurried along beside him, taking three steps for his one. Petrov was bare-headed, his face flushed pink, firing his Rykov wildly at groin level. The pair ran towards the burst-open strong car, out-distancing the others. Petrov shot a soldier who was rising to his knees, while the giant wrenched at the doors of the car, tearing the metal hinges, and climbed inside. It seemed improbable that he could fit himself inside such a small space, but he ducked into it as if it was a cupboard to hide in.

The others spread out across the square, firing and lobbing grenades. Pieces of flesh, human and horse, spattered the cobbles. There were soft messes of blood and snow and fluid. The screams of the injured sounded as remote to Josef Kantor as the distant cries of the gulls in the bay.

The revolutionary is doomed, he whispered across the Square. *The revolutionary has no personal interests. No emotions. No attachments. The revolutionary owns nothing and has no name. All laws, moralities, customs and conventions – the revolutionary is their merciless and implacable enemy. There is only the revolution. All other bonds are broken.*

The potato seller lay on her face in the middle of the square, her leg somewhat apart from the rest of her, her arm stretched towards a thing she could not reach.

A kind of quiet began to settle on the square, until the tall bronze doors of the bank were thrown open and a mudjhik came lumbering out, twelve feet high, the colour of rust and dried blood. Whatever small animal had given its brain to be inserted inside the mudjhik's head-casket must have been an exultant predator in life. This one was barely under control. It was smacking about with heavy arms, bursting open the heads of anyone who did not run. Behind the mudjhik, more militia came out of the bank, firing.

Whether it was the shock of the mudjhik or some more private and inward surge of life-desire, one of the horses attached to the strong-car twitched and jerked and rose up, squealing. Still harnessed to the car, its comrade dead in the traces alongside and its own bowels spilling onto the pavement, the horse lowered its head and surged towards the empty mouth of East Prospect. With slow determination it widened the distance between itself and the noise and smell of battle, pulling behind it thirty million roubles and Vaso the giant, who was still inside.

Kantor breathed a lungful of cold, clean air. The chill hit his hollow, blackened tooth and jolted his jaw with a jab of pain. Time to come down from the roof.

3

W hen Lom got back from placating Magadlovosk on the phone, Ziller was already in the office, writing up his report. Ziller wrote carefully, word by meticulous word, holding his chewed pencil like a jeweller mending a watch.

'Where are they?' said Lom.

'Who?'

'Briefcase,' said Lom. 'The soldier.'

Ziller put down his pencil. 'Oh,' he said. 'Them. Lasker had them taken across to the Barracks. The militia are going to sweat them a bit and then send them to Vig.'

'What?' said Lom. 'I'd have got what I needed in an hour. They won't survive a week at Vig. You saw them—'

Ziller looked awkward.

'Lasker wanted them off the premises. He said they were an embarrassment.'

'It was a contact,' said Lom.

'Yeah,' said Ziller. 'Well. Lasker thinks you fucked up. Actually, he just doesn't like you. But forget it; it doesn't matter anyway. You're going on a trip. There's a wire on your desk. There was no envelope, so I read it. So did Lasker.'

Lom spread the crumpled telegram out on the table, trying to flatten the creases with the side of his palm. A flimsy sheet with blue printed strips pasted down on it.

INVESTIGATOR VISSARION LOM MUST MIRGOROD SOONEST STOP
ATTEND OFFICE UNDER SECRETARY KROGH STOP 6PM 11 LAPKRIST
STOP LODKA STOP MANDATED REPEAT MANDATED ENDS

Lom read it three times. It wasn't the kind of thing that happened. A provincial investigator summoned halfway across the continent to the capital. They never did that. Never.

'Maybe they want to give you a medal, Vissarion Yppolitovich,' Ziller said.

'Or shoot me in the throat and dump me in the Mir.'

'Don't need to go to Mirgorod for that. There's plenty here would do it, not only Lasker, after what you did to Laurits.'

'Laurits was a shit,' said Lom. 'I saw the room where she was found. I saw what he did.'

'Sure. Only she was a non-citizen and a tart, and Laurits was one of *our* shits. He had a wife and daughters. That makes people feel bad. You're not a popular guy any more.'

'It wasn't a career move.'

'Better if it was,' said Ziller. 'They'd understand that.'

'I did it because he was a murdering bastard. That's what policemen do.'

'You shouldn't joke about this, Vissarion. Things could get serious. People have been asking questions about you. Turning over files. Looking for dirt. You should be careful.'

'What people?' said Lom.

Ziller made a face. 'You know,' he said. 'People.' He hesitated. 'Look, Vissarion,' he said. 'I like you. You're my friend. But if they come after me, I won't stand up for you. I can't. I'm not that kind of brave. I won't risk Lena and the children, not for that. It might be a good thing to be away for a week or two. You know, let things settle down.'

Lom folded the telegram and put it in his pocket. A trip might be good. A change of scene. There was nothing here he would miss. Maybe, just possibly, in Mirgorod they had a job for him. A proper job. He was tired of harassing students and checking residence permits while the vicious stuff went on in this very building, and they fucked you over if you did anything about it. He looked at his watch. There was time: an hour to pack, and he could still catch the overnight boat to Yislovsk.

'You can take the Schama Bezhin file,' he said to Ziller. 'Call it temporary promotion.'

Ziller grinned. 'And I thought you didn't appreciate me,' he said. 'Don't rush back.'

4

A messenger was standing near the back exit of the Sviatopolk, white-faced, gripping his bicycle. Kantor dragged the machine out of his hands and rode off in pursuit of the dying horse, the money and the giant. He found them in a lane off Broken Moons Prospect. Vaso had begun to unload the satchels of roubles, stacking them neatly in the gutter. The horse was dead. Vaso was inside the back of the car, filling it almost completely. Kantor leaned his bicycle against the wall and peered in.

Vaso looked back over his shoulder.

'They were waiting for us,' he said. His huge blue eyes peered into Kantor's face as if from deep under water. 'Inside the bank. They knew we were coming.'

'Yes.'

Kantor looked away a fraction too late. In some odd instant of rapport, some unprotected momentary honesty, there was a flash of communication between the giant and the man which neither had intended. Kantor saw the start of it in the giant's huge eyes and the changed way he held his massive shoulders.

'You,' said Vaso. 'It was you that told them.' He began to pull himself backwards out of the strong-car.

'Vaso,' said Kantor quietly, 'wait. It's not how you think.'

But even as he spoke, Kantor had already taken the grenade from his pocket and shoved it hard into the crevice between the thighs of the giant.

Three pounds of explosive filler encased in a sphere of brittle iron.

The release lever of a standard grenade is held in place by a pin. Once the pin is removed, only the grip of the bomber prevents the lever

17

from springing open, firing the primer and igniting the fuse, which detonates the main charge with a ten second delay. But when Kantor thrust the grenade between Vaso's legs, it was squeezed tight. The lever couldn't spring open.

Vaso, alarmed but uncertain what had happened, hastily tried to back out. Kantor retreated until he was pressed against the wall of the building behind him, watching the giant reversing into the light. At the last moment, the bomb dropped free, rolled forward into the vehicle, and exploded. The force of it struck Kantor like his father's fist used to. It cracked his skull backwards against the wall and the world slipped sideways. When it righted itself, the remains of Vaso were on the ground in front of him. The giant's head, as big as a coal bucket, was smouldering. There was no skin on his face, but his lidless eyes still had life in them. He looked up mutely at Kantor and the big gap of his mouth moved slightly.

Kantor reached inside his coat for the revolver tucked in his belt. He brought it out, showed it to the giant, and fired two shots into his head.

5

*T*he light of the broken moons, circling one another in their slow, wobbling dance, floods the forest. Archangel dominates the empty landscape, a thousand feet high, like a solitary hill. The huge slopes of his body have accumulated a thick covering of snow. When he struggles to move, he dislodges avalanches and rumbling slides of ice, but he cannot shift himself. His body is irredeemably stuck, the lower part of it plunged many more hundreds of feet deep into the heart-rock and permanently fused there by the heat of his fall. The blast of his impact burned the trees flat for miles around, but new trees are growing through the ashes. Fresh snowfall carpets the floor of the shallow crater ten miles wide whose centre is him.

Call him Archangel, though it's not his name, he has none. He is what he is. But call him Archangel. It is ... appropriate. The duration of his existence unfolds from everlasting to everlasting, measured by the lifespan of all the stars.

At least, that was how it seemed, until, in one impossible moment, the shadow fell across him. Now he's as you see him, caught, unable to escape, stuck hard in the planetary crust, at the bottom of the uncertainty well. He cannot adjust his density. He cannot extrude any part of himself by even a few inches. He cannot move at all. Only his perceptions can travel, and even that only within the limits of this one trivial, cramped, poisoned and shadowed planet. He is bound in a straitened prison, scarcely larger than his own self.

And he's afraid of dying.

He examines his fear carefully. Pain and surprise are its flanking attendants, but it is the fear that intrigues him. So this is what fear is like. It could be useful. If he is to live.

His attentive gaze, vast and cool and inhuman, moves restlessly across the surface of the planet, sifting through the teeming profusion of minds that populates it. So many minds. He opens them up, first one and then another, looking for what he needs. And he draws his plans.

6

L om took the overnight steamer down the Yannis and reached
the rail terminus at Yislovsk just after dawn the next day. There
was an hour to wait for the Mirgorod train. The waiting room
was crammed with fresh conscripts for the southern front, crop-
haired and boisterous, so he bought a bag of pirogi and settled on a
bench outside, sheltered from the blustering sleet. He shivered inside
his heavy black woollen cloak, his feet numb, the pirogi warm in his
hands. Stevedores, sacking tied round their shoulders against the rain,
were unloading barges. Passengers wandered across the wet quay, picking their way across the rails, squeezing between trucks and wagons.
A crane arm swept the sky, the grind of its winch engine competing
against the sound of the rain and the wash of the river against the
quayside. The first warning bell rang. Fifteen minutes to departure. On
a whim, Lom went across to the telegraph office and wired ahead to
Raku Vishnik, hoping to save himself the cost of a room in Mirgorod.

The train was a twelve-foot-gauge monster, the locomotive as high as
a house. The *Admiral Grebencho*, in the purple livery of the Edelfeld
Sparre line. Three cylinders, double Chapkyl blastpipe, sleek, rounded,
backswept prow, pulling thirty carriages. The *Admiral* could make a
hundred and fifty versts an hour on the straight, but they travelled
with meticulous slowness, stopping at every halt and crossing place,
sliding across vast flat country.

Krasnoyarsk. Novorossiysk. Volynovsk. Elgen. Magaden.

Lom had spent an entire week's salary on a first-class compartment.
He travelled in solitude, in a slow blur of daylight and darkness. His
only company was a framed photograph of the Novozhd and two

posters: CITIZEN! WHOM ARE YOU WITH? and COME TO LAKE TSYRKHAL! THE WATER IS WARM!

The unchanging landscape of birch forest made all movement seem an illusion. Time grew thickened and lazy, measured out in the glasses of tea the provodnik brought from the samovar at the end of the corridor. Lom watched the trees and slept, stretched out on the green leather upholstery. Five days of enforced inactivity ... the trundling of iron wheels and the slow passage of trees and earth and sky ... rest in motion ...

The birches bored him. They were unimpressive: widely-spaced chalk marks. Nothing like the forest east of Podchornok. That was proper forest. Dark. Mossy. Thick. He'd lived all his life in its shadow. Podchornok was the last town before the forest began: from Durnovo-Burliuk Street you could see the low hills of the tree edge. The measureless forest. No one knew how big it was, or what – if anything – lay beyond it. Normally, Lom tried not to think about the forest too much – it was addictive, it consumed the hours – but now, with nothing else to do, he imagined what it would be like to walk there, smelling the damp earth, digging his fingers into layers of mouldering leaves and rotting, mushroomy fallen wood. Swimming in the white lakes. Great wolves and giant elk moving through splashes of sunlight.

The Vlast mounted periodic incursions into the trees. Artel followed artel into the woods, only to find themselves caught in impenetrable thickets of thorn, their horses floundering up to their bellies in mud. River expeditions drifted through tangled shadow, feeling themselves shrinking, diminishing, losing significance as the world grew silent and strange. Aircraft flew over an illimitable carpet of trees flecked with the glint of rivers and lakes. The silence of the forest remained undisturbed.

Karka. Lapotev. Narymsk. Kaunats. Vorkutagorsk.

Having no money for the restaurant car, Lom carried with him a supply of bread and white crumbly cheese. Bored of this eventually, he got off the train at Chelyagorsk, where they had a two-hour stop, and spent a few kopeks on some mushrooms and dried fish and a newspaper. There was a wooden hut at the end of the platform. A sign said EXHIBITION OF PRESERVED ZOOMORPHS – 5 KOPEKS. A pale girl in a knitted headscarf was sitting on a flimsy chair by the door. She was shivering. Her eyes watery with the cold.

'Is it good?' he said. 'The exhibition. Is it worth seeing?'

The girl shrugged. 'I guess. It's five kopeks.'

'Do you get many visitors?'

'No. Do you want to go in? It's five kopeks.'

He gave her the money. She put it in her pocket carefully.

The hut was unheated and dim and filled with dusty stuffed animals: some drab wildfowl, a pair of scrawny wolves, a cringing bear. Feeble specimens compared to the forest beasts of his imagination. And there was a female mammoth, extracted from permafrost to the north. She had been mounted exactly as she was found, sitting back on her haunches, one forefoot set on the ground, as if she had fallen into a bog and was trying to climb out. Her hair was reddish, rough, worn thin in patches, and she squinted at Lom with mean, resentful eyes, small and black and glittering like sloes. Yellowing tusks arched up in supplication towards the pitch ceiling. For the rest of the journey she came to him in his dreams.

One incident broke the limpid surface of the long, slow journey. In the next compartment to Lom's an old man – clouded eyes, a thick spade of a beard combed with a central parting – was travelling with his wife and a dark-haired girl of six or so. Lom heard him through the partition, coughing, grumbling, swearing at his wife for letting the cold air in.

There was a commotion as the train was coming into Tuga. Lom found the wife in the corridor, wailing in dry-eyed distress, surrounded by guards and curious passengers. The girl was watching, silent and wary in the background. It turned out the old man had run from the compartment in his slippers, rushed down the length of the carriage and pushed open the door onto the small ledge at the end, just as the train was slowing. He'd fallen between the cars, and was dead.

Lom watched them bring a stretcher to carry off his shrunken old body. Blood was leaking from his mouth. The wife and child and all their baggage followed him off the train.

As Lom turned to go back to his compartment, a gendarme grabbed him by the arm.

'You,' he said. 'You.'

'What do you want?'

'What do you know about the man who died?'

'Nothing. Why?'

'You were watching.'

'So was everyone.'

'But not like you. Where are you from?'

'Podchornok. I joined the train at Yislovsk. But—'

The gendarme was standing too close, looking up into Lom's face. He thrust his hand forward, almost jabbing it into Lom's midriff.

'Papers. Your papers.'

'What papers?'

'Papers. Passport. Permission to travel. Certification of funds. Certification of sound health and freedom from infestation. *Papers*.'

'There was no time,' said Lom. 'And I don't need papers.'

'Everyone needs papers. If you've got no papers, you're coming with me. Unless—' The gendarme pushed his face up closer to Lom's. 'Unless you've got a big fat purse.'

'Fuck you,' said Lom quietly, and turned away.

The gendarme grabbed his shoulder and spun him round. 'You're coming with me. Now. Bastard.'

'You're talking to a senior investigator in the third department of the political police. You don't call me bastard. You call me sir.'

For a moment the gendarme hesitated; but only for a moment.

'I don't care if you're the fucking Novozhd himself. If you've got no papers, you're mine.'

'Like I said, I don't need papers.' Lom took off his cap to let the man see the irremovable seal, the small dark coin of angel flesh embedded in the bone of his forehead like a blank third eye. 'I have this. This is better.'

On the fifth day the birch trees thinned out, separated now by long tracts of flat and treeless waste, black mud under dirty melting snow, and on the sixth morning the train emerged abruptly into a flat watery landscape. Lakes. Rivers. Marshland. Low, misty cloud. And sometimes a glint of harder grey on the skyline that was the sea. Stops became more frequent, though the towns were still small. Rain trickled down the windowpane in small droplets. A large, stumpy, dark red mass appeared on the horizon. It looked like an enormous rock. The Ouspenskaya Torso.

Then, suddenly, without warning, the train was high above the landscape and he was looking down on houses: ramshackle wooden structures with pig yards and cabbage rows; yellow tenements; streets and traffic; the pewter glint of canals and basins. They were on the Bivorg Viaduct, hopping from island to island, closing on the Litenskaya. The rain gave everything a vivid, polished sheen of wetness. Lom felt a nameless stirring of excitement. Arrival. New things coming. The capital. Mirgorod.

7

J osef Kantor had a tiny office on the Ring Wharf, an unmarked
doorway at the top of an iron staircase among mazy yards and
warehouses, tucked away behind bales, vats, crates, barrels and
carboys. It reeked of coal and tar and the spice and citrus smells of
imported foodstuffs. There was room for a desk, a shelf for books and
a small grate for a fire. Kantor had a portable printing press hidden
under a blanket, and here he produced the leaflets he distributed along
the wharves.

Every day, he walked among the steam-cranes and the rail trucks,
the hammering, the waves of heat and showers of sparks, the supervising engineers with their oilskin notebooks, the collective industry of
men. He watched them work on the naked, propped bodies of ships
in dry dock and the towering frames of new ships rising. Day by day,
immense steel vessels took shape out of chaos, bigger and stronger and
more numerous than any before them. *Speed. Power. Control. This is
a new thing*, thought Kantor, and wrote it in his leaflets. *This is the
future. It requires new ways of thinking: new philosophy, new morality, a
new kind of person. All that is old and useless must be destroyed to make
way.*

Kantor slept on his desk, and on cold nights he built a wall of books
around himself to keep out draughts. He'd learned the books trick at
Vig, in a moss-caulked hut he shared with three families and the psycho-
path Vereschak. On winter nights in Vig, your breath iced on your
beard while you slept. Vig had taught Kantor the luxury of being alone.
He had learned the prisoner's way of withdrawing inside himself and
entering a private inner space the persecutors couldn't reach.

Kantor's life had been shaped by the dialectic of fear and killing:

if you feared something, you studied it, learned all you could from it, and then you killed it. And when you encountered a stronger thing to fear, you did it again. And again. And so you grew stronger, until the fear you caused was greater than the fear you felt. It was his secret satisfaction that he had begun to learn this great lesson even before he was born. He was an aphex twin: a shrivelled, dead little brother had flushed out after him with the placenta and spilled across his mother's childbed sheet. Before he even saw the light of day, he had killed and consumed his rival.

His father, the great Avril, hero of the Birzel Rebellion, had made his living packing herrings in ice. Avril Kantor loathed his work and himself for doing it. He came home stinking of brandy and fish. Josef heard the crude voice and saw his mother kicked across the floor. Felt the ice-hardened fist in his own face. He didn't hate his father. He admired his power to hurt and the fear he caused. Only later, when he understood more, did he come to despise him for hurting only weakness, and sacrificing his own life in a grand futile gesture of revolt.

The Kantor family name earned Josef a place at the Bergh Academy. He was safe then from the fish wharves that ruined his father, but Bergh's was a dull and vicious place. The masters spied on the students, searched their possessions, encouraged them to inform on each other. They beat him for reading prohibited books and lending them to the other boys. He studied the masters' methods and hated the unimaginative, unproductive purposes to which they put their dominance. On the day he'd grown strong enough, he went to find the mathematics master alone, gripped him by the hair and cracked his face down onto his desk.

'If I'm beaten again, I will come back and kill you,' he whispered.

The teacher wore the bruise for a week. Josef was left alone at Bergh's after that. He grew tall and lean and hard and full of energy. The first work the Lezarye Committee gave him was distributing leaflets to the railway workers. He was caught and badly beaten, while Anastas Bragin, Director of Railways, looked on, his face flushed rosy pink. Three nights later Josef Kantor climbed into Bragin's garden with a revolver. It was late spring, and the sun was still in the sky though it was after eleven at night. The air in the garden was heavy with warmth and bees and lime blossom perfume. Bragin was working by lamplight at a desk in a downstairs room with the window open. Kantor trampled fragrant earth to get to the casement. He leaned in.

'Remember me?'

He waited a moment before he shot Bragin in the head. He was seventeen then.

The police picked him up after the Birzel Rebellion. They wanted to know where his father was hiding. They broke his hands and burned his feet and kicked his balls until they swelled like lemons, but he didn't tell them. They gave up in the end, and left him alone, and then he told them where his father was. The police forced him to watch his father's execution. That was a pleasure. The icing on the cake. He was stronger than them all.

There was a rapping at the door of the office. Kantor swore under his breath. It would be Vitt. Vitt and the others. Vitt had said they would come, though Kantor had forbidden it. He hated people coming here. It compromised his security and invaded his private space. But they'd insisted. Vitt had insisted.

The knocking came again, louder. Determined. They were early.

'Come in then, Vitt,' he called. 'Come in if you must. This had better be good.'

They crowded into the room. Kantor surveyed their faces. So many useless, vapid, calf-like faces. He'd told them to lie low, that was the proper way, but after a few days they'd got restless and suspicious. Too frightened of the police, not frightened enough of him. Vitt had dragged them along.

'The banknotes are marked,' Vitt was saying. 'They've published the serial numbers in the *Gazetta*.'

'The roubles go to the Government of Exile Within,' said Kantor. 'You know that. Their problem, not ours.'

'They were waiting for us,' said Lidia. 'They knew we were coming. They knew when and where.'

'And we lost Akaki,' said Vitt. 'Akaki was a good comrade.'

'Deaths are inevitable,' said Kantor. 'Nothing worth having is got without great price. Be under no illusion, there is worse to come. Storms and torrents of blood will mark the struggle to end oppression. Are you ready for that?'

They stared at him sourly.

'But—'

'Is this a challenge, Vitt?'

Vitt stopped dead, his mouth open, the colour draining from his face.

'No. No, Josef. I'm only trying to …'

Kantor looked around the room, fixing every one of them, one by one, with hard eyes. It was time.

'Yes,' he said. 'They were waiting for us, and you know what that means, but none of you has the courage to say it. One of us is an informer.'

'Maybe it was—' Stefania began.

"Let's go over it again,' said Kantor. 'You, Vitt, threw a bomb that did not explode, and then you, Vitt, ran like a hare.'

'I—'

'I smell you, Vitt. I smell treachery and lies. I smell the policeman's coin in your pocket.'

'No, Josef! Maybe it was Petrov? Where is he today? Has anyone seen him? It was *Petrov*!'

'I smell you Vitt, and I'm never wrong. See how you crumble? This is how you crawled and squealed when the police took you. This is the traitor's courage. This is the disease within.'

Kantor took the revolver from his pocket and held it out in the palm of his hand.

'Who will do what must be done? Must I do it myself?'

'Let me,' said Lidia. 'Please, Josef.'

Kantor gave her the revolver. Vitt upped from his seat and made for the door, but Stefania stuck out her foot. He fell on his face with a sickening slap.

'Oh, no,' he murmured. 'No.'

Lidia put the muzzle to the back of his head.

'Bye, fat boy.'

She fired.

'I wish,' said Kantor, wiping a splash of something warm from his face, 'I wish you'd done that outside.'

No sooner had Kantor closed the door behind them than he felt the attention of Archangel enter the room. The furniture crackled with fear.

'No,' said Kantor quietly. 'No. I don't want this. Not again.'

Archangel opened him up and came into him. Ripping his way

inside his head. Occupying everything. Taking everything. Leaving nowhere private. His voice was a roaring whisper.

They fear you, it said. *But whom do you fear?*

Kantor lay on his back on the floor, his limbs in rigid spasm, his eyes fixed open, staring at nothing. Archangel's alien voice in his mind was a voice of shining darkness, absolutely intelligent, absolutely cold, like a midnight polar sky, clean of cloud and shot through with veins of starlight.

Whom do you fear?

Archangel allowed him a little room, in which to formulate his response.

'You,' whispered Kantor. 'I fear you.'

You are wasting time. Think like a master, not like a slave. Are you listening to me?

Kantor tried to speak but the muscles of his face were stuck and his throat was blocked with the inert flesh of his tongue. He tried to drive out the thing that had torn open his mind and come inside. It was like trying to push his face through raw and solid rock.

There must be fear. There must be war. There must be death. Everything is weak. Everything will shake. I will put this world in your hands. And others. Many many others. And you will do one thing for me. One small thing.

Destroy the Pollandore.

8

The platforms of the Wieland Station, enclosed under a wide, arching canopy of girders and glass, roared. Shrill whistles, shouts, venting steam, the clank of shunting iron. The smell of hot oil, hot metal, stale air, dust. The roof glass, smeared with sooty rain, cast a dull grey light. Train lamps burned yellow. Raucous announcements of arrivals and departures punctuated the 'Tarsis Overture' on the tannoy.

Lom collected his valise from the luggage car himself. It was heavy and awkward, a hefty oblong box of brown leather, three brass-buckled belts and a brass clasp. He'd dressed for the cold, his cap pulled down tight down over his forehead, but the station was hot and close. By the time he'd hauled his baggage down the wide, shallow marble staircase into the concourse, he was hot with sweat and the din was ringing in his ears.

He let the crowds part around him. Guards and porters shouted destinations. Droshki and kareta drivers called for business. A giant lumbered past, hauling a trolley. Everyone was in uniform, not just the railway workers, drivers, policemen and militia, but students and door-keepers and concierges and clerks, wet nurses and governesses, messengers and mail carriers. The only ones not in uniform were the wealthy travelling families, the labourers in their greasy jackets and the civil servants in their dark woollen coats. Lom scanned the passing faces for Raku Vishnik. There was no sign of him. Maybe the telegram hadn't reached him. Maybe, after fourteen – no, fifteen – years, Vishnik had read it and thrown it away.

'Clear the way there!'

Lom stepped aside. A ragged column of soldiers was shuffling through the central hall and up the shallow stairs to the platforms. The smell of the front came with them: they stank of herring, tobacco, wet earth, mildew, lice and rust. The wounded came at the rear. The *broken-faced,* they were called. It was a literal term. Men with pieces of their heads missing. One had lost a chunk out of the side of his skull, taking the ear with it. Another had no jaw: nothing but a raw mess between his upper teeth and his neck.

At the end of the column two privates were struggling to support a third, walking between them, or not walking but continually falling forward. Trembling violently from head to foot, as if he was doing some kind of mad dance, as if his clothes were infested with foul biting bugs. He had a gentle face, bookish, the face of a librarian or a schoolteacher. Apart from his eyes. He was staring at something. Staring backwards in time to a fixed, permanent event, an endless loop of repetition beyond which he could neither see nor move.

Lom felt his stomach tighten. The war was far away. You tried not to think about it.

The veterans went on and up, absorbed back into the crowd. Lom looked at his watch. It had stopped. He'd forgotten to wind it on the train. The station clock stood on a pillar in the centre of the concourse, its minute hand five feet long and creeping with perceptible jolts around its huge yellowed face. Ten past six. He was late for Krogh.

9

It took Lom an hour to get across the city to the Lodka. When he got there, he leaned on the balustrade of the Yekaterinsky Bridge, looking up at it. The momentous building, a great dark slab, rose and bellied outwards like the prow of a vast stationary ship against the dark purple sky, the swollen, luminous stars, the windblown accumulating rags of cloud. Rain was in the air. Nightfall smelled of the city and sea, obscuring colour and detail, simplifying form. He felt the presence of the angel stone embedded in the walls. It called to the seal in his head, and the seal stirred in response.

The Lodka stood on an island, the Yekatarina Canal passing along one side, the Mir on the other. Six hundred yards long, a hundred and twenty yards high, it enclosed ten million cubic yards of air and a thousand miles of intricately interlocking offices, corridors and stairways, the cerebral cortex of a stone brain. It was said the Lodka had been built so huge and so hastily that when it was finished, many of the rooms could not be reached at all. Passageways ran from nowhere to nowhere. Stairwells without stairs. Exitless labyrinths. From high windows you could look down on entrance-less vacant courtyards, the innermost secrets of the Vlast. Amber lights burned in a thousand windows. Behind each window, ministers and civil servants, clerks and archivists and secret policemen were working late. In one of those rooms Under Secretary Krogh of the Ministry of Vlast Security was waiting for him. Lom crossed the bridge and went up the steps to the entrance.

Krogh's private secretary was sitting in the outer office. Files were stacked in deep neat piles on his desk, each one tagged with handwritten slips of paper and coloured labels. He looked up without interest when Lom came in.

'You're late, Investigator. The Under Secretary is a busy man.'

'Then you'd better get me in there straight away.'

'Your appointment was for six.'

'I was sent for. I've come.'

'Pavel?' A voice called from the inner office. 'Is that Lom? Bring the man in here.'

Krogh's office was large and empty. Krogh himself was sitting at the far end, behind a plain wooden table in an eight-sided bay with uncurtained windows on every side. In daylight he would have had an almost circular view across the city, but now the windows were black and only reflected Krogh from eight different angles. The flesh of his face was soft and pouched, but his eyes under heavy half-closed lids were bright with calculation.

Lom waited while Krogh examined him. His head hurt where the angel seal was set into it. A dull, thudding ache: the tympanation of an inward drum.

'You're either an idiot or a courageous man, Lom. Which is it?'

'You didn't bring me all the way to Mirgorod so you could call me an idiot.'

'Yough!' Krogh made an extraordinary, high-pitched sound. It was laughter. He picked up a folder that lay in front of him on the desk.

'This is the file on you, Lom. I've been reading it. You were one of Savinkov's. One doesn't meet many. And you have talent. But still only an Investigator. No promotion for, what is it, ten years?'

'Eleven.'

'And three applications for transfer to Mirgorod. All rejected.'

'No reason was given. Not to me.'

'Your superiors in Podchornok refer to attitudinal problems. Is that right?'

Lom shrugged.

'There's room for men like you, Investigator. Opportunities. That's why you're here. Would you do something for me? A very particular task?'

'I'd need to know what it was.'

The ache in Lom's head was stronger now. Shafts of pain at the place where the angel stone was cut in. Patches of brightness and colour disturbed his vision. None of the angles in the room was right.

'You're cautious,' said Krogh. 'Good. Caution is a good quality. In some circumstances. But we have reached an impasse, Investigator. I can't tell you anything until I know that you're on my side. And mine only. Only mine, Lom.' Krogh spread his hands. Slender hands, slender fingers, pale soft dry skin. 'So. Where do we go from here? How should we proceed?'

'I've had a long journey, Under Secretary. I've been on a train for the last six days. I'm tired and my head hurts. Unless you brought me all this way just so you could not tell me anything, you'd better say what this is all about.'

Krogh exhaled. A faint subsiding sigh.

'I'm beginning to see why your people find you difficult. Nevertheless, you have a point. Does the name Josef Kantor mean anything to you?'

'No.'

Krogh sank back, his head resting against the red leather chair-back.

'Josef Kantor,' he began, 'was nineteen at the time of the Birzel Rebellion. His father was a ringleader: he was executed by firing squad. Here at the Lodka. Josef Kantor himself was also involved. He spoke at the siege of the Armoury, and drafted the so-called Birzel Declaration. Do you know the Declaration, Lom?'

'I've heard of it.'

'It's fine work. Very fine. You should know it by heart. One should know one's adversary.'

Krogh leaned forward in his chair.

'*We believe,*' he began in a louder, clearer voice. '*We believe that the Vlast of One Truth has no right in Lezarye, never had any right in Lezarye, and never can have any right in Lezarye. The rule of the Vlast is forever condemned as a usurpation of the justified government of the people of Lezarye, and a crime against human progress of the Other Rational Peoples. We stand ready to die in the affirmation of this truth. We hereby proclaim the Nation of Lezarye as a sovereign independent people, and we pledge our lives and the lives of our comrades-in-arms to the cause of its freedom, its continued development, and its proper exaltation among the free nations of the continent.*'

Krogh paused. Lom said nothing.

'Fine words, Lom. Fine words. Kantor was arrested, of course, but – and I cannot explain this, the file is obscure – his sentence was limited to three years' internal exile. To your province, Investigator. And there he might have sat out his sentence in relative comfort and returned to the city, but he did not. He made persistent attempts to escape. He killed a guard. So. For this he got twenty years at the penal colony of Vig. Such a sentence is rarely completed, but Kantor survived. And then, a year ago, for reasons again obscure, he was simply released. He came back to Mirgorod and disappeared from our view. And also about a year ago,' Krogh continued, 'we began to notice a new kind of terror in Mirgorod. Of course we have our share of anarchists. Nihilists. Nationalists. There is always a certain irreducible level of outrage. But this was a new sense of purpose. Daring. Destructiveness. Cruelty. There was a new leader, that was obvious. There were names, many names: eventually we discovered they all led to one person.'

'Kantor.'

'Indeed. This month alone he has been responsible for the assassination of Commissioner Halonen, a mutiny at the Goll Dockyard and only last week an attack on the Bank of Foreign Commerce. They got thirty million roubles. Can you imagine what a man like Kantor is capable of, with thirty million roubles?'

'I read about the bank raid in the papers,' said Lom. 'But why are you telling me this?'

Krogh waved the question away.

'I've been after Kantor for a year,' he continued. 'A year, Lom! But I never get anywhere near him. Why?'

'I guess he has friends,' said Lom.

Krogh looked at him narrowly. A glint of appreciation.

'Exactly. Yes. You are sharp. Good. I cannot get near Kantor because he is protected. By people in the Vlast – people here, in the Lodka itself.'

'OK,' said Lom. 'But why? Why would they do that?'

'I guess,' said Krogh, 'that some understanding of the international situation percolates even as far as Podchornok? You realise, for instance, that we are losing the war with the Archipelago?'

'I only know what's in the newspapers. Seva was retaken last week.'

'And lost again the next day. The Vlast cannot sustain this war for another year. Our financial position is weak. The troops are refusing to fight. The Archipelago has proposed terms for a negotiated peace, and ...' Krogh broke off. 'This is confidential, Lom, you understand that?'

'Of course.'

'The Novozhd is preparing to open negotiations. Peace with honour, Lom. An end to the war.'

'I see.'

'Yet there are ... elements in Mirgorod – in the Vlast – elements who find the concept of negotiation unacceptable. There are those who say there should be no end to the war at all. Ever. Warfare waged for unlimited ends! A battle waged not against people like ourselves but against the contrary principle. The great enemy.'

'But—'

'These people are mad, Lom. Their aims are absurd. Absolute and total war is an absurd aim. Exhaustion and death. Ruin for the winners as much as the losers. You see this, you're an intelligent man. The Novozhd understands it, though many around him do not. The negotiations must not fail. There will not be a second chance.'

'Surely these are matters for diplomats. I don't see—'

'The Novozhd's enemies are determined to bring him down. They will use any means possible, and they will work with anyone – anyone – who can further their cause.'

'Including Josef Kantor?'

'Precisely. Kantor is a one-man war zone, Lom. His campaigns cause chaos. He sows fear and distrust. People lose faith. The Novozhd is failing to control him. I am failing. We are all failing. The security services grow restless. People are already whispering against us. Against the Novozhd. Which of course means opportunity for those who wish to replace him. The time is ripening for a coup. This is not accidental. There is a plan. There is a plot.'

'I see.'

'Kantor is the lynchpin, Lom. Kantor is king terrorist. The main man. Bring him down and it all comes down. Bring him down and the Novozhd is safe.'

'I understand. But ... why are you telling me all this? What's it got to do with me?'

'I want you to find Kantor, Lom. Find him for me.'

'But ... why me? I know nothing of Mirgorod, I know nobody here. You have the whole police department ... the gendarmerie ... the third section ... the militia ...'

'These disqualifications are what make you the one I need. The only one I must have. Why have I got your file, Lom? What brought you to my notice?'

'I have no idea.'

Krogh picked up the folder again.

'There are enough complaints against you in here,' he said, 'to have you exiled to Vig yourself tomorrow. Serious charges. I see through all that, of course. Innuendo and fabrication. I see what motivates them. You're not afraid to make enemies, and they hate that. That's why I need you, Lom. The Novozhd's enemies are all around me. I know they are there, but I don't know who they are. I can trust nobody. *Nobody*. But *you*, Investigator. Consider …' Krogh ticked off the points on his fingers. 'A good detective. Loyal to the Vlast. Incorrupt. Independent. Courageous. Probably not stupid. You know nobody in the city. Nobody knows you. You see where I'm going?'

'Well, yes but—'

'You will probably fail, of course,' said Krogh. 'But you might just succeed. You find Kantor, Lom, and you stop him. By any means possible. Any at all. And more – you find out who's running him. Somebody here is pulling Kantor's strings. Find out who it is. You find out what the bastards are up to, Lom, and when you do, you tell *me*. *Only* me. Got that?'

'Yes.'

'You'll be on your own,' said Krogh. 'You'll have no help. No help at all. This is your chance, Lom, if you can take it.'

10

Josef Kantor was reading at his desk. The window of his room stood open. He liked how night sharpened the sounds and perfumes of the wharf. He liked to let it into his room. There was no need for the lamp: arc lights and glare and spark-showers flickered across the pages of his book. There was no better light to read by. The light of men working. The light of the future.

He heard the quiet footfall on wet paving, the footsteps climbing the iron staircase. One person alone. A woman, probably. He was waiting in the shadow just outside his door when she reached the top, his hand in his jacket pocket nursing his revolver. He made sure she was in the light and he was not.

'Who are you?' he said.

'I'm sorry,' she said. 'I meant never to come here, but I had no choice.'

A group of men just off their shift were coming up the alleyway, talking loudly. Curious glances at the woman on the staircase. She wasn't the kind you saw in the yard at night. They would remember. Kantor didn't need that sort of attention.

'Go in,' said Kantor.

He followed her into the room and lit the lamp. He saw that she was young – early twenties, maybe – and thin. Her hands were rough and red from manual work, her wrists bony against the dark fabric of her sleeves, but her face was filled with life and intelligence. Thick black hair, cut short around her neck, fell across her brow, curled and wet. It had been raining earlier, though now it was not. Her coat was made of thin, poor stuff, little use against the weather, but, fresh and flushed from the cold, she brought an outside air into the room, not the industry and commerce of the shipyards but fresh earth and wet leaves. She met his gaze without hesitation: her eyes looking into his were bright and dark.

There was something about her. It unsettled him. She was not familiar, exactly, but there was a quality in her that he almost recognised, though he couldn't place it.

'You've made a mistake,' he said. 'Wrong person. Wrong place.'

'No. You're Josef Kantor.'

Kantor didn't like his name spoken by strangers.

'I've told you. You're mistaken,' he said. 'You're confusing me with someone else.'

'Please,' she said. 'This is important. I'm not going until we've talked. You owe me that.'

She took off her coat, draped it over the back of a chair and sat down. Underneath the coat she was wearing a knitted cardigan of dark green wool. Severe simplicity. Her throat was bare and her breasts were small inside the cardigan. Kantor was curious.

'Since you refuse to leave,' he said, 'you'd better tell me who you are.'

'I'm your daughter.'

Kantor looked at her blankly. He was, for once, surprised. Genuinely surprised.

'I have no daughter,' he said.

'Yes, you do. It's me. I am Maroussia Shaumian.'

It took Kantor a moment to adjust. He had not expected this, but he should have: of course he should. He had known there was a child, the Shaumian woman's child, the child of the frightened woman he'd married all those years ago, before Vig, before everything. That affair had been a young man's mistake: but, he realised now, it had been a far worse mistake to let them live. He studied the young woman more carefully.

'So,' he said at last. 'You are that girl. How did you find me?'

'Lakoba Petrov told me where you were.'

'Petrov? The painter? You should choose better friends than Petrov.'

'I haven't come here to talk about my friends.'

'No?' said Kantor. 'So what is this? A family talk? I am not interested in families.'

Maroussia put her hand in the pocket of her cardigan and brought out a small object cupped in her hand. She held it out to him. It was a thing like a nest, a rough ball made of twigs and leaves, fine bones and dried berries held together with blobs of yellowish wax and knotted grass. 'I want you to tell me what this is,' she said.

Kantor took it from her. As soon as he held it, everything in the room was the wrong size, too big and too small at the same time, the angles dizzy, the floor dropping away precipitously at his feet. The smell of resinous trees and damp earth was strong in the air. The forest presence. Kantor hadn't felt it for more than twenty years. He had forgotten how much he hated it. He swallowed back the feeling of sickness that rose in his throat and moved to throw the disgusting thing onto the fire.

'Don't!' Maroussia snatched it back from him. 'Do you know what it is?' she said. 'Do you know what it means?'

'No,' he said. 'No. Where did you get it?'

'Mother has them. I stole this one from her. I don't know where she gets them from, but I think they come from the forest, or have something to do with it.'

'Nothing useful ever came from that muddy rainy chaos world under the trees. That's all just shit. So much shit.'

'I think these things are important.'

'Then ask your mother what they are.'

'She can't tell me.'

'Why not?'

'Do you really not know? Don't you know anything about us at all? You could have found out, if you wanted to.'

It was true. He could have taken steps. He had considered it while he was at Vig, after the Shaumian woman had left him, and later. But it would have meant asking questions. He had told himself it was better to share with no one the knowledge of their existence. That had been stupid. He could see that, now. Now, it was obvious.

'My mother isn't well,' the girl was saying. 'She hasn't been well for years. In her mind, I mean. She's always frightened. She thinks bad things are happening and she is being watched. Followed. She never goes out, and she's always muttering about the trees. For months now these things have been appearing in our room. I've seen three or four, but I think there have been more. She pulls them apart and throws them away. She won't say anything about them, but she keeps talking about something that happened in Vig. Something that happened when she went into the trees.'

'You should forget about all that,' said Kantor. 'Forget the past. Detach yourself. Forget this nostalgia for the old muddy places. Trolls and witches in the woods. These stories aren't meant to be believed. Their time is finished.'

'They're not stories. They're real. And they're here. They're in the city. The city was built on top of it, but the old world is still here.' She held up the little ball of twigs and stuff. 'These are real. These are important. They're from the forest, and my mother is meant to understand something, but she doesn't. Something happened to her in the forest long ago. And ...' She hesitated. 'She keeps talking about the Pollandore. I need you to tell me what happened then. I need you to tell me about the Pollandore.'

For the second time, Kantor was genuinely startled. Whatever he had expected her to say, it was not that.

'The Pollandore?' he said. 'It doesn't exist.'

'I don't believe that. I need you to tell me about it. And tell me about my mother. What happened to her in the forest? It's all connected. I need to understand it. I have a right to know. You're my father. You have to tell me.'

Kantor was tired of playing games. It was time to end this. End the pretence. Open her eyes. Peel back the lids. Make the child stare at some truth.

'I'm not your father,' he said.

She stared at him.

'What?' she said. 'What do you mean? Yes you are.'

'That's what your mother told you, apparently, but she lied. Of course she lied. She always lied. How could I be your father? She would not ... your mother would not ... She refused me ... For months. Before she became pregnant. She went into the trees. She kept going there. And then she abandoned me and ran back home to Mirgorod. You're not my child. I'm not your father. I couldn't be.'

There was raw shock in her face.

'I don't believe you,' she said. 'You're lying.'

But he saw that she did believe him.

'What does it matter, anyway?' he said. 'What difference does it make?'

'It matters,' she said. 'It matters to me.'

'Hoping for a cuddle from Daddy? Then ask your mother who he is. If you can get any sense out of the old bitch.'

The girl was staring at him. Her face was white and set hard. Blank like a mask. So be it. She would not look to him for help again.

'You bastard,' she said quietly. 'You bastard.'

'Technically, that's you. The forest whore's bastard daughter.'

'Fuck you.'

After she had gone Kantor extinguished the lamp again and sat for a long time, considering carefully. The girl's visit had stirred old memories. Vig. The forest edge. The Pollandore. He'd thought he had eradicated such things. Killed and forgotten them. But they were only repressed. And the repressed always returns. The girl had said that.

He should have done something about the Shaumian women long ago: that he had not done so revealed a weakness he hadn't known was in him, and such weakness was dangerous. More than that, the girl was a threat in her own right. She was rank with the forest, and surprisingly strong. She had caused him to show his weakness to her. He would have to do something: the necessity of that was clear at last. He must end it now. He was glad she had come. Laying bare weakness was the first step to becoming stronger. In the familiar dialectic of fear and killing, only the future mattered. Only the future was at stake.

11

Maroussia Shaumian walked out through the night din and confusion of the dockyard and on into nondescript streets of tenements and small warehouses. She was trembling. She needed to think, but she could not. There was too much. She walked. Wanting to be tired. Not wanting to go home. Scarcely noticing where she went.

There was rain in the air and more rain coming, a mass of dark low cloud building towards the east, but overhead there were gaps of clear blackness and stars. She didn't know what time it was. Late.

She came at last to the Stolypin Embankment: a row of globe lamps along the parapet, held up by bronze porpoises. Glistening cobbles under lamplight. Beyond the parapet, she felt more than saw the slow-moving Mir, sliding out into the Reach, barges and late water taxis still pushing against the black river. The long, punctuated reflections of their navigation lights trickled towards her, and the talk of the boat-men carried across the water, intimate and quiet. She couldn't make out the words: it felt like language from another country. A gendarme was observing her from his kiosk, but she ignored him and went to sit on a bench, watching the wide dark river, its flow, its weight, its still-ness in movement. She took the knotted nest of forest stuff out of her pocket and held it to her face, breathing in its strange earthy perfume. Filling her lungs.

And then it happened, as it sometimes did.

A tremble of movement crossed the black underside of the clouds, like wind across a pool, and the buildings of the night city prickled; the nap of the city rising, uneasy, anxious. Maroussia waited, listen-ing. Nothing more came. Nothing changed. The rain-freighted clouds settled into a new shape. And then, suddenly, the solidity of Mirgorod stone and iron broke open and slid away, vertiginously. The blackness and ripple of the water detached itself from the river and slipped upwards, filling the air, and everything changed. The night was thick with leaking possibilities. Soft evaporations. Fragments and intimations of other possible lives, drifting off the river and across the dirty pavements. Hopes, like moon-ghosts, leaking out of the streets.

The barges, swollen and heavy-perfumed, dipped their sterns and raised their bows, opening their mouths as if to speak, exhaling shining yellow. The porpoises threw their mist-swollen, corn-gold lamp-globes against the sky. The cobbles of the wharf opened their petals like peals of blue thunder. The stars were large and luminous night-blue fruit. And the gendarme in his kiosk was ten feet tall, spilling streams of perfume and darkshine from his face and skin and hair.

Everything dark shone with its own quiet radiance and nothing was anything except what it was. Maroussia felt the living profusion of it all, woven into bright constellations of awareness, spreading out across the city. She looked at her own hands. They were made of dark wet leaves. And then the clouds closed over the stars and it started to rain in big slow single drops, and Mirgorod settled in about her again, as it always did.

12

It was late when Lom got out of Krogh's office. The streets about the Lodka were deserted. Shuttered and lightless offices. The wind threw pellets of rain in his face. Water spurted from downpipes and spouts and overflowing gutters, splashing on the pavements. Occasionally a private kareta passed him, windows up, blinds drawn.

In his valise he had a folder of newspaper clippings – accounts of attacks and atrocities attributed to Kantor and his people, Krogh had said – and one photograph, old and poorly developed, of Kantor himself, taken almost twenty years ago, at the time of his transfer to Vig. And he had a mission. A real job to do. At last. Mirgorod spread out around him, rumbling quietly in the dark of rain and night. A million people, and somewhere among them Josef Kantor. And behind him, shadow people. Poison in the system. The ache in Lom's head had gone, but it had left him hungry. He needed something to eat. He needed a place to stay. He needed a way in. A starting point. He wished he'd asked Krogh about money.

In his pocket he had Raku Vishnik's address: an apartment somewhere on Big Side. He had a vague idea of where it was, somewhere to the north, beyond the curve of the River Mir. Not more than a couple of miles. He had no money for a hotel, and he didn't want to pay for a droshki ride, even if he could find one. He would go to Raku. Assuming he was still there. Lom buttoned his cloak to the neck and started to walk. A fresh deluge dashed against his face and trickled down his neck. A long black ZorKi Zavod armoured sedan purred past him, chauffeur-driven, darkened black windows, the rain glittering in its headlamp beams. White-walled tyres splashing through pools in the road. Lom hunched his shoulders and kept moving.

The hypnotic rhythm of walking. The sound of water against stone. As he walked, Lom thought about the city. Mirgorod. He'd never seen it before, but all his life he had lived with the idea of it. The great capital, the Founder's city, the heart of the Vlast. Even as a child, long before the idea of joining the police had taken shape, the dream of Mirgorod had taken root in his imagination. He remembered the moment. Memories rose out of the wet streets. He was back in Podchornok, at the Institute of Truth. Seven years old. Eight. It was another day of rain, but he was in the library, looking out. He liked the library: there were deep, tall windows, their sills wide enough to climb up onto and crouch there. Although it was grey daylight, he pulled the curtain shut and he was alone: on one side the heavy curtain, and on the other the windowpane, rain splattering against it and running in little floods down the outside of the glass. Beyond the window, the edge of the wood – not the forest, just an ordinary wood, rain-darkened, leafless under a low grey sky. And him, reading by rainlight.

He even remembered the book he had been reading. *The Life of our Founder: A Version for Children.* The chapter on the founding of Mirgorod. There was an illustration of the Founder on horseback, accompanied by his retinue on lesser horses. They had drawn to a halt on a low hummock surrounded by flat empty marshland, and the Founder had thrust his great sword upright into the bog.

'Here!' he said. 'Here shall our city stand.'

It was a famously preposterous location for a city. The ground was soft and marshy, scattered with low outcrops of rock like islands among the rough grass and reedy pools and soft, silken mud. No human settlement within two hundred versts. No road. No safe harbour. Nothing. Yet *here* the Founder had said, because he could see what all his counsellors and diplomats and soldiers could not. He could see the great River Mir reaching the ocean. He could see that the river was linked by deep inland lakes and other rivers and easy portages to the whole continent to the east. He could see that to the west lay great oceans. Only the Founder could see that this lonely place was not the back end of nowhere but a window on the world.

'We can't build a city in this awful place!' the Founder's retinue cried, splashing knee-deep in the mud, their horses struggling and stumbling.

'Yes,' the Founder had said. 'We can. We will.'

'Hey, you!'

Lom was passing a small shop of some kind, still open. A man came lurching out.

'Hey, come on. Drink with us.'

Lom ignored him.

'Wait. That's my cloak. Give it me, you bastard. You stole my cloak.'

Lom fingered his cosh. The length of hard rubber, sheathed with silk, rested in a specially tailored pocket in the sleeve of his shirt, near the wrist. He undid the small button that let it slip into his hand and turned.

'You'd better go back inside,' he said.

The man saw the weapon in his hand. Stared at him, swaying slightly.

'Ah, fuck you,' he said, and turned away.

Lom walked on, deeper into the city. Kantor's city. But his city too: he would make it so. He was the hunter, the good policeman, the unafraid. He passed a bar, but it was closed and dark. Its name written on the window in flaking gold paint. The Ouspensky Angel. When, in the last years of the Founder's reign, the first dying angel had fallen from the sky and crashed into the Ouspenskaya Marsh, it had been taken as a sign of acknowledgement and consecration. Over the centuries the stone of the angel's limbs had been used to furnish protection for the Lodka and other great buildings, and to make mudjhiks to garrison the city, but its torso had been left to lie where it still was, visible to all newcomers as they arrived in the city. The *Life of our Founder* had a picture of the falling angel and a simple sketch map of 'Mirgorod Today' showing the cobweb of streets and canals, the city like a dark spreading net. Lom remembered how he had stared at that map, and the picture of the falling angel, that time in the library. The strange, nameless longing the pictures had stirred in him. The sense of possibilities. Purposes. The adventures that life could hold.

And then Lom remembered ...

... now, for the first time ...

He had forgotten ... for a quarter of a century ...

... when he was reading that book, looking at that picture, imagination stirring ... he remembered ...

... the hand ripping aside the curtain from the library window and the hate-filled face stuck into his, the sour breath, the cruel hand snatching the book from his hand, the voice screeching at him.

'Here you are, you vicious little bastard! Now you're caught, you evil piece of shit!'

The claw-hand grabbed him by the neck, fingernails gouging his skin, and hauled him out of the window seat. He fell hard, down onto the library floor.

Lom stopped in the middle of the street, pausing for breath, letting the rain run down his face. The memory of that moment had shocked him. He had put it away so deep. Forgotten it. A hurt from a different world, it meant nothing to the policeman he had become. Put it aside again, he told himself, think about it later. Maybe. Now, immediately, he needed to get out of this rain and night. He wondered if he was lost. There were no signs. No sense of direction in the empty streets. He had been stupid not to take a ride.

Rain skittered down alleyways, riding curls of wind. Rain slid across roof-slates and tumbled down sluices and drainpipes and slipped through grilles into storm drains. Rain assembled itself in ropes in gutters and drains, and collected itself in watchful, waiting puddles and cisterns. Rain saturated old wood and porous stone and bare earth. Rain-mirrors on the ground looked up into the face of the falling rain. The wind-twisted air was crowded with flocks of rain: rain-sparrows and rain-pigeons, crows of rain. Rain-rats ran across the pavement and rain-dogs lurked in the shadows. Every column and droplet, every pool and puddle and sluice and splash, every slick, every windblown spillage of water and air, was alive. The rain was watching him.

Ever since the builders first came, the rain had been trickling through the cracks and gaps in the carapace of the chitinous city, sliding under the tiles and lead of the roofs, slipping through the cracks between paving slabs and cobbles, pooling on the floors of cellars, insinuating itself into the foundations, soaking through to the earth beneath the streets. Every rainfall dissolved away an infinitesimal layer of Mirgorod stone, leached a trace of mineral salts from the mortar, wore the sharp edges imperceptibly smoother, rounded off the hard corners a little bit more, abraded fine grooves down the walls and buttresses. Fine jemmies and levers of rain slid between ashlar and coping. Little by little, century by century, the rain was washing the city away.

The rain trickled down Lom's face, tasting him. The rain traced the folds of his skin and huddled in the whorls of his ears. The rain splashed against the angel-stone tablet in his skull. The rain tasted angel, the rain smelled policeman, the rain trickled over the hard certainties of the Vlast and the law, stoppered up with angel meat. While Lom walked on, oblivious, absorbed in memories, the rain was nudging him ever further away from the peopled streets, towards the older, softer, rainier places.

Memory hit him like a fist in the belly.

How was it he'd forgotten her? Buried her so deep? Never thought of her? Never. Never. Not till now.

She had dragged him down corridors and up stairways to the Provost's room.

'Here you are!' she shrieked at the Provost. 'I told you! He is corrupted. He is foul. He should never have been admitted. I said so.'

There was a fire of logs burning in the room. She had taken something of his, something important, and gone across to the fire and put it carefully in.

'*No!*' he'd cried. '*No!*'

He'd thrown himself across the room and scrabbled at the burning logs. He remembered her, screeching like an animal, punching him across the back of the head, and … Something had happened. What? He couldn't remember There was a door he couldn't open, and something terrible was behind it. What had he done? He felt the shame and guilt, the permanent stain it had left, but he didn't … he couldn't … he had no recollection of what it was.

But he did know that the next day they had cut into the front of his head and placed the sliver of angel stone there, and that had made him good.

Lom rested his valise and wiped the rain from his face. He was passing through narrow defiles between once-grand buildings that were tenements now, propped up with flimsy accretions and lean-tos. Gulfs of night and rain opened between the few street lamps. Mirgorod had withdrawn indoors for the night, and his sodden clothes had tightened around him, becoming a warm mould, wrapping him in his own body heat. The sound of the rain seemed to seal him in. Dark alley-mouths gaped. Broken wooden fences barricaded gaps of waste ground. Small doorways cut into high brick walls.

He might have seen something, some shape slipping back out of the lamplight. He felt again for the smooth weight of the cosh in his sleeve.

He came to the margin of an endless cobbled square, the far side all but invisible behind the night rain. There was a lamp in the middle of the square, and some kind of kiosk beneath it. Two horses standing against the rain, their heads turned to watch him. And a covered droshki waiting. He walked fast towards it, but he hadn't crossed half the wide open space when the driver appeared from the kiosk and climbed up into the seat.

'Hey!' shouted Lom. 'Hey! Wait!'

Lom started to run, awkwardly, hampered by a horizontal gust of sleet in his face, and his rain-heavy cloak, and his luggage. It was hopeless. The droshki drove away into the dark on the farther side.

'Shit.'

The rain fell harder and colder. It stung his face and pressed down on him like a heavy weight. Wind-spun rain gathered itself in front of him and resolved itself into a thing of rain, a man of rain – no – a woman of rain – taller than human, a hardened column of rain and air.

And then the rain attacked him.

Lom spun around and tried to hide from it, but when he turned it was in front of him still. It lashed out and struck him. A fist of rain. A hard smash of wind off the sea, filled with rain. A stinging punch of rain in his face. He fell to the ground, tasting rain and blood in his mouth. The rain became a great foot and stamped on him, driving him face-down into the stone, driving the breath from him.

He was going to die.

He hauled himself to his feet and tried to run, slipping and stumbling across the cobbles. But he was running towards his enemy, not away. The rain surrounded him, and met him wherever he turned, dashing pebbles and nails of rain into his face. He held up his hand to protect his eyes. The droshki kiosk was in front of him. He stumbled towards it and pulled at the door. It wouldn't open. He tried to barge into it with his shoulder, but the rain kicked his legs out from under him and he fell on his back, cracking his head. When the world came back into focus he was looking up into the face of the rain. His nose and mouth began to fill. He gasped for air and his throat filled with rain and blood. Rain kneeled on his ribs, driving the breath out of him. He was drowning in rain.

Something broke open inside him then. He felt it burst, as if a chain-link had snapped apart. A lock broken open. Some containment that had been placed inside him long ago had come undone.

He remembered.

He remembered what he had done that afternoon in the Provost's room.

He remembered how he had gathered up all the air in the room and thrown it at her, and she had screamed and fallen. He remembered the pop that had followed when the air recoiled, refilling the temporary vacuum. He remembered the Provost's papers flying about the room, the air filled with a cloud of hot embers and ash and smoke from the fire, the chair falling sideways, the picture crashing down from the wall. He remembered what he had done, and he remembered what it had felt like, and he remembered how he hadn't known, not then and not later, how he had done it.

He tried to do it again. *Now!*

He reached out into the squalling, churning air and gathered up a ball of wind and rain. He tried to compact it as hard as he could. And he flung it at the figure of rain.

It was a feeble effort. It made no difference. Nothing could. He was going to die.

The thing of rain was standing over him, suddenly gentler now. Lom felt the attention of its regard, appraising him, wondering. A hand of rain reached down and touched his forehead gently. Fingertips of rain stroked the shard of angel stone cut into his head. He seemed to feel a brush of kindness. Pity.

Poor boy, it seemed to say. *Poor boy.*

The thing of rain dissolved into rain, and he was alone.

He picked himself up off the ground, bruised, exhausted, soaked. He needed to get inside. Out of the rain. And quickly.

13

I t was almost midnight when Lom arrived, bruised, soaked and chilled to the core, at Vishnik's address. Pelican Quay turned out to be a canal-side row of houses, one among many such streets on Big Side, north of the river. The rain had paused. A damp and cave-like smell on the air and the heavy iron bollards and railings on the far side of the road betrayed the invisible night presence of the canal. Number 231 was a tall flat-fronted tenement squeezed between neighbouring buildings, the kind of house once built for grander families but partitioned now into many smaller, boxy apartments for the accommodation of tailors, locksmiths, cooks, civil servants of the lower ranks. Many pairs of eyes were observing him: although it was late, the dvorniks were out, each hunched in a folding chair under his own dim lamp in the lea of his domain. The dvornik of number 231 was drinking from a tin mug. His face gleamed moonily. His cheeks had collapsed to form loose jowls at the level of his chin.

'Raku Vishnik,' said Lom. 'Apartment 4.'

'No visitors after nine.'

'He's expecting me. He keeps late hours.'

The dvornik looked at Lom's scruffy valise. His sodden clothes. His dripping hair.

'No overnights.'

Lom fumbled in his pocket. 'I appreciate the inconvenience. Twenty kopeks should cover it'

'A hundred.'

'Fifty.'

The dvornik grunted and held out a hand. He wore thick fingerless woollen gloves: even in the sparse lamplight they looked in need of a wash.

'Second floor. Don't use the lift and don't turn on the lights.'

The stairs were dark and narrow, lit by street light falling through high small windows. Stale cooking smells. A thin carpet in the corridor. The bell of Number 4 sounded faint and toy-like, like it was made of tin.

Lom waited. Nobody came. He stood there, dripping, in the dark passageway. He realised that he was shaking, and not just with cold and hunger and the fatigue of carrying his case through the empty streets. The taste of the living rain was in his mouth. The smell of it on his face and his clothes. He had heard of such things, the possibilities of them. You didn't live at the edge of the forest without being sometimes aware of the wakefulness of the wilder things: the life of the wind, the sentience of the watchful trees. The memory of the damp, living earth. But not in Mirgorod. He had not expected to find such things here: Mirgorod was the capital of solidity, the Founder's Strength, the Vlast of the One Truth.

He needed Vishnik to open up. He rang the bell again. Nothing happened. Maybe Vishnik was already in bed. He rang twice more and banged on the door. There was a muffled sound of movement within, and it opened slowly. A pale, drawn face appeared. Dark eyes, blank and unfocused, looked into his own.

'Yes?'

'Raku?'

The dark eyes looked past him to see if someone else was in the corridor. Vishnik was dressed to go out: an unbuttoned gabardine draped from his shoulders, a small overnight bag in his hand. He was taller than Lom remembered, but the same glossy fringe of black hair flopped across his forehead. The same dark brown eyes behind rimless circular lenses. But the eyes were glassy with fear.

'Raku. It's me. Vissarion.'

Vishnik's hands were balled in tight fists. He was shaking with anger. 'Fuck,' he said. 'Fuck. What the fuck are you doing.'

'Raku? Didn't you get my telegram?'

'No I didn't get any fucking telegram. Shit. What are you doing? I don't see you for half a lifetime and then you're hammering on my door in the middle of the night.'

'I wired. Five, six days ago. I said I would be coming. I said it would be late.'

Vishnik held up his bag. Shoved it at Lom. 'See this? What's this? Clothes. Bread. So I don't have to go in my pyjamas when they come. How did you get in here anyway? The dvornik shouldn't have—'

'I gave him fifty kopeks.'

'Fifty? That's not enough. He has to report visitors to the police.'

'What's he going to report? I am the police.'

'Some fucking policeman. Look at you. Dripping on the carpet.' He looked at Lom's valise. 'You got dry things in there?'

'Yes.'

'Wait.'

Vishnik disappeared. Rain seeped out of Lom's hair and down his face. Rain dripped from the hem of his cloak and spilled from his trouser cuffs.

Vishnik came back carrying a towel.

'There's a bathroom at the end of the corridor.'

'Thanks.'

'Yeah. Shit. Well, get dry.'

Lom tucked the towel under his arm, picked up the valise and started down the corridor.

'Oh, and Vissarion.'

'Yes?'

'It's good to see you. I thought I never would.'

Fifteen minutes later Lom was sitting on Vishnik's couch with a glass of aquavit. There was food on the table. Solyanka with cabbage and lamb. Thick black bread. He leaned back and let the room wrap itself around him. Heavy velvet curtains of a faded brick colour hung across the window. Electric table lamps cast warm shadows. A paraffin heater burned in the corner. Bookshelves everywhere. More books piled on the floor and stacked on the desk. And on a side table, carefully arranged, a strange assemblage of objects: a broken red lacquer tea caddy; a grey and blue mocha mug with no handle; a china dog; a piece of stained wood, stuck through with bent and rusting nails; broken shards of ceramic and glass; a feather; a bowl of damp black earth. Odd things that could have been picked up in the street. Set out like the ritual items of a shaman of the city.

But it was the collection of art that made the room extraordinary. In plain dark frames, squeezed in between the bookshelves, hung in corners and high up near the ceiling, the paintings were like none Lom had seen before. They were of shapes and colours only. Sharp angular quadrilaterals of red and blue and green, smashed against a background of dark grey that reminded him of city buildings at twilight, but falling. Collapsing. Black lines slashed across jumbled boxes of faded terracotta. Thick, unfinished scrapes of paint – midnight blue – burnt earth – colours of rain and steel. Mad, childish clouds and curlicues and watery rivers of purple and gold and acidic, medicinal green. As Lom looked he began to see that there were objects in them – sometimes – or at least suggestions of objects. Bits and pieces of objects. A bicycle wheel. A bottle-cork. A bridge reflected in a river, exploded by sunset. A horse. The spout of a jug. Sometimes there was writing – typographic fragments, scrawled vowels, tumbled alphabets, but never a whole word.

Vishnik was sitting at the desk nursing a glass. He looked thin, almost gaunt. His hands were still trembling, but his eyes were warmer now, filled with the dark familiar ardour, missing nothing. It was the same clear serious face, illuminated with an intense intelligence. There was something wild and sad there, which hadn't been there when they were young. But this was Raku Vishnik still.

'You gave me a fright, my friend,' Vishnik was saying. 'I was ungracious. I apologise. I spend too much time alone these days. One becomes a little strung out, shall we say.'

'What about your work?' said Lom. 'The university.'

Lom had gone with Vishnik to see him onto the boat, the day he left Podchornok for Mirgorod. Vishnik was going to study history at the university, while Lom was to stay in Podchornok and join the police. Vishnik had dressed flamboyantly then. Wide-brimmed hats and bright bow ties. The fringe longer and floppier. They'd exchanged letters full of cleverness and joking and the futures that awaited them both in their chosen professions. Vishnik was going to become a professor, and he had. But the correspondence dwindled over the years and finally stopped. Lom had settled into the routine of the Provinciate Investigations Department.

'The university?' said Vishnik. 'Ah. Now they, they are fuckers. They don't let me teach any more. My background became known.

My family. Someone let the bloody secret out. Aristocrats. Nobility. *Former persons.* Some of the darling students complained. And then of course there was the matter of my connections with the artists. The poets. The cabaret clubs. I used to write about all that. Did you know? Of course not. Criticism. Essays. Journalism. The magazines could never afford to pay me, but sometimes they gave me a painting.' He waved clumsily at the walls. 'But that's all over. It appears I became an embarrassment to the authorities. The hardliners run the show now, on matters of aesthetics like everything else. These pictures are degenerate. Fuck. They closed the galleries and the magazines. The painters are forbidden to paint. They still do, of course. But it's dangerous now. And I am silenced. Forbidden to publish. Forbidden to teach.'

He emptied his glass and filled it again. Poured one for Lom.

'That's tough,' said Lom. 'I'm sorry.'

'I was lucky. Not completely cast into the outermost darkness. I think some of my fucker colleagues did have the grace to feel a little ashamed. They have made me the official historian of Mirgorod, no less. In that august capacity I sit here before you now. There's even a small stipend. I can afford to eat. Not that anyone wants a history of Mirgorod. I doubt it will ever be published. I'm not spoken to, Vissarion, not any more. And I'm watched. I'm on the list. My time will come. I thought it had, when you came banging at the fucking door. They always come in the night. Never the fucking morning. Never fucking lunchtime. Always the fucking middle of the fucking night.'

'I'm sorry. I didn't think—'

'Fuck it. Fuck them, Vissarion. Tell me that you haven't changed.'

'I haven't changed.'

Vishnik raised his glass.

'To friendship, then. Welcome to Mirgorod.'

Archangel studies his planet, his prison, his cage. He assembles the fragments, the minds he has sifted and collected, and comes to understand it better. The planet has a history, and history is a voice. The people of the planet serve their history as photons serve light, as agglomerations of massiveness serve gravity. The voice of history is a dark force.

And Archangel comes to understand that the voice of this planet's history is broken. In the future that is coming and has already been, the future that re-imagines its own antecedence, a catastrophic mistake is made.

And he learns something else, which is a danger to him. Cruel and immediate danger. Somewhere nearby there still exists a well of old possibility. The vestige of an older voice. The lost story that can no longer speak is tucked away somewhere in silent obscurity. It does not exist in the world but it is there. Beside it. In potential. A seed dormant. A storage cell untapped.

And this encapsulation of failed futurity is ripening, and breaking, and beginning to leak. It is beginning to wonder: maybe what is done will yet be undone?

Archangel roars.

'*THAT CANNOT BE ALLOWED TO HAPPEN!*'

Archangel must return to the space between the stars, which is his birthright and his stolen domain. Not merely return to it, but seize it, consume it, become it. Become the stars. Become the galaxies. Better than before. He sees how it can be done. This planet can do it for him.

'*Let the voice of the planet be my voice. Let the voice of its history be mine. A fear voice. A power voice. Make the voice of history be my larynx. Retell the broken story in a new way. Make the expression of the world unfolding be the planning, cunning, conscious, necessary, unequivocal expression of me, Archangel, voice of the future, voice of the world, speaking through all people always everywhere.*

'*Let the people take flight from this one planet to all the stars, all the galaxies, all the intergalactic immensities everywhere always – and let them speak me! A billion billion billion people always everywhere in glittering crimson ships across the black-red-gold recurving energy-mass-time seething scattered shouting me. The perpetual unfolding flowering of the voice of me. All filled with the angelness of me.*

'*So it will be.*

'*But first, for this to happen, that fatal other source – the fracturing egg of other possibilities that impossibly continues – must be destroyed.*'

This then is the first syllable of the first word of the first phrase of the first sentence of the voice of Archangel.

'*DESTROY THE POLLANDORE!*'

14

Lom woke early the next morning. As the first greying of the dawn filtered through the gaps in the curtains in Vishnik's study, he lay on his back on the couch, turning the question of Kantor over in his mind. How to find him. How to even begin. Krogh had told him he would have no help, no resources, no official support from the immense intelligence machine of the Vlast. Krogh's private secretary would fix him an access pass for the Lodka, and an office there, under cover of some suitably bland pretext to account for his presence, but that was all.

He had read Krogh's file of clippings on Kantor late into the night. It was an accumulation of robberies, bombings, assassinations. There was no pattern that he could find. The targets were indiscriminate, the victims seemingly random: for every senior official of the Vlast or prominent soldier or policeman killed, there were dozens of innocent passers-by caught in appalling eruptions of destructive violence. There was no clear purpose: responsibility for each attack was claimed by a different obscure and transient dissident grouping, or by none, and none of the perpetrators had ever been taken alive.

He had spent a long time staring at the photograph of the young Josef Kantor that Krogh had given him. He tried to find in that face the lineaments of calculating cruelty that could drive such a murderous campaign. But it was just a face: long and narrow, scarred by the pockmarks of some childhood illness, but handsome. Kantor looked into the camera with dark, interested eyes from under a thick mop of dark hair, uncombed. Although the picture must have been taken in an interrogation cell, there was the hint of a smile in the turn of his wide mouth. This was a confident, intelligent young man, a man you could like, even admire. A man you would want to like you.

Of course, the photograph had been taken two decades ago. Twenty years at Vig would change anyone. Because of this man, an atmosphere of anxiety and distrust and lurking incipient panic had settled on Mirgorod. Lom felt it in the newspaper accounts. He noticed also how in recent months, alongside the official condemnation of the atrocities, there was a growing tendency to criticise the authorities for failing to stem the tide of fear. And this criticism, though it was couched in carefully imprecise language, was increasingly directed towards the Novozhd himself. The hints were there: the Novozhd was old, he was weak, he was indecisive. Was he not, perhaps, even deliberately letting the terror campaign continue, as a means to shore up his own failing authority? These attacks on the Novozhd were always anonymous, but – in the light of Krogh's accusations – Lom felt he could sense the presence of an organising, directing hand behind them.

One thing was certain. Lying on the couch thinking about it would get him nowhere. He pushed his blanket aside. He needed to move. He needed to start.

In Vishnik's bathroom the plumbing groaned and and clanked and delivered a trickle of cold brown water into the basin. Lom shaved with his old cut-throat razor. Through a small high casement came the sounds of Mirgorod beginning its day: the rumble of an early tramcar, the klaxon of a canal boat, the clatter of grilles and shutters opening. He breathed the city air seeping in through the window, mingling diesel fumes, coal-smoke, canal water and wet pavements with the scent of his shaving soap. The city prickled and trembled with energy, humming at a frequency just too low to be audible, but tangible enough to put him on edge.

He dried his face on the threadbare corner of a towel and went back down the corridor to Vishnik's room. Vishnik was sitting at his desk. He had the newspaper spread open – the *Mirgorod Lamp* – but he was looking out of the window, sipping from the blue and white mug, his left hand fidgeting restlessly, tapping a jumpy rhythm with slender fingers.

Lom had laid his uniform out ready on the couch: black serge, silver epaulettes, buttons of polished antler. He pulled on his boots, also black, shined, smelling richly of leather. He stripped and cleaned his gun. It was a beautiful thing, a black-handled top-break Zorn service side-arm: .455 black powder cartridges in half-moon clips; overall length, 11.25 inches; weight 2.5 pounds unloaded; muzzle velocity, 620 feet per second; effective range, fifty yards. Like most things in Podchornok, it was thirty years out of date, but he liked it. He worked carefully and with a certain simple pleasure. Vishnik watched him.

'Vissarion?' he said at last. 'Just what the fuck is it that you are doing here, my friend?'

'Ever hear of Josef Kantor?'

'Kantor? Of course. That was a name to remember, once. A Lezarye intellectual, a polemicist, young, but he had a following. He knew how to please a crowd. A fine way with words. But he was silenced decades ago. Exiled. I assume he's dead now.'

'He isn't dead. He's in Mirgorod.' Lom told Vishnik what Krogh had said.

'There've always been sects and cabals in the Lodka,' said Vishnik. 'The White Sea Group. Opus Omnium Consummationis. The Iron Guard. Bagrationites. Gruodists. Some wanting to liberalise, some to purify. But why are you telling me this?'

'You asked.'

'Sure, but—'

'I need help, Raku. Someone who knows the city, because I don't. And I need somewhere to stay.'

'That's a lot to ask. A very fuck of a lot to ask, if I may say so.'

Lom reassembled the gun, put it in the shoulder holster and strapped it on.

'I know.'

'So,' said Vishnik eventually. 'OK. Sure. You are my friend. So why not. Where do you start?'

'I don't know. Somewhere. Anywhere. Find a thread and pull on it. See where it takes me.'

He picked up Vishnik's paper. It was that morning's edition. Idly he turned the pages, skimming the headlines.

GUNBOATS POUND SUMBER. ARCHIPELAGO ADVANCE STALLED OUTSIDE HANSIG. BACKGAMMON CHAMPION ASSASSINATED: LEZARYE SEPARATISTS CLAIM RESPONSIBILITY: LODKA PROMISES REPRISALS.

TRAITORS MUST BE SMASHED BY FORCE! the editorial thundered.

The verminous souks and ghettos where these vile criminals are nurtured must be cleaned up once and for all. Our leaders have been too soft for too long. Yes, we are a civilised folk, but these evil elements trample on our forbearance and spit on our decency. They are a disease, but we know the cure. We applaud the recent speech by Commander Lavrentina Chazia at the Armoury Parade Ground. Hers is the attitude our capital needs more of. We urge ...

Like Krogh's file of clippings, the paper was filled with traces of terror, of war, of Kantor and the nameless forces working against the Novozhd. But there was other stuff as well. Other voices, other threads, omitted from Krogh's selective collection.

An inside spread described new plans for massive monumental ossuaries to hold the corpses of the fallen soldiers, sailors and airmen of the Archipelago War: 'On the rocky coast of the Cetic Ocean there will grow up grandiose structures ... Massive towers stretching high in the eastern plains will rise as symbols of the subduing of the chaotic forces of the outcast islands through the disciplined might of the Vlast.' They were to be called Castles of the Dead. There were artist's impressions, with tiny, lost-looking stick families wandering in the grounds, inserted for scale.

MOTHER MURDERS LITTLE ONES. A lawyer, Afonka Voscovec, had suffocated her three children with a pillow and hanged herself. She'd left a note. 'The floors keep opening,' she'd written. 'Will no one stop it?'

Lom was about to throw the paper aside when he noticed a small piece in the social columns. A photograph of an officer of the militia shaking hands with the Commissioner of the Mirgorod Bank of Foreign Commerce. 'Major Artyom Safran, whose brave action defended the bank in Levrovskaya Square against a frontal terrorist assault, receives the congratulations of a grateful Olland Nett. Major Safran is a mudjhik handler.' Levrovskaya Square was, according to Krogh, Kantor's most recent atrocity. If this Major Safran had been there, that meant he had seen Kantor or at least his people. It was a connection.

Lom studied the photograph carefully. The legs and belly of the mudjhik could just be made out in shadow behind the Major's head. And in his head, in the middle of his brow, was a seal of angel flesh, the twin of Lom's own.

He stood up. It was time to go.

He took the lift down to the exit. The dvornik was in his cubbyhole. If the uniform impressed him, he didn't let it show. There was a cork board behind his head, with notices pinned to it: the address of the local advice bureau, details of winter relief collections, blackout exercises, changes to social insurance, a soap rationing scheme.

'Yes? What?'

'I'm going to be staying here for a few days. With Professor Vishnik.' Lom showed his warrant card. The dvornik glanced at it. Still not impressed. 'My presence here is authorised. By me. The Professor is under my protection. You are to report nothing. To no one. The fact that I am here – when I come – when I go – that's up to me. You notice nothing. You say nothing. You remember nothing.'

The dvornik had his tin cup in his hand. He took a sip from it and shrugged. Barely. Perhaps.

'Understand?'

'Whatever you say, General.'

15

L om found the office Krogh's private secretary had fixed for him at the Lodka. One office among thousands, a windowless box on an upper floor among storerooms, filing rooms, cleaning cupboards, boilers. It took him half an hour wandering corridors and stairways to track it down. There was a freshly typed card in the slot by the door handle: INVESTIGATOR V Y LOM. PODCHORNOK OBLAST. PROVINCIAL LIAISON REVIEW SECRETARIAT.

In the office there was a chair, a coat rack, a desk. Lom went through the drawers: stationery lint; a lidless, dried-up bottle of ink. Somebody had hung a placard on the wall.

Citizens! Let us all march faster
Through what remains of our days!
You might forget the fruitful summers
When the wombs of the mothers swelled
But you'll never forget the Vlast you hungered and bled for
When enemies gathered and winter came.

He laid out his notepad and sharpened his pencils. He gave the room two more minutes. It felt about a minute and a half too long. *Do something. Do anything. Make a start.*

Lom left the office behind and set himself adrift in the mazy corridors of the Lodka. There were floor plans posted at intersections, but they were no help: the room numbers and abbreviations in small print, amended in manuscript, bore little relationship to the labels on doors and stairwells. He knew that the place he wanted would be *down*. Such places were always near the root of things. Tucked away. Like death always was.

He came into a more crowded part of the building: secretaries in groups, carrying folders of letters, talking; porters wheeling trolleys of files and loose papers; policemen, uniformed and not; civil servants arguing quota and precedent, trading the currency of acronyms. The placards on committee room doors were syllables in a mysterious language. Hints and signs.

CENTGEN.

COMPOLIT.

GENCOM.

INTPOP.

POLITCENT.

He half expected someone to stop him and ask him what he was doing there, so he prepared a line about the urgent need to improve liaison with the Eastern Provinciates. He found he had a lot to say on the subject: it was an issue that actually did need attention. He began to think of improvements that could be made to the committee structure and lines of command. Perhaps he should write a memo for Krogh? He started to take out his notebook to write some thoughts down.

What the fuck am I doing?

He put the notebook back in his pocket. The Lodka was getting under his skin already, releasing the inner bureaucrat. Doors, wedged open, showed glimpses of desks, bowed concentrating heads, pencils poised over lists. Empty conference tables, waiting. The quiet music of distant telephone bells and typewriter clatter. The smell of polished linoleum and paper dust. Stairs and corridors without end. The Lodka cruised on the surface of the city like an immense ship, and like a ship it had no relationship with the depths over which it sailed, except to trawl for what lived there.

He let these thoughts drift on, preoccupying the surface layers of his mind, while the Lodka carried him forward, floating him through its labyrinths on a current you could only perceive if you didn't look for it too hard. This was a technique that always worked for him in office buildings: they were alive and efficient, and knew where you needed to go; if you trusted them and kept an open mind, they took you there.

On the ground floor he followed his nose, tracing the faint scent of sweetness and corruption down a narrow stairwell to its source. A sign on the swing doors said MORTUARY. And beyond the door, a corridor floored with linoleum, brick-red to hide the stains. The attendant led him to an elevator and closed the metal grille with a crash. They descended.

'You're in luck. We burn them after a week. You're just in time. They'll be a bit ripe though, your friends.'

The attendant gave him a cigarette. It wasn't because of the dead – they weren't so bad – it was the sickly sweetness of the formaldehyde, the sting of disinfectant in your lungs. That was worse. The harshness of the smoke took Lom by surprise: it scoured his throat and clenched his lungs. He coughed.

'You going to puke?'

'Let's get on with it.'

The Cold Room was tiled in white and lit to a bright, gleaming harshness. Their breath flowered ghosts on the stark air.

'Anyone else been to see them?'

The attendant ran his finger down a column in a book on the desk by the door.

'Nope. Wait here.'

Lom dragged hard on the cigarette. Two, three, four times. It burned too quickly. A precarious length of ash built up, its core still burning. The cardboard was too thick.

The attendant came back pushing a steel trolley. A mounded shape lay on it, muffled by a thin, stained sheet.

'You'll have to help me with the giant,' he said. 'They're heavy bastards.'

Lom let his cigarette drop half-finished on the white-tiled floor, ground it out with his boot, and followed the attendant between heavy rubber curtains into the refrigerator room. Many bodies on trolleys were parked along the walls, but there was no mistaking the bulk of the giant on its flatbed truck. Lom took the head end and pushed.

'You can leave me,' he said when they were done. 'I'll let you know when I'm finished.'

Sheets pulled back, the two cadavers lay side by side, like father and son. What was he hoping to find? A clue. That's what detectives did. Dead bodies told you things. But these bodies were simply dead. Very.

He checked the record sheets. The man had been identified as Akaki

Serov. 'Male. Hair red. Dyed brown. Age app. 30–35.' The face had matched a photograph on a file somewhere: there was a serial number, a reference to the Gaukh Archive. The face on the trolley was unmarked apart from a few small cuts and puncture wounds, but nobody would recognise it now. The flesh was discoloured and collapsed, the lips withdrawn from the teeth in the speechless grin of death. The torso was swollen tight like a balloon. The blood had drained down to settle in his back and his buttocks. A wound in his neck was lipped with darkened, crusted ooze – a nether mouth, also speechless. There were no legs.

Lom hesitated. He should take fingerprints. He should prise the jaws open to check for secreted … what? … secrets. In life, he could have worked with him. Serov dyed his hair: he was vain, then. Or trying to change his appearance. Human things. Things Lom could use. Serov might have felt a grudge against someone. Taken a bribe. Feared pain. Something. That was how Lom interrogated people: seducing, cajoling, threatening, building a relationship, coming to a conclusion. But the dead told you nothing. It was their defining characteristic, the only thing that remained to them: being dead.

He turned to the other corpse.

The giant had been found by the empty strong-car. There was no name for this one, no photograph to match his face on a file, not much face left to match. His flesh was hard and waxy white. Bloodless. Between his legs, where his lower belly and genitals and thighs should have been, there was nothing. A gouged-out hollow. Ragged. Burned. Vacant. The front of his body was seared and puckered. Flash burns. And there was a gunshot wound in his face that had exploded the back of his skull.

The bullet was a puzzle. He must have been dying already – the entire middle part of his body blown to mush – but someone had taken the trouble to shoot him anyway. Why? A kindness? A silencing? A message for others to read? There were too many stories here. Too many possibilities were the same as none. They took you nowhere. The dead, being dead, were of no help.

Lom put his hands in his pockets, trying to warm them. The cold of the room was beginning to numb his face. He needed to get out of there.

Do something else. Pull on another thread.

16

Maroussia Shaumian climbed the familiar stairs to Lakoba Petrov's studio and pushed open the door. Grey daylight flooded the sparse, airy room. Gusts of rain clattered against the high north-facing windows. She knew the room well: its wide bleak intensity, its smell of paint and turpentine, uneaten food and stale clothing. She used to come here often.

Petrov had been working on Maroussia's portrait, on and off, for months. He was painting her nude, in reds and purples and shadowed blacks of savage energy, her body twisted away from the viewer in a violent torsion that revealed the side of one breast under the angle of her arm. A vase of flowers was falling across a tablecloth behind her, as if she had kicked the table in the violence of the movement that hid her face. Petrov had said it was an important work: he was using it to feel his way out of conventional, scholastic painting of the female form, searching for a way to express directly his dispassionate desire and his indifference to the suffocating conventions of love and beauty. But he had lost interest in painting her since he'd got involved with Kantor. He had changed, becoming distant and distracted. Maroussia had come there less and less, and finally not at all.

She had met Petrov at the Crimson Marmot Club, where she had started going in the evenings after work. She had gravitated towards the place because she felt obscurely hungry for new things. New ways of looking at the world. But the Marmot's had been disappointing: a refuge where artists and intellectuals gathered to drink and boast instead of work. Everyone there had tried to get inside her skirts. Everyone except Petrov.

'What do you want from this place?' he had asked her.

'I don't know,' she'd said seriously. 'Something. Anything. So long as it's new.'

'Is anything ever really new?' Petrov had said. 'The present only exists by reference to the past.' That was the kind of thing you said at the Marmot's.

Maroussia had frowned. 'The past is a better place than the present,' she said. 'The present is a bad place, and the future will be bad too. Unless we can start again. Unless we can find a new way.'

Petrov had laughed. 'You won't find anything new at the Marmot's. Look at them. Every one a poser, every one a hypocrite, every one a mountebank. They talk about the revolution of the modern, but all they're after is fame and money.'

'Are you like that?'

'Not me, no,' Petrov had said. 'I mean what I say. One must begin the revolution with oneself. One must remove all barriers and inhibitions within oneself first, before one can do work that is truly new. One must do all the things it is possible to do. Experience the extremes of life. I don't care what other people think about me: I want to shock *myself*.'

She had liked him then. She hadn't seen then the danger of his words, the literal seriousness of his desire to shock and destroy. They had met again at the Marmot's, several times, talking earnestly. Maroussia had wondered if they might become lovers, but it hadn't happened.

And now, he scarcely looked up when she came in. The studio was bitterly cold, but he was working regardless, in fingerless mittens and a woollen cap, the paint-spattered table at his side set out with jars and tubes and brushes. He painted hastily, with bold, rapid strokes, stabbing away at the immense canvas that towered above him.

'Lakoba?' said Maroussia. 'I wanted to ask you something.'

Petrov didn't look round.

'I will not paint you today,' he said. 'That picture is finished. They're all finished. This is the last.'

'What are you doing?' she said. 'Can I look?'

He shrugged indifferently and turned away to busy himself at the table. Maroussia stared up at the picture he had made. It was colossal, like nothing he had made before. At the centre of it was a giant, laid out on a black road, apparently dead, his head and feet bare, surrounded by six lighted candles, each set in a golden candlestick and burning with

a circle of orange light. A woman in a white skirt – suffering humanity – threw up her arms in grief. Dark, crooked buildings, roofed with
blood, loomed around them. Behind the roofs and taller than all the
buildings a man walked past, playing a violin. He seemed to be dancing.
The lurid yellow-green sky streamed with black clouds.

'This is good,' she said. 'Really good. It's different. Has it got a title?'

'It's Vaso,' he said. '*The Death of the Giant Vaso, Killed in a Bank
Raid.*' But he didn't look round. Her presence seemed to irritate him.

'Lakoba?' she said. 'I want to ask you something. It's important. I
want to find Raku Vishnik.'

Petrov didn't reply.

'Raku Vishnik,' she said again. 'I need to see him. He didn't come to
the Marmot's last night.' She paused, but he didn't answer. 'Lakoba?'

'What?' he said at last. 'What did you say?'

'Raku Vishnik. I need to find him. Quickly. I need his address.'

'Vishnik?' said Petrov vaguely. 'You won't find him during the daytime. He wanders. He always wanders. He's on the streets somewhere.
He walks.'

'Where then? He wasn't at the Marmot's.'

'No. I haven't seen him there. Not for weeks.'

'Where then?'

'You must go to his apartment. At night. Late at night. Very late.'

'What's his address?'

'What?'

'Vishnik's address? Where does he live?'

'Oh,' said Petrov vaguely. 'He's on Pelican Quay. I don't know the
house. Ask the dvorniks.'

For the first time he turned to look at her. Maroussia was shocked
by how different he looked. He had changed so much in the weeks
that had passed. His hair was wild and matted, but his face was illuminated with a strange intense distracted clarity. His pupils were dilated,
wide and dark. He was staring avidly at the world, and at her, but he
wasn't seeing what was there: he was looking *through* her, beyond her,
towards some future only he could see. And he stank. Now that he was
close to her, she was aware that his breath was bad, his clothes smelled
of sourness and sweat.

'Something's wrong, Lakoba,' she said. 'What is it?'

Petrov opened his mouth to speak again but did not. He looked as if his brain was fizzing with images … ideas … words … purpose – what he must do. But he could say nothing. He tried, but he could not.

'Lakoba?' Maroussia said again. 'What's wrong?'

'Go,' he said at last. 'You have to go now.'

'Why? What's happened?'

'You have to go.'

'Why?'

'I want you to go. I won't need you again. Don't come here again. Not any more.'

'What are you talking about? What have I done?'

'Everything is finished now. I am leaving it behind.'

'Where are you going?'

'There is no more to say. No more words. Words are finished now. Personal things don't matter any more: my personal life is dead, and soon my body will also die.'

'Lakoba—'

'Go. Just go.'

Maroussia left Petrov to his empty room and the immense dead giant. Once again, for the second time in as many days, she walked away from a door that had closed against her. She didn't want to go to work, and she didn't want to go home – not home to her mother, trapped in quiet shadow, waiting silently, too terrified to leave the room, too terrified to look out of the window, too terrified to open the cupboards, too terrified to move at all – she didn't want to go anywhere. But it was still early, not even afternoon: she would have to wait till night to go to Raku Vishnik's. Vishnik might tell her about the Pollandore. He was the historian. He might know.

17

That morning, after Lom left, Raku Vishnik went to the Apraksin Bazaar. He liked the Apraksin, with its garish din and aromatic confusion, its large arcades and sagging balconies of shopfronts and stalls, the central atrium of market sellers and coffee kiosks. Areas of the Apraksin were reserved for different trades: silver, spices, rugs, clothes, shoes, umbrellas, papers and inks, rope and cordage, parts for motors and appliances, tools, chairs, tobacco, marble slabs. Poppy. One distant corner for stolen goods. And at the very top, under a canopy of glass, was an indoor garden littered with unwanted broken statuary: a dog, a child on a bench, a stained sleeping polar bear. Katya's Alley.

Vishnik wandered from stall to stall, floor to floor, making lists, drawing sketches, taking photographs, picking up discarded bits of stuff – a tram ticket, a dropped theatre programme. He recorded it all.

Mirgorod, graveyard of dreams.

He had roamed back and forth like this across the city every day for more than a year, a satchel slung over his shoulder with a fat oilskin notebook, a mechanical pencil, a collection of maps and a camera. The official historian of Mirgorod. He took his duties seriously, even if no one else did. He was systematically mining the alleyways, the streets, the prospects. Blue–green verdigrised domes. Cupolas. Pinnacles. Towers. Statues of horsemen and angels. The Opera. The Sea Station. The Chesma. The Obovodniy Bridge. It all went into his notebooks and onto his maps. He noted the smell of linden trees in the spring and the smell of damp moss under the bridges in the autumn. He photographed chalk scrawlings on the walls, torn advertisements, drinking fountains, the patterns made by telephone wires against the sky. A wrought-iron clock tower with four faces under a dome.

What he found was strangeness. Vishnik had come to see that the whole city was like a work of fiction: a book of secrets, hints and signs. A city in a mirror. Every detail was a message, written in mirror writing.

A wrong turning has been taken. Everything is fucked.

As he worked through the city week by week and month by month, he found it shifting. Slippery. He would map an area, but when he returned to it, it would be different: doorways that had been bricked up were open now; shops and alleyways that he'd noted were no longer there, and others were in their place, with all the appearance of having been there for years. It was as if there was another city, present but mostly invisible, a city that showed itself and then hid. He was being teased – stalked – by the visible city's wilder, playful twin, which set him puzzles, clues and acrostics: manifestations which hinted at the meaning they obscured.

Tying myself in knots, that's what I'm doing. There must be cause and pattern somewhere. I'm a historian: finding cause and pattern is what I do. And it's here, but I can't see it. I just can't fucking see it.

Vishnik was hunting traces: the trail of vanished enterprise, the hint of occupations yet to come, the scent of possibilities haunting the present. Such as this jeweller and watchmaker, whose wooden sign of business (S. LARKOV) was fixed over – but didn't completely cover – the larger inscription in bottle green on purple tiling RUDOLF GOTMAN – BOOKSELLER – PERIODICALS – FINE BINDINGS. Vishnik noted Gotman's advertisement on his plan of the Apraksin and took out his camera to photograph the palimpsest vitrine.

'You. What do you want? What are you doing?'

Oh my fuck. Not again.

A small man – slick black hair, round face polished to a high sheen – had come out of the shop. S. Larkov. He wore gold half-moon glasses on his nose and a gold watch chain across his tight waistcoat. Expandable polished-steel sleeve suspenders gripped his narrow biceps, making the crisp white cotton of his shirtsleeves balloon.

'I said, what are you doing?'

'Taking pictures,' said Vishnik, and offered him a card.

Prof. Raku Andreievich Vishnik
Historian of Mirgorod
City Photographer
231 Pelican Quay, Apt. 4
Vandayanka
Big Side
Mirgorod

The jeweller brushed it aside. 'This means nothing. Who photographs such places? Who makes maps of them?'

'I do,' said Vishnik.

'I'll tell you who. Spies. Terrorists. Agents of the Archipelago. Here, give me that!' He grabbed for the camera. Vishnik snatched it back out of his grip.

'Listen, you fuck. I'm a historian—'

Larkov's face was stiff with hatred. His tiny eyes as tight and sharp and cramped as the cogwheels in the watches he picked over at his bench.

'What if you are? Your sort are disgusting. Parasites. Intelligentsia. Only looking after their own. The Novozhd will—'

People were coming out of the neighbouring shops. Larkov made another snatch at the camera and missed, but caught the strap of Vishnik's satchel.

'Stay where you are. I haven't finished with you. Intellectual!' The man propelled the word into Vishnik's face, spattering him with warm spittle.

'You piss off,' said Vishnik. 'Piss away off.'

He jerked the satchel away from Larkov.

'Gendarme! Gendarme! Stop the bastard!'

Vishnik saw a green uniform coming from the other direction. Time to go.

18

From the mortuary Lom found his way eventually, via many corridors and stairs, to the Central Registry of the Lodka. He had wanted to see this place for years, and when he found it he stopped a moment in the entrance, taking it in.

It was a vast circular hall, floored with flagstones, ringed by tiers of galleries, roofed with a dome of glass and iron. It had the airy stillness of a great library and the smell of wood polish and ageing paper that a library has. Rows of readers' desks radiated outwards from the hub of the room like the spokes of a wheel. Each desk had a blue-shaded electric lamp of brass, a blue blotter, a chair upholstered in blue leather. Three thousand readers could work there at once, though not more than a tenth of that number was present now, bent in quiet study.

At the centre of the vast hall, rising more than a hundred feet high, almost to the underside of the dome, was the Gaukh Engine. Lom had seen a photograph of it once. It had been beautiful in the picture, but nothing prepared him for the reality. It was immense. An elegant nested construction of interlinked vertical wheels of steel and polished wood carried, like fairground wheels, dozens of heavy gondolas. The whole machine was in constant motion, its wheels turning and stopping and turning. The murmuring of its electric motors gave the hall a quiet, restful air.

A woman – pink arms, a round red face, hair wound in braids about her head, a white sweater under her uniform tunic – was watching him.

'Yes?' she said. 'Can I help?'

'I'm looking for a file,' said Lom. 'Name of Kantor. I haven't been here before.'

The archivist came around from behind the desk. She was shorter and wider than he had thought. There were crumbs in the lap of her skirt.

'Follow me,' she said.

She led him to one of the control desks. There were two arrays of lettered keys, like the keyboards of two typewriters.

'This one is for surnames, and this is for code names. Enter the first three letters of the name you want, then press the button and the engine will bring the correct gondola. Gondolas contain index cards. When you find the one you're looking for, copy the reference number in the top right corner and bring it to me. The index is phonetic, not alphabetical – sometimes a name is only overheard, and the spelling is uncertain. Cards are colour coded: yellow for students, green for anarchists, purple for nationalists, and so on. It's all here.' She showed him a hand-coloured legend pinned to the desk.

'How many cards do you have here?'

'Thirty-five million. Approximately.'

Lom keyed in the letters. K A N. Pressed the button. The wheels turned slowly, until the right car stopped in front of him. He lifted the hinged lid to reveal tray after tray of cards suspended from racks on an axle. He spun through the racks. There was a half-tray of Kantors, generations of them, but only two Josefs with a birth date in the last half-century. One card was white, indicating a minor public official included for completeness, against whom nothing was known. The other was lavender, creased and dog-eared, cross-referenced to at least twenty separate code names. Lom noted the reference on a slip of paper from the pad provided and handed it in.

While the archivist was gone, Lom wandered around the hall. There were card index cabinets, rows of guard-book catalogues. Newspapers, periodicals, journals, directories, maps, atlases, gazetteers, timetables. The publications, proceedings and membership lists of every organis-ation and society. The records of universities, technical colleges and schools. Galleries rose up to the domed ceiling. Swing doors led to the specialised archives and collections: keys, said a notice, could be col-lected from the desk by the holder of appropriate authorisation.

The foundation of any security organisation is its archives. That was what Commander Chazia had said in her address to the assembled police and militia of the Podchornok Oblast the previous year. Lom and Ziller had arrived late to find the room over-filled and over-hot. They had to stand at the back, craning to get a decent view between the bullet heads of a pair of gendarmes from Siflosk. Deputy Laurits had made a long and unctuous speech of welcome. The visit of the great Lavrentina Chazia, head of Vlast Secret Police, in all her pomp, was a momentous occasion, a moment for the provincial service to feel close to the heart of the great machinery of the Vlast.

Chazia had dominated the room: a small woman but, standing on the simple stage at the front of the hall, a pillar of air and energy, pale and intense, neat and slender and upright, her voice carrying effortlessly to the back of the hall. She had drawn and held the attention of every man there. *We are hers*, they found themselves thinking. *We are her soldiers. We are working for her.*

The reports they provided *mattered*, that was Chazia's message to them: they were *used*; they had to be done *right*. Lom listened intently as she unfolded the process by which raw intelligence from across the Dominions of the Vlast was gathered and sifted. It was a huge undertaking, rigorous, elegant, thorough: beautifully simple in its conception, dizzying in its scale and reach.

The Vlast's information machine was in fact three machines, or rather it was a machine in three parts: that was how Chazia expounded it. First, there was the soft machine, the flesh machine, the machine of many humans. They were the Outer Agents: uniformed policemen, plain-clothes detectives, infiltrators and provocateurs – tens if not hundreds of thousands of them – watching and listening, collecting information about the political activities, opinions and social connections of the population. The Outer Agents used direct observation, and they also employed their own informants – dvorniks, tram drivers, schoolteachers, children. Their primary targets were the shifting and fissile groups of dissidents, separatists, anarchists, nationalists, democrats, nihilists, terrorists, insurgents and countless other dangerous sects and cults that sought to undermine the Vlast. Naturally they also collected an enormous amount of collateral intelligence on the families, neighbours and associates of such people, and on public servants and prominent citizens generally, for the purposes of cross-reference, elimination and potential future usefulness.

The soft machine fed the second machine, the paper machine: tons and tons of paper; miles of paper; paper stored in the dark cavernous stacks that ramified through the basements and inner recesses of the Lodka. Nothing was thrown away: nothing had ever been thrown away in the history of the centuries-long surveillance. The technicians of the paper machine were the archivists and code breakers and, at the pinnacle of the hierarchy, the analysts. It was they who, working from summary observation sheets, prepared the semi-magical *Circles of Contact*. Finding cadres, plots and secret cells in the teeming mass of the population was harder than finding needles in haystacks. *Circles of Contact* was how you did it. You began by writing a name – the Subject – at the centre of a large sheet of paper and drawing a circle around it. Then you drew spokes radiating from the circle, and at the end of each spoke you put the name of one of the Subject's contacts or associates. The more frequent or closer the contact, the thicker the connecting spoke. Each associated name then became the centre of its own circle, a new node in its own right, and the process was repeated. The idea was to find the patterns – connections – linked loops – that would crystallise out of seemingly inchoate lists of names and dates and demonstrate the presence of a tightly knit but secretive connection. Lom found it exhilarating. It was like focusing a microscope lens and seeing some tiny malignant creature swimming in a bath of fluid. This was why he had become a policeman. To understand the pattern, to find the alien cruelty at its heart, to cut it out.

And the third machine, Chazia had said, the heart and brain of the operation, was the machine of steel and electricity: the famous Gaukh Engine, right at the heart of the Lodka. And now Lom was standing in its shadow.

The archivist came back.

'The material you ordered is unavailable,' she said.

'What does that mean?'

'It means you can't have it. You don't have the appropriate authorisation.'

'Where do I get authorisation? I mean urgently. I mean now.'

'This material is stored in Commander Chazia's personal archive. They are her personal papers, and her personal permission is required. In writing. I'm sorry, Investigator. There's nothing I can do.'

'Thank you,' he said. 'Thank you. I'm grateful for your help.'

Shit.
I'm running out of threads.
Pull another one.

19

The tattered pelmet of an awning fluttered in the wind. It was the colour of leather. Florid script crawled across it. *Bakery. Galina Tropina. Confections. Coff—.*

Vishnik went in.

The woman behind the counter frowned at him. She had arms the colour and texture of uncooked pastry, and her hair was artificially curled, sticky-looking, dyed a brash, desiccated copper. There were a couple of empty tables at the back.

'I would like coffee,' said Vishnik. 'Strong, please. And aquavit. A small glass of that. Plum. Thank you.'

His legs were trembling. He was getting sensitive: things were getting to him more than they should. *I've been spending too much time on my own.* He used to like being alone, when he was young. But that was a different kind of loneliness: the solitude of the only child who knows that he is free and safe and loved. That was the rich, enchanted solitude of *Before*. Before the purge of the last aristocrats, when the militia had come winkling them out of the obscure burrows they had made for themselves in their distant country estates.

That was a different world. The storms smashed it long ago. All I am now is fucking memories. I move through life facing backwards.

He checked the camera. It was a precise, purposeful thing. A Kono. When he was growing up in Vyra, a camera was a hefty contraption of wood and brass and leather bellows, which required a solid and man-high mahogany tripod to hold it steady. But the Kono was matte black metal, about the size of his notebook, and sat comfortably in the palm of his hand, satisfyingly solid and weighty. Vishnik had built a darkroom in the kitchen of his apartment, where he developed his own films and made his own prints, which he kept in boxes. Many, many boxes.

A girl came into the bakery and put a basket of provisions on the counter. Her black dress fell loosely from her narrow, bony shoulders. Her fine strengthless hair had parted at the back to show the pale nape of her neck. She wore thick grey stockings and scuffed, awkward shoes. The woman behind the counter smiled at her. The smile was a sunburst of love, extraordinary, generous and good, and in the moment of that smile it happened: the surface of the world split open, spilling potential, spilling possibility, spilling the hidden truth of things.

The sheen of the zinc counter top separated itself and slid upwards and sideways, a detached plane of reflective colour, splashed with the vivid blues and greens of the tourist posters on the opposite wall. The hot-water urn opened its eyes and grinned. The floorboards turned red–gold and began to curl and writhe. The woman's arms were flat, biscuity, her hands floated free, dancing with poppy-seed rolls to the tune of the gusting rain, and the girl in the black dress was floating in the air, face downwards, bumping against the ceiling, singing 'The Sailor's Sorrow' in a thin, clear voice.

O Mirgorod, O Mirgorod,
Sweet city of rain and dreams.
Wait for me, wait for me,
And I'll come back.

Cautiously, slowly, so as not to disturb the limpid surface of the moment, Vishnik raised his camera to his eye and released the shutter. He wound the film on slowly – cautiously – with his thumb and took another. And another. Then he opened his notebook and began to write, spilling words quickly and fluently across the page.

The Pollandore, buried beneath a great and populous upper cata-comb of stone in the heart of the city, waits, revolving.
In darkness, but having its own light, it turns on its axis slowly. Swelling and subsiding. Gently.
Like a heart.
Like a lung.
Like respiration.

Every so often – more frequently now, perhaps, but who could measure that? – somewhere inside it – deep within its diminutive immensity – a miniscule split fissures slightly wider – a cracking – barely audible, had there been anyone to hear it (there wasn't) – the faintest spill of light and earthy perfume.

Almost nothing, really.

The egg of time, ripening.

20

L om stopped in front of the Armoury and looked up. Narrow and needle-sharp, the One Column on Spilled Blood speared a thousand feet high out of the roof. The militia was head-quartered at the Armoury, not the Lodka, a distinction they carefully maintained. Being both soldiers and police, yet not exactly either, the militia considered themselves an elite within the security service, the Novozhd's killers of choice.

He climbed the splay of shallow steps and pushed his way through heavy brass-furnished doors into a place of high ceilings; black and white tiled floors; cool, shadowed air; the echoes of footsteps; the smell of polish, sweat, uniforms and old paper. There were texts on the walls, not the exhortations and propaganda that encrusted the city, but the core tenets of the committed Vlast.

ALL THAT IS COMING IS HERE ALREADY.

HISTORY IS THE UNFOLDING OF THE CLOTH, BUT THE CLOTH HAS ALREADY BEEN CUT AND EVERY STITCH SEWN.

A clerk behind a high counter was watching him.

'I'm looking for Major Safran,' said Lom

'Just missed him. He left about ten minutes ago.'

'How do I find him?'

'Try the stables. He'll be with the mudjhik. Never goes home without saying goodbye.'

The stables, when he found them, were a separate block on the far side of the parade ground. The doors, fifteen feet high and made of solid heavy planks, stood open. Lom stepped inside and found himself in a high-ceilinged hall of stone: slit windows near the roof; unwarmed shadows and dustmotes in the air. It didn't smell like stables. No straw. No leather. No horse shit. The mudjhik was standing motionless at the far end of the hall, in shadow. A militia man was sitting at its feet, his back against the wall.

'I'm looking for Major Safran.'

'That's me.'

Lom took a step forward. The mudjhik stirred.

'Come on,' said Safran. 'He'll be still.'

The mudjhik was a dull red in the dim light, the colour of bricks and old meat. Taller than any giant Lom had seen, and solider, squarer: a statue of rust-coloured angel stone, except it wasn't a statue. Lom felt the dark energy of its presence. Its watchfulness. The mudjhik's intense, disinterested, eyeless gaze passed across him and the sliver of angel stuff in Lom's forehead tingled in response. It was like putting the tip of his tongue on the nub of a battery cell: the same unsettled sourness, the same metallic prickling. The same false implication of being alive.

Safran waited for Lom to come to him. He was about thirty years old, perhaps, smooth shaven, his hair clipped short and so fair it was almost colourless. His uniform was crisp and neat. A small, tight knot tied his necktie. Without the uniform he could have been anything: a teacher, a civil servant, an interrogator: the joylessly nutritious, right-thinking staple of the Vlast. And yet there was something else. Safran seemed ... *awakened*. The life-desire of the mudjhik glimmered in his wash-pale eyes. His slender hands moved restlessly at his side, and the mudjhik's own hands echoed the movement faintly. And there was the angel seal, the third blank eye, in the front of his head.

'Well? I've got five minutes.'

Lom took off his cap. Letting Safran see his own seal set in his brow.

Safran grunted. 'You can feel him then.'

'It's watching me?'

'Of course.'

Lom looked up into the mudjhik's face. Except it had no face, only a rough and eyeless approximation of one. It wasn't looking anywhere in particular, not with its head sockets, but it was looking at him.

'They call them dead,' Safran was saying, 'and they use them like pieces of meat and rock, but that's not right, is it? You'd know what I mean.'

'Would I?'

'We know, people like you and me. The angel stuff is in us. We know they're not dead.'

Lom stepped up to the mudjhik and placed his hand on its heavy thigh. It was smooth to the touch, and warm.

'Is it true,' he said, 'that it contains the brain and spinal cord of a dead animal?'

'You shouldn't touch him. He has his own mind. He acts quickly.'

'With a dead cat for a brain?'

Lom didn't remove his hand. He was probing the mudjhik, as it was probing him. He encountered the distant pulse of awareness. Like colours, but not.

'Not cat,' said Safran. 'Dog. It's in there somewhere, but it's not important. You really should step away.'

It was like being nudged by a shunting engine. Lom didn't see it move, but suddenly he was lying on his back, breath rasping, mouth gaping, hot shards of pain in his ribs. Safran was standing over him, looking down.

Lom rolled over and rose to his knees, head down, retching sour spittle onto the floor. No blood. That was something. He felt the mudjhik pushing fingers of awareness into his nose, his throat, his chest.

Stop!

Lom repelled the intrusion, slamming back at it hard. He wasn't sure how he knew what to do, but he did. He felt the mudjhik's surprise. And Safran's.

Lom hauled himself unsteadily to his feet, wiping his mouth with the back of his hand.

'You're a crazy man,' said Safran.

Lom was becoming aware of the link between Safran and the mudjhik. There was a flow between them, a cord of shared awareness.

'Did you make it do that?'

'That's not how it works.'

'But you could have stopped it.'

'I don't know. Maybe. I didn't try.'

'And if I hit you, what would it do?'

'Defend me.'

'I saw your picture in the paper.'

'What are you talking about?'

'Levrovskaya Square. You were getting a handshake from a bank. I wasn't sure what for.'

'Protecting the money.'

'But you didn't. Thirty million roubles disappeared from under your nose.'

Lom was rubbing his chest and pressing his ribs experimentally. The pain made him wince but nothing felt broken. The mudjhik had judged it just right.

'It might have been worse,' said Safran. 'They didn't get into the bank.'

'They weren't trying to. The strong-car was the target.'

'Maybe. Maybe not. The bank was happy. It wasn't their money. Hadn't been delivered.'

'You were waiting for them. You must have known they were coming.'

'So?'

'You could have stopped it. You were meant to let them get away.'

'You should be careful, making accusations like that.' The mudjhik took a step forward. 'People have been killed wandering about in here. Accidents. It's dangerous around mudjhiks if they don't know you.'

'Were you paid off?'

'What's your name, Investigator?'

'Lom. My name is Lom.'

'And who are you working for, Lom? Who are you with? Does anyone know you're here?'

'You could buy a lot of militia for thirty million roubles.'

'And you should piss off.'

'So how did you know they were coming?'

'Detective work.'

'You had an informant. Someone in the gang, maybe. Who was it?'

'Don't they teach you the rules where you come from, Lom? What's the rule of informants? The first rule?'

Never reveal the name. Not even to your own director. Even you, you yourself, must forget his name for ever. Remember only the cryptonym. One careless word will ruin both your lives for ever.

'You're in trouble, Major. Corruptly receiving bribes. Standing aside to let thirty million roubles go missing.'

'You couldn't prove that. Even if it was true, which it isn't.'

'You were following orders then. Whose? Tell me whose.'

'Shit. You're not joking are you.'

'You want to stay a major for ever?'

'What?'

'Taking bribes is one thing. But nobody likes the ones that get caught. It's not competent. It's not commanding officer material.'

'I should kill you myself.'

The mudjhik's feet moved. A sound like millstones grinding.

'But you won't. You don't know who I'm working for. You don't know who sent me. You think I'm here for the hell of it?'

'Who?'

'No.'

Safran shrugged and looked at his watch.

'There was no informant.'

'Yes, there was.'

'No, there really wasn't. It was just some drunk. I have people who make it their business to be amenable in the bars where the artists go. They keep their ears open. It's not hard. Artists are always pissed. Neurotic. Boastful. Shutting them up is the hard thing. Anyway, there was this particular one, highly strung even in that company. Mild enough sober, but he likes a brandy and opium mix, and after a few of those he starts abusing anyone in range.'

'And?'

'So one evening this idiot starts broadcasting to the world that he's mixed up with some great nationalist hero, and he's got a sack full of bombs. You should all be shit scared of me, that was his line. One day soon there's going to be a rampage. He tells everyone how he and his new friends are going to rob a strong-car when it makes a delivery to a particular bank he mentions. Turned out it was true.'

'The name?'

'Curly-haired fellow. A woman's man. Studio somewhere in the quarter. I broke in to have a look. It stank. Obscene pictures too.'

'The name.'

'Petrov. Lakoba Petrov.'

21

Lom wanted to go back into the Registry to see if there was a file on Petrov, but when he got there he found the doors shut against him. The Gaukh Engine was closed to readers for the rest of the day. Shit. He looked at his watch. It was just past four. He considered going to his office, but what was the point? It occurred to him that he hadn't eaten since breakfast. To eat he needed money, and for that he needed Krogh.

Krogh's private secretary was in the outer office. He made a show of closing the file he was reading – *Not for your eyes, Lom* – and stood up. Making the most of his height advantage.

'Ah. Investigator Lom.'

'Nice office you got me,' said Lom. 'Thanks.'

'Thought you'd appreciate it. How's the Kantor case going? Anything to report?'

'Not to you.'

The private secretary picked up the desk diary.

'I can fit you in with the Under Secretary this evening. He's very busy. But I can find a space. As soon as you like, in fact. Soon as you're ready, Investigator. Just say the word.'

'I need money.'

The private secretary sat down and leaned back, hands behind his head.

'I see. Why?'

'Because I do this for a job. The idea is I get paid for it. Also, expenses.'

'Have you discussed an imprest with the Under Secretary? As I said, I can fit you in.'

'No. You do it. Sign something. Open the cash tin. I need two hundred roubles. Now.'

'What expenses, actually?'

'Rent.'

'But you're staying with your friend, aren't you. The good citizen Professor Vishnik at Pelican Quay. The dvornik there is a conscientious worker, not the type to be browbeaten, or bribed come to that. I have the Vishnik file with me now, as it happens.' He picked up a folder from his desk and made a show of leafing through it. 'His terms of employment at the university are rather irregular, I feel.'

Lom leaned forward and rested his hands on the desk.

'Vishnik's my friend. Something happens to him, I'll know who to come and see about it. Just give me some money, Secretary. I don't intend to live off my friends, or steal food, and I don't intend to pay bribes for informants out of my own pocket. Especially not unreliable ones.'

The private secretary gave him a friendly grin.

'Of course, Investigator. Anything for the Under Secretary's personal police force.'

'And who,' said a woman's voice behind Lom, 'is this fellow, to get special treatment?'

It was Lavrentina Chazia. Commander of the Secret Police.

'This is Investigator Lom, Commander,' the private secretary said. 'He is doing sterling work for the Under Secretary. On provincial liaison.'

Lom wondered whether he had imagined an ironic note in the private secretary's reply: some hidden meaning, some moment of understanding that had passed between him and Chazia. Whatever, Chazia was examining him shrewdly, and he returned the gaze. Indeed, it was hard not to stare. She was changed, much changed, since he had seen her last. The sharpness and predatory energy were the same, but there was something wrong with her skin. Dark patches mottled her face and neck. They were on her hands as well: smooth markings, hard and faintly bluish under the office light. He recognised the colour – it was in his own forehead – it was angel skin. But he had never seen anything quite like this. There had been rumours even in Podchornok that Chazia had been working with the angel-flesh technicians, experimenting, pushing at the boundaries. Lom hadn't paid them much attention, but it seemed they were true.

'So,' said Chazia, 'this is the notorious Lom. You're from Podchornok, aren't you?'

Lom was surprised.

'That's right,' he said. 'I'm flattered. I'd hardly have expected someone like you – I mean, in your position—'

'Oh I know everything, Investigator. Everything that happens in the service is my business.' Again Lom had the uneasy feeling that she meant more than she said. Her pale narrow eyes glittered with a strange energy that was more than confidence. Something almost like relish. Hunger. 'For example,' Chazia continued, 'I know that you were over at the Armoury this afternoon. Talking with Major Safran. No doubt you were ... *liaising* with him.'

Lom felt his stomach lurch. The private secretary was watching him curiously. Lom felt ... lost. Stupid. That was what he was supposed to feel, of course. Chazia was playing with him. It occurred to him that she hadn't turned up in Krogh's office by chance. She was showing herself to him. Letting him know who his enemies were. But why? What did it mean? Some political thing between her and Krogh that had nothing to do with him? Possibly.

'Safran and I are both products of Savinkov's,' he said, indicating the lozenge of angel stuff in his head. 'I don't get many chances to compare notes.'

He wondered whether Chazia had already talked to Safran herself, whether she knew of his interest in the Levrovskaya Square robbery, and Petrov. But there was no way to read her expression.

'Of course,' she said. 'I hope you got something out of it.' She smiled, showing sharp even teeth, and her pale eyes flashed again, but her face showed little expression, as if the patches of angel stuff had stiffened it somehow. The effect made Lom feel even more queasy. Out of his depth. He was relieved when she had gone.

22

Lom took a tram back to Vishnik's apartment.

The private secretary had signed him a chit. It took Lom more than an hour to find the office where he could get it cashed. It was only twenty roubles.

'I'd give you more, Investigator,' he had said. 'If I could. But this is the limit of my delegated expenditure authority.' He didn't even try to pretend this was true. 'Of course, if you'd prefer to see the Under Secretary ...'

At least now he had cash in his pocket. He stopped off on the way back to Pelican Quay and bought some onions, lamb, a box of pastries and a couple of bottles of plum brandy. Vishnik wouldn't take rent, but it was something.

When he got to the apartment, Vishnik was waiting for him, full of energy, strangely exultant, dressed to go out. Lom sat on the couch and started to pull his boots off. He shoved the bag of shopping towards Vishnik with his foot.

'Here. Dinner.'

'This is no time for fucking eating, my friend,' said Vishnik. 'It's only six. We'll go out. I want to take you to the Dreksler-Kino.'

'Another day maybe. I've got to work.'

'What work, exactly?'

'Thinking.'

'Think at the Dreksler. You can't be in Mirgorod and not see the Dreksler. It's a wonder, a fucking wonder of the world. And today is Angelfall Day. '

Lom sighed. 'OK. Why not.'

Lom didn't wear his uniform. On the crowded tram he and Vishnik were the only passengers without one. The Dreksler-Kino was draped with fresh new flags and banners, red and gold. Its immense marble dome was awash with floodlight. Vertical searchlights turned the clouds overhead into a vast liquescent ceiling that swelled and shifted, shedding fine drifts of rain. Inside, twenty thousand seats, ranged in blocks and tiers and galleries, faced a great waterfall of dim red velvet curtain. The auditorium was crowded to capacity. A woman with a flashlight and a printed floor plan led them to their seats, and almost immediately the houselights dimmed. Twenty thousand people became an intimate private crowd, together in the dark.

There were cartoons, and then the newsreel opened with a mass rally at the Sports Palace, intercut with scenes from the southern front. The war was going well, said the calm, warm voice of the commentator. On the screen, artillery roared and kicked up churned mud. Columns of troops marched past the camera, waving, smoking cigarettes, grinning. *Citizen! Stand tall! The drum of war thunders and thunders!* The crowd cheered.

The commentator was reading a poem over scenes of wind moving across grassy plains; factories; columns of lorries and tanks.

In snow-covered lands – in fields of wheat –
In roaring factories –
Ecstatic and on fire with happy purpose –
With you in our hearts, dear Novozhd –
We work – we fight –
We march to Victory!

There was stomping, jeering and whistling when the screen showed aircraft of the Archipelago being shot down over the sea. Corkscrews of oil-black smoke followed the silver specks down to a final silent blossoming of spray.

A familiar avuncular face filled the screen. The face that watched daily from a hundred, a thousand posters, newspapers and books. The Novozhd, with his abundant moustache and the merry smile in his eye.

Citizens of the Vlast, prepare yourselves for an important statement.

He's looking older, thought Lom. Must be over sixty by now. Thirty years since he grabbed power in the Council and gave the Vlast his famous kick up the arse. *The Great Revitalisation*. Eight years since he re-opened the war with the Archipelago. Three decades of iron kindness. *I go the way the angels dictate with the confidence of a sleepwalker.*

In the Dreksler-Kino everyone rose to salute, and all across the Dominions of the Vlast people were doing the same.

'Citizens,' the Novozhd began, leaning confidingly towards the camera. 'My brothers and sisters, my friends. It is now three hundred and seventy-eight years exactly, to the hour, since the first of the angels fell to us. There and then, in the Ouspenskaya Marsh, our history began. From that event, all that we have and all that we are, our great and eternal Vlast itself, took root and grew. We all know the story. I remember my mother when she used to sit by my bed and tell it to me. I was a child then, eyes wide with wonderment.'

The auditorium was in absolute silence. The Novozhd had never spoken in such intimate and fraternal terms before.

'My mother told me how our Founder came to see for himself this marvellous being that had tumbled out of the night sky. And when he came, our Founder didn't only see the angel, he saw the future. Some say the angel spoke to him before he died. The Founder himself left no testimony on that count, so we must say we don't know if it's true, although ...' The Novozhd paused and looked the camera in the eye. 'I know what I believe.' A murmur of assent and a trickle of quiet applause brushed across the crowd. 'On that day,' the Novozhd was saying, 'the Founder saw the shape of the Vlast as it could be. From the ice in the north to the ice in the south, from eastern forest to western sea, one Truth. One Greatness. That's what the first angel gave us, my friends, and paid for with the price of his death.'

Lom had looked up synonyms of Vlast once. They filled almost half a column. Ascendancy. Domination. Rule. Lordship. Mastery. Grasp. Rod. Control. Command. Power. Authority. Governance. Arm. Hand. Grip. Hold. Government. Sway. Reign. Dominance. Dominion. Office. Nation.

'You know this, friends,' the Novozhd was saying. 'Your mothers told you, just as mine told me. And this isn't all. Something else came to us with the first angel, and it kept on coming as other angels tumbled down to us like ripened fruit falling out of the clear sky.'

'All of them dead,' whispered Vishnik. 'Every single fucking one of them dead.'

'Brave warrior heroes,' the Novozhd was saying, 'fallen in the battles that broke the moon. Giving their lives in the eternal justified war. A war that wasn't – and isn't – against flesh and blood enemies, but against powers, against hidden principalities, against the rulers of the present darkness that surrounds us.

'And what else did the angels bring us? Didn't they give us the Gift of Certain Truth? Try to imagine, my brothers and sisters, my friends. Imagine if you can what it must have been like to live in this world before the first angelfall, when people like us looked up at the night sky and wondered – only wondered! – what might be there. They knew nothing. They could only guess and dream. Speculation, ignorance and superstition. Dark, terrible times. Until we were freed from all that. The long cloudy Ages of Doubt were closed. We were given incontrovertible, imperishable, touchable EVIDENCE. Ever since the first angelfall, we have KNOWN.' The Novozhd half-stood in his chair and smacked his fist into this palm. 'KNOWN! On this day, three hundred and seventy-eight years ago, the first of the Years of the True and Certain Justified Vlast began! May we live for ever in the wing-shadow of the angels!'

Roars from the twenty thousand. Shouting. Crowds on their feet, stamping. On the screen the image of the Novozhd paused, anticipating the ovation now being shouted and sung across five time zones. After a suitable period he raised his hand. Acknowledging, calming, requiring silence.

'And today a new chapter is beginning.'

The audience fell quiet. This was something different.

'We have been fighting our own war, friends, which is part of the great war of the angels, and not different from it. We too have been fighting against hidden powers and unsanctified principalities. The Archipelago – the islands of the Outsiders – the Unacknowledged and Unaccepted Lands – where no angels have ever fallen. Where even their existence is not taken for certain and true.

'Many brave warriors of the Vlast have fallen in the struggle. I know them all, I have felt the anguish of each one, and I've cried your tears – you who are listening to me now and thinking of your own sons and daughters, brothers, sisters, fathers, mothers, comrades and friends. Let's remember the fallen today. We owe them an unpayable debt. Don't be ashamed to weep for them sometimes. I do. But praise them also.

'I know you all. I am your friend as you are mine. The angels know you too. Friends, I am here to tell you that the time of Victory is close! The Archipelago is sending an ambassador to Mirgorod to sue for peace with us. The enemy weakens and tires. The light of truth dawns in their eyes. Yes, my friends. Victory draws near. One last push! One last supreme effort! The great day is soon.

'I want you to hear this from my own lips. Pay close attention now and remember. On this very day of Truth and Light I want you to hear it and be sure. Your love is with me. Our victory will be absolute and total. With the Truth of the Angel clear in our minds it cannot be otherwise. Goodnight.'

The image of the Novozhd at his desk faded out, replaced by a full close-up of his face. He was outside now. The sunshine was in his face, making him crinkle the corners of his eyes in laughter lines. A breeze teased his hair. As the opening bars of the 'Friendship Song' began to play, the words started scrolling slowly up the screen and twenty thousand voices sang.

> All join in our song about him –
> About our beloved – our Novozhd!
> And us his true friends –
> The people – his friends!
> Count us? You cannot!
> No more could you count
> The water in the sea!
> All join in our song about him!

'Fuck,' said Vishnik as they filed out slowly into the rain. 'We need a drink.'

23

It was almost midnight. After the Dreksler-Kino, Vishnik had dragged Lom to a bar where they drank thin currant wine. He would have stayed there all night if Lom hadn't insisted on going back and getting some food. And now Lom was sitting on the couch in Vishnik's room with his legs stretched out along the seat. His chest was sore and bruised where the mudjhik had hit him, but the stove had heated the room to a warm fug and the bottle of plum brandy was nearly empty. The apartment smelled of lamb goulash and burning paraffin, and also of something else – the sweet tang of hydroquinone. Lom recognised it from the photographic laboratory at Podchornok.

'That smell. Is that developer?'

'What?' said Vishnik. 'Oh. Yes. I was printing.' His face was flushed. He had been drinking steadily all evening. 'Photographs. Have you ever made photographs, my friend? Marvellous. Very fucking so. You're completely absorbed, you see. In the moment. Immersed in your surroundings. Watching your subject. Observing. How does the light fall? What is the shutter speed? Aperture? Depth of field? It is an intimate thing. Very fucking intimate. It drives out all other thoughts. Your heart rate slows. Your blood pressure falls. You are in a waking dream. Time is nowhere. Nowhere.' Vishnik lurched unsteadily to his feet. 'Wait. Wait. I'll show you. Wait.'

He was going towards the kitchen when there was a loud rapping at the outer door. Vishnik froze and stared at Lom. The fear was in his face again. His eyes went to the bag waiting packed by the door.

'I'll get it,' said Lom. 'I'll deal with it. You wait here.'

Lom opened the door, half expecting uniforms. But there was only a woman, her wide dark eyes staring into his.

'Oh,' she said. 'I was looking for Raku Vishnik. I thought this was his place. I'm sorry. Would you know, I mean, which—?'

Vishnik had come up behind him.

'Maroussia?' he said. 'I thought it was your voice. This is a good surprise. Don't stand in the doorway. Come in. Please. Come in.'

She hesitated, glancing at Lom.

'I'm sorry, Raku. I wanted to ask you something. But it can wait. You're not alone. Now's not the time. I'll come back.'

'Ridiculous,' said Vishnik. 'Fucking so. You can speak in front of Vissarion, for sure. He is my oldest friend, and he is a good man. If there is trouble, perhaps he can help. At least come in now you're here. Warm yourself. Eat something. Have brandy with us. '

'No,' she said. 'There's no trouble. It doesn't matter.'

Lom had been watching her carefully. The yellow light from Vishnik's room splashed across her troubled, intelligent face. She looked worn out and alone. Like she needed friends. She would be worth helping, Lom found himself thinking. He wanted her to stay.

'Don't mind me,' he said. 'Please. You look tired.'

She hesitated.

'OK then,' she said. 'Just for a moment.'

Lom stood back to let her in. As she passed he caught her faint perfume: not perfume, but an open, outdoor scent. Rain on cool earth.

'Well,' said Vishnik. 'How can I help?' He was pacing the room, eager and animated. 'What is it that I can do for you? There must be something, for you to come so late. Tell me, please. I am eager for gallantry. For me, the chances are few. Ask me, and it is yours.' His eyes were alive with pleasure. He was more than a little drunk.

Maroussia looked at Lom again.

'I don't know that I should …' she said.

'Oh for the sake of fuck, Maroussia,' said Vishnik. 'Tell us what you need.'

She took a breath. 'OK. I want you to tell me about the Pollandore, Raku. I want you to tell me anything you know about it. Anything and everything.'

Vishnik stopped pacing and stared at her.

'The Pollandore?'

'Yes.' Maroussia was looking at him earnestly. Determined. 'The Pollandore. Please. It's important.'

'But ... fuck, this I was not expecting ... of all things, this.' Vishnik fetched another bottle from the shelf and settled himself in a sprawl on the rug on floor. 'Why are you asking me this?'

'You know about it? You can tell me?'

'I've come across the story. It's an old Lezarye thing. Suppressed by the Vlast long ago. Nobody knows about the Pollandore any more.'

'I do,' said Maroussia. 'My mother used to talk about it. A lot. She still does.'

'Really?' said Vishnik. 'I thought ... those stories are forgotten now.' He turned to Lom. 'Did you ever hear of the Pollandore, Vissarion?'

Lom shrugged. 'No. What is it?'

'Maroussia?' said Vishnik. 'Will you tell him?'

'No,' said Maroussia. 'I want to hear it from someone else.'

'OK,' said Vishnik. 'So then.' He poured himself another glass. 'Do you ever think about what the world was like before the Vlast, Vissarion?'

'No,' said Lom. 'Not much.'

'Four hundred years,' said Vishnik. 'But it might as well have been four thousand, no? Our civilisation, if we might even call it that, has lived for so long in the shadow of the angels' war, our history is so steeped in it, we live with its consequences in our very patterns of thought. Who can even fucking measure the damage it has done?' Vishnik paused. 'That's what the Pollandore is about. The time before the war of the angels.'

'The Lezarye walking the long homeland,' said Maroussia quietly. 'The single moon in the sky, not broken yet.'

'The world had gods of its own, then,' Vishnik was saying. 'That's how the story goes. Small gods. Gentle, subtle, local gods. But those gods are gone now. They withdrew when the angels began. They foresaw destruction and a terrible, unbearable future. They couldn't co-exist with that. Their time had to end.'

Vishnik emptied his glass and poured another. Lom wondered just how drunk he was. And how long since he'd had an audience like this.

'But before they went,' Vishnik continued, 'one of them, a forest god, made a copy of the world, the whole world, as it was at the moment before the first angel fell to earth. It was a pocket world, a world in stasis. Everything squeezed up into a tiny box. A packet of potential that would exist outside space and time, containing not things themselves but the potential for things. Possibilities. Do you see?'

'Yes,' said Lom. 'I guess so.'

'The idea was,' said Vishnik, 'that this other future, the future that could not now be, in our world, was to be kept safe. Waiting. A reserve. A fall-back. A cupboard. A seed. That's the Pollandore. That's the legend, anyway.'

'But what happened to it, Raku?' said Maroussia. 'Where did it go?'

'The people of Lezarye kept it safe for a while, but in the end the Vlast took it.'

'Yes,' said Maroussia. She was leaning forward. Looking at Vishnik intently. 'But what did they do with it? Where is it now?'

Vishnik shrugged.

'They tried to destroy it,' he said, 'but they could not. It was lost. Why are you asking me this, Maroussia? These are old forgotten things.'

'I want to find it.'

'Find it?' Vishnik looked startled. 'Fuck.'

'Yes. And please don't tell me it doesn't exist. I don't want to hear that again.'

'But … It's a good story, yes. A symbol. Truth in a picture. But what makes you think this? That it actually exists?'

Maroussia hesitated. Lom tried to read her expression but couldn't. She was looking at Vishnik with a pale and troubled look.

'Things have been … happening,' she said. 'Things have been coming … to my mother. From the forest. She was there once, long ago, before I was born, and something happened. I don't know what. But she always used to talk about the Pollandore. And now … Things happen in the city. I see … stuff that isn't there … only it's more real than what is there. It's like glimpses of a different version of the world. It's as if the Pollandore was trying to open. That's what it feels like. That's what it is.' She stopped. 'I'm sorry. I'm not saying this right.'

But Vishnik was hardly listening any more.

'Oh, my darling girl!' he said. 'You see these things too? I thought I was the only one. And you think it's the *Pollandore*? That's … that's … I hadn't seen that, but it could be. It could be so. What an idea *that* is. Fuck. Yes. But—'

'Raku? Do you mean you know what I'm talking about?' said

Maroussia. 'Fuck,' said Vishnik. 'I could hug you. I could fucking hug you.'

'Could somebody tell me, please,' said Lom, 'just what the hell you two are talking about?'

'Tell you?' said Vishnik. 'Fuck. Show you.' He stood up and lurched unsteadily in the direction of the kitchen.

'Raku?' said Lom. 'What are you—'

'Wait,' said Vishnik. 'This is what I was going to show you anyway. Wait.'

Lom and Maroussia sat for a moment in awkward silence while Vishnik rummaged in the other room and came back with a large round hatbox. He dumped it on the low table and took off the lid.

'Here,' he said. 'Look.'

The box contained photographs. Hundreds of them. Vishnik shuffled through them, picking out one after another.

'See?' said Vishnik. 'See?'

The photographs were odd and beautiful. A light in a window at dusk, shining from a derelict building. A penumbra of gleaming mist about a house. A great dark cloud in the sky. There was a sad magic in them all. It was in the sunlight on a street corner, in the ripples in a pool of rain on the pavement, in the way the light caught the moss on a tree. Gleams and glimpses. Tracks and traces. There was a purity of purpose in Vishnik's work that was strangely moving.

'I'll tell you something,' said Vishnik, pointing to one picture. 'That building there. See it. It does not exist. It never did. I photographed it, but it's not there. I have been back. Nothing.' He picked up another. His face was flushed. His breath ripe with brandy. 'See this burned-out store? There was no fire. See this alleyway? Its not on any map. See this island? There is no island in this water. And this couple has no children. I know them, Vissarion. They live here. But see ... there ... that child?'

Maroussia was looking through the photographs intently, staring at each one with a frown of concentration. She said nothing.

'And these,' Vishnik was saying, opening a small package and laying the contents out on the table. 'These are my specials. My very fucking absolutely specials.'

The first picture was a street scene, but the familiar world had been torn open and reconstructed all askew. The street skidded. It toppled and flowed. All the angles were wrong. The ground tilted forwards, tipping the people towards the camera. It wasn't an illusion of perspective, the people knew it was happening. A bearded man and an old woman threw up their arms and wailed. A baby flew out of its mother's arms.

Maroussia picked up the picture and stared at it for a long time.

'Oh Raku,' she whispered. 'This is it. Yes. This is it.'

Raku went to sit next to her.

'How often do you see this?' he said quietly.

'Not often,' said Maroussia. 'Sometimes. You?'

'All the fucking time. But then I look for it. Every day.'

'How long have you been doing this, Raku?'

'Two years,' said Vishnik. 'Maybe more. Other people are seeing it too, I'm sure of it. It's not the kind of thing you talk about though.'

Lom remembered the woman in the paper, the mother who had killed her children. *The floors keep opening,* that was what she'd said. *Will no one stop it?* He looked through the other pictures. Vishnik's specials. One showed an interior, a hotel bar, but the walls of the room were broken open to the elements and the ceiling was studded with stars. A woman's head was floating upside down in the corner of the picture, smiling. The barman, from the waist up, floated in mid-air, while his legs – were they his? – danced at the other end of the room. In another, a girl was descending like a messenger from the sky to milk a luminous cow. In her ecstasy at the lights blazing across the black night, she had left her head behind. The whole city was ripping open at the seams.

'You made these?' said Lom.

'All the time,' said Vishnik.'Always.' He picked one out and showed it to Maroussia. 'This is today's. It's a good one.'

She looked at it and passed it to Lom. The print was still damp. It had been taken in a café or a bakery, something like that. There was a girl in a black dress floating in the air. Up near the ceiling. The top had come off the counter: it was up there with her.

'These are good,' said Lom. 'How do you do it?'

'What, you think these are fakes?' said Vishnik.

'Well—'

'Fuck off with fakes. Of course they're not fucking fakes. This is

what's happening. Out there. This is the city. Maroussia has seen this.'
He looked at her. 'No? Am I not right?'

'Yes,' said Maroussia. 'It's the Pollandore.'

'See?' said Vishnik. 'Shit. Why would I make such stuff up? Why do
fakes? Fuck, Vissarion. You've been a policeman too long.'

Maroussia stared at Lom.

'What?' she said. 'What did he say? You? You're the *police*?'

Lom didn't say anything.

'Well,' said Vishnik. The colour had drained from his face. 'Yes, I
suppose he is a policeman. Of a sort. But a good policeman. Not really
a policeman at all.'

'Raku?' said Maroussia quietly. 'What have you done?'

'It's OK,' said Lom. 'Don't worry, I won't—'

But Maroussia was on her feet, gathering her coat. Her face was
closed up tight. She looked … alone. He wanted to reach out to her.
He didn't want her to go, not like this.

'Maroussia—' he said.

'Leave me alone. Don't say anything to me. I've made a mistake. I
have to go.'

Vishnik was aghast.

'No.' he said. 'Don't go. Not when we've just … Fuck. Fuck. But it's
fine. Vissarion is a friend. Your friend.'

'Don't be an idiot, Raku,' said Maroussia. 'That could never be.'

Lom watched her walk out of the room, straight and taut and brave.
He felt something break open quietly inside him. A new rawness. An
empty fullness. An uncertainty that felt like sadness or hunger, but
wasn't.

24

In a train travelling west towards Mirgorod there is a first-class compartment with its window blinds drawn, which the guards think is empty and locked. The guards know – though they couldn't say how they know – that there's something wrong with it, something ill-defined which needs a mechanic, which makes it unsuitable for occupation, and which they themselves should keep clear of. That's fine. No inconvenience for them. It's the end compartment of the furthest carriage, and first class is barely a quarter full. When they arrive in Mirgorod there'll be the fuss of detraining, and by the time that's done the episode of the closed compartment will be forgotten. When the train's ready to leave again, the compartment will be fine, except – should anyone notice, which isn't likely – for a lingering trace of ozone and leaf-mould in the air.

Just at the moment there are two figures sitting opposite each other in the darkness of the closed and blinded compartment. They are making a long journey. Should anyone happen to see them – which nobody does – they would appear to be human: two women, not young, riding in composed, restful, silent patience, swaying slightly with the movement of the train. Both appear to be dressed in layers of thin cloth in muted woodland colours of bark and moss. Their heads are covered, their faces lost in shadow. Or they would be, if they had faces, which – strictly speaking – neither does.

One of them – the one facing the direction of travel, as if eager to reach her destination, for her purpose is to arrive – is a paluba. The word is complex: its possible meanings include old woman, witch, hag, female tramp, manikin, tailor's dummy, waxwork, puppet and doll, none of which is exactly accurate here, though all have some bearing on the true nature of the figure, which is an artefact carefully constructed of birch branches and earth and the bones of small birds and mammals. The paluba is a kind of vehicle, a conveyance, currently travelling inside another conveyance, artfully made to carry the awareness of its creator and act as a proxy body for her, while she herself remains in the endless forest, in the safety of the trees which she can never leave.

The paluba's maker has placed a little gobbet of herself, a ball of bees' wax nestled inside the paluba's chest cavity, approximately where the heart would be. The wax has been mixed with many intimate traces of its maker – her saliva, her blood, her hair, a paring of fingernail, smears of sweat and other fluids, a condensation of breath – and many intimate words have been whispered over it, as the maker kneaded it between her warm palms for many hours over many days, making it well, making it strong, so that she would remain connected with it as the paluba travelled ever further westward. The maker doesn't stay with the paluba all the time. That would be exhausting and unnecessary. She can find it when she needs to. She can guide its steps, perceive with its senses and speak with its tongue, which is the tongue of a hind deer. When she needs to. For now, the paluba is empty. It's waiting, endlessly patient, facing its direction of travel. Facing westwards. Facing Mirgorod.

The paluba's companion faces opposite, eastwards, back towards the border of the endless forest. And whereas the paluba has a hand-made body, a material caricature of the living human form, the companion is the opposite of this also. For while she is not an artifice but a living creature, she has no body at all. Inside her shrouds of cloth there is nothing but air, only air – collected, coherent, densely-tangible forest air. She is the breath of the forest, walking.

As the train edges slowly closer to Mirgorod, the paluba's companion feels the widening distance between herself and the forest as an ever-increasing pain. She wants to go home. She needs to go home. Nothing would be easier for her than to leave, but she cannot. It is only her presence close to the paluba that enables it to continue to hold together and function so far from the forest. If she were to abandon the paluba it would fall apart. It would become inert, nothing more than the heap of rags and stuff of which it is made. Without her, the paluba's mission would fail, and with it would fail the hope of the forest, the only hope of the world.

25

The next morning, Lom took the tram back to the Lodka. He had a lead from Safran – the name of the painter, Petrov, who was one of Kantor's gang and had betrayed the Levrovskaya raid – not much of a lead, but something. A link to Kantor. Lom tried to keep his focus on Kantor, but his thoughts kept sliding sideways. Chazia was a presence in the background, unsettling him. A dark, angel-stained presence. She had showed herself to him deliberately. Playing a game with him. He was sure of that, though he didn't understand why. Yet it wasn't her face he kept seeing in the street on the other side of the tram window, but Maroussia Shaumian's. She had got under his skin. He hadn't liked the way she looked at him as she left last night: the mixture of fear and scorn in her face had cut him raw. For the first time, it didn't feel so good, being a policeman.

The tram had come to a stop. The engine cut out. A murmuring broke out among the dulled morning passengers.

'We're going nowhere,' the driver called. 'They've cut the power. Traffic's all snarled up. I guess there's another march somewhere up ahead.'

Lom sighed and got out to walk. It wasn't far.

A few hesitant snowflakes twisted slowly down out of the grey sky and littered the streets. People kept their heads down. As he got nearer the Lodka, Lom noticed the crowds getting slower and thicker. There was a sound of distant music. Hymns. He turned a corner and was brought up short by a mass of people passing slowly down the street.

They were singing as they came, not marching but walking. There were old men in sheepskin hats and women in quilted coats. Students in threadbare cloaks. Workers from the Telephone and Telegraph

Office and the tramcar depot. Schoolchildren and wounded soldiers, bandaged and hobbling. There were giants, shuffling forward, struggling to match the slow pace. Faces in uncountable passing thousands, following a hundred banners, shouting the slogans of a dozen causes. STOP THE WAR! PAY THE SOLDIERS! FREE TRADE UNIONS! LIBERATE THE PEOPLE OF LEZARYE! The finest banners belonged to the unions and free councils. They were made of silk, embroidered in beautiful reds and golds and blacks and hung with tassels. Each took three men to hold the poles and three more to go in front, pulling the tassels down to keep the banner taut and straight against the wind. The banner men wore long coats and bowler hats.

They were going his way, so Lom stepped into the road and walked along beside them. These people weren't terrorists or even dissidents. They were ordinary people, most of them, ordinary faces filled now with energy and purpose and an unfamiliar sort of joy. Lom felt the warmth of their fellowship. It was a kind of bravery. He almost wished he was part of it. A few people in the crowd looked at him oddly because of his uniform, but they said nothing. The traffic halted to let them pass. People on the pavement watched, curious or indifferent. Some jeered, but others offered words of encouragement and a few stepped off the kerb to join them. Gendarmes in their plywood street-corner kiosks fingered their batons uncertainly and avoided eye contact. They had no instructions.

Lom scanned the faces in the crowd automatically, the way he always did. Looking for nothing in particular, waiting for something to grab his attention. There was a man striding with the crowd, not keeping his place but weaving through them, working his way slowly forward towards the front, handing out leaflets as he went. He was wearing a striking grey fedora. His overcoat flapped open and his pink silk shirt was a splash of colour in the crowd. He came within a few feet of Lom, singing the chorus from *Nina* in a fine tenor voice.

Lom felt a lurch of recognition. The man's face meant something to him, though at first he couldn't make a connection. Then it came to him. Long and narrow and pockmarked, with those wide brown eyes, it could have been Josef Kantor. This man was older – of course he would be – and his face was filled out compared to the lean features in Krogh's old photograph. But it could have been Kantor. Lom was almost certain it was.

Lom's heart was pounding. He could hardly go up and seize him. Apart from any doubts about the man's identity, if he – in his uniform, with few other police around – tried to seize someone by force out of this crowd, things would get nasty. He'd be lucky to get out of it with his life. Certainly, he wouldn't get out of it with Kantor. Lom walked on, watching the man who might have been Kantor make his way expertly through the crowd.

For a while Lom tried to keep up with him. The man was tall, and in his fedora he was hard to lose sight of. But he was working his way steadily deeper into the crowd. As Lom went after him, his uniform began to attract attention. People jostled him and swore. Twice he was almost tripped. If he fell, he would have been kicked and trampled. He was sure of it.

A strong hand gripped his arm and squeezed, dragging him roughly round. A fat, creased face was shoved close to his.

'Idiot. Get the fuck out of here. What are you trying to do? Start a fucking riot?'

The man shoved him towards the edge of the crowd. Lom bumped hard against someone's back. Something sharp hit him on the back of the head, momentarily dizzying him.

'Hey,' said another voice behind him. A quiet voice, almost a whisper. 'Hey. Look at me. Arsehole.'

Lom turned in time to see the glint of a short blade held low, at waist level, in someone's hand. He lurched sideways, trying to get out of range. He couldn't even tell, in the crowd, who had the knife. Most of the walkers were still ignoring him, still walking on, ordinary faces wanting to do a good thing. Kantor, if it had been Kantor, had disappeared from view.

Shit. He needed to get out of there. Warily, watchfully, trying not to be jostled again, he edged himself sideways until he could step out of the slow tide of people, back onto the pavement. Lom realised he was sweating. He paused for a moment to catch his breath and tried to find his bearings, looking for a side street or alley that would let him get to the Lodka without getting caught up in the march again.

26

Unaware of Lom's abortive pursuit of him, Josef Kantor continued to weave his way through the moving crowd. Kantor wasn't the leader of the march. Nobody was. A dozen separate organisations had called for the demonstration and claimed it as theirs. There was a vague plan of sorts: to march up Founder's Prospect to the Lodka and hold a vigil there, with speeches from the steps, then on to the Novozhd's official residence in the Yekaterinsky Park to present a petition at the gates.

The chiefs of each marching organisation walked apart from the others, following their own colours, suspicious of spies and provocateurs. Kantor moved from coterie to coterie with a word of encouragement and support. He was everyone's friend. Some of them wondered who he was. Some thought they knew him, though each one knew him by a different name – Pato, or Lura, or David, or Per, or simply the Singer. Some knew him as the go-between and negotiator who had drafted their petition, a masterpiece of inspiring words and lofty demands that meant different things to different people.

The size of the crowd grew as it went, exceeding all expectation, even of Kantor himself. Runners moved through it, passing back instructions and bringing forward news of the swelling numbers, until those at the front began to wonder what they had unleashed, and felt nervous. They were beginning to sense that something more momentous than they had intended was preparing to happen.

The song changed from *Nina* to the Lemke Hymn. Their breath flickered on the air, but their hearts were warm. They were no longer a hundred thousand separate, accidental people but one large animal moving forward with a strength and purpose of its own. A newly-formed being whose moment had come.

And then a hesitation began somewhere in the crowd, no one knew where, and spread, a gathering wave of silence and concern. The singing died away but the crowd kept on walking.

Kantor shoved his way to the front.

'What is it?' he said. 'What's happening?'

'Dragoons are gathering at the Lodka. They have mudjhiks, and orders to fire.'

'Rumours. There are always rumours.'

'Maybe.'

Kantor moved on to another group. The Union of Dockers and Tracklayers was always up for a fight. He grabbed their Steward, Lopukhin, by his sleeve.

'It's only a rumour,' said Kantor. 'Keep them going. Get them singing again.'

'Who cares if the dragoons are waiting for us?' said Lopukhin. 'They won't attack us. We are fellow citizens. What a moment for us! Imagine. The dragoons refusing a direct order!'

But Lopukhin's was only one voice among the leaders. Others were for turning aside and making straight for the Park. The argument continued all the way up Founder's Prospect, and they were still arguing when they found themselves at the edge of the Square of the Piteous Angel.

The square was empty. On the far side, the huge prow of the Lodka rose against the sky. And between the marchers and the Lodka were two lines of mounted dragoons. A mudjhik stood at each end and another in the middle.

Those at the head of the march tried to halt and turn back, but the great mass of the crowd had a momentum of its own, and those behind, unaware of what was happening, kept on coming. The shoving and jostling started. Kantor found Lopukhin again and seized him by the shoulder.

'Come on!' he shouted. 'This is your moment! Lead them, Lopukhin! Face the soldiers down!'

'Damn, yes!' cried Lopukhin. His face was flushed, his eyes bright and unfocused. 'I will!'

Lopukhin shoved his lieutenants in the back, making them stumble forward into the empty square. He grabbed the colours of the Union and jogged forward, yelling and waving it over his head.

'Come on, lads! Come on! They won't shoot us!'

Some of the men followed Lopukhin willingly and others were pushed forward by pressure from behind. Kantor slipped away to the edge of the crowd and took up a position in the doorway of a boot shop. At first nothing happened. The dragoons didn't respond, and the demonstrators grew confident. More and more spilled into the square. Then Kantor heard what he had been waiting for. From the back of the crowd a swelling noise rolled forward. At first it sounded like they were cheering. Then the screams grew clearer, and the crack of shots.

All was as it should be. The troops that had been waiting out of sight in the side streets, letting the crowd pass by, were attacking the flank and rear. The killing had begun.

27

Threading through back streets and alleys, Lom made his way round to a side entrance of the Lodka and back into the great Archive. He called up the file on Lakoba Petrov without difficulty – unlike the Kantor file, it was there, and there was no sign that it had been tampered with. He sat reading it at one of the long tables under the dome while the Gaukh Engine rumbled and turned quietly behind him. He'd switched on the desk lamp. It pooled buttery yellow light on the blue leather desktop. But he found it hard to concentrate on the file. His head was hurting, as it had done in Krogh's office. Patches of faint flickering colour disturbed his vision.

Lom rubbed at his forehead, feeling the seal of angel skin smooth and cool under his fingers, tracing the slight puckering of the skin around it. He was keyed up and unsettled after his dangerous encounter with the marching crowd. The glimpse of Kantor – it was him, he was sure of it – haunted him: the sureness with which he had moved through the jostling people, the easy confidence on his face. He hadn't looked like a hunted man.

But there was something else that troubled Lom, something deeper: watching the crowd marching, he had been drawn towards them. He had launched himself unthinkingly among them to follow Kantor. He had, he now realised, wanted to be one of them. He was, at some instinctive level, on their side. And yet ... the hostility, the contempt, even the hatred they had turned on him when they noticed him. Not him, the uniform. For the second time, it didn't feel so good, being a policeman.

Lom turned his attention to the papers on Petrov. It was a thin file. Petrov was a painter, one of the modern type, not approved by the

Vlast. Petrov wasn't popular, it appeared, not even among his fellow artists. He was a marginal figure: there was only a file on him at all because he came into contact with bigger figures. Artists. Composers. Writers. *Intelligentsia*. They gathered at a place called the Crimson Marmot Club, where Petrov seemed to be a fixture. He had a temper: the file contained accounts of arguments at the Crimson Marmot, scuffles he was involved in. And there had been a dispute with a picture framer. Petrov claimed he'd left a dozen of his works to be framed, the man denied all knowledge of them, and Petrov accused him of having stolen and sold them. He'd made a formal complaint. The framer said Petrov owed him for previous work, and there were no documents on either side. The investigating officer could resolve nothing. He'd filed a report, though. Must have been a quiet day.

Petrov appeared to have few friends of any kind, the report noted, apart from one woman, a life model who worked in a uniform factory near the Wieland Station. Her name was noted for thoroughness, though there was no address and no file reference. The name was Shaumian. *Maroussia Shaumian*.

Lom sat back in his chair and drew a deep breath. *Circles of Contact.*

He tried to imagine Petrov. The registry file gave only a vague outline, a man seen only through the lens of surveillance. He wondered what Petrov's pictures were like. There was one scrap of newsprint pinned inside the cover, clipped, said a manuscript note, from *The Mirgorod Honey Bee*, dated early that spring: a review of an exhibition at the Crimson Marmot Club. He'd ignored it before, but he looked at it now.

'It would be remiss,' the reviewer said,

> to overlook the work of Lakoba Petrov, though most do. This young painter is developing a fine individualism. His prickly personality, which is perhaps better known than his canvases in the city's advanced artistic circles, manifests itself in the three likenesses shown here as a reckless energy. He is impatient with the niceties of style – surely a trait to be admired – and he is not a tactful portraitist, but his use of colour is original and his brush strokes have a fierce movement. He captures through his sitters something of the essence of the modern Mirgorod man. A troubled anxiety lurks in the eyes of his subjects, and their surroundings seem jagged, uncertain, about

to fall away. A young man's work, certainly, but there is bravery and promise here. *The Honey Bee* hopes for good things from Lakoba Petrov in the future.

The review was by-lined Raku Vishnik.
Circles of Contact.

There was a high-pitched frightened shout from somewhere above him.

'Soldiers! There are soldiers in the square!' All across the immense reading room, readers looked up from their work. Lom searched for the cause of the commotion.

'They're charging!' the voice called again. And then Lom saw where it was coming from: somebody was leaning over the balustrade of the upper gallery, where the high arched windows were. He was waving frantically. 'The dragoons are charging!' he was shouting. 'They're going to kill them all!'

Lom ran up the gallery stairs. The upper windows of the Archive, under the dome, were crowded with people watching the demonstration. He squeezed in among them and looked out across the rooftops, through grey air filled with scrappy lumps of snow.

A line of dragoons was moving out across the square, the mudjhiks loping forward, drawing ahead of the riders. Some of the demonstrators broke away from the crowd and started to run for the side streets but stopped in confusion, seeing more troops emerging from there. The dragoons had them bottled up tight. A strange collective tremor passed through the demonstrators as the horsemen picked up speed and raised their blades and whips. Then the heads of riders and horses were moving among the crowd, arms high and slashing downwards. The mudjhiks, moving with surprising speed, waded into the thick of it, striking with their fists and stamping on the fallen.

The dragoons withdrew, circled around and attacked again. And again. Lom saw a group of men grab hold of one of the riders and pull him down until his horse was forced to stumble. Once they had him on the ground, they kicked him and stamped on him and hacked at him with his own sword.

And something else was happening, though nobody but Lom seemed to see it. *There were too many people in the square.* Among the demonstrators and the dragoons, Lom could see others walking there: a sifting crowd, soft-edged, translucent, tired and unaware of the killing all around them. They were not old, but their hair was already turning grey. Their shoulders were frail, their faces drawn unnaturally thin and their skin was as dry and lifeless as newsprint. If they spoke at all, they spoke only when necessary; their voices had no strength, and didn't carry more than a few paces. Whisperers. The dragoons rode through them as if they weren't there at all. Because they weren't.

Above the massacre the sky tipped crazily. Out of the low leaden cloud another sky was breaking through, bruised and purple. An orange sun was tumbling across it like a severed head, its radiance burning in the cloud canyons. Behind the muted grey and yellow facades of the familiar buildings in the square there was another city now. High, featureless buildings rising against the livid sky. One immense white column of a building dwarfed all the other blocks and towers. Ten times taller than the tallest of them, fifty times taller than the real sky-line of Mirgorod, it climbed upwards, tier upon tier, half a mile high, its lower flanks strengthened by fluted buttresses that were themselves many-windowed buildings. The top quarter of it was not a building at all, but an enormous stone statue of a man five hundred feet tall. He was standing, his left foot forward towards the city, his right arm raised and outstretched to greet and possess. He was bare-headed, and his long coat lifted slightly in the suggestion of wind. Although the statue was at least a mile away across the city, Lom could make out every detail of the man's lean, pockmarked face. His eyes were fixed on the visionary distance yet saw every detail of the millions of insect-small lives unfolding beneath his feet. He would be visible from every street in Mirgorod. He would rise out of the horizon to lead incoming ships. He was uncle, father, god. The city, the future, was his.

The statue was the man he had seen weaving his way through the demonstration that morning. The man whose more youthful face gazed confidently into the camera in the photograph in Krogh's file. Josef Kantor.

Tucked in its pocket of no-time and no-space, the Pollandore feels the nearness of the deaths in the Square of the Piteous Angel. Feels the footfall of mudjhiks, the spillage of blood. The panic.

To the Pollandore it is a hardening, a sclerosis ... and a loosening of grip. Something slipping away. Its surface growing milky and opaque. The silence that surrounds it darkening into distance.

From its well of silence the Pollandore reaches out.

Lom stood for a long time at the window, staring at the immense white statue of Kantor half a mile above the blocky, featureless city. What he was seeing, he knew, wasn't there. Not yet. It was a city that wasn't there, but could be. Would be. He could feel it taking shape and solidifying. He was seeing for himself one of the glimpses that Maroussia and Vishnik had talked about last night. A scene from one of Vishnik's photographs. But this was different: Vishnik's was a city of soft possibilities, sudden moments of opening into inwardness and truth; this city was hard and cruel and silent. Closed up. Uniform. A city of triumphal fear. The city of the whisperers and dominion of Kantor, imperial and immense. Mirgorod was a battleground, a contention zone: two future cities both trying to become. The hard city was winning.

And which side was he on?

But that wasn't the question, not yet. The question was, what were the sides? Kantor was an enemy of the Vlast, yet his statue presided over the dragoons at their murderous business in the Square of the Piteous Angel. Vishnik and Maroussia were feeling their way towards the softer city under the iron and stone of Mirgorod, and went in fear of the Vlast's police. Fear of him. The feel of his uniform against his skin disgusted him. What kind of policeman was he? He pushed the question aside. Of one thing he was sure. Kantor had to be stopped, and that was his job. Lom turned away from the window. He had made a decision. He had something to do.

When he came back down the stairs from the gallery window, the great reading room was almost empty. Only a few had stayed at their desks, head in hands, or staring into space, or pretending to work, trying to ignore the sounds of killing. Shutting it out. None of them was going to take any notice of him.

Instead of turning left at the bottom of the staircase and going back to his own desk, Lom went right, following the perimeter of the reading room until he reached a door of varnished wood. It was inset at face height with small square windows of rippled glass.

CLOSED ARCHIVE! AUTHORISED ACCESS ONLY!

He pushed through the door and let it close quietly behind him. His hands were sweating.

The corridor beyond was empty. Lit with dim electric bulbs in globes suspended from the high ceiling, it was lined with more doors, each with a small square of card in a brass holder with a hand-written number. Occasionally a name. Lom went slowly down the corridor reading them. It took for ever.

CMDR L Y CHAZIA.

Lom gripped the brass doorknob, turned and pushed. It was locked. He shoved, but it didn't shift. He thought of trying to kick it down, but the door was solid and heavy. The noise would bring someone. In his pocket he had a bunch of thin metal slivers. His hands were clumsy, slick with sweat. It took him three, four attempts to pick out the right tool. He had to bend down and put his ear close to the door so he could hear what he was doing above the sound of blood in his own ears.

At last the tumblers slipped into place.

He closed the door before he flicked the light switch. Illumination flared dimly. Green-painted walls, an empty desk, rows of steel-framed racks holding files and boxes of papers. Lom forced himself to move slowly down the aisles between the racks, reading the file cards. It wasn't hard to find what he was looking for. Chazia had been methodical. The lavender folder for Josef Kantor was in its place on the K shelf. It was fat and full. He took it and pushed it inside his tunic.

As he was leaving, something made him turn back and go round to the L shelf. It was there. A much slimmer folder, pale pink. LOM, VISSARION Y, INVESTIGATOR OF POLICE. He stuffed it inside his tunic next to Kantor's.

He was halfway across the still-deserted floor of the reading room, almost at the exit, before he realised he hadn't switched off the light inside the room. An archivist was watching him curiously. No way to go back.

Lom stepped out into the square. The snow had stopped falling, leaving the air damp with impending rain. The smell of burned cordite and the dead.

People were moving across the square, alone or in small groups, pausing to look at each body, searching for a familiar face, hoping not to find it. Their feet splashed and slipped across cobbles wet with slush and blood. The dragoons had gone, and the militia, uncertain what to do, were ignoring the searchers. Nobody seemed to be in charge. The grey whisperers were there still. Walking by on their own withdrawn, secretive purposes.

But a couple of blocks away everything was normal. People pursued their business. Trams came and went. Lom boarded one, taking the Vandayanka route, heading for Pelican Quay. When he got there, he stopped at a chandlery to buy a small rubberised canvas sack with a waterproof closure. Then he wandered over to a bench and sat watching the boats at their moorings, idly kicking at the pavement. When he'd managed to loosen a cobble stone, he bent down casually to prise it out of the ground. And slipped it into his pocket.

28

Half the city away, in a room in the House on the Purfas, the paluba sat at the end of the table under the gaze of the Inner Committee of the Secret Government of Lezarye in Exile Within. The windwalker stood behind her, filling the air with woodland scents, ozone and leaf mould and cold forest air.

The five men of the Committee were drinking clear amber tea from glasses in delicate tin holders, waiting for her to begin. They waited patiently, taking the long view, as their fathers had, and their fathers' fathers. Their room, their rules. They were the ones who carried the weight of the past. Theirs, the great duty to keep the traditions. One day they would overturn the Vlast and bring back the good ways. The rebellions of Lezarye, the Birzel among them, were theirs. They worked and thought in centuries, but their day would come, and they would be ready.

'Madam,' said the man at the far end of the table. Elderly, white hair clipped short and thick, a gold pin in the lapel of his thick dark suit. 'Please. It's been many years since we were honoured by an emissary from the forest. We are anxious to hear your news.'

'Stasis,' said the paluba. 'Balance. Archipelago. Continent. Forest.'

Her voice was quiet, leaves stirring in the wind. The men leaned forward slightly to catch her words.

'For centuries,' she continued, 'balance has prevailed.'

White hair nodded. 'This Novozhd is weak,' he said. 'His position is attacked from without and from within. He is losing his war with the Archipelago. Our moment is coming.'

She knew he was a liar. *Stasis is good*, that was what he meant. *Balance is satisfactory.*

The paluba rested her hand of twigs and earth and wax on the table. It settled like a moth on the pale surface of polished ash and drew their eyes.

Take it away, she felt these men thinking. *This is a foul and horrible thing. Get it off our table.*

Pay attention to me! That was what she wanted the hand to say. *I am the Other, the Unlike You. But I am here. Listen to me. Your world is not what you think.*

'Everything is different now,' she said aloud, looking around the table and fixing each man in turn with the sockets where her eyes would have been. 'Your stasis is broken. An angel has fallen in the forest, and lives. It is alive.'

'Impossible.'

'It is injured. It cannot move, though it struggles to free itself and may yet succeed. It is the strongest there has ever been. By far.'

'There hasn't been an angelfall for eighty years,' said the man on White Hair's right. 'And none has ever survived the impact. The war in heaven is over. Even some in the Vlast's own council say so.'

'Wait, Efim,' said White Hair. 'Let her speak.'

'The angel's power flows from it into the rock that holds it. It is killing the forest. The greater trees are failing.'

'Even if this is true—' said Efim.

The paluba ignored him. 'But the angel is frightened,' she said. 'It feels itself weakening. Failing. It has been looking for a way to defend itself. Or escape.'

'Peder! Surely we're not going to listen to this?'

'And now the angel has found a way,' said the paluba. 'It is building an alliance. Here in Mirgorod.'

Another man leaned over to speak in White Hair's ear. 'Can't we get rid of these awful creatures? The smell ...'

The paluba could hear the whisper of a moth's wing.

'Efim's right,' said a small man in a waistcoat. 'We don't have time for this. Tomorrow we'll have thirty million in our hands.'

'I've already said we shouldn't touch that money,' said another, a soft, round, moon-faced man in spectacles. 'Kantor's Fighting Organisation is too vicious, too wild. Our reputation suffers by association.'

'Ridiculous!' said the man in the waistcoat. 'This is war! We can't afford to be fastidious. While we do nothing our people are dying.

Pogroms are growing worse. Show trials. Executions. Whole streets are being cleansed while we sit here and talk and do nothing.'

They were voices, just voices, so many useless, chattering, indistinguishable, male, redundant, broken voices. The paluba hardly troubled to hear them. She already knew that she had failed here. She had known it when she saw the little glass of amber tea and smelled the fear in the room. Nonetheless, she must not give up. Everything must be attempted.

'There is no time!' said the paluba. 'None at all. We can stop what is coming. But we must move now. Now! The alliance of Lezarye and the forest—'

'And what are we to do, exactly?' said Efim. 'Send in the Fighting Organisation? Could they blow this angel up with their grenades?'

'The answer lies in the Pollandore.'

Efim stood up. 'I've had enough of these fairy tales. And of these disgusting ... things. Call me when this rubbish is over.'

The paluba felt the finality of the room turning against her.

'The Pollandore is stirring,' she said. 'It is beginning to have effects. It is beginning to spill, perhaps even to break apart. Even in the forest we have felt it.'

'The Pollandore is nothing. More stories. More nonsense.'

'The time has come.' The paluba was whisper-roaring at them. 'Open the Pollandore. This is the message from the forest. The time is now. You have to open it.'

'What you ask is impossible. Even if we knew how to open it – whatever it is.'

'Even if it existed, even if this wasn't all absolute rubbish ...'

'I bring you the key,' said the paluba. 'I offer it to you now. This is my message to you, the gift I bring you from the one who sleeps.'

'The Pollandore is in the keeping of the Vlast,' said Peder. 'Unless they have already destroyed it. I'm sorry, madam. We cannot help you in this. Not at all.'

She had failed. She had known it as soon as she came in, and it had proved to be so. But there was another way. The Shaumian women. She had hoped it wouldn't be necessary. It was not ... reliable. That had been shown already, many times. But she would have to try. If there was time.

29

When Lom got back to the apartment, Vishnik was out. Lom turned on the lamp, poured a glass of aquavit and opened the dossier on Kantor. The early stuff was standard: student records, informants' reports of domestic life, associates and contacts. There was an extracted account of the Birzel Rebellion court proceedings and the Executive Order of Internal Exile. Notes on the subject's conduct in the camps. Something about a wife. She had followed him to the camp, but once there she had become pregnant by another man, abandoned Kantor and come back to the city.

Lom read the whole file through from cover to cover, but the papers only filled out what Krogh had told him without adding much, until he got to the end. In a separate pouch at the back, attached with a string tag, were some loose pages with manuscript notes on them in a tight, spidery hand. Some of the notes were initialled. *LYC.*

Lavrentina Chazia.

Lom sat up and began to read more carefully. This was something else. There was an account of Kantor's repeated escape attempts. Violent attacks on other inmates. He had crushed an informant's hand in a vice. '*A resourceful man,*' Chazia had scribbled across it. '*He dominates the camp. The guards fear him. Commandant reluctant to discuss the case.*'

On another page, in a different ink, were the words '*Spoke to Kantor today. He has agreed.*' Attached to the same report with a paper clip was a single sheet of lined paper torn from a bound notebook. It was covered in Chazia's scrawl, apparently written in haste, in pencil, and in parts illegible. It took him a long time to puzzle out the words, and some whole passages defeated him. '*It spoke to me at Vig! It is an angel, a living angel! There can be no doubt of it. We are acknowledged, we are acceptable. The power of it! The power is ...'* The next few lines were not readable. *'... hands trembling. I can't hold it all ...'* Illegible. *'... write before it fades. Not words – ideas, impressions, understandings – roaring floods of light. Much lost ...'* Illegible. *'... magnificent. This is the day! The new Vlast begins here. It speaks to Kantor also. It does.'*

There were a few more notes in Chazia's scrawl. They seemed to record further meetings with Kantor, but they were undated. Only a few unconnected words and figures. Lom could make nothing of them. Chazia had written across the bottom of one, *'It speaks to him. Always to him. Never to me.'*

30

There was a way to enter the Lodka revealed only to the most secret and trusted servants of the Vlast. It was a small shop, occupying the ground floor of a grimy brick house. The shop window, glazed with small square panes of dirty glass and lit by dim electric bulbs, displayed photographs of naked dancing girls. Books in plain yellow covers. Packets in flimsy paper wrappers marked with prices in spidery brown manuscript. The dried-out carcases of flies and moths.

The proprietor was a fat bearded man in gloves and striped shirt-sleeves, known only as Clover. If you spoke certain words to this Clover, he would nod, lift the partition in the counter and show you through a dusty glass door into the back parlour. From there you went through a curtained back exit, across an interior courtyard and down a narrow stairway into a mazy network of tunnels and cellars. It was easy to lose yourself in that subterranean labyrinth, but Josef Kantor knew the way well.

It was an unpleasant route. Kantor disliked it and used it as rarely as he could. The way was damp and dark, and stank of stale river-water. The tunnels and passageways were faced sometimes with stone, more often with rotten planks, and always with slime and streaks of mud. The floor was treacherous with dirty puddles and scattered rubbish. These underground passageways extended under much of inner Mirgorod. They were remnants of the original building work, if not – as some said – remains of some much more ancient settlement that pre-dated the coming of the Founder. Kantor tended to believe the latter. Sometimes he heard things – the shuffle of slow footsteps, mutterings and echoes of shouting – and saw the trails of heavy objects dragged through the mud. Not all the original inhabitants of the marshlands had been driven away by the coming of the city, and some that had left had returned. He wasn't nervous, threading his way through the maze, but he found it … distasteful.

He came eventually to a locked metal gate that barred the way. He had a key, and let himself through onto an enclosed walkway slung beneath one of the bridges that crossed to the Lodka. Out of sight of the embankment and the windows of the building, it led into the upper basements of the vast stone building. Once inside, Kantor traced a circuitous route that led him gradually upwards, through unused corridors and by way of service elevators and blank stairwells, to the office of Lavrentina Chazia.

Kantor picked up a chair, placed it in front of her desk and sat down. Chazia ignored him and carried on working. Her face had always reminded Kantor of something reddish and cruel. A vixen. And the dark, smooth blemishes where her skin was turning to stone. They were spreading. It was getting worse. He watched her unconsciously scratching at the angel mark on the back of one hand. *She dabbles too much.*

'It was a complete success,' he said.

'What?' She didn't look up.

'The march. On the Lodka.'

'Oh. That. But we must talk about something else, Josef. Your position is compromised. Krogh knows who you are. He has the name. Josef Kantor.'

'Krogh is old and tired.'

'Krogh is clever,' said Chazia. 'He knows we're working against him and he knows he can't trust his own people. He's taken steps against you. An investigator. From the east. Someone with no connections here. He's set him to track you down.'

Kantor grunted. 'One investigator? That can be taken care of. You'll do that?'

'Of course.'

'We can't afford distractions.'

She looked up from her papers at last.

'You and I cannot meet again, Josef. Our plans must change. At least in so far as they involve you.'

'I'm not *dispensable,* Lavrentina. The angel speaks to me. Not you.'

Kantor saw Chazia's vixen head lean forward, her eyes widen a fraction. She scratched at the stone-coloured back of her hand again. Delicately wet her lips with the tip of her tongue. *How transparent she is. She gives herself away. She doesn't know she's doing it. How she wants to be close to power! How she desires it! She longs to feel power's hot breath on her skin, and open her legs for power. She is jealous of me, because the angel comes inside me, not her. She felt it once and she wants it again. She's hooked like a fish.*

'What does it say?' said Chazia. 'What does the angel say to you?'

He saw how weak she was. *Desiring to be near power is not the same as desiring power. It is the opposite.*

'It is impatient,' he said. 'It urges haste. It makes promises.'

'Promises?'

'To me, Lavrentina. Not to you. To me.'

'Of course you would say that. To save yourself.'

'One cannot lie about the angel. One cannot deceive it.'

Chazia showed the tip of her tongue again, pink between pale thin lips.

'Is it here? Is it with you … now?'

'Of course not. I couldn't speak to you if it was.'

'Why does it choose you, Josef? Why doesn't it come to me again?'

Kantor said nothing.

'Do you know why not?'

'No.'

'You could ask it.'

'No.'

Chazia sighed and leaned back in her chair.

'So. What does it promise you, Josef?'

'Stars. Galaxies. Universes. The red sun rising.'

'Meaning? Meaning what?'

Kantor looked at her and said nothing.

'Meaning nothing,' said Chazia.

'It has given me an instruction. The Pollandore must be destroyed.'

'It knows about that?'

'It knows everything.'

'Then it knows we cannot destroy the Pollandore. We have tried and failed.'

'It must be done'

'This doesn't change your position, of course,' she continued. 'The logic is inescapable.'

'I do not see it.'

'Think, Josef. See it from my perspective. Soon the Iron Guard will step in and put things right. This weak and backsliding regime will fall. The One Righteous War will recommence with renewed vigour.'

'With me alongside you, Lavrentina. That is the agreement. It must stand.'

'But consider this, Josef. How would it be if Krogh makes the connection between you and me? If he can *prove* it? If he takes this to the *Novozhd* before we are ready? Surely you see the impossibility of this?'

Kantor watched her steadily. He said nothing.

'What would you do, Josef?' she said. 'In my position?'

He shrugged. 'It is not complex,' he said. 'Krogh must be killed.'

Her eye flickered.

You are transparent to me. You garrulous intoxicated mad old foxbitch.

'Nothing is easier than death,' he said. 'The more deaths there are, the better for our purpose.'

'But—'

'The solution is clear,' Kantor continued. 'Krogh must be killed. Of course ...' He looked her in the eye. Held her gaze. 'If you don't have the stomach for that, I will do it myself. It doesn't matter so long as it is done.'

Chazia glared at him.

'It will be done,' she said. 'It's not a problem.'

'Thank you,' said Kantor. 'Good. Of course, that isn't why I came to see you.'

'So why did you come?'

'I have a couple of requests.' He smiled. 'No doubt these also will be no problem.'

Chazia bridled.

'Be careful, Josef. Don't go too far. You are not ... safe.'

'No one is safe, Lavrentina. Such is the world. But there are some favours you could do for me.'

'What?'

'My former wife, the slut Feiga-Ita.'

Chazia looked at him in surprise. 'What about her?'

'Kill her. Kill that bastard daughter of hers too.'

'I see,' said Chazia. 'But … surely you could do this yourself? You have people.'

'They would want to know why. That would not be helpful.'

Chazia sat back and considered.

'I see no objection,' she said eventually. 'But you will owe me, Josef. The service is not your personal execution squad. Is that all?'

'No. I want you to take me to the Pollandore. I want to see it.'

31

In Vishnik's apartment, Lom poured another glass and reached for the file with his own name on it. It was a standard personnel file, tied with ribbon. The registry slip on the front showed it had been referred to Commander Chazia only the day before. The day he had arrived in Mirgorod and seen Krogh. The referring signature was Krogh's own private secretary.

The file itself contained all the paperwork of an unexceptional career. Good but not brilliant academic achievement. Stalled promotions and rejected applications. The criticisms, complaints and accusations. And one other thing. The earliest document. A letter. Lom read it over and over again until he had it by heart. It was addressed to the Provost of the Podchornok Institute of Truth.

Righteous and Excellent Provost Savinkov
  I bow to you deeply from the white of my face to the damp earth, and I commit to your care this boy, gathered in by my artel when, in pursuance of the Forest Extirpation Order, we removed the village and nemeton of Salakhard. The boy does not speak to us, but is believed to be a child of uncouth persons, and consequently now parentless. He is apparently not above six years old, and in all conscience we hesitate to end the life of one so young. But his remaining with us is not by any means practicable. Our orders take us further eastwards, under the trees. Perhaps he may be closed up, in the way you know how, and enfolded in the One Truth? He is yet young.
  Your servant,
  S V Labin, Captain

Lom leaned back on Vishnik's couch. Deeply buried memories: first memories, beginnings. He was lying under a tree, a thickened old beech that thrust torsos of root deep into the earth and rose high over his head, spreading its leafhead, casting a pool of blue shade on the spring-green grass. The sun hung above the tree, a moored fiery vessel, and small things moved in the thickets. The air was filled with strong, sour, earthy smells, and he could feel the ground beneath his back. He heard the leaves of trees and bushes moving as if in a wind. He was looking upwards, tracing the boughs of the tree where the trunk bifurcated and reached high into the mass of foliage, the million leaves, fresh and thick, bright with the green liquid fire of sunlight that was pouring through them. The tree was eating light and breathing clouds of perfume.

The perfumed tree-breath was its voice, its chemical tongue. It was speaking to the insect population in its bark and branches, warning and soothing them. It was speaking to its neighbour trees, who answered: tree spoke to tree, out across the endless forest. And it was speaking to him. Psychoactive pheromones drifted through the alveolar forests of his human lungs and the whorled synaptical pathways of his cerebral cortex.

At the institute at Podchornok they'd given the silent boy a name, Vissarion Lom, and all this they had taken from him.

Memory left him. For a while Lom simply sat, tired and empty, thinking of nothing, listening to the evening call of the gulls in the sea-coloured sky. Surfacing. It was almost dark when he finally moved. Lom gathered up the files and his notes, put them in the waterproof bag, weighted it with the quayside cobblestone and slipped it into the cistern in the bathroom. He settled down to wait for Vishnik to return. That night they would go to the Crimson Marmot Club. To see Lakoba Petrov.

32

The music got louder with each step down the alleyway. Letters in electric red flickered on and off above a door shut tight against the blowing rain and cold. *The Crimson Marmot.* Lom pushed the door open. A blast of thick, heated air, tobacco smoke and noise hit his face. Inside was a hot, boiling cauldron of red. Red, the colour of the Vlast, the colour of propaganda, the colour of blood, but also the colour of intimacy and desire. Loud voices shouting into excited faces.

Vishnik led the way through the crowd to a table. A young man was dancing nearby, an absorbed, solitary dance with unseeing eyes. His face was powdered chalky white. As his face caught the light Lom saw a ragged wound scar down his cheek. At the next table a snaggle-bearded man was smoking with his eyes closed. The woman with him looked bored. Her jacket shimmered as if it was silk. She was naked from the waist down. She laughed and drained her glass and got up to dance with the young man with the powdered face, swaying her hips and moving her hands in complicated knots. The young man didn't notice her. On a bench in the corner a couple were making love.

Lom leaned across to shout in Vishnik's ear: 'Who are these people?'

Vishnik shrugged.

'That doesn't matter here. They come to leave all that behind. Outside, in the daytime, they are clerks. Waiters. Former persons who used to be lawyers or the wives of generals. But this is the night side, a place without history. They come here for the now of it. Keep raising the level. Another notch. Another glass. Another powder. Here you make the most of your body and anyone else's you can. Does that shock you?'

'No,' said Lom. 'No. It doesn't.' He'd been to places in Podchornok where fat rich men went to get drunk and touch young bodies, but this was different. There was a version of himself that could be comfortable here. He looked around again. Searching the faces. 'Can you see Petrov? Is he here yet?'

'No, but it's still early.'

A waiter brought a bottle of champagne and two glasses. Lom watched him uncork and pour.

'Relax,' said Vishnik. 'Enjoy the evening.'

Lom's eyes were adjusting to the rich, dim redness of the Marmot's. The walls were crimson plush and hung with vast gilded mirrors that made the room seem larger than it was. Tables crowded one another in a horseshoe around a central space where dancers moved between people standing in noisy, excitable groups. At the back of the room was a small stage, its heavy curtains closed, and in one corner, musicians played instruments of the new music. Lom recognised some of them: a heckelphone, a lupophone, a bandonion, a glasschord. Others he couldn't identify. He sipped at the champagne and winced. It was thick, with a metallic perfume.

He'd expected something different of the Crimson Marmot: an art gallery, perhaps, with intense talk and samovars. There was art here, though. Wild, angular sketches on the walls. A larger-than-life humanesque manikin hanging from the ceiling, dressed as a soldier with the head of a bear. A figure, crouched high in the corner, with eight limbs and six pairs of woman's breasts. Lom realised it was meant to be an angel. It was made out of animal bones, old shoes, leather straps and rubbish. Candles burned in its eyes and a scrawled placard hung from its neck. *Motherland*. Beneath it, someone had pinned a notice to the wall.

ART IS DEBT! LONG LIFE TO THE MEAT MACHINE ART OF THE FORBAT!

With a crash of drums, the musicians fell silent and the curtain was drawn aside to reveal the small stage. A red banner unfurled. *The Neo-emotional Cabaret*. An ironic cheer went around the room, and a smattering of applause. Vishnik leaned across to Lom.

'You'll like this. This is different. This is new. This is fucking good.'

On the stage a man was crouching inside a large wooden crate, shouting nonsense words into a tube connected to a megaphone on top of the crate. 'Zaum! Zaum! Baba-zaum!' he chanted. The musicians hacked away with atonal enthusiasm. Lom caught some longer phrases of almost-coherent verse.

Wake up, you scoundrel self-abusers!
Materialists! Bread eaters! Mirgorod is a cliff –
bare snow in banked-up drifts – daybreak.
Winter's late dawn – worn out – shivering –
descends the river like smallpox.

Lom was relieved when it finished. The curtain closed and the band struck up again. Pink spotlights lit the dance floor. Lom hadn't noticed the dancer enter, but she was there. Her breasts were bare and she wore a long flickering skirt, divided to give her legs room for movement. The dancer's body was thin and muscular, her breasts small and narrow, her black hair cut short, and she danced fast and thoughtlessly, shouting and jerking to the music, advancing towards the audience and then retreating with a shrug. Pleasing herself. Not trying. Just doing.

And then, to cheers and applause, she was gone. Most of the band stood up and went to the bar, leaving the glasschord player alone to unwind some kind of drifting, song-like melody.

Vishnik took him by the arm and whispered in his ear, 'Petrov's come. At the table by the bar. The green shirt.'

Lom looked across to where a group of men were listening to a large bearded fellow talking loudly, his wet red mouth working, banging the table with his fist to punctuate his periods. Petrov was a silent bundle of energy in a corner seat, staring with obvious resentment at the talker. Lom studied him carefully. He was all wild, dark curly hair, a long sharp nose and dark eyes, wide and round, full of passionate need and intelligence and a crazed, intent sort of anger. His lips, pressed tight together, were full and almost bruised-looking. He looked as if someone had punched him and he was trying not to cry. When he leaned back in his chair, as if he was trying to get further away from the bearded shouter, his loose green shirt gaped open halfway to his waist, revealing the white, almost skeletal bone structure of his upper chest.

'Take me over, can you?' said Lom. 'I want to talk to him.'

Vishnik picked up the half-empty champagne bottle and the glasses and went across. Lom followed. Some of the men at the table nodded. The beard ignored them. So did Petrov.

'The city as a whole,' Beard was saying in a deep, resonant voice, 'is instinct with energising power. It inspires me. The more marches and strikes and riots – the more confrontation – the better it is for art. The agitation in the squares and factories is like the revving of the engines of the vehicles in the street. It provides heart. It is marvellous. Wonderful. I must have it, at all times, in order to work. It's the fuel my motor burns.'

Beard paused to take a drink.

'Did you hear?' said the young man with the powdered face. 'The Novozhd has said that from now on all his rallies will be held after dark. Isn't that perfect? It is already evening across the Vlast. Midnight! The Novozhd is an artist himself, though he won't admit it.'

Beard spluttered.

'The Novozhd! Do you know what he said about my picture of Lake Tsyrkhal?' He stared around the table, daring them to speak. 'I made the water yellow and black, and this is what the Novozhd said: *As a hunter, I know that Lake Tsyrkhal is not like that.* So now he forbids us to use colours which are different from those perceived by the normal eye. What is the point, I ask you, of a painter with a normal eye? Any idiot can see what's normal. But do I fear this Novozhd? No!'

'Does he fear you, Briakh?' said Petrov fiercely, uncoiling from the tense crouch he'd wound himself into. He was nursing a small glass of something thick and dark. 'Does the Novozhd fear you? Isn't that the question? I think he does not.'

Briakh glared at him.

'Meaning?'

'Meaning your paintings are nothing. All our paintings are nothing. This club is nothing. It's not even so much shit on his boots, so far as the Novozhd cares. We're only still here because he hasn't noticed us yet.'

'He put three of my pictures in his Exhibition of Degenerate Art. Three.'

'They get people to laugh at us, that's all. It's a distraction. Do you think the Novozhd lies awake at night because you made Lake Tsyrkhal black and yellow?'

Powdered Face giggled. '*The most perfect shape,*' he quoted, '*the sublimest image that has ever been created didn't come out of any artist's studio: it is the infantryman's steel helmet. The artists ought to be tied up next to their pictures so every citizen can spit in their faces.'*

Briakh ignored him. He was staring at Petrov.

'And you, Petrov?' he said. 'Is the Novozhd scared of you? How many of your pictures does he have in his exhibition?'

'Painting's finished,' said Petrov quietly. 'I told you. There will be a new art. And he will know my name soon enough. He will know Petrov by his works. You all will. Yes, he should fear me.'

'Why?' said Lom into the silence. 'What are you going to do? Rob a bank?'

Petrov stared at him.

'Who are you?'

'He's my friend, Lakoba,' said Vishnik. 'He's from out of town.'

'Anyone can see that,' said Petrov. He turned to Lom. 'And do you like this place? It is our laboratory. We are all scientists here. We are studying the coming apocalypse.'

'Sounds to me you're planning to start it.'

'You shouldn't laugh at me.'

'As long as you bring us champagne,' said Briakh, 'you can laugh as much as you like.' He reached a heavy paw across to Vishnik's bottle, took a pull from the neck, emptied it and waved it at the bar. 'Another!' he boomed. 'Two more! Dry men are desperate here! Friend Vishnik's paying.'

Petrov stood up.

'Drink till you vomit,' he said. 'The crisis is now, but you wouldn't know it if it bit your arse.' He went unsteadily towards the exit.

'You're crazy drunk yourself, man!' Briakh shouted after him. 'Crazy drunk on that crazy-man syrup you drink.'

Lom got up and followed Petrov. He got entangled with a boy in a spangled crinoline and jewelled breast-caps who wanted to dance with him. By the time he got free and caught up with him, Petrov was halfway down the street.

'Can I walk with you a while?' said Lom.

'Why?'

'Curiosity. I agree with what you were saying in there. I wanted to hear more.'

'I don't believe you understood a word of it.'

'Maybe I don't know about painting. But I do know about blowing things up.'

'What's that got to do with anything?'

'That was fighting talk in there.' The rain was heavier now, whipped along on a bitter wind. Petrov, wearing only his half-buttoned green shirt, seemed oblivious to it. Lom wished he had brought his cloak out with him. His head was ringing with the noise and heat of the club. 'Unless it was just bluster,' he added. 'Like Briakh.'

'You're right about Briakh. Ha! Blusterer Briakh.'

'What about you?'

Petrov's face was close to his. His eyes were wide and black and shiny. Lom smelled the fumes of sweetness and alcohol on his breath.

'*I* have an *idea*,' said Petrov. '*I* have an *intention. I* have a *purpose*.'

'I'd like to hear about it.'

'You will. When it's done.'

'Why not tell me now? Perhaps I can help you. Let me buy you a drink somewhere out of the rain.'

'Help doesn't come into it. Help isn't necessary. And neither is talk. One can either talk or do, but not both, never both. You should tell that to Briakh. Tell all of them back there. They can't tell talk from do, any of them. That's their problem.'

Petrov walked on. Lom followed.

'We should talk though. We have a friend in common, I think.'

Petrov didn't stop walking. 'Who?' he said.

'Josef Kantor.'

'Kantor?'

'You know him then?'

'You said I did.'

'I guessed.'

'Kantor the Crab. Josef Krebs. Josef Cancer. The smell of the camps is in his skin. He can't wash it off. I think he made himself a shell when he was there and climbed inside it, and he has sat inside it for so long that now he's all shell. Nothing but shell, shell, and lidless eyes on little stalks staring out of it, like a crab. But people *like* him. Do you know that, Vishnik's friend? They think he has *charm*. They say those crab eyes of his twinkle like Uncle Novozhd. But they're idiots. There's no man left in there at all. He's all crab. Turtle. Cockroach. And shall I tell you something else about him?' Petrov stopped and turned to

Lom, swaying slightly, oblivious of the rain in his face. He began to speak very slowly and clearly. 'He has some other purpose which is not apparent.' He began to tap Lom on the chest with a straight forefinger. 'And. So. Do. You.'

'Me?'

'I don't like you, Vishnik's friend. I don't like you at all. Your hair is too short. You look around too much. You keep too many secrets and you play too many games. Vishnik should choose his friends better. You wear him. Like a coat. No, like a beard.'

'I—'

'He knows it, and he lets you. *That's* a friend. And you'll kill him because of it. You think I don't know a policeman when I see one?'

33

It was long after midnight, but not yet morning. Lom lay on the couch in Vishnik's apartment under a thin blanket, trying to force sleep to come, but it would not. The couch was too small and the stove had gone out long ago. All heat had seeped from the room, along with the illusion of warmth from the Crimson Marmot's champagne and brandy, leaving him cold and wakeful. Moonlight flooded in through a gap in the curtains: the glare of the two broken moons, wide-eyed and binocular, searchlighting out of a glassy, starless, vapourless sky. The room was drenched in it. The effect was remorseless: every detail was whited, brittle, monochrome. Petrov's drunken accusation cut at him again and again.

You think I don't know a policeman when I see one?

One day when he was about fourteen he'd been sent out on some errand, and there was a girl in a green dress in the alleyway by Alter's. Town boys were gathered around her. Shoving. Tripping. Touching. *What's in your bag? Show us your bag.*

Lom could have walked away, but he didn't.

'Hey!' he shouted. 'Leave her alone!'

They'd beaten him. Badly. The big one kept punching him in the face: a boy with a pelt of cropped hair across his skull. Every time the boy punched him in the face Lom fell over. And every time that happened, he shook his head and stumbled back to his feet. And the big one punched him again. And he fell. And got up. At first Lom had shouted at them. Yelled.

'Fuck off! Leave me alone! I haven't done anything to you!'

But that soon passed. He'd fallen silent. Fallen into the rhythm of it. Punch. Fall. Stand up. Punch. Fall. Stand up. There was no room for yelling. No breath for it either.

'I love this,' one of the boys was saying. 'Do it again, Savva. Hit him more. Go on. Yes. I love it.'

There was blood on Lom's face and he hardly knew what was happening. Everything was weightless and distant. The punches hardly hurt now. Every time he fell, he stood back up. It was mute, pointless resistance. His face was numb. He'd been beaten beyond the capacity for thought. There was nothing left but the automatic determination to get back up on his feet.

Eventually there would have come a time when he could not have got up again, but before he reached it Savva stopped. He was looking at Lom with something like fellowship in his eyes. And then one of the smaller ones, one of Savva's shoal, stepped in and punched at Lom's chin himself, but he didn't have Savva's power and Lom was numb to anything less. He didn't stumble or fall this time, but turned to look in the little one's feral, weasel eye, disinterestedly.

'Leave him,' said Savva. 'That's enough.'

Lom had felt something like friendship for Savva then, a feeling which had shamed him secretly ever since. That moment of instinctive friendship, he thought afterwards, had taught him something. The victim's gratitude toward his persecutor. How it felt so much like love.

Savva had taken his money. The Provost's money. Lom had been made to clean the lavatories every morning for a month. But a letter had come from the girl's father to thank the unknown boy in the uniform of the Institute who had come to his daughter's help. The father was Dr Arensberg the magistrate, and the Provost had given him Lom's name. An invitation arrived, addressed to Vissarion Lom himself. He was asked to the Arensbergs' house for tea, and the Provost had made him go. After the first time he'd become a regular visitor on weekend afternoons.

The Arensbergs' house was well known in Podchornok. It was large, steep-gabled, wooden, with clustered chimneys of warm red brick, set in its own orchard. The rooms were full of dogs and flowers, the smell of baking, and the Arensberg children at music practice. The family taught him to play euchre and svoy kozyri: Dr and Mrs Arensberg, the girl, Thea, and her brother Stepan, who was seventeen and going to be an officer in the hussars, sitting together, playing cards in the dusty sunlight. The smell of beeswax and amber tea.

Lom's visits to the Arensbergs were his first and only encounter with family domesticity. A private life. The warmth and decency that came with secure money. He'd known nothing of such houses before, or the families that lived in them, except what he saw through townhouse windows at dusk, when the lights were lit and the curtains not yet drawn.

One day in summer Dr Arensberg called him into his study.

'What will you do, Vissarion? With your life, I mean? Your career?'

'Career? I don't know. I expect I will become a teacher.'

'Do you want to do that?'

'I've never considered it from that angle. It's what boys in my position do.'

'What would you say about joining the police? It's a good life, solid, a decent salary, a career in which talent can rise. One of the few. You could hope for a good position. In society I mean.'

And so Lom's future had been settled. He would be a policeman. The private decency of houses like the Arensbergs' was worth protecting. He was a fighter and he could keep it safe, and one day perhaps he would rise high enough in the service to have such a house himself, like the Deputy's on Sytin Prospect.

He passed the entrance examination without difficulty. It was in the very same week that he took the oath of commitment to the Vlast that the terrible dark blade fell. The knife went in.

Gendarmes came from Magadlovosk to the Arensbergs' house and took the doctor away. He was denounced. A profiteer. An enemy of the people. A spy for the Archipelago. They took him down the Yannis and he never returned. The house was seized, declared forfeit to the Vlast and granted to the new Commissar for Timber Yards. Stepan's commission was revoked. Mrs Arensberg, Stepan and Thea moved into a single room above a stationer's shop off Ansky Prospect.

Lom couldn't believe in Arensberg's guilt. It was a mistake. It would be cleared up. Someone had lied. A magistrate made his share of enemies. Lom would prove Arensberg's innocence one day, when he'd finished his training. He said as much to Thea when he went to see her, wearing his new cadet uniform, in the room off Ansky Prospect, with its yellow furniture and thin muslin curtains. She had tied a scarf around her hair and she was scrubbing layers of fat and dust off the kitchen shelves when he arrived.

Thea had thrown him out.

'Get out of here, policeman,' she said bitterly.

'Thea – I want to help you – all of you.'

'Don't you see you're one of them?'

'But only for you … for him …'

'That uniform makes me sick,' she said. 'Don't come here again.'

He stayed away for a few days to let her calm down, but when he went back, Mrs Arensberg – distant, polite, formal – told him Thea had left Podchornok. She was going to live in Yagda. She had cousins there, or aunts, or something. She planned to study and become a doctor like her father.

That same week Lom saw Raku Vishnik off to the University. In one week he'd lost them both, and the Arensbergs' house was gone for ever.

Lom had immersed himself in police work. As soon as he could, he called up the magistrate Arensberg's file. The evidence against him was overwhelming. He'd been sent to Vig, and died there. No cause of death was recorded. There was nothing to be done.

Fifteen years.

It hadn't been difficult. There was always someone to tell you what to do. Someone like Krogh. Krogh wasn't a bad man. But he wasn't a good man either. He wasn't any sort of man.

Detectives make nothing happen. They do the opposite, repairing the damage done by events: desire, anger, accident and change. Stitching the surface of things back together. But events break the surface open anyway. Inside you. Transforming the way you feel and see things. Taking an axe to the frozen sea inside us. Detectives can't clear up after that.

Sleep would not come. Lom lay there and listened to the rumble of the darkened city.

And then there was something else in the room. There had not been and now there was.

It was a dark and sour presence, a thing of blood and earth. No door had opened. No curtain had stirred. It had arrived. Somehow.

It was coming closer. Lom could see it now, at the edge of vision, soaked in the light of the moons. Standing, looking at him, sniffing the air. Lom dared not move his head to see it more clearly, but he knew what it was. He had seen such a thing before, once, laid out dead on the earth under a stand of silver birch. That one had been shaped like a man, or rather a child, short and slender, with a small head and a lean, wiry strength. But this one was different, and not only because it was alive, and stalking him. The body he had seen was naked and entirely white, with the whiteness of a thing that had never felt the light of the sun. This one wore clothes of a kind and the skin of its face and hands was oddly piebald. Large irregular blotches of blackness marked the pallor. It was a killer, an eater of blood.

Suddenly the thing was not where it had been, ten feet away between the window and the door. It was standing over him, leaning forward, opening its black mouth. Lom had not seen it cover the intervening space. He was certain it had not done so. It had simply ... moved.

Such creatures cannot bear to be looked at. They hate the touch of the human gaze. When it saw that Lom was awake and staring into its eyes it flinched and staggered a step backwards. It recovered almost immediately, but it had given Lom the moment he needed to screw up all his fear and revulsion into a ball and cast it at the thing. In the same instant he threw off the blanket, leapt to his feet and lunged forward. But the thing was no longer where it had been. It was to his left, at his side, jumping up and gripping his shoulder, scrabbling at his neck. He felt the heat of its breath on his face. Smelled the cold wet smell of earth. In desperation Lom threw at his attacker all the air in the room. The creature staggered back and fell. Photographs scattered and a chair fell loudly sideways. A lamp crashed to the floor.

It was the surprise as much as the force of the attack that was effective. The piebald thing fell awkwardly. As it struggled to its feet, the back of its head was exposed. Wisps of thin hair across its surprisingly slender, conical skull. Lom stepped forward, the cosh from his sleeve gripped firmly. He wouldn't get another chance.

But it was not there. It was gone. Lom whipped round, braced for an attack from behind that he was unlikely to survive, but the moonlit room was empty.

The door from the bedroom opened.

'Vissarion? What the fuck are you doing?'

Vishnik lit the lamp. The study was in chaos. Heaps of books scattered everywhere. A picture fallen from the wall, its glass shattered.

'What happened? What have you done?' He saw the rips in Lom's shirt, the smears of blood from deep scratches on his face and neck, the delicate nastiness of the small cosh in his fist.

'It was a vyrdalak,' said Lom. 'A strange one.' He sat down heavily on the couch. Now that it was over, his legs were trembling and he felt emptily sick. He knew what the bite of such a creature could do. 'I guess the Commander wants her files back.'

34

Lakoba Petrov didn't go home after leaving the Marmot's. He no longer needed a place of his own. He hadn't eaten for so long, he no longer felt hungry. He threw away what remained of his money and walked through the night, drinking sweet water copiously wherever he could find it. The clear coldness of it made his soul also clear and cold. His Mirgorod burned. It was awash with cool, glorious rain and the rain washed him clean.

Again and again the night city detonated for him, bursting into roses of truth. He was walking through paintings, truer and better than any he had painted. He could have painted them if had chosen to do it. But why should he? There was no need. He had a better idea. As he walked the streets in a pyrotechnical excitement of fizzing synapses, he developed in words his new principle of art. An art that would leave painting behind altogether and become something new and pure and clean. The art of the coming destruction.

He did carry one tube of paint with him, though, in his pocket. A beautiful lilac–turquoise. In the lamplight, looking at his reflection in the mirror in a barber's shop window, he squeezed the paint onto his finger and wrote on his forehead. '*I, Petrov*.' It wasn't easy, mirror writing. He had to concentrate.

When he grew tired he lay down to sleep, and in the dawn when he woke his clothes crackled with the snapping of ice.

35

Maroussia Shaumian got out of bed in the chill grey of dawn. She lived in a one-room apartment with her mother out near the Oyster Bridge. There wasn't much: a bed to share, some yellow furniture, a thin and faded rug on bare boards. Her mother was sitting upright on a chair in the centre of the carpet, wearing only her dressing gown. Her thin hair, unbrushed, stood up round her head in a scrappy, pathetic halo. It was icy cold in the room, though the windows were closed tight. Her small breaths and Maroussia's own were tiny visible ghosts in the chill air.

'Come on,' said Maroussia, holding out her hand. 'I'll get the stove lit. Come and get dressed.'

Her mother flapped at her to be silent. Her hands were as soft and pale and strengthless as the empty eggshells of a small bird.

'What is it?' said Maroussia. 'What's the matter?'

'Come away from the window. They'll see you. They're watching.'

'There's nobody there. Just people in the street.'

'They're there, only you can't see them.'

'Where then? Show me.'

Her mother shook her head. Stubbornness was the only strong thing left in her. 'I'm not coming over there.'

'Get dressed at least.' Maroussia went towards the wardrobe.

Her mother whimpered quietly. 'Don't open it,' she breathed. 'Maroussia. Please. Don't.'

Maroussia began to set out food on the table for their breakfast. There'd been a time when she would have dragged her mother across to the window or even out into the street, to show her that what she feared wasn't there. Hoping to shake her out of it. Sometimes she had literally grabbed her and shaken her by the shoulders, hard, until it must have hurt, and shouted into her face. *It's all right. It's all right. There's nothing there. Please, just be normal.* But it made no difference. Nothing did. The nights were the worst. Maroussia would wake to find her mother piling up their few bits of furniture against the door. 'They're coming back,' she would be muttering. 'The trees are coming back.'

She still called her 'mother', though the word had long ago stopped being even the empty shell of an exhausted, bitter joke. 'Mother' was the faded inscription on an empty box.

Maroussia touched her mother on the shoulder.

'Come over to the table,' she said. 'You must be hungry.'

There was bread, sausage, a potato. Her mother looked at it. 'Where's it from?'

'Issy and Zena's'

'Oh no, I couldn't touch anything from there.'

Maroussia couldn't say that the falling of the shadow across her mother's life had come as a surprise. Although she had never been sat down and told the story of their lives, she had pieced it together over the years.

Her mother had been Feiga-Ita Shaumian, and then Feiga-Ita Kantor, and then Feiga-Ita Shaumian again. The Shaumians had been one of the great families of Lezarye, and Feiga-Ita's marriage to Josef Kantor was a grand occasion: he the firebrand orator and Hope of the Future, she his loving and industrious amanuensis. When Josef was sent into internal exile in the aftermath of the Birzel Rebellion, Feiga-Ita had gone with him, though she didn't have to. But then, suddenly, she'd abandoned her husband, even though she was pregnant, and gone back to the city. She endured the long journey to Mirgorod alone and ill. It had been a difficult pregnancy. In Mirgorod she had reverted to her former name, borne the child, called her Maroussia, cut off all contact with her old life, her family, the dreamers of Lezarye, brought up the daughter in a succession of obscure and shabby attics.

At first there had been good times. Maroussia remembered the games and stories, the small adventures out into the city and beyond, to the sea and to the suburban parks that ringed the city, but Feiga-Ita had lapsed at last into this permanent darkness of the heart. Maroussia had got used to sharing their room with the dark predatory walking shadows of trees and the spies and accusers that followed her mother down the street and waited in the darkness of alleyways, stairwells and wardrobes.

She cut a slice of hard black bread and some sausage and ate it herself.

Her mother, feeling herself watched, looked across at her with wide, watery eyes.

'Maroussia?' she said.

'Yes?'

You won't tell them, will you?'

'What?'

'Don't ever tell them what I did.'

'I have to go now,' said Maroussia. 'I have to go.'

36

Lom sat at the desk in Vishnik's apartment, turning over the pages of the Kantor folder again. Wondering where to go from here. Chazia wanted her file back. She was a dangerous enemy: she had tried to kill him once, and she would try again. Kantor was Chazia's agent. So much was obvious from the file. It was proof – enough to take to Krogh and let him deal with Chazia. But it was unsatisfactory. Would Krogh deal with Chazia? Could he? And Lom wanted more. He wanted Kantor.

He was about to close the folder when he noticed a paper he had overlooked before, because it was out of date order, torn loose and tucked inside the flap at the back of the file. It was just a routine official instruction, concerned with Kantor's removal to Vig. The accompanying report said that his wife had already returned to Mirgorod. Wife's name: Shaumian, Feiga-Ita. Chazia had added a note in pencil: '*There is a daughter. Not his. KEEP IN VIEW.*' The last three words triple underlined. Pinned to the back of the instruction sheet was a typed half-sheet with an address:

Shaumian, Feiga-Ita & Shaumian, Maroussia
387 Velazhin, Apt. 23
Oyster Bridge
White Side

Chazia had written against each name a series of letters and numerals. Lom recognised them as file references for the Gaukh Engine.

Kantor had a wife, and Maroussia Shaumian was her *daughter*?

Circles of contact.

Shit.

37

The paluba and her companion of forest air stood in the doorway of an empty building, watching the entrance to the Shaumians' apartment block across the street. They were waiting for the daughter to leave. They wanted to find the mother alone. It was the mother they knew. From many years before. She was their better hope.

When they saw the daughter go, they crossed the road and climbed the stairs. No one saw them. There were people there, in the street, but they were not seen.

The paluba paused outside the apartment door, on the tiny landing at a bend in the stairs. She could feel the Pollandore as a strong presence in the room and seeping out of it. She could feel its thrilling touch. New things were possible here. She scratched and tapped at the door with her fingers of birch twig and squirrel's tendon.

'Feiga-Ita Shaumian, let me in.' Her voice buzzed and rattled like gusts of air in the strings of a wind harp. There was no answer. Nothing moved behind the door, but the paluba sensed a listener in the dark.

'Feiga-Ita Shaumian, open the door.'

Silence.

'Feiga-Ita Shaumian. You know me. Let me in. I have a message. From him.'

Silence.

'Feiga-Ita Shaumian!'

'He's dead.'

It was quieter than a whisper. The old woman was talking to herself, her words drained of energy by a fear so old and heavy it was like listening for the trickle of dust under stones. But the paluba heard.

'No,' she said. 'He is alive.'

'He is dead.'

'No. He sent you letters, but you never replied.'

'There were no letters.'

'He is your daughter's father.'

Silence.

'Feiga-Ita Shaumian, open the door.'

Silence. No, not silence. Short, harsh breathing. The scraping of furniture across a wooden floor. Bumping against the other side of the door. Being piled up.

'Feiga-Ita Shaumian, I have a message for you.'

'There are trees in my room. Get them out of my room. Leave me alone.'

'He needs you now. He needs his daughter. You must hear his message. Let me in.'

'I am standing by the window. If you try to come in I'll jump.'

The paluba heard the casement opening. Heard the faint sounds from the street become louder. Felt the stir of air from outside.

'You could come with us. We will take you with us. Back to the woods.'

Silence. Quiet, ragged gulps of breath.

'We will take you both, the daughter too, when what must be done is done.'

Silence.

The figure of air made a slight motion and the door blew inwards, splintering off its hinges, but the furniture piled behind it budged only a few inches. Inside, Maroussia's mother moaned.

'Please don't make me jump,' she said. 'Make the trees go away. Please.'

'The Pollandore must be opened, Feiga-Ita. The time has come. You or she must do it. There is no one else now. It needs to be done.'

Inside the room there was only breathing.

Silence.

The paluba laid her dry simulacrum of a hand against the door as if she were going to push it aside. But she didn't.

'Do this thing, Feiga-Ita Shaumian. Or tell the daughter. The daughter can do it. Will you tell her?'

Silence.

The paluba brought a small object out from under her garment. It was an intricate hollow knot of tiny twigs, feathers and twine, somewhat larger than a chicken's egg, with a handful of dried reddish berries rattling around inside it. Globules of a yellowish waxy substance adhered to the outside. She put it to her mouth and breathed on it, then laid it on the floor in front of the broken door.

'When you see your daughter, Feiga-Ita, give her this. It is a gift from him. It is the key to the world.'

She waited a moment longer, but there was only silence. The paluba turned away. Her time was ebbing. And so was hope. She and her companion descended the stairs.

Some time later – an hour – two hours – there came the sound of furniture scraping across the floor inside the room. Slowly. Hesitantly. Then nothing.

Then the broken door was pulled aside and Feiga-Ita Shaumian came out.

She saw the small object left for her on the landing, picked it up gingerly with her fingertips and slipped it into a small, flimsy bag. Holding the bag carefully in both hands she went slowly down the stairs and out into the street.

38

An hour later Lom arrived at the Shaumians' apartment and found the door broken off its hinges and thrown to one side. He went in and looked around. Furniture was overturned and the window stood wide open: thin unlined curtains stirred in the cold breeze. He pulled open a drawer in the table. There was nothing inside but a few pieces of cheap and ill-matched cutlery. What had he expected?

'You've missed them. They just left.'

The woman was standing behind him in the doorway. She was wearing slippers and a dressing gown belted loosely over some kind of undergarment. Her hair, bright orange, showed grey roots. She held out her hand to him with surprising grace.

'Good morning sir. Avrilova. I am Avrilova.'

The way she said her name implied she thought it should mean something to him. He smelled the sweet perfume of mint and aquavit on her breath.

'They went out and left it like this?' he said.

'I mean, you've missed the other police. Or were they militia? What *is* the difference? Could you tell me please?'

'Madam ...'

'I told you, I am Avrilova. You must have heard me sing. Surely you did. I was at Mogen's for many years.'

'What did the police want here? The other police.'

'The same as you, of course. Looking for the Shaumian women.'

'And did the police do this to the door?'

'Of course not. Police don't break down doors. It was like that before. She's mad, the old one. She never goes out, but you hear her all the time, shouting to herself. You wouldn't think she had the voice for it.'

'But she has gone out. She is not here now.'

'Well, obviously.'

Lom walked round the room some more. There wasn't much else to see. A bed. A few books. Poetry. That surprised him. And *Modern Painters of Mirgorod*, a cheap-looking edition with poor-quality plates. The author was Professor R. t-F. M. S-V. Vishnik.

When he looked up from the book Avrilova was still there.

'What does she shout?' he said.

'I beg your pardon?'

'You said you hear Madam Shaumian shouting to herself. So what does she shout about? What does she say?'

Avrilova shrugged. 'Does it matter? Rubbish. Craziness. I told you, she's mad.'

'Mad enough to wrench her own door off its hinges?'

Avrilova shrugged again. 'It would be a mad thing to do.'

'There must have been some noise when that happened to the door. Did you hear anything?'

'I sing every morning without fail. The house could blow up while I am singing and I'd know nothing about it.'

'Madam Avrilova, I need to talk to them. It's a police matter.'

'It's the daughter you want.'

'Why would you say that?'

'Well, she's the *trouble*, isn't she? She's the *intellectual*.'

'Do you know where she is?'

'Why ask me? Haven't you read the file? I've told Officer Kasso all about her several times. He gave me money and wrote it down.'

'What did you tell Kasso?'

'He knew the value of good information. Those other ones hadn't read the file either, but they gave me ten roubles. You only just missed them. You might catch them if you run. Then you could ask them, couldn't you? So many policemen for one broken door.'

Lom fished a handful of coins from his pocket.

'Madam Avrilova—'

'The daughter sews. At Vanko's. The uniform factory.'

39

Maroussia Shaumian worked without thinking, and that was good. She let the dull weight of work squat in her mind, smothering memory.

Vanko's uniform factory had been an engine shed once, but it was a hollow carcase now, a stone shell braced with ribs and arches of old black iron, the walls still streaked with soot, the high windows filmed with grease and dust. Parallel rail tracks sliced across the stone floor and the ghost of coal haunted the air, mingling with newer smells of serge and machine oil. The cutting machines clattered and shook under an old tin sign pitted with rust: MIRGOROD—CETIC AMBER LINE. From the iron arches Vanko had slung a net of cables sparsely fruited with bare electric bulbs, but he only switched them on when it was too dark to work by the dirty muted light of day. Vanko himself sat in his high glass cabin underneath the clock, warmed by a paraffin stove, drinking aquavit from a tin mug and watching the women work.

Maroussia was on buttons. The serge roughened and cracked the skin of her hands. She sat at a trestle with a tin of threaded needles and a compartmented tray of buttons – heaps of cheap brass discs and ivory pellets – while the endless belt of rubberised cotton jerked slowly past her. She had to pick a garment, sew four buttons on it, and replace it on the belt before the next one reached her. If she looked up, she saw the hunched back of the woman in front, who would add the next four. The row of women's bent heads and backs stretched away before her and behind, mirrored by an identical row across the conveyor belt, facing the other way. On the other side they worked pedal-powered sewing machines, black and shiny as beetles. They did pockets, collars, seams. Each woman worked in silence under the thin shelter of her own woollen scarf or shawl. You couldn't make yourself heard above the clatter of the belts and the cutting machines, and if you tried Vanko saw you and docked your time. He kept a plan of the tables on his desk and he knew the name of every woman by the number of their position.

'Hey!' Vanko's voice squawked on the tannoy. 'Get that old witch out of here! Who let her in? Blow away, Granny! Hey, Fasil! Where the hell is Fasil?'

Maroussia looked up. The small woman coming down the aisle was her mother. Her hair was a wild, sparse corona of grey, and she was clutching a small bag in both hands, holding it high against her chest as if it would defend her against the indifference of the women and Vanko's yelling. Scattered melting flakes of snow on her face and in her hair. She had no coat. Fasil was working his way towards her from the direction of the cutting machines.

Maroussia stood up, spilling a tin of pins across the floor. By the time she reached her, her mother had come to a bewildered halt.

'Mother? What are you *doing* here?' said Maroussia. 'Do you want to lose me my job?'

Her mother's eyes wouldn't focus properly. She was pressing the little bag to her breasts. Fasil was coming closer. Maroussia put her mouth against her mother's ear and shouted.

'Come on. We have to get outside.'

Her mother didn't move. She was saying something, but her voice couldn't be heard. Maroussia put her hands on her shoulders – they felt as soft and strengthless as a child's – and turned her towards the way out, pushing her gently forward. They had reached the door and Maroussia was pulling it open when Fasil gripped her roughly by the elbow and pulled her backwards.

'You're holding up the line. Will you pay for the pieces?' He turned to Feiga-Ita. 'Will you?'

'Look at her, Fasil. She's ill.'

Fasil pulled Maroussia closer against him. His cheeks were striated with fine red veins. His small eyes were narrowed, his mouth slightly open. There were damp flecks of stuff in his heavy tobacco-gingered moustache.

'Superior little whore,' he breathed. 'You think we're shit.'

'Fasil, please, I just need a moment ...'

He moved his hand down her back. She felt him trace the curve of her spine down into the valley of her buttocks, probing with his fingers through the thin material of her coat.

'Whore,' he hissed in her ear. 'You can pay me later.'

Maroussia shoved her mother out and followed, pushing the door shut behind her and leaning against it, her eyes closed. Fasil was a bastard. There wouldn't be an end to that, now.

Her mother was talking rapidly.

'They've come for me. He's back. We have to go. Run. Hide.'

'What are you talking about?'

'He's alive. He's come back. He sent a message. He wants us. He says for us to go with her. To the forest, Maroussia. Back to the trees.' She held out the bag she was clutching. 'Take it,' she said. 'Take it. It's here. You can feel it here.'

Maroussia pushed the shabby little bag aside.

'You shouldn't have come here, Mother. I have to go back inside now.'

'No!' Her mother was pleading with her. She held the little bag forward again, her thin white fingers like frail claws. 'There were trees in the room. He wants you.'

'He's not in the forest! Josef is in Mirgorod. And he doesn't want us, Mother, of course he doesn't. And we don't want him.'

Her mother looked at her, puzzled. 'Josef? No. Not him – not Josef – the other one.'

Maroussia felt the door move behind her. Somebody was trying to push it open. She heard Fasil's voice.

'Go home, Mother!' It was hard enough without this. 'Please. Whatever it is, you can tell me later. At home.'

Maroussia turned and pulled the door open, surprising Fasil. She shoved past him and walked back to her trestle, looking neither right nor left, feeling the eyes of the women watching her. She picked a uniform from the line and began to work.

It took her two minutes, perhaps five, to realise that her mother would never find her way home by herself. It was a miracle she'd managed to get herself to Vanko's in the first place.

Maroussia picked up her coat and walked back down the aisle, out into the Mirgorod morning. There were other jobs. Probably.

When she got outside she looked up and down the street. There was no sign of her mother.

40

Lom came round a corner against soft wet flurries of snow and stopped dead in his tracks. Twenty yards or so ahead of him two militia men were standing in the long alleyway that cut down between warehouses towards Vanko's. They had their backs to him. One of them was Major Safran.

The other had laid a hand on Safran's shoulder and was pointing out an elderly woman coming up the alley towards them, walking slowly, talking to herself. Her hair was a wild wispy mess and she was holding her hands cupped in front of her, carrying something precious. Safran took some papers out of his pocket – photographs – glanced at them and nodded. The militia men moved down the alley to meet the old woman. When she saw them coming she clutched her hands tighter against her chest and turned back.

'Hey!' shouted Safran. 'You! Stop there!'

She ignored him and walked faster, breaking into a kind of scuttling hobble. Safran took his revolver from his holster and levelled it.

'Militia! Halt or I shoot!'

'No!' shouted Lom, but he was too far away to be heard above the traffic noise.

Safran fired once.

The woman's legs broke under her and she collapsed. She was still struggling to crawl forward when Safran reached her. He hooked the toe of his boot under her ribs and flipped her over onto her back. She lay, her left foot stuck out sideways at a very wrong angle, looking up at him. Her other leg was shifting feebly from side to side. Safran compared her to the photograph in his hand, said something to the other militia man, and shot her in the face. Her head burst against the snowy pavement like an over-ripe fruit, spattering the men's legs with mess. The one with Safran flinched back in disgust, and dabbed at his trouser-shins with a handkerchief. After a cursory check that she was dead, they continued towards Vanko's.

Lom felt sick. Another senseless killing in the name of the Vlast. Another uniformed murder.

The woman's body, when he came close to it, was a bundle of rags. Around her broken face the cooling blood had scooped hollows in the snow, scarlet-centred, fringed with soft edges of rose-pink, and in one of the hollows lay the object she had held so tightly: a little bag of some thin, rough material. Hessian? Hemp? Lom picked it up. The side that had lain in the snow was wet with blood. He untied the cord that held the mouth of it pursed shut. Inside was a fragile-looking ball of twigs. He closed the bag and slipped it into his pocket

'Get away from her! Leave her alone!'

Lom looked round. Maroussia Shaumian was staring at him with wide unseeing eyes.

'She's my mother,' she said. 'I have to take her home.'

'Maroussia,' said Lom. 'I couldn't stop this. I was too late. I'm sorry.'

'I have to take her home,' she was saying. 'I can't leave her here.'

'Maroussia—'

'Perhaps I could get a cart.'

She was losing focus. He'd seen people like this after a street accident: together enough on the surface, but they weren't really there, they hadn't aligned themselves to the new reality. You had to be rough to get through to them.

'Your mother has been shot,' he said harshly. 'She is dead. That is her body. The militia killed her deliberately. They were looking for her. Do you understand me?' Maroussia was staring at him, her dark eyes fierce, small points of red flushing her cheeks. 'I think they're looking for you too. When they find you're not at Vanko's they'll come back, and if you're still here they'll kill you as well.'

'You,' she said. 'I know you. You did this.'

'No. I didn't. I wanted to stop it. I couldn't—'

'You're a policeman.'

He took her arm and tried to turn her away from her dead mother. 'I want to help you,' he said.

'Fuck you.'

'I'll take you somewhere. We can talk.'

She jerked her arm away. She was surprisingly strong. Her muscles were hard.

'I said *fuck you.*'

Safran had appeared at the far end of the alley.

'Maroussia, I want to help you,' said Lom. 'But you have to get away from here. Now. Or they'll do that to you.'

'Why would you help me? You're one of them.'

'No,' said Lom. 'I'm not.'

Safran was coming.

Maroussia looked at her mother, lying raw and dead under the high walls of the alley and the sky.

'I can't just leave her,' she said. 'The rats … the gulls …'

'Listen,' said Lom. 'You have to go now. I'll make time for you.'

'What?'

'Go now. Do you hear me? Don't go home. Go to Vishnik's and wait for me there.'

But she was glaring at him. Her face was hard and closed.

'You don't want to help me. You're a liar. Leave me alone. Leave my mother alone.'

Hey!' Safran had begun to jog, drawing his revolver as he came. 'Hey, you!'

Lom stepped into the middle of the alley and held up his hand, hoping that behind him Maroussia was walking away. Hoping that his own face wasn't on one of Safran's photographs.

'What the hell are you doing here, Lom?'

Safran's face was tight with anger.

'No mudjhik?' said Lom. 'Doing your own killing today?'

'Who was that woman? Teslev, stop her.'

'Wait,' said Lom. 'I want to talk to you. Both of you.'

Teslev ignored him and hurried after Maroussia, who had reached the end of the alley, walking fast. Her back looked long and thin and straight in her threadbare coat. The nape of her neck, bare and pale between collar and short black hair, was the most vulnerable and nakedly human thing Lom had ever seen. He felt as if a fist had reached inside his ribs and taken a grip on his heart, squeezing it tight.

41

Maroussia's legs were shaking so much it was hard to walk. Her spine was trickling hot ice, waiting for the impact of the militia man's bullet.

Keep going, she told herself. *Don't look back. Get out of sight. Think!*

Her world was compressed into the next few seconds, She imagined the bullets smashing into her spine. Her legs. Breaking.

Think! Do something! Now!

There were no limits. No rules. Just *do something*.

An alleyway opened up to her left, narrow between tall buildings. No one had been down it since the snow started. She knew where the alley went. Nowhere. A dead end. She cut into it. At least for a few moments she was out of their sight.

One side of the alley was a blank brick face, the other a wall of rough stone blocks stained with grime. Dark windows looked out over it, but high overhead, out of reach. No doors. The building was, she thought, an old warehouse. If she could get inside it ... inside was better ... she could run ... weave ... find a way out again ... into the crowded streets ... lose herself in the crowd ...

She took a few steps into the middle of the alley, turned, ran at the wall, jumped ... Her fingers stretched for the window ledge ...

Her weight crashed hard against the wall. Her knee, her elbow, smashed against it. Her fingers scrabbled at the rough face of the stone, well below the window, and she fell.

She pulled off her shoes and forced the bare toes of one foot hard into the crevice between two blocks of stone, drove her fingers into the gap at shoulder level, and pulled herself up. It worked. She was off the ground, barely, her body flattened, her cheek pressed against the cold wall, her fingers trembling. She tried to dig them further into the stone, tried to gouge out holds by sheer effort of will. She raised her good leg, gasping as her weight pressed on her injured knee, lifted one hand, pulled herself a little higher. It worked. And again. She was almost half her own height above the snow and crawling slowly up the vertical face of the wall. She stretched upwards and got the fingertips of one hand onto the stone ledge of the window. With a desperate lunge she got the other hand next to it. Her feet slipped but she scrabbled with her toes and got purchase again, half pulling and half walking upwards until her backside was sticking out, her knees tucked under. There was a groove in the window ledge she could hook her fingers into. If she could just get one knee up there—

'Are you going to come down, or do I shoot you up the arse?'

42

Lom turned his back on Safran and walked over to the old woman's broken body. She had been so fragile. He could have picked her up and tucked her under his arm. It was taking all his effort not to look behind him, back up the alley, to see if Teslev was coming back.

'Who gave you the photographs, Safran? The pictures of the Shaumian women? Who turned you loose on them?'

Safran stared at him. 'This has nothing to do with you.'

'I mean,' Lom continued. 'You'd hardly come after them on your own initiative, would you? You probably don't even know who they are. I mean, who they really are.'

'What are you getting at?'

'I hope for your sake the order came directly from Chazia herself.'

'And who are *you* working for, Lom?'

Lom shrugged. He kicked at a stone. *Keep him off balance. Don't let him have time to think.*

'So did you find the object Chazia wanted?'

This time Safran looked genuinely puzzled.

'What are you talking about?'

'Never mind. Don't worry about it.'

The crack of a pistol shot echoed off the high walls. It sounded a few streets away.

Safran smiled. 'Teslev found her.'

Another shot. And then another.

'Ah,' said Safran. 'The *coup de grâce*.'

43

Maroussia, clinging to the window ledge, looked down under her arm and stared into the face of the militia man. He was standing below her, his pistol in his hand. He'd obviously been there a while, watching her trying to climb. He thought it was funny. It was in his face. She pushed herself away from the wall and crashed down onto him. He collapsed under her weight. The pistol fired. Something slapped, hard and burning, against her calf and her whole leg went numb.

'You. Stupid. *Bitch.*'

She was lying on her back on top of him. His breath was hot against her ear, his voice close, almost a whisper. She whipped her head forward and sharply back, smashing it into his face, and felt his nose burst. The militia man swore viciously and smashed his gun against the side of her head. And did it again. And again. She felt something jagged open a rip in her cheek. Then his other hand was scrabbling around in front of her, trying to pull at her, trying to roll her off him.

'I'm going to kill you,' he whispered. '*Bitch.*'

He was strong. She couldn't fight him. In another second he would be able to get his gun against her back or her ribs and fire without risk of hitting himself. She dug her hand back and under herself, pushing it down between their struggling bodies, scrabbling for his testicles, and when she found them she squeezed and twisted as viciously as she could. The militia man yelled and arched his back, trying to throw her off, trying to club at her hand with the pistol. She jerked her head backwards again and again, smashing it recklessly into his face. She felt it strike a sweet spot on his chin, smashing his skull back against the pavement. She felt him go slack.

Maroussia rolled away from him and raised herself up on her hands and knees. The militia man was lying on his back, trying to raise his head, his eyes struggling to focus.

'Bitch,' he mumbled. 'Bitch.' He raised his pistol towards her. It seemed heavy in his hand.

She grabbed at the pistol with both hands, twisting and wrenching it. It fired a shot but she barely noticed. She felt the man's finger snap and the gun came away in her grasp. 'Oh no,' he said quietly. 'No.'

She pressed the muzzle against his thigh and pulled the trigger.

44

In the mid-morning quiet of his apartment Raku Vishnik cleared his desk and spread across it a large new street plan of Mirgorod. The city – crisp black lines on fresh white paper – looked geometrical and rectilinear, a network of canals and prospects laid out like electrical cabling, connecting islands to squares and squares to islands; a civic circuit diagram for the orderly channelling of work and movement. It was nothing, or almost nothing, but wishful aspiration. A flimsy overlay of civilisation, the merest stencil grid over marsh and mist and dreams.

Next to the map Vishnik set out his neat pile of filled notebooks, a box file of newspaper cuttings, a sheaf of other maps and plans. The maps all showed the city or parts of it, and all of them were creased, much re-folded, and covered with faint pencil marks: lines and symbols and Vishnik's own cramped and scarcely legible annotations, from single words to entire paragraphs. The hatbox of photographs was on the floor beside his chair. On the other side of the window the city breathed and rumbled. Snow flurries smudged the distance, yellow and grey and brown.

He was looking for shape and pattern.

Methodically he sifted through his notes, looking for anomalous events. Times and places when the city slipped and shifted. Like it had in the Bakery Galina Tropina. Like it had in his photographs. Like it had when he went back to a familiar place and found it different. Others had seen such things in the city. He picked them up in newspapers usually, but also in conversations overheard on trams and buses, in shops, in the street. He'd kept a record of every one. They were in his notebooks. Date, place, time.

Ever since Maroussia Shaumian had come to him the other night a new idea had been taking shape in his mind. A new possibility. Maroussia had pushed him across a threshold. Until then it had never occurred to him that he could do more than accumulate notes and records. He had been an archivist of glimpses only. The thought had never struck him that what he was seeing had a cause. A source. That he could act.

But now, slowly, carefully, thoroughly, he went through the notebooks, one by one, and for each event he made a pencil mark on the map. All morning he worked, attuning his breathing to the slow pulse of the rain and the city.

The pattern began to emerge. It started to resolve itself under his gaze like a photograph in a developing dish, a sketchy outline first, then the richer finer details. But he resisted it. He didn't want to jump to conclusions. He didn't want to mislead himself. He kept calm. He stuck to his method.

I should have done this long ago. This has always been here for the finding and I never thought to look.

By mid-afternoon he'd finished. He pinned the map to the wall and stood back. There was no doubting it. There could be no mistake. The spattering of pencil marks looked like a black sunburst, a carbon flower blooming, a splash – as if a ball of black flakes had been thrown at the city and splattered on impact. The rays of the sun-splash pattern thinned out in all directions towards the edges of the city, but at the centre they were clustered, overlapping, intense. They were concentrated around one place. It looked like an impact point, a moon crater, the focal point of an explosive scattering. It was the source. There was something there. Causing the surface life of the city to shift and tremble. And the effect was growing stronger. He had found it.

Vishnik went to the bookshelf by the stove and took out the old book with the sun-faded, water-stained cover. The spine was detaching itself, the gilt lettering rubbing away, the thin translucent pages grubby and bruised. It was a forbidden work now, under the interdiction of the Vlast for more than a century, ever since its existence had been noticed. He'd found this copy tucked behind a heating pipe in the library of the Institute of Truth at Podchornok more than twenty years ago. He'd shown it to no one, and he'd never found another copy since. No reference to it in any library. So far as he knew, his was the only one in existence. *A Child's Book of Wonders, Legends and Tales of Long Ago*.

Once more he opened it at the familiar page. Once more, sitting on the floor by his bookshelf in the dimming light of late afternoon, he began to read.

'How They Made The Pollandore.'

45

Lom left Safran and the body of the executed woman, and walked. Anywhere. Nowhere. He hated the city. He hated the way you could just walk out of an alley and into the flow of crowds and traffic. Faces in the street. Faces behind windows. Faces that knew nothing about the dead body of an old woman a few yards away. That was in another city, not theirs. He needed to *breathe*. Needed to *think*.

He bought a ticket and got on a tram at random. The circle line, orbiting the city centre. The car was almost empty. Two thin men with clean-shaven angular faces were talking about horses. Round-brimmed hats, heeled ankle boots, woollen suits with trouser cuffs. Signs shouted at him: CITIZENS! BEWARE BOMBS! REPORT SUSPICIOUS PACKAGES! LEAVE NO LUGGAGE UNATTENDED!

A young man in the rear corner seat was staring at him. Frowning. A long thin nose. High cheekbones. Greasy hair in thick strands across his forehead. He had a book open but he wasn't reading. When his gaze met Lom's he de-focused his eyes and pretended he was looking past him, out of the window. Lom shrugged inwardly. Just a student. He wondered what book he was carrying. It was heavy and thick and looked old. Not mathematics or engineering, not with hair like that. He considered going across to find out what it was. Shake the tree. See what fell out. Once, not long ago, he would have. But not now. Leave him be. Leave him to his thoughts. Lom realised he was staring, and the young man was suffering under it: he'd buried himself in his book, pretending to be absorbed in it, but his neck and the edges of his cheekbones were flushed. When the tram stopped he would get up and leave, carefully, avoiding eye contact.

The snow had stopped falling. Nothing but wet grey slush on the pavements already. Mirgorod unfolded on the other side of the window but Lom hardly saw it. It was too close, pressed right up against his face. It was too big and too dirty. It made no sense. What you saw from a tram window were the small things. Random, fragmentary things: a narrow alleyway disappearing between shopfronts; the sign of a drawing master's school; fresh perch on ice outside a fishmonger's; the hobbles on a dray horse; a bricked-up window. The city was vast beyond understanding. It replenished itself infinitely, teeming beyond count. People lived their lives in Mirgorod by choosing a few places, a few faces, a few events, to be the landmarks of their own imagined, private city. Interior cities of the mind, a million cities, all interleaved one with another in the same place and time, semi-transparent. Onion-layer cities, stacked cities, soft and intricate, all of them tied together by the burrowing, twining, imperceptible threads of the information machine. Flimsy cities, every one. All it took was a militia bullet, the hack of a dragoon sabre. But the tissue cities carried on.

And underneath them all, two futures, struggling against each other to be born.

Lom slipped his hand into his pocket and met something sticky and rough: Feiga-Ita Shaumian's bag, tacky with her clotting blood. He untied the cord and looked inside. It was like the hedge-nest of some bird, just the kind of thing a crazy old woman might carry around, but it wasn't a nest. The sticks were tied together with thread. He eased it out of the bag for a closer look. Some of her blood had soaked through and clotted on it, dark and viscous, and there were globs of some other stuff, some kind of yellow wax, and dry, maroon-coloured berries. He held it up to the light. There were fine bones inside, parts of the skeleton of some tiny animal. A mouse? A mole? A small bird? There was a strong scent too, some sweet warmth stronger than the iron of blood. He remembered the whiteless brown eyes of the soldier in the street in Podchornok, out in the rain.

Some instinct made Lom hold the thing up close to his face and sniff at it. And the world changed. It was as if the skin of his senses had been unpeeled. The hard line between him and not-him, the edge that marked the separateness of himself from the world, was no longer there. Until that moment he had been tied up tight inside himself, held in by a skin as taut and tense as the head of a drum, and now it was all let go. It was as if he had fallen into green water and gone down deep, turning and tumbling until he had no idea which way was up. At first he panicked, lashing out on all sides, struggling to get control, but after a moment he seemed to remember that you shouldn't do it like that. He stopped struggling and allowed himself to drift, letting his own natural buoyancy carry him back to the surface.

He was a woman in the woods in winter. He wasn't *seeing* her, he *was* her, crunching her way among silent widely-spaced trees, going home, tired and alive in the aftermath of love, her mouth rubbed sore, the man's semen pursed up warm inside her. She sniffed at her fingers. The scent of the man clung to them, as strong as memory. She remembered the weight of his belly on her, the warmth of his bed by the stove. Her collar, her sleeve, the fur of her hood, everything had soaked up the smell of his isba, rich and strong, smoke and resin, furs and sweat. Oh hell! *He* would notice when she got home! Even *He* couldn't miss the smell of him on her skin. Did she care? No! This was a new kind of madness and she liked it.

The vision faded. Lom closed his eyes and watched the patterns of muted light drift across the inside of his eyelids. Thinking was tiring. His thoughts were too heavy to lift. He stared out of the window, trying to think as little as possible. In the reflection he saw Maroussia Shaumian's wide dark eyes. Her long straight back as she walked away.

Three shots. There were three shots.

I've achieved nothing. Every thread I follow leads nowhere, or to a corpse.

No, not nowhere. To Chazia.

Kantor was Chazia's agent. All the killing, the bombs, the robberies, inspired not by nationalist fervour or revolutionary nihilism, but by the Chief of the Vlast Secret Police. Safran was Chazia's too. Chazia had sent him to kill Maroussia and her mother.

And I am Chazia's too.

Except that wasn't true. Not any more.

Chazia would kill him now for what he knew, and take the file back. She had sent the vyrdalak. It must have been her.

The file.

He saw it tucked away in the bathroom of Vishnik's apartment. He saw Vishnik beaten by militia night sticks. He saw Vishnik, dead in his room, bleeding from Safran's bullets.

The file. Shit. The file.

46

Josef Kantor followed Chazia along empty passageways seemingly cut through blocks of solid stone. They clattered down steep iron flights of steps lit by dirty yellow bulbs. The treads were damp and treacherous. She was leading him deep into the oldest, lowest parts of the Lodka, where he had never been before, down into ancient, subterranean levels.

'No one comes here,' she said. 'Only me. You're privileged, Josef. Remember that.'

When had she become so pompous? She was weaker than he had thought. Failing. Not to be trusted. She had agreed, reluctantly, to show him the Pollandore, but she had made him wait. 'Come back tomorrow,' she'd said. 'Let me prepare.'

Kantor felt suddenly annoyed with this terrible old fox-bitch who pushed him around. He wanted to bring her down a bit.

'Is Krogh dealt with, Lavrentina?'

She was walking ahead of him and didn't look round.

'You were right about him,' she said. 'He's an annoyance. It is in hand.'

'But not done yet, then. And what about the other matter?'

'The other matter?'

'The women,' said Kantor impatiently. Chazia had not forgotten – she never forgot anything – she was prevaricating. 'The Shaumian women. You were going to deal with them too. Is it done?'

'Oh that,' she said. 'Yes. Your wife is dead.' He caught a slight hesitation in Chazia's reply.

'And the daughter?'

Chazia said nothing.

'The daughter, Lavrentina?' said Kantor again.

'She is not dead. She escaped. We've lost her. Just for the moment. We'll find her again.'

'What happened?'

'She had help, Josef. Krogh's investigator was there.'

'Lom?'

'He interfered,' said Chazia. 'Safran let him get in the way. Your daughter shot one of Krogh's men and disappeared.'

'Did she, then?' Despite himself, he was impressed. But it would not do.

'You must kill them both,' he said. 'Krogh's man and the daughter. Do it now. Do it quickly, Lavrentina. And Krogh too. No more delays. Kill them all.'

Chazia turned to face him.

'Don't try to bully me, Josef. I won't accept that. Remember our respective positions. I have other things to do apart from clearing away your domestic mess. Today we are going into the Lezarye quarters. That will raise the temperature. And you have your part to play too. Remember that. The Novozhd—'

'You can leave that to me,' said Kantor. 'You don't need the details. Better you don't ...' He felt that Chazia was going to argue the point, but just then they reached a narrow unmarked door in the passageway, and she stopped.

'Here,' she said, reaching in her pocket for a bunch of keys.

The door looked newer than the rest. Shabby institutional paint, but solid and heavy with several good locks. Chazia opened it and Kantor followed her inside.

The first impression was of spacious airy dimness. Grey light filtered down from high – very high – overhead: muted daylight, spilling through a row of square grilles set into the roof. But they must have been far below ground level. The grilles were the floors of light wells, he realised: shafts cut up through the Lodka to draw down some sky. As his eyes grew accustomed to the dimness he saw that they were in a high narrow chamber that stretched away on both sides. He could not see the end of it in either direction. It might have been a tunnel. Parallel rails were set into the floor, for a tram or train.

The floor of the chamber was heaped with boxes and sacks and pallets. Large shapeless lumps of stuff shrouded under sacking and tarpaulins. And there were machines, on benches or on the floor. Some he recognised: lathes and belt saws, pulleys and lifting chains and other such contraptions. Others, the majority, meant nothing to him: complex armatures of metal and rubber and wood and polished stone. The impression was of a workshop, or a warehouse, but its purpose escaped him. There was an oppressive mixture of smells: iron filings, wet stone and machine oil. The atmosphere unsettled him. He felt on edge and slightly disoriented, as if there was a low vibration in the air and the floor, a rhythm and resonance too deep to hear.

'Where is it?' he said. 'Where's the Pollandore?' He didn't know what he was expecting the Pollandore to look like, but nothing he could see seemed likely to be it.

'It's not far,' said Chazia. 'I need another key.' She switched on a lamp at a work table and began to search through drawers. 'I haven't needed this for a while.' The table she was searching was spread with small implements, scraps of paper and chips of stone. Its centrepiece was a large brazen ball with tiny angled spouts protruding from its dented, fish-scaled skin. It floated in a dish of some heavy silver liquid that might have been mercury. Its surface shimmered and rippled faintly in the lamplight.

'So what is this place?' said Kantor.

Chazia glanced up. Light from the lamp glinted in her foxy eyes and slid off the dark marks on her face and hands. Did they cover her whole body, Kantor found himself wondering. He was beginning to feel uneasy. He felt for the revolver in his pocket.

'This is my private workplace,' said Chazia.

The lamp threw light into some of the nearer shadows. Kantor started. He thought he had seen someone else in the room, standing watchful and motionless against the wall. It was a shape, draped in oilcloth, almost seven feet tall. Curious, Kantor went across to it and pulled the sheet away.

At first he thought he was looking at a suit of armour, but it was much cruder, larger and heavier than any human could have worn and moved in. There was some kind of goggle-eyed helmet and clumsy-fingered gauntlets with canvas palms that made the effect more like a deep-sea diver's suit. The whole thing was a dull purplish red. He realised it was constructed from pieces of angel flesh. The woman had made herself a mudjhik! But one you could climb inside. One you could wear. He had underestimated her. Badly. His mind began to work rapidly. What you could do with such a thing, if it worked. If it worked.

'Come away from that,' said Chazia sharply.

She didn't want me to see this. So this is what she does. This is her dabbling.

'You *wear* this?' he said. 'You put yourself *inside* this thing?'

'It's nothing,' said Chazia. 'Come away from it. Do you want to see the Pollandore or not? We haven't much time. I need to get back. Come, it's this way.'

She led him to an iron door in the side wall, unlocked it and went through. Kantor followed her and found himself standing on a narrow iron platform suspended over space.

Whatever he had expected, it was not this. They were looking across a wide circular pit, a cavern, and in the middle of it was a wrought iron structure. It must have been a hundred and fifty feet high. In the depths of the Lodka. An iron staircase climbed up round the outside. There were viewing platforms of ornate decorative ironwork, pinnacles and spiracles, and within this outer casing an iron helix spiralling upwards. It reminded Kantor of a long thin strip of apple peel. And inside it, held in suspension, touching nowhere, the Pollandore.

The air of the cavern crackled as if it was filled with static electricity. It made Kantor's head spin. The Pollandore hung in blankness, a pale greenish luminescent globe the size of a small house, a cloudy sphere containing vaporous muted light that emitted none. Illuminated nothing. A smell of ozone and forest leaf. It revolved slowly, a world in space: not part of the planet at all, though it was following the same orbit, describing the same circumsolar trajectory, passing through the same coordinates in space and time, tucked in its inflated sibling's pocket but belonging only to itself. There was no sound in the room. Not even silence. The Pollandore looked small for a world, but Kantor knew it wasn't small, not by its own metrication.

He turned to say something to Chazia, who was standing beside him staring across at the uncanny, terrible thing. Kantor opened his mouth to say something to her, but nothing came out. The space in the cavern swallowed his words before they were spoken. He grabbed her arm and pulled her roughly back off the platform and pushed the door shut.

'We must destroy it,' he said. 'Get rid of that repellent thing.'
'Don't you think,' said Chazia, 'don't you think we have tried?'

47

Maroussia Shaumian sat on the slush-soaked ground under the trees at the end of her street, leaning her back against one of the trunks. Watching for uniforms. Watching for watchers. Her whole body was trembling violently. She had almost not made it. The militia man's first bullet had gouged a furrow of flesh in the calf of her left leg. It was a pulpy mess of blood, but it held her weight. Her knee, which had crashed against the wall in her first wild jump, stabbed bright needles of pain with every step, and the hair at the back of her head was sticky with blood – hers, and his. She could feel pits and flaps of skin where his teeth had cut her scalp. There was a ragged stinging tear in her cheek, wet with blood. Her neck was stiff. It hurt when she tried to turn her head. The pistol lay black and heavy in her lap.

She knew it was stupid to return home. The policeman. Lom. He had warned her not to. But then that was reason enough to do the opposite. Distrust of the Vlast and all its agents went deep. And yet … this one had helped her. He had let her get away. Without him she would already have been taken.

She could not think about that now. She needed to go home. Where else could she go? She needed to be clean of all this blood. She needed fresh clothes. She needed the little money that was there. She needed to rest. And she needed to think through her plan. She waited until the street was quiet, stood up stiffly and limped up the road to the entrance to her building.

There was a small bathroom up a flight of stairs at the end of the corridor. It had a basin and a bathtub and cold running water. A tarnished mirror. The walls were painted a pale lemon-yellow. Maroussia locked herself in, took her clothes off and washed herself, all over, slowly and without thinking. She let trickles of icy water take the blood and dirt from her skin. Out of her hair. She caught some water in cupped hands and drank from it: it tasted faintly of blood, but it was cold and sweet. She left her dirtied, bloodied clothes in a heap on the floor, wrapped herself in a thin rough towel and went barefoot back to her room as quickly as her stiffening injuries would let her, not wanting to encounter Avrilova on the stair. She found the door broken down, and assumed the militia had done it.

She dressed carefully, taking her time, not only because of her vicious and stiffening wounds, but also because she felt there was something ceremonious about it. *Here begins the new life.* She found clean under-wear. A cotton slip. A plain grey dress. A black scarf for her hair. Shoes were a problem: her left shoe was sticky with the blood that had run down her leg. Her mother had saved a pair of boots from better times. They would do. And there was a clumsy woollen coat, also grey, which her mother had left behind that morning. She must have frozen.

When she'd dressed, she wandered around the room stuffing things into a bag. A few spare clothes. Soap. Their bit of money, about thirty roubles. That wouldn't last long. After some thought she put in the book of Anna Yourdania's poems. Someone at the Marmot's had given it to her. *The Selo Elegies.* She loved the quiet, allusive, suffering voice.

> The sun is dropping out of the sky, the orchard
> breathes the taste of pears and cherries,
> and in a moment the transparent night
> will bear new constellations –
> like salt berries – glittering – harsh.

> Why are our years always worse?

Yourdania's son, who was nineteen, had died in the camp at Vig. Her husband was shot on the basement steps of the Lodka.

As she dressed and packed her few things, Maroussia went over her plan. Like so many people in Mirgorod, she had lived for years with the thought that one day such a time would come. The militia would come for her, and it would be necessary to run. She had decided long ago that when this day came she would make for Koromants, the Fransa Free Exclave on the Cetic shore, three hundred miles to the south of Mirgorod.

The whole world to the west of the forest was divided between Vlast and Archipelago, locked in their endless war. But wherever there was war, there must be bankers, financiers, traders in weapons – wars were fought on credit – and so the Fransa free cities, which belonged neither to the Archipelago nor to the Vlast, existed. Sealed off from the dominions by guarded perimeters. Everyone was stateless there, everyone was free, money and information the only power. Spies and criminals and refugees of every kind gravitated to such places – if they could get in, through the wire or over the walls. Exiled intellectuals gathered there to plot and feud, and she had heard of other, stranger figures, not human, forced out of the ghettos, margins and northern wildernesses of the Vlast, who found places to live in the older, darker corners of the Fransa exclaves. Ones who might understand about the Pollandore and help her.

The nearest Fransa port to Mirgorod was Koromants. Maroussia had seen a photograph once of the seafront there: a wide boulevard of coffee shops and konditorei looking out over clear dark waters, and behind it, rising against the sky, the sheer jagged mountains of the Koromants Massif. There, she had decided, that was where she would go, when the time came. Though how she would get there she didn't know.

Maroussia decided not to take her identity card. It would be no help where she was going. She placed it carefully on the table in clear view, for the police to find when they came. It was time. She had delayed too long.

She turned towards the doorway and saw the figure of madness and death standing there, regarding her with shadowed fathomless eyes.

'Maroussia?' it said. 'Maroussia. Are you ready?'

The paluba's voice was thin and quiet in the room, a breeze among distant trees. The air was filled with the scent of pine resin and damp earth. Flimsy brown garments shifted about the creature, stirring on a gentle wind. There was a mouth-shape in the hooded shadows that moved as it spoke.

The creature stepped forward across the threshold. Only it wasn't a step. The thing seemed to fall slowly forward and jerk itself backwards and upright at the tipping point. It appeared flimsy, held together by fragile joints. Its limbs were articulated strangely. Behind the creature another one came, its follower, its companion double, more shadowy, more shapeless, more airy, more ... nothing. Just a shadow, waiting.

'What are you?' said Maroussia, at the ragged edge of panic. And hope.

'I can smell wounds here,' the paluba said. 'You're bleeding. You've been hurt.'

'Who are you?' said Maroussia again. 'What do you want from me?'

'You don't have to be frightened,' the voice said. 'I am your friend. Your mother's friend. But your mother wouldn't listen to me. Did she tell you nothing?'

'She's gone now. She's dead. The police killed her.'

'Oh.' There was a moment's stillness in the shadow where the paluba's face was suggested. Maroussia thought she could hear grieving in its voice. 'She took what we left for her. Did she give it to you?'

'No. She gave me nothing.'

'It was an invitation. A key. Your father sent it.'

'I never had a father.'

'Of course you did. Everyone does.'

'My father was a lie. I come from nothing.'

'Did she tell you that? Poor darling, it wasn't so. Do you want to know?'

'Know what?'

'Everything.'

'Yes.'

The paluba reached up and pushed back her thin hood, showing her beautiful, terrible face. Her waiting mouth.

'Kiss me, Maroussia.'

'What?'

'Kiss me.' In the shadow the companion stirred. 'Kiss me.'

Maroussia stepped forward and rested her hand on the paluba's slender shoulders. Sweet air was drifting out of its upturned mouth. It tasted of autumn. Maroussia put her own dry mouth against it, slightly open, and drank.

In the paluba's kiss there were trees, beautiful complex trees, higher and older than any trees grew, and everything was connected.

Maroussia was walking among them. She placed her hand on the silent living bark and felt her skin, her very flesh, become transparent. She became aware of the articulation of her bones, sheathed in their muscle and tendon. Eyes, heart and lungs, liver and brain, nested like birds in a walking tree of bone. A weave of veins and arteries and streaming nerves that flickered with gentle electricity.

She heard the leaves and branches of the trees moving. Whispers filling the air with rich smells. The trees reached their roots down into the earth like arms, and she reached down with them, extending filament fingers, pushing, sliding insistently, down through crevices in the rock itself.

And breaking through.

The buried chamber of the wild sleeping god was furled up tight but immense beyond measuring. The restless sleeping god, burdened with tumultuous dreams, had extended himself outwards and inwards and downwards, carving out an endless warren, an intricate dark hollowing. Its whorls and chambers ramified in all directions, turning and twisting and burrowing, spiral shadow tunnellings of limitless extent, unlit by the absent sun but warmed by the heart of the earth. It was all rootwork: the roots of the rock and the roots of the trees. It was matrix and web. Fibrous roots of air, filaments of energy and space, knitted everything to everything else in the chamber of the sleeping god's dream.

He was lying on his back and great taproots drove down through his ribs. A tree limb speared up out of his groin. Water trickled over him. Rootlets slipped down, fingering his pinioned body, brushing and touching gently. The roots of the great trees drank from the buried god as their leaves drank the sun.

Up in the light the trees mingled their crowns in one great leafhead and exhaled the good, living air of the world. The air she drank on the paluba's breath.

And there was a man walking among the trees. She knew that he was her father and he knew that she was there, and he greeted her, and she understood why her mother had loved him and why she had to leave and how the leaving had been her death.

48

Lom sat bolt upright in his seat on the tram. The file! Chazia would come for it, and she would find Vishnik. Maroussia.

He had to do something. Now.

The tram had stopped. An anonymous place somewhere away from the centre of the city. Across the street was a hotel, a telephone cable running to it from a pole in the centre of the square. Lom ran across. THE GRAND PENSION CHESMA. Wet zinc tables under a dripping wrought-iron veranda. Steep marble steps up to a chipped, discoloured portico. A handwritten card propped in a small side window: *Closed For Winter*. Lom hammered on the door.

'Open up! Police!'

The paint on the door was peeling, revealing sinewy bleached grey wood. There was an ivory button in a verdigrised surround. BELL, it said. PORTER. He pressed it, more in hope than expectation, and kicked at the door.

'Police! Open or I break it down.'

There was a noise of bolts being pulled back. The door opened. A porter in sabots and a brown overall eyed him warily.

'You don't look like police.' *We wouldn't take you as a guest.*

Lom shoved the door open and shouldered his way past the porter into the dim hall. A suggestion of wing-backed chairs and ottomans draped with grey sheets. A smell of old cooking and older carpets. Dampness, dust and the sea. Lom unbuttoned his cloak.

'This is a uniform,' he said. 'And this is a gun. I need to telephone. Now.'

The porter led him into a back room. There was a phone on the desk. The porter lingered uneasily.

'Don't stand there gawking. I'm hungry. Get me some sausage. And a mug of tea.'

It took Lom for ever to negotiate his way past a series of operators, getting through first to the Lodka and then to Krogh's office. The private secretary's voice came on the line.

'Yes?' he said. 'Who is this?'

'It's Lom. I need to speak to him. Now.'

'Ah. Investigator Lom. The Under Secretary was beginning to wonder whether you might not have taken a train back to Podchornok. You haven't, have you? Where exactly is it you are calling from?'

'Just put me through to him.'

'I'm afraid he's not available at the moment. His diary is very full. If you'll tell me where you are, or give me the number, I'll arrange for him to return your call some time this afternoon. Unless you'd like me to make you an appointment to see him. I'm sure he would be most—'

'Stop pissing me about and put me through.'

There was a hiss of indrawn breath and the line went dead. *Fuck.*

He was about to hang up when he heard the tired dry voice of Krogh.

'Yes, Investigator. Something to report?'

'Can I speak?'

'Of course.'

'I mean, this call is private? Bag carrier not listening?'

'Just give me your report, Lom. I was playing this game when you were at school.'

'Perhaps you're getting complacent. Are you sure you're secure?'

'Of course I am, man. There are systems. Arrangements.'

'That's what Chazia thought, but she was stupid. She relied on the systems because she'd made them, but getting in wasn't even hard.'

There was a pause.

'What are you talking about?'

'Maybe she's listening now.'

'That's ridiculous. You're hysterical. Perhaps I made a mistake about you.'

'If she is, it doesn't matter. I'm not saying anything she doesn't already know I know.'

'What exactly *are* you saying?'

'Kantor isn't the story. Kantor's an agent. Chazia's agent. Chazia's the one moving all the pieces.'

'Can you prove it? Are you sure?' Lom listened for indignation. Disbelief. But there was only guarded interest in Krogh's voice. 'Is there proof, Lom? Certain proof I can take to the Novozhd?'

'Oh yes,' said Lom. 'I've got a bag full of proof. Her own files. Her own handwriting all over them. But she knows I've got them.'

'I see.'

'And if she is listening to your calls – and if I were you I wouldn't bet my life she's not – she knows I've told you. Of course, even if she doesn't listen to your calls, she'll assume I've told you anyway.'

'Ah. I see. Yes.' Pause. 'And how did you come by these sensitive papers?'

'I broke into her private archive and took them.'

'Did you, indeed? You've exceeded my expectations, Investigator.'

'And now you know, and she knows you know. So you have to do something about it. Action this day, Under Secretary. Action this hour.'

'What exactly did you have in mind?'

'You're her boss. Roll her up. Reel her in. Have her killed. I don't know – it doesn't matter – just get her, and do it now. Get her and you get Kantor too.'

'I'll need the proof. I'll need the papers.'

'There's no time for that. You need to move now. And I'd take care of your private secretary as well, if I were you.'

'That's wild talk, Lom.'

'Chazia had my personal file, Krogh. She had it from your office less than an hour after we met. Referred to her by your private secretary. He even signed the fucking thing out to her. They're running rings round you. They're so confident they don't even try to hide their tracks.'

'I still need to show the Novozhd the proof.'

Krogh sounded old and tired. The fatigue was seeping down the line. Lom remembered the big office. The plain neat desk. The windows. Quiet traffic noise. Long corridors. This wasn't going to work.

'I'll get the files to you, Krogh. But you can't wait for that. You need to act.'

'When can you bring me the files?'

'Soon. Soon. I'm not saying any more on this line.'

'Investigator Lom. Be calm. You're asking me to risk a huge amount – everything – on—'

'A telephone call from a junior policeman from Podchornok. Your rules, Under Secretary. You got me into this.'

'I did.'

'Oh, and there's one other thing.'

'Yes?'

'There's an angel in the forest somewhere beyond Vig. It's alive.'

'That's preposterous.'

'Chazia and Kantor – mainly Kantor, I think – are in communication with it. I just thought you should know.'

Lom hung up.

The porter brought a tray with a glass of black tea, a plate of rye bread and a length of dark purple sausage.

'The dining room is closed. You can take it here. Or there is the garden.'

'Forget it,' said Lom. 'You have it.'

There was half an hour yet till the tram to Pelican Quay. Back at the tram halt, Lom sat alone under the canopy, sick and dispirited. His clothes and skin stank of hopelessness and self-disgust and other people's blood.

Image: Safran killing the old woman in the street.

Image: Maroussia Shaumian walking away alone. Pistol shots. Three.

Image: Chazia overturning Vishnik's flat and finding the file.

Image: Vishnik dead.

All caused by him. His responsibility. His fault. Because every step he'd taken had been wrong. Because he'd been a blundering, half-hearted, self-indulgent, piss-poor idea of a detective, and now he wasn't even that. He was loose. He was alone.

It would take him hours to retrieve the file and get it to Krogh, even if it was still there. He had no confidence that Krogh would move against Chazia before he had the file in his hands, or even when he did have it. Lom had done what he could, but it hadn't been good enough. It hadn't been good at all. It had been shit.

The sky had grown dark and livid. Fat cold drops of rain began to explode on the ground, bursting at first like fallen overripe fruits but then like bullets from a mitrailleuse, rapid and hard and shattering, mixed with shards of ice. Over the sea a storm was coming.

*

Out in the Sound a high tide had been building. The two broken fragments of moon tugged at the weight of water, dragging its dark bulk shouldering against the land. A twisting black surge of foam-flecked ocean forced its way in through the Seagate towards the city, scouring the foundations of the Halsesond martello forts as it came. The rivers and canals of Mirgorod were already high and swollen, pregnant with weeks of rain and snow. Inside Cold Amber Strand the column of brackish tidal waters confronted and commingled with the rivers in flood. In Mirgorod the waters rose quickly when they came.

49

The rain pounded the city and darkened the sky. Soaked, Vishnik stepped out of the shabby crowded street and closed the louvred door behind him, and the House on the Purfas enfolded him in its familiar melancholy civilised quietness. The entrance hall was faded, airy, spacious. Empty but for dust motes, pools of shadow and the sweetness of wax polish and age. Grey window-light and the sound of rain. Somewhere a clock was ticking slowly. Doorways and corridors opened in all directions, and a wide staircase climbed upwards into indistinctness.

Now, the House on the Purfas was home to the Lezarye Government in Exile Within, but once it had been the Sheremetsny Dom, a low expansive sprawl of wood and brick, skirted with peeling loggias and leaking conservatories. The country estate for which it was built had disappeared long ago under the tenements and courtyards of the expanding city, but for Vishnik the corridors of the House on the Purfas led away into the lost domain of his childhood. If he could go deeper into the house, he felt, he would be back among it all. Back in his own boundless childhood house at Vyra, with its world of passages and stairs. Daylight slanted in through high narrow windows panelled with stained glass, splashing lozenges of colour across dusty floorboards and threadbare rugs. The tall furniture and heavy fabrics of drawing rooms, salons, dining rooms, bedrooms, box rooms and attics. The strange devices and spiced air of kitchens, pantries and sculleries. If he went to a window in the House on the Purfas and looked out, he was sure he would see, not the Moyka Strel, but balustraded pathways, formal parterres, weathered statuary, great heaps and mounds of foliage overgrowing walls of old brick and, in the furthest distance, a slope of wooded hills.

There was a brass hand-bell on a side table. Vishnik picked it up and rang it. A woman in a black dress and a white cape came.

'Yes?' she said. 'Sir?'

A domestic servant. Another dizzying time-tumble. The whole place was a museum. A case of butterfly specimens, dried out and pinned; their dusty wings spread under glass in a parody of summer flight, but if you opened the glass and picked one up it would crunch and collapse between your fingers.

In the centuries after the coming of the Founder, the people of Lezarye had learned to accept the end of their annual migrations and settle into the static life of the Vlast. The elder families had absorbed the ways of the aristocrats, a choice that was only the latest in the long history of tragic turns and counter-turns that left them with nowhere to go when the Novozhd gripped power and the aristocrats fell.

'I need to see Teslom,' said Vishnik to the woman.

'What name shall I say?'

'Prince Raku ter-Fallin Mozhno Shirin-Vilichov Vishnik.'

'Will you wait in the library, please, Excellency.'

Teslom was the Curator of Lezarye. He kept the records of the old families and tended the artefacts, regalia and memories that survived from their proud ancient days of hunting and herding, and the long slow rhythms of their decline: the systole of assimilation, the diastole of segregation and pogrom. Although Vishnik had visited the House on the Purfas to consult Teslom several times before, he had never been admitted to the Curator's collection. No one who was not born into the long families ever was. The exclusion irked him. Lezarye had few enough friends in Mirgorod.

The room he was put in to wait was not part of the Collection, it was only the Secular Library. It was a dim quiet place of heavy bookcases shut away behind glass doors and curtains. Vishnik opened one of the cases and looked at the spines of the books. The ones here were merely miscellanea, marginal outriders of the true library, but still there were some things here that could be found nowhere else in the Vlast.

Lyrics From The Moth Border
Hunting Cold Beasts
Peace Of Mind Among Cold Beasts

Pigments, Tints
Life On The Water Ways
The Geometry Of Clouds, Steams and Vapours
Jurisprudence In The Archipelago

Vishnik took a book from a shelf, carried it across to a table and opened it. *Shaw's Atlas of the Archipelago*. It contained page after page of maps in muted colours and a gazetteer of place names: a world, but not his; other countries, other islands, strung out across the face of the blue, with vertebrae and ribs of snow-capped mountains. The poetry of unfamiliar shorelines. A great bridge had been built across the sea to join them, thousands of miles long, but it was broken in several places. The orthography of the place names was familiar, but the names themselves ... He didn't recognise them – they were strange and wonderful. Morthern. Foerd. Mier. Gealm. The Warth. Horrow. Sarshalls. It was an atlas of elsewhere.

Teslom had come in quietly while he was reading. When Vishnik noticed him, the Curator made the formal gestures of acknowledgement and permission.

'Welcome, Prince Vishnik. The princes of Vyra and Turm were always friends of Lezarye in the former days of the long homelands. There is a place for you in our hearts and at our tables. How can I help you?'

Teslom was a small man, neat, spare, kempt, with dark-shadowed eyes behind rimless circular glasses and glossy brown hair flopped across his forehead. He wore a double-breasted suit of dark blue; a soft white shirt with a soft turned-down collar and faint pattern of squares; a dark tie held in place with a pin.

'I want you to tell me about the Pollandore, Teslom my friend. Every fucking thing you can.'

'The Pollandore? Why?'

'I found a story about this thing. It was in a book. An old and rare book. I asked myself, is it real? Is it true?'

'What story is this? Where did you find it? What book?'

Vishnik opened his satchel and handed it to him. *A Child's Book of Wonders, Legends and Tales of Long Ago*. Teslom took it carefully and opened it, his dark eyes shining.

'I had heard of it, but even we don't have a copy.' He held it close to his face, examining the stitch binding and inhaling its paper smell.

'Tell me about the Pollandore, Teslom, and I will give it to you. My gift to the People.'

Teslom handed the book back to him.

'A good gift. But why the Pollandore? There are other stories here.'

'Because of these.'

Vishnik opened his satchel again, took out a sheaf of photographs and spread them across the table. Teslom lit a lamp and studied them for a long time in silence.

'Where did you get these?' he said at last.

'They are mine. I took them. These things happen. I've seen them. This is the proof. And now I ask myself, what does Teslom know about this?'

'But what makes you connect these pictures with the story of the Pollandore?'

'Why? Always fucking why? Because it is a possibility, Teslom my friend. Because I have a feeling. A hypothesis. Because it would fit the case. So. What do you tell me? What do you say?'

Teslom hesitated.

'I would say,' he said at last, 'that you are not the first to come to this house and speak about the Pollandore. A paluba came here yesterday.'

'A paluba.'

'Indeed. From the woods. It talked of the Pollandore and now you come with these questions about the same thing.'

'The Pollandore is real then. It was actually made.'

'I don't know that. There is a record that Lezarye once held such a thing in care, that one of the elder families was appointed warden, but it was seized by the Vlast soon after the Founder came north. Attempts were made to destroy it in the time of the Gruodists, but they failed. That is what is said.'

'And this paluba spoke of it? That implies it exists.'

'It implies only that our friends in the woods believe so. Some of the Committee also think it is real. Others do not.'

'What else did it say, this paluba?'

'It asked to address the Inner Committee. It spoke of an angel, a living angel that had fallen in the forest and was doing great damage. The woods fear it will poison the world. The paluba wanted us to open the Pollandore. That is the way the legend goes, is it not? The Pollandore, to be opened in the last extremity, when hope is lost.'

'Exactly. Yes. Fuck yes. Do you see what this means, Teslom? Do you see?'

'The paluba also said the Pollandore itself was broken, or leaking, or failing, or something. The point was unclear, I think. I was not there myself.'

'What did the Committee do?'

'Nothing. They refused to countenance the paluba's message at all. They wanted nothing to do with it. They sent it away.'

'So ...'

'I was appalled when I heard what they had done. But they're too frightened to act. The pogroms have begun again, worse than ever. Did you know that? The Vlast is clearing the ghettos. People are being lined up and shot. Lezarye is being rounded up and put on trains to who knows where. Whole neighbourhoods are being emptied.'

'I didn't know. I've seen the rhetoric in the papers, but I didn't ... What are you – I mean the Committee ...?'

'The Committee is too frightened to move. There is talk of arming ourselves and fighting back. Getting money and mounting a coup. Young men on the rooftops throwing down bombs on the militia. Others, of course, hope that if we keep quiet the troubles will fade away again, like they have done before. But already people are dying.'

'And you? The Collection?'

'My duty is to protect it. It has survived such times in the past. I've begun to pack it away, but ... it is so much work for one man. The Committee offers no help. They will not consider departure.'

'Where would you go?'

'I don't know. Perhaps the woods, if I can find a way to transport the collection there. Or one of the exclaves. Koromants. Or maybe I will get it on a ship and go across the sea to the Archipelago. But with the winter coming ...'

Vishnik held out the *Child's Book of Wonders*.

'Here,' he said. 'Take it.'

'But you know I can't ... it may not be safe ...'

'Take it, Teslom. Find a way. And if you think I can help you, my friend, ask me. Ask me.'

50

Maroussia must have fallen. She was lying hunched on the floor of her room. Aching, exhausted, she pulled herself carefully, with steady deliberation, up onto the chair. The feel of the trees, the buried sleeping god, swam in her head. The paluba was watching her.

'That's real,' she said. 'It's there. Isn't it? I didn't know.'

The paluba said nothing.

Maroussia saw it and the companion now for what they really were: a weaving of light and will and contained, living air. The moulded breath of forest trees. Trees rooted in the body of the buried god.

But her mother was still dead. The militia would come. They were already coming. That was real too.

'How long was I ...? I mean, when did you come? How long have I been lying here?'

The paluba shrugged jerkily. The question meant little to her.

'I've done what I can for your wounds. They will heal quickly now.'

Maroussia pulled up her skirt and looked at her leg. The raw gash had crusted over. The pain was dulled.

'Who was he?' she asked. 'The man I saw?'

'Your father?'

'Yes. My father. He must have a name.'

'Oh, he's Hasha.'

'Hasha?'

'Hasha. He can't come to you here. He can't leave the forest.'

'Will I ... Could I go there, to him?'

'Eventually. Perhaps. It is possible. But ... I'm sorry, there's something more.'

Maroussia stared into the paluba's wild, fathomless eyes. 'Show me.'

51

Rain was tumbling out of the sky. A heavy black downpour. Lakoba Petrov the painter had walked a long way, out to the northern edge of the city, no longer Mirgorod proper but the Moyka Strel, in the wider Lezarye Quarter, out beyond the Raion Lezaryet itself, an ageing halfway place where the houses were made of wood. Although they had been there for centuries, they were skewed, temporary-looking buildings of weathered planking, with shuttered windows and shingled roofs. Their eaves and porches and windows were mounted with strips of intricately carved wood, pierced with repeating patterns and interlaced knotwork. It was like embroidered edging. Like pastry. Like repeating texts printed in a strange alphabet. The woodwork was salt-bleached, and broken in places, but even so the houses looked more like musical cabinets or confectionery than dwellings. They were made from trees that had grown on the delta islands long before the Founder came.

Petrov had been born in this place, but he hardly knew that now. New thoughts filled him so full of wild energy that he could not keep body or mind still, he couldn't even walk straight. Uncontainable and superabundant, he tacked back and forth across the road, advancing only slowly and zig by zag in stuttering steps, muttering as he went, hissing random syllables under his breath in a new language of his own.

Lost in his fizzing new world, he walked smack into the line of soldiers that blocked his path.

In the face of one a mouth was moving, but Petrov heard no words, only the soft swaying of the sea and the hissing of the rain, until the soldier struck him in the shoulder with the butt of his rifle, hard, and he fell.

'Go down there. Get in line with the others.'

Petrov struggled to his feet, his shoulder hurting. The soldier who had hit him was young, not more than a boy, his face white as paper. He seemed to have no eyes.

'Get in line.'

'No,' said Petrov. 'No. I can't.'

The soldier jabbed the muzzle of the rifle hard into his stomach.

'Do it. Or we shoot you now.'

Some of the soldiers had circled round behind him. A hand shoved Petrov sharply in the back, so that he stumbled forward, almost falling again. The soldiers in front of him moved aside to let him through.

'Down there. Walk.'

Petrov realised then that he knew this place. It was a piece of waste ground, cut across by a shallow gully. Boys used to play there when he was one of them. They had called it Red Cliff, having never seen cliffs. There was a small crowd of people there now, lined up on the lip of the slope, in silence, in the rain. Soldiers to one side, waiting. Three army trucks drawn up in a line. Soldiers unloading stuff from the tarpaulined backs. An officer, fair-haired, neat and pale, was giving orders. Petrov knew he smelled of soap.

Some of the people were naked, and others were in their under-clothes. Some were undressing under the soldiers' gaze. Women crossed their arms over their breasts and shivered. The rain soaked them. There was a pile of rain-sodden clothes. Alone, at some distance, an earth-coloured mudjhik stood, sightlessly swaying, attendant. The soldiers were arranging their mitrailleuses in a row on a raised mound.

Petrov realised that one of the soldiers from the street had followed behind him, and was standing at his shoulder.

'Go over there and join the others, citizen,' the soldier said in his ear. His young voice was drab with shock. 'Leave your clothes on the pile. If we can, we will be quick.'

The people smelled wet and sour. They were as silent as trees. Petrov was aware of bare feet, his own among them, cold and muddy in the rain-soaked, puddled red earth.

Time widened.

Somewhere – distant – it seemed that someone, a woman, was

berating the soldiers with loud, precise indignation. Three echoless shots repaired the silence and the rain.

Then the mitrailleuses began to fire.

52

Maroussia was in a terrible place. The paluba's kiss had taken her there. A dreadful nightmare place in the shadow of a steep hill. Only it wasn't a hill, it was alive. It was an angel, fallen.

There were trees here too, but here the trees were stone, bearing needles of stone. Maroussia was walking on snow among outcrops of raw rock. In parts the earth itself, bare of snow, smouldered with cool, lapping fire under a crust of dry brittleness. Dust and cinders, dry scraping lava over cold firepools. Walking over it, Maroussia's feet broke through the crust into the soft flame beneath. Flame that was cold and didn't burn.

Stone grew and spread like vegetation. There were strange shimmering pools of stuff that wasn't water.

Everything was alive and watched her. No, not alive, but the opposite of life. Anti-life. Hard, functional, noticing continuation without existence, like an echo, a shadow, a reflection of what once was. But everything was aware of her. Everything.

The hill that was an angel had spilled its awareness. It was bleeding consciousness into the surrounding rock for miles. Like blood.

She wasn't alone. Sad creatures wandered aimlessly among the trees. Creatures of stone. Creatures that had become stone. They were broken, cracked, abraded, but they couldn't die. From the shelter of stunted stone birches, a great stone elk with snapped antlers and no hind legs watched her pass. There was no respite for it. It could only wait for the slow weathering of ice and wind and time that would, eventually, wear it away and blow its residuum of dust across the earth. But it would be watching, noticing dust. Cursed with the endlessness of continuation.

Stone giants were digging their way up out of the earth and walking across the top of it, breaking waist-high through stone trees. If they fell they cracked and split. Headless giants walking. Fingerless club-stump hands. Giants fallen and floundering in pools of slowed time.

The corruption was spreading, seeping outwards through the edge-less forest in all directions like an insidious stain, like lichen across rock, like blood in snow. It would never stop. It would creep outwards for ever. The forest was dying.

The angel had been shot into the forest's belly like a bullet, bursting it open, engendering a slow, inevitable, glacial, cancerous, stone killing.

The angel was watching her. The whole of the lenticular stone waste was an eye, focused on her. She felt the gross intrusion of its attention like a fat finger, tracing the thread from her to the paluba to the great trees of the forest.

It knew. And without effort it burst the paluba open.

The explosion of the paluba drove sticks and rags and meat across the apartment, smashing furniture and shattering glass. The air companion was sucked apart like a breeze in the hurricane's mouth.

Maroussia felt a scream in her head as the paluba tried to tuck her away in a pocket of safety. There were fragments of voice in the scream – the paluba's voice – desperately stuffing words into the small space of her head.

The Pollandore! Open it! Open it, Maroussia! You have the key!

And in the moment of ripping and destruction she also sensed the angel's fear. Fear of what was in Mirgorod waiting, and fear of what she, Maroussia, could do.

Maroussia walked out of her apartment and down the stairs. Out into the street and the rain.

53

Lakoba Petrov lay among the bodies of the dead. A dead face pressed against his cheek. The smell and the weight and the feel of killed people were piled up on his chest – he couldn't breathe he couldn't breathe he couldn't breathe – the trench was filling up with the bodies of the dead – one by one in rows they jerked as the bullets struck them and they died – they fell – they died. Water, percolating through the stack of the dead, brimmed in his open mouth. He coughed and puked. His mouth tasted bitter and full of salt.

The soldiers clambered among the bodies, finishing off the ones who were not yet dead, the ones who moaned, or hiccupped, or moved, or wept. Petrov, who had fallen when the firing began, untouched by any bullet, lay as still as the dead under the rain and the dead.

The soldiers began to cover the bodies over with wet earth. Petrov felt the weight of it and smelled its dampness. It was as heavy as all the world. He could not draw breath. He waited.

When the time came he pulled himself out from among the bodies and the red earth and turned back towards the city. But there was no escape: the dead climbed out after him in countless number; sightless, speechless, lumbering. Dripping putrefaction and broken as they died, they climbed out from the pit and followed him, walking slowly.

What he needed now could be got only from Josef Kantor.

54

By the time Raku Vishnik got home from the House on the Purfas he was soaked, but he hardly noticed the rain. He was certain that he had found the Pollandore. What Teslom had said confirmed it. It was real, it existed, he knew where it was. He wanted to tell someone – he would tell Vissarion – he would tell Maroussia Shaumian – they would share his triumph. They would understand. And together they would make a plan. His head was turning over scenes and plots and plans as he opened the door to his apartment and walked into nightmare.

The room was destroyed. Ransacked. His furniture broken. Drawers pulled out and overturned. Papers and photographs spilled across the floor. A man in the pale brick colour uniform of the VKBD looked up from the mess they were sifting when he arrived. Two other men were sitting side by side on the sofa. Rubber overalls and galoshes over civilian clothes. Neat coils of rope put ready beside them. Two large clean knives.

'My room,' he said. 'My room.'

It was the room he thought of first, though he knew, some part of him knew, that this was madness. When he'd arrived in Mirgorod twenty years before, to begin his career, he'd been able to obtain this small apartment, just for himself. The first time he closed the door behind him he had almost wept for simple joy. One afternoon soon afterwards he'd found on a stall in the Apraksin a single length of hand-blocked wallpaper – pale flowers on a dark russet ground – and put it up in the corner behind the stove. It was there now. And he'd accumulated other treasures over the years: the plain gilded mirror, only a little tarnished; the red lacquer caddy; the tinted lithograph of dancers. He looked at it now, all spilled across the floor.

'Fuck,' said Vishnik quietly, almost to himself. 'Fuck.' A tired resignation settled over him. None of it mattered now. He had known this time would come. He picked up the holdall, waiting packed by the doorway. 'OK,' he said to the VKBD man. 'OK. Let's go.'

The VKBD man took the bag from Vishnik's hand and shut the door.

'You won't be needing that,' he said. 'We're not going anywhere. All we need is here.'

'What?' said Vishnik.

'Where is Lom? Where is the girl? Where is the file?'

'What the fuck is this?' Vishnik was angry. Livid. 'Who the fuck are you, with your fucking questions? Look at my room. Look what you have done. You can go fuck yourself.'

'Where is Lom? Where is the girl? Where is the file? Please answer.'

'Number one,' said Vishnik. 'I don't know. Number two. What girl? Number three. What fucking file?'

The two men in rubber overalls were standing now. They picked up the couch and moved it to the middle of the room. The VKBD man repeated the questions. And then the fear came. Vishnik stumbled and almost fell. But he would not fall. He would not.

'You,' said Vishnik, 'can piss for it.'

The VKBD man indicated the couch in front of him.

'Sit down, Prince Vishnik. No, lie down. Close your eyes and think. We have plenty of time. Shout all you like. No one will come. The dvornik will have told them we are here and they'll keep quiet until we are gone. You know this is true. No one will come to help you. Now …' He put a hand on Vishnik's shoulder and propelled him gently forward. 'Please don't feel you must attempt to endure. Prolongation of your pain is needless and inconvenient.'

'Fuck you,' said Vishnik. 'Fuck you.'

55

Lom's tram forced its way against the rising storm. The other passengers sat tightly silent, staring out through the rain-streaming windows. The air grew bruises, purple and electric. Wind burst upon the streets in panicky, erratic bellows. Ragged whorls and twisters of wind-lashed rain threw hard gobbets against roofs and windows. Within moments floodwater was gushing up through the gratings of the sewers.

The tramway was raised above it, running on embankments and viaducts. Lom watched the mounting flood through blurred glass. People caught in the streets wrapped their arms over their heads and waded for shelter. The embankments of the city overbrimmed. Canal barges and ferries were tipped out of their channels into the streets and surged about helplessly before the wind, thumping hollowly against the walls of buildings, smashing through the windows of shops and theatres and restaurants. Pale faces looked out from upper windows. Droshki drivers struggled in the teeth of the storm to cut their horses loose from their traces and let them swim. It was impossible to tell street from canal. Some people had taken to boats and sculled their way slowly between tenements and shopfronts. A few souls swam, making little progress against the currents and churn.

The tram trundled on, deeper into the city, until at last the inevitable confronted it and it lurched to a halt in a shower of sparks from the power cable overhead, up to its wheel-tops in mud-thickened surging water. In the aftermath of the engine's surrender, wind and rain filled Lom's ears. His first instinct was to wait where he was, but the driver was shouting at them that they had to get out.

'The water is rising! The car will tip!'

They could already feel her shifting uneasily under the pressure of the flood. One by one they climbed down. The water was almost up to his waist, brown and icy cold.

The passengers from the tram stood in a huddle in the water, ineffectually wiping at the rain streaming down their faces, at a loss. There was a small bakery nearby, its door open, the flood lapping dully at the counter lip. Baskets and sodden loaves and pastries floated low in the water. From an upstairs casement a man in a pink shirt was beckoning, mouthing, his words lost in the rain. The others moved towards the shop, but Lom ignored him. He had to get to Pelican Quay.

56

When Lakoba Petrov came to his room, Josef Kantor's first instinct was to shoot him out of hand. Petrov stank like shit in a ditch. He had shaved his head, and his body, always thin, was a bundle of sticks. He was sodden, weighted down with water, a drowned rat. There were smears of what looked like paint or ink on his face, as if he had been writing on himself. His pupils were dilated, wide and dark.

'You told the girl where to find me,' said Kantor. 'You are an idiot, a useless fool. What are you doing here now?'

But Petrov only looked puzzled.

'Girl?'

'The Shaumian girl.'

Petrov waved the issue aside.

'I have come,' he said. 'I am prepared. What we spoke of earlier. The great inflagration, when all things will burn. I have decided. Let it come.'

Kantor withdrew his hand from his pocket. He had been fingering his revolver, but he let it lie. Instead he sat back in his chair and regarded Petrov with an interested benevolence. He had given up on this plan, and intended to use Lidia or Stefania, but he had not been able to overcome his doubts about their reliability. Their commitment to the sacrifice that was required. If Petrov had come back to him, that was better. That would be much more satisfactory.

He smiled at Petrov.

'Good,' he said. 'Very good. I'm glad you came to me, my friend. Let us discuss what you need.'

57

Walking against the flood was a perilous business. The water was slicked with oil and foulness. A dead rat nudged against his chest and caught there. Lom slapped it away with a shudder. The cold numbed his feet; hidden kerbs and obstructions underfoot threatened to trip and duck him at every step; his cloak spread sluggishly about him on the water. There were fewer and fewer people about. The streets were being abandoned to the rising waters. Lom rounded a corner and saw a flat-bottomed boat making slow headway away from him. Lom surged ahead, shouting. The boat, already low in the water with the weight of hunched bodies, was being poled effortfully forward by a man standing in the stern. Someone saw Lom and tugged at the boatman's sleeve. He paused to rest and let Lom catch up. Lom grabbed the gunwale with both hands and hauled himself over the side, falling heavily into the bottom among feet and sodden belongings.

'Thank you,' he breathed. 'Thanks.'

'Fifty roubles,' said the boatman.

Lom fumbled for the money with chilled, clumsy fingers and leaned across to pay him – not fifty roubles, but all he had – rocking the boat and elbowing his neighbour. She glared at him in mute protest. The boat punted forward in silence, past the Laughing Cockerel Theatre and the sagging balconies of the Apraksin. The wind was getting up, whipping the rain into their faces, raising low, choppy waves and flecks of spray. Lom found himself shivering. At least the floods gave him time. Chazia's people couldn't move in this.

An argument broke out among the passengers. A group of conscripts wanted to be taken to the Armoury and were attempting to commandeer the vessel. The boatman had had enough and wanted to go home. He poled stubbornly onwards, ignoring the soldiers' attempts to issue orders and impress upon him the urgency of his duty. The rest of the passengers looked on disconsolately, having given themselves up to events, indifferent to where they were carried as long as they stayed out of the icy, dirty water. Lom kept out of it. Neither direction suited him.

The boat was crossing a wide inundated square when the arguing soldiers fell quiet. Lom followed the direction of their gaze. There was something in the water. A smooth coil of movement. It came again, and then again: a slicker, surer movement than the wavelets chopping and jostling in the wind. Lom glimpsed a solid, steely-grey, oil-sleeked gun barrel of flesh. He thought it was an eel, but larger. Blackish flukes broke the surface without a splash and a face was watching him. A human face.

Almost human. It was the almost-humanness of the face that made it so shocking, because it wasn't human at all. It was a soft chalky white, the white of human flesh too long in the water, with hollow eye-sockets and deep dark eyes, the nose set higher and sharper than a human nose, the mouth a straight, lipless gash. The creature raised its torso higher and higher out of the water, showing an underbelly of the same subaqueous white as the face, and heavy white breasts, with nipples like a woman's but larger and bruise-coloured, bluish black. Below the almost-human torso, the dark tube of fluke-tailed muscle was working away. The creature's face was watching him continuously. It knew he was there. It knew it was being watched. There was no expression on its face at all. None whatsoever.

The creature swam swiftly towards the crowded boat, its white face upturned, watching Lom intently. He saw its hollow dark eyes, its expressionless mouth slightly open. He heard a faint hiss, like an expulsion of breath. It came right up to the boat and put its hands up on the sides, and began to tug and rock it, trying to pull itself in. It had a smooth, square, white upper back, like a man's, with a faint raised ridge the length of its spine.

'Rusalka! Rusalka!'

The boatman was yelling, panicked, and striking at the creature with his long heavy pole. One of the conscripts shouted in protest and lunged across the thwarts to grab at his arm, but it was too late.

The boatman caught the rusalka a heavy blow full on its head, and it withdrew under the water.

The soldier jumped in after it.

'Come back!' he was shouting. 'Please! Come back!'

He splashed about until he was exhausted and sobbing and gulping for air. At last he let his companions pull him back into the boat. While the passengers' attention was distracted Lom slipped over the side and waded away towards the edge of the square.

58

Krogh barely looked up when his private secretary came into the office carrying another stack of files. As always, the files would be placed in the in-tray and the completed work from the other tray would be cleared. It would be done without speaking. That was the routine. Minimal disturbance. Krogh was slightly surprised when the private secretary lingered, and walked around behind the desk to stand in the bay and look out of the windows. The rain was pouring in sheets out of the ruinous, bruised sky.

'The floods are rising,' the private secretary said.

Krogh grunted. The interruption irritated him. He was already unsettled following the call from Lom.

'I won't go home tonight,' he said. 'I'll sleep in the flat. I may need to speak to the Novozhd later. There's no need for you to stay, Pavel. Go home now before the bridges are closed.'

'It's too late for that.'

There was something in the private secretary's tone that surprised him.

'Well,' said Krogh, 'get them to find a launch to take you. Tell them I said so. I don't want you any more, not till tomorrow.'

'There was a message from Commander Chazia.'

'What did she say?'

'That you were a stupid old fucker.'

Krogh realised too late how close behind him the private secretary had come. The loop of wire was round his neck before he could react. It tightened, cutting into the folds of his flesh. He felt it slicing. Felt the warm blood spill down his neck inside his collar. It splashed the papers on his desk. He tried to get his fingers inside the wire, but could not.

His fingers slipped on the blood. He felt the wire cut them. He tried to stand up, he tried to fight, he tried to call out, but the private secretary was leaning away from him, pulling at his neck with the wire loop, tipping him backwards, unbalancing him. He tried to throw himself sideways but the private secretary hauled him upright. No sound could escape from his constricted throat. He could get no air in. He felt the back of his chair digging into his head. It hurt. Then he died.

59

When Maroussia Shaumian reached the building where Raku Vishnik lived, she found the street door shut against the rising waters. She pushed it open and waded into the dim, flooded hall. Her splashing echoed oddly. She felt the weight of her sodden clothes dragging at her as she climbed the stairs to Apartment 4. The door was ajar.

'Raku?' she called softly. 'Raku? It's Maroussia.'

There was no answer. She pushed the door open and went in.

What was left of Vishnik lay on the couch, adrift on a sea of littered paper and broken household stuff. He was naked, on his back, his arms and legs lashed by neat bindings to the legs of the couch. There was blood. A lot of blood. Three fingers of his right hand were gone.

She must have made some sound – she didn't know what – because he turned his pulped and swollen face in her direction. He was watching her with his one open eye. She had thought he was dead.

She went across the room to him. He was moving his mouth. He might have been speaking but she couldn't hear him over the sound of the rain against the windows. She knelt down beside him. The water from her dress soaked the drift of notebooks and scattered photographs.

'Maroussia—' he said. 'I didn't ...'

What should I do? she thought. *What should I do?*

'It's OK,' she said. 'I'll help you.' *What should I do?* She tried to undo one of the knots, but it was tight and slippery with blood. Her fingers tugged at it uselessly. 'What happened?' she said. 'Who did this? What can I do, Raku?'

'I found it,' said Vishnik. He was staring at her with his one remaining eye. They had taken the other one. 'It's here and I found it. I didn't tell them what I know.'

'It's OK, Raku,' she said. 'It's OK.'

'No. I want to tell you. I wanted to. I was going to.' He tried to raise his head from the couch. There was blood in his mouth. 'I found it. I found it. And they were here ... But they didn't get it. Even they ... even they are human. And stupid.'

'Raku?'

He laid his head back against the couch. His mouth fell partly open. His face was empty. He was gone.

Maroussia stood up. She was trembling.

I need to get out of here. I need to get out of here now.

The horror of the thing on the couch – what they had done to him ... She could not stay. It was impossible. But the storm was raging outside, and the floods ... She had almost not made it here. Where could she go? How?

She went to the window, parted the curtains and looked out into storming darkness. The casement was rattling in its frame; the reflection of the room behind her flexed as the panes bowed under the force of the wind. She pressed her face against the glass, trying to see.

The street lamps were out. The only faint light came from the windows of neighbouring houses, but she could see by their glimmering reflection on the waves down below that the flood had risen further. There must have been ten to fifteen feet of surging water in the street, whipped into choppy, spray-spilling peaks.

And there was a boat.

A diesel launch was nosing its way up the flooded street, half a dozen uniformed men in the open stern, hunching their shoulders against the rain, MILITIA OF MIRGOROD in white lettering on the roof of the cabin.

She heard a movement in the room behind her, and spun round, thinking wildly that it was Vishnik, raising himself somehow from the couch.

But it was Lom.

'We have to get out,' said Maroussia 'We have to go. They're outside now. They have a boat.'

'I know,' said Lom. 'I saw them.' He was looking at Vishnik. 'I came for him.'

'Raku's dead,' said Maroussia. 'He was … He spoke to me when I got here, he said … he said he told them nothing.'

'He had nothing to tell. They didn't need to do this.'

From down below there came the sound of hollow thumping, wood striking against wood, heavily. Glass breaking.

'There's no time,' said Maroussia. 'We have to go now.'

Lom stood looking at Vishnik for a moment.

'Take the stairs,' he said. 'Not the lift. Go up. In houses like this the roof space is usually open from house to house. All the way to the end of the row if you're lucky. Keep going up. You'll find a way.'

'What about you?' she said. 'Aren't you coming?'

'I'll keep them occupied. You can find a boat on the quay.'

'They'll kill you,' said Maroussia.

'They won't,' said Lom. 'Not straight away. They need to know what I've done. They need to be sure.'

Maroussia shook her head. 'Come with me,' she said.

'No,' said Lom.

Maroussia hesitated. There was another crash from downstairs. A shout.

'Shit,' said Lom. 'Just go. You need to go. Please.'

There was nothing else to say. She turned away from him and went out of the door.

60

When Maroussia had gone, Lom went to the lift cage and pressed the button to summon the car. The mechanism juddered loudly into life. The lift was on one of the upper floors, and it took agonising moments to descend. When it reached him, he pulled open the cage and stepped inside, pressed the button for the basement and stepped back out again. There was a splash when it hit the water below. It wouldn't be coming back, not with the weight of water inside it. That left only the stairwell.

He went to the top of the stairs. He would see down one flight and the landing below. He checked the gun. Checked it again.

A quiet voice. The sound of boots. A face peering up from the landing below.

Lom fired high. The shot struck the wall above the man's head, and he ducked out of sight.

'Lom?' It was Safran's voice. 'Lom? Is that you? What are you hoping to achieve?'

Lom fired another shot down the stairwell.

'Don't try to come up,' he called. 'I'll shoot anyone I see. I won't fire high again.'

'There are six of us, Lom. You haven't got a chance.'

'I've got boxfuls of shells. I'm very patient.'

'You're mad.'

Lom said nothing. The longer he could hold them here, the more time he would give Maroussia.

'We can rush you, Lom. Any time we want. You can't shoot us all.'

'Who's first then?'

'How's your friend, Lom? How's Prince Vishnik?' Lom felt the anger rising inside him. 'He liked you, Lom. Did you know that? He called your name a lot. When he wasn't squealing like a pig.'

'You bastard—' Lom stopped. Safran was goading him. He mustn't let it distract him. He waited. 'Safran?' he called. But there was no answer. The silence stretched. Nothing happened. Lom waited.

Someone appeared on the landing below. A face. An arm. Throwing something. Lom fired too late.

The grenade bounced off the wall and skittered towards him. Instinctively he kicked out at it, a panicky jab of his foot that almost missed completely, but the outside edge of his shoe connected. The clumsy kick sliced the grenade against the skirting board. It bounced off and rolled back down the stairs, two or three steps at a time. Lom lurched back, protecting his face with his arm.

The explosion sucked the air down the stairwell and then burst it back up. The noise was too loud to be heard as sound; it was just a slamming pain inside his head. Lom stumbled dizzily.

As he leaned against the wall, trying to clear his head, trying not to vomit, it dawned on him that the sawing, hiccupping sounds he was hearing were someone else's pain.

He looked up in time to see a uniform looming up the stairs. He fired towards it wildly and the uniform retreated.

Something – a sound, a glimpse of movement in the corner of his eye – made him turn. Safran was behind him, only a few yards away, his revolver raised.

Shit. The lift shaft. He climbed it.

As Lom swung round, he saw the satisfaction in Safran's pale eyes. There was no time to react. Safran clubbed him viciously on the side of his head. On the temple. And again.

Lom's world swam sickeningly, his balance went and he fell.

Two militia men were holding his arms behind his back. Safran's pale eyes were looking into his. Lom tried to tense the muscles in his midriff, but when the blow came, hard, he folded and tried to drop to his knees. The men held him up.

Lom hauled at the air with his mouth but no breath would go in. Safran pulled his head up by the hair to see his face and hit him again. And again. When the men dropped his arms, he went down and curled up on the floor, knees tucked in against his chin, trying to protect himself. At last he was able to suck in some air, noisily. A sticky line of spit trailed from his mouth to the floor.

'You,' said Safran, 'are nothing. You are made of shit.'

61

The room they left him in was stiflingly hot. It must have been somewhere deep inside the Lodka: there were no windows, just shadowless electric light from a reinforced glass recess in the ceiling. Some sort of interview room. A wooden table in the centre of the floor, two chairs facing each other across it, another two along the wall. Green walls, a peeling linoleum floor and, around the edges of the room, solid, heavy iron pipes, bolted strongly to the wall and scalding hot to the touch. Leather straps were wrapped loosely around them, and there were stains and dried stuff stuck on the pipes. There were stains on the floor too. Dark brown. Through the door came the sound of a distant bell, footsteps, muffled yelling and shouting. It was impossible to tell what time it was. Whether it was night or day.

Every part of him hurt. His left eye was closed. It felt swollen and tender to the touch. His fingers came away sticky with drying blood. His head was throbbing. There was a dull pain and an empty sickness in his midriff. A sharp jabbing in his ribs when he moved. No serious damage had been done. Not yet. He had been lucky or, more likely, Safran had been careful.

He tried the door. It was locked. He sat at the table, facing the door, and waited, trying to keep the image of Vishnik on the couch – what they had done to him – out of his mind. He would settle with Safran for that.

He found himself thinking about Maroussia Shaumian. Her face. The darkness under her eyes. She had been holding herself together but the effort was perceptible. There had been a ragged wound across her cheek. He hoped she was far away. He hoped he would see her again.

When he heard the key turn in the lock, he thought about standing up to face them, but didn't trust his body to straighten, so he stayed where he was. The man in the doorway was wearing a dark fedora and a heavy grey coat, unbuttoned, over a red silk shirt. His face was thin and pockmarked under a few days' growth of beard.

Lom had seen him before. In the old photograph on Krogh's file. In the marching crowd. As a statue half a mile in the sky, looking out across another Mirgorod, a city that didn't exist, not yet. The whisperers' Mirgorod. *His* Mirgorod. This was him.

The half-mile-high man laid his hat on the table, hung his coat on the back of the other chair and sat down facing Lom. His hair was straight and cut long, thickly piled, a dark of no particular colour, unusually abundant and lustrous, brushed back from his face without a parting. The red silk of his shirt was crumpled and needed washing. Close up, his eyes were dark and brown, with a surprising, direct intensity. It was like looking into street-fires burning. The man let his hands rest, relaxed and palm-down on the table, but all the time he was watching Lom's face with those deep, dark brown eyes in which the earth was burning.

'Kantor,' said Lom. 'Josef Kantor.'

'You're an interesting fellow, Investigator,' said Kantor. 'Stubborn. Clever. Courageous. A policeman who steps outside the rules.' He paused, but Lom said nothing. Every word was to be wrung from him. Nothing offered for free. He regretted he'd spoken at all. He'd given too much away already. In interrogations, there was as much to learn for the subject as for the interrogator. What did they know? What did they not? What did they need? The silence in the room continued. It became a kind of battle. Eventually, Kantor smiled. 'You react as I would,' he said. 'Observe, learn, give nothing away. That's good.'

Lom said nothing. Kantor leaned back in his chair.

'So. Here we are. I wanted some time alone with you before Lavrentina comes. She'll be here soon, I'm afraid, and after that it won't be possible for us to speak like this any more. Which for me is genuinely regrettable.' Kantor looked at his watch. 'You've impressed me. Do you want to know what time it is? Ask me, and I'll tell you.'

Lom said nothing.

'Would you like to smoke?' He laid a packet of cigarettes on the table. 'Oh please, say *something*. We both know the game. I've been beaten myself, in rooms like this one. You ask yourself, will I be brave? But it doesn't matter. It makes no difference. Lavrentina will come soon, and that won't be the kind of roughhouse you and I are used to.'

The strangest thing about Kantor, thought Lom, was that, despite all he knew about him, he was attractive. He turned interrogation into a teasing game. He made himself charming, fun to be with. You sensed his strength and power and his capacity for cruelty, but somehow that made you want him to look after you. He might kill you, but he might also love you.

'Perhaps you're still hoping you'll be able to deliver Lavrentina's stupid file to Krogh. Perhaps you're thinking, *Krogh is arresting Chazia even as we speak. He will come through the door any moment now and rescue me.* But that isn't going to happen.' Kantor paused, and looked into Lom's eyes with warm sympathy. 'We found the files in the bathroom. And Krogh is dead. She had to do that, didn't she, after that telephone call?'

Lom felt his defences crumbling. He was tired and scared and weak and sick.

'You killed him, actually,' Kantor was saying. 'Of course you did. You knew you were doing it at the time. At least, you were indifferent whether it happened or not. See why you interest me, Lom? I see something of myself in you, as a matter of fact. And you killed Vishnik too.'

'No!'

'What do you want to know, Lom? Go on, ask me something and I will answer, I promise, even if only to repay the pleasure of having finally got you to speak. I have to get something out of you before Chazia does. You have the advantage of me: you've seen my file. Tell me about it. What does it say?'

It was as if he had been reading Lom's thought processes in his face.

'Chazia thinks she can use you,' said Lom. 'But she's wrong, isn't she? You're using her. The question is, what for? What do you want, Kantor?'

'Ha!' cried Kantor. 'You wonderful man! You do see to the heart of things, don't you? You're right, that is the biggest question. No one, not even the angel, has asked it until now.'

'You owe me an answer.'

'I do.'

'So answer.'

'Have you ever wondered where the angels come from?'

Surprised, Lom shook his head. 'The stars, I guess,' he said. 'The planets. Outer space. Galaxies.'

'Exactly. And what about that? We hardly consider it, do we? They arrive, and we take them for signs and wonders. Messages about us. Who is justified, who not? What clever machines can we make of their dying flesh? It's all so narrow and trivial, don't you think? As if this one damp and cooling world with its broken moons was all there is. The Vlast looks inwards and backwards all the time. But we're seeing angels the wrong way round. What they tell us is, there are other worlds, other suns, countless millions of them; you only have to look up in the night to see them. And we can go there. We can move among them. Humankind spreading out across the sky, advancing from star to star.'

'Impossible,' said Lom.

Kantor slammed his hand on the table. 'Of course it's possible. It's not even a matter of doubt. The engineering is straightforward. Like everything else, it is only a matter of paying the price. A few generations of collective sacrifice is all that's needed. The fruit of the stars is there to be harvested. That's our future. I know it. I've seen it in the voice of the angel. A thousand thousand glittering vessels rising into the sky and unfolding their sails and crossing the emptiness between stars. All it requires is ingenuity. Effort. Organisation. Purpose. Sacrifice. The deferment of pleasure. Imagine a Vlast of a thousand suns. That would be worth something. Can you see that, Lom? Can you imagine it? Can you share that great ambition?'

It seemed to be an honest question. It might have been a genuine offer, a door out of the torture room.

'No,' said Lom. 'No. I can't.'

'Ah,' said Kantor and shrugged. 'Pity.'

The door opened and Lavrentina Chazia came in.

Archangel unfurls his mind like a leaf across the continent.

The dead dig trenches to bury themselves.

The dead ride long slow cattle trains eastwards, the streets behind them empty, the walls fallen from their houses, their wallpaper open to the rain,

their home-stuff spilled across the streets. The smell of wet, burned build-
ings enriches the air.

Grey-haired young men with ears turned to bone.

A naked corpse lies at the foot of the slope; a lunar brilliance streams
across the dead legs stuck apart.

Conscripts in trenches kiss their bullets in the dark and drink the snow.

Corpses awaiting collection stiffen like thorn trees.

Men and women hang by the neck from balconies on long ropes, like
sausages in a delicatessen window.

I becoming We.

The clock and the calendar reset to zero.

Everything starts from here.

Archangel – voice of history, muse of death – reaches out across his
world – the is and the will-be-soon – touching its unfolding – tasting its
texture with his mind's tongue – testing it with his mind's fingers – it
is satisfaction – it is joy – it is hope. The stars are coming, and the space
between them.

And yet – and still – nearby but out of reach – the tireless egg of time
glimmers diminutively in the massy dark – his future tinctured still with
the edge of fear.

Chazia had brought a carpet bag with her, which she set on the table
and began to unpack. Lom watched as she unrolled a chamois containing an array of small tools: blades, pliers, a steel-headed hammer.

Kantor picked up his hat and cigarettes and withdrew to a chair at
the edge of the room. He laid the hat on his lap and folded his arms
across it. It seemed like an instinctive act of self-protection. It wasn't
deference. It might have been distaste.

'There is only one subject of interest to us, Investigator,' said Chazia.
'The whereabouts of Maroussia Shaumian, the daughter of Josef's late
wife. That is all. There is nothing else. The sooner we have exhausted
that topic, the sooner we can leave this unpleasant room.'

His flimsy constructions of hope and defence crumbled. He said
nothing.

'Major Safran saw you talk to her, and now we can't find her. I think
you know where she has gone.'

'He won't speak,' said Kantor. 'He's playing dumb.'

Chazia came round to Lom's side of the table and knelt beside him.

She began to bind him with leather straps like the collars of dogs. She fixed his hands to the legs of the chair, so that his arms hung down at his sides, and then she bound his ankles to the chair legs as well. Her face was close to his lap. Her breasts were pressing against the rough material of her uniform blouson. The patches on her skin didn't look like stone, they *were* stone. Angel stone.

She worked with methodical care, her breathing shallow and rapid. The fear was a dry, silent roaring in Lom's head. He wanted to speak *now*, to tell her *everything*, but his mouth had no moisture in it and he could not.

'You were a promising policeman, Investigator,' she was saying as she worked. 'Krogh thought he'd been clever, spotting you, but it was my doing, actually. Didn't you guess? I keep track of all Savinkov's experiments. You'd never have been able to get at Laurits if I hadn't let you. We fed you the evidence, of course. Laurits was lazy, and brazen with it. I thought it would be a good idea to let you take him down, if you could. Keep the others on their toes. I had it in mind to bring you to Mirgorod myself, if you succeeded. A career open to talent, that's what the Vlast should be. But Krogh got you first, and it has come to this. A pity.'

Lom tried to focus on her, but his vision was blurry. What was she saying? He wasn't sure. His gaze was drawn back to the line of implements ready on the desk.

'Oh no,' said Chazia. 'It won't be like that. Excruciation has many uses, but collecting information quickly isn't one of them. Torture is good for encouraging demoralisation and fear – for every one person put to pain, a thousand fear it – and it binds the torturers closer to us. But none of that is relevant in your case. Such methods were ineffective on your friend Vishnik, and I doubt they would be more so with you. On this occasion I require the truth quickly, and there is a better way. You may find the method professionally interesting.'

She took a piece of some dark stuff from her bag and pulled it onto her right hand. It was a long, loose-fitting glove made of a heavy substance something like rubber, but it wasn't rubber. She held it out for him to see. It had a slightly reddish lustrous sleekness like wet seal fur.

'Angel skin,' she said, though he knew that already. He had read of such things. This was a Worm. Chazia took a flask out of her bag and held it up to Lom's face. He jerked his head aside.

'It's only water,' she said. 'Drink a little if you like.'

He nodded, and she unscrewed the cap and held the flask to his dry lips, tipping it up to let him take a sip. He sluiced the water around carefully in his mouth and let it trickle down his throat as slowly as he could. Without warning, she tipped the rest of it over his head. It was ice-cold. Lom shouted at the shock of it.

'It helps,' said Chazia. 'I don't know why.'

She brought her chair round from the other side of the desk and sat beside him, placing her angel-gloved hand on his face. He flinched. His skin crawled.

'Ask him, Josef,' she said quietly, with suppressed excitement. 'Ask him.'

Kantor came and stood by him. His eyes were hard and dispassionately curious. The smouldering earth flickered deep inside them.

'Where is my wife's bastard daughter, Vissarion? Maroussia Shaumian? Where is she now?'

Lom felt something disgusting slithering about on the surface of his mind, and pushed it instinctively away. He closed his thoughts against it and concentrated on Kantor's face. He imagined himself drawing it, like a draughtsman, meticulously. He examined its lines, contours and shadows.

See it as an object. See the surface only.

Chazia grunted in surprise, and Lom felt her push the Worm harder against the defences he had built. Her hand inside the obscene glove tightened, gripping his face where before she had only touched. He shut his mind more firmly against her. Kantor asked the question again.

Fall back to the second line of defence. Tell them something they already know. Let them believe they are making progress.

He ignored Chazia and looked into Kantor's eyes.

I can do this.

'I saw Miss Shaumian this morning, for the first and last time. Or perhaps it was yesterday, I've lost track of time. I saw her on the occasion of the summary execution in the street of her mother, Feiga-Ita Shaumian, wife of Josef Kantor, by Major Safran of the Mirgorod Militia. Miss Shaumian also observed this execution, and afterwards she walked away. I do not know where she went. I have not seen her since.'

Kantor returned his gaze impassively. If the words meant anything to him he did not show it. Lom felt Chazia remove her hand from his face.

'Nothing,' she said to Kantor. 'Hold his head please.'

Kantor walked around the desk to stand behind him and put his arm across Lom's throat, under his chin, pulling him backwards until he was choking, and all he could see was the recessed light in the ceiling. Kantor's other hand gripped his hair so that his head was held firmly.

Chazia's face came into his line of view. He saw the fine blade in her hand, but it was only when she placed it against the skin of his forehead that he realised what she was going to do.

Repel! Repel!

He drove his mind against her with all his strength, trying to ball up the air in the room and throw it at her.

Nothing happened.

'The vyrdalak reported that you could do that,' said Chazia. 'No wonder Savinkov sealed you up.' She touched the stone rind in her face and smiled. 'Quite useless here, of course.'

He felt her begin to cut.

Chazia didn't find it easy to get the embedded piece of angel stone out of his forehead. She had to dig and gouge and pry with considerable force. She tried several different implements. The pain went on for ever. Lom choked and fought for breath and closed his eyes against the blood that pooled in their sockets and seeped under the lids. He might have screamed. He wasn't sure.

At last it stopped. Kantor released his hold on Lom's head and let it fall forward. Lom was gasping for breath. His eyes were blinded with blood and his nose was filled with it, but his hands were bound at his sides and he could do nothing about that. He hadn't fainted while it was happening, and he didn't faint afterwards. Fainting would have been easier, but it didn't come.

Kantor was leaning over him.

'Is that the brain in there?' he said to Chazia.

Kantor's finger probed the hole in his forehead.

'It's firmer than I would have thought.'

He jabbed harder. Lom felt no pain, only a deep, woozy sickness.

'Don't, Josef,' said Chazia. 'Don't damage it yet.'

Then Lom fainted.

62

'**N**ow we must try again,' Chazia was saying, somewhere far away. Nothing had changed. It must have been only minutes. Seconds, even. 'Quickly, before we lose him.'

Still blinded, Lom felt the glove of angel substance on his face again, and this time there was nothing he could do to defend himself. She came right inside him, roughly. Invading. Violating. He was naked and broken.

He gave Chazia everything.

She was in there, inside his mind, and she *knew*. Nothing could be hidden from her. She went everywhere, and he gave it all up. Everything that had happened. Everything he had heard. Everything he knew. Krogh. Vishnik. The Archive. The massacre. The whisperers in the square. The Crimson Marmot. Petrov. Safran. The mudjhik. Maroussia. Everything.

'He desires her, Josef!' Chazia crowed with genuine wonderment and pleasure. 'The poor idiot desires her.'

And then – how much later was it? how much time gone? nothing seemed to take very long—

'He knows nothing,' she said. 'Nothing. He's of no use at all. Kill him.'

They left him alone in the interrogation room, still tied to the chair. After an unmeasurable amount of time it seemed that other men came and released him. He might have been sick. One of the men might have been Safran. He might have imagined that.

They were leading him along corridors. He could see from one eye: linoleum, worn carpet, flagstones, his own feet. It didn't matter.

A shock of cold and space and early morning light. The smell of water. A *bridge*. They were crossing a *bridge*.

He jerked himself out of the grip of the men, who were holding him loosely by the arms, and lurched away from them towards the bridge's low parapet.

For a moment, a half-second, no more, he looked down at the dark, swollen current. He wanted the water to wash the blood and mess and memory away. A clean, cold, private death. He tipped himself over the edge.

The water reached up to take him as he fell.

The moment between tipping over the parapet and hitting the water seemed to go on for ever. Lom hung head downwards in air. The surface of the river rose slowly to meet him, freighted with the debris of the flooded city. The water had a particular smell: dark, cold, earthy, cleansing.

He crashed into green darkness and the noise churned in his ears. The shock of the cold seized his lungs in ice fists and squeezed. Bands of freezing iron tightened around his head and his chest.

He tried to scrabble his way to the surface of the river, not knowing the direction where the surface was. His clothes, water-heavy, wrapped round his body. The weight of his boots pulled at his legs, slowing their struggle to a nightmare of running. His mouth fell open in a silent O.

And yet he was happy.

After the first rush of panic, he felt his pulse-rate slowing. The icy river reached inside his ribs with cool gentle fingers and cupped his heart kindly. Calmness returned. This was now, and he was alive, and the river was his friend.

He let the dark and freezing absolution of the Mir wash away the stink and shame and failure of the interrogation room. The river let him understand.

There is no blame. There is no judge but you. Forgive yourself.

He had been ... *violated* ... by alien, brutal intruding fingers. The fat, poking stubs of Kantor, Chazia's in her foul dead-angel glove. He had given up nothing. It had been ripped out and taken, that was all. And that was not the same.

The waters cleansed the hole in the centre of his forehead where the piece of angel stone had been ripped away and the river now entered.

He felt the cool currents of its touch directly against the naked cortex of his brain, bursting long-dead synapses into light and life. Unplugged at last, for the first time since childhood, Vissarion Lom perceived the world as it was, fresh and new and timeless, flooded with truth. He smelled the light and tasted the space between things.

The Mir was filled with watchful awareness and intelligence. Lom opened wide his arms and felt himself rising. He broke the surface into early morning air. His cloak unfolded and spread itself around him like a huge black lily pad, rotating slowly in the current. His face, upturned in the cloak's dark centre, was the lily's pale flower, opening to the grey light. Breathing.

The river was in full spate. As he turned slowly, tilted upwards, he saw the wharves and quays and rooftops of Mirgorod passing against the cloud-grey sky. Nearer to his face, pieces of wood and broken things came with him. He was the flagship of a debris flotilla, being carried towards the edge of the city and beyond it the sea, on the surge of the withdrawing flood.

Waves splashed against his face and trickled into the open hole in his forehead.

The sentient water had a voice that was speaking to him. It told him that the city was an alien tumorous growth, formed around the plug with which the Founder had tried to stop the river's mouth. Yet there had been a time before the city, and there could be such a time again: when it was gone, when trees grew up between the buildings, and moss and black soil breathed the air again.

The kindly waters of the Mir brushed against his skull and reached inside to calm his heart and whisper reassurance. The voice was telling him who he was. He was a man of muscle and lung and love and understanding. He was a vessel and a flowering on the seaward flow. There were people it was right to love and there were people it was right to loathe and bring to destruction.

Yes, if I have time. I need more time.

Only there was no more time.

As he rotated slowly on the current, the ice-cold waters of the river were draining all the feeling from his body. Lom no longer knew where his arms and legs were, or what they were doing. The muscles of his face were numbed into immobility, his mouth frozen in its permanent open O.

Helplessly, from a great distance, he observed the rippling water work at the bulges and pockets of air that had been trapped in the folds of his cloak. The movement of the river was easing them slowly to the edges of the heavy fabric. One by one they bubbled out and surrendered themselves to the sky.

There was nothing he could do.

What his lily-pad cloak was losing in buoyancy it gained in weight, and slowly it was sinking, and taking him down with it. The river was already lapping at his chin and spilling over into the waiting uncloseable O.

The river brimmed against his nostrils and covered them over. At last he inhaled the cold waters deeply and sank for the second and last time. It felt like sleep. As he closed his eyes he saw against the shadows the face of Maroussia, pale and calm and serious, looking down on him hugely out of the sky, like the moon made whole.

Close by (so close!) – but also not – neither in this world, nor very far away at all – the other O – the pocketful of second chances, the waiting second mouth, the tongue of different lives – is listening to the river, listening to the rain.

63

Maroussia Shaumian found Lom's body floating face down, lodged against a squat stone pillar of the Ter-Uspenskovo Bridge among planks and branches, lost shoes and broken packing cases. She tried to pull it into the boat but she could not. Several times she almost tipped herself into the river before she gave up and knotted a line to his leg and towed him, an inert, lifeless weight, to a place where there were stone steps in the embankment. All the time she worked, she expected the shouts, the bullets, to start.

She had found the boat – an open, clinker-built, tapered skiff, her oars neatly stowed on board – bumping against the wall at the end of Pelican Quay. Ignoring the oars, she'd crouched in the bottom and edged it slowly, hand over hand, along the house-fronts until she came in sight of Vishnik's building, and she'd watched from the shadows as Lom was taken into the militia vessel. When the police boat left, its searchlight stabbing the night, raking darkened street frontages and swirling water, she followed it all the way to the Lodka, and moored against a telegraph pole.

Cold and wet and shivering, she waited. She could have left, but she did not. Lom had saved her twice. She thought of Vishnik, his ruined body and his terrible lonely death. She thought of her mother, shot in the back in the street. She would not let the Vlast take another. Not if she could prevent it.

When dawn began to seep across the city and other boats began to appear, she felt it would be less conspicuous to be moving, and so she started a slow patrol, circling the Lodka through flooded squares and across re-emerging canals. It was sheer luck that she saw, from the cover of a stranded fire-barge, the uniforms come out of a side door, and Lom stumbling along in the middle of them as if he was drunk. She saw his lurch for the parapet and heard the warders' shouts and the splash when his body hit the water. But she couldn't go to look for him straight away. She had to wait, watching the killing party linger near the bridge, shouting to each other and shining torch beams on the dark water. It was fifteen minutes before they gave up and another fifteen before she spotted the sodden hump of his back floating low in the water among the rubbish.

She dragged the body up the steps and laid it on its back. Water seeped out and puddled on the stone. The eyes were open and glassy, the pupils darkly dilated. In the dim grey dawn the face and hands were tinged an ominous blue. She made a desperate, rushed examination. There was no pulse at the wrist or neck, and no breath from the stiffened, cyanotic mouth.

'He's *not* gone,' she said to herself. 'He's *not* gone.' She was surprised how much it mattered.

With a desperate energy Maroussia pumped the lifeless chest with the heel of her hand and forced her own breath into the waterlogged lungs. Every time she paused to rest, she saw the ragged-edged hole in Lom's forehead. It oozed a dark rivery fluid.

She worked and worked, pounding the inert chest, forcing breath into the cold mouth. At last she collapsed across him, her chest heaving.

It was no good.

But at that moment Lom gave a powerful jerk and twisted out from under her weight. He rolled over onto his side, retching and vomiting black river water.

Emptied of the river, Lom sank back into unconsciousness, but he was breathing now, and the blue of his face began to flush faintly in the rising light of morning.

Somehow she managed to heave him back into the boat. There was nothing else to do. She could not carry him, and she would not leave him.

She unshipped the oars and pushed the boat free of the landing place and out into the current. Pulling out into midstream she felt the force of the current seize her. The subsiding flood waters were pouring out of the city, down towards the marshes and the sea. The boat took its place among the detritus, the floating wreckage and the crewless vessels drifting, bumping and turning on the dark foam-flecked current. There was no need to row. It would be better – less conspicuous – if she did not. But Lom's body was icy to the touch. He needed warmth, and quickly, or he would die.

Maroussia pulled Lom's cloak over his head, stuffed it away at the stern, and got his shirt, boots and trousers off. His body, naked but for his underclothes, was white as chalk. She took off her own coat and dress and lay down next to him, pulling the clothes over them both and taking him in her arms like a lover. His body was cold, clammy, inert, like something dead, and the cold seeped from him into her. She shivered uncontrollably, but she pushed herself closer against him and closed her eyes.

The Mir surged forward in the cold of the morning, taking their small vessel in its grasp, carrying them onward, downstream on turbid waters under a dark pewter sky, past the waterfronts of the waking city.

Archangel probes a sudden strangeness, and realisation almost shatters him.

He is appalled.

He is brittle.

A new fact bursts open, flowering into his awareness, staining it with a rigid poison.

Blinded by the profusion of the millions – he has not noticed – not until this moment – the faint, brushing touches – the trails – the spraints – of those he cannot see. There are time streams, and people in them – story threads, small voices – that are not part of his future.

He begins to sense them now. He detects – faintly, peripherally – the tremor of their passing and knows what it means for him. Suddenly, disaster is near. At the very moment of his triumph, failure is becoming possible.

In the forest he heaves and struggles, desperate to release the embedded hill of himself from his rock prison. He pulls and shudders, straining at the crust of the earth. Stronger now, he feels the give of it, just a little, a fraction, and the snow roars and slides off his shoulders. For a moment he believes he might succeed. But it is not enough. He cannot move, he cannot rise, he cannot fly.

He sends his mind instead, the whole of it, the entire focused armoury of his attention forced down one narrow beam, ignoring everything except the hint of one small boat and its impossible cargo of change.

He cannot see them, he cannot find them, not himself: they are somehow hidden. But they are there, and there are – he reasons – others who will be able to see them with their jelly-and-electromagnetism oculars.

He bursts his way into first one human mind, then another, and another, a roaring angel voice.

WHERE ARE THEY? WHERE ARE THEY?

A sailor falls, bleeding from the eyes. Archangel jumps to another.

WHERE ARE THEY?

A typist collapses to the floor, fitting, speaking in tongues. Archangel jumps to another.

WHERE ARE THEY?

An engineer splatters vomit across the floor and tears at his ears until they hang in tatters and bleed. Archangel jumps to another.

Archangel leaps from mind to mind, faster and faster, finding nothing. Yet they must be found. Now. Before it is too late.

Part Two

64

The giant Aino-Suvantamoinen lay on his back on the soft estuarial river-mud of the White Marshes. It was almost like floating. It was more like being a water-spider, resting on the meniscus of a pool, feeling the tremor of breezes brushing across the surface. He kept his eyes closed and his hands spread flat and palm-downward on the drum-tight, quivering skin of the mud. He was listening with his hands to the mood of the waters, feeling the way they were flowing and what they meant. He drew in long slow lungfuls of river air, tasting it with his tongue and nose and the back of his throat. There was ice and fog and rain on the air, and the exhalations of trees. He knew the savour of every tree – he could tell birch from alder, blackthorn from willow, aspen from spruce – and he could taste the distinctive breath of each of the great rivers as they mingled in the delta's throat: the Smaller Chel, the Mecklen, the Vod, and above all the rich complexity of the Mir, with traces of the city caught like burrs in her hair. Everything that he could taste and hear and feel spoke to him. It was the voice of the world.

He was floating on the cusp – the infinitesimal point of balance – between past and future. The past was one, but futures were many, an endlessly bifurcating flowering abundance of possibilities all trying to become, all struggling to grow out of the precarious restless racing-forwards of *now*.

Aino-Suvantamoinen sat up in the near-darkness – his heart pounding, his head spinning – and scooped up handfuls of cold mud. Cupping his palms together, he buried his face in the slather for cool-ness and rest. There was something on the Mir that morning such as he had never known before. The river was excited, it was strung out and buzzing with promise. In three centuries of listening, no other morning like this one. A boat was coming, the river told him: a boat freighted with significance, freighted with change. New futures were adrift on the Mir, and also – astonishingly – he'd never felt, never even conceived of anything like this – a new past.

The giant picked himself up from the mud. He had to hurry. He had to reach the great locks and set his shoulder to the enormous ancient beams. He had to open the sluices and close the weir gates before the rushing of the flood carried everything past. Before it was too late.

65

Maroussia lay in the bottom of the skiff, wet and cold, holding the unconscious Lom in her arms. The boat rocked and turned in the current, colliding from time to time with other objects drifting on the flood: the bodies of drowned dogs and the planks of Big Side shanties. Maroussia kept her face turned towards the wooden inside freeboard, staying low and out of sight, risking only occasional glances over the gunwale. If anyone saw the skiff, it would look like one more empty boat adrift from its moorings. Lom was breathing loudly, raggedly, the terrible wound in the front of his head circled with a fine crust of dried blood and weeping some cloudy liquid.

The river had breached its banks in many places. The current was taking them west, towards the seaward dwindling of the city. They passed through flooded squares. Lamp posts and statues sticking up from the mud-heavy, surging water. Pale faces looking from upper windows. Later, at the city's edge, they drifted above submerged fields, half-sunken trees, drowned pigs. The swollen waters carried them onwards, out of Mirgorod, into strange territories. As the morning wore on, the waters widened and slowed, taking them among low, wooded islands and spits of grass and mud. By now they should have been following one of the channels of the Mir delta, but the channels were all lost under the slack waters of the flood. Maroussia couldn't tell where the river ended and the silvery mud and the wide white skies began.

Maroussia had been as far as the edge of the White Marshes once or twice, years ago. She remembered walking there, just at the edge of it, lost, exhilarated, alone. That's where the water would take them. There was no other choice.

It was a strange, extraordinary place. Inside the long bar of Cold Amber Strand, the huge expanse of Mirgorod Bay had silted up with the sediment and detritus of millennia, deposited there by slow rivers. The commingling waters of the four rivers and many lesser streams, stirred by the ebb and flow of the brackish water entering through the Halsesond, had created behind the protecting arm of the Strand a complex and shifting mixture of every kind of wetland, a misty tract of salt marsh, bog and fen. It was a place of eel grass and cotton grass, withies, reed beds and carr. Pools of peat-brown water and small shallow lakes. Winding creeks shining like tin. Silent flocks of wading birds swept against the sky, glinting like herring shoals on the turn.

The sun was hidden behind cloud and mist. Maroussia had no way of measuring the passing of time, except by growing hunger and thirst. Lom was breathing more easily, but she had no food or water. She needed to find a landing place soon. Eventually – it might have been early in the afternoon – she unshipped the oars and began to row. The little skiff was the only vessel to be seen, conspicuously alone in the emptiness. Cat's-paw ripples and veils of fine mist trailed across the flatness, ringed by the wide horizon only. Waterfowl flew overhead or bobbed in small rafts. A mist was gathering and thickening around them, and Maroussia was glad of it. Mirgorod was a fading stain on the horizon behind them. It began to seem to her that they were nowhere at all.

She rowed clumsily, learning as she went. At least the work warmed her and loosened her stiffened muscles. Lom lay at her feet in the bottom of the boat, heavy and still. Shorelines loomed at them out of the mist. The skiff seemed to be passing between islands, or perhaps they were following channels between mudflats. It was impossible to say. After a time – it might have been only an hour, it might have been much more – she began to feel that the shores were closing in around them. They were approaching slopes of mud and stands of tangled tree growth coming down to the water's edge. An otter slipped off a mudslope and slid away through the slow waters. A heron, motionless, regarded them with its unblinking yellow eye. At last she saw that, without realising it, she had been following the narrowing throat of a backwater, and now they had reached the end of the passage. They came up to a broken-down jetty of weathered, greyish wood. She managed to bring the skiff up against it with a gentle jolt, clambered up onto the planks with the bow line in her hand, and stood there, looking down at the inert shape of Lom, wondering how she was going to get him out of the boat. At a loss, she glanced back the way they had come.

A giant was wading towards them, waist deep in the dark waters.

In the city, in their labouring clothes, the giants were diminished and made familiar by the human context. This one was different. It was as if the river itself and the mud and silt of the estuary had gathered into human-like form – but twice as large – and risen up and started walking towards them.

The slope of the giant's belly broached the waters like a ship as he came. His chest was as deep and broad as a barrel, but far larger. Unlike the city giants, who wore their hair tied back in queues, his hair was long and thick and spread across his shoulders in dark, damp curls. The giant waded right up to them and gripped the gunwale of the skiff with both hands, steadying it. The hands were enormous. Fingers thick as stubs of rope, joined with pale webs of skin up to the first knuckle. Wrists strong and round as tree branches. His huge face was weathered dark and his eyes were large and purple like plums, with something of the same rounded protuberance.

'Your boat is named *Sib*,' he said. 'She's a good boat.'

His voice was deep and slow, with the cool softness of estuarial mud, but ropes of strength wound through it. His clothes were the silvered colour of mud, with a faint shimmer of grainy slickness. Brown or grey, it was difficult to tell the difference. He was neither wholly of the land nor wholly of the water, but in between, estuarial, intertidal, partaking of both.

'She's not our boat,' said Maroussia. 'I stole her. She was floating loose, so I took her. We needed her. Badly. My friend is hurt.'

'You make fast here,' said the giant. 'You climb out, and I will bring him.'

The giant scooped Lom up in his arms, settled him into a comfortable position against his chest and waded across to a place where he could climb out. The water sluiced off him. His legs up to the knee were sleek with mud. Maroussia hesitated. The giant walked a few paces, then stopped and turned. Maroussia hadn't moved.

'Well?' said the giant.

'What?' said Maroussia.

'Follow me.'

'Where?'

But the giant had already gone ahead.

66

Vissarion Yppolitovich Lom – that part of him which is not made of tissues and plasma, proteins and mineral salts – is floating out in the sea, buoyant, awash in the waves. And Vissarion Yppolitovich Lom – this is not his true name, he knows that now, but he has no other – is puzzled by his situation.

He is alive.

Apparently.

Evidently.

Yet he has no recollection of how he got here, how he came to be in this …

Predicament?

Situation.

And he is … changed.

This is not his body.

His body is elsewhere.

He is aware of it, distant, separate, yet not *entirely* detached.

And this sea that he is in, it is the real sea, but also …

… not.

The sky is too clear. Too close above his head. There appears to be no sun in the sky. Everywhere he looks, it is …

… just the sky.

Time is nothing here.

The sea shines like wet slate. Numbing slabs of sea-swell hammock and baulk him. He rides among the bruising hollows and feels the touch of salt water pouring over his face, and when he runs his fingers through it, it is like stroking cool hair. Fulmars scout the wave valleys and terns squall overhead. He sees the faint distant smudge of a cliff shoulder to the north, and the low beach-line curving away southwards into mist and indeterminacy. He sees the shore of Cold Amber Strand. He can see it, but he can't reach it. He lacks the strength to swim so far. It doesn't matter.

Time is nothing here.

His head is wide open – there is a hole in it – the sea is pouring in – and the fluid from inside him is seeping out, pluming away into the wider water. Part of him is part of the sea. Part of the sea is taking its place. And then ...

Time is nothing here.

The sea is slow and always. Days graze its surface and the sea's skin rises and falls with the barely perceptible pulse of the tide. He can feel the unseen pull of the moons: a gentle lunar gravity tugging at his hair and palpating with infinite slowness the ventricular walls of his heart. But days and nights touch only the thinnest surface of the sea, and all the while, below the surface, beneath the intricate, flashy caul, there is darkness: coiling and shouldering layers inhabited by immense, death-less, barrelling movers.

Time is nothing here.

He imagines he is already sinking. The abyssal deeps open below him like a throat. He dives, pulling the surface shut behind him, nosing downwards, parting the layered muscles of the dimming waters' body. Sounding. Depth absorbs him.

As he descends, the light fails. Layer by layer the spectrum is sucked dry of colour: first the reds fade and the world turns green, then the yellows give up the ghost and the world turns blue, and then ... noth-ing, only the fuliginous darker than dark, the total absence of sight.

The waters are deep. It takes only seconds to leave the light behind, but the descent will be many hours. Every ten yards of depth adds the weight of another atmosphere to the column of water pressing on his body. He imagines going down. Fifty atmospheres. A hundred. A thousand. More. More. The parts of his strange new body which contain air begin to rupture under the weight. Long before he reaches the bottom, his face, his chest, his abdomen, implode. Fat compresses and hardens. The finer bones collapse. Broken rib ends burst out through the skin.

He imagines he hears himself speaking to the hard cold darkness. 'You are the reply to my desire.'

67

Maroussia slept late the next morning, and woke in the giant's isba. It smelled of woodsmoke, lamp-oil and the smoked fish that hung in rows from the rafters. Rafters which, now that she looked at them up there in the shadow, weren't the branches of trees as she had thought, but salt-bleached and smoke-browned whale bones.

The isba was twice as tall as a human would make it, but it felt warm and intimate, lit with fish-oil lamps and firelight from the open stove. Although it was morning outside, inside was all shadow and quiet. The whale-skeleton frame was covered with skins and bark, the gaps caulked with moss and pitch. Iron boiling-pots and wooden chests stood along the sides. From the middle of the floor rose a thick pillar of ancient-looking wood, its base buried in the compacted earth. Every inch of it was carved with the eyes and claws and heads of animals – elk, horses, wolves, seals – their teeth bared in anger or defiance – and inscribed with what looked like words in a strange angular alphabet. The pillar seemed meant to ward off some threat, some doom that was waiting its chance. What kind of thing was it, out here in the marsh, that a giant would be afraid of?

The stove was made of iron, large and elaborate, with panels of white and blue tiles. It was the kind that had a place for a bed on the top of it. Lom lay on it now, breathing quietly. Inert.

Maroussia remembered the night before only in snatches and fragments. She had been too cold. Too tired. Too hungry. The giant had given her food, a broth from his simmering-pot. Fish, samphire, berries. Food that tasted of the river and the sea and wide open spaces. And then he'd left her and gone out into the night and she had slept.

When she woke, the morning was half gone, and she was alone with Lom.

She stood up stiffly and crossed the floor to look at him. The stove was taller than her but his face, roughened with a growth of reddish stubble, was near the edge and turned towards her. He wasn't sleeping, he was ... gone. But his body breathed and seemed to be repairing itself. The giant had tended to the wound in the front of his head and left it bound in a cloth soaked with an infusion of bark and dried leaves. Now that she was close to him, the clean, bitter scent cut through the fish-and-smoky fug in the hut.

She had lain alongside him in the cold of the boat, the warmth of their bodies nurturing each other, keeping each other alive. That meant something. That changed something. She knew the smell of his body close up, the smell of his hair and skin, the feel of his warmth. She touched his face. Despite the stove and the furs he felt cool and damp, like a pebble picked up from a stream.

Wake up. Please wake up. We can't stay here.

She needed to go. She had something to do. It was a weight. A momentum. A push. What she needed to find was somewhere in the city. Vishnik had found the Pollandore. She was certain now, that's what he'd meant to tell her. He had died and hadn't told her where. Yet surely it would be in Mirgorod, if he had found it. She needed to get back there.

The giant came in, pushing his way between the skins across the entrance gap. His bulk filled the space naturally and made her feel that humans were small.

'Has the sleeper woken?' he said.

'No. No, he hasn't.'

The giant walked with a surprisingly soft and quiet tread across to where Lom lay, and looked down on him in silence. He placed a huge hand on the small head and put his huge face near Lom's small mouth, as if he were inhaling his breath, which – she realised – he was.

'He has been like this all morning?'

'Yes. He hasn't changed.'

The giant went to a wooden chest and took out something wrapped in dark cloth, which, sitting cross-legged on the floor by the stove, he unwrapped and began to eat. It looked like a piece of meat, except that it was dark grey, soft and satiny, with a strange oily sheen. He tore off a large chunk with his teeth and chewed it, his head on one side, his massive jaws working like a dog's, up and down.

'Does anyone else live out here?' Maroussia asked. 'In the marshes, I mean. I didn't see any sign ... when we were coming here. It all seemed so empty. Are there villages?'

'Why?'

'I was wondering where the clothes came from.' He had found dry clothes for her, not city clothes but leggings and a woven shirt. Soft leather boots.

'There are no humans here now. There used to be a village on the smaller lake.' He waved his arm vaguely in no particular direction.

'You've been kind to us,' she said.

'The rivers brought you. Why would I not be kind?'

'I don't even know your name.'

'My name is Aino-Suvantamoinen, and yours is Maroussia Shaumian, and you are important.'

'What do you mean? How do you know my name.'

'You are someone who makes things happen. Different futures are trying to become. You have something to do, and what you choose will matter.'

She stared at him. 'You know?' she said. 'About the Pollandore?'

The giant made a movement of his hand. 'I know,' he said, 'some things.'

'You know where it is?'

'It was taken. Long ago.'

'Where is it now?'

'That I do not know.'

'I have to find it,' said Maroussia. 'I can't stay here. Time is running out.'

'Yes.'

'But I don't know what it is. I don't know what to do when I find it. I don't *understand*.'

'Understanding is not the most important thing. Understanding never is. Doing is what matters.'

The giant turned away and sat down in a corner to concentrate on his meat, as if he had said all he would say. It was like talking to a thinking tree, or a hill, or the grass, or the rain.

'What exactly is that stuff you're eating?' said Maroussia.

'Old meat,' the giant said. 'The marsh preserves. Trees come up whole after a thousand years. This meat ... I put it in, I leave it, I find it again. It tastes good.'

'What kind of meat?'

He held the chunk at arm's length, turned it round, inspected it.

'No idea.' He took another bite. Then he laid it aside and stood up. 'Come with me,' he said. 'Let us walk.'

Maroussia looked at Lom, sleeping on the stove.

'What about him?' she said. 'Will he be all right on his own?'

'No harm will come today.'

Maroussia walked in silence beside the giant. The floods had receded during the night, revealing a wide alluvial land, a cross-hatch of creeks and channels punctuated by rocky outcrops, islands and narrow spits of ground. Reed beds. Salt marsh. Sea lavender and samphire. Withy, carr and fen. There were stretches of water, bright and dark as rippled steel. Long strips of pale brown sand, crested with lurid, too-green, moss-coloured grass. Reaches of soft, satiny mud. Wildfowl were picking and probing their way out on the mud. Maroussia knew their names: she had watched them rummaging on the muddy riverbanks near her home. Curlew, plover, godwit, redshank, phalarope. The quiet progress of geese at the eelgrass. A kestrel sidled across the sky: a slide, a pause, a flicker of wings; slide, pause, flicker of wings.

This was a threshold country, neither solid ground nor water but something liminal and in between. The air was filled with a beautiful misty brightness under a lid of low cloud. There was no sun: it was as if the wet land and the shallow stretches of water were themselves luminous. The air smelled of damp earth and sea, salt and wood-ash and fallen leaves.

'This is a beautiful place,' Maroussia said. 'It feels like we are in the middle of nowhere, but we're so near to the city. I didn't know. I never came this far.'

'It will be winter soon,' the giant said. 'Winters are cold here. The birds are preparing to leave. In winter the snow will lie here as deep as you are tall. The water freezes. Only the creatures that know how to freeze along with it and the ones who make tunnels beneath the snow can live here then.'

'But it's not so cold in Mirgorod,' said Maroussia. 'It's only a few versts away.'

'No. It is colder here.'

'What do you do when the winter comes?' said Maroussia.

'When the ditches freeze and the marshes go under the snow I will sleep. It will be soon.'

'You sleep through the winter like a bear? The giants in Mirgorod don't do that.'

'Their employers do not permit it. They are required to work through the year, though it shortens their lives.'

The giant fell silent and walked on. Maroussia began to notice signs of labour. The management of the land and water. Heaps of rotting vegetation piled alongside recently cleared dikes. Saltings, drained ground, coppiced trees. Much of it looked ancient, abandoned and crumbling: blackened stumps of rotting post and plank, relics of broken staithes and groynes, abandoned fish traps. The giant paused from time to time to study the water levels and look about him, his great head cocked to one side, sniffing the salt air. Sometimes he would adjust the setting of some heavy mechanism of wood and iron, a winch or a lock or a sluice gate.

They stopped on the brink of a deep, fast-flowing ditch. The giant stared into the brown frothing surge that forced its way across a weir.

'The flood is going down,' the giant said. 'Every time the floods come now, the city builds its stone banks higher. But that is not the way. The water has to go somewhere. If you set yourself against it, the water will find a way, every time.' He stooped for a moment to work a windlass that Maroussia hadn't noticed among the tall grass. 'I tried to tell them,' the giant continued when he had done his work. 'When they were building the city, I tried to tell them they were using too much stone. They made everything too hard and too tight. You have to leave places for the water to go. But I couldn't make them listen. Even their heads were made of stone.'

'You remember Mirgorod being *built*?'

'I was younger then. I thought I could explain to them, and if I did, then they would listen. They tried to drive me out, and every so often even now they try again.' He grinned, showing big square teeth. Incisors like slabs of pebble. Sharp bearish canines. 'I let them lose themselves.'

'What do you mean?'

'The marshes are bigger than you think, and different every day. Every tide brings shift and change. All possible marshes are here.'

'I don't understand.'

'Yes,' said the giant. 'You do.'

Maroussia hesitated. 'If you remember the city when it was being built—' she said.

'Yes.'

'—then you would remember the time before? You remember the Pollandore?'

'You don't need to remember what is still here.'

Maroussia hesitated.

'I need to go back,' she said. 'But I don't want to leave Vissarion. He helped me.'

'You should not leave him,' said the giant. 'He is important too.'

'What do you mean?'

The giant stopped and looked down at her.

'I don't know, and neither does he. But it is on the river, and the rain likes him. That's enough.'

'But what if he never wakes up?' said Maroussia. 'Or he wakes up but he isn't … right. He almost drowned, and there's that hole, that terrible hole, in his head.'

'He is not hurt,' said the giant. 'At least, his body is not. But he doesn't know how to come back.'

'I don't understand that either.'

'I can fetch him back, if you want me to. Tonight. After dark. When the day is over. Your choice.'

'Do it,' she said. 'Do it.'

68

Vissarion Yppolitovich Lom lies face down, floating on the glass roof of the sea. He presses his face against the water as if it were a pane of glass. Looking down into clarity. A landscape unrolls beneath him.

Time is nothing here.

This is the drowned, memorious land. Mammoths' teeth, the bones of bear and aurochs and the antlers of great elk litter the sea's bed. The salt-dark leaf mould of drowned forests. It is a woodland place. Lom sees the sparrowhawk on the oak's shoulder and he sees the bivalves browsing the soft stump's pickled meat. Sea beasts move across the floor of it. Their unhurried footfalls detonate quiet puffballs of silt as they go, slow without heaviness, shoving aside fallen branches, truffling for egg-purse, flatworm and urchin, their eyes blackened like sea beans and gleaming in the half-light.

Time is nothing here.

Except … something touches him. The merest graze of an eye in passing. An alien gaze, cold and empty, vaster far than the sea, star-speckled. It passes away from him.

And pauses.

And flicks back.

And takes him in its grip.

Lom closes himself up like a fist, like a stone in the sea, like an anemone clenching close its crop of arms, like a hermit crab hunching into its shell. He wants to be small. Negligible. He wants to pull himself tight inside and withdraw or sink out of sight. But it is hopeless. He knows the touch of the angel's eye for what it is.

Archangel begins to prise him open for a closer look.

No! Lom dives, pulling the surface shut behind him, nosing downwards, parting the layered muscles of the dimming waters' body. Sounding. Depth absorbs him. He is strong. Very strong. Stronger than he had ever known. Lom slips with a writhing kick out of the angel's grasp. He hears, very faint and far away, the yell of its anger. And feels its fear.

In his room on the Ring Wharf, Josef Kantor felt Archangel rip a hole in his mind and step inside. Archangel's voice filled his head. The cold immensity separating stars. He fell.

THEY ARE IN THE MARSH! THEY ARE IN THE MARSH! THEY LIVE!

KILL THE TRAVELLERS! DESTROY THE POLLAN-DORE!

As soon as he was able to stand and wipe the spittle from his face and stem the blood that was spilling from his nose, Kantor went to find a telephone. He needed to speak to Chazia.

69

Night came, a thick and starless black. Inside the isba the smoke from the burning bog-oak in the stove and the fumes from the boiling-pot made Maroussia's head swim. Afraid she would be sick, she tried to retreat into the shadows at the edge of the room and would have squatted there, watching, but the noises from outside drove her back. There were voices outside in the dark, voices that barked and growled and called like birds and argued in unintelligible words. The skin covering of the isba shook as if something was pounding on it and tugging at the door covering. She crawled back towards the centre of the room and crouched as near to the iron stove as she could get. Blue fire was burning hot and hard as a steam-engine's firebox, roaring heat into the air.

'Do not be alarmed by anything you see or hear,' Aino-Suvantamoinen had said. 'But do not touch me. And do not go outside.'

Yet now he lay on the floor, immense, like a felled bull. His arms and legs trembled as if he was having a fit: their shaking rattled and clattered the antlers, vertebrae, pieces of amber and holed stones tied to his coat. The hood of the coat hid his face, but she could still see his eyes. They were open, but showing white only, as sightless and chalky as seashells. He'd put a piece of leather between his teeth, and now his mouth dripped spittle as he chewed and ground on it with an unconscious concentration that seemed like blank rage.

Lom lay on his back in the centre of the floor.

'No matter how bad it gets,' the giant had said, 'you can do nothing. Understand? Nothing. Whatever happens, do nothing. and do not touch me.' Yet he had been like this – collapsed, growling, fitting – for … how long now? Half an hour? An hour?

The wall of the isba bulged inward, as if some heavy creature outside had thrown itself against it. There was a screech of anger. Surely whatever was outside would break in soon. The carvings on the central pillar flickered in the fierce firelight as if they were alive and moving.

Five minutes. Five more minutes, and if nothing has changed ...

Vissarion Yppolitovich Lom is lying on his back in the sea, looking up into the night sky. He feels the gentle pull of the moons in his belly. All around him the sea glows with a gentle phosphorescence. A fringe of luminousness borders his body. Light trickles down his arms when he holds them in front of his face.

The hole in the front of his head is open to the starlight. A little cup of phosphorescence has gathered there. So much has flowed in, and so much flowed out, washing across the folds of his cerebral cortex. He is merging with the sea. His pulse is the endless passing of waves. His inward darkness is the darkness of the deep ocean.

Time is nothing here.

He hears the sound of splashing. Rhythmical. Sweep, sweep, through the waves. It is a sound he remembers, but he cannot place it now. The drift of water through the kelp forests below him is more interesting.

Idly, with the last remains of merely human curiosity, he turns to look. Something very large and human-shaped, an outline darker than the sky, a starless mass against the stars, is wading towards him. That is what the sound is. Legs. Wading through water. Did he not once do such a thing himself?

The wading person is growing larger and larger as he comes closer. He is watching. He has a purpose. His purpose is to bring Lom back.

But Lom doesn't want to go back.

He gathers the weight of the sea and throws it against the giant in immense curling waves that crash against him. Lom fills the waves with the teeth and jaws of eels and the stings of rays. He tangles the giant's feet in ropes of weed. The giant stumbles and the undertow of the waves pulls at him, dragging him towards the edge of the deep trench that opens and swallows him.

The giant Aino-Suvantamoinen feels the viciousness of the sea's antagonism. Ropes of water form within the water and wrap themselves around his arms and legs, tugging him down towards the pit that is opening beneath him. Bands of iron water squeeze his ribcage, forcing the breath from his lungs. Ice-cold water-fingers grip his face, hooking claws into his nostrils, stabbing into his ears with water-needles, gouging his eyes, tearing at the lids. *This isn't how it is meant to be.* The man he is trying to bring home is fighting him. He's too strong. All the futures in which he will rescue this man and return home safe are fading and dying one by one. Something is putting them out like lamps.

I will drown here, and with me the marsh will fail.

With one last push of effort he begins to swim for the surface.

Pulling the water-fingers from his face he peers up and sees the dim light above him, the greenish star in the shape of a man, glowing dimly. It is not far. The giant kicks and hauls himself towards it. The seawater clamps itself about him, heavy and chill as liquid iron, squeezing like a fist. He fights it, dragging himself upwards out of the ocean pit. But it is too far. He is tiring. He cannot reach it. The thread of river-water that links him to his body in the isba is failing, and when it breaks he will be lost.

Desperately he lets go of a part of himself and sends it back up the river-thread, squirming and writhing for home like a salmon against the stream. The silver thought-salmon flickers its tail and disappears into the dimming green.

Maroussia was kneeling over the still body of the giant, her ear against his mouth. He was trying to say something.

'Wake him ... wake the man ... call him back ... do it ... now ...'

The hoarse whisper faded. The giant's face collapsed.

Maroussia lurched across to where Lom was lying and took his face in her hands, turning it towards her.

'Vissarion!' She was shouting to be heard. The voices outside in the night were screeching and yammering, hurling themselves against the walls of the isba. 'Vissarion! It's Maroussia! Listen to me! You have to wake up now! Oh, you have to. Please.'

Vissarion Yppolitovich Lom hears a voice calling, faint above the noise of the sea and very far away. He opens his eyes and sees against the shadows of the sky a face he knows, a familiar face, a face with a name he half-remembers, pale and calm and serious, looking down on him, like the moon made whole. He lifts his arm towards it, and as he does so he feels a tremendous blow against his back, lifting him up out of the water, and a huge fist seizes him by the neck and begins to pull him back towards the shore.

Lom woke in the giant Aino-Suvantamoinen's isba, aware of the warmth and the fire and the quiet shadows and the giant sitting near him, waiting, patient, large and solid. Lom knew where he was. Completely. He felt the moving water nearby, and grass, and trees, and the sifting satiny mud. The sea, some distance off, was still the sea, and the river that surged towards it was a great speaking mouth. The air around him was a tangible flowing thing, freighted with a thousand scents and drifting pheromone clouds, just as the space between the stars was filled with light and forces passing though. Everything was spilling myth, everything was soaked in truth-dream.

'You are awake,' said Aino-Suvantamoinen gently. His voice was slow and strong and estuarial.

'This will fade,' said Lom. 'Won't it? This will not last. Will it? Will it?'

He tried to raised his head from the leather pillow.

'No,' said the giant, 'this feeling that you have now will not last. But it will not altogether fade. There is no going back to the way you were before.'

'I don't want to.'

'You need to rest.'

'I hurt you, didn't I? I didn't want to come back, and I hurt you.'

'Yes.'

'I almost killed you.'

'Yes.'

'I'm sorry.'

'Not your fault. You were stronger than I thought. You did not know.'

'No.'

'I bear you no grudge. '

'But you are hurt.'

'Only tired now. I will recover. But I need to sleep. it will be winter soon.'

Lom tried to push the covers back and sit up.

'You can't sleep yet,' he said. 'You know that. There is something wrong. There's something coming. It's very close.'

'Ah. You felt that?'

When the giant left him, Lom went outside to sit by himself some distance from the isba, on a stump of wood. The stiffness of his bruises was scarcely noticeable. He touched his forehead tentatively. In the centre of it, just above the eyebrows, he found a small and roughly round hole in the bone of his skull, like a third eye socket. It had a fine, smooth covering of new skin, slightly puckered at the edge. With his fingertip he felt the fluttering of a pulse.

The world he had seen in all its oceanic myth-ridden fullness was already diminishing, but still he smelled the dampness in the air, the woodsmoke, and heard the flow of water in the creek, and he knew what they meant. It was all traces and memories now, a faint trembling of presences: possibilities almost out of reach. But still real. Still there. The plug in his head was gone, and he was alive.

The world and everything in it, everything that is and was and will be, was the unfolding story of itself, and every separate thing in the world – every particle of rock and air and light, every life, every thought and every event – was also a story, its own story, the story of everything becoming more like itself and less like anything else. The *might-be* becoming the *is*. The winter moths on their pheromone trails, intent on love and flight, were heroes. Himself, Maroussia, Vishnik, Aino-Suvantamoinen, they were all like that, or could be: living out the bright significant stories of their own lives, mythic, important.

But Vishnik was dead. Vishnik, what was left of him, mutilated and killed, his ruined body laid out naked on the couch; Chazia had done that.

Lom remembered Chazia and Kantor bending over him in the interrogation room – Chazia's knife, Kantor's indifferent finger poking at his opened brain. It was all coming back, riding a hot rushing tide of anger. He could not stay here, in this timeless watery place. He had to *do* something. He had to go back.

And then – only then – the question occurred to him. The last thing he remembered, vaguely, a blur, was throwing himself from the bridge into the flooding Mir. What had happened to him after he fell? How had he come to be here? He didn't know.

71

Elsewhere – far away, but not so far – in an empty side room in the Lodka, Lakoba Petrov was preparing himself for his one great moment. He had obtained all he needed – all the materials for his new, wonderful art – from Josef Kantor, impresario of destruction. And now the time was almost come for the performance.

From a canvas holdall Petrov extracted three belts of dynamite and nails, enwrapped his person with them, buckled the straps. Also from the canvas holdall he drew forth a capacious overcoat of dark wool, threaded the detonator cords through the sleeves so he could grip their terminations in his palms, and put on the coat to drape and obscure his death-belted torso.

Petrov did what he did with care. Fully. With absolute clarity and certainty of purpose. Every movement a sacrament. Every breath numbered. Rendered aesthetic. Invested with ritual luminance.

When he tugged the detonators, nails would fly outwards from him explosively. Omnidirectional. Flying in the expulsive, expanding, centrifugal cloud of his own torn and vaporised flesh. He would be the heart of the iron sunburst. Going nova.

And so I am become the unimaginable zero of form. The artist becomes the art. Total creation. Without compromise. Without hesitation. Without meaning, being only and completely what it is. The gap between artist and work obliterated.

His own unneeded coat he closed up in precise folds and set in the middle of the empty floor. Adjacent to this he placed the now-empty canvas holdall.

They would be found so. The only extant work of the Petrovist Destructive School: members, one.

A thought struck him. Awkwardly, on account of the bulk of the explosive girdles, he bent to withdraw items from his former coat. A tube of paint. A piece of polished reflective tin to use as a mirror. One final time, with the facility that came with practice, he inscribed his forehead. And then, with an unexpected flourish, one last tweak of originality, he unbuttoned his shirt and wrote on his bare, white, fleshless, hairless (because shaven) upper chest, the same two splendid words.

I, Petrov.

He was calm. He was prepared. All was ready.

At the other end of the same long corridor as the room in which Petrov prepared himself, in a much larger chamber, there was a large gathering of persons of importance. The Annual Council of the Vlast Committee on Peoples. Josef Kantor was there, thanks to the arrangements of Lavrentina Chazia. He stood anonymously at the back of the room, one more nondescript functionary among many, watching. Waiting for what would come. For what he knew would happen. His toothache, which had not troubled him for weeks, was back, and he welcomed it, prodding at the hurt again with his tongue as he examined the scene.

The large room was dominated by one long narrow heavy table of inlaid wood. A line of electric chandeliers hung low above it like frosted glittering clusters on a vine, and creamy fluted columns made an arcade along one side, where secretaries sat at individual desks with typewriters. For all its spaciousness the room was warm, and filled with muted purposeful talk. The places at the table were occupied by men in suits and full-dress uniforms, absorbed in their work, assured of their importance and the significance of what they did.

On the far wall from where Kantor stood hung a huge painting of the Novozhd, life size and standing alone in an extensive rolling late-summer landscape. Sunlight splashed across his face, picking out his plush moustache and the smile-lines creasing his cheeks, while behind him the country of the dominions unrolled: harvest-ready fields crossed by the sleek length of express trains, tall factory chimneys blooming rosy streamers of smoke against the horizon, the distant glittering sea – the happy land at its purposeful labours.

And beneath the portrait, halfway down one side of the table, sat the Novozhd himself, in his familiar collarless white tunic, drinking coffee from a small cup.

There was a shout from across the room.

'Hey! You! Who are you?'

Kantor looked across to see what was going on. It was Petrov. He was pushing past flustered functionaries, his shaven head moving among them like a white stone. He was wearing an oddly bulky greatcoat and there were fresh scarlet markings on his face. He was right on time. Kantor stepped back towards the wall. He needed to be as far away from the Novozhd as possible.

Petrov paused and surveyed the room for a moment.

The militia who lined the walls, watchful, were not approaching him. Those nearest him were retreating. Giving him room. They were Chazia's Iron Guard, every one: they would not interfere.

A diplomat near Kantor took a step forward. 'What is that man doing—?' he began.

'Stay where you are!' hissed Kantor. The diplomat looked at him, surprised, and seemed about to say something else. Kantor ignored him.

Petrov had seen the Novozhd, who had risen from his seat, cup in hand.

High functionaries were murmuring in growing alarm. A stenographer was shouting. There was rising panic in her voice. 'Someone stop him!'

Petrov moved towards the Novozhd, blank-faced and purposeful.

The ambassador from the Archipelago was on her feet, trying to push through a group of Vlast diplomatists who did not know what was happening and would not make way. She was shouting at the guards: 'Why won't you do something!' But the guards were moving away, as Kantor knew they would.

Petrov made inexorable progress through the crowd. When he got near the Novozhd, his arms stretched out as if to embrace him.

And the explosion came. A muted, ordinary detonation. A flash. A matter-of-fact thump of destruction. A stench. The crash of a chandelier on the table. Silence. More silence. Ringing in Kantor's ears.

Then the voices began: not screams – not shouts of anger – just a low inarticulate collective moan, a sighing of dismay. Only later did the keening begin, as the injured began to realise the awful permanent ruination of their ruptured bodies.

*

Pushing through the crowd, stepping over the dead and dying, Kantor found himself looking down at the raw, meaty remnants of the Novozhd, and Lakoba Petrov fallen across him like a protective friend. Petrov's head and arms were gone, and some great reptilian predator had taken a large bite of flesh from his side. The Novozhd, dead, was staring open-mouthed at the ceiling that was spattered with his own blood and chunks of his own flesh. His moustache, Kantor noticed, was gone.

Someone touched his arm, and Kantor spun round. He knew the guards would not bother him, but there was always the possibility. But it was only Chazia.

She leaned forward intimately, speaking quietly under the din and panic of the room. Her blotched fox-face too close to his.

'Good, Josef,' she said. 'Very good.'

Kantor took a step back from her in distaste. There was too much of angels about her. It was like a stink. She was rank with it.

'I do my part, Lavrentina. You do yours. What about the girl, and Krogh's man? Lom?'

'That's in hand,' said Chazia. 'It is in hand. Though I don't understand why you set so much store—'

Kantor glared at her.

'I mean,' Chazia continued, 'after today—'

'The angel needs them dead, Lavrentina,' Kantor heard himself say, and struggled to keep the self-disgust out of his voice. *It uses me like a puppet. A doll. A servant.* He was getting tired of the angel. More than tired. He feared and hated it. The situation was becoming intolerable.

I am bigger than this angel. I will make it fear me and I will kill it. I will find a way. I have killed the Novozhd and I will kill the angel. Kill Chazia too.

But now was not the time. He needed to prepare. He needed to focus on the future. Only the future mattered.

'Just get rid of them,' he said. 'Lom and the girl. Don't foul it up again.'

'I told you,' said Chazia. 'It's already in hand.'

72

It was night outside the isba, under clear stars. Aino-Suvantamoinen was a massive dark bulk crouching over the flickering wood-fire. It was crisply, bitterly cold, and the light of the moons was bright enough to see the shreds of mist in the trees at the edge of the clearing. A hunter's night. Lom sat wrapped in sealskin, drinking fish stew from a wooden bowl. He'd slept all day – a proper, resting, dreamless sleep.

'I can't stay here,' Maroussia was saying. 'I have to go back. To the city. There was a paluba. And someone else. She ... showed me ...'

The giant shifted his weight. 'You saw a paluba?'

'Yes.'

Lom watched her as she talked. She held herself so straight and upright, her face shadowed in the firelight. Lom saw her now as she was, a point of certainty, uncompromised, spilling the flickering light of possibilities that surrounded her. She was clear, and defined, and alive. She rang like a bell in the misty, nightfall world. She was worth fighting for.

'I have to do this thing,' she said. 'I don't have a choice.' She paused. 'No, that's not right. I do have a choice. And I'm choosing.'

She lapsed into silence, watching the fire.

'Maroussia?' said Lom.

'Yes?'

'I wanted to thank you.'

'What for?' she said.

'You came back for me, didn't you? You didn't have to.'

She didn't look round. 'You didn't need to help me either. But you did. Twice.'

'I'll come back with you to Mirgorod,' said Lom. 'If you want me to.'

She turned to look at him then.

'Would you do that?' she said quietly.

'Yes.'

73

Major Artyom Safran stood at the edge of the trees by the giant's isba, watching it from the moonshadow. Muted light spilled from a gap in the skins draped across its entrance. His quarry was inside. The mudjhik was motionless at his side, a shadow-pillar of silent stone.

Safran held the fragment of angel stuff that Commander Chazia had cut from Lom's head tight and warm in his hand. Using the mudjhik's alien senses he felt his way along the thread that still joined it to Lom until he touched the other man's mind with his own. He felt the faint, startled flinch of an answering awareness and hastily withdrew. Lom was unlikely to have known what the contact meant, if he had even registered it, but it was better to be cautious.

There were three of them, then. Lom, a woman – *the* woman, it must be – and something else: a strange, complex, powerful, non-human presence. He put himself more fully into the mudjhik, inhabiting its wild harsh world. The mudjhik needed no light to see by. It had other senses through which Safran felt the hard sharpness of thorns, the small movements of leaves on branches, the evaporation of moisture. Bacteria thrived everywhere, and the mudjhik was studying them with simple, purposeless curiosity. Something had died and was decomposing near their feet, under a covering of fallen leaves.

Safran felt the watchfulness of small animal presences pressing against him. One in particular was close by, drilling at him with a hot, bitter attention. A fox? No, something smaller and crueller. A weasel? Its mind was like strong, gamey meat. Every mind had its own unique taste, that was one thing he had learned. And here, in the wetlands, it was not only animals: ever since he and the mudjhik had entered the marsh territories, Safran had been aware of the semi-sentience of the trees themselves, and the rivers, even the rain. There was a constant, vaguely uncomfortable feeling that everything around him knew he was there and did not welcome his presence. He ignored it, as did the mudjhik, which disdained trees and water as beneath its notice. Safran, through the mudjhik's senses, probed the interior of the isba. The third presence was a giant, then. That too was unexpected.

For all its physical stillness, Safran sensed the mudjhik's eagerness to rush forward and attack. It enjoyed human fear and death. It fed on it. Some of the mudjhik's bloodlust leaked into Safran's mind. It made him hungry to charge and stomp and crush. He fought to keep the urge in check. He hadn't anticipated the presence of the giant. It could be done, of course, but the position was not without risk. It needed thought.

His target was Lom. Chazia had been clear on that. And the Shaumian woman, if he found her there. There had been no mention of others, human or giant, but the strategic purpose of his mission was to draw a line. No loose ends. No continuation of the story. What that meant was without doubt. Leave none alive.

Mentally he checked through his equipment: a heavy hunting knife; two incendiary grenades; the revolver that Chazia had given him (a brand new model, the first production batch, a double-action Sepora loaded with .44 magnum high-velocity hunting rounds, power that would stop a bear mid-charge). The Sepora should be enough to handle the giant. And then there was the Exter-Vulikh, a stocky and wide-muzzled sub-machine gun with a yew stock, modified to take hundred-round drum magazines, of which he carried four.

The Vlast employed killers who prided themselves on the precision and refinement of their technique: they affected the exactitude of assassins, with high-velocity long-range hunting rifles and probing needle blades. But Safran was not one of those. He preferred brutally decisive weapons, muscular weapons that did serious, dramatic damage. Handling the Exter-Vulikh gave him powerful gut feelings of pleasure. He liked the weight and heft of it, the fear it provoked, and the noise and mess it made. Just thinking about using it stirred a feeling in his belly like hunger. Desire. And with the mudjhik, it was even better: the strength of the mudjhik was his strength, its power his power. The fear it caused was fear of *him*. Safran loved the mudjhik, with its barrel head and reddish brown stone-hard flesh. It was the colour of rust and dried blood, but it could glow like warm terracotta in the evening sun.

Years of training and long experience had built the connection between Safran and his mudjhik, until their minds were so closely intermixed there was no longer a clear distinction between them. Most mudjhiks passed from handler to handler and brought traces – *stains* – of their previous relationships with them, including the memories of deaths, fears, failures, human aging; but Safran's had been a virgin, the last of them. Another reason to love it. But he feared it, too. Sometimes he dreamed it was pursuing him. In his dreams he tried to run and hide. In empty streets it followed him. Crashing through walls. Pulling down houses. Wherever he went it found him. In one dream he took refuge inside the Lodka itself, and the mudjhik was beating on the ten-foot-thick walls of stone, trying to break through. The *boom-boom-boom* of its heavy blows made the ground he stood on shake and tremble. He knew the mudjhik would never stop. Each blow chipped a fragment of the wall away. Hairline fractures opened and spread through the immense walls.

A mudjhik was tireless. If the man ran, the mudjhik would follow. Relentless and for ever. It was only a matter of time. There was no escape.

'You'll go alone,' Chazia had said. 'Travel light. Move fast. It'll be better.'

The march had taken longer than expected. The mudjhik kept sinking into the soft ground and floundering in streams and shallow pools. Safran had become confused about direction, distance, time. The territory seemed larger than was possible. A day's travel seemed to bring them no nearer the target. As time passed, Safran had felt his mind merging more and more completely with the mudjhik. He had thought they were close before, but this was overwhelming, as if the mudjhik were using him, not the other way round. It was a good feeling. He embraced it. He felt the Vlast itself, and all its authority and power and inevitability, flowing through him. He was not a single person any more. He was history happening. He was the face of the hammerhead, but it was the entire force of the arm-swing of the hammerblow that drove him forward. He didn't have questions, he had answers. And, at last, after uncountable days of arduous marching, the onward flow of angel-sanctified history and the piece of angel stuff he held in his hand like a thread brought him to the isba.

The mudjhik was restless, knowing its quarry was close. It wanted to wade in and crush his skull and stamp his ribs in. Now. Even in the dark it would not miss. But Safran was tired after the long days of marching. His hands trembled with cold and fatigue. He would not fail, he could not, yet he knew the dangers of overconfidence. Once again he surveyed the lie of the operational zone.

The isba stood, stark in the moonshine, on a slightly raised shoulder of ground in a clearing about a hundred yards across. On the far side of the clearing from where Safran stood some kind of canal or nondescript river was running. With the mudjhik's senses, he could smell its dark, cold and slow-moving current. On every other side of the isba there were thickets of thorn and bramble and low trees, cut through with narrow wandering pathways. Safran was satisfied that the targets could not escape. They could not cross the open ground without him knowing. In daylight, if they tried, he could cut them down with the Exter-Vulikh before they reached the cover of the trees. But in this light? The cloud cover was thickening, the last moonlight fading.

Working only by feel, Safran stripped down the Exter-Vulikh and reloaded the drum magazines one more time.

Wait. Let them sleep.

74

Lom was dreaming, dark, ugly, disturbing dreams of gathering hopelessness and death, and when the giant woke him he found them hard to shake off. Slowly he focused on the giant's heavy hand on his shoulder, the huge figure leaning over him, the dim face close to his, the deep soft voice whispering in the stove-light.

'The enemy is come. Wake up.'

'What?'

'You must go quickly. Both of you.'

'What? I don't ...' He struggled to separate reality and dream.

'There is a hunter outside in the trees. A killer. An enjoyer of death.'

'Yes,' said Lom. 'I know.'

And he realised that he did know. He'd felt the presence of them in his dream, and he could still feel it now.

'There are two of them,' he said.

'He has a *follower* with him. A thing like stone.'

A mudjhik? Could that be?

Lom, fully awake now, climbed down from the bed on top of the stove.

'You must make no noise,' said the giant. 'They listen hard.'

It was viciously cold. Lom stood as close to the stove as he could. He had the slightly sickened feeling of being awake too early. Maroussia was preparing with pale and silent efficiency.

'My cloak?' whispered Lom. 'Where is it?'

Aino-Suvantamoinen had it ready and handed it to him. Lom wished he could have felt the weight of the Zorn in its pocket, but that was still somewhere in the Lodka, presumably, where Safran and the militia would have left it when they brought him down. He'd lost his cosh too.

And then they were ready. But for what? He found he could sense the hunters outside in the darkness. They were out there watching. Waiting for dawn, presumably, a better killing light, and that would come soon. Lom considered their options for defending the isba, or getting to their boat, or escaping into the woods; but without weapons there were none. They were caught. Helpless.

Aino-Suvantamoinen stepped across to the great iron stove, pressed his belly against it and, stooping slightly, embraced it. The isba filled with the smell of damp wool singeing as the giant grunted, lifted the entire stove off the ground, spilling red embers against his legs, and carried it, staggering, a few paces sideways. The stove had been standing on a threadbare rug with an intricate geometrical pattern, much worn away and scarred by spills of ash and charcoal. The giant kicked the rug aside to reveal an area of rough planks. He knelt and fumbled at it, trying to get a grip with his huge fingers, then leaned back and pulled. The area of floor came up in his hands, releasing a chill draught of air that smelled of damp earth and stone. A patch of darkness opened like the cool mouth of a well.

'Go down,' he said. 'Quickly!'

'You want us to hide down a pit?' said Lom.

'Not a pit. A tunnel. The old lake people built souterrains. Follow the passageway until you find a side opening to the right. That will bring you out in the woods behind the enemy. When you are past them, then you run.'

'What about you?' said Maroussia.

'I don't fit down there.'

'So ... ?'

'So I will destroy our enemies if I can.'

'You can't fight a mudjhik,' said Lom. 'Not even you.'

'There are ways,' said the giant.

'You can run too,' said Maroussia. 'You don't have to fight. Not for us.'

The giant didn't reply. He lit a lamp from the stove embers and handed it to Lom. His face in the flickering light looked mobile, distorted and strange.

'You must be quiet,' he said, 'or you will alert the enemy. And you must go now.' He knelt and scraped a heap of compacted earth from the isba floor and scooped it into the stove, dousing the flames and burying the embers. In the near-darkness they heard the swish of the entrance covers and knew that he was gone.

The souterrain passageway was narrow and low. Lom, stooping, the lamp flickering in his hand, went first. The walls and roof of the passage were lined with rough wet blocks of stone. The floor was of damp compacted earth. The feeling of immense weight above their heads, pressing down and pressing in sideways against the passage walls, was oppressive. Unignorable. It seemed impossible that there should be underground constructions at all in such a place of soft and shifting, saturated ground, but the tunnel they were following was evidently old. Perhaps even ancient. It had survived. Lom led the way forward as quickly as he could.

They felt the rush of scorching air almost before they heard the explosions. The surge extinguished the lamp in Lom's hand. The concussions themselves, when they came, were muted, abbreviated, like heavy slabs being dropped from a height, and it took them a moment to realise what they had heard.

'Oh, shit,' said Lom. 'Grenades. He's got grenades.'

There was a longer, liquid-sounding, sliding slump, another rush of hot air, then silence and profound darkness. The tunnel had collapsed behind them.

'Keep going,' said Maroussia. 'I'm right behind you. Don't stop.'

Lom edged forward, his right hand on the rough stone wall to feel his way along, his left hand stretched out ahead of him. The darkness was total. More than the simple absence of light, it was a tangible presence. It closed in around them and pushed against them, touching their faces with soft insistent fingers, pressing itself against their eyes, feeling its way into their nostrils, the whorls of their ears, slipping down their throats when they opened their mouths to breathe, thick with the rich and oppressive smell of being underground.

Lom kept moving. He had to push his way through the insistent jostling darkness, filled with the presence of the long-departed souterrain builders, alert, curious and resentful. He felt the hairs rising along the back of his neck.

There was nothing to measure their progress by, nor the passage of time, except the sound of their own bodies moving and breathing. Raw root-filled earth and rock were all around them now, just the other side of this thin skin of stone. This flimsy, permeable wall. The wall was nothing. Negligible. With one push he could put his hand through it and make an entrance for the slow ocean of mud. Why not? Mud was only a different air. They could breathe it, if they wanted to, like the earthworms did. They could swim through it, slowly, working their limbs through the viscous, slow-yielding, supportive stuff. They could do that. If they wanted to.

'Vissarion?' Maroussia's voice reached him from somewhere far away. 'Why have we stopped?'

He had lost the wall. He had taken his hand off it. When? Sometime. He waved his arms to left and right, over his head, and encountered nothing.

'Can you feel the wall?' he said.

'What wall?' she hissed.

'Either side. Any wall. Can you?'

'No.'

'Shit.'

Think. Figure it out.

They must have come into some larger chamber that the giant hadn't mentioned. He would have assumed they'd have the lamp.

He was standing on the very edge of a bottomless pit. A narrow tapering well. One more step ... any step ...

No. It was a tunnel not a cave. They were not lost, only disoriented. Taking a deep breath he turned to his right and began to walk steadily forward. Four or five paces, and he barked his knuckles against the cold damp stone. Its roughness was familiar now, and comforting.

There was another concussion. It made the ground sound hollow, and it seemed to have come from just above their heads. Then the ground shook again. And again. A rhythmical pounding that was obviously not grenades, not this time. Trickles of cold stuff fell across their faces and shoulders in the darkness. It might have been earth or water or a mixture of both. The pounding stopped, and a regular scraping took its place.

'It's the mudjhik,' said Maroussia. 'It's found us. It's trying to dig us out.'

*

Lom felt the mudjhik's presence. Felt the pleasure it was feeling. The anticipation. It would haul them out of the earth like rabbits. Burst their heads between its thumbs, one by one.

'Keep moving!' hissed Maroussia. 'Come on! There's no point waiting here till it gets through.'

Yes, thought Lom, *but which way?* He felt sour panic welling up at the back of his throat.

Which way?

His eyes were stretched wide, straining to see in the absolute dark that pressed in against them. When he realised what he was doing, he closed them.

We are too rational, he thought. *We overvalue sight.*

'Get low!' he hissed. 'Lie down and get out of the airflow. And keep still.'

'Lie down?' said Maroussia.

'Just do it.'

Lom breathed deeply, concentrating on the air around them, ancient and cold and thickened and still. Almost, but not entirely, still. The hole in his head was open, and he was open with it. He could feel the air circulating slowly in a hollow space, and he let himself ride with it, feeling its moves and turns. There was a current eddying slowly towards a gap in the wall. Another passageway. Sloping gently upwards towards an opening into the world outside. In the darkness he crossed directly to Maroussia and took her hand.

'Come on,' he said. 'Follow me.'

He was hurrying, almost running through the dark, pulling Maroussia behind him. She swore as she smashed her elbow against an outcrop of stone and almost stumbled, but he kept hold of her and pulled her on. Behind them the sound of the mudjhik's digging had stopped. It knew they were moving. Lom felt its uncertainty. Frustration. For the moment it was at a loss. But it would find them. And it would keep coming. It always would.

The walls of the passageway were closing in. The roof was getting lower. But Lom led them on at a desperate shambling run. Then there was light ahead of them. The grey light of dawn. Slabs of stone fallen sideways. A gap half-blocked with brambles and small trees. They pushed and scrabbled their way through, ignoring the scratching of thorns and the gouging of branches. And then they were out. Standing among fallen leaves in pathless undergrowth.

Lom looked for cover, any cover, any place to hide or make a stand against the mudjhik. Nowhere. Only a tangle of low trees and undergrowth and moss in every direction.

But what sort of stand could they have made? You needed a trench mortar to stop a mudjhik in its tracks. If it came, it came.

There was an acrid smell in the air. A big fire, burning. The isba!

Maroussia went crashing off towards the scent of burning. Lom was leaning against a tree, doubled over, gasping and trying desperately to get enough breath in to refill his spasming lungs.

'Shit,' he gasped. 'Shit. Wait!'

Maroussia stopped and turned.

'Come on,' she said. 'Just keep up.'

75

Minutes later they were crouched side by side among the trees at the edge of the clearing. The isba was in flames. Its skin covering was gone. The whalebone frame still stood, blackened and skeletal in the middle of a wind-tugged roaring fire of wood and furs and wool. White and grey smoke and clouds of sparks poured into the sky, swithering and whipping in the wind. The smoke was blowing away from them but they could smell it.

The mudjhik was a dark shape slowly circling the fire. From time to time it paused, its massive neckless head tilted to one side, as if it were listening to something. Sniffing the air.

There was no sign of Aino-Suvantamoinen. There was no sign of their human hunter either. They watched the mudjhik in silence.

Lom felt something dark touch his mind. It was the same intrusive triumphant contact he had felt in the souterrain. His hands prickled as if the flow of blood were returning to numbed extremities. His mouth was dry. He felt himself sinking into a pit of blank hopelessness. Despair.

The position is hopeless. We're going to die.

No. That's not my voice.

The mudjhik's blank face whipped around towards where they were hiding, driving its eyeless gaze into the tangle of branches.

'Fuck!' hissed Lom. 'It's seen us. Run!' He caught a glimpse of the mudjhik beginning to move towards them. A kind of lurching fall that was the beginning of its accelerating charge. They turned and fled.

They ran thoughtlessly, stumbling and crashing through the undergrowth. Lom's chest was tight, his stomach sickened. Already he was feeling the thud of the stone fist against the back of his head that would be the last thing he ever felt.

After twenty or thirty yards they broke out of the thorny scrub onto a path, a narrow avenue filled with pale dawn light like water in a canal. It led gently downhill between taller trees towards the mudflats. Picking up speed they ran along it. Lom had no plan, no hope, except the wild thought that if they could reach the soft expanses of mud the mudjhik would be unable to follow them. It would flounder and sink. How they themselves would cross the treacherous flats he didn't know.

He didn't look back. He didn't need to. He could hear the mudjhik following. The rhythm of its heavy footfalls shook the earth beneath them. And he could feel the taunting, the almost casual mockery of its leisurely pace. It would not lose them now.

Then Lom was almost knocked sideways off his feet by a slap of wind against his body. Flying leaves and small pieces of twig and thorn stung his face, half-blinding him. He half-felt and half-saw in the corner of his eye a small and indistinct figure flow out of the woods and back up the path behind them. It was almost like a woman except that she was made of twigs and leaves and twisting wind. Behind him he heard Maroussia cry out and stumble. He stopped and turned to grab her and pull her upright.

'Don't stop!' he shouted into the rising noise. 'Don't look back!'

The wind rose, dissonant and maddening: it was almost impossible to walk against it, let alone run. A heavy bough fell at their feet with a dull thud. It didn't bounce. Big enough to have killed them.

'Just keep going!' Lom yelled.

A series of tremendous crashes came behind them, one after another. Four. Five. Six. Accompanied by the squeal and groan of tearing wood. The wind died.

'Vissarion!'

It was Maroussia. He stopped and looked back.

There was an indistinct shape on the path, at once a woman and a vortex of air and tree fragments, standing on the air a foot above the earth. It seemed as if her arms were spread wide to embrace the wood. Beyond her, huge trees had toppled across the track. Half a dozen of the largest beech and oak lay as if hurricane-flattened. Swirls of wind still stirred among their fallen, near-leafless crowns. The mudjhik had almost managed to evade them, but the last of them had come down with the immense weight of its trunk across its great stone back. The mudjhik was trapped under it, its face pressed deep into the scrubby grass and dark earth. It was not moving.

The wind-woman let her arms drop to her sides in a gesture filled with tiredness and relief. Aino-Suvantamoinen stepped out of the woods. He was walking towards the mudjhik where it lay.

'No!' yelled Lom. 'Wait! Don't!'

The giant didn't hear him, or else he took no notice. He walked across to look down on the mudjhik's motionless head. Its face was pressed inches deep into the mud. It could not have seen or heard or breathed. But it did not need to. As soon as the giant came within reach the mudjhik's free arm whipped forward in a direction no human or giant could have moved. But it was not human or giant: it had no ligaments and skeletal joints to define the limits of its moves. Its fist of rust-red stone smashed into the front of the giant's knee and broke it with a sickening crack. The giant shrieked in shock and anger and pain as he fell. The wind-woman seemed to cry out also, and shiver like a cat's-paw across still water. A storm of twig-fragments and whipped-up earth clattered ineffectually about the mudjhik's half-buried head.

The mudjhik's arm struck out again, almost too fast to be seen, punching towards the fallen giant's body, but he was just out of reach. Groggily, Aino-Suvantamoinen began to crawl away to safety, shaking his great head and dragging his snapped and twisted leg. Lom could hear his laboured breathing, deep and hollow and harsh. He sounded like a huge beast panting, a dray horse or a great elk. The mudjhik was moving purposefully under the weight of the fallen tree. Unable to raise itself with the trunk on it back, it was rocking its body from side to side and scooping at the earth under its belly with its hands. Gouging a deepening groove in the ground. Digging its way out. Soon it would be free.

He turned to Maroussia, but she wasn't there. He looked around wildly. Where the hell had she gone?

Then Lom saw her. Up the path, at the edge of the trees. She was heading for the stricken giant. Aino-Suvantamoinen was waving her away, but she was taking no notice.

'Maroussia!' Lom yelled. 'Get down! Get out of sight!'

There was a sharp ugly rattle of gunfire. An obscene clattering sound, flat and echoless. *A sub-machine gun.* Lom saw the muzzle flashes among the trees up and to the left, on the side of the path away from Maroussia. Bullet-strikes kicked up the mud, moving in a line towards the crawling, injured bulk of Aino-Suvantamoinen. A row of small explosions punched into the side of the giant's chest from hip to shoulder, each one bursting open, sudden rose-red blooms in little bursts of crimson mist. The huge body shuddered at the impacts. Then the top of his head came off.

Lom heard Maroussia's sigh of despair. Then the gun turned on her. A spray of bullets ripped into the trees around her, splattering the branches like heavy rain. He saw a splash of blood across her cheek, red against pale, as she fell.

'Maroussia!'

She wasn't moving.

No, thought Lom. *Not her. No.*

He began to move. He needed to get to her. He needed to draw the fire. Give her time to get into cover. If she could.

The gunfire turned towards him. He yelled and threw himself sideways into the trees, falling heavily.

Silence. The firing had stopped.

Keeping low, expecting the hail of bullets to fall again at any moment, Lom began to slither along the ground, hauling himself along on his elbows, driving forward with his knees. He felt the low mat of brambles and the roots of trees scraping his lower belly raw. He winced as a sharp branch dug into him under his belt: it felt as if it had pierced his skin and gouged a chunk from his flesh. He ignored it. He was trying to work his way up the hill to where she had fallen. Keeping his head low, he could see nothing. Where was the gunman? Waiting for him to show himself. Moving to a new position? Coming up behind him? No point in thinking any of that. *Move!* The only thing in his mind was reaching Maroussia. He reached the shelter of a moss-covered stump. Pushing aside a thicket of small branches, he risked a look.

Twenty yards ahead of him, Maroussia, looking dazed and lost, was trying to stand. He saw her stumble into the cover of the trees.

And then the mudjhik was free of the fallen tree and on its feet, and coming straight towards him.

Lom ran, ducking low, ignoring the thorns and brambles that slashed his face and hands until they ran wet with blood, heading for where the trees grew densest, squeezing between close-growing trunks, wading brooks. Anything that would slow the mudjhik. Anything that would give him the advantage.

The mudjhik was relentless. It would not give up. It would keep on coming. But it could not move as fast as a man through a wood. Lom could hear it behind him, crashing its way through the trees, but he was getting further ahead. Widening the gap.

Lom ran. There was nothing before this moment, nothing after it; there was only *now* and the *next half-second after now*, where he had to get to, by running as fast as he could make his body run and by *not falling*. The world narrowed down to one single point of clarity, the hole through which he had to pass to reach the moment on the other side of now. Behind him was the hunter. Ahead of him ... calling him, wanting him as much as he wanted it ... the safe hiding. The dark place. The mothering belly. The hole in the ground.

Lom hunched in the souterrain. He was sweating and shaking with cold. Thick darkness pressed against his eyes and seeped into his skin. He could smell his own blood, smeared on his hands and face; he could smell the damp earth and stone; and he could smell his own fear. Fear, and despair. Where was Maroussia? For the third time he did not know. For the third time he had left her to face her enemies alone. Vissarion Lom, protector of women. His own death would surely come and find him here. The mudjhik would sniff him out and dig. Drag him out and snap his neck. He had a little time to wait. But no hope. The souterrain was not a refuge but a trap. A dark hand reached inside his skull with stone fingers and squeezed his brain in its palm. Cruel and stupid and certain. *I am coming. I will be with you soon.* Again Lom felt the prickling clumsy numbness in his fingers and the gut-loosening dread. *It will not be long.*

He repelled the touch with all his force and slammed his mind shut against it.. He had more strength than he had expected. This was something new. And good. He felt a moment of surprise, his adversary's mental stumble as he lost his footing, and then ... silence. He was free of it.

Only when it was gone did Lom realise how long it had been there: the fear, the lack of confidence, the constant unsettling feeling of alarm and threat moving at the barest edge of his awareness. It had been with him ever since he'd woken in the giant's isba, but it was gone at last. He'd driven it out. He was stronger than he thought. Stronger than his enemies knew.

Lom waited a moment, collecting his strength. He took stock. The hunters knew where he was, and he couldn't keep the mind-wall in place for ever. But it was a chance. And Maroussia might be alive. She was alive. He was sure of it, though he couldn't have said how he knew. Somehow he could feel her presence out there somewhere in the woods.

It was time to fight back.

When he was ready, Lom called back all the feelings of defenceless-ness and despair. He let himself be defeated, hopeless, hurt. Bleeding and weeping and broken in the dark.

It is finished. Over.

He let the one thought fill his mind.

I am finished. No more fighting. No more running. Everything hurts.

And deliberately he lowered his defences and let the mudjhik in. He felt its touch flow into his mind, and let it feel his defeat.

And then – when he had it, when he felt its triumph – Lom began to edge away within his mind.

Carefully, slowly, reluctantly, so it would feel to the mudjhik like energy and will draining away, he slipped beneath the surface of his own consciousness, retreating behind a second, inner, hidden wall he had built there. Barely thinking at all, moving by instinct only, he began to crawl away down the souterrain passage, further and deeper into the earth.

76

Maroussia watched the militia man step past Aino-Suvantamoinen's body with relaxed, fastidious indifference. He was another uniform, another gun. After the mudjhik had lumbered off under the trees in pursuit of Lom, he had stepped out of cover. Coming for her.

He was casually confident now, the squat ugly weapon slung from his shoulder and held across his body, pointing to the ground. He stopped for a moment to look at the dead giant. A defeated humiliated hill of flesh. The carcase of an immense slaughtered cow. She could tell by the way the man held himself that he was pleased. Gratified by the demonstration of his own power. He was walking across to where she lay. Not hurrying. She was no threat to him. Simply a matter of tidiness. A job to finish neatly. An injured woman to kill, while the mudjhik hunted down the fleeing man. He was a man who had succeeded.

She saw him close up. He was bare-headed. She could see his pale, insipid face. Fine fair hair, close-cropped, boyish. A piece of angel stone in the centre of his head. Then it came to her. Like a blow to the head. Anger knotted its fingers in her stomach and pulled, tight, making her retch. *It was the same man.* The one who had shot down her mother was the same one who was sauntering across to her now to finish the job.

'No,' she said quietly. 'No.'

She began to crawl away towards the trees. She was not badly hurt. Splinters of wood, smashed from the trees by the machine-gun fire, had sprayed her face, leaving her stung and bleeding from small cuts, and something heavy had struck her on the back of the head, leaving her momentarily dizzy, but that was gone now. She could have stood up and tried to run, but the militia man would simply have cut her down. She wanted to draw him closer. Get him into the woods, where she could spring at him from behind a tree. Knock the gun aside. Claw at his eyes with her fingernails. She needed him close for that. Careful to make no sudden movement that might cause him to raise his gun and rake her down from where he was, she crawled with desperate slowness towards the thickets.

The image of her mother dead came vividly into her head. Another slack and ragged body lying in the pool of its own leaking mess. That was three of them. Aino-Suvantamoinen. Vishnik. Mother. Just three among many of course: the Vlast was heaping up the corpses of the dead in great hills all across the dominions, tipping them into pits with steam shovels and bulldozers, and no one was counting. Soon she would be another.

She was not going to make it to cover. Her chance was no chance at all. In less than a minute – in seconds – he would do it. It was his job. His function. He was an efficient man, and even here in the woods the day belonged to efficient men. She was about to get up and run, knowing it would only hasten the end, when she heard him cry out in anger behind her. The noise of his gunfire shattered the silence that had settled on the morning. But no bullets struck her.

She looked back. For a second she thought he had been surrounded by bees. Little black insects were swarming all over him and he was firing wildly, the gun held one-handed while he tried to protect his face with the other and beat the bees away. Only it wasn't bees. It was leaves and pieces of twig and thorn. He was at the centre of a wildly spinning vortex of wind. The woman-shaped column of air that she had glimpsed earlier was upon him. Embracing him with her arms of wind. The hunter was panicking, blinded, shouting in anger and fear, lurching from side to side, trying to punch the wind away, firing his gun at the air that was assaulting him.

Maroussia could see, as he could not yet, that the wind-woman was losing her strength. Dissipating. The man was keeping his feet. The wind-woman who had brought down huge trees on the mudjhik could not even floor him now. She was exhausted. But she had done enough. She had made time. Maroussia ran.

She pushed her way through the undergrowth, following a path she hoped was taking her back to the isba. It wound between trees and turned aside round boulders. Sometimes it failed altogether, and she had to squeeze between close-growing trees until she found it again. Or found a different path. There was no way of telling. She might have been doing no more than following random trails made by wild animals. She had a vague notion of where the isba lay, but no way of knowing whether she could trust her sense of direction in this world of moss and leafless branches and strange hummocks in the ground.

The wind-woman had given her time. She should use it. She stopped running. Stood. Listened. Heard the sound of her own ragged breathing, the beating of her heart, the air moving through the trees – a sound as ancient and constant as the sea. She rested her hand on the smooth grey skin of a young beech tree. Trying to feel the life in it. She could feel nothing, but she imagined the tree welcomed the effort. She felt that maybe the warm touch of her palm had quickened it somehow. Imagination. But it was a good thought anyway, her first good thought in a long time. Progress. The territory would help her if she let it. Her pursuer would not think like that.

Once more she followed the smell of burnt wood and bone and wool to the remains of the isba. Much of the whalebone framework had fallen, but a few blackened lengths stuck upwards out of the mess. Heaps of rug and fur still smouldered, clotted and blackened and ruinous. The smell of it caught at the back of her throat. The iron stove was canted sideways, heat-seared and filthy with ash and soot. Some of its tiles had fallen away. It looked diminished and pathetic. Everything looked smaller now. There had been so much room inside the isba when she was in it, but the burnt scar it had left on the ground seemed too small to have contained so much space. Maroussia had seen plots like this in Mirgorod, sites where condemned houses had been cleared away and new ones not yet built. The gaps they left always seemed too small. All interior spaces were bigger than their exterior. Living inside them made it so.

The *Sib* was still tied to the little jetty on the creek at the edge of the clearing where Aino-Suvantamoinen had brought it the day after they arrived, while Lom had lain lost in his fever and she had sat with him. She considered untying the skiff, climbing in and drifting away. But Lom was out there somewhere in the woods. Perhaps not dead. Perhaps the mudjhik had not found him.

What would the hunter do? Come here of course. Check the isba. Check the *Sib*. Maybe he was watching her now from the trees. Maybe the mudjhik was there. No. Not that. They would not wait. They would attack immediately. They were not here yet. But they would come.

Think.

The territory will help you, if you let it.

The hunter would come here. He would walk where she had walked. Cross the ground that she had crossed. Stand on the jetty where she had stood, to look down into the boat. Sooner or later, he must do that. How much time did she have? Perhaps hours. Perhaps minutes. Perhaps none.

Near the isba was a neat stack of Aino-Suvantamoinen's fishing gear, untouched by the fire. A hauled-out salmon trap. A mud-sled. Leather buckets for cockles. And, leaning neatly against a stack of firewood, a shaft of wood thicker than her arm and as long as she was tall, with a flat metal blade like a long, narrow spade, lashed firmly to one end. She tested the blade edge. It was sharp on both sides and at the end. She had seen implements like this before, in the whalers' harbour. Flensing tools, used to slice long ribbons of flesh from porpoises and small whales as they hung from hooks. This was the same, but bigger, of a thickness and weight for the giant to heft. Unwieldy for her. But it was all she had.

The territory will help you, if you let it.

There was a little inlet by the jetty, where a stream flowed into the creek. The ground all around it was flat, grassy, empty but for a few saplings all the way back to the isba and the wood's edge. But the bank of the inlet was undercut by the stream, creating an overhanging ledge a couple of feet above a small expanse of soft, grey, semi-liquid mud. Maroussia threw a stone out onto the mud and watched it slowly settle for half its depth into the slobs.

She threw the heavy flensing blade after the stone, marking its position by a large bluish tussock of rough grass. Then she took off her clothes. All of them. They would be useless for what she intended; they would only hamper her movements. Slow her down.

She shivered. The touch of the wintry morning raised tiny bumps on her skin. She would be colder soon, much colder, but that was nothing. She could ignore it. Rolling her clothes into a bundle she dropped them into the bottom of the boat and threw a tarpaulin over them. Then she went back to the overhanging bank and slipped carefully down onto the mud within reach of where the blade had sunk almost out of sight. She pressed it down with her foot until the mud closed over it.

Maroussia knelt on the mud. Her knees sank immediately into the chilly ooze. Its touch was soft and slightly gritty against her skin. She began to scoop out a narrow channel the length of her body, plastering the mud over herself. Water began to puddle in the bottom of the shallow trench. But she couldn't cover herself entirely with the mud. She couldn't reach her back. There was no time. She lay down in the hollow she had made and rolled, covering every inch of her pale skin with the cold grey mud. Rubbing it into her hair and over her face. She lay flat, trying to wriggle her body down into it as much as she could, until she was firmly bedded in. Lying still, she could feel herself sinking slowly deeper as the mud opened to take her down. Gradually she felt the cold softness rising higher. She had chosen a place where a notch in the bank gave her a view of the jetty ten feet away. It would have to do. She waited. The hunter would come.

Time passed. Maroussia felt her body stiffening in the cold. She felt the tiny movements of the soft mud oozing against her. Water puddling underneath. The mud on her back began to dry and itch. She closed her mind against it. *Do not move.* Slowly the terrain closed in about her, absorbing her presence until she was part of it. Scarcely there. A heron flapped along the creek on loose flaggy wings and alighted close by. She watched it stand motionless, a slender sentry, probing the water with its intent yellow gaze, oblivious of her only a few feet away. She could not let it stay. If she startled it later, when the time came, it would alert *him*.

'Go!' she hissed. 'Move it! Shift!'

The heron didn't react. She risked moving a hand. Flexing her fingers out of the mud. The heron's yellow eye swivelled towards the movement instantly, alert for the chance of a vole or a frog. Their gazes met. For a moment they stared at each other. Then the heron lifted itself slowly away to find a more private post.

Some time later – how long, she had no idea – an otter came browsing along the creek and passed near her face. It had no idea she was there.

And then the hunter came.

She didn't hear him until he was almost on her. He was good. He was taking care. She heard his boots in the grass when he was ten steps away. He was standing where she had known he would stand. Checking out the *Sib* as she had known he would. Holding the gun cradled and ready, as she had pictured him doing. With his back towards her.

The territory will help you, if you let it.

She took a firm grip on the heavy shaft of the flensing blade that lay alongside her in the mud. Now was the time.

She was certain that the sounds of the river masked the sound of her rising out of the mud – a thing of mud herself – and the tread of her bare muddy feet on the grass, but some peripheral sense must have alerted him He was turning towards her and raising the muzzle of the gun when she swung the blunt end of the flensing tool at his head. It caught him across the side of his face. The momentum of the blow knocked him sideways and his booted feet slid from under him on the wet planking of the jetty. He went down heavily, losing his grip on the gun, and ended up on his back, looking up at her, blankly surprised.

Afterwards she wondered whether it had been her startling appearance, naked and plastered with mud, her face distorted with effort and hate, that slowed his reaction, as much as the mis-hit blow and the awkward fall. But whatever the cause, he was too slow, and she had played this scene through in her imagination a thousand times while she waited, anticipating every variation, every way it might go. Without stopping to think, she reversed the tool in her grip, set the vicious leading edge of the blade against his neck between sternum and chin, and shoved it downwards with all her weight, as if she were digging a spade into heavy ground. It sliced into his neck with a gristly crunch. She felt it parting the flesh and lodging against his vertebrae. He tried to scream but could manage only a wheezing, frothing gargle. She pulled back an inch or two and thrust again. The shaft was at an angle now, and she leaned the whole of her weight onto it. She felt the blade find its way between two vertebrae. It was sharp. She pushed again. His head came clean off and rolled a few feet across the planking, leaving a mess of flesh and tubes and gleaming white glimpses of bone between the man's shoulders. A widening pool of purple blood.

77

Lom walked fast through the souterrain tunnels. There was no light, but he didn't need it: the fear had gone and he was strong. He was going back to where they had first come down, under the giant's isba. He knew the way. He knew how to avoid the earth fall caused by Safran's grenades. The tunnels weren't dark and cramped; they were bright, airy, perfumed, luminous, beautiful. He knew his way by the smell of the earth, the trickle of dislodged earth, the stir and spill of air across the dampness of stone. He felt it all – he felt the roots of trees in the earth and the sway of their leafheads in the wind – as he felt the rub of his cuff against his wrist, the sock rucked under his foot, the sting of the grazes on his belly. There were other things too, things he could not quite focus on, not yet, but he felt their presence: they were like flitting shadows, hunches, hints. He was a world in motion – a borderless, lucid, breathing world. The seal in his head was cut away. The waters of the river and the sea had washed him clear.

This would not last. He knew that. Aino-Suvantamoinen had said that. It would fade, but it would not altogether go, and it would come again.

As he passed through the dark tunnel without stumbling, he tried to reach out with his mind into the woods above him. He didn't know yet what he could do. What the limits were. Further and further he pushed himself.

He found Safran. Safran was nearby. Moving with careful confidence almost directly above him.

He found the mudjhik, pushing its way through thorns. It was hunting but it had no trail. It was lost.

Lom reached out for Maroussia, but he couldn't find her. He felt her presence, but she was … withdrawn. Barely breathing. Waiting. Still. She was *hiding*. But not from him.

And then he felt Safran's death …

Lom needed to get out of the souterrain. Now. He needed to get to Maroussia.

He came to the place where the giant had let them down, but when he pushed up against the wooden hatch it would not shift. It was high above his head: he could just about touch it with his hands but he couldn't get his full strength into the shove. It seemed as if there was something heavy on top of it – the stove had fallen across it, perhaps.

He needed to get out.

There was another way. Perhaps.

Lom gathered all his strength into himself. Breathing slowly, focusing all his attention on what he was doing, he reached out around him into the perfumed earthy darkness, pulling together the air of the tunnel, making it as tight and hard as he could. He waited a moment, gathering balance. The earth above his head was cool and dark and filled with roots and life. It was another kind of air. Thicker, darker, richer air, and that was all it was. And then he pushed upwards.

78

Maroussia sat on the edge of the jetty and considered her situation. She had killed a man. She thought about that. When she had shot the militia man near Vanko's, although she had not meant to kill him and didn't think she had, afterwards she had been filled with empty sickness and self-disgust. But this time, though she had killed, she hadn't felt that. There was only a pure and visceral gladness. Satisfaction burst inside her like a berry. She had wanted to do it. Now it was done. That was good.

She slipped off the jetty edge into the deep icy water of the creek. It came up to her chest and the coldness of it made her gasp. She wished she knew how to swim but she had never learned. She waded out into the middle of the stream, feeling the slippery mud and buried stones and the tangle of weeds beneath her feet. The strong current pushed at her legs. She ducked her head under the water, eyes open, letting it wash the clotted mud from her hair. Cleaning everything away, the mud and the fear and the blood that had splashed her legs. Surrendering herself, she let her body drift downstream, turning slowly, until she came to a place where the branches of a fallen tree reached out across the creek. There she climbed out.

When she got back to the jetty she kicked the severed head over the side. It fell in the water with a plop and disappeared. Then she put her clothes back on and prepared the skiff to leave: laid the oars ready in the rowlocks; made sure the lines were loosely tied so one tug would release them. She would give Lom till dusk to find her, and if he had not come, she would go alone. She drank a little water and wished there was something she could eat. She had not felt so hungry for days. But that was tomorrow's problem. For the moment it was enough to sit with her back against a jetty post and wait.

She tried to keep her eye on the edge of trees that enclosed the wide clearing, watching for any sign of movement that would signal the coming of Lom. Or the mudjhik. But her gaze kept being drawn back to the burned-out remains of the isba. The outward sign of her desolation and grief. Killing the militia man had not healed that. Not at all. Desultory snowflakes appeared, skittering in the grey air.

And then the wreckage of the isba erupted. It was as if a shell had fallen, or a mine exploded. A column of dark earth and roots and stone and the remains of the isba spouted ten – twenty – feet up and slumped back down in a crump of dust. She saw the giant's stove bounce and break open. A wave of dust-heavy air rolled over her, smelling of the raw, damp underground.

As the air cleared she saw something, a man-shaped figure, climbing up out of the earth. Its face was a mess of dirt and blood. A heavy cloak hanging from its shoulders. It stood for a moment as if dazed, looking around slowly, then it began to walk slowly towards her.

'Vissarion?' she said. 'Vissarion? Is that you.'

The figure stopped to wipe its face with its sleeve. It was Lom. He looked lost, disoriented, stunned. She saw that the wound in his forehead had opened. It was seeping blood into his eyes and down across his mouth. He kept wiping at his face, vaguely, again and again.

'Maroussia?' said Lom. 'There's dirt in my eyes. I can't see properly.'

'What ... what happened? Was that another grenade?'

Lom wiped his face again and looked at her, blinking.

'That?' he said. 'That was me.' He paused, and she saw that he was grinning at her. Grinning like a child. 'This is going to be fun.' Then his legs crumpled and he sat down heavily beside her with his hand to his forehead. 'Ow,' he said, looking at her balefully. 'My head hurts. You haven't got any water I could drink, have you?'

'Vissarion?' said Maroussia. 'Where's the mudjhik?'

79

Artyom Safran wondered where he was. Dead, certainly. But also ... not. As the terrible flat blade had begun to slice into his neck and he knew that he would certainly die there, he made one last reckless throw of the dice. He grabbed at the mental cord connecting him to the mudjhik and hurled himself along it, all of himself, wholeheartedly, holding nothing in reserve. It was easy and instant, like jumping from a window to escape a fire. The mudjhik had been pulling at him insidiously for years, and the pull had been growing stronger all the time they were in the wetlands. More than once in the last few days he had felt himself slipping away, and it had required an effort of will to hold himself separate. Now he stopped trying, and threw himself instead at the door, and it was open, and he stumbled through. The mudjhik, reacting instantly, pulled him inside. Greedily. It felt like a great hunger being fed at last. In the last moment of his separateness, Safran had felt a surge of crude, ugly, inhuman satisfaction enfolding him.

What have I done?

It was his last purely human thought.

He was not alone. Dog-in-mudjhik came at him hard, scratching and tearing and spitting, before he had a chance to find his balance. Dog-in-mudjhik would tolerate no rival. It was a territory thing. Only the death of the interloper would do.

Safran tried to put up some sort of defence, but he had no time to work out how. He tried curling himself into a tight ball with his back against Dog-in-mudjhik's ripping jaw. Hugging himself to protect his vital organs. But it was the merest persiflage. Dog-in-mudjhik cut through all that. Dog-in-mudjhik was shredding him, tearing him off in chunks, snarling. Dog-in-mudjhik made himself as big as a house and started to dig. Safran was going to die a second time.

But the mudjhik's angel stuff knew what it needed, and it was not dog thoughts any more. In the gap between two instants the space inside the mudjhik that Dog-in-mudjhik occupied ceased to exist. It closed up completely, solid where space had been. Dog-in-mudjhik went out like a snuffed candle. Dog-in-mudjhik was extinguished, leaving only a faint and diminishing smell of dog mind in the air.

What had once been Safran lay still, curled up tight, quivering like hurt flesh. Trying to close himself off. Trying too late to renege on the deal. Far too late. The angel-stuff encompassed him, fitting itself around him until there was no space between them. Then it moved in.

Safran-in-mudjhik felt sick and dizzy with horror. He was in a cold red-grey world. Seeing without eyes, hearing without ears, overwhelmed and confused by the mudjhik's alien angel-senses, he couldn't grasp where he was. Or who. Or what. But even then, in the moment of his profoundest and most appalling collapse, he began to feel something else. A new kind of triumph. He sensed the first glimmerings of an immense new power. The angel stuff was feeling it, but so was he. He was going to be a new thing in the universe. A first. A best. Immortal. Safran-in-mudjhik was strong.

Experimentally he swept an arm sideways. It cracked against a tree and broke it. The tree toppled towards him and he fended it off effortlessly. A long-eared owl, half-stunned and dislodged from its roost, struggled to get purchase on the air with its wings. Safran-in-mudjhik caught it in flight and smashed it against his own stone chest. Felt it break. Felt it die. So good. This would be fun. There were so many things to do. Sweet freedom things.

First and sweetest, revenge.

Safran-in-mudjhik began to explore his new self. There were angel-senses here, and angel memories that Dog-in-mudjhik could perceive nothing of. The bright immensity between the stars. Existence without time. He could remember. He belonged there. And now he was on his way back.

Somewhere in the rust-and-blood-red corridors of his new mind he could feel the connection with Lom. Faint but still there. He fumbled towards it, but he was still too clumsy to hold on to it. He couldn't get it clear enough to know where Lom was. Not yet. But soon. Finesse would come. In the meantime, he certainly knew where she was. The Shaumian woman. The Safran-slicer. Creator of Safran-in-mudjhik. Kill her first. He turned towards the isba clearing and the creek. It was going to be a good first day.

80

The swollen river surged ahead, thick and brown and heavy. It carried the skiff onwards and widened as it went. Lom, cradling Safran's sub-machine gun, stared mesmerised at the surface. It was scummed with ragged drifts of foam, littered with dead leaves and matted rafts of grass and broken branches. He felt drained. His head hurt. The new skin across the hole in his skull had split, and though a crust of dried blood had formed, it throbbed in time with his pulse and wept a clear sticky liquid. It was sore, and all the muscles of his body ached. The effort of pushing his way out of the souterrain had exhausted him, and the world around him felt diminished, distant and separate. He wondered if such easy power would ever come back to him again.

Maroussia handled the oars. She had little to do but steer the skiff with occasional touches, avoiding the larger obstacles floating along with them and keeping them clear of eddies and backwaters.

'The waters are rising,' said Lom. 'It must have been raining in the hills.'

Maroussia shook her head.

'The giant is gone,' she said. 'Without him to work the sluices, the waters are running wild. All this wetland will go. There'll be nothing left but the city and the sea.'

A dark mossy floating lump of tree nudged heavily against the bow and rested there, travelling alongside them in the current. Lom stared at it. It was a mass of little juts and elbows of branch-stump and bark canker. Every crook and hole was edged with a dewy fringe of spider's web. Lom shifted the weight of the gun, which was pressing into his leg. The death of Aino-Suvantamoinen, and the weight of all the other deaths before him, had left him feeling numbed and stupid. The boat was taking them into a darker, emptier future.

Maroussia pulled hard at the oars, skewing the *Sib* sideways. She rowed in silence, looking at nothing. Lom watched her hands on the oars. Large, strong, capable. She'd pushed back her sleeves. Her hands were reddened but her forearms were pale and smooth. He could see the tendons and muscles working as she rowed. Her black hair was slicked with river mist: it clung to her face and neck in tight shining curls.

'It's not your fault,' said Lom.

'What?'

'The giant. It was Safran that killed him. Not you.'

'He tried to help,' said Maroussia.

'He thought it was important. So did Raku.'

'Yes.'

'So it is important.'

For a long time Maroussia didn't say anything. She just kept rowing. Then she looked up at him.

'I'm going to find the Pollandore,' she said. 'The angel is destroying the world. The Pollandore can stop that.'

Lom noticed how thin she was, though her arms were strong. As she rowed, he watched the shadow play on the vulnerable, scoop-shaped dip at the base of her throat. The suprasternal notch. She was human and raw and beautiful. She rowed in silence for a long time. Lom watched the empty mudbanks pass by. He wiped his weeping forehead.

'Vissarion?'

'Yes?'

'That thing in your head ...'

'It's gone now.'

'What was it? How did it get there?'

'I was young. I don't know how old. Eight maybe. Eight or nine. A child.'

'That man I killed ...'

'Safran.'

'He had one the same.'

'Savinkov's Children. They call us that. Ever heard of Savinkov?'

'No.'

'You should have. Everyone should know about Savinkov.'

'I don't.'

'He was provost of the Institute at Podchornok when I was there. Vishnik went there too. He was my friend.'

'But he didn't ... he didn't have anything like that.'

'No. Only a few of us. Before he came to the Institute, Savinkov was a technician of angel-flesh. His specialism was the effect of it on the human mind. Putting a piece of it in direct contact with the human brain.'

'They put that stuff in people's heads?'

'And the other way round.'

'You don't mean ...'

'It's common practice with mudjhiks to put in an animal brain: naturally they tried with human brains too, but it doesn't work that way. The mudjhiks become uncontrollable. Insane. But there are less dramatic methods than full transplant. Angel flesh has a sort of life. Awareness. It *affects* you. And it encourages loyalty. The sacrifice of the individual for the sake of the whole. It's a way of binding you to the Vlast.'

'But ... you ... They did it to you when you were a *child*.'

'That was Savinkov's subject. His research. Were children more or less susceptible? Did the effect grow or diminish with time? How could you measure and predict it? The skull insertion technique was Savinkov's invention. It used to go wrong a lot. The children died, or ... well, Savinkov put them to work. In the gardens. The stables.'

'But ... the *parents*?'

'We didn't have parents. None of us did. Savinkov used to take waifs and strays into the Institute for the experiments. I never knew who my parents were.'

'Oh ...'

'Savinkov saw nothing wrong with it,' said Lom. 'He had some successes too. Some of them became excellent mudjhik handlers and technicians with the Worm. Servants of the Vlast of great distinction.'

'But not you.'

'No. I was one of Savinkov's disappointments in that respect.'

Walls rose on either side of the river. The channel narrowed. A roar of rushing water. The skiff rolled and yawed, rushing ahead out of control.

'Hold on!' yelled Lom.

Maroussia almost lost the oars as the *Sib* pitched over a low weir and spun out into wide grey water. The Mir Ship Canal. The skiff settled, drifting slowly with the current.

It was a bleak, blank place after the edgeless mist and mud of the wetlands: a broad channel cut dead straight between high embankments of stone blocks and concrete slopes, wide enough for great ships and ocean-going barges to pass four or six abreast. Featureless. There was nothing natural to be seen, not even a gull in the sky. The trees were out of sight behind the great ramparts and bulwarks built by armies of giants and serfs. Built by the Founder on their bones. The water was deep: Lom felt it fathoming away beneath them, dark and cold. A bitter wind, freighted with flurries of sharp sleety snow, was pushing upstream off the sea, smelling of salt and ice, slowing their progress. It had been autumn when they entered the wetlands. It felt like winter coming now.

'It'll be easy from here on,' said Lom. 'Downstream to the sea lock. We can leave the boat there and walk back along the Strand to the tram terminus. Let me take the oars for a while.'

Maroussia wasn't listening. She was staring over his shoulder up towards the embankment. He followed her gaze. The mudjhik was standing on the crest, a smudge of dried blood and rust against the grey sky. Grey snow. Grey stone. It was watching them. As the current took them downstream, the mudjhik began to lope along the top of the high canal wall, keeping pace. Lom looked for an escape. On either side of the canal the embankments rose sheer and high. No quays. No steps cut into the stone. Nowhere to go. The mudjhik had only to follow them.

'Maybe we'll find a place on the far side where we can get out,' he said. 'It can't cross the canal before the sea lock. We can be miles away by then.'

As if in answer, he felt the dark touch of the mudjhik's mind in his. It felt stronger than before, much stronger, and different now. There was an intelligence there that had been absent before, with a sickening almost-human edge to it. It was almost a voice. No words, but a cruel demonstration of existence and power. It was a voice he recognised. *Safran.* But it wasn't quite Safran: it was something more and something less than he had been. Lom felt he was being touched intimately by something ... disgusting. Something strong but inhuman, broken and foul and ... wrong. A mind that stank.

He slammed his mind-walls closed against it. The effort hurt. His head began to ache immediately. He felt the pulse in the socket in his forehead flutter and pound.

'We have to destroy that thing,' he said. 'Somehow. We have to end it. Here.'

Safran-in-mudjhik considered the pathetic little rowing boat sitting there helplessly, a flimsy toy on the deep flowing blackness. The two frail lives it carried, cupped in its brittle palm, flickered like matchlights. He had shown himself deliberately so he could taste their fear. Their deaths would be … delicious. Especially hers. The one that had taken his head when part of him was in the man.

That part of him wanted to be back in the man. It wasn't happy any more. But it would learn, or he would find a way to silence what he did not need. The angel-stuff was coming awake. Learning to remember. Learning to think. Now it had learned it could soak up human minds, absorb them, grow, it wanted to do it again. The first one had come willingly. More than that, it had come by choice, pushed its way in. Regretted it already, though. Would have preferred extinction. Too late! Too late, impetuous companion! Stuck with it now. But willingness was not essential. There were many minds here. Take them. Harvest them. Fed with such nutriment, what could angel-stuff not become? It remembered swimming among the stars. Why not again? But better. Stronger. More dangerous.

Start with the two in the boat. There was history there. Bad blood.

81

Lom pulled hard on the oars, racing the skiff seaward, scanning the far embankment for a scaleable escape. There was none. His head was hurting worse: tiny detonations of bright light flickered in his peripheral vision; waves of giddiness distracted him. He couldn't maintain his defences indefinitely. He hadn't the strength.

Maroussia went through Safran's equipment. There was the pistol, useless against the mudjhik, but not negligible.

'Here,' she said. 'You'd better have this.'

Lom put it in his pocket.

There was also the Exter-Vulikh that had cut down the giant. Its magazine was half full and there were two more besides, but it was nothing that would worry a twelve-foot sentient block of angel flesh, not even for an instant. Maroussia laid it aside with an expression of distaste.

'Wouldn't it be better if we just stopped?' she said.

'What do you mean?'

'We could wait. I know we can't make headway upstream, but we could try to hold our position out here. Or maybe we could make the boat fast somehow against the far embankment. Sooner or later a ship will come along.'

Lom considered.

'Maybe,' he said. 'If there is a ship. We haven't seen any. Don't they try to clear port before the freeze? I think the season's over.'

'Something must come along, one way or the other.'

Lom turned the skiff and began to row against the stream.

The mudjhik understood what they were doing instantly. It stopped loping forward and began to jog up and down on the spot, stamping heavily. Then it bent forward and began to pummel the ground with its fists. For a moment Lom thought it was raging impotently, but it straightened up with a large chunk of stone in its hands and lobbed it towards them.

The first throw fell short. A boulder as large as a man's torso whumped into the canal, jetting up a column of white water. Short, but close enough for them to feel the sting of the spray on their faces. The ripples reached the *Sib* and set her rocking. The next shot was closer. The mudjhik was finding its range.

'Shit,' said Lom and turned the boat again.

As soon as the boat started heading downstream, the mudjhik halted its bombardment and went back to pacing them along the embankment.

'It's herding us,' said Lom. 'It could sink us anytime, but it wants to get in close.'

I will not let you touch her. Weak as he was, he tried to force the thought towards the mudjhik, against the flow of its onslaught. *I will bring you down.*

They heard the sea gate before they saw it. The light was failing. Twilight brought sharp fresh squalls of sleet off the sea. There were gulls now, wheeling inland to roost. The Ship Canal swung round the shoulder of a small hill and narrowed, channelling the flow of the Mir in flood into a bottleneck of concrete, and ahead of them rose the great barrier. On one side, the left as they approached it, were the lock gates themselves, three ship-breadths wide, and to the right a roar of gushing water hidden in a cloud of spray. The grand new hydroelectric turbine, turning the pressure of water into power to light the streets of Mirgorod.

The immense lock gates were shut against them. They could make out the silhouette of the Gate Master's hut at the far end, between the lock and the turbine, but no light showed there. Of course not. Night was falling. No shipping traffic would come now. None, probably, till the spring. They were alone except for the mudjhik, standing in plain sight next to the massive stubby gate tower, waiting for them.

Lom fought the surging water with the oars, but there was nowhere to go. The skiff would either be brought up hard against the bottom of the gate or carried into the turbine's throat.

'A ladder!' Maroussia shouted above the noise of the water. 'Over there.'

Lom could just make out in the gathering gloom a contraption of steel to the right of the turbine, away from the mudjhik, designed to give access to the weir at water level. All he had to do was take the *Sib* across the current without getting dragged into the churning turbine mouth.

He could see nothing of what happened under the curtain of spray. There would be a grating, probably, to sift detritus from the canal. Maybe that's what the ladder was for. To clear it. But even if there was a grating, the boat would surely be smashed against it. The whole weight of the river was passing through there: the force would be tremendous; nobody who went into that churning water would come out again.

He let the current carry them forward and tried to use the oars to steer a slanting course across it, aiming for a point on the embankment just upstream from the bottom of the ladder. His arms ached. His head was pounding. There would be no second chance. The mudjhik was attacking his mind hard, not constantly but with randomly timed pulses of pressure, trying to knock him off balance.

The skiff crashed against the wall, caught her bow on a jut of stone and spun stern-first away from the embankment towards the deafening roar and dark, blinding spray. Lom dug in with the left-hand oar, almost vertically down into the water, and turned the skiff again. She crashed against the foot of the ladder and Maroussia grabbed it. The boat kept moving. Lom crouched and leapt for the ladder. The impact jarred his side numb, but he managed to hook one arm awkwardly round a steel strut. He had slung the Exter-Vulikh across his back by its webbing strap and the Sepora was in his pocket. The *Sib* continued sliding away from under him. She left them both clinging to the metal frame and disappeared into the shouting darkness and mist. Lom scrabbled desperately for a foothold and barked his shin against a sharp-edged metal rung. Then he was climbing, following Maroussia up the sheer embankment side.

There was nowhere to go. They were standing on a railed steel platform overlooking the turbines. A narrow walkway led across plunging water and slowly turning turbines to the lock gate tower, and beyond that was the lock itself, and the mudjhik. There was no other exit.

Lom looked over the seaward side with a wild idea of diving into the sea and swimming for the beach. If there was a beach. But down there, there was no sea, only a cistern to receive the immense outflow from the turbines. It was a deep, seething pit of water. Hundreds of thousands of gallons burst out from the sluice mouth every second and poured into what was basically a huge concrete-walled box. You wouldn't drown in there, you'd be smashed to a bloody pulp before the air was gone from your lungs.

Across the walkway a door led into the lock gate tower. With a crash of masonry it shattered open and the mudjhik shouldered its way through. It stood there a moment. Its face was blank. No sightless eyes. No lipless, throatless mouth. Just a rough lump of reddish stone sat on its shoulders. But it was watching them.

Lom raised the Exter-Vulikh and fired a stream of shells into the mudjhik's belly. The clattering detonations echoed off the surrounding concrete, deafening even above the roar of the turbine sluice, but the shells had no discernible effect. Lom had not thought they would. It was a gesture. The magazine exhausted itself in a few seconds and he threw the gun over the rail into the water below.

For a moment nothing happened. Stalemate. The mudjhik watching them from its end of the walkway. Lom and Maroussia staring back. Waiting. Then the mudjhik turned sideways and began to edge its way across the narrow steel bridge, squeezing itself between the flimsy rails. Lom reached for Maroussia's hand – it was the time for final, futile gestures – but he didn't find it. Maroussia had darted forward, running straight at the mudjhik. Lom felt its surge of raw delight as it grabbed for her, reaching sideways, swinging its leading arm wildly. He felt it reaching for her with its mind at the same time. Opening itself wide. Drawing at her. It was like a mouth, gaping.

It's trying to suck her in.

Understanding slammed against Lom's head like a concussion. And with it another thought. Another piece of insight.

It's too confident. It fears nothing at all.

And he saw what Maroussia was trying to do.

The mudjhik's swing at her was too awkward a move for its precarious position on the walkway. She ducked and the arm missed her, sweeping through the air above her head. The impetus of the move overbalanced the mudjhik slightly. It stumbled and leaned against the walkway rail, which sagged under its weight.

Lom pulled Safran's Sepora out of his pocket and fired, again and again, aiming high to clear Maroussia, aiming for the huge eyeless head. The recoils jarred his hand and shoulder. He flung all his rage and defiance and disgust and hatred at the mudjhik's undefended, questing, open-mouthed mind. He was still tired and weak – the power of his push was nothing compared to what he had done under the ground – but he felt the jar as it impacted. It was enough. Together, the mental onslaught and the heavy magnum rounds confused the mudjhik and added momentum to its stumble. The narrow guard rail collapsed under its weight and the mudjhik fell into the churning, roaring waters of the cistern below.

82

Maroussia was lying on the narrow iron walkway. She wasn't moving. Lom ran across. He knelt down beside her and laid his hand on her head. She stirred, raised her head and looked at him.

'Is it gone?' she said.

'Yes. It's gone. Are you … are you OK?'

'If that thing is gone then we can go back. I need to go back.'

'It's almost dark,' said Lom. 'And it's a long walk back. There won't be any trams till the morning. We'll have to stay here.'

She sat up slowly. She looked dizzy and sick.

'No. I …' But she had no strength for a night journey. No strength to argue even.

'Just for tonight,' said Lom. 'We can stay in the Gate Master's cabin.'

The Gate Master's lodge was an incongruous wooden superstructure on the lip of the sea gates. The lock on the door gave easily at a shove from Lom's shoulder. Inside was near-darkness. The smell of pitch and lingering tobacco smoke and tea. Maroussia found a lamp and matches. In the yellow lamplight the interior had a vaguely nautical flavour: large-scale charts of the harbour and the inner reaches were pinned to the walls, and more of the same were spread out on a plan table under the seaward window, with instruments, pencils, a pair of binoculars. There was a chair, the kind with a mechanism that allowed the seat to revolve and tip backwards. A long thin telescope on a tripod stood on the floor; heavy oilskins hung from a hook on the back of the door; a pair of large rubber boots leaned against the foot of a neat metal-framed bed. The Gate Master had left everything prepared to make himself comfortable when he returned: firewood stacked in the corner, water in the urn, a packet of tea, a box of biscuits. Lom pulled the heavy curtains across the window while Maroussia lit the stove and the urn. There were even two mugs to drink from. Maroussia sat on the edge of the bed and Lom took the swivelling chair, leaning back and putting his feet up on the table.

'What if someone sees the light?' said Maroussia.

'There's no one for miles. Anyway ...' Lom shrugged. 'Shipwrecked mariners. Needs must.' But he took Safran's heavy revolver from his pocket and laid it on the table within reach.

'Any bullets left in that?'

'No.'

Maroussia was looking at him. Her eyes were dark in the lamp shadow. Uncertain.

'Before the mudjhik fell ...' she began, and stopped. He waited for her to continue. 'I felt something. Inside my head.' She paused again. Lom didn't say anything. 'I don't know ... There was a kind of sick feeling, like I was going to faint. Everything seemed very far away. And then ... it was like a fist, a big angry punch, but inside my head. It didn't feel aimed at me, but it almost knocked me over anyway. And then the mudjhik ... went.'

'What you did was crazy. Running at it like that. You were lucky. If it had caught you when it swung—'

'It was you, wasn't it? The mind-punch thing. It felt like you. You did it.'

Lom said nothing.

'And when you blew yourself out of the ground ...' said Maroussia. 'How do you do that? I mean, what is it?'

'I don't know. It's something I used to be able to do. When I was a child. Then it stopped when Savinkov sealed me up. But since the seal was taken – actually before then, when I came to Mirgorod. It's been coming back. I just ... I just do it.'

There was a long silence. Pulses of sleet battering at the window. Maroussia was examining the woollen rug on the bed. Picking at it. Removing bits of fluff.

'Who *are* you?' she said eventually. 'I mean, what are you? Where do you *come* from? I mean, where do you really *come* from?'

'I don't know,' said Lom. 'But I'm beginning to think I should try to find out.' He took a biscuit from the box. It was soft and stale and tasted of dampness and pitch. He swallowed it and took a sip of tea. Cooling now. Bitter. He chucked the box of biscuits across the room onto the bed next to her. 'Here,' he said. 'Have one.'

'No.'

'Sleep then. We need to clear out early tomorrow. You can have the bed.'

'What about you?'

'I'll take the floor.'

'We could share the bed,' she said. 'There's room.'

She was sitting in shadow. Lom couldn't see anything in her face at all. Another scatter of sleet crashed against the window. The door with the broken lock stirred in the wind.

'Yes,' he said. 'That would be better.'

83

Lom lay on his back, pressed between Maroussia and the wall. He was tired but sleep hadn't come. As soon as he had got into the bed, Maroussia had pulled the blanket over them both, turned on her side, away from him, and apparently gone straight to sleep. He felt her long back now, pressed against his side, the length of her body stretched against his.

The wind and rain had died away. He could hear the slow rhythm of her breathing and the quiet surge of the sea. And it seemed to him that somewhere at the edge of his mind he could hear Safran under the water, crying in his pain. But if he tried to reach for the thread of it, it wasn't there.

'Vissarion?'

'Yes?'

But she said nothing more. Only the gentle ebb and flow of her breath. The rising and falling of her ribs against him. He turned on his side so that his face was against the back of her neck. He could smell her dark hair. The moment of rest at the end of the pendulum's swing, before it fell back and swung again. They would have time. Later. Or they would not.

The mudjhik lay pinned under a hundred thousand gallons a second. On its back. It pounded the concrete floor beneath it, the floor built to take the brunt of the Mir in flood, pounded it with its fists and heels and head. The mudjhik would never sleep. Never die. No matter how long, no matter what it took. It would pound its way out.

Somewhere, deep inside the angel-stuff, what remained of Safran wanted to scream but had no voice. Wanted to weep but had no tears. No mouth. No eyes.

They overslept. Lom surfaced eventually to the sound of Maroussia making tea. She had drawn back the curtains and filled the cabin with grey dawn light. Lom stumbled out of bed and found the Gate Master's shaving kit – a chipped bowl for water, soap, a razor and a small square of mirror – all set out neatly ready for use. He washed and shaved for the first time in … how long? He had lost count of the days. The mirror showed him the hole in the centre of his forehead with its crust of blood. He washed it clean and watched it pulsing faintly with the beating of his heart. He touched it with his finger. The new, healing skin felt smooth and young. The pulse inside it was a barely palpable fluttering.

'Here.'

Maroussia nudged him gently and handed him a mug of strong, sweet tea. She had found sugar. As he sipped it, she kissed him, once, quickly, on his freshly shaven cheek. He caught once more the scent of her hair and felt the cool bright touch of her mouth fading slowly from his skin.

With the Gate Master's razor he cut a strip of cloth from the bottom of his shirt, knotted it bandanna-fashion round his head to hide the wound of the angel mark, and checked the result in the mirror. The effect was odd but not unpleasing. Gangsterish. Buccaneering. Conspicuous, but not as instantly-identifying as a hole in the head. After a moment's hesitation, he folded the Gate Master's razor, slipped it into his pocket and turned to find Maroussia appraising him.

'You'll do,' she said. 'I've seen worse.'

'And you look … fine,' said Lom. She had washed her hair. It was damp and lustrous. Her cheeks were pink. 'But you're going to freeze out there.'

'I'm too hungry to notice.'

'We'll find a café,' he said. 'When we get back. We'll have breakfast.' Coffee. Eggs. Pastries. That would be normal. That would be simple and good. Then a thought struck him. 'Have you got any money?' He had none. Nothing but a razor and an empty gun.

Maroussia dug in her pockets and came up with a few coins. Enough for tram fares to the city, perhaps. Not much more.

'I wanted to leave something,' she said. 'For the Gate Master.'

'We'll send it to him,' said Lom. 'Afterwards.'

They stood for a moment in the middle of the neat cabin. They had set things as straight as they could, and Lom had made a temporary repair to the lock. It would hold.

'We'd better go,' said Maroussia.

'Yes.'

TRUTH AND FEAR

The salt stars melt in the barrel –
The ice-water turns coal-black –
Death is getting purer, hard times saltier,
The planet edging closer to truth and to fear

OSIP MANDELSTAM (1891–1938)

Part One

Part One

1

In the debatable borderland between night and day, the city of Mirgorod softens. A greyness that is not yet dawn settles on rooftops and gathers in wide empty avenues and squares. Yellow lamp-lit windows grow bleak and drab. Things move in the city, but surreptitiously, in the margins, with a muted, echoless quietness of speech. Mud-footed night-shapes pad away down alleys. A boatman winces at the raw gunning of his barge engine. A waiter eases the iron shutters of the Restaurant Hotel Aikhenvald carefully open so they will not clatter.

Low on the city's eastern horizon, a gap opens in the growing milky bruise of morning and a surprising sliver of sun, a solar squint, spills watery light. The River Mir that has flowed black through the night kindles suddenly to a wide and wind-scuffed green. An exhalation of water vapour, too thin to be called a mist, rises off the surface. The breath of the river quickens and stirs, and on its island between the Mir and the Yekaterina Canal, moored against the embankment of the Square of the Piteous Angel, the Lodka condenses out of the subsiding night, blacker and blacker against the green-tinged yellowing sky. Its cliff-dark walls seem to belly outwards like the sides of a momentous swollen vessel. The jumbled geometry of its roofscape is forested with a hundred flagpoles, and from every pole a red flag edged with black hangs at half mast, draped and inert. Banners hang limply from parapets and window ledges: repetitious, identical fabrics of blood and black, the officious, unwavering, requiring stare of collective mourning.

Within the walls of the Lodka, the unending work of the Vlast goes on. Its skeleton crew, the three thousand watchkeepers of the night – civil servants, diplomats, secret police – are completing their reports and tidying their desks. First light is falling grey through the grimed glass dome onto the still-empty galleries of the Central Registry, where the great wheel of the Gaukh Engine stands motionless but expectant. On hundreds of yards of unlit shelving, the incoming files – the accusations and denunciations, the surveillance records, the intercepted communications – await the archivists of the new day. The stone slabs of the execution yards are being scrubbed and scoured with ammonia, and in the basement mortuary the new arrivals' slabbed cadavers seep and chill.

In the Square of the Piteous Angel the morning light loses its first bright softness and grows complacent, ordinary and cold. Along the embankment the whale-oil tapers, burning in pearl globes in the mouths of cast-iron leaping fish, are bleached almost invisible, though their subtle reek still fumes the dampness of the air. The iron fish have heavy heads and bulging eyes and scales thick-edged like fifty-kopek coins. Their lamps are overdue for dousing. The gulls have risen from their night-roosts: they wheel low in silence and turn west for the shore.

And on the edge of the widening clarity of the square's early emptiness, the observer of the coming day stands alone, in the form of a man, tall and narrow-shouldered in a dark woollen suit and grey astrakhan hat. His name is Antoninu Florian. He takes from his pocket a pair of wire-framed spectacles, polishes with the end of his silk burgundy scarf the circular pieces of glass that are not lenses, and puts them on.

It is more than two hundred years since Antoninu Florian first watched a morning open across Mirgorod. Half as old as the city, he sees it for what it is. Its foundations are shallow. Through the soles of his shoes on the cobbles he feels the slow seep and settle of ancient mud, the deep residuum of the city-crusted delta of old Mir: the estuarial mud on which the Lodka is beached.

The river's breath touches Florian's face, intimate and sharing. Cold moisture-nets gather around him: a sifting connectedness; gentle, subtle water-synapses alert with soft intelligence. Crowding presences move across the empty square and tall buildings not yet there cluster against the skyline. The translucence of a half-mile tower that is merely the plinth for the behemoth statue of a man. Antoninu Florian has seen these things before. He knows they are possible. He has returned to the city and found them waiting still.

But today is a different day. Florian tastes it on the breath of the river. It is the day he has come back for. The long equilibrium is shifting: flimsy tissue-layers are peeling away, the might-be making way for the true and the is. And in Florian's hot belly there is a feeling of continuous inward empty falling, a slow stumble that never hits the floor: he recognises it as quiet, uneasy fear. The breath of the river brings him the scent of new things coming. It tugs at him. Urges him. Come, it says, come. Follow. The woman who matters is coming today.

Florian hesitates. What he fears is decision. Choices are approaching and he is unsure. He does not know what to do. Not yet.

The curiosity of a man's gaze rakes the side of his face. A gendarme is watching him from the bridge on the other side of the square. Florian feels the involuntary needle-sharpening of teeth inside his mouth, the responsive ache of his jaw to lengthen, the muscles of neck and throat to bunch and bulk. His human form feels suddenly awkward, inadequate, a hobbling constraint. But he forces it back into place and turns, hands in pockets, narrow shoulders hunched against the cold he does not feel, walking away down Founder's Prospect.

The gendarme does not follow.

2

I n her office high in the Lodka, on the other side of the Square of the Piteous Angel, Commander Lavrentina Chazia, chief of the Mirgorod Secret Police, put down her pen and closed the file.

'We are living in great days, Teslom,' she said. 'Critical times. History is taking shape. The future is being made, here and now, in Mirgorod. Do you feel this? Do you taste it in the air, as I do?'

The man across the desk from her said nothing. His head was slumped forward, his chin on his chest. He was breathing in shallow ragged breaths. His wrists were bound to the arms of his chair with leather straps. His legs, broken at the knees, were tied by the ankles. His dark blue suit jacket was unbuttoned, his soft white shirt open at the neck: blood had flowed from his nose, soaking the front of it. He was a small, neat man with rimless circular glasses and a flop of rich brown hair, glossy when he was taken, but matted now with sweat and drying blood. Not a physical man. Unused to enduring pain. Unused to endurance of any kind.

'Of course you feel it too,' Chazia continued. 'You're a learned fellow. You read. You watch. You study. You understand. The Novozhd is dead. Our beloved leader cruelly blown apart by an anarchist's bomb. I was there, Teslom. I saw it. It was a terrible shock. We are all stricken with grief.'

The man in the chair groaned quietly. He raised his head to look at her. His eyes behind their lenses were wide and glassy.

'I've told you,' he said. 'A hundred times ... a thousand ... I know nothing of this. Nothing. I ... I am ... a librarian. An archivist. I keep books. I am the curator of Lezarye. Only that. Nothing more.'

318

'Of course. Of course. But the fact remains. The Novozhd is dead. So now there is a question.'

The man did not reply. He was staring desperately at the heavy black telephone on the desk, as if its sudden bell could ring salvation for him. Let him stare. Commander Chazia stood up and crossed to the window. Mirgorod spread away below her towards the horizon under the grey morning sky. The recent floods were subsiding, barges moving again on the river.

There had been rumours that when the recent storms were at their height sentient beasts made of rain had been seen in the city streets. Dogs and wolves of rain. Rain bears, walking. Militia patrols had been attacked. Gendarmes ripped to a bloody mess, their throats torn out by hard teeth of rain. And rusalkas had risen from the flooded canals and rivers. Lipless mouths, broad muscular backs and chalk-white flesh. With expressionless faces they reached up and pulled men down to drown in the muddied waters. The rumours were probably true. Chazia had made sure that the witnesses and the story-spreaders were quietly shot in the basement cells of the Lodka. It was good that people were afraid, so long as they feared her more.

She had left Teslom long enough. She turned from the window and walked round behind his chair. Rested her hand on his shoulder. Felt his muscles quiver at her gentle touch.

'Who will rule, Teslom? Who will have power? Who will govern now that the Novozhd is dead? That's the question here. And you can help me with that.'

'Please ...' said Teslom. His voice was almost too quiet to hear. 'Please—'

'I just need your help, darling. Just a little. Then you can rest.'

'I ...' He raised his head and tried to turn towards her. 'I ... I can't ...'

Chazia leaned closer to hear him.

'Let's go over it again. Tell me,' she said. 'Tell me about the Pollandore.'

'The Pollandore ... ? A story. Only a story. Not a real thing ... not something that exists ... I've told you—'

'This is a feeble game, Teslom. I'm not looking for it. It isn't lost. It's here. It's in this building. I have it.'

He jerked his head round. Stared at her.

'Do you want to see it?' said Chazia. 'It would interest you. OK, let's do that, shall we? Maybe later. When we can be friends again. But first—'

'If you already have it, then …'

'The future is coming, Teslom. But who will shape it? Tell me about the Pollandore.'

'I will tell you *nothing*. You … you and all your … you … you can all *fuck off*.'

Chazia unbuttoned her uniform tunic, took it off and hung it on the back of Teslom's chair. He was staring at the telephone again.

'Do you know me, Teslom?' she said gently.

'What?'

'I think you do not. Not yet.'

She rolled the sleeves of her shirt above the elbow. The smooth dark stone-like patches on her hands were growing larger. Spreading up her arms. The skin at the edges was puckered, red and sore and angry. The itching was with her always.

'Let's come at this from a different direction,' she said. 'A visitor came to the House on the Purfas. An emissary from the eastern forest. A thing that was not human. An organic artefact of communication. You're surprised that I know this? You shouldn't be. Your staff were regular and thorough in their reports. But I'm curious. Tell me about this visitor.'

She was stroking him now. Standing behind him, she smoothed his matted brown hair. He jerked his head away.

'No,' he said hoarsely. 'I choose death. I choose to die.'

'That's nothing, Teslom.' She bent her head down close to his. She could smell the sourness of his fear. 'Everyone dies,' she breathed in his ear. 'Just not you. Not yet.'

As she spoke she slid her stone-stained hand across his shoulder and down the side of his neck inside his bloodied shirt, feeling his smooth skin, his sternum, the start of his ribs. She felt the beating of his heart and rested her hand there. Closing her eyes and feeling with her mind for the place. She had done this before, but it was not easy. It needed concentration. She let her fingers rest a moment on the gap in his ribs over his heart. Teslom was still. Scarcely breathing. He could not have moved if he wanted to: with her other hand she was pressing against his back, using the angel-flesh in her fingers to probe his spinal cord, immobilising him.

She had found the place above his heart. She dug the tips of her fingers into the rib-gap, opening a way. It needed technique more than strength, the angel-substance in her hand did the work. Teslom's quiet moan of horror was distracting, but she did it right. She reached inside and cupped his beating heart in her palm. And squeezed.

His eyes widened in panic. He could see her hand deep in his chest. He could see there was no blood. No wound. It was not possible. But it was in there.

'Are you listening to me, Teslom?'

He was weak. Cold sweat on the dull white skin of his face, livid blotches over his cheekbones. Chazia released the pressure a little. Let his heart beat again.

'Are you listening to me?'

He shifted his head almost imperceptibly to the left. An attempt at a nod.

'Good. So. This strange living artefact, this marvellous emissary from the forest. Why did it come? What did it want? Did it concern the Pollandore?'

'It ... I can't ...'

Chazia adjusted her grip on his heart.

'There,' she said. 'Is that better? Can you talk now?'

'Yes. Yes. Oh please. Get it out. Get it out. Stop.'

'So tell me.'

'What?'

'The messenger. From the forest.'

'It ... addressed the Inner Committee.'

'And what did it say?'

'It said ... it said there was an angel.'

'An angel?'

'A *living* angel. It had fallen in the forest and it was trapped there. It was foul and doing great damage. Oh. Please. Don't ...'

Chazia waited. *Give him time. Let him speak. Patience.* But his head had sunk down again and there was a congested bubbling in his chest. Perhaps she had been too harsh. Overestimated his strength. The silence lengthened. She lessened the pressure on his heart but kept her hand in place. It was the horror of seeing it in there, as much as anything, that made them speak.

'Teslom?' she said at last. 'Tell me more. The forest is afraid of this living angel? Afraid it will do terrible things?'

'Yes.'

'And so? This emissary. Why did the forest send it? Was it the Pollandore?'

'Of course. Yes. Open the Pollandore, it said. Now. Now is the time. Before it's too late.'

'Too late? For what?'

'The Pollandore is breaking. It is failing, or leaking, or waking, or ... something. I don't know. I didn't understand. It wasn't clear ... I can't ... I need to stop now ... rest ... please ... for fuck's sake ...'

He coughed sour-smelling fluid out of his mouth. Viscous spittle stained with flecks of red and pink. It spilled on her forearm. It was warm.

'You're doing fine, Teslom. Good. Very good. Soon it will be over. Just a few more questions. Then you can rest.'

He struggled for breath, trying to bring his hands up to push her off. But his hands were strapped to the chair.

Chazia sensed his strength giving out. He was on the edge of death. She tried to hold him there, but she didn't have complete control. There was a margin of uncertainty. But they had come to the crisis. The brink of gold. Crouching down beside him, she rested her head on his shoulder, her cheek against his.

'Just tell me, darling,' she said quietly. '*How* was the Pollandore to be opened?'

'There was a key.' He was barely whispering. 'The paluba – the messenger – it brought a key.'

'What kind of key?'

'I don't know. I didn't see it. I wasn't there. I heard. Only heard. Not a key. Not exactly. Not like an iron thing for a lock. But a thing that opens. A recognition thing. An identifier. I don't know. The paluba offered it to the Inner Committee. Oh shit. Stop. Please.'

'And what did the Inner Committee do?'

'*Nothing.*'

'Nothing?'

'They refused the message. They were afraid. What *could* they do? They didn't *have* the Pollandore. They lost it. The useless fuckers lost it long ago. Please—'

'So?'

'So they sent it away. The paluba. They sent it away.'

'What happened then? What did the paluba do? Where did it go? What happened to the *key*?'

He closed his eyes. His head sank forward again. She was losing him.

'Your daughter, Teslom. You have a daughter. You should think of her.'

'What?'

'She is pregnant.'

'No ... not her ... Leave her alone!'

'If you fail me now, I will reach inside your daughter's belly for her feeble little unborn child – it's a girl, Teslom, a girl, she doesn't know this but I do – and I will take its skull between my fingers ... like this ...' She paused. 'Are you listening to me?'

'Yes.'

'Do you know that I will do this? Do you know that I will?'

She squeezed his heart again, gently. He screamed.

'It's all right, darling,' she whispered in his ear. 'Nearly finished now. Think of your daughter, Teslom. Think of her *child*.'

'Oh no,' he gasped. 'Oh no. No.'

'Where is the key to the Pollandore? Tell me how to find it.'

'I don't *know*!'

'Then who? Who knows?'

'The woman,' said Teslom, so quiet Chazia could hardly hear. 'The woman,' he said again. 'Shaumian.'

'What? Say it again, darling. Say the name again.'

'Shaumian. The key. It would go to the Shaumian woman next. If not the Committee ... then Shaumian. *Shaumian!*'

Chazia felt her own heart beat with excitement. *Shaumian*. She knew the name. And it led to another question. The most important question of all.

'Teslom?'

'No more. Please. I can't—'

'Just one more thing, sweetness, and then you can have some peace. There are two Shaumian women. Was it the mother? Or the daughter? Which one was it, darling? Which one?'

'I don't know. It doesn't matter. Either. What's the difference? It makes no difference. It doesn't—'

'Yes, it matters. The mother is dead. The mother dead, the daughter not. That's the difference, darling. Mother or daughter?'

Teslom choked and struggled for breath. He was mouthing silence like a fish drowning in air. Chazia waited. Everything depended on what he said next.

'Mother or daughter?' whispered Chazia gently. 'Mother or daughter, darling?'

'Daughter then.' His voice was almost too quiet to hear. 'Daughter. The key would be for the daughter.'

'Maroussia Shaumian? Be sure now. Tell me again.'

'*Yes!* For fuck's sake. I'm telling you. That's the name. Shaumian. *Shaumian! Maroussia Shaumian!*'

He was screaming. Chazia felt his heart clenching and twitching in her hand. Shoving the blood hard round his body. He was working his lungs fast and deep. Too fast. Too deep.

It didn't matter. Not any more. She squeezed.

When she had killed him, she withdrew her hand from his chest, wiped it carefully on a clean part of his shirt and went back round to her side of the desk. Turned the knob on the intercom box. Pulled the microphone towards her mouth.

'Iliodor?'

'Yes, Commander.' The voice crackled in the small speaker.

'There is a mess in my office. Have it cleared away. And I need you to find someone for me. A woman. Shaumian. Maroussia Shaumian. There is a file. Find her for me now, Iliodor. Find her today and bring her to me.'

3

Vissarion Lom and Maroussia Shaumian took the first tram of the day into Mirgorod from Cold Amber Strand. Marinsky Line. Cars 1639, 1640 and 1641, liveried in brown and gold, a thick black letter M front and back on each one. Four steep clattering steps to climb inside. Slatted wooden benches. *Standard class, single journey, no luggage: 5 kopeks.* There were few other passengers: in summer holidaymakers came to Cold Amber Strand for the bathing huts, the pleasure gardens, the bandstand, the aquarium, but now winter was closing in. Signs above the seats warned them: CITIZEN, YOU ARE IN PUBLIC NOW! BEWARE OF BOMBS! WHOM ARE YOU WITH?

They went to the back of the car and Lom took a seat opposite Maroussia, facing forward to watch the door. He kept his hand in the pocket of his coat, holding the revolver loosely. A double-action Sepora .44 magnum. It was empty. But that was OK. That was better than nothing.

The tram hummed and rattled and accelerated slowly away from the stop. Maroussia huddled into the corner and stared out of the window, eyes wide and dark. Flimsy shoes. Bare legs, pale and cold.

'The Pollandore is in Mirgorod,' said Maroussia. 'It must be. Vishnik knew where it was – he found it, and he was looking in the city. So it's in the city. That's where it is.' She frowned and looked away. 'Only I don't know where.'

'We'll start at Vishnik's apartment,' said Lom. 'He had papers. Photographs. Notes. We'll go and look. After we've eaten. First we need to find some food. Breakfast.'

'I left my bag at Vishnik's,' said Maroussia. 'I've got clothes in it. Clothes and money and things. Maybe the bag's still there.'

'Maybe,' said Lom.

'I can't go back to my room,' said Maroussia.

'No.'

'They'll be waiting. Watching. The militia ...'

'Possibly,' said Lom. 'Don't worry. We'll be fine—'

Lom broke off. A woman with two children got on the tram and took the seat behind Maroussia. Maroussia withdrew further into the corner and closed her eyes. She looked tired.

The city opened to take them back. A fine rain greyed the emptiness between buildings. It rested in the air, softening it, parting to let the tramcars pass and closing behind them. The streets of Mirgorod were recovering from the flood. River mud streaked the pavements and pools of water reflected the low grey sky. Businesses were closed and shuttered, or gaped, water-ransacked and abandoned. People picked their way across plank-and-trestle walkways between piles of ruined furniture stacked in the road. Sodden mattresses, rugs, couches, wardrobes, books. A barge, lifted almost completely out of the canal and left beached by the flood, jutted its prow out into the road. A giant in a rain-slicked leather jacket was shouldering it off the buckled railings and trying to slide it back into the water. Gendarmes and militia patrols stood on street corners, checking papers, watching the clearing-up. They seemed to be everywhere. More than usual.

Lom leaned forward and slid open a gap in the window, letting the cold city air pumice his face. He inhaled deeply: the taste of coal-smoke, benzine, misting rain and sea salt was in his mouth – the taste of Mirgorod.

Maroussia's shoulder was raised protectively, half-turned against him. Her face was almost a stranger's face, at rest and unfamiliar in sleep. She *was* almost a stranger to him. He knew almost nothing about her, nothing ordinary at all, but he knew the most important thing. She had set her will against the inevitability of the world. The Vlast had come for her, for no reason that she knew – not that the Vlast needed reasons – but Maroussia hadn't gone slack, as so many did, numbed by the immensity and inertia of their fate. She had seized on the vague and broken hints of the messenger that came from nowhere – from the endless, uninterpretable forest – and she had turned them into the engine of her own private counter-attack against ... against what? Against unchangeability, against the cruelty of things.

But the energy of her counter-attack was Maroussia's own. It came from dark inward places. She was alone, unsanctioned, uninstructed. Lom couldn't have said with certainty what she thought she was going to achieve, or how, and it seemed not really possible, in the cold grey light of the morning return to the city, that she could do anything at all: Mirgorod was the foremost city of the continental hegemony of the Vlast, four hundred years of consolidated history, and they were two alone, without a map of the future, without a plan. But what struck him was how irrelevant the impossibility of her purpose was. It was its asymmetric absurdity that gave it meaning and shape. The undercurrent of almost unnoticed fear that he was feeling now was fear for her. He had none for himself. He had never felt more alive. He was relaxed and open and strong. He would do what he could when whatever was coming came; he would stand with her side by side. Her mouth was slightly open in sleep, and she was doing the bravest, loneliest thing that Lom had ever seen done.

The healing wound in the front of his skull pulsed almost imperceptibly under fine new skin with the beating of his heart. He pulled off the white scrap of cloth he'd tied round his forehead. It was unnecessary and conspicuous. As he stuffed it into his pocket, he felt the touch of something else: a quiet stirring under his fingers. He brought the thing out and cupped it in his palm. A small linen bag stained with dried blood. He'd forgotten he had it. He opened it and took out the strange small knotted ball of twigs and wax, tiny bones and dried berries. Brought it up to his face and breathed its earthy, resinous air. A woodland taint. He slipped the small thing back into its bag. It was a survivor.

The tram got more crowded as they approached the city centre: squat, frowning women with empty string bags; workers going to work, each absorbed in their own silence. More than half the passengers were wearing black armbands. Lom wondered why. It was odd. Looking out of the window, he saw checkpoints at the major intersections. Traffic was backed up in the streets and people were lining up along the pavement to show their papers. The pale brick-coloured uniforms of the VKBD were out in force. Mirgorod, police city. Something was happening.

'Pardon me please. May I?'

A man with thinning hair and a crumpled striped suit slid onto the seat next to Maroussia. He rested a cloth attaché case on his knees, opened it and took out a paper bag. Nodding apologetically at Lom, he started to eat a piece of sausage.

'Sorry,' the man said. 'Running late. Crowds everywhere. I've had my cards looked at twice already. The funeral, I guess. Back to normal tomorrow.'

Lom gave him a *What can you do?* shrug and went back to watching through the window. The sausage smelled strongly of garlic and paprika.

Fifteen minutes later the tram pulled up at the terminus and the engine cut out. People started to stand up and shuffle down the aisle. The man sitting opposite Lom put his empty sausage bag into his attaché case and clicked it shut. He glanced out of the window and swore under his breath.

'Not again,' he said. 'I'm going to be late. Damn, I don't need this, not today.' He got up with a sigh and joined the back of the line.

Lom stayed where he was and took a look out of the window to see what the problem was. There were four gendarmes on the platform. Two were stopping the passengers as they got off – looking at identity cards, comparing photographs to faces – while the other two stood back, watchful, hands on their holsters. One of the watchers was a corporal. The checkpoint was set up right. The men were awake and alert and doing it properly. The corporal knew his stuff.

Lom had to do something. He needed to *think*.

Maroussia stirred and woke. Her cheeks were flushed and her hair was damp. Stray curls stood out from the side of her head where it had pressed against the window. She looked around, confused.

'Where are we?' she said.

Lom began buttoning his cloak. Taking his time, but making it look natural. Not like he was avoiding joining the queue.

'End of the line,' he said quietly. 'Marinsky-Voksal. But there's trouble.'

Maroussia turned to see, and took in at a glance what was happening. She bent forward to adjust her shoe.

'Are they looking for us?' she whispered.

'Not necessarily. But possibly. Can't discount it. I've got no papers. Have you?'

'No.'

'OK,' said Lom. 'We'll separate. I'll go first. Give them something to think about. You slip away while I've got them occupied.' Maroussia started to protest, but Lom had already stood up and joined the end of the resigned shuffling queue.

He was getting near the exit. There were only two or three passengers ahead of him, waiting with studied outward patience, documents ready in hand. One of the gendarmes was examining identity cards while the other peered over his shoulder into the tram, scrutinising the line. Lom saw his eyes slide across the faces, pass on, hesitate, and come to rest on Maroussia with a flicker of interest. He checked against a photograph in his hand and looked at her again, a longer, searching look. He took a step forward.

Shit, thought Lom. *I can't let us be taken. Not like this. That would be stupid.* His fingers in his pocket closed on the grip of the empty Sepora .44.

He felt an elbow in his ribs.

'Excuse me, please!'

It was Maroussia, pushing past him and heading for the gendarme.

'Excuse me!' she said again in a loud voice.

'What are you *doing*?' hissed Lom, putting his hand on her arm.

'Making time,' she said. 'Not getting us killed.'

She pulled her arm free, pushed past the waiting passengers and spoke to the gendarme.

'You must help me, please,' she said firmly. 'Take me to the nearest police station. At once. My name is Maroussia Shaumian. I am a citizen of this city. A militia officer murdered my mother. He also tried to kill me. I want protection and I want to make a statement. I want to make a complaint.'

The gendarme stared at her in surprise.

'You what?'

'You heard me,' said Maroussia. 'I want to make a complaint. What is your name? Tell me please.'

Lom stepped up beside her.

'Stand aside, man,' he said to the gendarme. Peremptory. Authoritative. 'I'm in a hurry. This woman is in my custody.'

The gendarme took in his heavy loden coat, mud-stained at the bottom. The healing wound in his forehead.

'And who the fuck are you?' he said.

'Political Police,' said Lom.

'You don't look like police. Let's see your ID.'

'I am a senior investigator in the third department of the Political Police,' said Lom. 'On special attachment to the Minister's Office.'

'You got papers to prove that?'

'Vlasik,' said the corporal, 'this is a waste of time. Bring them both.'

4

In the pre-dawn twilight two thousand miles north and east of Mirgorod, Professor Yakov Khyrbysk stepped over the coaming and out into lamplit fog on the deck of Vlast Fisheries Vessel *Chaika*. Sub-zero air scraped at the inside of his nose and throat. Despite the two sweaters under his oilskin slicker the freezing cold wrapped iron bands round his ribcage and squeezed. He dug out his petrol lighter and a packet of Chernomors, cupped his hands to light one and inhaled the raw smoke deeply.

The *Chaika* stank of diesel and fish. During the night sea spray had frozen in glassy sheets on every surface. Ice sheathed nets and hawsers and hung like cave growths from cleats, winches and davits. Crewmen, working under lamps, waist-deep in thunderous clouds of steam, were hosing the ice off the deck with hot water from the boilers. The men wore mountainous parkas and wrapped scarves across their mouths to keep from inhaling the foul spray. They sent gleaming slicks of slime, fish guts and oil sluicing across the planks and out through the bilge holes. *Citizen Trawlermen, you are frontline workers! By feeding the people you strengthen the Vlast! Strive for a decisive upsurge in the production of fish protein!*

The *Chaika* heaved and dipped, her hull moaning with the low surge of her engine. Khyrbysk threaded his way across the treacherous deck and climbed the companionway. Captain Baburin was waiting up on the platform outside the wheelhouse.

'There is low pressure coming in, Yakov Arkadyevich,' said Baburin. 'Then it will be cold enough for you, I think.' In the yellow light from the wheelhouse his heavy black beard and the folds of his greatcoat and cap glittered with frost.

'Is she there?' said Khyrbysk. 'Can you see her yet?'

Baburin shrugged towards the starboard bow.

'She's there,' he said. 'Exactly where she should be. We'll come up with her soon enough.'

Khyrbysk peered in the same direction. Fog and black water were emerging out of the night. The glimmer of scattered pieces of ice.

'I can't see anything,' he said.

'She is coming,' said Baburin.

Khyrbysk waited, leaning on the rail, smoking and watching the grey dawn seep out of the fog and the sea. The day came up empty and sunless. Fog blanked out distance and brought the horizon near. Coal-black swells rose, marbled with foam, and surged forward, shouldering the *Chaika*'s prow upwards. She heaved and dipped. Rafts of sea-ice scraped against her hull. Every so often she hit a larger piece and shuddered. This was the grey zone: the crew of the *Chaika* might see the sun once or twice in three months. If they were lucky. Khyrbysk felt an involuntary surge of excitement. Was he himself not the igniter of a *thousand* suns?

'There!' shouted Baburin from the wheelhouse, pointing. Khyrbysk could just about make out a wedge of darker grey in the fog, a triangle embedded in black water. The triangle loomed larger and resolved itself into a head-on view of the factory ship *Musk Ox* steaming towards them, twin stacks brimming dark heavy smoke. The blunted prow and swollen skirts of an icebreaker.

Ten minutes, and Baburin had swung the *Chaika* right in under the lee of the factory ship. The *Musk Ox*'s huge hull towered overhead, a sheer and salt-scoured cliff of bleeding rust, battered and dented from twenty years of unloading trawlers in bad weather. Khyrbysk stared down into the narrow channel between the two vessels. The water was so cold it had a thick, sluggish sheen, laced with soft congealing slush-ice. A shout from above told him the *Musk Ox*'s side crane was ready.

The transport cage was descending, swinging gently from its cable, four tyres fixed to the underside to soften the landing. In the cage, Kolya Blegvad rested one gloved hand on the rectangular wooden crate that stood on its end beside him, taller than he was, and with the other he kept a tight grip on the cable chain. A crewman on the *Chaika* leaned out with a gaff to guide the cage in.

Khyrbysk went to find Zakopan, the *Chaika*'s mate.

'I want the box in my cabin,' he told him. 'And quickly. The machinery is delicate. It will not tolerate the cold on the deck.'

In Khyrbysk's overheated cabin, the crate took up all the space between his bunk and the pale green bulkhead. Khyrbysk locked the door, drew the curtain across the porthole and lit the oil lamp. From the same match he lit another Chernomor. Kolya Blegvad watched him with clever soft brown eyes.

'You came to meet me, Yakov,' he said. 'I am touched.'

'Were there any difficulties?' said Khyrbysk.

'With transit papers signed by Dukhonin himself? No. How could there be? Our friend in Mirgorod was as good as his word.'

'I want to see it,' said Khyrbysk. He produced a crowbar.

'Now?'

'Now,' said Khyrbysk. 'Yes. Now.'

He prised off the lid. Inside the crate was thirty million roubles in used notes of miscellaneous denomination.

5

In Levrovskaya Square the gendarmes drew their revolvers and moved towards Lom and Maroussia. Lom considered the position. All the angles. Staying calm, staying relaxed. *Assess and evaluate. Think and plan.* Like he'd been trained to do. It took him a second. Maybe a second and a half.

The misting rain softened edges and blurred distances. He felt in his face and across his shoulders the weight of massive slabs of high cold air sliding in off the sea. The temperature was dropping. Freezing cold snagged at the back of his throat and in his nose. His visible breath flickered. Tiny vanishing ghosts. Stone slabs slick and slippery underfoot. The Marinsky-Voksal Terminus was a double row of tram stops, low raised platforms under wrought-iron canopies. Tramcars were pulled up at three of them, including the one they'd arrived at, and waiting passengers crowded at the other three. Beyond the terminus, Marinsky Square was a grumbling tangle of traffic, street sellers and pedestrians.

Lom wasn't too worried about the four gendarmes pressed in close around them. Gendarmes, with their uniforms of thick green serge, their shiny peaked caps, polished leather belts and buttoned-down holsters, were street police: efficient enough at traffic and checkpoints and petty crime, but not used to serious trouble. They carried 7.62mm Vagants: heavy service revolvers, the seven-cartridge cylinder unconverted single-action version. Lom had carried a Vagant himself for three years and he'd never liked it: loud and clumsy, with a wild kick, a Vagant made a nasty mess at close range, but it was hopelessly inaccurate over more than ten yards.

These four weren't the problem. The problem was the other four–

man patrols at the other five tram halts and the VKBD truck pulled up at the kerb twenty yards away, two men in the cab and an unknown number in the back. Shit. They shouldn't have stayed on the tram till the end of the line. They should have got off at some suburban stop and walked in. He'd made a mistake. The only thing now was to get out of Marinsky Square as quickly as possible with the minimum number of police in tow. Maroussia had seen that quicker than he had. Second mistake of the day. *Wake up. This is serious.*

Maroussia was standing silent, upright and fierce, waiting while the gendarmes briefly debated their next move. The one who'd spotted them wanted to take them across to the VKBD truck, but the corporal vetoed it.

'I'm calling it in myself. We'll get no thanks from Vryushin if the VKBD gets credit for this. Take them across to the section office. Quickly, no fuss, before anyone notices what's going on. Move. Now.'

They split into pairs, two walking ahead with Maroussia between them, the corporal and the other one following with Lom. They didn't wait to search him. Traffic cops.

But the corporal stayed ten feet behind him with his Vagant aimed at the small of Lom's back. It was efficient enough. Lom might have got away, perhaps, but he couldn't see a way to take Maroussia with him, so for the moment he rode with it. Things could have been worse. Perhaps.

Something else nagged at him. He couldn't shake a small insistent pressure at the back of his neck. The familiar feeling that he was being watched.

Two floors above the street on the other side of Marinsky Square, Antoninu Florian crouched on the sill of a bricked-up window, enfolded by scarves of rain-mist drifting down off the roof slates. He licked the living moisture from his upper lip and savoured it on his tongue, sharing with it the city, the engine fumes and sweat and the dark strong silt-green surge of the living River Mir. The mist tasted of fires not yet burning and blood not yet spilled, traces of the passing touch of the living angel in the forest. But there was also the bright sharp resinous hint of something good, scents of earth and green currents stirring: all morning Florian had been following the trail of it, and now with yellow-flecked eyes he watched the woman who mattered walking between policemen. And he watched the man who was with her. He gripped them with the teeth of his gaze, sifting their particular scents out of the city tumult.

The man who was with the woman was spilling bright shining communication, all unawares. Florian could have found him a mile away in a dark forest at night in a thunderstorm, and the man did not even know it. Though he did have some vague sense of Florian's presence: Florian watched him hesitate and look around. But the man did not look up. Nor did the police look up. They never looked up. Not until they learned. If they ever did.

Experimentally, Florian shifted and adjusted the bone structure of his face. Slid musculature into new places under warm sleeves of flesh. His hair moved like leaves under water. He tested thickness and shade, melatonin and refraction. It was enough. He was confident. When the woman and the man and the four policemen had passed beneath him, Florian leaped down from the second-floor ledge, landing lightly on all fours on rain-skinned cobbles, rose up and followed.

6

*T*housands of miles east of Mirgorod, deep in the endless forest, the immense, mountainous body of Archangel rises against the skyline like a storm cloud approaching. His consciousness bleeds into the surrounding country, not life but anti-life, oozing out through the forest like lichen across rock. Like piss in snow. In the lower skirts of his body, dead-alive giants of ice and stone with eroded faces lumber waist-high through crumbling stone trees.

A wonderful thing is happening to Archangel. He is beginning to recover.

He has wormed and rooted tendrils of himself down through the planetary crust and deep into the hot seething places. He has spread vapours of himself thinly on the upper layers of the atmosphere, sifting solar radiation. And now, at last, slowly, slowly, the clouds of forgetfulness grow thin and dissipate in the growing heat of his renewed interior sun.

Far down inside the painful solid rock of himself, Archangel feels gobbets of mass spark into energy. Tiny bright cold shards of pure elation spark and shatter. Crushed clods of light stretch and breathe. Fragments of dead processes, imploded and squeezed to appalling density by his flight and fall, are unpacking themselves and restarting. Raw spontaneous networks unfurl and new possibilities trickle across them, glittering into self-awareness. Archangel, ancient as all the stars, old and hurt, wrapped in scraps of memory and stunted relics of ambition, is growing young again.

He makes an inventory of his inward terrain. Scraps of brightness in a dark country. He hadn't realised how much of himself he had lost and forgotten. How far gone dead he'd been. Even now the greater part of him remains useless. Eclipsed. Obscure. Inert. And much that was lost will never return, not while he remains trapped here on this small dark planet.

He cannot escape. He hasn't the strength for that, not yet. But he can, at last – at last! – begin to move.

With a roar of agony and joy, thunderous and tree-shattering, Archangel grinds and slides forward, forcing extrusions and pseudopodia of himself out across the landscape. He is a rock amoeba, a single-cell life-form mountain-high. It hurts. With painful slowness at first, millimetre by screaming millimetre, a metre by day, a metre by night, onward he goes. The ground for miles around him trembles. The flanks of his momentous body shed fresh avalanches. He is anti-life rock mountain slowly moving, leaving in his wake a slug-trail of seething, crippled waste. As he goes he screams out in his agony and joy and desperate purpose. It is a fear voice. A true power voice. The voice of history.

And in Mirgorod Josef Kantor hears him.

7

Lom was in a cell in the local gendarme station down a side street just off Marinsky Square. It was barely a cell at all, more of a windowless cupboard: brick walls painted a pale sickly green, worn linoleum lifting from a concrete floor; it was hardly big enough for the table and two chairs. The door was plain, unpainted wood, panelled, not solid, with a standard domestic lock. There was a single caged lamp in the ceiling. They still hadn't searched him; they'd locked him in without a word; they weren't interested in him. Maroussia had been taken to another room. But somebody would come in the end. Somebody always did.

He climbed on the table, unhooked the lamp cage and smashed the bulb, plunging the room into darkness, then climbed back down, felt his way to the door and took up a position beside it, back against the wall. The darkness inside the room would give him half a second. Whoever came would hesitate. Wonder if they'd come to the wrong cell. Then caution and alarm would kick in, but not immediately. He would have half a second at least, and that would be all he needed.

He waited, but nobody came. The narrow line of brightness seeping under the door was the only light. Somewhere in the distance a door slammed shut.

He'd noticed on the way in that the station was almost deserted. Everyone who could be spared was out on the streets. He thought about that. The whole of the city centre was locked down and under surveillance. It couldn't possibly be all for him and Maroussia. Something else was happening. Something bigger. He listened for footsteps coming down the corridor but none came. A muffled telephone rang three times and broke off. That and his breathing and the quickened beating of his heart were the only sounds he could hear. He focused all his attention on the corridor on the other side of the door. Ready for the sound of the key in the lock. The handle beginning to move.

The air in the room was warm and thick and oppressively close. All interrogation rooms smelled the same: the acrid tang of disinfectant failing to mask the faint stale sweetness of vomit and urine and sweat. Lom had been in cells like this one many times before. For years, when he was an investigator of police in Podchornok, such rooms had been comfortable spaces for him. They were his working environment, a place to do what he did well: uncovering truth, extracting truth, the skilled and delicate practice of peeling back surfaces, evasions, pretences, assertions, lies.

In Podchornok Lom had considered himself a subtle, accomplished interrogator. He'd admired himself for his delicacy of touch. He didn't use the crude and brutal techniques that many of his colleagues used. He'd never done that. Well, hardly ever, and only when urgently necessary. He used to think that his tools were persistence, empathy, imagination, patience and preparation. He had a nose for the hidden core of fact and an instinct for the detours and false constructions people used to obscure it. Everybody left traces. Lom used to think he was clever. Perceptive. He'd never realised, it had simply never dawned on him, not in Podchornok, that the tool he used – the only effective tool in his box – was fear. When prisoners looked up as he stepped into the interrogation room, they never saw Lom the sympathetic, imaginative man, the disinterested investigator nosing for facts. All they saw – all there was to see, because that's all he was – was an avatar of fear. A black serge uniform, belt and boots and antler buttons polished, a sliver of angel flesh in his forehead; the cropped fair hair and frank blue eyes of a man who could, if he chose, at his own inclination, break their bodies and break their families, break their careers and break their lives. They'd sweated and felt sick while they waited for him to come, and when he did come they all wanted to piss themselves and some of them did. And he had done that to them, not by what he said or what he did – not often – but simply by being what he was: not a man with a job to do, but an expression of the Vlast in human form.

You couldn't be a man who happened to be a policeman. Not in the Vlast. You could cling, in the stories you told yourself about yourself, to the evasions, the illusions, the fictions of somebody drawing interior lines, keeping it clean: that could be how you saw yourself, but it wasn't what you *were*. What a prisoner saw when you walked into the interrogation cell, that and only that, that was what you *were*. All those dead and wasted years in Podchornok that's what he had been, Vissarion Yppolitovich Lom the unselfconscious torturer, excavating truth with fear. Vissarion Lom, one of Chazia's men.

Until Chazia herself had left him waiting in an interrogation cell. Lavrentina Chazia, who – when she'd come at last – had used that angel worm glove thing to slither around inside his mind, rummaging about, turning him inside out, pulling out half-known intimate private things. Lom flinched at the memory of having her inside his mind. It had been ... disgusting. And she had dug into his skull with a blade, prising the lozenge of angel flesh from his forehead while Josef Kantor stood behind her. Kantor had leaned in for a closer look. *Is that the brain in there?* Kantor had said, probing the bleeding, kopek-sized hole with his finger. *Firmer than I'd have thought.*

Lom was surprised to find that he felt almost no antagonism towards Josef Kantor. Kantor was cruel and murderous and charming, and no doubt in the end a more lethal enemy than Chazia was, but in some way that troubled Lom even as it half-seduced him, Kantor was – Lom struggled with the word, but it was true – Kantor, at least as Lom had seen him, was *honest*. Kantor had become completely what he had chosen to be. He was *all* of something, like an animal was all of what it was. Lom felt in some odd way a bond with Josef Kantor. Kantor was his adversary, still. For some reason that he couldn't explain to himself, Lom felt he had not laid down the task of hunting him. But he didn't hate him.

Chazia, though, Chazia was unwholesome. She was one thing on the surface and another thing inside. Lom had looked up the public details of her record once, and found nothing there except ordinariness: the ordinary successes and advancements of an assiduous career. She had risen smoothly from comfortable family beginnings to the top of her profession. The sickness and poison that Lom had smelled on her breath in that interrogation room and seen breaking out in dark patches on her skin, that came from nowhere, that was all her own. She was unfeedable hunger, unsatisfiable desire. She would draw and draw on power and pain and never be full. It was Chazia who was responsible for what he had been in Podchornok, Chazia who had wormed his mind, Chazia who had sent men for Maroussia and for him, Chazia who had sent the men who killed his friends … With Chazia, Lom felt a different sort of bond. Unfinished business of a different kind.

Don't think about this. Not now.

Outside in the street Antoninu Florian took off his astrakhan hat and combed the thin fine blond hair on his head. His overcoat was too large on the slight frame of the body shape he was using. He undid the buttons to let it hang loose so it wouldn't show. When he was ready, he strode up the steps and into the gendarme office. Closing the outer doors carefully behind him. Slipping the bolt quietly into place.

The desk clerk looked up in surprise. Recognised him. Registered a reflex of alarm. Stood straighter and tugged at his necktie.

'Captain Iliodor!' he said. 'We weren't expecting you. We weren't told—'

'No,' said Florian quietly. 'Not Iliodor. I am so sorry.'

8

L om waited in the darkness. The muffled telephone rang and stopped and rang again. Time passed. Once, he thought he heard a voice in the distance, a man's half-shout of anger or surprise, cut off by silence. How long had he been standing there, behind the door? Five minutes at least. More.

The telephone was ringing again. Incessantly now. Urgently. It jangled his nerves. *For fuck's sake somebody answer it.* He tried to measure out the time by counting the rings of the telephone but lost patience after thirty.

Nobody was coming for him. It was Maroussia they were interested in. The corporal would have made his glory phone call by now, reporting the successful capture of the fugitive. Somebody would come for her. They might take her away and leave him here. He had to get out. Now.

Lining himself up by feel, he kicked at the door, aiming for underneath the handle. It shook in its frame but didn't give. The noise was shockingly loud in the dark. Surely it would bring someone. He kicked again. And again. No progress. The geometry of the attack was all wrong: kicking the door just made him stagger back, off balance. He put down his shoulder and crashed all his weight against the wooden panel and heard something split. It sounded like it was inside the door near the hinge, but when he tested it, it was as solid as before. The pulse in the wound in his head was pounding now. The darkness surrounding him was a sour, suffocating stillness. Impending panic. He had to get *out*. Desperate, attentive senses felt the air pressing in around him like a tangible, mouldable, moveable substance. He reached out with his mind and gathered the dark air up like a fist and shoved it, threw it,

343

forward. It was like a fierce silent shout. The door burst open, tearing its hinges out of the frame and crashing to the ground.

Lom stepped back behind the gaping doorway, leaning against the wall, recovering his breath, letting his eyes adjust to the light. Now someone would come. The noise would bring them. He had to be ready. Surprise lay in not rushing out into the corridor. He counted off a whole minute. Still no one came. Halfway through the count, he realised the telephone had stopped ringing. When the minute was up he went out into the corridor and checked the other cupboard-cells one by one. None was locked. All were empty. Maroussia wasn't there.

He went up the passage into the office area. At first he thought there was nobody there, that they'd all just gone away, leaving chairs pushed back, filing drawers pulled out, lights burning, doors open, empty. Then he saw the gendarme lying on his back on the floor between two desks. It was probably the one who'd first spotted them on the tram, but it was hard to be sure, because there was a pocket of bloody mess where the man's throat used to be, and the lower half of his face was gone. Dark blood pooled on the linoleum under his head: a neat pool, almost perfectly circular, except where a chair leg had interrupted the flow. The spilling blood had separated to pass round it and come together on the other side. The obstruction had caused a notch, an irregularity in the circumference of the shiny crimson dish. Not a big dish. No heart had pumped it out. The man been dead when he went down.

A murmur of traffic noise drifted in through the open front doors. The cry of distant gulls. Lom found the desk clerk curled behind the counter. His neck was broken.

Maroussia!

He ran back across the open area, dodging between the desks. In the first office he tried, he found the corporal propped in the chair, his body slumped across the desk. Lom lurched backwards out of the office and shouted.

'Maroussia!'

He waited a second and called again.

'Maroussia!'

There was no answer.

All the other ground-floor offices were empty. On a desk in the middle of the big room a telephone began to ring again. *For the love of fuck, shut up.* A swing door opened onto a hallway and a staircase climbing up. Lom raced up, heart pounding, taking the stairs two at a time. There was a uniformed body slumped on the first landing. He jumped it without slowing.

'Maroussia!'

At the top of the stairs was another passageway. Doors, some standing open, some locked.

'Maroussia!' It was almost a scream.

And then he heard her voice. Cautious. Hesitant.

'Vissarion?'

'Where are you?'

'Here.' He heard a thump against one of the doors halfway down the passage. 'I'm in here. It's locked. I can't get out.'

Lom barged against the door. It was solid. He would break it down eventually, but it would take time. *Wasted time.* He ran back down the stairs to where the desk clerk lay in a foetal huddle and hauled him over onto his back. Ignoring the look in the dead, staring eyes, he went through his pockets. Found the bunch of keys by their weight.

The telephone was still ringing, loud and demanding and persistent, as he ran back up the stairs. Then, abruptly, it stopped. It took him three or four goes to find the right key to let Maroussia out. She was fine. She wasn't hurt.

'What—' she began. Lom held up his hand to cut her off.

'Don't talk,' he said. 'Move. We need to clear out. Now.'

They had to step across the body on the stairs. Maroussia looked but said nothing.

They passed the open door to the office where the corporal's body lay across the desk. The telephone started to ring. On impulse, Lom went in and picked it up.

'Yes?' he said.

'Mamontov? Is that Mamontov?'

It was a woman's voice.

Lom recognised it.

Chazia.

'I must speak to Mamontov,' she said. 'Immediately. It is a matter of great urgency.'

'Mamontov is the corporal here?' said Lom.

'Of course. Who is this? Who am I speaking to?'

'Mamontov can't come to the phone. He's dead.'

'Who is this?'

'This is Lom.'

A moment's silence in the receiver. Then Chazia spoke.

'Safran was supposed to kill you.'

'He fucked up. I'm coming for you.'

'I'm not hard to find.'

'So wait for me.'

Lom put the phone down.

Maroussia was waiting outside the office. She'd found two more bodies. She stared at Lom, her face drawn tight and blank.

'Vissarion?' she said quietly. 'Did you ... ? Did you do this?'

'Of course not.'

She exhaled deeply.

'No,' she said. 'Of course you didn't. But ... what happened here?'

'I don't know. I was locked in a room. I didn't hear anything.'

'Then—'

'Think later. Now, immediately now, we have to get far away, completely clear of here. We have to do that very quickly.'

9

Lavrentina Chazia hung up the telephone and reached for the intercom.

'Iliodor?'

'Yes, Commander.'

'The Marinsky Square gendarme post. There is a problem there.'

'Marinsky Square? That's where the Shaumian girl is being held. A patrol is on its way to collect—'

'There is a problem there. Lom. Lom is the problem. Lom is there.'

'Lom? That's impossible. Safran was—'

'I have just spoken to him, Iliodor. To Lom himself. On the telephone, from Marinsky Square. He threatened me, Iliodor. He threatened *me*. The Marinsky Square station is down. I want them found, Iliodor, him and the girl. Found and brought to me. No more gendarmes. No more militia. No more mistakes. I want the SV involved.'

'But this afternoon is the funeral—'

'This is the priority, man! This matters more! Deal with it yourself, Iliodor, and do it now.'

Chazia switched off the intercom and sat back in her chair, scratching irritably at the itching dark patch on the side of her neck. She didn't like being threatened. And she needed the Shaumian girl *found*.

Taking a deep breath, she pushed her anger and frustration aside. *Focus. Focus.* She had work to do. Her desk was heaped with files, reports, photographs, telegrams. The walls of her office were hung with maps. Nothing happened in the Vlast that Chazia didn't know about. Nothing moved and nothing was agreed. All significant intelligence reports passed through her office before anyone else saw them and were only acted on if and when she let them out again. She knew more about criminals, dissidents and revolutionaries than the police. More about the ongoing war against the Archipelago than the military commanders. She knew it was a war the Vlast could not win.

Since the death of the Novozhd and subsequent collapse of the peace conference the junior officers had taken to hanging their generals and taking their men across to the enemy. In Herkess and Gorkysk the populace had risen against their land colonels. The aristocrats were coming out of their tenements and moving back to their estates. Eleven oblasts had been lost in the last week alone. The fleet at Remontin had mutinied. The divisions and war fleets of the Archipelago were within striking distance of Mirgorod itself. They could be at the gates of the city in a matter of days. The city's defensive line looked impregnable on the map but it was brittle. When the enemy came with their armoured and motorised artillery like movable fortresses and the nine-hundred-rounds-a-minute drum magazines of their Whitfield-Roberts automatic rifles, the political commissars would not hold the army together. The hundred-foot war-mudjhiks which still remained viable might delay the advance for a few days but that was all. One sharp blow and the western Vlast would crumble. Dust.

Good. Let them come. Let them destroy the aging, desiccated Vlast. Let them sweep it aside. Its collapse was both inevitable and necessary, and the Archipelago would do it more quickly from outside. It would make her task all the easier.

A New Vlast.

History was on her side. The enemy could not hope to hold what it took. Weakened by the war and by its own internal contradictions and fault lines, its stupid plurality, that loosely bound argumentative club of island nations would soon retreat back beyond the Cetic Ocean. They would have no stomach for the terror to come. And while they were here, she would be building a new and better Vlast in the east, protected from the Archipelago occupation by five thousand miles of rolling continental plain. The New Vlast would be strong. Modern. Purposeful. Cleansed of all the impurities, weaknesses and compromises accumulated under generations of feeble Novozhds. And united under her.

And yet it was taking too long. She had no illusions. She knew that failure was possible. The others had been cleverer than she had expected. Dukhonin. Khazar. Fohn. Particularly Fohn. Within hours of the Novozhd's death they had pulled together this *Colloquium*. They had gathered to themselves the reins of power in the Vlast. The generals and officials of the Inner Council had signed up to it before she even knew what was in the air. Fohn had done that. He had been ready. Polished, metropolitan, underestimated Fohn.

Fohn had made himself Chairman. Dukhonin was General Secretary. Khazar was … what? She could not remember. Khazar was negligible.

Chairman Fohn had wanted to keep her out of it altogether – her! Chazia! Excluded from power! But Dukhonin and Khazar had not dared shut her out. So it had become the Colloquium of Four, and they made her Secretary of Security. She had insisted on keeping the police under her direct control and retained the title of Commander. But she hated and despised the whole thing. It was a useless, bastardised, temporary compromise going nowhere. She would bring it all down. Set them one against another, take them down, one by one.

But it was taking too much time.

Chazia was not patient. She was hungry and sleepless. She itched and fretted and burned. She sat in her high office and read the reports and scratched at the dark itching patches on her arms and face. The worms and insects moving under her burning skin. She needed more *strength*. More *power*. An edge to cut them down. A massive fist to crush them.

She needed the Pollandore. The Pollandore was power, she was convinced of that. There was no doubt. But she couldn't use it because she didn't know how. For that she needed the Shaumian girl.

There was a quiet sound behind her. Chazia jerked her head round. The hidden door in the panelling of her office opened and Josef Kantor stepped in.

Chazia hated the way he would just come in like that, with his pockmarked face, dirty red silk shirt and preposterous fedora, presuming access and attention. She regretted ever giving him the key to the bridge gates.

'I wasn't expecting you, Josef,' she said.

'Of course not. You sent me no word, Lavrentina. Since the Novozhd died I have heard nothing from you. Nothing at all.'

'Were you expecting to? I am busy. I have many new responsibilities now.'

'Responsibilities? You are a bureaucrat. This Colloquium was not the plan.'

'It is temporary,' said Chazia. 'Fohn's position is stronger than I had anticipated, but this phase will pass. Everything is in hand.'

Kantor pulled out a chair and sat down in front of her.

'This was not the plan,' he said again.

'There is no need for you to be concerned, Josef. I keep my promises. Let's talk about you, since you're here. You need a change, my friend. You played your part well, but you've lived too long among thieves and terrorists. I've been thinking about you. I have an offer for you: land colonel of Vassaravia. The current incumbent is insufficiently diligent. You would be a good replacement.'

'*Vassaravia!* A flat empty landscape three thousand miles away. Horse meat and wool.'

'It is in the south, yes. But to be land colonel in such a place is no small thing. A population of two million, and Kirtsbergh is a substantial capital. You would have scope to flourish there, Josef. There is work there for a man of your quality. The Donvass cavalry is wavering. The defences are unprepared. If Vassaravia fell, the whole of the Pienau river basin would be open.'

'The armies of the Archipelago are half a continent from the Donvass and the bulk of their navy is already off the Bight of Gatsk. They wouldn't waste a single gunboat on Kirtsbergh. They have no need.' He leaned forward. 'I won't be shuffled off to Vassaravia, Lavrentina.'

'Then name your oblast, Josef. What about Stari-Krasnogorsk? Or Munt? Land colonel is a handsome offer. Or would you prefer a less public role? Munitions production in Susaninograd is 60 per cent behind target—'

'I will remain here. In Mirgorod.'

'But distance is necessary, Josef! We've talked about this before. You are the great Kantor, king of terrorists! You cannot take a place in public among us. It is impossible. You can't be—'

Kantor waved the objection away.

'That is being dealt with,' he said. 'Josef Kantor will disappear and the people who know my face will die. Is this not so? Did we not agree?'

'Josef...'

Kantor paused. Looked at her sharply.

'The girl,' he said. 'The Shaumian girl? The bastard daughter of the

whore who was my wife? You have done this, Lavrentina? It *matters*.
It is *important*.'

'Yes.' Chazia lied with facility. It was a talent of hers. 'Yes. It is done.'

'You found her? And the Investigator? Lom? They are cleared away?
They are killed?'

'Yes. Of course. I have told you.'

'Good. I will take a new name. An alias. A sobriquet. A *nom de
guerre*. I'm thinking of *Rizhin*. Rizhin the red man. The crimson man.
Rizhin. I think the name has a ring to it. *Rizhin*. What do you think?'

'I think we must go more slowly, Josef.'

'*Slowly?* Everything with you is always *slowly*! This is not satisfactory, Lavrentina. Do you know where you are going?'

Chazia glared at him.

'And do you share your plans with me, Josef?' she said. 'No. You do
not.'

Kantor leaned back in his chair and put his hands behind his head.

'You're making heavy weather of this, Lavrentina. You seem tired.
You grow weak when the moment has come for strength. You delay
when the time has come to act.'

'Be careful, Josef. Remember who you are speaking to. I have made
you a good offer. A very fair offer. You should take it.'

Kantor's gaze locked with hers. His expression didn't change, but in
his dark brown eyes she saw black earth burning.

'I'm beginning to think,' he said, 'that you're not the right person
for the angel's purpose.'

Chazia felt her face grow hot.

'You wave this angel at me like a shroud!' she said, slapping her hand
hard against the tabletop. 'Yet it hides itself from me. Why, Josef? Why
does it not speak to *me*? It spoke to me once at Vig but never again.'

'I will remain here in Mirgorod, Lavrentina. As *Rizhin*. And you,
you will arrange it. You will make me a general. You will make me
Defence Commissar.'

'City Defence Commissar? I am offering you an oblast of your own!'

'I will remain in Mirgorod. As Defence Commissar.'

'But Mirgorod is lost. It can't be defended, the Novozhd saw to
that. The Archipelago will take it, and soon. Mirgorod is worth nothing now.'

'Then give it to me.'

Chazia shrugged.

'Very well,' she said. 'If you wish. It means nothing to me. I will be leaving the city soon. You are welcome to it.'

Kantor stood up.

'It is settled then,' he said.

10

Once they were clear of the gendarme station, Maroussia led the way. Lom followed. It was her city. She set a fierce pace, striding in silence. Lom loped along beside her with a steady, comfortable rhythm. The violence of what had happened in the gendarme station was a third presence between them, strange and raw and dark. A gap in the world had opened up and something new had reached through it and touched them: something sourceless and reckless and inexplicable. It set Lom on edge. It was like a thin whining noise in his ear: pitched too high for hearing, it reached into his unsettled belly and clenched there, an uneasy knot, a fist. An unspoken, liminal intimation of blood fear. He could sense that Maroussia felt it too, but they didn't speak of it. The shadow of a separation walked between them.

And then Lom realised what the separation was. There was something else that he was feeling: not fear, but something deeper than fear; the nameless, surprising visceral exhilaration of violence, and a taste in his mouth that reminded him of mudjhiks: the aliveness of angel flesh.

They walked on through the city, keeping to side streets and quiet backwaters because away from the main thoroughfares and intersections there would be fewer gendarme patrols. The temperature was still dropping fast. A front of freezing air was rolling straight in off the Cetic Ocean. The freezing wall of atmosphere came on slowly, rolling through the streets, pouring into alleyways, folding round buildings and spilling in through open doors and windows. Meeting the residual warmth of the city, it condensed in tongues and low thin drifting pillars of fog. A crisp delicate edging of frost formed on lamp posts and railings and wet sandbags stacked in doorways.

Mirgorod felt different. Something had changed. Where before the carapace of the city, its chitinous exoskeleton, had been hard and shiny and black, subject to sudden fractures, now everything was softer, more elastic. Fluid shifting changes of grey. Currents of possibility and change rippled and collided and slid across one another. There were tiny openings everywhere. Nothing was fixed. Apparent reality felt like a thin skin easily torn. Lom felt the watchfulness of the tenuous drifting fog. Wakeful, attentive presences inhabited it. Ice-cold fingers brushed his cheek and investigated the opening in his forehead. Sifting river voices whispered in his ear. The speech of strange tongues.

And he felt something else, something not of the cold air and the soft rain and the city. A hot animal pressure. An urgent attentive hunter's gaze drilling into the small of his back, dangerous, intelligent and wild.

Lom spun round suddenly but there was nothing to be seen, only warehouses and alleyways and solitary pedestrians hunched and muffled against the frosting cold.

'What is it?' said Maroussia. 'What are you doing?'

'I don't know,' said Lom. 'Nothing. Probably nothing.'

They walked on in silence.

'We still need to eat,' said Lom after a while.

Maroussia shook her head.

'I'm not hungry.'

'Nor am I,' said Lom. 'All the same, we should eat when we can. Is there somewhere we could go? Somewhere quiet.'

Maroussia frowned. 'OK,' she said. 'OK.'

She led them to a place in a basement, down a narrow flight of steps next to the stage door of the Mogen-Balterghen Music Theatre. There was no sign outside: if you didn't know it was there, you'd walk right past. A shabby door opened into a kind of one-room café-bar. Maroussia had been there once, a year or so before, she said. The place was known as Billroth's among the painters and theatricals and yellow-press journalists who spent their after-show evenings there. She hadn't liked it much – a stale, noisy jostle, everyone shouting-drunk on cheap sweet wine – and she'd never gone back there again.

But at this time of the morning Billroth's was just opening and almost empty: only a couple of plump-armed women in floral print blouses sharing a plate of cakes and a bottle of raspberry brandy, and a sallow ageing man with ink-black hair behind the bar, counting up the till. There was a coal fire in the grate and the smell of frying onions mixed with the reek of stale tobacco from the thick carpet and the dirty plush upholstery.

Lom found a table in the shadows away from the fire while Maroussia went across to the counter. He took off his coat and laid it beside him on the soft, sagging banquette. The brown velvet of the seat was rubbed smooth and dark. Sticky. There was thick flocked wallpaper everywhere, not on the walls only but also on the back of the doors and even the panels of the upright piano in the corner: florid blooms and intricate curlicues of dark blue against gold. It looked sticky too, with a thick patina of smoke and grease. Purple-shaded brass lamps flickered on the tables. Lom liked the place. It was cosy. To pass the time till Maroussia came back he read the yellowing show posters on the walls – THE GREEN-GOLD HYACINTH REVUE, MAIDENS ALL!, THE SCUTTLE-BUG, THE HERRING HARVEST – and studied the clutter of framed and autographed photographs among them. Studio-lit faces of actors, singers, dancers in greasepaint and costume or crisp evening wear.

One portrait in particular caught his attention. A beautiful young woman was leaning forward towards the camera, kohl-rimmed eyes wide, bright and eager, long silver-blond hair flowing from under a headdress made of birds' wings. Her body was squeezed into a spectacular confection of feathers and fruit and flowers and bead-covered concertina sleeves, and she held some kind of stick or staff in her hand, wound round with ivy. There was a typed caption set into the mounting card: 'AVRIL AVRILOVA as the BEREHINYA QUEEN in YOU UNDER THE LEAVES WITH ME! Produced and directed by Captain T Y Lebwohl'. There was a date, more than twenty years before, and a signature scrawled in a rounded girlish script, written big and bold across the girl's overspilling, fruit-bedecked bosom: '*To Billroth. For the Friends and the Memories. Avrilova*'.

Maroussia came back from the counter with a pot of coffee on a dented pewter tray. Bowls of red pork soup. A heap of apricot pastries.

'Yesterday's pastries,' she said. 'They were cheap. I don't think they're too stale.'

'Good,' said Lom. 'Wonderful.' He meant it. The coffee was thick and strong, and he found he was hungry again. He heaped in sugar and scooped out the cream from a couple of pastries and stirred it in.

Finished the first mug in one long gulp and poured himself a second.

'Vissarion?' said Maroussia. 'Why did we survive? Whoever killed those gendarmes, why didn't they find *us*?'

'OK,' said Lom, wiping crumbs from his mouth with the back of the hand. 'Let's think about it.' In the warm fug of Billroth's, his belly filled with coffee and pastries, what had happened was no longer an impossible irruption of uncanny violence. It was a problem to analyse. There were likelihoods to be appraised, improbabilities to be peeled away, kernels of fact to be rooted out into the light. Pragmatic decisions to be made. And he was good at that. He was trained. 'There are three possibilities,' he said. 'One.' He ticked it off on his finger. 'The attack was unconnected to us. We just happened to be there. Whoever did it, they did what they came to do and then they left.'

Maroussia made a face.

'You think that was nothing to *do* with us?' she said. 'You think it was a *coincidence*?'

'It's a possibility.'

'I don't think so. Nor do you.'

'OK,' said Lom. He folded down another finger. 'Second possibility. They were looking for us. We were the target. But they didn't find us. So why didn't they find us? We weren't hard to find.'

'They could have been disturbed,' said Maroussia. 'Interrupted before they finished.'

'Disturbed by what?' said Lom.

'I don't know. Anything.'

Lom shook his head.

'I can't see it,' he said. 'If they were after us, why did they fail? No reason to fail. Nothing stopping them. So ...' Another finger. 'Third possibility. We have an ally. Or allies. The attack was meant to be help us. After all, that's what it did. It got us out.'

'In that case, why did they disappear?' said Maroussia. 'Why didn't they stay and let us out and take us with them?'

'Presumably so we wouldn't see who they were,' said Lom. 'Our ally wants to remain anonymous.'

'Is that what you think?' said Maroussia.

Lom shrugged.

'I don't know,' he said. 'Coincidence? Enemy? Ally? It's all speculation. None of this is information we can work with. All we can do is carry on. Get to Vishnik's apartment as quickly as possible. But be more cautious. Stay away from patrols and checkpoints. Keep off trams. Walk.'

Lom paused and looked up as a tall slender man in a grey astrakhan hat came in, pulled off his hat and slumped into a deep chair next to the fire on the other side of the room. He was grey-faced and gaunt almost to the point of emaciation. He waved the barman over to give his order, then leaned back in the chair and closed his eyes. The dark shadow-rings under his eyes looked like bruises.

Maroussia picked at a stale pastry. She hadn't touched the coffee. Lom's rationalised anatomy of the situation hadn't dispelled the silence in the gendarme station. The torn bodies. The smell of blood. The insistent ringing of the telephone.

'What you said to Chazia,' she said at last. 'On the phone. You threatened her.'

'Yes.'

'You didn't have to do that,' said Maroussia. 'You didn't have to say anything at all.'

'No.'

'I need to find the Pollandore,' said Maroussia. 'That's all I'm interested in. Nothing else.'

'Chazia had your mother killed,' said Lom.

'Did she? It was Safran that shot her.'

'On Chazia's orders. And she's still looking for you. Those gendarmes had your picture.'

'But why? It makes no sense. I'm nothing. Why would Chazia even know or care that I exist?'

'Because of the angel. Because of the Pollandore.'

Maroussia stared at him.

'You don't know that,' she said.

'No,' said Lom. 'But I think it. There's a connection. Chazia. Angel. Pollandore.'

'So you reached into the Lodka and yanked Chazia's tail?' she said.

'To see what she does.'

Maroussia glared.

'It was a spur of the moment thing,' said Lom.

'I'm still going to Vishnik's apartment,' said Maroussia.

'Then finish the pastries and have some coffee before we go. It's going to be a long cold walk.'

11

Antoninu Florian, at rest in the wing-backed chair by the fire in Billroth's, listened to Lom and Maroussia's whispered talk with a corner of his mind. Eyes closed, he heard it all, as he heard the crackle and hiss and slip of coals in the fire, the stir of smoke, the steam from the samovar on the counter. The tick of spoon against side of cup. The breathing of the man behind the counter. The bark of the pink women's laughter.

He leaned forward and picked a fragment from his plate. Fingernails clicked against ceramic. The apple cake exploded on his tongue, a shattering of acid and sugar and cinnamon and orchard earth. He sipped at his lemon tea. It was hot and sour. He crushed sugar-grit against the bottom of the glass with a spoon. The teeth in his mouth were sharp. He took another sip of tea and listened to the murmuring traffic roar of the city rumbling overhead. He discriminated a hundred, a thousand, ten thousand separate sounds. Each one was heard. Nothing was merged and muddy, everything was distinct: every engine cough and rumbling wheel, every footfall, every shout. The brush of every sleeve. The sifting fog.

Florian detested the city and wished he had not come back again. He resented the press of human crowds against his sense of privacy and solitude. He was tired of worrying away at the weight of what had been done and straining at the looming, muttering shadow-gates of what must be done next. The weight of choice and consequence had long ago grown wearisome. All he wanted to do was fill his lungs with cold clear air and stretch out his limbs and run among trees. He wanted to sleep out the heat of the day in the grass by a lake with a belly full of meat. He wanted to clear his mind of *words*.

He hated Mirgorod, but he had returned. The call had come, insistent, almost below the threshold of cognition, and he answered, as he always did. He'd sensed the mind of the living angel fallen in the forest, the terrible widening horror of its seeping poison, and he'd felt the movement in the Pollandore, the opening of many new possibilities. He had no choice but to make the long journey to Mirgorod again, because this was a moment of turning.

And now he considered his own choices once more, as he had done already several times that morning. The woman mattered – she was a maker of difference, an agent of change – but it wasn't yet clear what her effect would be. Influences from the forest were driving her towards the Pollandore, and that made him uneasy. They wove their stories around her and told her their tales; they gave her what they needed her to hear, but the consequences could be disastrous. While the Pollandore remained where it was, in the world beyond the border, the border stayed permeable: forest breathed in the world, world in the forest. But if the Pollandore was ... touched, that would be the end of it, the green wall would be shut. The angel, its contact severed, would die, and the forest would live, but there could be no reopening: the forest would be gone from the world.

Was that what the minds from the forest at work here intended? He would not let it happen. He would intervene first. If necessary he would kill the woman. Yet the Pollandore itself drew the woman forward, for purposes of its own. It was murky. Florian could not see. He didn't know what he should do.

The woman and the man who was with her got up to go. They didn't look at him as they left, and he didn't move to follow. There was no need. He could find that man again, any time he needed. He was *opened up*. There was no other word for it. It was shocking to encounter.

This man's involvement in the unfolding pattern had thrown Florian off balance. He was something completely unexpected, something new and unpredictable, a mixing of forest and the stain of angel flesh such as Florian had never known before. And there was strength in him. He was new and frail and oblivious, and could easily still fade and fall back, lapsing into wherever and whatever he had been before. But he might not fall. He might grow stronger. Stronger, perhaps much stronger, than Florian himself. Strong enough to drive a living angel out of the world?

Florian finished the lemon tea and found he'd come to a decision, of a kind. A temporary decision, until a clearer pattern emerged. In fact, he realised, he'd reached it even before he entered the gendarme station. There was too much uncertainty to act. So. Let the man and the woman find their own paths. Maximum openness. Close nothing down. Keep the borders open. At least for now.

One of the women at the other table said something, and the other erupted in a cackle of laughter. Then they were both laughing, raucous, blowsy and wild. Their mouths gaped. Lipsticked lips pulled back from poor, ragged teeth. The pink flesh of their throats and upper arms shook, spilling the scent of powder compacts and thick-sweet scent and stale underclothes. And then something happened.

A stir of air in the room, a flicker of shadow from the lamp on their table, and Florian glimpsed the whole trajectory of each woman's life in her face: each was at once and all together a child, a lover, a sleeper in the dark of dreams, and an older – not much older – face, drawn thin and grey and hard by terrible loss to come. Each woman was the same as the other and also resembled her not at all; resembled no one else ever out of all the millions of millions of women who lived and ever had lived or ever would live. But in that moment, now and in Mirgorod, the women were together and laughing with the raspberry brandy in their stomachs at some small ripe obscenity, and the floor fell away under them and they stayed where they were, suspended.

The women in their squat upholstered chairs, their lamp-bearing table, Florian in his chair, and all the furniture in Billroth's hung, turning slowly, held in formation by their own gentle gravitation, above a beautiful dark well of endless coldness and depth, an abyss scattered with fat and golden stars. The walls of the room receded and grew endlessly tall, rising towards more nightfallen sky. The dark-purple flowers and twisting stems in the wallpaper were mouths to see night through. The room turned and tumbled at moon-slow pace, and the women, their faces illuminated from within by copper-yellow light, turned with it. Light poured from their open laughing silent mouths. The barman, red and green, standing on a patch of carpet canted at thirty degrees to the rest of the room, sang a quiet private song with the voice of the wallpapered, star-intestined piano.

The Pollandore was stirring.

12

Lom and Maroussia crossed the Brass Cut by an unwatched footbridge and followed the canal-side north in the direction of Big Side, where Vishnik's apartment was. Mailboats were unloading at a jetty in the lee of a huge wood-framed warehouse. The Fransa-Koromantsy Postal Depot. There were still huge areas of the Vlast, thousands of miles of bog and lake and birchwood, where the railways didn't run and the roads were rutted dust in summer and thick impassable mud in winter. Long slow rivers connected by lakes and stretches of canal and overland portage were the only way to cover distance. Place names were crudely stencilled on the sacks and pallets. Solovits. Onyeg. Voitsogorad. Shar-Dudninsk. Plestovosk. Way stations on the inland waterways. A litany of strangeness and distance. The men in bulky coats and rubber boots, talking quietly among themselves as they shifted their cargoes, knew such places and the long wildernesses in between.

Lom studied the boatmen curiously. They were all men. Women sometimes worked the mailboats, and even whole families, but he saw none here. Many of the men had the broad, flattened faces and squat strength of the people from beyond the ice edge, but others were lean and wiry, with straw-coloured hair and colourless eyes. They all had the same quietness, the same hard-weathered distant look. Interior voyagers, one or two to a boat, moving slowly through non-human landscapes. The country of giants. Man-wolves. Great elk. Rusalkas.

Sailors discharged from the navy sometimes took work on the river mail, and so did disillusioned politicals: zeks who had survived a sentence in the hard camps. It was something you could do, if you had no place to go. If you'd never had a home. Or you had lost it. It was something Lom had once thought he might end up doing himself, one day. But he didn't want to be alone. Not always. Not for ever.

Past the postal depot, they turned away from the canal into the Bronze Sturgeon Quarter. There was not enough traffic in the road. Lom didn't like it. He felt exposed: him in his mud-streaked cloak-like loden, Maroussia bare-legged and shivering in her thin summer coat, they were too *visible*.

'Isn't there another way we could go?' he said. 'We stick out a mile.' Maroussia shook her head.

'Not without crossing the Lilac Bridge, and they always check papers there. We'll be in Starimost soon. It'll be better there.'

As they approached Starimost the buildings got bigger and grander, the roads more crowded: trams, horse-drawn karetas, the occasional private automobile. The street they were following widened and became a Prospect. Houses gave way to shops, department stores and hotels. Yellow light glowed in the windows and made soft halo-edges in the cold fog, as if it was later than it was. There were no checkpoints here, and no traces of the floods any more. Good property in Mirgorod was above the high-water line.

Maroussia stopped at a milliner's window. 'Look,' she said. 'Look at this.'

Lom came and stood next to her. Her cheeks were pink with cold, her short black hair, slicked damp and glossy from the fog, lay in tight curls across her forehead and stuck to the back of her neck. The window display was swathed with elegant lengths of mourning cloth. Among the homburgs, fedoras and astrakhans, the fascinators, cloches and cocktail hats, was a photograph of the Novozhd framed in overwrought gilt and draped with ribbons of black silk.

'He must be dead,' she said. 'The Novozhd is dead. It doesn't seem possible. Maybe it's something else. His wife, or ...'

But other shops carried similar displays. Businesses had closed their doors in grief and left black-edged handwritten cards in their doors: '*The proprietors and staff of Blue's Tea Importation Company weep together for our beloved Novozhd.*' They had to step off the pavement to avoid the small crowd that had gathered round a stall selling mourning flags and tokens of remembrance. The stuff was hastily made and shoddy. Brass medal-pins. Red and black silk lapel-flowers. Lettered jugs and teapots. Black-rimmed cake plates with the Novozhd's profile in the centre, his face looking strangely pink. Lom stopped at a newspaper kiosk to read the headlines. The front pages shouted in heavy black capitals, PEOPLE OF MIRGOROD, LINE THE STREETS WITH MOURNING BLACK! JOY FOR HIS LIFE! SORROW FOR HIS DEATH! HATRED FOR HIS KILLERS! MORE IS REQUIRED OF US NOW! RALLY TO THE STANDARD OF THE COLLOQUIUM! The funeral was to be held that afternoon. That explained the police lockdown in the centre of the city. Lom picked up a paper and read the front page.

'He didn't just die,' said Lom; 'he was killed. Assassinated. A bomb.'

'Then everything is changed,' said Maroussia. 'Nothing will be the same now.'

Lom realised she was right. For twenty years – more – the Novozhd's face, familiar, benevolent, paternal and determined, had looked out on the Vlast, smiling or stern, from posters, newspapers, cinema screens, history books, the wall of every office and school and home. Every person in the Vlast read about him, thought about him, dreamed of him all the time. The Novozhd was everyone's constant interior conscience and companion, the interlocutor of a thousand imagined conversations, confessions and tirades. Even if you despised him he was always *there*. Even his enemies needed him, to give their enmity shape and meaning. And now he was gone. Something permanent had shifted, something unthought-of had come into the world. A wall had fallen down, a door had opened. A gap.

'What's the Colloquium?' said Lom. 'You heard of it before?'

Maroussia shrugged.

'Somebody new will take over now,' she said.

'There'll be trouble first,' said Lom. 'This will stir things up.'

Half an hour later, they were standing side by side outside the Hotel-Pension Koromantsy Most in Marzelia Vovlovskaya Prospect. An expensive place. Plate-glass windows. OYSTERS. FRUITS DE MER. The temperature was still falling. A brisk gusting wind from the north-west straight off the Cetic Ocean had scattered the fog. It sliced through their clothes and threw scant handfuls of snow in their faces. Sharp flakes caught on their shoulders and sleeves. In Maroussia's hair. They watched the moneyed classes of Mirgorod taking early luncheon.

Warm white light, white table linen, white napkins. MINERAL-VODA. SOURCE VAKUL. Fat men of business at their coquilles and perch. Hard, watery eyes blinked through flashing lenses. Women in furs and red shoes drank chocolate and ate cakes with pursed, dissatisfied lips. A clatter of lipstick and pastry crumbs, flickering tongues, complaints. The restaurant door opened and a sullen group pushed past them out into the street. Lom caught the smell of the dining room on their clothes. Garlic and gravy and eau de toilette. They'd left an unopened eighth of cherry aquavit on their table. RANEVSKAYA'S ORCHARD.

Lom was using the plate-glass window as a mirror. He caught a glimpse of something thirty yards back. Maybe. Too far for details. When he turned round to look there was nothing. But the edgy feeling was back, the pressure at the top of his spine, the certainty that he was being watched.

13

Josef Kantor, master terrorist, was alone in his room on the Ring Wharf, listening to the voice of Marfa-Anna Priugachina. She was singing the 'Apple Harvest' from Lefalla's *Five Evening Songs*.

The autumn orchard drowsing
In the honey-warm windfall sun.

The phonograph, a portable ODZ *Pobedityel,* was a new acquisition. When it was closed, the heavy, rexine-covered wooden cabinet looked like a briefcase, and when you unlatched and lifted the lid to reveal the turntable with its mat of red felt, it released a rich unnameable scent of components and dust. The neat iron crank handle was clipped inside the lid. All it needed was a disc on the felt, a few turns of the crank in the slot on the side of the box, and the machine was ready. A neat, precise lever dropped the meticulously balanced tone-arm into position and Lefalla's melody, coming rich and full from the perforated grille on the sides of the casing, filled the room. The gramophone was modernity in a box. The contrast between the precision of its components and the nostalgic melancholy confection of Priugachina's voice stimulated and soothed him.

One sweet last fruit for Ninel
Before the salt stars come.

Kantor had treated himself to the phonograph the week before: one small gift to himself, one negligible handful of roubles skimmed from the thirty million before they went north to Yakov Khyrbysk. It was a rare departure from his iron principle that all money was for the cause and none for himself, except the most frugal of necessary living expenses. But the deviation from his own discipline didn't trouble him. It was justified. Looked at clearly, it was no deviation at all. The spirit must be nourished, just as much as the body must, because Kantor was a poet: his greatest resource was the force of imagination, and imagination must be given space to stretch and breathe, or else it grew tired and constrained, and then he missed opportunities and made mistakes.

So he sat in his chair and listened to music. It was a moment of pause, a widening of the spirit, a gathering of forces. The preparations for his new life were almost complete: his books were packed away in a wooden case and the ashes of his papers were smouldering in the grate. All his pamphlets and leaflets and speeches, all the incendiary paragraphs over which he had laboured in the long nights, they were all burned. *Citizens! Sisters and brothers! New times are coming. The blood of the Vlast is thin and cold. A fragile skull under a paper face. Young Mirgorod will smash it with a fist!* He had believed it in a way, and he believed it still, because it was true: in distant workshops far to the north, amid the pounding of steam hammers, the detonation of rivet guns, the blazing spark-showers of foundries spilling streams of glowing molten iron, new things were being built. Crimson seeds to scatter across the stars. Radiant humankind.

But Kantor let the papers burn without regret, feeling the fading warmth of the fire on his face like the evening sun in Lefalla's orchard. A new phase was beginning for him now: there was new work to do, and he was ready. More than ready. He had long outgrown the tedious conspiracies of factions and cells, movements and tendencies and futile terrorist acts. The assassination of the Novozhd had been the last and greatest of his triumphs.

Kantor used explosives as an engineer did, with an engineer's precision and strategic purpose, to loosen rock, to clear a blockage and blast a passage, as in a mine, a quarry, a tunnel, and the bomb that destroyed the Novozhd was the one that had broken through. It had released the landslide. Things were on the move. It was time for direct action now, and for that he needed different tools: he needed armies and police, he needed a city, he needed his own hands on the levers of power. And now he had that: the fox-bitch Chazia had given him Mirgorod in the end, as he knew she would. All he had to do was waft the scent of the living angel under her nose and she was avid for it, blind. She surrrendered the tool of her own destruction to him in her hunger for a sniff of the angel's rancid piss.

Chazia was a hunter after power in her own way, but her way was weak. She wanted to be near power, to wash herself in it, to smell it on her fingers, but she had no idea what power really was. Chazia had the heart of a bureaucrat. She was insane – there was no doubt of that – but hers was the insanity of the mad administrator. She would *give herself* to power, when power was to be *taken*. Power was to be *used*. And to use power, you needed a poet's purpose, not an administrator's.

Kantor despised Chazia as he despised the rest of the authors of this pathetic Colloquium that sought to ride the rockfall of history let loose by the Novozhd's death; he despised her as he despised the politicking conspirators and secret coterists he had been obliged to deal with for so long: the factionalisms of anarchists, nationalists, nihilists, social democrats, Birzelists. He despised them all. Weak-minded, they considered their goal to be the administrative implementation of ideas, principles, policies. They pleasured themselves in perpetual debate about ends and means and slogans, contending the disposition of property and labour, the organisation of schemes for the provision of sewerage and justice. They built and broke alliances, they disbursed compromise and patronage and money. Kantor understood their world – he had exploited it when he needed to – but he hated it. It absorbed energy and purpose and hope. *Policies!* The word itself was small-minded. Pusillanimous. It made him feel tired, nauseous, sleepy and bored. There was only one thing that mattered. *Energetic force of personality.* That was all there was to it, everything else was illusory, bones thrown to dogs. There was nothing of greatness in *policies*, and Josef Kantor was nothing if not great. He was a visionary. A poet. He saw the shape and sweep of things.

Chazia had given him Mirgorod, and Mirgorod would be his beginning. He would weld the city into one single weapon with a simple, efficient, basic, robust system of control. Fear. Terror. The Vlast had wandered in the foothills of terror but Josef Kantor would climb terror mountain. The city would be a Kantor-machine, and then the continent, the entire planet, would be a Kantor-machine. And still that would only be the beginning. Beyond the world were other worlds, other stars, the angels themselves. The Kantor-machine would force itself ever outwards with one simple beautiful poetic purpose, with an abstract beauty of its own. Perpetuation. Propagation. Expansion. Total universal integration.

And yet there was a problem, an obstacle: the living angel that came from time to time and screamed at him inside his head. For the moment, the angel's direction and Kantor's direction were the same, and it was useful to him. The angel was the leash that hauled Chazia to him again and again. But a machine could not have two engines. Kantor feared the angel, and the thing you feared must be confronted. It must be killed. In the end that time must come, and he would find a way.

The recording of Marfa-Anna Priugachina reached its end in a hiss of crackle. The metronome-click of the needle rebounded and rebounded at the limit of its groove.

14

The further north into the city Lom and Maroussia went, the smaller and poorer the houses became. Narrow streets smelled of rendering fat, cabbage and potatoes. There were shops selling black bread and dried fish, packets of dusty tea, sour kvass, second-hand linen. Pawn shops and moneylenders. In small yards groups of men smoked rank tobacco and tossed quarter-kopek coins against walls. Fat snowflakes flocked thicker in the air. They stopped at a second-hand clothes stall in the street. Bought a grey scarf and a pair of woollen gloves for Maroussia. A knitted cap for Lom. He pulled it low over his forehead to cover the wound there. They got the lot for a single rouble. Apart from a few kopeks, it was the last of their money.

Ten minutes later they came to the first smashed windows. Pieces of broken glass and shattered roof tiles littered the pavement. Lom felt the tension of violence and fear in the air. It was a tangible thing. A taste. Outside a ransacked clothing shop a white-haired woman was gathering up the ruins of her stock. She'd made a neat little heap of dislocated, broken-backed umbrellas at the roadside, and in her arms she held a pile of white undergarments, torn and trodden with mud. Her face was closed up tight. Nobody helped. Further down the street, other shops were the same. Words were daubed on walls and windows in red paint.

FUCK OFF LEZARYE!

A thin young man in a peaked felt hat was handing out printed fliers. Lom took one. It was badly printed on a cheap portable press.

'Friends, remember Birzel!' it read. 'The government of the Colloquium is not legitimate. The Archipelago is not our enemy. All angels are dead. Let us unite with our brothers the giants and all free

369

peoples everywhere. Wear the White Freedom Rose of Peace! Support Young Mirgorod and bring an end to this pointless war!'

The young man looked cold and scared and vulnerable. Lom wanted to stop and say something to him, but what could he say? Not all the angels are dead?

The part of the city they were walking through was like nothing Lom had experienced in daylight before. It felt both small and immensely extensive. Streets led into other streets, turned into alleyways, went blind and died, or opened suddenly into expansive paved squares. It was like the place he'd wandered into when he was lost on his way to Vishnik's in the rain, the evening he first arrived in Mirgorod. Through open windows he could see the shadowy profiles of people at work in kitchens. In workshops open to the street men in overalls bent over dismantled engines, and from somewhere out of sight came the sound of a lathe. Every so often there was a street name, but the names were strangely anonymous, interchangeable, perfunctory. Meat Street. Polner Square. Black Pony Yard. A woman flapped a rug from an upstairs window: she caught his eye and looked away. Lom felt he had intruded on something private.

Before he came to Mirgorod, Lom had been only in towns which had a centre and a periphery, and that was all. But this place was neither middle nor edge, but some third thing that could exist only in the gaps and interstices of a great city. It was a part of the huge fabric of Mirgorod, yet Lom had the feeling that for the people they passed, these ordinary fractal streets were the core of their lives, the stage for their dramas, and they seldom left them. It was both somewhere and nowhere, a familiar alienness, the kind of place you saw – if at all – from the window of a tram or a train. The otherness of someone else's ordinary places. Yet history found its way here, just as much as it came to the wide central prospects and the great buildings of the capital: you felt the presence of it, its strength and its anxiety, the possibility of dark murderous events and love and wonder. For the first time Lom realised the strangeness of what history was: a physical force that acted from a distance on the granular substance of life, like gravity, like inertia. Everywhere was obscure and elsewhere, non-existent until you found yourself in the middle of it, and then it was local and overwhelmingly specific. Everywhere history operated, everywhere there were things to be afraid of and choices to be made. Because history was gravity, but you could choose not to fall.

'Where is this place?' said Lom. 'What's it called?'

'I'm not sure,' said Maroussia. 'I don't think I've been here before. We must have taken a wrong turning somewhere back there.'

They turned to retrace their steps, only what they'd passed before wasn't there any more. Different traders, different names. Maroussia slowed and looked around, puzzled.

'I thought there was an umbrella shop on this corner,' she said. 'We haven't passed that stationer's before. I would have remembered. Still. It doesn't matter. We just need to keep going north and east and we'll come into Big Side in the end.'

There was a burned-out building on the corner of a broad cobbled square. It stank of wet ash and charred wood. A girl of fifteen or sixteen was sitting in the middle of the square under a statue of Admiral Koril. She had a box eubandion on her knees but she wasn't playing, just resting her arms on the instrument and staring up at the raw darkness of glassless windows, the mute gape of a broken doorway, the jagged roof beams against the sky. She wore long black skirts and a black scarf drawn up over her head. Pulled low, it shadowed her face. Maroussia went across to her.

'Was that your place?' she said, nodding to the burned ruin.

The girl looked at her narrowly. She had dark intelligent eyes. Watchful. A strand of dark hair fell across her face. Her hands were red and raw with the cold.

'No,' she said. 'That's the Internationals.'

'The what?'

'The Peace and Hope Meeting Rooms For All Nations. Or it was.'

'What happened here?'

'Who are you?' said the girl. 'Why're you asking?'

'We're not anybody,' said Maroussia. 'We're just walking through.'

The girl glanced at Lom.

'He's not nobody. He's police.'

'No,' said Lom. 'No. I'm not.'

The girl closed her face against them and looked away.

'Leave me alone,' she said. 'I don't want to talk to you.'

'It's OK,' said Maroussia. 'He's OK. Really, he is. My name's

Maroussia Shaumian. I live by the Oyster Bridge. And this is Vissarion. He's my friend.'

'Oyster Bridge? Isn't that in the raion?'

'Just this side of the gate. We only want to know what happened here.'

'The Boots burned it in the night,' said the girl.

'Boots?' said Lom.

'Thugs,' said Maroussia. 'Vlast Purity rabble rousers. Why?' she said to the girl. 'Why would they do that?'

'They're saying Lezarye killed the Novozhd,' said the girl. 'The government said that, so the Boots attacked the Lezarye shops and the hotheads came to fight the Boots, which is what the Boots wanted. Because the Novozhd is dead now, and they want to make trouble.'

'Who did kill the Novozhd?' said Lom. 'Who is the government now?'

The girl stared at him.

'It's not a trap,' said Lom. 'It's just a question.'

'But everyone knows.'

'We don't,' said Maroussia. 'Honestly. We've been away. Travelling. We don't know what's happened here.'

'Where could you travel where they don't have the Novozhd?' The girl stood up and hoisted the eubandion across her shoulder. 'I'm going. Don't follow me. I've got brothers. They're just over there. I'll call them.'

'We won't follow you,' said Maroussia. 'Please. We just want to know what everyone knows. It can't do you any harm to tell us.'

The girl studied Maroussia for a moment. Lom hung back.

'The Colloquium is the government now,' she said. 'There's four of them. Fohn. Dukhonin. Chazia. I forget the other one. They say it was the Lezarye that killed the Novozhd, but some people say it was a spy from the Archipelago, and others say it was a loner. A madman. Who do you believe? Everyone says what they want to be true.' The girl lowered her voice. 'I even heard someone say the Colloquium did it themselves, to get him out of the way. I don't know. Whoever did it, it was bad. Look at what happened here. Everything's getting worse. The Boots—'

She stopped short as a heavy horse-drawn wagon trundled into the square, a gang of young men crowded in the back, bawling 'Blood of Angels'.

Vlast! Vlast! Freedom land!
My heart a flag in winter –
The drum of my blood
In storms of rain.

'They came back,' the girl said bleakly.

15

*A*rchangel sends a node of sentience out beyond the forest border and snatches a bird in the air.

HELLO, BIRD.

He flies in bird a while, becoming bird, savouring the alien taste of bird mind. When he withdraws, bird falls, heart-stopped, out of the sky.

GOODBYE, BIRD.

Archangel isolates a tiny piece of his own rock-hard substance and puts into it all that he has learned of bird. He replicates bird. When he has finished, he pulls the tiny chunk of angel flesh out of himself and throws it into the air.

It flies. For a while it is bird and he is bird in it. Archangel-bird. Almost.

Archangel-bird flies and flies, and then the shadow falls. Archangel-bird stutters, stumbles out of the air and collapses in on itself, reverting into nano-quantum-slime that slaps down onto the earth.

Never mind. First steps. He is learning as he goes.

He returns to original bird. Dead bird. He sniffs and prods the corpse and slips back into it. Repairs it and makes it fly again.

HELLO, BIRD.

It is almost as good.

It is almost better.

But it is not enough. One bird. Or one man. It does not even begin to be enough.

Archangel needs EVERYTHING. If he is to escape this dark con-stricting suffocating world – if he is to regain his birthright across the uncountable stars and the spaces between the stars – he must have it

ALL. *Every mind on the planet must speak with HIS voice and speak always and only HIM.*

The unfolding future of the planet, its coming history, must be HIS. He must understand it all in every intricate detail and inhabit it all and transform it all.

Remake it all.

No secret private thought. No life outside HIS life.

Archangel. Always and only and everywhere Archangel.

Total Archangel.

That will be the beginning.

16

L om watched the horse-drawn wagon pull up outside a bookshop seventy yards away across the square. SVENNER CIRCULATING LIBRARY. TEXTS. PERIODICALS. A bed sheet hung from the side of the wagon, a slogan painted on it in blocky letters: *STUDENTS OF MIRGOROD! MARCH AGAINST UN-VLAST THINKING!*

The men climbed down. Lom counted nine. They were all in some kind of uniform: black trousers, heavy black workboots, vaguely naval waist-length pea coats of dark blue wool. Short haircuts. One was older than the others, red-faced, with iron-grey hair. He looked like he was giving the orders. The rest were young. None of them looked like students. A couple were carrying batons, swinging them loosely by their sides.

Three of them went into the bookshop. They came out dragging an old man between them and hauled him over to the wagon. Two held his arms while the third started in on his beard, hacking at it with scissors. The old man stood there, blank-eyed and confused, letting them do it. Waiting till it would be over. No one else was in sight. The stink of charred wood was sour in the air. There was a crash of broken glass and a ragged cheer went up. The others were scooping books out of the shop window. Some of them went inside and came out with their arms full. They dumped the books in a growing pile on the pavement. Somebody fetched a jerry can from the wagon and started splashing paraffin. The leader took the glasses from the shopkeeper's nose and put them in his own pocket. Then he punched him in the face.

The old man crumpled to his knees, cupping his mouth in his hands.

Lom felt anger tightening in his stomach, and with it the edge of excitement came again: the hot exhilaration of violence that had come in the gendarme station, only this time it was stronger. This time it was justice, this time it was him, this time it was edged with fear.

'Wait here,' he said and set off across the square.

'No,' said Maroussia. 'I'm coming.'

When they were twenty yards out the Boots saw them coming. Seven peeled off to meet them. Two hung back with the old man. Snow flurries gusted across the square. Lom tested his footing. The cobbles were slick with slush. Not so good. But he would manage.

The Boots should have spread out to meet him, come at him from the side, got in behind him: he'd have had no chance then. Seven against one. But they clumped together. They were a herd.

Stay calm. Analyze. Plan.

The leader was at the front, flanked by the two with straightsticks. The one on the left was a couple of inches over six feet tall, blond, with a wide neck and a thick bull-chest. The other was a couple of inches smaller. Lom's height. Straggles of brown hair. An edge of smile on his thin ratty mouth. Of the other four, the second rank, two were big and broad and walked with a wide-legged shoulders-back swagger, and the other pair were skinny, with bad complexions and pink excited faces, hoping to see someone hurt but not likely to do much damage themselves. Lom waited for them. He felt Maroussia come up beside him. Her face was pale and tight.

There was a snigger from the Boots. When they were close enough that he didn't need to raise his voice, Lom said, 'Get back in the wagon. All of you. Get back in the truck and ride away.'

The leader stopped. The others gathered in behind him. He was smiling.

'Who the fuck are you?' he said.

'Concerned bystander,' said Lom. 'Leave the old man alone.'

'Him?' said red-faced grey-hair. 'Fuck him.'

Lom met the man's gaze with absolute confidence.

'You should go now,' he said. 'While you still can.'

There was one tiny flicker of uncertainty in red-faced grey-hair's eyes. But he was the leader and his men were watching him. If he backed down he'd lose them for ever.

'There are nine of us,' he said. 'We're going to take you apart. We're going to fucking kill you. Then we'll take the woman back with us for later. The boys will like that.'

A couple of faces behind him grinned.

'Let's do it, Figner,' said one of the skinny ones. He had thin yellow hair. A narrow pink nose. A face like cheese. 'Go on. Do him now. Cut off his fucking dick and stuff it in his mouth.'

'Stick it in the whore's mouth!' said another.

The boys were starting to enjoy themselves. Warming to their work. This was better than shoving a half-blind old bookseller around. A gust of wind threw snow in Lom's face.

'I don't see nine,' he said. He stared into grey-hair's eyes. 'I see seven, and only four that might be any use. That's not enough. You need to get in the wagon and drive away. You need to do that now.'

'Bullshit.'

Rat-mouth stepped forward and took a swing at Lom with his stick.

It was a standard militia-issue baton. Twenty-four inches of black polished wood, thickening slightly from the cloth-wrapped handle to the rounded tip. A six-inch length of lead in the striking end. The lead weight was a mixed blessing. It multiplied the kinetic force of the blow, but it made the stick unwieldy. Once you started a swing you were committed.

Lom knew the drill with batons. Basic police training. If you wanted to put an opponent out of action you aimed for the large muscle areas. The biceps. The quadriceps. There was a nerve in the side of the leg above the knee. A good blow to any of those would leave the limb numbed and disabled for five, ten minutes at least. But if you wanted to really hurt someone, you went for the skull. The sternum. The spine. The groin.

Rat-mouth came in high and hard, swinging for Lom's head. A killing blow.

Which suited Lom fine. It cleared the air.

Lom had been in fights when he was a young policeman in Podchornok. Street fights. Bar-room brawls. Gangsters looking for revenge. Knives. Clubs. Broken bottles. The first fight he was ever in he'd lost, badly. He'd been lucky to get out of it alive. After that, he didn't lose any more. He'd learned that what lost you a fight was inhibition. Decency. Restraint. Civilised values had their place, but you had to know when you'd stepped outside all that, because when your opponent went somewhere else, you had to go there too. Completely.

Rat-mouth went for a really big swing. A barnstormer. A skull-smasher. That was his first mistake. Men like him got used to hitting people who didn't fight back. Mostly, if you come at someone with a baton they'll try to duck it or they'll hold up their arm to fend it off, which is a broken femur for certain. Game over. But Lom stepped forward inside the swing. He watched the arc of it coming and reached up and caught it in both hands when it was barely a foot past rat-mouth's shoulder. The impact stung his palms but that was all. He pivoted left and jerked the stick down and forward. In the same movement he stamped down hard on the side of rat-mouth's knee. Felt the joint burst open. Rat-mouth screamed. Lom tore the straightstick out of his grip before he hit the ground. He should have used the wrist strap. Second mistake.

The thug on the leader's left was fast as well as big. By the time Lom straightened up he was already coming for him. Lom jabbed rat-mouth's stick into the side of his head. No swing, just a quick jab. But hard. Very hard. The big man's skull snapped sideways against his shoulder. Blood sprayed from his nose. He stayed on his feet for half a second, but his face was empty. Then he collapsed and lay still. His eyes were open, and there was blood and mess all over his face. Pink fluid coming out of his ear.

Two seconds, two down, five to go. So far so good. Lom felt hot and calm and alive. His anger was a quiet, efficient engine.

There was a dry click. Someone had opened a knife. A couple of the others had brass knuckles out and were putting them on. They were starting to fan out. Getting their act together. Another few seconds and he could be in bad trouble.

The one with the knife was the immediate threat. Lom stepped forward and crashed the tip of the baton down on his wrist. Felt the bone snap. He flicked the stick up and smashed it hard under the attacker's chin. There was a warm spattering of blood as his head jerked back and he went down, jaw broken.

The leader lumbered in then, head hunched between his shoulders, swinging wildly. Lom let the meaty white fist buzz past his ear, matched his charge and crashed his left elbow horizontally into the big red face.

Five seconds, four down.

Someone from Lom's right jabbed at his cheek with a knuckle-duster, grazing his ear. It might have done some damage but the boy had stayed too far out and mistimed it. Lom spun and smashed his left fist into the man's belly at the same time as Maroussia clubbed him viciously on the back of the head with the stick the big fellow had dropped when he fell.

The leader was getting clumsily to his knees, coughing and snorting clods of blood from his nose. Lom kicked him hard in the ribs. His elbows caved in under him and he slumped face down on the ground.

Five down, four still standing, but it was over. The rest only needed an excuse to get out of there. Lom let the baton clatter to the ground and pulled the empty Sepora .44 from his pocket.

'Like I said. Get in the wagon and drive away.' He gestured to the five men on the ground. 'And take this rubbish with you.'

There was a moment when they hesitated and a moment when he knew that's what they would do.

'I'm sorry,' said Maroussia when they'd got clear of the square.

'You were fine,' said Lom. 'You were more than fine. You were great.'

'No,' she said. 'Not that. I told that girl who we were. I gave her our names. I shouldn't have. It was stupid and now it's a risk. I'm sorry.'

He was only half listening to her. His hands were sore – there was a gash on one of his knuckles, seeping a little blood – and his legs felt weightless and slightly out of control as the adrenaline worked its way out of his system. For the second time, the day was stained with violence. Violence clanged in the air, hateful and sour. Now that the fighting was over Lom felt uncomfortable and slightly sick. He'd hurt people before, when he had to, but he hadn't enjoyed it, not like that. Today he'd done it gladly, efficiently, well, and he felt faintly ashamed.

'You were being kind,' said Lom. 'I guess we can't afford too much of that.'

'You helped that bookseller,' said Maroussia.

'Did I?' said Lom. 'They'll come back, them or others like them, for him or some other old guy. It won't be better because of what I did. It might be worse. Putting boys in hospital doesn't make the world a better place.'

Maroussia stopped and turned to face him. She stood there, pale, troubled and determined. Holding herself upright, shivering a little in the snow and bitter cold that whipped round the corner. She looked so thin. The sleeves of her coat too short, her wrists bony and raw against the dark wool. She had kissed him that morning at the sea gate lodge. On the cheek. The cool graze of her mouth against his skin.

'You didn't start it,' she said. 'You chose a side, that's all. There are only two sides now. There's nowhere else to stand.'

They walked a little way in silence.

'I didn't know you could fight like that,' said Maroussia.

'That wasn't fighting,' said Lom. 'That was winning. Different thing altogether.'

17

They came out abruptly on the side of the Mir opposite Big
Side. The river was a broad green surge, a wide muscular shoulder of moving water knotted with twists of surface current.
Low waves and backwash slapped against the bulwarks of the stone
embankment. Canopied passenger vedettes jinked between ponderous
barges nosing their way seawards.

They crossed the river by the crowded Chesma Bridge. The bronze
oil-lamps on the parapet, shaped like rising fish with lace-ruff gills and
scales like overlapping rows of coins, were already lit. Each one draped
in ribbons of funeral black, they burned pale flames in the grey afternoon. Light flecks of snow speckled the air. Not falling, just drifting.
Lom felt again the familiar pressure on his back. The follower was still
there. He was certain of it now. It was time to do something about it.

On the other side of the river, after the embankment gardens and
cafés, was the jewellers' quarter, and galleries selling artefacts from the
exotic provinces. Carpets and cushions and overstuffed couches. Vases
and urns and samovars. Plenty of traffic. Plenty of crowds.

'Will you do something for me?' said Lom.

'Of course.'

'I mean, do exactly what I say?'

'What do you want me to do?' said Maroussia.

'We're being watched,' he said. 'Someone's following. I think. I
want to be sure. No, don't look back. Not yet.'

'Is it the police?'

Lom shook his head.

'Whoever it is has been with us on and off since Marinsky-Voksal.
They're just watching. I wasn't sure. I thought they'd gone, but they're

back. There's not many of them, maybe only one. I want to have a look. Make sure. Then decide what to do.'

'So what do I do?'

'We walk on together for a while. Then I'll duck out of sight and you go on alone. Keep visible and don't try to lose them. Stop and start. Cross the street at random, but stay with the crowds. Always be among people. Make it hard for them, make it so they have to come in close, to keep in touch with you.'

'What if they don't follow me? What if they look for you?'

'Then we'll know something. After ten or fifteen minutes find somewhere you can go inside and sit down. Somewhere with lots of people. I'll find you there.'

Maroussia nodded. 'Now?' she said.

'I'll be watching you the whole time,' said Lom. 'I can do this kind of thing. I'm good.'

'It's fine. Let's go.'

They rounded a corner and Lom ducked into an alleyway and stepped quickly back into the shelter of a service door. He waited there for a slow hundred count then stepped back out into the street.

Maroussia was still in sight a block or so ahead. Lom stayed back and matched his pace with hers. He watched the traffic in the road. Most of it was horse-drawn: a few carts and karetas, a shabby droshki waiting outside a shuttered pension. He ignored them. You didn't run mobile surveillance with a horse. Maroussia was crossing the street between traffic, stopping to look in a window, starting to cross back, seeming to change her mind, then suddenly going anyway.

Don't overdo it.

She swung up onto the back of a moving tram, rode it fifty yards back towards Lom, then jumped off at the intersection and walked back the way she'd come. And Lom saw him.

A man had started to jog after the tram, then he came up short and turned away, abruptly absorbed in studying a poster. He was obvious. Clumsy. Not professional. And he was on his own. Definitely. If it was a team, he'd have taken the tram and left the others on Maroussia till he could double back.

Lom hung back, just to be sure. But there was no doubt about it. He wondered how the man had managed to stay out of sight for so long if he wasn't better than this. It was almost as if he wanted to be seen.

Lom pushed the thought aside. *Later. Do the job now.* He started to close in. He wanted a look at the man's face. From behind he was tall and wide-shouldered, wearing a long dark coat, a red wine-coloured scarf, a pale grey astrakhan hat. He walked with a faint hitch in his right hip. There was something familiar about him.

The follower was starting to slow, looking left and right, letting Maroussia get ahead of him. *He knows I'm here.*

Lom increased his pace, reeling him in. He'd got within thirty yards when the man spun on his heels and looked behind him. Straight at Lom. It was like he'd been punched in the chest. All the breath gone out of him. A constriction in the throat.

The face looking at Lom was his own face.

They locked gazes. The follower made a curt nod, spun on his heel and walked rapidly away.

The shock cost Lom a second. Then he reacted. He started forward but got tangled up with an old woman with a dog on a leash and a bag of groceries. By the time he got free the astrakhan hat was disappearing into a side street. When Lom reached the turning there was no sign of him.

Halfway down the street was a café with tables outside. Lom pushed the door open and went in. It was a long dark place, full of shadowed nooks and crannies and booths, thick with the smell of coffee and peppery, meaty stew. Lamps and candles spilled pools of yellow light and deep brown shadow. Most of the tables were empty. A radio was playing a big band march, 'Ours Are the Guns'.

Almost at the back of the room a man was sitting alone with his back to the door. A pale grey astrakhan hat. A wine-coloured woollen scarf. He was writing by the light of a flickering oil lamp. There was nothing else on the table. No cup. No plate. Lom threaded his way between the tables.

'Hey,' he said.

The man stood up and turned round. It was a different person, taller and older, with narrower shoulders. A long oval face under the grey astrakhan. A face full of serious openness. Deep dark eyes looked into Lom's from behind black wire-rimmed spectacles, wise and a little sad. He had a vaguely military bearing, but it wasn't a soldier's face. A doctor's perhaps. Or a poet's.

'Yes?' he said. 'Can I help you?'

'Sorry,' said Lom. 'I thought you were someone else.'

'Ah. Then excuse me, please.'

Lom stepped aside to let him pass and scanned the rest of the café but there was no one else. As he was turning to go, he saw the man had left something on the table. A single sheet of paper, folded once. A name was printed on it in a large clear hand. In capitals. Meant to be noticed. '*VISSARION LOM*'.

He picked up the note and read it.

'*Keep her safe. I will watch when I can.*'

It was signed '*Antoninu Florian*'.

Lom snapped his head round but the man had gone. Shit. He hustled back out into the street and looked both ways, but there was nothing to see. He refolded the note and tucked it into his pocket.

On Captain Iliodor's desk the telephone coughed into life. He picked it up first ring.

'Yes?'

'Glazkov, Captain. There was an incident an hour and a half ago in Braviknaya Square. A fracas with some young patriots outside a Lezarye bookshop. Four men are in the Bellin Infirmary—'

Iliodor interrupted him impatiently.

'Why are you telling me this? This is hardly unusual.'

'It was done by one man, Captain. One man against many. A man competent in violence. And there was a woman with him. The name Shaumian has come up. Shaumian and Lom.'

'This was *an hour and a half ago*? And I'm only hearing about it *now*?'

'The victims were unable to make an identification. A witness was found, a girl, but her testimony was … reluctant. The interrogation took some time.'

'*An hour and a half?*'

'The subjects are reported to be walking north. Towards Big Side. I'll get the written report across to you immediately.'

'You will tell me yourself, Glazkov. Tell me all of it. Now.'

18

*T*he underground chamber deep beneath the Lodka is lit by the
bluish flicker of fluorescent tubes. The gantry stands a hundred
feet high and drips with decorative ironwork. Life-size figures of
pensive women with long braided hair; plump naked children riding dol-
phins. An obelisk crowns the dome, and the entire construction is painted
burgundy and green. Within the outer framework the alloy containment
helix winds upwards like a single strip of orange peel.

Inside the gantry the Pollandore hangs, a perfect globe high as a house,
revolving slowly, touching nothing. It glows with is own vaporous lumi-
nescence but casts no light. It has no weight. No temperature. Frictionless,
it turns on its own axis and follows its own orbit, parallel to but no part
of this world, not in this universe but its own, tainting the air of the
chamber with a faint smell of lake-water and damp forest floor.

The gantry is almost four hundred years old. It was built soon after the
Vlast captured the Pollandore from Lezarye. There was a plan to show it
in public – a trophy, a holiday wonder, a kopek to climb to the viewing
platform and look down into the heart of strangeness – but this never
happened. Perhaps it was never meant to. Perhaps one of the madder
descendants of the Founder had the gantry made for his own private
pleasure. Perhaps he came down to it alone, at night, driven by some urge
to reach out and touch the Pollandore, to run his palm along the underside of another world. And his hand would slide across the skin between
alternative possibilities, feeling nothing and leaving no impression.

Whatever. Soon after the gantry was made, the Pollandore was
consigned to the lowest basement of the Lodka, its existence denied and
redacted from the files. Through the centuries that followed, the Vlast
periodically tried to destroy it. The Pollandore survived fire and furnace,

explosives, the assault of war mudjhiks. Subtler methods were attempted: corrosives, vacuums, the agonisingly slow insertion of invisibly fine needle-points. Nothing affected it. Nothing at all.

The only thing they didn't do was take it out to the deepest trenches of the ocean and sink it. They would not do that. If they could not destroy it, the Vlast preferred to know where it was.

And the Pollandore went on turning on its own axis.

Being other.

Being something else.

But now inside the Pollandore planetary currents are stirring. Masses are shifting.

It watches and waits.

Its time is close.

19

It was almost three in the afternoon when Lom and Maroussia reached the street where Vishnik had his apartment. Where Raku Andreievich, formerly Professor Prince Raku ter-Fallin Mozhno Shirin-Vilichov Vishnik, one-time historian of Mirgorod and city photographer, had lived among his books and paintings. Where he had died, slowly and painfully, under the interrogation of Chazia's police.

They surveyed the building from the shadow of a shuttered droshki kiosk on the corner. There was no sign of militia surveillance. The dvornik was at his station outside, slumped in his folding wooden chair, chin buried in a dirty brown muffler, nursing a tin mug in gloved hands. The subsiding flood water had left a smashed-up handcart with no wheels lying canted against the canal-side bollards. A couple of boys were kicking at it, trying to break it up for firewood, but they didn't have the weight to make an impact. After a while they gave up and dragged the whole thing away. The dvornik's small black eyes watched them resentfully. He looked like he'd been pulled up out of the canal mud himself and left outside collecting snow.

'He can't stay there all day,' said Maroussia. 'He has to move sometime. Everyone has to piss.'

'We haven't got time for this,' said Lom. 'Come on.'

The eyes of a dozen other dvorniks followed them from their chairs and lobbies. Informers every one, watchers and listeners, recording comings and goings in their black notebooks. The dvornik at Vishnik's building recognised them. His little berry-black eyes widened even more when Lom pulled his hand partly out of his pocket to show him the grip of the Sepora .44.

'This is pointing right at your belly. We're coming inside.'

The dvornik threw a panicked glance sideways.

'Make one sign to them,' said Lom, 'and I'll shoot your bollocks off. Or you can let us in. It's a fair offer. A trade.'

The dvornik didn't move. He shook his head.

'You'll kill me inside.'

'Maybe,' said Lom. 'Only if you piss me off.'

The man still didn't move. Pig-stubborn, or too scared to think. Probably both. A couple more seconds and the watchers would know something was wrong.

'He won't shoot you,' said Maroussia. 'Really he won't. We've come to see inside Professor Vishnik's apartment, not to kill you. We only need a few minutes. Then we'll be gone.'

The dvornik's raisin eyes squinted up at her. He nodded, stood up slowly and went ahead of them up the steps and into the building. Lom followed close behind. When they were inside, Maroussia pushed the heavy outer door shut. Latched it. Pushed the bolts home, top and bottom.

The dvornik turned to face them, blocking the hallway.

'It wasn't my fault,' he said. 'It wasn't me. I didn't—'

Lom shoved him in the shoulder. Hard. He stumbled back.

'Get the key,' Lom said. 'Number 4. Hurry.'

The dvornik went behind the counter into his little office. Lom followed him, the Sepora clear of his coat. The office was in a filthy state: the rug sodden, the linoleum floor still wet from the flood. A greasy leather armchair slumped in the corner, oozing and ruined. The whole place reeked of canal. The dvornik rummaged about in a box under the counter and brought out a labelled key. Held it out to Lom.

'Here,' he said. 'Second floor.'

'Bring it. Take the stairs, not the lift.'

'We can't. The lift's still out. The flood … the electrics …'

'I said the stairs, arsehole. You first.'

On the way up Lom saw the gouges in the plaster where he'd fired at Safran and his men when they came for him. The wreckage the grenade had made of the landing. It seemed for ever ago. As the dvornik put the key in the lock, Lom had a premonition that Vishnik's body would still be there, still tied to the couch, eyes open, wounds crusted and gaping. Left by Chazia's interrogation team to rot and seep and dry out where he had died.

But the body was gone, though the couch still stood where it had been dragged into the centre of the room. It was covered in dried blood. And other stuff. The leakage of death.

The room had been thoroughly, violently searched. The filing cabinets were open and empty. Desk drawers pulled out, their contents spilled, the desk smashed open. Faded brick-red curtains pulled off the wall along with the rail that held them. Bookshelves emptied and torn from the wall, the books scattered across the floor. All the strange, inconsequential objects that Vishnik had collected in his solitary city walks – the red lacquer tea caddy, the pieces of wood and brick, the discarded tickets and printed notices, the shards of pottery and glass – swept into a heap in the corner. The paintings that had filled every gap on the wall ripped from smashed frames. Vishnik's lonely absence hung in the air, bereft, accusing and sad.

'I haven't had time ...' the dvornik said.

'What?'

'The floods ... I've been too busy. The room has to be re-let, but I can't—'

'Sit there,' said Lom. 'On the couch. Don't move and don't speak. I may just shoot you anyway.'

In a corner of the room there was a small heap of women's clothes and a threadbare carpet bag. Maroussia pounced on them

'My things!'

She started to stuff them back into the bag. When she had finished, she knelt among Vishnik's scattered books, sifting through them, riffling the pages.

'There's nothing here,' said Lom. 'If there was, they've taken it.'

Maroussia shook her head.

'There must be something. He told me. *They didn't get it*. That's what he said. *They didn't get it. Even they are human and stupid.*'

'But they searched again,' said Lom. 'More thoroughly. After he was dead.'

'They looked all over,' said the dvornik. 'The halls. The stairwell. The bathroom. They pulled the cistern off the wall.'

'You shut up,' said Lom.

'He just wants us out of here quickly,' said Maroussia. 'We need to search. We don't have another option.'

Lom pushed the dvornik ahead of him into the kitchen. Vishnik's

darkroom was still set up in a corner. Bottles of chemicals opened
and spilled down the sink. The room reeked of metol and hypo. The
enlarger head had been unscrewed and opened up. The red safety light
smashed. Packets of photographic paper ripped open and ruined.
Unexposed films, pulled from their canisters, lay on the floor in curls
and spools of grey-black cellulose ribbon. The boxes where Vishnik
kept his prints and negative strips were gone.

Lom searched for a while randomly. After a few minutes he went
back into the other room. Maroussia was sitting on the floor in the
wreckage of Vishnik's desk. She would have stayed there for days,
sifting every last piece. Opening every page of every book. But it was
hopeless. They didn't even know what they were looking for.

'We have to go,' said Lom.

She looked up at him, suddenly angry.

'Where?' she said. 'Where else would we look? Do you know? I
don't know. Here. This is the place. Here. There's something here. You
knew him. He was your friend. Work it out.'

'Please ...' said the dvornik.

'Sit back down on that couch,' said Lom, 'and shut the fuck up.'

'Does he have to sit there?' said Maroussia.

Lom looked at the awful object, stained by torture and dying.
Vishnik had lain there. *Shit.*

'I know where it is,' he said.

They didn't get it. Even they are human, and stupid.

The interrogators had searched thoroughly. While Vishnik's body
was still there on the couch. And the one place they didn't look was
the same place he and Maroussia hadn't looked. Because of what was
on it. Because of what had happened there. They blanked it out. Even
the Vlast torturers blinded themselves. Avoided seeing the work of
their own hands. Forgetting as soon as they had done it.

'It's in the couch,' said Lom.

He pulled the dvornik off it roughly and knelt to look underneath.
There was nothing. He felt with his hands all over the bloody and still
faintly sticky leather seat and up the back of it, slipping his hands into
the crevices. Looking for something. Anything. An opening. A lump
in the stuffing. There was nothing.

The couch was a kind of chaise longue with a seat-back rising at
one end. Lom went round behind it, down on his knees. The back was

covered with a single panel of leather, sewn at the top and pinned tight with a row of black metal studs along the bottom. He ran his finger along the studs. Picked at a couple of them with his fingernail. One came loose. Then another. They weren't completely tight. As if they had been levered out and pushed loosely back into place. They held, but only just.

Lom took the razor from his pocket and sliced a long, arcing cut across the leather back panel. Stuck his hand inside. Pulled out a large brown envelope stuffed with paper and sealed down tight.

20

The Colloquium of Four sat on the high platform at the north end of the All-Dominions Thousand Year Hall on chairs of plush red velvet. Chazia was in the centre with Chairman Fohn. Dukhonin, the General Secretary, was on Chazia's left, and Khazar – negligible Khazar, the Minister for Something – sat at Fohn's right hand. The platform, raised high above the crowd, had room for a hundred, but the Four sat alone, a wide frosty space gaping between each chair. To the crowd we look small, Chazia thought. Unimpressive. Vulnerable. Fohn had planned the Novozhd's funeral and he had fucked it up. Every part of it.

Fohn would make the speeches. Reading the exequies of the lost leader. Chazia had not objected. Let Fohn lick the dead man's arse; she wouldn't wrap herself in his corpse-shroud. They would know her for other reasons soon enough.

Behind the Four on their chairs, Fohn had hung immense waterfalls of red and black fabric and, bathed in a golden spotlight, a portrait of the Novozhd fifty feet tall. Fine words picked out in letters of gold.

WE WILL REMEMBER HIM, AND IN REMEMBERING, VICTORY!
STAND TOGETHER, CITIZENS, AGAINST ENEMIES WITHIN AND WITHOUT!

Beneath the platform the corpse itself was displayed. It lay on crimson silk in an open casket of black wood polished to a mirror shine. The embalmers had done their work thoroughly: repaired his bomb wounds, given his face a waxy apple flush, blacked and glossed his hair and moustache. A man in the prime of life. The image of his portrait. Only the drab khaki uniform that Fohn had insisted on – *We must remember, colleagues, that we are, after all, in a state at war* – spoiled the fine effect. The four mudjhiks faced outwards, one at each corner of the catafalque, motionless and watchful, the colour of dried blood.

From the Thousand Year Hall, after the funeral, the body was to be carried in solemn procession to the Khronsk-Gorsk Mausoleum. Factories had been closed for the day so the workers could line the avenues for the cortège. Free meals were being served at the municipal canteens. On the way to the funeral Chazia had seen huge crowds of people in mourning black. Karetas, droshkis and cars, black ribbons and pennants fluttering.

Chazia's attention was fixed on the crowd in the hall. The first rows of seating were reserved for war veterans. They sat in rigid silence, holding up their crutches, pointing with them towards the leaders on the podium like arms raised in salute. And behind them, row after row, dissolving into shadow, one hundred thousand persons dressed in black with touches of red, standing to attention in perfect rank and file, not one speaking a word. So many feet, so many shoulders, so many lungs breathing. The noise of a hundred thousand silences – the small shuffle for balance, the rub of cloth against cloth, the swallow and stifled cough – roared against the platform like the sea. One hundred thousand faces, one expression. The sombre gravity of grief. It was *one* body. One *mass*. It had heaviness. Inertia. An existence all of its own. It was the Vlast.

Chazia pictured how it would be when she stood alone before them, speaking in a fine clear amplified voice. Two hundred thousand shining eyes fixed on her. The roar of their cheering. The rhythmic stamping of two hundred thousand feet. They would chant her name. She would throw her arms wide to embrace their acclamation, and her hair would lift and stir in the wind of their breath.

In the Thousand Year Hall, the waiting dragged on too long. The hundred thousand people waited. On their platform the Colloquium of Four waited. Dead time. Chazia felt the *mass* dissolving. Atomising. A hundred thousand separate thoughts. Fucking Fohn. He was surely finished after this.

There was a deep loud crash from outside the hall. Another. And another. The distant explosions roared on and on, ceaselessly, merging into a rolling brutal thunder. The veterans were standing to attention, right hands clenched against their chests. Somewhere in the crowd a woman was screaming. *The Archipelago! The Archipelago has come!* But it was only the five hundred guns of the fleet at the Goll Dockyards doing their bit.

At last the thundering guns subsided into silence and a magnified rustling came over the tannoy. The Combined Services Orchestra in the gallery was getting ready to play. Chazia could see them across the vastness of the auditorium, minute figures in a splash of stark white light for the kinematograph camera. When Colonel of Music Vikhtor Vanyich Forelle raised his baton, all other lights in the hall fell dim. Everything disappeared in shadow, apart from the orchestra and the corpse itself, isolated under a single spotlamp. The effect drew murmurs of appreciation from the mourners. *Well done, Fohn. They can't see us at all now.*

The music began. The slow movement from Frobin's *Lake Horseman Suite*. The massed voices of the Navy Choir singing the 'Blood of Angels' chorus from *Winter Tears*.

Vlast! Vlast! Freedom land!
My heart a flag in winter –
The drum of my blood
In storms of rain.

Music was of no interest to Chazia. She waited for it to end.

Someone edged across the platform towards her, taking advantage of the dimness that hid them from the hall. It was Iliodor. Ignoring Fohn's ostentatious disapproval, he crouched behind Chazia and whispered in her ear.

She smiled.

'Good,' she said when he had finished. 'Good. When you have her, bring her to me.'

21

L om pulled the envelope from the back of the bloody couch
and ripped it open. It contained a sheaf of glossy monochrome
photographic prints. He shuffled through them quickly. He
knew what they were. Vishnik's Pollandore moments, the photographs taken with his beloved Kono on his long wanderings around
Mirgorod. Photographs of moments when the world broke open and
new things were possible. He'd kept them safe at the cost of his life.

Lom sat back, flooded with disappointment.

'There's nothing new here,' he said. 'We've seen all this before.'

'Maybe he saw something else in them,' said Maroussia. 'Something
specific. Something we missed.'

'It's possible,' said Lom. 'I guess.'

'So let's have another look.'

Maroussia spread the photographs out on the floor and they went
through them together. Most were gentle, beautiful images, full of an
oblique magic: sunlight on a street corner, ripples in a pool of rain, the
way light caught the moss on a tree. Some were passionate, dramatic,
apocalyptic even: the curtain torn aside, the whole of the city ripping
open at the seams. The people in them knew what was happening to
them. They looked into Vishnik's lens, their mouths open as if they
were laughing, their faces filled with ecstatic joy.

Sorting through the pictures, Lom felt a sharp pang of loss. He felt
the loss of Vishnik, and also of the city as Vishnik had seen it. Vishnik's
Mirgorod was beautiful: these things happened and were perhaps still
happening, somewhere in the city, but Lom had never seen them. For
him too the city had opened to show him glimpses, possibilities, but
he saw blank-faced buildings, a tower half a mile high crowned with

an immense brutal statue of Josef Kantor, the Square of the Piteous
Angel crowded with grey withdrawn people, their downturned faces,
their drab whispering voices. A future crushed under the weight of its
own fear, far heavier even than the weight of the Vlast today. Kantor's
future. Chazia's future. It had to be stopped, and if he could stop it he
would. Maroussia's way, or his way.

Maroussia picked up a handful of photographs from the pile.

'These are new,' she said. 'I haven't seen these before.'

'Show me,' said Lom.

He went through them one by one. A couple walked naked on
the surface of a river, the river glowing with an inward radiant light.
A giant stood on a harbour side, silhouetted against the sky, his hair
rising in a cloud around his head. A parade marched down a street
towards the lens, only the street was above the rooftops and wrapped
in chimney smoke and the people carried blazing candelabras and
some of them were only heads and had no bodies at all. They were
exhilarating, uncanny pictures, but they added nothing. No help at all.

'Maybe if we knew where they were taken?' said Lom. 'Vishnik
had notes, but without them ... It would take us days to find all these
places. Weeks.'

Maroussia slipped her hand inside the couch, feeling around towards
the top of the backrest.

'Wait,' she said. 'There's something else in here. Hang on ... yes!'

She pulled it out and held it up. A large map, printed on thin paper
and folded to make a compact packet, the creases strengthened with
strips of glued linen.

'That's more like it,' said Lom.

Lom cleared a space on the floor and they laid it out flat. The map
was a standard large-scale street plan of Mirgorod, but Vishnik had
made marks all over it. Hundreds of small circles in black pencil. The
pattern was instantly discernible: a few outliers in the outer quarters,
growing denser towards the centre of the city. The marks clustered
most thickly at a point on the River Mir where it made an elbow-bend
southwards and the Yekaterina Canal joined it.

'It's the Lodka,' said Maroussia. 'The Pollandore is in the Lodka.'

The Lodka. The stone heart and cerebral cortex of the Vlast. The immense island building, the thousand-windowed palace of bureaucracy,
the labyrinth of linoleum-floored corridors, entranceless courtyards,

stairwells without stairs. The offices of uncountable clerks and archivists and diplomats and secret police. The basement cells, the killing rooms, the mortuary. Vishnik had traced the Pollandore to there.

Lom refolded the map, scooped up the photographs, stuffed the whole lot back into the envelope and gave it to Maroussia.

'Take it,' he said. 'We need to get moving. We've been here too long.'

She pushed the envelope into her carpet bag and they hurried out of the apartment, Maroussia first, then Lom hustling the dvornik ahead of him. At the bottom of the stairs they turned left into the narrow entrance hall and walked straight into two militia men coming the other way, 9mm Blok 15 parabellums in their hands.

22

The men confronting Lom and Maroussia were officers, a captain and a lieutenant. Crisply turned out uniforms, neat haircuts under their caps, pale steady eyes. Their cap badges said SV. *Spetsyalnaya Voyska*. Political Police operating within the armed forces. The militia picked the best from the army and the gendarmes, and then the SV picked the best of the militia. The SV were supremely competent, tough and absolutely ideologically loyal.

'We'll do this step by step,' the captain said. He pointed at Lom. 'You. Four steps back and face the wall. Put your hands against it, high, and shuffle your feet back.'

Lom did as he said.

'You –' the captain pointed to the dvornik '– come past me on the left, go into the office and stay there. Keep back from the door. Don't come out.'

The dvornik looked back at Lom. A leer of triumph. Arsehole.

Maroussia was still standing in the centre of the corridor.

'Now you,' the captain said to her. 'On the floor.'

Maroussia didn't move. Lom couldn't see her face.

'Maroussia,' he said over his shoulder. 'You need to do what he says.'

She put her bag on the floor and lay face down, hands on her head. The captain stepped forward and took the envelope out of her hand. The lieutenant came up behind Lom and patted him down, keeping the muzzle of the Blok 15 pressed hard against the base of his spine. He patted down Lom's pockets. Took out the empty gun and the razor.

'OK,' the captain said. 'Now let's get out into the street.'

A covered truck waited outside, an unmarked GPV in generic military olive, the tailgate open. The driver saw them coming and started the engine. Lom and Maroussia got in the back and sat side by side on the bench. The lieutenant sat opposite. Covered them with his gun. The captain came last, carrying Maroussia's bag. He closed the tailgate and sat at the far end of the truck, away from them. Nobody spoke. It was all measured, practised, competent. The lieutenant slapped the back of the cab and the truck moved away.

'Where are we going?' said Lom. He had to speak loudly above the noise of the engine. The SV men ignored him. Maroussia sat ramrod straight. Expressionless.

'OK,' said Lom. 'If that's how you want it.'

He leaned back and stretched his legs in front of him. Closed his eyes and let his mind open, focusing on nothing.

Listen. Feel. Breathe. There is plenty of time.

He felt the faint, steady pulsing in the skin-covered gap in his skull. Focused all his attention on it.

Lom used to imagine his unconscious mind as a dark, irrational place, an airless primeval cave where monsters moved. But the opposite was true. The unconscious mind was immense. Bright, airy, perfumed, luminous, borderless, beautiful. The outside world poured into it constantly, without ever filling it up. Everything was felt, everything was noticed.

And all you had to do was pay attention.

Now, at this very moment, there was the street noise outside, the faint calling of seagulls, the rumble of the truck's wheels on the road, the working of the engine, the whisper of cloth against cloth, four people breathing. The smell of leather and sweat, hot steel and engine oil. The lieutenant's shaving soap. Maroussia's hair. Her skin. And there was the rub of his cuff against his own wrist, the sock rucked under his foot, the pressure of the hard bench seat against his back and thighs. In the subliminal mind's timeless empire nothing was diminished. Nothing wore thin by tedium and habit. Nothing was ignored, nothing judged trivial. Nothing was forgotten. The luminous inner world contained everything he was and everything undiscovered that he might still become. His forest birthright. His strength and his power.

Lom opened his eyes and looked across at Maroussia. She was still sitting straight-backed and staring ahead. How long did they have? Fifteen minutes? Twenty? Then they would reach the Lodka, or the

Armoury, or wherever they were going. Then all chance would be gone. *Listen. Feel. Breathe. There is plenty of time.*

The GPV came to a halt. An intersection, or a traffic hold-up. Lom reached out into the air around him. Carefully he began to assemble it, to gather it together. He'd never tried to work with such precision before. Always, previously, he'd done what he'd learned to do in haste. In desperation. Recklessly. This time the task needed subtlety: blow out the back of the truck, take down the SV men. But not hurt Maroussia. And try not to draw the attention of everyone in the street. He wasn't sure if he could do it but it was time to try. He was as ready as he would ever be.

But Lom never made the move. Something else happened. The sudden crash of breaking glass from the cab of the truck. A shout. A scream.

Open to the world as he was, Lom felt the driver die.

23

L avrentina Chazia had another place in the Lodka, a place few knew of, deeper than the deepest of the interrogation cells, reached by steep iron stairs and locked corridors to which she had the only key. It was not a room but a high, narrow tunnel, running under the immense building and out beyond it. Sometimes, when she was working alone, Chazia heard faint sounds and echoes from the dark tunnel mouths. The skitter of footfalls. Mutterings and distant shrieks. Heavy objects being dragged across stone and mud. She took no notice. Mice and rats in the city's loft.

The section of tunnel where she worked was filled with cool grey morning light, spilling downwards from smeared light wells in the roof. Parallel steel rails set into the flagstone floor disappeared in both directions into shadow. The air smelled of damp stone and river water and machine oil and the faint iron-and-ozone scent of angel flesh. The tunnel hummed and prickled with the muted almost-life of the angel stuff. It was a low vibration at the threshold of perception. Chazia had collected blocks of it, in slabs and rolls and drums: offcuts from the Armoury workshops where they maintained the mudjhiks. For years she had been working here, at her bench, at night, under the bleak illumination of fluorescent tubing. She worked with lathes and belt saws and finer, subtler tools. It had taken her years to acquire the skills and equipment. Years of trial and error. Years of developing techniques. Years moving towards ever greater power.

The substance dug from the bodies of the immense dead angels varied in consistency. Some of it was as dense as lead and as hard as rock, but it could be soft and fibrous, like meat, or a viscous semi-liquid, or a fine and weightless lustrous diaphane. It ranged in colour from heavy blood-purples, almost blacks, through reds to alabaster orange-pinks. The theoreticians of the Vlast had no idea how the angels' living bodies might have functioned: there were no apparent internal organs, and no two carcases had the same shape or inner structure.

Unlike the Armoury engineers, Chazia didn't wear protective clothing. She didn't work from behind thick glass, her hands in clumsy rubber mittens. She didn't mask her face with gauze. Unafraid, she immersed herself in angel stuff and breathed its dust. She tasted it. She let it stain and merge with her flesh. Absorbing and being absorbed. It was strength, it was vigour, it was a heady prospect of joy. There had been failures, of course, false starts and disappointments and near-disasters. No one had ever attempted anything so ambitious as this work of hers. No one had dared imagine it or face the risks. But she had driven herself onward relentlessly. And in the end she had succeeded.

She had made herself a suit of angel flesh to wear.

And now, in the grey subaqueous wash of light, she pulled the oil-cloth shroud from it.

The thing she had made looked like a mudjhik, but smaller and slighter. A matte reddish-purple carapace of interlocking pieces. And a mudjhik would have had the brain and spinal cord of an animal embedded in it, to give it cerebration, whereas this had none: it required none. She had made an angel headpiece to encase her own head, and angel gauntlets for her hands.

She stared at it, trembling with excitement. Its crude face stared into hers. The sense of power and life in it prickled across her skin, raising the hairs on the back of her neck. She felt the tightening in her throat. The stirring in her belly and between her legs. For weeks she had come down here daily to look at it. To be with it. To stand before it. She had not yet dared to put it on. Fear, or the delicious prolongation of desire, had held her at the brink. The tipping point.

She knew the risks. The science of angel flesh was a thin crust of bluster over vertiginous ignorance. Many had ruined their minds and died. She was not reckless. She would proceed cautiously and step by step. But she had already delayed too long.

No more delay. She must begin.

24

In the first second and a half of the attack on the truck the SV men reacted slowly. They needed time to readjust. Lom was faster. He slid forward on the bench and kicked at the lieutenant's right hand. The Blok 15 went spinning from his grip and clattered to the floor. Lom punched him in the face. Hard. He went down.

The captain hesitated, caught between the unknown threat outside and what was happening inside the truck. Then he was swinging his gun towards Lom, and Lom was scrabbling towards him, knowing he had no time, knowing he had failed and it was over, when Maroussia grabbed the captain's wrist and forced it down. The revolver went off, firing into the floor of the truck. The shot was deafening in the enclosed space. The smell of burned powder. Lom clubbed the captain with his fist in the side of the head and he fell sideways.

The tailgate crashed open. A face looked in. A long, oval, serious face under an astrakhan hat. Round wire-rimmed glasses. A doctor's face. A poet's.

'You!' said Lom.

'Come with me, please,' said Antoninu Florian. 'There is little time to lose. A gunshot will attract attention.'

Maroussia stared at him.

'Who—' she began.

'Please,' said Florian. 'Please hurry.'

Maroussia looked at Lom. He nodded. *Get through the next two minutes.* Maroussia grabbed her carpet bag and climbed down from the back of the truck, clutching it tight in her hand. Lom picked up the lieutenant's gun from the floor at this feet. Checked the magazine. It was full. He followed Maroussia out of the truck and into the street.

It was snowing hard. Lom spun round, checking on all sides. No visible immediate threat. People on the pavement were looking. One man in particular, bareheaded, open shirt, was staring hard. Considering getting involved but hadn't made his mind up yet. Florian was already pushing his way through the gathering crowd, moving fast.

'Go!' Lom hissed in Maroussia's ear. 'Go!'

They followed Florian until he ducked through an arched brick entrance leading into shadow. At the corner by the entrance was a bakery. A torn awning. Curlicues of white script. *BAKERY. GALINA TROPINA. PASTRY. COFF--.* The archway opened into a long gully between high buildings. It was at least two hundred yards long, and deserted. There was no sign of Florian.

'Do you know this place?' he said to Maroussia. 'Do you know where it goes?'

'It leads to the back entrance to the Apraksin,' said Maroussia. 'The indoor market. There'll be crowds.'

'OK,' said Lom. 'Let's go.'

They were about fifty yards into the gully when Lom felt the unmistakeable zip of a bullet passing close to his ear. There was a sharp crack behind them. The echo followed. Lom swung round, pulling the Blok 15 from his pocket. The SV captain was silhouetted just inside the entrance, lining up for a better shot.

'Hey! You! Captain!'

The shout came from somewhere up above them.

Antoninu Florian jumped from the high window ledge and landed with a heavy skid between them and the SV captain, crouching like an animal. He rose and charged with astonishing, loping speed. But there was too much ground to cover and not enough time.

The captain shot him in the belly.

Florian spun round with the force of the bullet hitting him. His knees went first. He staggered and collapsed almost at their feet in a hunched foetal curl, his hand at his stomach. Dark blood spilling out between his fingers and pooling on the ground.

'Oh,' said Maroussia quietly. 'Oh.'

The SV captain raised his gun again, straight-armed for a careful aim. They had no cover. Nowhere to go. Lom shot him. The captain's skull burst open in a spray of blood and fragments of bone. His lifeless body smashed back against the wall and toppled sideways to the ground.

There was a moment of stillness. Silence. Lom didn't move. Nor did Maroussia. They were watching Florian. He was getting unsteadily to his feet. Maroussia ran forward. Lom followed. By the time they reached Florian he was standing, swaying, head bowed and holding his hands cupped together at waist level as if he was inspecting the sticky mess on the front of his coat. The thick spill of blood. Then he looked up at them, his eyes unfocused. Glassy surprise.

'Shot, then,' he said, almost to himself. 'Shot again.'

His legs gave under him and he would have fallen if Maroussia hadn't caught him. He managed to get himself upright again.

'Sorry,' he said. 'Sorry. Blood. On your coat now.'

'Can you walk?' said Maroussia.

'Honestly don't know. Let's give it a try.'

Lom put his shoulder under Florian's arm and lifted him, getting the weight off his feet, drag-carrying him along. His face against Lom's cheek felt cold and damp. His lungs were dragging at short, fast, shallow breaths.

'We have to get out of here,' said Lom.

Stumbling awkwardly, they retreated down the long alley towards the Apraksin, the injured man a sagging, limping weight on Lom's shoulder. As they got near the far end, Florian tried to pull away from Lom. He seemed to have recovered some strength, enough to stand unaided, though blood was dripping down the front of his coat and splashing the ground at his feet.

'This is not right,' he said. 'I just need to sit down. Sort myself out. Could you? Find me somewhere? You can leave me there.'

'No,' said Maroussia.

'Yes,' said Florian. 'Really.' He leaned against the wall, took off his glasses, wiped them on his sleeve and put them back on. His face was papery white, his forehead beaded with sweat. 'I'll be fine. In a minute.'

'You've been *shot*,' said Maroussia.

'True,' said Florian. And for a second his face seemed to readjust itself. Looking at Maroussia, he reflected her own face back at her, mirroring her expression. Concern. Indecision. Shock. The dark bright eyes widening. He gave her a pained, sympathetic grin. 'I am in some pain. And so for now I cannot walk. I must sit down. Or lie down. Even better. You can leave me. You need to go.'

'He's right,' said Lom.

'Vissarion—' Maroussia began.

'It's true. We can't take him with us. He can't walk in that condition.'

'But ... we can't just leave him here.'

'No. So we need transport. And we need somewhere he can stay while we find it.' Lom turned to go. 'Wait here.'

Near the exit from the gully was a wide high wooden gate, peeling black paint, with a small wicket door set into it. Lom tested the wicket. It was unlocked, and opened into a wide linoleum-floored passageway. Bare electric bulbs hanging from the ceiling cast a bleak light on a clutter of stacked boxes and pallets. Shuttered entrances, grilles, closed doors. A porter's trolley. A service entrance for the Apraksin market. There was no one about. Lom was thinking two minutes ahead. Maximum. Get through that. Then worry about the next. The only thing now was to get off the street.

Twenty feet into the passageway was a half-glazed door. Small panes of frosted glass. No light showing. Lom tried the handle but it was locked. He smashed a pane with his elbow, reached in past the sharp broken jags and unlatched it. Inside was a room for the porters, something like that: several tables and chairs littered with unwashed mugs and plates. In the corner was a small sink and an urn for hot water. He hustled back out into the alley.

'I've found somewhere,' he said.

Florian was drowsy, unsteady on his feet. Lom didn't like it. A bullet in the gut was a killing wound, not immediately, but soon: bleeding out or infection, death either way.

They got him into the porters' room somehow. Florian sat in a chair at one of the tables, his face pale, his eyes wide and dark behind their lenses. Sweat slicked his forehead. He took off his coat and unbuttoned his shirt to the waist. Blood smeared his ribs, matted the thick hair on his chest, gathered in the thin folds of his belly. The entrance wound was a dark ominous leaking hole. His face tight with pain and concentration, Florian pushed his finger inside it and poked around, hooked something out and placed it on the table. A distorted fragment of brass sticky with blood. A bullet.

'You got it *out*?' said Maroussia.

'Bad idea to leave it in,' said Florian. 'It hurt. A lot.'

He hauled himself to his feet, staggered and leaned against the table.

'If you could just ... pass me my coat.'

Maroussia hesitated.

'You can't …' she said. 'You don't look—'

'I am quite well.' He shrugged the coat on painfully. 'Thank you. I will go now.'

He took a step forward and slumped to the floor, sending the chair crashing over.

Between them Lom and Maroussia hauled Florian, a heavy dead-weight, awkwardly up into a chair and let him slump forward across the tabletop, head cradled on folded arms. To a cursory glance he would look like someone sleeping.

Working quickly, Lom went through his pockets. There was a hand-ful of coins, a leather wallet with a few rouble notes, a fountain pen and a soft leather notebook, the kind with an elastic strap to hold it shut and a thin black ribbon to mark the page. The pen was expensive, a squat and solid turquoise Wassertrau. Nothing else. No identity papers.

'Vissarion!' hissed Maroussia. 'Hurry!'

'One second.'

The astrakhan hat had a purple silk lining and a maker's crest, a double-headed eagle. A tag sown into the crown said, *Joakim Sylwest. Superior Outfitters. 144 Ulitsa Zaramalya. Koromants.*' Lom riffled the pages of the notebook, but there were only illegible scribbles and scrawls.

'We need transport,' said Lom when he had finished. 'There must be trucks or wagons somewhere near a place like this.'

'I know someone who works here,' said Maroussia.

Lom looked at her doubtfully. He didn't want to involve anyone else, just find what he needed and steal it. But that would take time, and how much did they have before the place was crawling with mili-tia? Not enough.

'Who?' he said.

'A friend. She works here on the fourth floor,' said Maroussia. 'I trust her.'

Lom hesitated.

Get though the next two minutes.

'OK,' he said. 'Let's find her.'

25

L avrentina Chazia worked the pulleys and lifting chains that swung the heavy angel skin away from the wall and into position. Stood on a stool to reach the headpiece, unhook it and bring it down. When she put her head inside it the weight of its edge cut into her shoulders. Enclosing, suffocating darkness. The iron-and-ozone tang of angel flesh in her mouth.

She waited.

Nothing.

Chazia opened her mind, greedy and desperate, hunting for the link, the connection that didn't come.

Nothing.

She had put her head inside a casket of stone meat. That was all.

But she could *not* fail. She *needed* not to fail.

Her legs were weak and trembling. She knelt on the ground and bent forward, resting her head against the stone to relieve the weight, stretching her arms out to the side. Closed her eyes. Focused all her attention on the dark purple surging inside her.

And waited.

And felt the barest touch of something at the back of her head, moving under her scalp. Like cool, tapered fingers brushing the surface of her mind. Tentatively feeling their way. Pausing. Teasing. Waiting.

Chazia screamed.

Hot blades stabbed deep into the core of her brain. The burning needle-bite of jaws snapped shut. Her body spasmed. Rigid. Jerking. She was on her back, staring unseeing up towards the roof, and the rock, and the earth, and the piled up floors and roofs of the Lodka, and the vaporous open sky. Her senses caught fire and burst into strange, alien life. The world poured into her.

She knew every contour and texture of the walls and the ground beneath her. Every object in the workshop. She sensed the tunnel leading away, its slight downward gradient. She was aware of Mirgorod around and above her, the weight and structure of its buildings. She felt the flow of the river as a surge of brown light. A heavy solid sound. She perceived the presence of people. Fuzzy patches of sentience. She could distinguish them from dogs or cats or birds. It was like a taste. They offered themselves up to her, all those teeming, unprotected, vulnerable points of life: they were naked before her alien angel gaze. She could have reached out and plucked one of them for herself, like a fruit from a bush. The sharp, dark, edgy points of meat scuttering away down the tunnel, those were rats. There were other things underground as well: ways and chambers unconnected to the tunnel, and lives inhabiting them. Older, stranger lives she could not identify, which felt her touch and slithered and shied away. And below her, deep and going down for ever, was the warmth and torsion and slow pressure of planetary rock. Sedimentary silt of seashell and bone. Extrusions of heart-rock: seams of granite and lava, dolerites, rhyolites, gabbros and tuffs, all buckled, faulted, shattered and upheaved under the weight of their own millennial tidal shifting.

It was uncontainable. Tumbling overwhelming floods of perception. In some detached and peripheral corner of her mind Chazia noted that it might be possible to master this torrent of percipience. With practice, it might be ordered and arranged into some approximation of consistent conscious understanding. But that was for another time. She didn't even try to control it. She didn't want to perceive: she wanted to *be perceived*.

She pushed back against the deluge of incoming sensation. Trying to use the power of it. She gathered together all the yearning and loneliness and frustration and humiliation and desire for power and control that she had carried inside her for so long. For always. All her will and purpose. Her sense of self, her towering, essential, unignorable self. She gathered it all into a tight ball and hurled it upwards and outwards into the world, powered by the energy pouring into her. A yelling, shrieking scream.

I am here! Notice me!

Recognise me! See what I have done!
Speak to me again! Speak to me!
Touch me!

Time after time she spurted and jetted herself out into the world. She was a blade of light stabbing up through clouds into the bright emptiness beyond. She was a loud voice calling above the storm. A scream of demand rolling across the continent. Again and again she shouted, until she was empty. Drained. Exhausted. And when she could do no more she stopped and listened.

Listened to the echoless silence. The unresponding emptiness behind and below the world.

She does not know that she has been noticed. That from nearby she is watched.

The Pollandore – enclosed in its little room but not enclosed – a world – a sphere of perfumed light – earth and leaf and forest air – turning on its quiet axis in no-time and no-space – the Pollandore knows what she is.

And senses what she could be.

Sees the trails of future possibilities spilling like ghosts around her.

And stirs uneasily in its patient waiting.

Deep inside it something that was balanced, slips.

Something that was silent, calls.

26

Maroussia led Lom to the far end of the passageway and up the stairs at the end. Swing doors at the top opened into the Apraksin: four levels of balconies and shopfronts rose around a wide central atrium crowded with stalls and bathed in blazing electric light. There was nothing you could not find in the Apraksin. Rugs, shoes, papers and inks, sheaves of dried herbs, spice boxes, taxidermy, mirrors, telescopes and binoculars, caged parrots and toucans. Fruit. But today there were few customers, and nobody seemed to be buying. It was a paused, subdued mortuary of commerce. Quiet funereal music played from the tannoy. Massed male voices singing from *Winter Tears*. Many concessions had closed for the day, and the bored stallholders who remained watched incuriously from behind their counters. They all wore black armbands.

On a fourth-floor balcony, squeezed between a leather stall and a tea counter, was a concession filled with wardrobes, cupboards and dressers of reddish brown wood. There was rich smell of wax polish and resin. A sign said CUPBOARDS BY CORNELIUS. The furniture was tall and solid and carved with intricate patterns of leaves and bunched berries. Doors were left open to show off shelves and drawers, rails and hooks. Compartments. Cubbyholes. On a side table was an arrangement of smaller boxes made of the same red wood, with lids carved and pierced and polished to a high shine.

'I don't see Elena,' said Maroussia, looking round. 'Shit. Where *is* she?'

A voice called across to them.

'Maroussia? It *is* you!'

A woman came across from the tea counter, wiping her hands. She was about thirty. Dark blue work clothes. A tangle of thick fair hair roughly cut. Her eyes were full of life and intelligence but she looked tired. Harassed.

She gave Maroussia a hug.

I'm so glad you came,' she said. 'I was worried. Your mother ... I heard. I'm so sorry. I went to your apartment, but you weren't there and nobody knew where you'd gone. Are you all right? You look pale ...' She glanced curiously at Lom.

'Elena,' said Maroussia. 'This is my friend Vissarion.'

The woman held out her hand.

'Elena Cornelius. Pleased to meet you. '

Then she saw the blood on his coat. And on Maroussia's.

'Maroussia?' she said. 'What's going on? Are you *hurt*?'

'No,' said Maroussia. 'But—'

'You're in trouble. What's happened?'

'Elena, I'm sorry. We shouldn't have come. I wouldn't have, but we ... There wasn't anywhere else to go, and I thought ...'

'What do you need?' said Elena.

'Transport,' said Lom. 'A cart or something like that.'

'There's someone else,' said Maroussia. 'We left him downstairs. He's hurt. He's been shot. It was just outside here, in the alleyway.'

'*Shot?*' said Elena. She looked hard at Lom. 'Shot by who?'

'The militia,' said Maroussia. 'They shot my mother and they're trying to kill me. They'll come here looking for us.' She stopped. 'Elena, I'm sorry. We shouldn't have come. I've brought you trouble. I wasn't thinking straight. We'll go. They won't ever know we were here.'

She turned to go.

'Don't be silly,' said Elena. 'We can use my cart. I can take you somewhere. I can take you home.'

Maroussia shook her head.

'I can't go home. Not ever.'

'Then come to my place,' said Elena.

'No,' said Maroussia. 'No, I couldn't. I can't ask you that. I'm sorry I came.'

'Just for now. Until you have a plan.'

Maroussia shook her head.

'Why not?' said Elena. 'Have you got anywhere else to go?'

'No.'

'Then come with me.' Elena Cornelius paused a beat, then she added, 'Both of you. For now. We'll work something out.'

Lom studied Elena Cornelius. He liked her. She was sensible. Purposeful. Tough.

'Where do you live?' he said.

'The Raion Lezaryet.'

Lom let it happen. *The next two minutes.* The raion was as good a place as any. Better than most. Gendarmes didn't patrol the raion.

He nodded.

'Thanks,' he said.

Elena ignored him.

'Where's the one who's hurt?' she said.

Maroussia told her.

'This way,' said Elena. 'There's a service elevator.'

She took Maroussia by the hand. It was an instinctive, almost motherly gesture.

When they reached the porters' room the chair was on its side, the table and the floor smeared with blood. Florian was gone.

'Somebody must have found him,' said Maroussia quietly.

'Or he got up and walked away,' said Lom. 'Either way, we need to get out of here. Now.'

Elena Cornelius kept her cart in a place that was part warehouse, part garage, part stables: a cavernous shadowy space with a flagstone floor scattered with wisps of straw.

'You ride up front,' she said. 'I'll walk with the pony.' She found a grey woollen blanket and insisted that Maroussia wrapped herself in it against the cold. It smelled of fresh-cut wood. 'Sorry about the sawdust.'

She pushed open the heavy sliding doors onto the street. Grey snow was shawling thickly out of a darkening sky. She took the pony's halter and said a word in her ear. The cart lurched forward and they were out and moving. There was hardly any traffic. It was freezing cold. A bitter wind whipped snow into their faces.

27

*T*housands *of miles east of Mirgorod, beyond the continental plain, the endless forest begins. The forest that has no centre and no farther edge. The absolutely elsewhere, under an endless sky.*

There are pools in the forest: pools and lakes of still brown water; streams and slow rivers, surrounded on all sides by brown and grey columns that disappear upwards into shadow and leaf. Ivy and moss. Fern. Liverwort. Lichen. Mycelium. Thread. There are no landmarks, only the rising and falling of the ground, and trees becoming dark in the distance. Low cloud and morning mist: breaths of cool air moving, chill and earthy and damp. There is rustling and sudden small movement. There are broad hollow ways, paths and side paths, ways trodden clear. Large things walk there: boar and aurochs, wisent and wolf. Lynx and wolverine. Elk and sloth and woolly rhinoceros. War otter and cave bear. Dark leopard and fox.

Somewhere in the forest it is winter. The long night settles; predators bury carrion in the snow; bear sows sleep with their cubs and the old fighting males wander in the dark. And somewhere in the forest it is spring, with the deep roaring of rutting deer, the air filled with the musk of females in season, and trees, trembling and flaring with blossom, pouring out scent and colour, ignited with life.

The forest is larger than the world, though the world thinks the opposite. Going in is easy: it's coming out that's hard. Time stops in the forest. People walk into the forest and never come out. They feel lost. They drift. They walk round in circles. They stop wanting.

The forest is the first place, original, primeval, primordial, primal. It is the inexhaustible beginning, direct, instinctual, unmediated, real. The land before the people came. This land. Old and bright and dark and full of dreams and nightmares. It is not an empty place. People live here, human and not so: free giants and tunnel dwellers; windwalkers, rusalkas, vyrdalaks, shapeshifters, hamrs, fetches, man-wolves; disembodied watchful intelligences, wild and cruel, that might be called witches and trolls. Many things are lost and buried in the forest: old things, perdurable, and new things, potential, unrealised yet, and waiting. All things are possible here, and here is everything. Growth and change. Here everything freely, abundantly begins, and becomes itself: the multiplicity, variousness, potential, myriadness, wanderability, wellspring and wilderness of forest. The trees are sensitive to light and earth. They taste and listen. Their roots go deep, and touch, and interweave. They spill pheromone language on the air. The trees are watchful. The rain, the air, the earth are watchful. The forest is borderless mind. It is aware.

Across the forest Archangel grinds his way, immense and alien and poison.

28

Minister of Armaments and General Secretary of the Colloquium Steopan Dukhonin's car took him home after the Novozhd's funeral. From a window in the building opposite, Bez Nichevoi watched the long ZorKi Zavod saloon arrive. It rode low, weighed down by two tons of steel plate. Assassination-proof. Bez could make out Dukhonin's head in the back, a dim featureless shape behind two inches of hardened glass. An underwater profile, bowed forward as if he were absorbed. Reading. The car pulled up at the wide double gates and the driver spoke into the intercom grille. The gates swung open to let the ZorKi edge through and closed behind it. Bez knew the routine. Dukhonin would not leave again before morning.

The house was a squat stone block, blank-windowed, in its own grounds, an enclave carved out of Pir-Anghelksy Park. The driver would ignore the steps up to the front door. He would follow the gravel driveway round to the back and into the courtyard. Walls within walls. One of the indoor guards would be waiting. The driver would see Dukhonin inside, then take the ZorKi across to the garage, lock it in for the night, and go into the house himself. Dukhonin would go to his study and work there until the early hours of the morning. He would have supper brought to him on a tray. Dukhonin worked prodigiously. Secretively. Since becoming one of the Four he had given up his office in the Lodka and worked solely from home.

Apart from the driver and the housekeeper, there were two guards inside the house and two in the grounds. And dogs. Lean, black, heavy-jawed killers left to roam free within the outer wall. Dukhonin also had a private secretary, a new man, Pavel, who arrived at 7.30 every morning and normally remained until 7.30 in the evening, but he was not in the house. He had been at the funeral, and Dukhonin had told him he wouldn't be required again until the morning. Dukhonin liked to observe such niceties – they were of consequence to him.

That evening's leave of absence was a propriety Pavel would come to appreciate. It had saved his life.

It took Bez five minutes to walk to the place where he could cross the perimeter wall without being seen from the street. The wall was ten feet high, but he climbed it without difficulty. His body was light as a small child's. He dropped to the ground inside the compound. There was fifteen yards of clear space before the laurels began, snow-mounded in the gathering darkness. The snow was falling thickly. It blurred his senses a little, muffling sound and muting scent, but he could feel the presence of the dogs nearby, three of them. They had his scent. He felt their alertness, the way they moved a few paces towards him, heads up, but they were hesitating, the strangeness of his smell making them uncertain. No sign of the guards.

Bez stood with his back to the wall and waited. It would be better if the dogs came to him. Neater that way. Simpler. He opened his mouth and let out a long plume of breath. A visible steam-cloud on the snow-thick air. He put into it the taint of carrion. Death. That would bring them, curious and eager but not alarmed. A few moments later the dogs broke through the laurels and saw him, not the dead thing they were expecting but a tall man standing.

When they came for him Bez killed them quickly. He absorbed their small deaths and started towards the house. He was leaving a trail of footprints, but it didn't matter. It would make no difference.

Because of the snow, the guards were within thirty yards of him before he was aware of them. They were not alert. Just a routine patrol. Bez dropped on them from the low branches of a fir tree, taking the head of one and piercing the eyes of the other, spearing his brain. He allowed himself a moment to digest their deaths and moved on. Entered the house through an upstairs window.

Inside, he took his time, walking through cool shadows, looking into all the empty rooms. Running his hands across tables and along the backs of chairs. Sharing in the quiet of the house, unbroken but for the slow ticking of a clock on a landing and the distant murmur of a radio. He found what must have been the housekeeper's sitting room. A chintz-backed armchair next to a purring stove. A shelf of china figures. A postcard from Lake Tsyrkhal. Nice things.

Dukhonin was in his study, at his desk, working on papers. He was smoking, a bottle of aquavit open at his elbow, a single glass. The radiogram in its cabinet against the wall playing quiet music. Absorbed, Dukhonin didn't see Bez Nichevoi watching him from the doorway.

Bez left him there for the moment. The others – the indoor guards, the driver, the housekeeper – were downstairs in the kitchen, gathered at the table, drinking tea. None of them noticed Bez until he was in the room with them, and by then it was too late. For them it had always been too late.

Now it was only him and Dukhonin in the house.

As Bez was going back upstairs, he heard a small sound. A door quietly opening. Dukhonin was on the move. Slowly. Bez sensed something uneasy about him. An edge of tense energy. Fear. He must have heard, or half-heard, what had happened in the kitchen. The housekeeper's interrupted scream. Bez moved soundlessly into the shadow of a doorway and waited.

Dukhonin was coming down the corridor in carpet slippers, a small pistol in his hand. He walked right past the doorway where Bez was. Bez stepped forward and gripped the wrist of the hand that held the gun. Dukhonin jerked round, lashed out, shouted – some harsh meaningless syllable – then saw what had come for him. Bez felt him collapse inside. Smelled that he had pissed himself. The pistol dropped to the floor.

Dukhonin stood in the corridor, arms dropped to his sides, resigned, hopeless.

'The guards?' he said in a flat voice. 'You killed them.'

'Yes.'

'All of them?'

'Yes.'

'And Mila?'

'Housekeeper?'

'Yes. The housekeeper.'

'Yes.'

A flicker of something – sadness? grief? – passed across Dukhonin's face and died.

'Who sent you?' he said. 'Khazar? Chazia? Fohn? Not Fohn? Surely not Fohn?'

'Chazia.'

Dukhonin nodded.

'Of course,' he said. 'Well. Go on then. Do it.'

Bez looked at him.

'Kill me,' said Dukhonin. 'Kill me, then. That's what you're here for. So. Do it, fuck you. I'm not going to fucking beg.'

Bez turned and started down the corridor.

'Come,' he said.

'What?'

'Your car,' said Bez Nichevoi. 'You drive.'

29

The Raion Lezaryet rose out of the surrounding city of Mirgorod on a steep angular hill of raw black rock. When the Lezarye's long wandering brought them to the shore of the Cetic Ocean in the time of the Founder's grandson, the hill of the raion had been an island in the marsh miles distant from Mirgorod. It seemed to surge out of the ground, a solid dark thunderhead glowering against the westering evening sky, the weathered root of a larger mountain. Some of the Lezarye families travelled on, taking ship onwards to the Archipelago and never returning, but the rest stayed and settled the black rock hill. Through the centuries that followed, Mirgorod flowed out across the waterland mud in a tide of suburbs and factories, surrounding the raion, pressing up against it and spilling past across the further islands one by one. On the steep black hill people crowded together, more and more of them squeezing into the narrowing streets. Every new Novozhd brought new restrictions, new laws, new arrests, new pogroms. *Why are our years always worse?* the poet Yourdania asked, because every decade that came hurt more than the last.

Other peoples came to settle in the raion, building their wooden shacks and shanties along the river and against the walls of the old Lezarye houses. Kyrghs and Mazhars, Esterhaziers, Samoys from the ice grass, shadowy relics of the proto-peoples who had lived in the Mir estuary before the Founder. Refugees from former countries that had been declared unVlast and erased from the maps. The memory of those sunken countries was written in the faces in the streets: men in long black coats and wide-brimmed hats or furs and boots and braided beards; women in embroidered linen shawls and headscarves made from the colour-stained skins of mice; stark-eyed children with beaded hair and ringlets under caps of felt, carrying little books on straps hung round their necks. No one remembered who had built the wall round the raion, or knew for certain whether it was built to keep Mirgorod out or the Lezarye in. But built it was, with one gate only, which opened through a stone arch onto the Purfas Bridge.

The pony walked slowly, head down and shoulders bunched against the weight of the cart. Maroussia hugged her carpet bag in her lap. Lom shivered and pulled his loden tighter against the cold. An early twilight was closing in and the snow was coming down in a dense steady flow, settling thickly, when they crossed the Purfas by the narrow wooden bridge and entered the raion.

The failing of the day brought the dusk bells ringing, the last circling of rooks, the first evening flicker of bats, lamps and candles in the windows. From narrow passageways came the smell of food: frying fish and spiced meat. Paprika. Onions. Livestock wandered and rooted in the cramped alleyways. There were animals in every tiny courtyard and fenced-in patch of cottage ground. Small stunted orchards, leafless and snow-covered, crouched behind walls. The chill darkening air was rich with woodsmoke and the reek of pigs, chickens and cows.

They climbed the winding streets between ravines of red-tiled roofs and smoking chimneys, jutting windows and arched doorways, weather-blackened wood and stone. Here and there angular outcrops of raw black rock shouldered the crowded buildings aside. Small cottages and wooden shanties jostled in the shadow of tall old houses with peeling louvred shutters at their windows and carved coats of arms on their gable ends: spread-winged eagles, prowling bears, running wolves. The antlers of a great elk were mounted over a courtyard arch. The raion was a place of gaps and crannies, steep angular lanes, small doorways and purposeless openings barred with rusted iron gratings.

Elena Cornelius walked ahead, leading the pony.

'Elena's a good woman,' said Maroussia, breaking a long silence.

'Yes,' said Lom.

'We can't stay here. We'll bring her trouble. She doesn't understand. She has children. I don't want to get her involved. This is my thing. People have died already.'

'It's not your fault,' said Lom. 'It happened.'

'If anything happens to Elena, it will be my fault. I went to her. I shouldn't have.'

'It'll be OK,' said Lom. 'It'll be fine. It's just for tonight.'

Wooden signs announced places of business – an estaminet, a pension, a tailor, an apothecary, a notary public – all crowded in among the houses and cottages. The names above the shops were names from lost, remembered countries, long ago obliterated under the hegemony of the Vlast. SYLWEST. NIKODEM. TILL. CZESLAW. ONUFRY. KAZIMIERZ. WHITE. The poetry of distance and difference.

Lom had known of the raion since childhood, though it wasn't mentioned in the books of the library at the Podchornok Institute of Truth. There were students at the Institute who said that Podchornok, within sight of the endless forest, had been one of the Lezarye way forts once, in the great days of their wardership of the border, under the Reasonable Empire long ago. Some even made whispered claims to family connections with the aristocrat families of the raion, though saying so risked denunciation by the Student Council. Lom, knowing nothing of his own family and remembering nothing before the Institute, toyed with the idea that he too was one of them. But Raku Vishnik, his one true friend, had mocked him. *The Lezarye, Vissarion, never gave birth to a great blond clumsy bear like you!*

Nevertheless, Lom stared about him now and wondered if it felt like coming home. But it didn't. Not for him.

Elena Cornelius pulled the cart off the road into a small yard.

'We'll go in this way,' said Elena. 'Our neighbours watch and talk as much as anyone else's do.'

She unlocked a door in the brick wall of the yard and led them through into a small private garden. In the gathering darkness Lom caught a vague impression of the side of a tall house: walls of mossy brick and crumbling stucco, precarious vine-tangled wrought-iron balconies, steep roofs and high crowded gables. The ground floor was skirted with a glass-roofed pillared loggia. Yellow light spilled through gaps in the curtains. They rounded the corner of the house and descended a narrow flight of basement steps. Elena rattled at a storm door of pierced zinc and wire netting until it jerked open and they squeezed inside, past buckets and mops and a rack of oilskins. A dog appeared at the end of the passageway, a black and yellow coarse-haired thing, standing stiff-legged and growling at the back of its throat. It was some kind of spitz or laitka, Lom didn't know what and didn't care. He preferred dogs at a distance.

'Vesna!' called Elena gently. 'It's OK. They're friends.'

The dog padded forward and inspected them. Lom offered his hand to be sniffed. The dog ignored it and went out into the garden.

'This is a big place,' he said.

'It's Sandu Palffy's house,' said Elena. 'Count Palffy. He and Ilinca have an apartment at the back. The rest is let out. But it is Count Palffy's house. At least, morally it is his, as he is morally a Count.'

There was a warm fug in the kitchen. Black and white tiles on the floor. Curtains drawn. A hefty old stove against the wall, its fire door open, shedding the heat of fast-burning logs. Two girls at the scrubbed deal table – thick black curly mops of hair and bright clever eyes – looked up when they came in. The older was about thirteen, school books spread in front of her amid the remains of their supper. The younger, who must have been ten or eleven, had a piece of reddish wood and a big clasp knife. She was carving something. An animal. A cat maybe. Lom thought it was probably good.

'Galina, Yeva, this is my friend Maroussia from the city,' said Elena. 'And this ...'

'Vissarion,' said Lom. 'I'm Vissarion. That's a good cat.'

'It's a lynx,' said Yeva. 'Not a cat.'

'Oh yes. Of course. Sorry.'

'There's rassolnik on the stove,' said the older girl. Galina. 'We got pigeons from Milla's. It was four kopeks for two, and Ilinca gave us a loaf of black bread. And kvass. There's plenty left.' She looked doubtfully at Lom and Maroussia. 'I think.'

'It'll be fine,' said Maroussia. 'Thanks.'

'You girls need to go and see to the pony, ' said Elena. 'Then go upstairs. Both of you. Go and sit with Ilinca. You could get her to put the phonogram on.'

Yeva made a sour face.

'Oh, but we haven't—'

'Upstairs,' said Elena. 'Now. I need to talk to Maroussia in private. Tell Sandu there'll be people in the attic tonight. Don't forget that.'

*

Elena brought a big iron pot from the oven. On the table she set out plates, a loaf of bread and a small blue jug of soured cream, and spooned out the thin rassolnik. Onions and cucumber. A few scraps of grey meat.

'I'm sorry,' said Maroussia. 'We should never have come. We'll go tomorrow.'

'It doesn't matter,' said Elena. 'It makes no difference.'

'You're not safe while we're here. The girls—'

'Safe?' said Elena. 'Nobody is *safe*. Not anywhere. One day they come for you, and that's it. That's all. Every day the girls go to school and I never know if they'll come back. Last week they shot thirty people at the Red Cliff. They lined them up in the rain and shot them. Buried the bodies in the ditch. A *reprisal*. Reprisal for what? Who knows? They didn't care who they took. Old men. Women. *Children*. They took their clothes first and then they shot them. They made them stand *naked*. Then they burned the houses.'

'Who?' said Lom. 'Who did that?'

'What difference does it make?' said Elena. 'Police. Militia. Gendarmes. Army. What's the difference? *Uniforms* did it. And it'll be worse now. Much worse.'

'Why?'

She stood up and went across to the sideboard, took a piece of paper from a drawer and shoved them across the table towards him.

'See this? Look at this.'

'Colloquium Communiqué No. 3'. Its corners were torn as if it had been ripped off a notice board or a telegraph pole.

Men and women of the Vlast!

Again the counter-revolution has raised its criminal head. Revanchists are mobilising their forces to crush us. The bloodstained pogrom-mongers, having slaughtered our beloved Novozhd, intend to cause more killing and terror in the streets of Mirgorod! They have deluded the minds of certain weaker elements within our army and navy and betrayed the heroic sons and daughters to the Archipelago. Staunch resistance is needed. Now is the time for action and clear-eyed sacrifice.

Justified by angels, the Colloquium for the Protection of Citizens and the Vlast agrees to take upon itself the defence of Perpetual

Revolution. The Administrative Government of the CPCV is hereby declared.

People of the Lezarye cannot be citizens of the Vlast. They have no rights in law.

It was signed with four names. Dukhonin. Khazar. Chazia. Fohn.

'See?' said Elena Cornelius. 'They're blaming us for the death of the Novozhd. They'll come for us all. *No rights in law.* You know what that means? It means anyone can do anything to us. Put us out of our houses. Loot our shops. Kill us, kill our children. Any time they want to, any time at all, and no police to protect us. The police are for citizens.

'And that is not all. Look at what happened to the men at the Saltworks Foundry. They took them all, hundreds of men, and their families. All of them.'

'Took them?' said Lom. 'Took them where?'

'Who knows? The Saltworks Foundry was the first. They come for more every day – whole factories and whole streets every time. They put them on trains and we never see them again. One day they will come here. It is only a matter of time. You should run, Maroussia. Get away from the city while you can. Don't tell me what trouble you're in, it doesn't matter. If the Vlast wants to kill you, then they will kill you. You have to get far, far away from here.' She looked at Lom. 'Take her away,' she said. 'If you are her friend, get her out of Mirgorod. Go to the exclave. Go to the ice. Go to the forest. Find a ship to the Archipelago. Go anywhere. There's nothing to keep you here. You should run.'

'No,' said Maroussia. 'I'm not going to run.'

30

Chazia left General Secretary Steopan Dukhonin alone for most of the night in the interrogation room where Bez Nichevoi had put him. *Let him stew. Let him think. Let him wonder.* She had other work to do. And she wanted to prepare for the interview: get the facts and figures straight in her head. Dukhonin was a sly little shit, but she would skewer him. She was going to skewer them all one by one: Dukhonin, Khazar, Fohn, all the vicious, patronising, conspiring little men who thought they could use her and keep power for themselves. The men who did not know her and did not see who she was. She would start with Dukhonin. Industrious, cautious, greedy, tiny, frightened Dukhonin. He was the worst. Start with him.

When she went down for him he was sitting at the table in his shirt and carpet slippers. The skin of his face was grey and patched with sparse white stubble. He smelled faintly of urine.

'Lavrentina, what the fuck ...' he said. 'What the fuck is this? Am I *arrested*? That ... that *thing* of yours *killed my people*. My fucking *housekeeper*! Fohn will destroy you for this. *Destroy* you!'

His small watery eyes glared at her, sour with fear. His thin little face was tight and full of bone. Chazia sat down across the table from him.

'We need a little talk, Steopan Vadimovich,' she said. 'Just a little talk.'

'You want to talk, make a fucking appointment.'

'Let's start with the steel from Schentz.'

'Does Fohn know I'm here?' said Dukhonin. 'He doesn't, does he? You're finished, Lavrentina. You're nothing. We should never have let you in. I told Fohn ... I told him you were—'

'Fohn?' said Chazia. 'What does Fohn matter? Look around you, Steopan. Where is Fohn? Is he here?'

'You've overreached yourself, Lavrentina. You're dead. Finished. What is this situation? It is preposterous, that's what it is. I am the *General Secretary*. I am one of the *Four*. You don't question me and I certainly don't fucking answer.' He stood up. 'I'm going home and you're fucking dead.'

'The steel, Steopan. Tell me about the steel from Schentz. The Mirskov Foundry invoices the Treasury for forty million roubles and the Treasury pays forty million. But only thirty-six million shows up in the Mirskov accounts.'

'So? Is that it? You think you can bring me down with that? Ten per cent for my trouble? Who fucking cares? You've got shit. Big mistake. You're dead.'

'I'm not interested in the money, I'm interested in the steel. Forty million gets a lot of steel. How much steel is worth forty million?'

'I don't know. Who fucking cares?'

'At a thousand roubles a ton that's forty thousand tons. Minimum. A hundred tons per wagon. Four hundred wagons. If you moved it in one train it would be four miles long.'

Dukhonin shrugged.

'So?'

'So why send forty thousand tons of steel to Novaya Zima?'

'Nothing to do with me. Why would I care where it went?'

'But you ordered it, Steopan,' said Chazia. 'You did it. You. Forty thousand tons of steel to Novaya Zima and a nice four million roubles for you. It was the cut that got noticed, but as you say, so what? Still, I'm curious. I ask myself, why is Steopan Vadimovich sending so much steel to Novaya Zima? What is there at Novaya Zima? A shit-hole on an island in an icebound sea? Nothing is happening there. We're losing a war, yet Steopan finds enough steel to make a thousand main battle tanks and sends it north-east to the edge of the ice?'

'This is outside your sphere, Lavrentina,' said Dukhonin. 'Way outside. You shouldn't be touching this. It's serious stuff. Dangerous stuff. You need to back away.'

'I made enquiries about Novaya Zima, Steopan. And what did I find? Nothing. Not a record of nothing, but no record. No file. An empty shelf where Novaya Zima should be. So I asked a different question. What else has my friend Steopan Vadimovich Dukhonin been buying with Treasury money? It wasn't easy to track that either, but I found traces. Coal. Rare earths. Machinery. Small quantities of metals I've never heard of. Seventy tons – seventy *tons* – of reclaimed angel flesh. Every scrap of angel flesh that could be found in the Vlast. All arranged by Steopan Vadimovich Dukhonin, who incidentally takes his little ten per cent. And people too. Eighty thousand conscript labourers diverted from war work, all for Novaya Zima. You're even taking them from here! From Mirgorod! So. Steopan. This is the question. *What is happening at Novaya Zima?*'

'Nothing,' said Dukhonin. He was confident now. The stupid man was confident. 'Like you said. Nothing.'

Chazia smiled.

'Actually, I considered that possibility. Maybe, I thought, it is all a scam. Paper transactions only. Money paid but nothing sent. Maybe Steopan's little scheme is a big scheme. But no, the shipments are real, and they really go to Novaya Zima. So what happens when they get there?'

'You've got shit,' said Dukhonin. 'Dangerous shit, but shit. You think you know it all, with your files and your informers and your useless lickspittle secret police? You know *nothing*, Lavrentina! Nothing of *importance*. You know nothing and you are no one. Who are you? What are you? You're meat, you're disgusting, a diseased, repellent little cow-bitch. Novaya Zima will kill you. Shit. You send that thing to scare me and you kill my *housekeeper* and you keep me locked up *all night* in this pathetic stinking toilet. Fohn will kill you slowly and I will piss on your shitty corpse.' He stood up. 'I've had enough. I'm going home.'

'The door,' said Chazia, 'is not locked.'

Dukhonin stood up, raised himself to his full five foot six, shuffled across in his carpet slippers and pulled the door open. Bez Nichevoi was standing in the corridor, patient and still. A shadow in the shadows. Dukhonin didn't see him until he moved. Bez dislocated Dukhonin's left arm at the shoulder and Dukhonin screamed.

Bez did something to Dukhonin's face, too fast for Chazia to see, and pushed him back into the room. Dukhonin fell forward hard on the floor and lay there, his left arm at a wrong angle, useless, his right hand holding his face.

'Oh shit,' he murmured. 'Shit.'

Bez followed him into the room and looked to Chazia for instructions.

'Help him back into his chair.'

Dukhonin sat slumped forward, twisted sideways with the pain in his shoulder, blood trickling down his cheek from his ruined left eye. The socket was a jellied, swollen mess.

'There cannot be *four rulers,* Steopan,' said Chazia. 'There can only be *one.* Power shared isn't power at all. This Colloquium you and Fohn and Khazar cooked up is an abortion. It is an arena for battle only – it is a *war* – but none of you is a soldier and none of you will win. I am going to take it all.'

Dukhonin didn't look at her. His one good eye was fixed on Bez Nichevoi, motionless and watchful in the corner of the room. Nichevoi seemed to be exuding the shadows that gathered around him despite the flat glare of the overhead lamp. Tall and thin, he wore a neat dark suit made of shadows. Dark hair, a dark inexpressive gaze, a stark face white as chalk. He made the angles of the room around him seem wrong.

'You're just like the rest of them, Steopan, when they come in here,' Chazia said. 'The ground you walked on was always fragile, and now it has broken and you've fallen through. You're in my world now.'

'But we can do a deal, Lavrentina,' said Dukhonin. 'Listen. We can do a deal. You're right about Fohn, of course you are. Completely. He's weak. A bureaucrat. A committee man. A compromiser. But not *me,* I'm not like that. You and I – we can make an alliance. Don't let that thing... You don't need to kill me, Lavrentina. There's no call for that. I can help you. You want to come in on it? I'll let you in. Of course I will. It's a perfect idea. Perfect. I should have thought of it before. We'll be good together, Lavrentina. We don't need Khazar and Fohn. You don't need to kill me. I'll share.'

'Share? What have you got that I need, Steopan Vadimovich?'

'Novaya Zima! Shit. *Novaya Zima!* You need it. You need *me.*'

'So what is Novaya Zima? Tell me what it is.'

'Not tell you. I'll show you. You need to *see.*'

31

When Elena Cornelius had left them alone in the attic, Maroussia went across to one of the mattresses and sat down. She put the carpet bag she'd brought from Vishnik's on the floor next to her and opened it. Started pulling things out, one by one and setting them out on the quilt. The envelope with Vishnik's photographs. A dark woollen skirt. A couple of thin cotton blouses, faded and softened from frequent washing. A blue knitted cardigan, neatly mended at the elbow with slightly mismatched thread. A linen nightshirt. A bar of soap, wrapped in a piece of brown waxed paper. A thin book in a grey card cover. *The Selo Elegies and Other Poems* by Anna Yourdania. The clothes were crumpled. They'd been fingered by Vishnik's killers and thrown aside until Maroussia had grabbed them off the floor and stuffed them roughly, hastily, back into the bag. Lom watched her set out each one, smooth it down and refold it, neatly.

She felt him watching her and looked up.

'I don't want to wear these again,' she said. 'Not after where they've been. Not after what happened there.'

'No,' said Lom. 'I guess not.'

'They're not ... they're not mine, not any more.'

She picked up the packet of soap and went across to the table under the window. There was a large pitcher of water and a wide shallow washbowl: chipped yellow enamel with a thin black rim. A rough brown towel hung from a hook. Maroussia poured some water into the bowl, rolled up her sleeves, leaned forward and splashed her face with tight cupped hands. Rubbed her dripping hands across her eyes, her mouth, her forehead, her throat, the back of her neck. Ran wet fingers through her hair. Then she straightened up, unwrapped the soap and

431

lathered her hands, her arms up to the elbow. She turned the soap over and over in her fingers, rubbed it again along the length of her arms and let it slip back into the bowl. Scooped a double handful of water and jammed the heels of her palms into her eyes. Not rubbing but pressing, gently pushing. She stood like that, not moving, breathing.

Lom went up behind her. He could smell the soap and the warmth of her skin and hair. Her hands, her face, her neck were flushed from the icy cold of the water. He could smell the scent of her on the thin blouse she'd been wearing the day the boat took them into the White Reaches and was still wearing now. He could still feel the warmth of her long back against his side, where she had lain pressed against him in the bed in the gate keeper's lodge the night before. Twenty-four hours ago. He picked up the towel and dipped a corner of it in the icy water in the pitcher. Began to wipe the soap from her neck and her arms.

When he took her two hands in one of his and drew them gently away from her face, her eyes were screwed tight shut. He wiped the soap from them, one by one. She turned into his arms, opened her eyes and looked into his. Held his gaze for a long, quiet time. There was a faint sweetness of brandy on her breath.

She was a stranger to him. Again, he felt the otherness of her. A part of her was very far away, behind her eyes, not wanting to be reached.

He moved the rough damp edge of the towel across her mouth, wiping the soap away. She moved her body against him. He felt the patch of damp cold where she had spilled water down her neck. She opened her mouth and put her lips against his.

Hours later, Lom lay wakeful in the dark, listening to the quiet creaks and ticks of the roof beams under the accumulating weight of snow. Maroussia was lying next to him, sleeping, the warmth of her breathing against his cheek. He listened to the rattles and groans in the pipes, the scratch and skitter of small animals. Felt the presence of dark, amorphous, inky, shifty, scuttling night-things that lived in the shadows and ceilings and whispered. Cool, filmy presences. Watchful creatures of fur and dust. The delicate new skin across the hole in the front of his skull fluttered in response with gentle moth-wing beats.

Slowly and carefully so as not to wake her, he slipped out from under the quilt and padded barefoot across to the window. It was bitterly cold in the room. He was instantly shivering. The vapour of his and Maroussia's breath had crystallised in whorls and ferns of frost across the windowpanes, and through it a faint snow-glimmer filtered into the room. He cleared a patch with the side of his palm and looked out: dense, swirling snowfall still coming down; the tumbled, tightly packed rooftops of the raion falling away down the hill. Lamps burning in a few isolated windows, their light reflecting off the snow.

Lom used to think, once, that snow was frozen rain, that snowflakes were raindrops that turned to ice as they fell through freezing air. But then, he'd forgotten where, he discovered the truth. Snow wasn't frozen rain, it had never been rain. Snow was the invisible vapour of water – the slow and distant breath of lakes, of rivers, of oceans – crystallising suddenly out of thin air. A billion billion tiny weightless dagger-spiked ghosts, materialising. From the first time Lom heard this, the thought had electrified him: he'd realised that all around him, all the time, all the year, always, there existed in the air, unseen, the latent possibility of snow. Even the warmest summer day was haunted by snow. The memory of how to be snow. All that was required to make it real was cold. And when the cold moment came, snow manifested itself suddenly out of the air in a kind of chill ignition, the opposite of flame.

Somewhere in the city was a man who had worn his face. A man who pulled bullets out of his belly and walked away. And Chazia was out there too. And so was Josef Kantor.

'Vissarion?' said Maroussia. Her voice was quiet in the dark.

'Yes? I thought you were asleep.'

'No.'

'Are you OK?'

'Yes. Only ... I was thinking.'

'What?'

'Do you think Elena's right? Do you think we should get out of Mirgorod? Do you think we should run?'

'Do you?' he said across the dim snow-shadowed room.

'No.'

'Then don't. Don't run.'

'But ... I don't know what to do,' she said. 'I mean, say we could get into the Lodka and find it, find the Pollandore ... All I've got is fragments. Garbled messages. It's not enough.'

'So what do you want to do?'

'I don't know,' she said. 'I need more. I need the forest to talk to me again.'

'OK,' said Lom.

'OK what?'

'OK, so talk to the forest again.'

'Do you know how to do that?' said Maroussia.

'No.'

She said no more, but Lom could hear her breathing. Lying awake in the dark.

She was taking the righting of the world on her shoulders. The weight of it, the pressure and hopelessness of what she was choosing, squatted heavily in the room. He went across to the bed and got in. Pulled the quilt up around them both. Made a warm dark private place, simple and human, like people's lives should be. Just for now.

32

Lavrentina Chazia had never believed that she knew every room in the Lodka. No one could. The route Dukhonin led her, shuffling slowly in his carpet slippers, his left arm stiff and useless, his thin bony face sticky with drying blood from his ruined eye, was new to her. They climbed stairs and took lifts, ascending and descending, until she had no idea where in the building they were, or even whether they were above or below ground. They passed no one.

'Here,' said Dukhonin, stopping at a heavy anonymous door with a combination lock. 'This is the place.'

He fumbled with the tumbler. His hand was trembling. He pulled at the door but it didn't shift.

'Shit,' he muttered. 'Shit.'

He started again. Chazia pushed him aside.

'I'll do it,' she said. 'Tell me the numbers.'

He did.

Beyond the door were more corridors, deserted in the early hours. Bez Nichevoi followed a few paces behind them. Silently in his soft leather shoes. They passed rooms that showed signs of current occupation. Handwritten notices: *ESTABLISHMENTS*; *ACCOUNTS*; *TRANSIT*; *PROCUREMENT AND SUPPLY*. Telephone cables trailing across the floor. Green steel cabinets. A telegraphic printing machine – a contraption of brass and cogs with a board of black and white keys like a piano, the kind that printed out endless spools of paper tape – stood inactive on a heavy wooden table. There was a basket to catch the tape as it passed out, but it was empty. This was a significant operation. Dukhonin set it all up and kept it running without even a whisper reaching her? But it was all support functions. Generic. The substance was elsewhere.

Dukhonin brought them to a small windowless room. The card beside the door said *PROJECT WINTER SKIES*. Inside were eight chairs set round a plain meeting table and on the wall was a map showing the rail and river routes of the north-eastern oblasts: wide expanses of nothing but a patchwork of small lakes and emptiness, railheads and river staging posts, the coast of the Yarmskoye Sea; and beyond that the irregular fringe of permanent ice, and blankness.

At one end of the room was a small projection screen, and at the opposite end a Yubkin film projector on a sturdy tripod.

'Sit, Lavrentina,' said Dukhonin. 'Please. Sit.' He looked at Bez. 'Is he ... staying? This is ... What you're going to see is ... I would not recommend that he remains.'

'He stays.'

'Lavrentina. Please. Nothing is more sensitive than this. And ... and I will need to extinguish the lights.'

'He stays.'

Dukhonin, his breathing loud and ragged, unclipped the twin reel covers and checked the film spool was in place. One-handed and trembling, it took him a long time. At last he got the projection lamp lit and set the cooling fan running. He brought up a test image and spent some time selecting a lens and adjusting the focus. There was a heavy radiator blasting heat into the cramped stuffy room. Chazia smelled Dukhonin's stale sweat. The sourness of his fear. The piss on his trousers. She shifted in her seat and scratched in irritation at the angel stains on her arms.

'What you're going to see,' Dukhonin began, 'needs no introduction. It speaks for itself. The culmination of years of work. Years of patient—'

'Get on with it.'

He switched off the room light and set the projector running. It clattered and whirred, casting flickering monochrome images on the screen. White letters, jittering almost imperceptibly on a dark background under a faint snow of dust and scratch-tracks:

TRUTH AND FEAR

A series of serial numbers and acronyms. A date about two months before.

The only sounds in the room were the clattering of the projector and Dukhonin's heavy breathing. From time to time he gave a quiet moan. He probably didn't know he was doing it.

Chazia watched the screen.

Men in heavy winter clothing were working outside in the snow. They were making adjustments to a large and heavy-looking metal object, a squat, solid, rounded capsule about ten feet high and twenty feet long. It resembled a swollen samovar turned on its side. Tubes and rivets and plates. One of the men turned to the camera and grinned. Thumbs up. Then the men had gone and the screen showed the thing alone. The camera dwelled on it for a moment or two and a caption came up. UNCLE VANYA. Then the scene cut to a wide expanse of windswept ice. A tall metal gantry, a framework of girders rising into a bleak sky. Tiny figures moving at the foot of it gave a sense of scale.

Another scene change: the heavy, swollen capsule being winched up the gantry and set in place at the top. More snow-bearded technicians gurning excitedly at the lens. And then nothing. Only the flat emptiness of the winter tundra: mile upon mile of grey icefields under a grey sky. Chazia waited. Nothing happened. Thirty seconds. A minute. Nothing.

Chazia shifted in her seat.

'Steopan—'

'Wait,' he hissed. Tension in his voice. Excitement. 'Wait.'

The entire screen lit up, a brilliant, dazzling white. A blinding flash erasing the tundra and the sky.

Dukhonin let out a small ecstatic sigh.

'You see?' he said. 'You see what I can give you?'

Chazia was sitting forward in her chair, gripping the armrests. There was a knot in her stomach of joy and excitement and desire. As the blinding light faded, the screen showed a huge burning column roaring into the sky. There was no sound but she could hear it roaring. A thick pillar of destruction surging thousands of feet upwards. The air itself on fire. Boiling. The base of the column must have been five hundred yards across, and thickening steadily. It looked like an immense tree in full summer leaf, half a mile high. A mile. At the top it flattened and spilled outwards, its leafhead a canopy of roiling power and destruction. Cataclysm. The force of it left her breathless.

At the base of the mile-high tree a wind began: an expanding circular shout of power, racing outwards from the centre, scouring the snow off the ice, scouring the ice itself, whipping it into a tidal wall hundreds of feet high, hurtling at tremendous speed towards the watching camera. When it struck the lens the picture stopped. The screen went blank. The film clattered to a halt.

Dukhonin switched on the room light and extinguished the projector lamp.

'Did you see? Did you see? One of these – just one of them! – can obliterate an entire city. And at Novaya Zima they are building hundreds. And that's just the beginning. We have plans ... Imagine, Lavrentina ... There is no limit. No limit at all.'

Chazia felt a constriction in her throat. Power on this scale ... Her legs and arms felt weak. She did not trust herself to stand.

'Who *knows*, Steopan?' she said.

'What?'

'Who *knows*? Does *Khazar* know? Does *Fohn*? Was it only me that did not know about this?'

'No, no,' said Dukhonin. 'Of course not. This is all mine. My doing. They brought this idea to me alone. And I have made it real! But you can join me, Lavrentina, and—'

'Who brought it Steopan? *Who brought you this knowledge?*'

'Technicians. Professors. Scientists. They're at Novaya Zima, all of them.

'But where is this *from*? *Where did they get this knowledge from?*'

'What kind of question ...? They are very brilliant men.'

'And they came to you?'

'Of course they came to me. An undertaking like this needs resources. Materials. Workers. *Organisation* of the highest order. They had gone as far as they could on their own. They needed help. Who else would they come to?'

'You're saying these scientists and professors did this?' She waved her hand towards the blank projection screen. '*This?* On their *own*? They worked on it, knowing what they had, and never told anyone. Never sought official sanction? Never came to the Novozhd in Council for recognition and protection and support. And then, when they had gone as far as they could on their own they came to *you*? To you *alone*? Who approached you? Some *professor*? Some *engineer*?'

'Not at all. Of course not. They were frightened men. Out of their depth. They knew the importance of what they had, and the risks … the risks that it would get into the wrong hands. You couldn't trust an idiot like Khazar with a thing like this. There was a middle man. An intermediary.'

'Who?'

'His name was Lura.'

'*Lura?*' Chazia stared at Dukhonin. She wanted to hurt him. Gouge out his other eye. Tear out his throat. 'Shall I describe to you this *Lura*?' she said. 'Tall and thin? A pockmarked complexion? Thick shiny hair and big brown eyes like a fucking cow? A red silk shirt?'

'Yes. That's right. That's Lura.'

'It is Kantor,' said Chazia. 'Josef Kantor.'

Chazia turned to Bez, waiting like a shadow behind Dukhonin.

'Kill this useless idiot,' she said.

Bez moved so fast that Chazia barely saw what he did.

'Find Iliodor, wherever he is,' she said when he had finished. 'I want these offices closed. The whole thing completely gone. Everyone who works here is to be dealt with. No trace. He is to do nothing about Novaya Zima, not yet, but I want a list of all the personnel there. Tomorrow. I want this tomorrow. In the morning. Tell Iliodor this.'

Bez nodded.

'And when you have done that, there is a woman. Maroussia Shaumian. Iliodor has the file. The SV were to pick her up this evening, but they did not succeed. There have been previous failures. Find her and bring her to me.'

'Of course,' said Bez. Something lopsided happened to his face. Chazia realised it was a smile.

'I want her alive,' she said. 'And in a condition to speak to me.'

33

In cloud-thickened moonless snow-glimmered darkness, in the hard bitter coldest part of the night, three miles east of the Lodka, crooked in a sharp elbow-bend of the River Mir, pressing hard against the south embankment, lay the eight flat, tangled, overgrown, neglected, lampless and benighted square miles of the Field Marshal Khorsh-Brutskus Park of Culture and Rest.

Three centuries earlier, the Park had begun life as the gardens of the Shurupinsky Palace, landscaped by Can Guarini himself, and the shell of the palace – its grounds long since appropriated to the greater needs of the citizens of Mirgorod – still stood, encircled (*girt* is the only word that will actually do) by an elegant, attenuated, over-civilised gesture of a moat, slowly succumbing to decay and sporadic, unenthusiastic vandalism. Long before the expropriation, the successive princes Shurupin in their financial prime had provided for themselves handsomely. In the high summer of the palace's splendour, the *Ladies' New Magazine* had produced a special supplement devoted to describing in detail, with tipped-in lithographs by Fromm, the thirty-two bedrooms, the eleven bathrooms, the glorious ballroom, the galleried library, the palm court, the orangery, the velodrome, the stabling for fifty horses, the private hospital, the theatre, the extensive Cabinet (in truth, a *Hall)* of Curiosities, the observatory with its copper revolving roof and huge telescope, and the artificial island in the lake where, on summer afternoons, tea might be taken under a lacy canopy of ironwork.

And when the grounds of the Shurupinsky Palace were expropriated and became the Park of Culture and Rest it happened that, by some oversight or unresolved quirk of administrative demarcation, no provision whatsoever of any kind was made for the great house and its

440

contents. No possessor or use for it was found. It was never emptied of its furnishings and equipment. Its library was never catalogued and relocated, its paintings never removed and rehung or stored away, and surprisingly little from the house was even stolen; at the time of the expropriation, and ever since, not only was there was no market for the cumbersome extravagances of the former aristocracy, they were dangerous to own, dangerous to be discovered with, and hideously inconvenient to export to the Archipelago, where buyers might still have been found though at a price that would scarcely have covered the illicit transportation cost. So the palace was simply abandoned, more or less in the condition the last prince left it, to moulder and slowly collapse.

Antoninu Florian had visited the Shurupinsky Palace once, before the expropriation, as a guest of the last prince. Prince Alexander Yurich Shurupin, landowner, moral philosopher, social reformer and author of prodigiously enormous, compendious, subtle novels, had shown Florian over the house and walked with him in the grounds, not in pride but in some bemusement and shame, because the Palace troubled him. An old man by then, his privilege troubled him. His own brilliant writings troubled him.

'You have no idea how restful it is for me, talking to you, my friend,' the Prince had said to Florian, striding along the avenue of yellow earth, hands in the pockets of his brown linen overalls, work boots flapping unlaced against his shins, beard and long grey hair flickering on the lilac-scented summer breeze. 'It gives me a wonderful freedom to speak fully and truly, your not being tainted with *humanness*. In my experience, one can never talk to another human person with complete honesty, not really. It is impossible. Even the best of them, they take the truth so *personally*. But you, you have a fine intelligence but you stand completely apart. You are not *engagé*, you are not *parti pris*. You hear my words simply as words. My thoughts are simply thoughts, not the thoughts of wealth and fame and a name. Not the thoughts of one who could be of help to you, or could wound and insult you with a careless dismissive phrase that is intended to be of general application, not personal at all. You bring the disinterested clarity of perspective that comes from standing elsewhere. I value that, my friend. I value it tremendously.'

The last prince had died soon after Florian's visit in obscure circumstances, but Florian, who had barely listened to Prince Shurupin's words at all but paid close attention to the man, returned to the abandoned palace from time to time, to prowl its fading rooms and read in the library, until large parts of the roof had collapsed, the floors became unsafe and the stench of damp and mildew and fungal growth too depressing to bear. Even when he'd stopped going into the palace, he still made visits to the park. Too large by far for the two men employed by the city to maintain them, the greater part of the former gardens had reverted to thicketed, brambled wilderness, the marble temples and mythographical statuary imported from the Archipelago by the early princes soot-blackened and mossy green, submerged under a tide of thorn and glossy mounds of rhododendron. For Florian it was a cool, earthy, leafy, sap-rich, owl-hunted refuge from the city.

And he had come there now, in the dark and snow-muffled night, to nurse the gunshot wound in his belly.

Relieving himself of the discomfort of human clothes and human form, Florian nosed his way into the shelter of a stand of pine trees in the centre of the park and curled himself up on a patch of bare earth. The wound was a dull ache. It was almost healed, only a tender puckered crust remained, but the effort of driving the bullet out had cost him energy and he needed rest. He rasped at the place with his tongue until the last taste of dried blood had gone, then stretched out and closed his eyes.

The watchfulness of the world was all around him, the living awareness of earth and trees reaching out in all directions to the edge of streets and the river and beyond. The connective tissue of the park and the city was earth and water and air and roots, and Florian merged himself into the flow and tangle of it, surrendering, letting the constant work of holding together a pseudo-human consciousness relax and blur away. No words, no structured thoughts. No names for things. He was what he was, and only that. The hurt in the belly was not *his* hurt, it was simply *hurt,* a thing that was there, that existed, but without implication. No before-time and nothing to come: and without that, no fear.

34

Lom woke in the morning to find the curtain pulled back and the attic filled with brilliant early light. The sky in the window was a bright powdery eggshell blue. Maroussia was already gone. He got up and dressed. There was broken ice in the washbowl. He splashed his face and looked out of the window. Snow mounded the rooftops of the raion and filled the silent streets. Nothing moved but wisps of smoke from chimneys. The broken moons, faint and filmy, silver-blue against blue, rested at anchor, day-visible watermarks in the liquid paper sky.

Lom went out into the corridor and tried to retrace his steps back to Elena's kitchen but found himself in parts of the house he hadn't seen before. A wide staircase took him down to an entrance hall: red tiles and threadbare rugs, a stand for coats and hats, umbrellas and galoshes. Fishing rods. The scent of polish and leather. Morning sun streamed in through the coloured-glass skylight over the door, kindling dust motes and splashing faint lozenges of colour across the floor. He unbolted the door and opened it onto foot-thick snow. Crisp bitter air spilled inwards, caught at his nose and throat and made his breath steam. He stepped out into crisp blue illumination. Every colour was saturated. The snow glistened, translucent, refracting tiny diamond brilliances. He stomped his way round the side of the house, looking for the entrance they'd used last night. Nothing moved in the streets. The snow muffled all sound, except for the morning bells, the calling of the rooks and the rhythmic crunch of his own feet.

He made his way round to the gate into the garden and pushed it open. As he was passing the wide low loggia, a figure stepped out to confront him.

'Yes? Who are you?'

It was a man of about sixty, leaning on a malacca cane. Wisps of un-combed grey hair, a heavily embroidered morning coat, gold-rimmed spectacles. An ugly intelligent face. He was standing on the step under the canopy. Worn, turned carpet slippers on his feet.

'Sorry,' said Lom. 'I'm staying in the house. We're with Elena Cornelius. I got myself lost. I was trying to find my way back to her apartment.'

'Ah,' said the man. He lit a black cigarette with a match. Wraiths of cheap rough tobacco smoke drifted in the cold air. 'That's it then. You are one of our guests in the attic. I fear it will have been cold for you up there among the rafters.' He came down the step and held out his hand. 'I am Sandu Evgenich ter-Orenbergh Shirin-Vilichov Palffy and this is my house. You are welcome. Of course.'

Lom took the offered hand.

'Lom,' he said. 'Vissarion Yppolitovich Lom.'

Palffy made a slight, formal bow.

'You were taking a walk in the snow before breakfast, perhaps?' he said.

'I guess,' said Lom. 'You don't see snow much, where I come from. Just rain. Always rain.'

'Where is that? Where you are from?'

'East,' said Lom, gesturing vaguely. 'East. Way east. On the forest border. I doubt you've heard of it. A small town called Podchornok.'

'I believe I do know Podchornok, as it happens. Some cousins of mine had an estate in that country once.'

Lom grunted.

'Small world.'

'Not such a coincidence,' said the Count. 'I had cousins in every oblast of the Dominions once, but that was a lifetime ago. A differ-ent world. The people I'm talking about were at Vyra. They had a fine house. A good lake for pike. The place is gone, now, of course, alas.' He coughed and looked sourly at the cigarette in his hand. 'In those days, when I was a child and went to Vyra, the Vlast was more ... what? Moderate? Sensible? Willing to overlook small independences, let us say, so long as they were far from their own front door and paid their taxes and didn't draw attention to themselves.'

'Vyra was the Vishniks' place,' said Lom.

'It was! Exactly so!' Palffy looked at him with a new interest. 'You *knew* them then?'

'I knew Raku. We were at school.'

'Raku?' Count Palffy frowned. Then he remembered. 'Of course! There *was* a Prince Raku. The Vishniks had a son, an only child. But that was long after my visit. We could not have met, Raku and I. So where is this Prince Raku now? What does he do with himself? Perhaps I might write to him. Families should keep up their connections, don't you think?'

'Raku died.'

'No!' said the Count. 'He couldn't have been more than thirty. Was he ill? What happened?'

'The militia happened.'

'Ah. How shit. How very shit.' Palffy dropped his cigarette on the step and crushed it out with the brass ferrule of his cane. Not an easy trick, but he speared it first shot. 'This is a heavy blow. But we should not be making ourselves sad on such a splendid morning, my friend. Come inside with me, Vissarion Lom, and have breakfast. The snow makes one hungry, don't you find?'

'Thanks,' said Lom. 'But I should be getting back— '

'Some coffee then. I have good coffee. Red beans from the Cloud Forest, roasted to my personal specification by Mandelbrot's in Klepsydra Lane. How does that sound to you?'

'I'd appreciate that,' said Lom. 'But not now. Maybe later.'

'I will hold you to that, Vissarion Yppolitovich. A bond of honour.'

Lom found Maroussia in Elena's kitchen, sitting on a stool against the warmth of the stove. She was wearing different clothes. She must have borrowed them from Elena: a plain grey woollen dress and a thick dark cardigan that was too big for her. She had the cardigan buttoned up to the neck, her fingers peeping from the cuffs. She gave him a quick wry smile when he came in, cold and fresh from outside, brushing the snow from his trousers. When the smile faded, her face was pale and drawn, but her eyes when they met his were bright with energy and fierce determination.

Elena was clearing breakfast off the table and the girls were laying out a backgammon board. The younger one, Yeva, was staring at Lom curiously.

'What's wrong with your head?' she said. 'There's a hole in it.'

Lom touched the wound on his forehead.

'Oh,' he said. 'Sorry.'

'What happened? Was it a bullet?'

'No.'

'There's a man at Vera's who was shot in the head by dragoons. He's not dead, but he doesn't talk and one of his eyes is gone. He dribbles his tea.'

'Be quiet, Yeva,' said Elena. 'Leave Vissarion in peace. And you can't start on a game now. There's no time. You need to go to school.'

'What? No!' said Galina. 'Not today. The snow. There's snow—'

'You're not missing school for a bit of snow. Kolya will take you in the cart. He'll be waiting already.'

'But—'

'Go. School. Now. He'll be waiting.'

'Nobody goes to school when there's snow. We'll be the only ones …'

'You're not missing school. That's not what we do. That's not who we are.'

Elena hustled the girls out of the kitchen. Lom sat at the table next to Maroussia.

'OK?' he said. 'You look tired.'

'I'm fine,' she said. 'I'm ready to go. Are you?'

'Go where?'

Elena came back into the kitchen and attacked the breakfast things in the sink.

'Elena?' said Maroussia.

'Yes?'

'I need to find out about the forest. Who is there in the raion that I can talk to about the forest?'

'The forest?'

'Yes.'

'Why? Why the forest?'

Maroussia brushed the question aside impatiently.

'This is important,' she said. 'I want to find someone who knows about the forest and what happens there. Someone who's actually been there.'

'Is this anything to do with the trouble you're in?' said Elena. 'No. Don't answer that. I don't want to know.'

'Is there someone?' said Maroussia again. 'Anyone who might be able to tell me something? Anything?'

Elena hesitated.

'I don't know,' she said. 'I don't think so. There was Teslom at the House on the Purfas. But he was arrested. And there's the Count – he used to travel once. But not any more. Not for a long time. And I don't know if he ever actually went into the forest himself.'

'Not the Count,' said Lom. 'I've run into him already. He's not the man, not for this.'

'Isn't there anyone else?' said Maroussia.

Well,' said Elena after a moment's thought, 'there is Kamilova. You could go and see her, I suppose. Eligiya Kamilova. She is a friend of mine, in a way. But ... well, she's not an easy person to talk to.'

'Kamilova?' said Maroussia. 'Who is she?'

Elena shrugged, as if she wasn't sure how to answer.

'No one knows much about her,' she said. 'She comes and goes. She goes into the forest, into the wild places under the trees. She brings back specimens for the Count's collection sometimes, but she's not easy—'

'I'll go and see her,' said Maroussia.

'I can't promise she'll even talk to you.'

'Where does she live? Is she here in the raion?'

'Yes,' said Elena. 'Down by the harbour.'

'I need to see her.'

'Now?' said Elena.

'Yes. Now.'

35

The Colloquium for the Protection of Citizens and the Vlast met at ten o'clock every morning, not in the Lodka but in a room in the Armoury, as befitted a War Cabinet. Chazia was there first, as she always was. Prepared. Colloquium Chairman Etsim Fohn and his sidekick, Fess Khazar, the Secretary of Finance, arrived together, five minutes late and already deep in conversation. Sharing a joke. Fohn surveyed the room. Saw the empty chair.

'Where is our General Secretary?' he said. 'Where is Dukhonin? I haven't seen him this morning. My office has been trying to raise him, but no one is answering at his house. He didn't come to ... Well, never mind. Where is he? We need him here.' The three of them – Fohn, Dukhonin, Khazar – always met in Fohn's office before the formal Cabinet, to prepare their lines. To take the real decisions. Chazia was never invited. They thought she did not know.

'The Minister for Armaments will not be joining us,' she said. 'Steopan Vadimovich is dead.'

Khazar sat down at the end of the table, his face white as chalk. He looked at Fohn, to see what he would do. Fohn was glaring at Chazia.

'What?' said Fohn. 'When? Why wasn't I told? Why do you know this, Lavrentina, and I do not? I am the *Chairman*. I should have been informed. I should have been told immediately. You should have ... I should have been the *first* ...'

Chazia ignored him.

'There was an attack on his house last night,' she said. 'The Lezarye were responsible, there is no doubt of that. Dukhonin and all his household were hacked to death in their beds and the house ransacked.'

'Last night?' said Fohn. 'Last night! We should have been informed immediately. A member of the Colloquium assassinated, and the Chairman not even told? Who was in charge of Dukhonin's security? I want names. I want them punished. Heads on spikes. And an overhaul. A thorough review. Action this day and a report on my desk this afternoon.'

'Absolutely!' said Khazar. 'If Steopan Dukhonin can't sleep safe in his bed then who is safe? It might have been any of us! Internal dissidence is your responsibility, Lavrentina. I cannot understand—'

Chazia held up her hand for silence.

'As you rightly say, gentlemen, this is my area. I will be making a speech in the parade ground as soon as this meeting is over. I will be announcing new measures. We have tolerated the presence of the Lezarye in this city for too long. We cannot afford an enemy within. An enemy at our backs. The raion will be closed and cleared. The Lezarye will be transported to the east. Conscripted labour is needed there.'

'No,' said Fohn. 'This is too hasty. There will be trouble. They will resist.'

'I will deal with that,' said Chazia. 'Leave it to me.'

'No. We should have been consulted. I am—'

'We need to move on, gentlemen,' said Chazia. 'This is a War Cabinet and we have more urgent business. Time is short. When I was at Steopan Vadimovich's house last night, clearing up the mess, I learned a disturbing thing. The situation is worse than we thought.' She paused and looked each man in the face, one by one. 'We have all been kept in the dark.'

Khazar turned to Fohn.

'What's going on, Etsim?' he said. 'What is she talking about?'

Fohn said nothing. He was watching Chazia narrowly. He was a bureaucrat, but not entirely stupid. She would have to deal with him soon.

'The war situation is much more desperate than we have been led to believe,' she said. 'Dukhonin's desk was piled high with reports. Complaints. Telegrams. A catalogue of inadequacy and failure. The army has no munitions. The navy has no fuel. The armament manufacturers have no materials. We are hopelessly in debt to the finance houses of the Fransa, and the Treasury is within a week of bankruptcy. The front at Brazhd is crumbling. An Archipelago fleet has been sighted off the Aanen Islands.'

'The Aanens—!' Khazar began.

'The enemy,' said Chazia, 'will be at the outskirts of Mirgorod within days.'

Khazar slumped forward, his head in his hands.

'Then we are ruined and it is over,' he muttered. 'I knew! I always knew!'

Fohn ignored him. He was glaring at Chazia.

'Lies,' he said. 'These are lies. The Novozhd would never have—'

'The Novozhd knew,' said Chazia. 'Of course he knew. Why else did he start negotiations for peace? Dukhonin knew. The admirals and the generals knew. Every foot soldier in the infantry knew. Only we did not know. We have been playing a charade of government since the Novozhd was killed, but now we know. And now we must act.'

'What?' said Khazar. 'What can we do?'

'The current military command cannot be trusted and must be purged. The necessary action is already in hand.'

'This is happening *now*?' said Fohn.

'It began,' said Chazia, ' as soon as you entered this room.'

'On whose *orders*?'

'On mine. Your personal staffs are also being replaced. You have been misled and betrayed. I will give you more trustworthy people. I will arrange it myself. But our first priority is the defence of Mirgorod. The city must not be allowed to fall to the Archipelago. Dukhonin has made no adequate preparations. None at all. However, I have taken matters in hand now. I have appointed General Rizhin as the new City Defence Commissar. He will begin work immediately—'

'*Rizhin?*' said Khazar. 'Who is this *Rizhin*? Fohn? I don't know the name. Do we know this man Rizhin?'

Fohn was on his feet, red-faced and trembling. His chair tipped backwards and crashed to the floor behind him.

'This is a *coup*!' he shouted. 'A filthy fucking *putsch*! I'm not going to—'

Chazia pressed the intercom buzzer. The door opened and Captain Iliodor entered the room, followed by three armed militia officers. They took up positions inside the door.

'Arrest this woman,' said Fohn. 'Arrest her now.'

The militia officers ignored him.

'Sit down, Chairman,' said Chazia. 'Please, Etsim Maximich, my friend. Sit.'

'So this is how it is,' said Fohn. 'You're mad. You can't sustain it. You have no strength. The people will not allow it. The army will stand behind me. I'll have you dragged through the streets.'

'Calm yourself, Etsim. Please. Of course this is not a coup. You are overwrought. This is shocking news, I know. I understand your feelings. I felt the same way myself last night. You will recover soon, and see things clearly again. You are my colleague, Etsim, my valued friend and my Chairman. We continue as before. Of course we do. I have made a plan. You and Secretary Khazar will leave Mirgorod immediately. It is too dangerous for you to remain here. The enemy is at the gate. You will go east, to Kholvatogorsk, and establish our new capital there. The Vlast continues. A new Vlast. A Vlast reborn. It will not matter then whether Mirgorod falls or not. The Vlast is more than one single city. Go to Kholvatogorsk and build anew. Prepare to strike back at our enemies. I will join you there shortly. I have somewhere else I must go first. '

36

Lom and Maroussia stepped out of Count Palffy's house into snow-bright cold.

'Eligiya Kamilova lives in a wooden house on the fish wharf,' Elena had said. 'You need to climb the Ship Bastion and take the covered steps down to the harbour.'

The Ship Bastion was a massive granite outcrop, the highest point in the raion, the highest in Mirgorod. Street sweepers were out – giants shovelling snow with easy strength – and some people were clearing the paths outside their houses and shops, but it was hard climbing. They had to pick their way across rutted, compacted stretches of ice and wade knee-deep through heaps and drifts of snow.

There was a small cobbled square at the top of the Bastion rock, with a parapet where you could lean and catch your breath. Below them, the canyons and ravines of the raion fell way in a tumble of steep roofs, stepped gables, leaning pinnacles and slumping chimneys; and beyond lay the expansive, grey, snow-dusted, smoking vista of Mirgorod. The city roared quietly under the wheeling of the gulls. In the distance the thousand-foot-high needle-sharp spire of the Armoury, the One Column On Spilled Blood, speared the belly of the sky. The Lodka was a massive squat black prow, and the steel ribbon of the Mir rolled westwards, crossed by a dozen bridges, towards the skyline smudge of the sea.

In the far corner of the Bastion Square was a wooden door set in a pointed arch of weathered grey stone.

'That must be the way,' said Maroussia. 'Down there.'

The door in the arch opened onto a steep winding flight of stone steps enclosed by wooden walls and a wooden roof. The stairway was in shadow, lit only by narrow slits cut at intervals in the wood, and the treads were worn smooth and hollow in the centre by centuries of footfall. It smelled cool and damp, like the mouth of a well. The steps wound and switchbacked steeply down. Hundreds of steps. Several times they had to stop and press themselves back against the wall to make room for someone coming up.

They came out into a huddle of warehouses, wharves and jetties. Boats crowded against the harbour edge, idle under a covering of snow. The River Purfas was a pale green porridge of slush and fragments of ice. Rigging clattered in the brisk river breeze. Nets were draped, black and reeking, from the weather-bleached warehouse walls, and the smell from gibbeted racks of drying fish and smokehouses hung heavy on the air. Yellow-eyed seabirds called from canted masts and rooftops, swooped on scraps and stalked the walkways, poking at the chum-buckets. Chalk-boards at the wharfside fish market promised eel and crab, flounder, zander, garfish, herring, bream and cod. But fishing was done for the winter. Harder times were coming. The market trays were empty, the sawdust swept and the shutters up. Men hung about, smoking, talking quietly in the throaty, fricative languages of the raion.

Lom and Maroussia picked their way between stacked baskets, salt barrels and coils of rope. They found the tall narrow building where Kamilova lived at the far end of the wharf, squeezed between a chandlery and a smokehouse. A frontage of overlapping timbers of tar-black pine and dark lopsided windows with many panes of thick green glass. Maroussia knocked. Lom pulled his woollen cap lower over his forehead.

The woman who opened the door must have been sixty years old, but she was tall and straight and wiry-muscular, with a traveller's sparse, defined, weathered face. Iron-grey hair, tied severely back. Bright pale intelligent eyes. She was wearing a knitted sweater, dark canvas trousers, boots.

'Eligiya Kamilova?' said Maroussia.

'Yes? Who are you?'

'My name is Maroussia Shaumian.'

'Shaumian?' Kamilova studied her with narrowed eyes. 'I see. *Shaumian.*'

'Can we come in? We want to talk to you. We want to ask you about the forest. I think you can help me—'

'No,' said Kamilova. 'I can't help you.'

She began to close the door. Lom stepped forward and leaned against it.

'We need to talk to you,' he said.

Kamilova looked at him steadily.

'You,' she said, 'should get off my door.'

'We just want to come in for a while,' said Lom. 'To talk. That's all.'

'I said get away from my door.'

Kamilova's eyes widened. There was a strangeness there. Wild distant spaces. Lom felt the air stirring. Responsive. Forest smells. Resin and earth. And suddenly the air around him was no longer stuff to breathe, it was his enemy. Heavy in his lungs, hard and cold about him. A stone fist of air punched him in the back of the head, sickening, dizzying, and he stumbled forward. The weight of solid air on his shoulders and back pressed down on him. All the mile-high heaviness of the air. Forcing him to his knees. A sudden wind whipped the snow from the ground. It smacked and scraped at his face, a bitter freezing hail, blinding him. He could hear Maroussia somewhere far away, shouting, but the wind destroyed her words. Panicking, he struggled for breath. He could not fill his lungs. He was drowning in the hostile air.

But he did not drown. There was a sentience in the air. It was alive and knew what it was doing. And he knew what it was.

Lom reached out towards it. Opening himself. Taking the barriers down. Not breathing in but breathing out. Remembering.

He was in the centre of a small hardened whorl of fierceness, but beyond it were oceans of atmosphere. Eddies and tides and deeps, layer over layer, air from the forest, air from the river, air from the sea, freighted with life and scent and the stories of themselves. He climbed higher. The air grew thinner, colder, clearer, more beautiful, bright and electric the higher he climbed. He opened himself to it. He was air himself, air in the air. The squalls that battered him were part of him and he was in them. He let them pass through where he was. He rose and stood and waited patiently for the assault to calm and stop.

Kamilova was looking at him with surprise and frank curiosity. And something else. Lom could not tell what it was. It might have been recognition.

'Who are you?' she said.

Lom tried to answer but found he could not. Not yet. His heart was hammering. He needed all the capacity of his aching lungs to breathe, tearing mouthfuls of breath out of the sparse, thinned air.

'Who is he?' Kamilova said to Maroussia. Urgently. 'Who is this man?'

'This is my friend. His name is Vissarion.'

Kamilova frowned.

'No,' she said. 'No. Not Vissarion. That's not a forest name. He's strong, but I didn't know him. He carries himself like a bear, but something's not right.'

'Can't we just ...' Lom breathed painfully. His whole body felt bruised and abused. 'Can't we just come in?'

37

Look to the south of Mirgorod and see hundreds of miles of frontierless grass. Sandy soil. Marshes and small lakes, slow yellow rivers, thorn thickets and sparse scatterings of birch. Collectivised farms of drab herds, two-strand fences, cabbages and potato fields. Hapless towns, dirt roads and one-platform railway halts. A long indeterminate coastline of gravel and mud. A country without features.

Across this country war is coming.

Onward the enemy's armies churn, at the pace of markers being moved across a map in an operations room, at the speed of terse conversations on field telephones, converging on Mirgorod, capital of the Vlast. The armies of the enemy find the opposition melting away.

It is a matter of machine logistics now. Statistics and arithmetics of steel. A calculation of armoured divisions. The sound is the sound of diesel engines droning and the clatter of iron tracks, the rattle of ammunition belts, the thunder-crash of heavy guns. The smell is the smell of hot oil and hot metal, the burning of rubber, the hot piss the gunners use to cool their overworked weapons. The light is the light of arcing sprays of burning gasoline, the flicker of rocket batteries firing, the daytime darkness of shadows under smoke-filled air. Not in one place, but in a hundred places: five separate fronts, all rolling forward, thirty or forty miles a day, converging on Mirgorod.

In rain-sodden fields and bypassed towns, people stand mute and look on as the logarithms of steel, too intent on the future to notice them, surge by. Seventy-ton tanks chew up the ground. The pale faces of motorised infantry stare back at the watchers without expression from the back of armoured half-tracks. Under the watchers' feet the earth trembles. The deep geologies of history are upheaving. The maps by which they have always lived are being torn up and trodden into the mud. The old certainties are dissolving like bones in an acid bath.

The ones who look on are not even frightened yet.

And over their heads the featureless sky is marked out with the high patchwork geometries of aircraft formations sliding north towards Mirgorod.

38

Lom followed Maroussia and Eligiya Kamilova up the staircase to Kamilova's room. It was a wide, airy, almost empty space at the top of the house: the scent of woodsmoke and damp earth mixed with the harbour reek. Thick leaded panes filtered the morning light, and harbour sounds drifted in through an open casement. The room was austere, like the woman herself. Stripped back. Only what was essential. Bare floorboards darkened with age. A large rug spread in the centre, leather cushions and bolsters ranged around the edge. A pair of low, carved stools.

A small fire was burning in the corner, logs stacked neatly nearby: the logs looked like they'd spent time in the sea. A bleached animal skull rested on the floor near the hearth. It was big like an elk but broad-browed and feline, with front-facing eye sockets and a pair of long curved incisors. A hunting beast. It was enormous. Colossal.

Kamilova brought them tea in china cups. It was made from forest leaves, muddy and bitter. She folded herself neatly onto a cushion. Maroussia sat near her and Lom squatted awkwardly on one of the stools, facing her across the rug.

'So?' said Kamilova. 'Why come to me?'

'My friend Elena Cornelius told me you've made journeys in the forest. I hoped ... maybe you might talk to us. You might know something that could help us. Help me.'

'Elena Cornelius?' said Kamilova. 'You should have said. But ... help you with what?'

Lom watched Maroussia hesitate. Take a deep breath. Make a decision.

'There was a paluba,' she said. 'It was looking for me and it found

458

me. It showed me things. The forest. A terrible living angel, and the damage it was doing. The paluba wanted me to find something. The Pollandore. Do you—?'

'*Air-daughter made a new world,*' said Kamilova, '*to displace the old one from within. World in the forest, forest in the world. What makes you look, and what you find. The wound, and what made the wound.*'

'That's it!' said Maroussia. 'That's what my mother used to say. I haven't heard that for years. Yes. And the Pollandore is—'

'A story. A riddle game. A children's tale. I have heard others.'

'No,' said Maroussia. 'It's real.' She reached inside her coat and brought out the bundle of Vishnik's photographs. Handed them across to Kamilova. 'Here it is. Here is the proof.'

Kamilova looked at the pictures one by one, carefully. Moments in the city, times and places opened up like sunlight in a rain-dark sky, like berries bursting.

'And this,' she said at last, 'you think this is the Pollandore?'

'No, it's what the Pollandore is *doing*,' said Maroussia. 'Here in Mirgorod. It's active. It's leaking or something. I don't know. I've felt it myself. I've *seen* these things. It's waking up. The Pollandore itself is a *thing*. It's an *object* in a *place*. The paluba ... she told me to find it. She wants me to open it.'

'Open it like a box, or open it like a door?'

'I don't know.'

'To let something out, or for you to go in?'

'I don't *know*!'

'But you're going to do it?'

'Yes. If I can.'

'Why?'

'Because of the angel. The paluba showed me—'

'The paluba,' said Kamilova, 'showed you nothing. The paluba was a vehicle, nothing more. The speaker but not the voice.' She paused, watching Maroussia closely. Studying her. 'So,' she said at last. 'You want me to tell you about the forest?'

'Yes,' said Maroussia. 'Please. Just ... just talk to us.'

Kamilova pulled back her sleeves and held out her arms. They were thin, muscular and berry-brown. Intricate knotted patterns wound across her skin, reaching down towards her wrists, drawn in faded purple and green. Like roots. Like veins. Filaments. Growth.

'Yes,' she said. 'I've been into the forest. I've taken my boat up the rivers. I've travelled with fur traders and shamans and women with spirit skins. I've lived with giants and lake people. I've slept with them and hunted with them and some of them showed me ... they showed me things. They taught me, and I listened. I learned. I'm talking about the deep forest now. Deep in under the trees.' She looked at Lom. 'He knows what I mean.'

'No,' said Lom. 'I don't.'

Kamilova made a crude derisive gesture and spat into the fire. Lom had seen traders on the Yannis do the same thing when offered an insulting price. She turned away from him, back to Maroussia.

'What you need to understand about the forest,' Kamilova continued, 'is this: there is no end to it, and no certain paths. It is not *a* forest, it is all forests. It contains all forests. Woods within woods, forests within forests, further in and further back, deeper and deeper for ever. Anything that *could* be in the forest *is* there. Anything you have ever heard about the forest – any forest – it is all there, somewhere. The Vlast is nothing, the world is nothing, compared to the forest.' She paused. 'And the point is, most of what lives in the forest has no interest in the human world at all. The forest has its own purposes. Not everything that comes out of the forest can be trusted.'

'You think the paluba lied to me?' said Maroussia.

'I think that, whoever was using it, they have purposes of their own, of which you are a part. Palubas speak to you like dreams. They draw things out of your mind, use images and ideas they find there, change them, put thoughts to you in ways that you can understand and believe.'

'But that's the point. I *don't* understand'

'You're doing what it needs you to do.'

'But the Pollandore is real,' said Maroussia. 'It's here. It's near. I've seen what it can do. It can make a difference. It can make things ... *change*. And I know where it is, only it will be hard to get to. And I am going to reach it.'

'Why?' said Kamilova. 'I ask you this again. Why?'

'Because ...' said Maroussia. She frowned. Hesitated. 'Because there's a terrible hole in the centre of everything. It's like a mouth, a gaping mouth that swallows up life and spews out shadow and cruelty and sadness. Not just for me, for everyone. There's this *gap*, this awful *gap* that you feel all the time, between how things are and how they could be. There's something really close to me, almost in the same place as I am, and it's my life, my real life as it's meant to be, only I'm not living it because I'm here instead. '

Maroussia was leaning forward, back straight, dark eyes fixed on the fire in Kamilova's grate. She was fierce and hurting and determined. Lom watched her intently.

'Do you understand?' she said urgently to Kamilova. 'Do you know what I mean?'

'Yes,' said Kamilova. 'Yes. I do.'

'I will reach the Pollandore,' said Maroussia. 'I know where it is. But I don't know what to do when I get there. The paluba said there was a key. Not a key, but something like it. It thought I already had it. It thought I knew more ... but I don't.'

Kamilova stood up.

'Come with me,' she said. 'I will show you something.'

The boathouse was a few yards down from Kamilova's building. She let Lom and Maroussia in through a small wicket in a larger door.

'This is my boat,' she said. '*Heron.*' It was under a tarpaulin, a varnished clinker hull. The rest of the space in the boathouse was filled with a clutter of bundles and stacked boxes. A canoe hung suspended from the ceiling, skins on a wooden frame. 'This is where I keep my collection. Things I've brought back from the forest.'

It was impossible to make out much in the shadows. There were carvings on the wall. Crude wooden masks. Bottles and boxes on shelves. Lom felt something stirring. Hunting animals with rain-wet fur. Leaf mould and shadow under trees. Watchfulness. Life. He was in an open space among the trees. Fern and briar and clumps of thorn. Earth and rain. A small stream, barely trickling its way over silted accidental dams of mud and stone and banked-up branches and leaves. A beech fallen in a pool of green water. Rain-mist erasing the further slopes and hillsides. He was young, and something was watching him, a bad dark thing, and he was frightened.

Kamilova disappeared into the back of the boathouse and came back holding something small cupped in her hand. A loosely knotted ball of twigs and dried leaves stuck with gobbets of wax-like stuff, dried brown and brittle. Dull, desiccated berries. The bones and fur-scraps of small animals. She held it out to Maroussia.

'Have you seen one of these before?' she said.

Maroussia took it and turned it over in her hand. Held it up to her face and breathed the scent.

'Yes,' she said. 'My mother had them all over the house. She said the forest brought them to her. But she ... she was weak and frightened all the time. She was terrified of trees in the street. She said they waited for her and watched and followed her. She wasn't ... well.'

'This is what the volvas, the wise women, call a solm, or a khlahv, or a bo. Sometimes they call them keys. It's a vessel for air. It can hold and carry a breath, and the breath is the message. The voice. That one in your hand is empty now. Old and dead.'

Maroussia handed the object back.

'What my mother had, they were *messages*?' she said. 'About the Pollandore?'

'About it. Or for it.'

'But they're all gone now,' said Maroussia. 'They're all lost. Or destroyed.' She paused. 'No, wait. Mother used to hide them sometimes in the apartment. Vissarion, we have to go back there. We have to go back and look.'

'No,' said Lom. He brought out from his pocket the bloodstained hessian bag he'd taken from her mother's body in the street by Vanko's. The survivor. It felt alive in his hand. Quiet and watchful. Breathing. 'I've still got this.'

Maroussia snatched it from him and opened it. Brought out the knot of twigs and forest stuff. Held it up to her face. Her hands were trembling slightly. But nothing happened. Nothing came.

'Is it still good?' she said to Kamilova. 'Is it OK?'

'I think so. Yes.'

'But ... what do I do with it?' Maroussia held it out to her. 'Can you tell me?'

Kamilova shook her head.

'Not if it's meant for you.'

'But I don't know how ... There's nothing. Nothing's happening.'

'You have to learn that for yourself. You have to listen. Keep it with you. Hold it. Breathe it. Pay attention. Don't push it. It's all about openness. Wakefulness. Give it time.'

'Time?' said Maroussia. 'There is no time. Time is what we haven't got.'

Kamilova kissed Maroussia on the mouth when they left.

39

Maroussia said nothing when they emerged from Eligiya Kamilova's boathouse. They walked in silence along the harbour edge and began the ascent back up towards the Ship Bastion.

Lom kept pace alongside Maroussia. Leaving her space. Letting her think. He wasn't sure, himself, what they had learned from Kamilova. In Kamilova's presence he'd felt the forest, its realness and closeness, its watchfulness, its urgency. But ... perhaps there wasn't anything else to know. Perhaps it wasn't about learning, but doing. The Pollandore was in the Lodka, right in the cruel stone centre of the Vlast. Bring Maroussia to the Pollandore and ... it would happen. *Something* would happen. Trying to learn, trying to explore, trying to figure out what she had to do when the moment came and what it might mean: that was nothing, only passing time. An avoidance strategy. A rationalisation of fear. The task was simpler than that.

Maroussia stopped and turned to face him.

'What Kamilova said ...' she began. 'About the people who sent the paluba having a purpose of their own, that I couldn't know ...' She paused. 'It doesn't matter, does it? None of that matters. The angel in the forest is real. The Pollandore is real. The rest of it doesn't matter. There are only two sides, and everyone has to choose. I'm not trusting the paluba, I'm trusting *myself*. It's about feeling and instinct and knowing what to do, when the time comes.'

'Yes,' said Lom. 'I guess that's right.'

'We have to get into the Lodka and find the Pollandore. What happens after that ... that's something else. We just have to get there.'

You can't just walk into the Lodka, thought Lom, but he said nothing. That was his problem, not hers. Getting her inside, that was his job. What happened afterwards would be up to her.

Consider the question in its widest aspect.

The Lodka: it was where the Pollandore was, and it was where Chazia was. And *Josef Kantor*. The Lodka was the last place Lom had seen Kantor. Kantor was more than a terrorist. Much more. Lom didn't fully understand Kantor's connections with Chazia and the Lodka, but he knew that Kantor was deeply and intricately meshed in it all. That made Kantor a way in. So. *Find Kantor*. It was back to that.

They climbed back up the winding covered steps to the Ship Bastion and emerged into winter light. The sky was pale powder-blue, airy and vertiginous, wisped with sparse cloud-feather, achingly elsewhere, achingly high. They leaned on the parapet and looked out across the city. Mirgorod, spreading out towards the horizon under an immensity of height and air, seemed almost small. A humane settlement. Containable. A place where people lived. The winter sun, already westering, burned with a blinding whiteness that gave no heat. There was something wrong. A buzzing in the air, an edgy vibration, like unseen engines racing. Too quiet and distant to be a sound, you heard it with your skin, your teeth, the bones of your skull.

'Look,' said Maroussia 'Look.'

She was squinting towards the sun.

Lom looked but saw nothing. The sun was cold and dazzling. When he shut his eyes against it, colour-shifting after-images and shadow-filaments floated across the blood-warmth inside. When he looked again, some of the specks were still there. Strings of dots across the sun in wavering horizontal lines. Faint punctuation.

Others had stopped to watch them. Nobody spoke.

More and more rows of specks resolved out of the sun. Coming into focus. Dozens. Scores. Hundreds. Coming in pulses. Waves. Formations.

The noise escalated to a thundering, rattling roar, not from the west where Lom was looking but from behind. He jerked his head round. The aircraft was low and descending and coming straight for them. It was immense. Three fat-bellied fuselages hung from wide, thick wings. Each wing carried eight – no, *ten* – propellers. The fuselages were as large as ships. The bomber was so big it seemed to be suspended in the sky, an impossible motionless thing. It was descending slowly straight down onto them, onto the rock hill on which they stood. It was going to crash.

At the last moment the plane lifted its nose fractionally and roared slowly overhead. They saw its swollen triple bellies of unpainted metal. Lettering on the underside of its wings. The insignia of the Archipelago. It was low enough to see faces looking down from its windows as it trundled over them and sailed out across the city, its engine noise climbing to a roar beyond hearing, its array of speed-blurred propellers chopping and grinding the air.

A trail of insignificant silver shapes spilled from its triple belly mouths.

A pause. A suspended moment. Maroussia's hand was gripping Lom's arm so tight it hurt.

The bombs splashed into the upturned face of the city and flowered into small blossoms of flame and smoke puffs.

And then came the sound.

The world lurched sickeningly and Lom's stomach with it. A new door had opened and everything was utterly changed.

Wave after wave of huge triple-fuselaged bombers unloaded their cargoes. The engines roared relentlessly and the detonation-thuds burst in short fast shattering series. Fat columns of black oily smoke rose everywhere and drifted in low, thickening banks. The smell of it reached them: an industrial smell, like engine sheds and factories. Hot metal and soot.

Higher in the sky, smaller wasp-like aircraft circled, buzzed and droned, drawing tracks and spirals of vapour trail.

'Which ones are ours?' said Maroussia. 'Can you tell?'

'None,' said Lom. 'None at all.'

Twenty thousand pounds of high explosive per minute, minute after minute after minute, spilled out of the sky in sticks and skeins of bombs. Whistling formations of aerodynamic tubular steel casing. A spattering rain of incendiary parcels. When their bays were empty, the heavy bomber squadrons swept round again for a fresh approach. They lumbered in low. Autocannons in fishbowl noses and underbelly gun-pods punched out 50mm phosphorus shells at thirty rounds per minute. The disciplined, practised attacks concentrated on the wharfs and harbour yards to the west of Mirgorod and the steelworks and factories to the south, but the seeds of destruction and burn were scattered widely.

A stick of two-thousand-pound bombs splashed across Levrovskaya Square: three crashed through the roof of the Hotel Sviatopolk and erupted inside, two more hit in the square itself. Shockwaves swept through the Teagarden, smashing rubble and fragments of traffic and restaurants and people through the citizens taking tea. The blast buckled the heavy bronze doors of the Bank of Foreign Commerce and shattered the plate windows of Rosenfeld's, blowing a hurricane of tiny glittering blades through customers and staff. Lacerating the polished mahogany panels and counters.

A five-thousand-pound barrel of explosive demolished the Ter-Uspenskovo Bridge. The river erupted, drenching the Square of the Piteous Angel and leaving the riverbed temporarily naked. The shock waves rocked the Lodka: glass and stone from its high roof-dome crashed down on the readers in the hall of the Central Registry and the great wheel of the Gaukh Engine canted six inches sideways, its motors seized up and screeching.

Incendiary clusters set the roofs of the Laughing Cockerel Theatre and the Dreksler-Kino burning.

Vanko's Uniform Factory was a crater of rubble and dust.

Mirgorod, city burning.

Fire-flakes licked at blistering paint and smouldering furniture and blew from house to house and street to street on gusting breezes of fire. Fire-clusters spread and merged and sucked in streams of air. Roads became channels for fire-feeding streams of air, hurricane inflows that reached the burning centre and columned up, high swaying pillars of uproarious flame. The walls of high buildings burning within toppled forward and came crashing down in billowing skirts of dust and flying brick and glass.

Rusalkas screamed and giants stumbled in the streets with burning hair. People saw other people hurt and die. Hurt and died themselves.

The warehouses and shipyards of the Ring Wharf burned. The timber yards and oil storage tanks and coal mountains burned. The bales and barrels and pallets in the lading sheds burned. The fires of the Ring Wharf roared like storms of wind and merged into one great fire, half a mile across: one bright shivering dome of burning under a thin canopy of smoke. The smoke-shell glowed from within as if it was itself on fire. Wavering curtains of orange-red flame opened and closed across the blinding heart of outrageous glare. Firefighters, walled off from the central blaze by bastions of heat, scrabbled at the outer edges of the Ring Wharf fire. They sucked water from the canals and harbour basins and pumped it in feeble arcs of spray that turned to steam on the air. If they got too close, their clothes and hair caught fire.

Josef Kantor, his own room gone, stands among the firefighters at the Ring Wharf, warming himself in the glow of the dockyards burning. Sweat greases his face. His skin is smeared with soot-smuts. He watches the thick column of oil-black smoke rising mile-high into the sky. A signal fire to the future. Heat and shadow flicker across his face, and the voice of Archangel whispers in his ear. Archangel has learned to whisper now.

40

Walking in silence, weighted with a heavy, sick emptiness, Lom and Maroussia saw almost no one as they made their way back from the Ship Bastion to Elena Cornelius's house after the bombing raid on the city. The raion had closed its shops and shut its doors and gone indoors. Belated air-raid warning sirens wailed in the distance. In the sky anti-aircraft shells were bursting, too high and too few and too late. The attackers had drifted away. Blue and yellow-brown smoke-streaks smudged the sky. Smuts drifted down and settled on the snow. The smell clung to their clothes: the faint, sickening smell of the city frying.

Elena met them in the hallway. The girls were with her.

'There's to be an announcement on the radio,' she said. 'We're going up to the Count's room to listen. Come with us.'

The Count opened the door. He had a newspaper in his hand.

'Ah, Elena!' He waved the paper at her. 'These are terrible times. Fohn is to speak at four. And did you hear? Dukhonin is dead. He was killed. An attack on his home. Terrorists. Assassins. *We* are blamed of course. *We* are behind it, apparently. This is very bad. But Vissarion Yppolitovich is with you! Marvellous. Come in, my friend. Come in.' He noticed Maroussia standing behind them. 'Ah, and you, you are Elena's friend and Vissarion's friend, and now our friend also.' He started towards her, holding out his hand.

'This is Maroussia, Sandu,' said Elena. 'Maroussia Shaumian.'

The Count stopped mid-stride.

'Shaumian? There is a *Shaumian* in my house? And nobody told me?' He took Maroussia's hand in both of his, his eyes devouring her face. 'Elena! How could you not tell me?'

Maroussia was looking at him in alarm.

'I'm sorry,' she said. 'I don't—'

The Count turned and shouted over his shoulder into the apartment, 'Ilinca! Ilinca! Say you do not believe this! A Shaumian is here! Feiga-Ita's daughter is come to our house!' He turned back to Maroussia. Took her by the hand like a child. 'Come in. Come in. Enter.' His face was pink with pleasure and excitement.

Count Palffy ushered them all through into the Morning Room. That was what he called it, though no doubt it was the afternoon and evening room as well. French windows with white louvred shutters gave a fine view over the snow-loaded lilacs in the garden, and there was a handle to crank down the awnings for summer afternoons in the sun. There were bears' heads and antlers on the walls and animal skins on the floor, no longer glossy, abraded by moth. The fine chairs and sofas still retained a few strands of their original fabric.

Ilinca came in with a tray of tea in glasses. A jug of lemonade for the girls. Ilinca was small and dumpy. She swished and shuffled noisily across the parquet in a tight skirt of funereal bombazine that reached the floor. She had forgotten to change out of her green house slippers, but her hair was pinned up and she wore a small, defiant turquoise brooch pinned on her chest. *Let enemies come*, it said. *We are aristocrats of proud and ancient family. We have survived and will survive again.*

A radio was set up on a table in the middle of the room. A fine old Piagin Silvertone in a highly polished wooden case. The tuning dial was illuminated. An orchestra was playing the 'Hero March' from *Ariadna Triumphs,* the volume turned low.

Palffy made the introductions.

'You *see*, Ilinca!' he said. 'Of *course* she is a Shaumian. Of course. No doubt of it. She has the look. She is Feiga-Ita come back to us, and here in my house! And I might never have known. Oh Elena! I might have missed her.'

'Did you know my mother?' said Maroussia. 'I'm sorry. She never talked about her friends in the raion. We never came here.'

'Know her?' said the Count. 'Of course we knew her!'

'Many years ago,' said Ilinca. 'She would have been the age you are now, perhaps, or younger. Then she married that hothead Kantor boy, and when he was sent to Vig she went with him. She came back of course, but not here, not back among her friends here in the raion.'

'A disaster!' said the Count. 'A catastrophe for Lezarye. We should not have left her so. We should have gone to her. We should have reached out. Insisted. I am ashamed. For myself and for all of us, I am ashamed.'

'And then ...' said Ilinca. 'We heard she was killed.'

'Yes,' said Maroussia. 'She was.'

'I am so sorry,' said Ilinca. 'So sorry.'

'But this is a *gift*,' said the Count. 'Your coming here now, it is a *sign*. The times darken, but opportunity comes.'

Maroussia frowned. 'I'm sorry,' she said. 'I don't—'

'Sandu!' said Ilinca. 'Leave the poor girl alone. Come and sit with me, Maroussia. Let's have tea. It is almost time for the broadcast.'

'But Vissarion Yppolitovich must have coffee!' said the Count. 'I promised him some of my coffee!'

'Tea's fine,' said Lom.

'Coffee,' said the Count. 'I will have some also. Ilinca, stay here. Talk to our guests.' He hustled out to fetch it.

Lom left Maroussia and Elena with the Countess Ilinca and wandered across to the window. Columns of thick black smoke on the skyline. A sudden dizzy unreality obscured his view of the raion. Could it really be that the war had come to Mirgorod? For a decade, for most of his adult life, war had been distant. Elsewhere. The Vlast at war was a permanent condition, the symptoms of which were glimpses of veterans and conscripts on the streets and accounts in newspapers of campaigns and salients across a geography that existed only on maps. War was background noise: you knew it was there, but only if you listened for it. Most of the time, unnoticed, it affected the taste and tone of things. Somewhere beneath consciousness it grew like a slow tumour and stained the world, an unease, a discomfort, but ignorable, and you carried on from day to day as if it was not there. Until, suddenly, between moment and moment, like a fist in the face, like a train crash in the night, bombs fell out of the sky. Buildings fell and burned. Everything changed.

Lom turned away from the window. Not wanting to join the murmuring conversation around the tea things, he prowled the room restlessly. It was a museum. There was a Kurzweiler baby grand piano in the corner. Its lid was down and crowded with framed photographs of officers in shakos and pelisses, guests at balls and shooting parties, a boy who might have been the young Count Palffy in a carriage. On the sideboard there was a rack of smoking-pipes on display and a collection of silver cigarette cases, all engraved with coats of arms and monograms. Lom drifted across to the bookcase. It was filled with directories, almanacs, bound volumes of the poets of the Silver Age. He picked one out. The pages were drilled through by insects.

But the coffee when it came was everything Count Palffy said it would be. Hot and bitter and strong, in a fine blue china mug. And sugar, dark brown and sticky in a matching lidded bowl. The mug was identical to one he'd seen Raku Vishnik drink from in his apartment. Before he was dead. It seemed a lifetime ago: another world, where Raku Vishnik was not dead and war had not come.

Time in Mirgorod, Lom realised, would for ever now be counted by the coming of war. *Ah, that was before the war*, people in the city would say, and, *Since the war* ... If there *was* an *after the war*. That was a new thought, possible only now. Nothing endured for ever. Not even Mirgorod. Not even the Vlast. Past and future were dissolving out of the city, leaving only a raw and shocking perpetual now. Ever since he had come to Mirgorod, Lom had felt the presence of other possibilities, other futures, drifting in the alleys: hints and glimpses, scraps of mist and half-heard voices. But now, he felt, all that was suddenly burned away, bleached out in a shocking sunburst glare. Everything was old and everything was new. It was vertiginous and horrifying. It was – he realised with a start of surprise – *exciting*. It was a *promise*. The vicious promise of war. The clock and the calendar reset to zero. *Everything begins again, thought* Lom. *Everything starts here.*

The Count offered him a cigarette.

'No,' said Lom. 'No thanks.'

'Well, I will smoke,' said the Count. 'Permit me.' He took Lom by the elbow and steered him across the room. 'Let us men stand over here with our coffee and our talk, and I will smoke. Ilinca disapproves, you see.' He lit a cigarette and inhaled it deeply, with satisfaction.

Count Palffy talked and Lom let him. Beneath the surface politesse, Palffy was agitated. Over-animated. Rambling. He talked without direction of neighbours in the raion and other people he had known in other places long ago. Balls and duels and amours. He pointed to photographs on the walls.

'Ah. Yes. Now that is Amah. The Graefin Blegvad. Eight thousand acres in the Konopy Hills. Her great-grandfather was ambassador to the Feuilleton Court of Oaks. Did you know, the wolf's head in their crest was awarded for some hunting exploit or other with the Bazharev Ride? She married a Tsyprian. He was the Archduke's second when he duelled with the Mameluke and he was wounded himself, in the leg. An idiot, of course, but he had the most comfortable kastely in all of the south Hertzbergen. Part of the Detlevsk oblast now, more's the pity. A military college. Such a waste.'

Count Palffy talked on. His world had gone fifty, a hundred years ago, but the Count was in it still, despite, or perhaps because of, the fact that the city around them was burning and war had come. Lom, only half-listening, found they had somehow moved on to lepidoptery.

'I'm something of a collector,' the Count was saying. He led Lom over to examine display cases mounted on the walls. Moths and butterflies and beetles, some drab, some gaudy, some as large as Lom's palm, others so small you could hardly see them. All labelled in a clear and careful hand. 'My specialism is winter moths. Ice moths. Strategies for surviving the deep winter cold. It's a fascinating area. You know about this, perhaps?'

'I've never thought about it. I assumed they laid their eggs and then they died.'

'That is the common strategy, Vissarion Yppolitovich, of course. But there are some – like this one, you see, this shoddy-looking fellow here, this Faded Birchmoth – now, he survives the winter by allowing himself to become frozen solid. But only externally. He prepares himself for the temperature drop by excreting all the water in his body. His internal fluids become extremely concentrated. They resist freezing inside. You see the brilliance of this? Dead on the outside, alive within. He endures! He can survive temperatures as low as minus forty. More. And for months at a time. His wings blacken and drop off, of course. But he grows fresh wings in the spring.'

'We're not talking only about moths here, are we?' said Lom.

The Count looked at him sharply.

'Of course not, man.'

'Sandu!' Ilinca called from the other side of the room. 'The radio. It's starting.'

The clock on the mantelpiece showed seven minutes past four. It was growing darker outside, though the curtains were not yet drawn. Early winter twilight. Palffy went across to turn the volume knob higher.

'Citizens of Mirgorod! Prepare yourselves for an important announcement!'

'Ah!' he said. 'Now we have it.'

'Citizens,' Fohn's unfamiliar voice began. 'Comrades. Friends. The Great Patriotic War has come to our city.' He started to speak of fronts and salients. Unexpected advances. The fall of southern cities. The sinking of ships. He spoke hesitantly. He sounded out of breath, baffled and hurt. Lom struggled to follow what he was saying. And then, suddenly and it seemed too soon, he was finishing. 'This afternoon I have given our commanders new orders. The enemy's air force is to be smashed. Their armies annihilated. We will defend our beloved city. General Rizhin will lead the counter-attack. Our cause is good. We are ratified by the angels. The enemy will be defeated all along the line and victory will be ours.'

The orchestra started up again with a crash of brass and drums. The Count snorted in disgust and switched the radio off.

'Well!' he said. 'So there we have it! There we have nothing at all! Who is this General Rizhin. We have heard nothing of him till now. And what kind of a name is Rizhin? These idiots will do nothing. They will let the country burn and the raion with it. The time has come for action. Maroussia, we must talk. We look to you. You must step forward.'

'Me? Why? What are you talking about?'

'Because you're a *Shaumian*. You're *the* Shaumian, now. The Vlast is crumbling and the Council of Lezarye is nowhere. And if the Council fails, then what is left but Shaumian? The name alone will be enough.'

'What does my name matter? I have no idea what you mean.'

'But of course you do. You must. You are Shaumian of the House of Genissei. Protosebasta. Porphyrogenita. You have a claim, a reasonable claim, there is no doubt about it. It goes by the female descent.'

Maroussia stared at him, pale and silent. She opened her mouth to speak but found nothing to say.

'Sandu? said Elena Cornelius. 'What are you talking about?'

'We must do something,' said the Count. ' And now –' he looked at Maroussia '– now we have an opportunity. We must take it.'

'Do what, Sandu?' said Elena. 'What, exactly? What are you thinking of?'

'Resist! The raion must rise! There has never been a better time. The Novozhd is dead, and there is no obvious successor. The enemy is at the gates. Don't you see? People of courage are ready to act, and now is the time. The aristocrats will come forward again, united under the ancient Shaumian name. We are not all dead. The people remember us. They haven't forgotten. We can make peace with the Archipelago. The Vlast itself will melt away and dissolve like mist in the heat of the sun.'

'No!' said Maroussia. 'I know nothing about my family, this *name*, and I want nothing to do with whatever you're talking about. Nothing at all.'

Lom saw that her hands were trembling slightly. He went across and stood beside her.

'Of course things must be handled carefully,' the Count was saying. 'There are men who will know what to do. Men of courage. I will call them together. You must meet them.'

'This is madness,' said Lom. 'Worse, it's lethal madness.'

The Count flushed.

'Certainly it is not madness. She has a legitimate claim. I know of no other.'

'Sandu,' said Elena. 'Please stop this. This is the kind of talk that gets young men ruining their lives. Making bombs. Killing innocent people.'

Maroussia stood up.

'I have to go now,' she said.

'But you'll come back?' said the Count. 'Come up this evening. Dine with us. You also, Vissarion Yppolitovich. I will invite some people. You will feel differently if you meet them. Hear what they have to say. When you know their quality—'

Lom gripped Palffy's arm. Hard.

'You can't tell anyone she's here,' he said urgently. 'You see that, don't you?'

'These are men I would trust with my life. Men of purpose and experience—'

'For fuck's sake,' said Lom. 'You can't tell anyone she's here. No one at all.'

41

Captain of Police Vorush Iliodor, assistant to Commander Chazia, was busy in his office. Outside his night-dark uncurtained window, snow was falling, and bombs. More bombs. From time to time a close impact shook his desk. He forced himself to ignore it. He had much work to complete and he was a man who stuck at his duty. He was preparing detailed orders to put into effect the evacuation from Mirgorod of the Government of the Vlast. He had almost finished.

Iliodor prided himself on unquestioning efficiency. His job was to take the broad instructions of his superiors and translate them into the detailed, precise and unambiguous practical orders that made for effective implementation. It required a certain kind of pragmatic imagination, at which he excelled. It required him to understand not just what was required, but why. He liked to call this, in his own mind, his strategic comprehension. But it emphatically did not require him to have personal opinions: these he rarely formulated, even in his own mind, and never expressed. It was precisely this quality of non-judgemental receptiveness which, as he well knew, had caused Chazia to appoint him to his post and made her comfortable in his presence, and even occasionally talkative.

The instruction to evacuate, which she had given even as the first bombs fell, came as no surprise. He knew, as Chazia had known, that in the last weeks of his life the Novozhd had accepted that if the tentative peace talks failed and the Archipelago pressed home their advance, Mirgorod was indefensible. He knew, as Chazia had known but Dukhonin, Khazar and Fohn did not, that the Novozhd had secretly approved the withdrawal of the Third, Seventh and Eighth armies from the provinces to the east and south of the city, leaving only a skeleton force to slow but not stop the enemy's advance. He also knew that Chazia saw the loss of Mirgorod as an advantage not a disaster.

'We will build a new Vlast, Iliodor!' she had said more than once. 'A renewed Vlast, young and strong and pure, safe in the east behind thousands of miles of empty steppe and plain. We will strip the factories and carry the plant eastward on trains. We will empty the Lodka and move the government out. Take what files we need and burn the rest. Mine and booby-trap the Lodka itself.

'Let the Archipelago bring Mirgorod down around their ears. We will have new cities, with marvellous modern buildings, taller and finer and fitter for the modern world. New towns, new factories, connected by the best roads and railways. With airfields in the centre! Around the towns we will build handsome, spacious farms for citizen peasants to work on, and delightful, hygienic villages. We will clear out all the *rubbish,* and grow a new, pure, wholesome and modern Vlast. Let the Archipelago wear themselves out in the west and overstretch themselves, and when we're ready we'll roll them back into the Cetic Ocean and rebuild Mirgorod as a vacation resort.'

So Iliodor had anticipated that one day the evacuation orders would be required. He had made his preparations. Outline plans and diagrams, kept in a sealed folder in the safe. When the moment came, he simply had to fetch out his folder and begin the process of filling out the necessary memoranda of instruction and orders of movement. The work was already nearly done. Chazia had suggested he should co-opt some assistance, but he had not done so. There was no need. Quicker to do it himself than to explain, and more certain to be done accurately and correctly.

Nevertheless it was arduous, absorbing work. The air raid on the city was an annoying distraction and the effort of ignoring it was wearing. Still, he had done well. And he had not forgotten his other, smaller duties. The file on the woman Shaumian was waiting, out of the way on the corner of his desk, ready for the creature Bez Nichevoi to collect that night. Including the note on where to find her, based on information recently received. No loose ends there.

Iliodor did not at first look up when he heard someone quietly enter the room. A figure pausing before the desk, waiting for attention. Iliodor held up his hand for silence and continued to copy a list of departmental branches from his notes onto a printed Consolidate-and-Remove proforma in a neat, precise script. Only when he had finished did he glance up to see who had come, and found himself staring into his own face. His own face watching him from under an astrakhan hat.

'How did you get in here?' said Iliodor. It struck him, even as he spoke, that this wasn't the most urgent, nor the most rational, of all the questions he might have asked.

'I'm afraid,' said the intruder with Iliodor's face, 'what with the bombs and all, security was rather cursory in the matter of credentials. A familiar appearance ...'

He spoke with a cultured, almost diffident voice that resembled Iliodor's own but was not, Iliodor thought, the same. There was a deepness, a throaty undertone, that struck him as odd. His neck was thicker than Iliodor's own, and roped with muscle under the skin. There were flecks of tawny amber in the green of his eyes.

'And of course,' the mirror-Iliodor continued, 'by the same token, given the destruction wrought across the city, one more unidentifiable body found in the street will be unlikely to cause much excitement.'

Only then did Iliodor notice the large kitbag in the intruder's hand, which was obviously empty.

'Oh ...' said Iliodor. 'No.' There was an emptiness in his stomach. An unhealable sadness. 'No. You don't have to ...'

The face watching him was raw. Gold-flecked eyes looked into his, dark almost to tears, reflecting Iliodor's own hopeless sadness back at him, distilled and magnified.

'But I am a soldier,' said the man who was not Iliodor. 'And this is a war.'

42

After Fohn's broadcast, Lom and Maroussia went back down with Elena Cornelius and her girls to their apartment. The air-raid sirens were wailing again in the distance. They could hear the muffled *crump* of falling bombs.

'I'm afraid you're stuck with us,' said Maroussia. 'For tonight.'

'It doesn't matter,' said Elena. 'No. I'm glad.'

The two of them, Elena and Maroussia, made a soup. Cabbage. An onion. Kvass. While they worked, Lom picked up the newspaper that Elena had brought with her from the Count's room. He skimmed idly through the account of the attack on General Secretary Dukhonin's house: the brave defence mounted by his guards and a passing militia patrol; the fall of Dukhonin himself in the struggle; the death of the firebrand convict Josef Kantor and all of his murderous gangster squad.

Lom read and reread the sentence. It didn't change. Kantor was dead. He had led the attack on Dukhonin and died in the ensuing gun battle.

Kantor was dead.

He read the story to the end. Chazia had made a speech about a renewed determination to rid Mirgorod and the Vlast of the disease of anarchic nationalist terrorism and those who harboured it. There was nothing more about Kantor. In the rest of the paper there was almost no mention of the war and the enemy coming towards the city. It might have been news from a year ago. A decade. Except that Kantor was dead.

Lom sat and nursed the news of Kantor's death like a wound. This was new disaster. Lom's thread into the Lodka; his plan – if it was ever a plan, not just a half-baked impossibility – was shredded. He would have to start working at it all over again. And war was come. The city burning.

'Maroussia?' he said at last.

'Yes?'

'You should see this.' He held the newspaper towards her, folded open at the page. Watched her read it twice.

'Oh,' she said. 'OK. So that's that.' She put the paper down and started laying the table.

When they had finished eating and Lom had helped the girls clear away, Elena Cornelius brought out a box and put it on the table. It was made of a reddish fibrous wood, heavy and roughly made, the size of a large book, with a tight-fitting lid. The lid was covered with carvings of leaves and intertwined curling thorny stems.

'I've been saving these,' she said. 'I brought them with me when I came to the city. I want to have them now.'

She took off the lid. Inside was a heap of dark shining fruit. Berries of purple and red. Wild strawberries, blackcurrants, raspberries. Elderberries, night-blue, luminous, as fat and fresh and full as the day they were picked. Other berries Lom didn't recognise.

'Here,' said Elena, offering the box to the girls. 'These are from the forest. I've kept them twenty years. There used to be more. The box was full when I came to Mirgorod. Your father and I had some, when each of you were born.'

Galina hesitated.

'Go on,' said Elena. 'They're good to eat. I promise.'

'But … they're for celebrations.'

'I want us to have them now.'

When the girls had taken a couple she pushed the box over to Maroussia and Lom.

'You too. Please.'

Lom took a single elderberry and put it in his mouth. Burst it against his tongue. The fruit was fresh and sharp and sweet, with a slight taint of resin that was not unpleasant but made the juice taste dark and wild and strange.

'It's a property of the tree,' said Elena. 'It's a kind of red pine: the breath of the wood keeps things fresh, not for ever, but longer. There was a giant called Akki-Paavo-Perelainen who used to come every autumn to our timber yard. He would always come just before the river froze, riding a great raft of red pine down the river. He gave me this box, and I carved the lid.

'That was the year my father was accused of crimes of privacy, and they made us leave the yard and the house. We weren't allowed to take anything with us. Not a thing. Not even our name. They said our family was dissolved. *Relations annulled.* My father was to be called Feliks Ioannes, my mother was Teodosia Braun, and I was Elena Schmitt. I remember my mother shouting at the official, "She is my daughter. It is a fact of nature. Nothing you say can change it." And the man was saying to us over and over again, "Your thoughts and your strength belong to the Vlast, just like the rest of us."

'They let us carry on living together for a while, in a room above a shop in the town. When we got there it was filthy. Disgusting. Every surface was covered in some kind of sticky grease, and the blankets smelled of illness. The day we moved in my mother set about cleaning it, and my father sat in a chair by the window, smoking, not saying a word. I sneaked away and went back to our old house. I broke in through a window and I just walked from room to room. Just touching things. While I was there some men came, and I had to hide in my bedroom. I heard them in the corridor. One of them pissed on the wallpaper. I heard it splashing on the rug. When I got away from the house I brought this box away with me, the only thing I had left from the old life, and when I came to work in Mirgorod I brought it here. These are the same berries Akki-Paavo-Perelainen gave me. You can't hang on to things for ever. Let's finish them now.'

43

Bez Nichevoi returned to his body at nightrise. He came back into it gradually, curled in its nest of earth and leaves and moss and chewed-over bones high among the roof beams of an empty warehouse in the city. As the planet turned its continent-face slowly away from the sun, the netted nerve-threads of his body snagged the touch of darklight and twitched and quietly sang. The settled sump of its blood unthickened, the secretions of its glands began to seep, interstitial lymph condensed like honeydew and capillaries, deconstricted, stirred. Ligatures of skeletal articulation re-clenched. In the slack pale slubs of jelly in the chambers of its skull, synaptic pathways undissolved. Bez Nichevoi warmed slowly through. And took breath. The body jack-knifed, spasming, choking, retching, vomiting acidic slews of gluey, gobbetty brown stink across its mushroom-pale and bone-thin chest. The waste products of a day of death.

Awakened, he lay back and opened his eyes, drinking in the beautiful darkness like water. The air around him was freezing. His first breaths hung in pale ghosts above his face, slowly dispersing. He surrendered himself to the pleasures of his nest, sweet and warm and crumbly-rotting, matted with perfumed fungal threads. The familiar musty smell of crusted salt and hawthorn blossom, rotting fruit and strong meat. A smell to awaken desire and dark, hidden feelings. Parts of his body were covered with skin-like papery stuff. He picked and peeled it carefully away with his fingernails and ate it.

When he was fully warmed through he rolled lazily out of his nest, swung himself up to the ceiling and skittered across it to the skylight, slipped through and climbed onto the lead of the roof. Naked, he squatted under the sky, bathing in starlight. There was something new on the air. The night was wired with it. The residue of burned city and upturned earth, the traces of two thousand deaths. The touch of war.

Bez Nichevoi, light of heart, unstrung the bundle of clothes he'd left hidden in the lea of a chimney stack, dressed, and set off across the rooftops to the Lodka, to read the file of papers Iliodor had left for him on Maroussia Shaumian.

44

Josef Kantor, king terrorist, buttoned the tunic of his Colonel-General's uniform with fat, stiff fingers. Josef Kantor, agitator, pamphleteer, bomb-maker, assassin and robber of banks, his fingers swollen and hardened by decades of labour with shovel and pick, bare-handed scrabbling at rock, freezing cells, interrogation rooms, did up his uniform buttons one by one. Josef Kantor, author of the Birzel Declaration, survivor of Vig, leader of the Fighting Organisation of Lezarye, forced awkward buttons of gleaming brass through virgin buttonholes with ruined fingernails.

The uniform was green, thick serge and factory-new. More brass at shoulder and collar. Hammers and stars. Boots shone like coal.

New times require new forms of thought.

The telephone on the desk rang. He picked it up.

'General Rizhin? They are ready for you. The Operations Room—'

'Let them wait.'

He opened the drawer and took out his revolver. A Ghovt-Alenka DK9. An unremarkable service firearm. It felt comfortable in his hand, a familiar, useful thing, like a spade to a peasant.

I'll dig with it.

He checked the cylinder and slipped it into his holster. Left the flap unbuttoned. A handful of loose shells in his pocket. It was time.

There is no past. There is only the future.

He walked out of the room into the corridor where Rizhin's future began.

It cost him nothing to let Josef Kantor die.

*

They were waiting for General Rizhin in a ground-floor conference room on the far side of the Armoury parade ground. *Operation Ouspensky Bulwark*. Maps and charts and telephones. The six officers at the table stood when he entered. The fat one stepped forward and saluted. The flesh of his neck bulged over his collar. Small, worried eyes squinted at Rizhin with wary hostility. The distrust of the career officer for the man he'd never heard of till that very morning. The political man. Chazia's man. Chazia's ears.

'I am Strughkov,' he said. 'Major-General Strughkov, Commander, City Defence. Welcome, General. We have prepared a presentation. The current situation, and our plans. We have proposals to make for—'

'The situation, Strughkov, is shit. Your plans are also shit.'

Strughkov flushed.

'General Rizhin—'

'Where are the divisions?' said Rizhin. 'Where are the guns? The Bukharsk Line is broken. When the enemy comes, will you blow up their armies with presentations and sink their ships with plans?'

'Our orders,' said Strughkov, 'are to hold the city for forty-eight hours. A week at most. We are to delay the enemy for long enough to allow the orderly evacuation of government. The Vlast is moving east. Plant and stocks from the factories are to be relocated. We have made our dispositions. Khalturin's Corps of Horse stands ready in the Ouspensky Marsh. Five infantry regiments at Satlivosk. We have the 23rd Engineers. We have stockpiled arms for the militia. Raised twenty thousand volunteers—'

'Untrained conscripts,' said Rizhin. 'Old men and boys. Policemen with antiquated rifles.'

'We make the best of what we have.'

'Where are the fortifications? The outer lines of defence? Artillery? Aircraft? More mudjhiks guard the Novozhd's bones than guard the city. Where are the gunships in the Reaches? Why do the bridges at Nordslavl still stand?'

'We will hold the line between Kropotlovsk and Yatlavograd for forty-eight hours. That will be enough. Then we will withdraw eastward, fighting as we go. We are to destroy everything we cannot take with us. Not a sack of grain, not a horse and cart, not a gallon of engine oil is to be left. We are to join the Third Army at Strom.'

'Mirgorod,' said Rizhin, 'is the capital city of the Vlast. The Founder's city, built at the site of the first angel fall. The heart of the Dominions for four hundred years. And you, General Strughkov, are proposing to abandon it without a fight.'

Rizhin watched with curiosity the working of Strughkov's fat, tired face. The reddening anger and, in his eyes like tears held back, the strange beginning of grief. The war been stalemated for so long, the fronts locked in entrenched positions far from Mirgorod to the south and south-east, that even to the men who led the armies of the Vlast it had come to seem permanent. Stable. Familiar. Inevitable. Like the authority of generals. Like the Vlast itself. A few miles lost and gained here and there, year by year, decade by decade, paid for with statistical quantities of death, changing nothing. And yet, behind it all, the whisper unheard. The myth dispersing. The possibility of failure and total collapse.

In the room a fundamental psychological turn had been taken. Rizhin felt it. The men withdrawing. Strughkov standing alone.

'The Novozhd ...' said Strughkov. 'He would not ... I asked, of course. I pressed the case for strengthening the defences of the city a hundred times. He refused to allow it. He would not admit the possibility of the enemy getting this far. He would not countenance the alarm and dismay that defensive preparations might cause among the population. He would not *listen* to me. And then, when he was killed and Commissioner Dukhonin was appointed, I hoped for a better response, but it was no different. Nobody would listen. They would not act. The orders to defend the city never came.'

'And now Dukhonin is dead and I am here. And you, General Strughkov, were charged with the defence of Mirgorod. What other orders did you need?'

'I am a soldier,' Strughkov shouted. 'I know my duty. I don't need a man like you—'

'What kind of man am I?' said Rizhin. 'Do you think?'

Strughkov glared at him, his face purple, his eyes full of hurt. A man who had done his best. He took a deep breath and puffed out his chest.

'Why don't you tell us, General Rizhin?' he said. 'None of us knows who the fuck you are.'

'Speculate,' said Rizhin.

'A uniform,' said Strughkov viciously, 'doesn't make you a soldier.'

Rizhin smiled thinly and looked around the room. One by one, he stared every officer present in the eye. Strughkov was still glaring at him – angry, but with the beginning of a gleam of triumph. None of the others met his gaze.

'There is a foul stink in this room,' said Rizhin quietly. 'I smell it, gentlemen. It is ripe and rank. I smell deviation. I smell revisionism. I smell conspiracy. I smell you, Strughkov. You are an enemy of the Vlast. A class enemy of all citizens. A traitor and a spy. Your treacherous failure to defend the city is an act of sabotage.'

Strughkov roared with anger and indignation.

'*You* say this to *me*!' he screamed. '*You* ... how *dare* you! You know *nothing* about—'

Bored, Rizhin drew his Ghovt-Alenka and shot him in the groin.

Strughkov collapsed, clutching the spurting wreckage between his legs, squealing in horror like a hurt, indignant child. Moving his legs slowly like a swimmer in a spreading pool of blood. Rizhin had to shoot him twice more to shut him up.

The five remaining officers were staring at him. None of them moved. None of them spoke. They were waiting to see what he would do. He swept all Strughkov's plans and charts to the floor, went over to the wall, tore down the large-scale map of the city and spread it out on the table.

'You need to start again, gentlemen,' he said. 'From the beginning. Battles are won by killing the enemy. Anyone with a gun is a soldier. And we will not surrender Mirgorod to the enemy.'

'But—' a major of cavalry began.

'Yes?' said Rizhin mildly.

'The Archipelago is only fifty miles away. We can hear their guns.'

'You need to understand something, my friends,' said Rizhin. 'We are at war. War is not a conflict between soldiers, it is a conflict between ideas. Conflict is not an accident or an aberration, conflict is essential and fundamental. War is not a sign of failure but of success. The Vlast *is* conflict. The Vlast *is* war. War is the engine, the locomotive of history. There can be compromise and armistice between armies, but not between truths. In the realm of ideas there is only win or lose, existence or annihilation.' He paused. 'Here is the essential point. Live by it and die by it. Mirgorod must be saved. Not the soldiers, not the people, the *city*. The death of citizens and soldiers does not matter. The loss of the city does. The city is a symbol. Tell me, what is this city of ours? The people? No. The buildings? No. Mirgorod is an *idea*. It is a thing the enemy does not have. The idea is to prevent them from winning. We must have a victory. The fact of victory is all that matters.'

'But the government is leaving,' the major said. 'Commander Chazia has already given the order to evacuate.'

Rizhin waved his hand dismissively.

'Let her go. Mirgorod is mine. I intend to keep it.'

Back in his office Rizhin picked up the telephone. Dialled a long number. Transcontinental.

'Get me Khyrbysk,' he said when it was answered. 'Professor Yakov Khyrbysk. Now.'

45

Bez Nichevoi stood in the centre of the empty office of Assistant Commander of Police Iliodor Voroushin. The items he needed were there, the room was in order. But he didn't move. He was breathing. Listening. Opening himself to the place around him. Paying attention. A hunter's attention. The trace of recent violent death brushed against him, exciting, prickling across his skin, making his jaw tense, his hungry belly stir. And there was something else. Dark animal pheromones on the air.

The scent of wolf.

There was a cardboard box on the table and a file of papers. *Shaumian*. He read the file quickly then turned to the box. Opened the lid and sorted through the things inside. Personal items from the Shaumian apartment. It was poor stuff: thin and much-worn undergarments, torn stockings and flimsy shoes marked with dried blood. Knotted balls of twigs and wax and animal bones that stank of the forest. They turned his stomach when he sniffed at them. It was enough. He fingered them idly for a moment or two, then put them back in the box, went across to the window, opened it and climbed out onto the sill.

He was only six floors above ground level: above him the huge flank of the Lodka rose into the night, spilling tiny splashes of lamplight from the occasional window where some official was working late. And below him was the slow breadth of the River Mir. The edges of the river were shut away under a crust of ice, but in the centre an open current still flowed darkly. Even above the stench of the city burning, the water smelled cold and earthy, like the mouth of a deep well. Bez heard the mutter and slap of little wavelets against the ice. He turned away from the river in disgust and scuttered rapidly up the outside of the building, climbing with wild easy leaps and swings until he reached the snow-covered roofs.

This was his world, a wide lonely landscape of ridges and slopes, slates and lead. Seen from up among the rooftops, it was obvious that the Lodka was many buildings jammed together and twisted. Where they collided, buildings rose out of buildings, extruding new turrets and towers, oriels, gables, corbels, parapets, catwalks, cornices and flagpoles; and where they pulled apart flagstoned quadrangles and courtyards stretched out, and ravines and canyons split open. Windows looked out across the Lodka's roofworld, but the rooms to which the windows belonged could not be reached from inside at all. No staircases climbed to them. No doorways opened into them. The rooms had been built, then closed up and left. Bez knew this, because he had entered them all.

The tallest turret on the roof did have an iron staircase spiralling up inside it, though it wasn't climbed any more. The observatory, a cupola of latticed iron and glass, still held the Brodsky telescope, built to watch the sky for dying angels. Occupied nightly for three centuries, abandoned a human lifetime ago. Bez climbed lazily onto the top of the rusting, snow-dusted dome and sat cross-legged to savour the night. He took off his shirt. The dark chill air fingered his ribs and his back. Kissed his small belly. He closed his eyes and held his arms wide, loosening the drapes of chalk-white skin that hung from forearm to waist, letting them hang relaxed and easy, windless sails unfurled, absorbing the cool of nightside.

Far below him lay the city by night. It was a good night. One of the best. A lid of thick low cloud shut out the moons and the stars and closed in the scent of fallen snow. The street lamps were extinguished. Fires started by the bombing raid still smouldered: the air was freighted with their fragrance. Reddening coals. Broken houses and apartment buildings spilled their intimate human smells. Under heaps of rubble unfound corpses were ripening.

The older city was wide awake. Doors that were often closed stood open: small, unnoticed doors. The things in the tunnels were moving and some of them were coming out. The wide cold waters of the Mir were alert and watchful. The rusalkas swam restlessly, nosing along the canals beneath the ice and sometimes breaking through. Hauling up onto river mudbanks and the ledges under bridges. Bez Nichevoi could hear their uneasy cries. There were quarters of Mirgorod that would be dangerous for Vlast patrols that night. Dangerous even for him.

Bez considered his choices. The last report of the Shaumian woman placed her north and east, in the Raion Lezaryet. But then there was wolf. Wolf had been in Iliodor's office and killed someone there. Iliodor? Bez thought probably yes. And wolf had lingered. Read the papers. Sifted through the box. Wolf knew. Wolf interested him. Wolf would be a good kill. Bez held that thought for a moment. Considered it. Tested the air, the night and the city. Yes, he thought, yes. Wolf had left the Lodka and wolf had gone north. North and then west.

The choice was woman or wolf. And wolf was an enemy and wolf would be good killing. So. There was plenty of time. Connect purpose with desire. First, let it be wolf.

He bent to pick up his shirt, tied it round his waist and slipped from the roof of the observatory cupola, spreading his moth-pale wingfolds, letting the cold night air take him in a long and dream-slow fall across the river. One time in three he could land on his feet, but not this time. He stumbled when he hit the cobbles, fell and rolled lightly in the snow, picked himself up and began to run north, following wolf spoor.

Wolf was easy hunting. There was a strong taint of wolf threading north, a clear track easy to follow. Bez loped after him. Mostly, wolf had kept to the streets and alleyways. Bez found places where he had lingered. Quiet places where he had rested, perhaps. Not hurrying. The wolfpath took him away from familiar territories, the avenues and parks and prospects, and out into the shabbier quarters, deep into the cramped tenements and estaminets of Marosch and the Estergam. Following wolf, he passed along twisting streets, so narrow the opposing buildings almost touched, and crossed nameless insignificant canals by iron walkways. Always wolf headed north. Bez had expected the track to turn eastward at some point and head for the raion but it did not.

He came to a place where a stick of bombs had gouged wide shallow craters in the street. The scent of upturned earth and exposed roots. A broken watermain welled up and made the street a shallow, muddy river flowing between houses with shattered roofs and fallen walls. A dead horse lay on the churn of earth and snow in the cooled spillage of its own entrails. Bez sensed a life nearby. A human sound. Spidering up the slope of a collapsed brick wall, he looked over the edge into an open cellar. A mother was crouched in the rubble over her dead children. Bez called to her. The face she lifted towards him was smeared with grey dust. It was too dark for her human eyes to find him. He could see them, wide and staring in the darkness. He dropped down into the cellar and stroked her dust-caked hair as he pulled out her throat.

Wolftaint was stronger now. Close by. Bez climbed to the roofs to make a cautious, circular approach. The human death, his first kill of the night, had calmed him, as it always did. Taken the edge off his need. He had abandoned the idea that wolf was leading him to the Shaumian woman. Wolf was stupider than he had thought and now he was simply prey. Take him quickly, then go to the Apraksin and pick up a trace from there. It was only a few minutes after midnight – hours yet till the sun.

Bez crested the ridge of a tenement roof and saw him. He was standing in the middle of a cobbled square in the form of a man, his back turned to where Bez was. Wolf seemed at a loss. Waiting. Wolf spoor streamed from him onto the air, bright unmistakable scented clouds. Bez settled in the lee of a chimney to watch. Wolf was doing nothing. Just standing out in the middle of the square. And then Bez realised his mistake. He'd been careless. Overconfident. This night he wasn't hunter, he was hunted. Wolf had led him out here into the waste places of the city, away from the Shaumian woman, and was calling him, baiting him with the trap of himself. *Come down. Come down.*

Bez grinned in the darkness as he slipped away.

46

Maroussia was awake in the night. She lay still, breathing slowly. Listening. The attic window framed a flickering sky: gunfire on the distant horizon, flashing against low-hanging cloud. A new kind of weather.

Lom lay next to her, warm and heavy under the quilt, eyes clenched fiercely in sleep.

There were trees in the room. The room was full of trees.

Count Palffy's house was full of trees.

The streets of the raion were full of trees.

Watchful trees, waiting for her.

Maroussia turned back the quilt and crawled out of the bed. Her dress was draped over a chair. From the pocket she brought out the bag, stained with her mother's blood, that held the thing of twigs and tiny bones. She opened the bag and took it out. It stirred in the cup of her palm restlessly, as if a small animal was in there, moving. There were tiny berries inside it, fresh and purple-bright. She leaned forward and brought it up to her face. Listening. Quiet voices whispered. Calling her.

Come out. Come out under the trees.

She pulled her coat on over her night shirt and, holding the knot of twigs and forest breath cupped gingerly in her palm, went down into the house and made her way through tree-crowded landings and passageways out into the street. Bare feet in the snow. The moons spilled white luminance through gaps in the cloud. The vapour ghosts of her breath glittered. It was so cold. Bitter cold.

There wasn't much left of the streets; it was mostly trees. She walked among them, her feet freezing, pushing onwards, deeper and deeper

493

into the trees. Eventually she remembered the bag in her hand and stopped. Undid the string at the bag's tight mouth and pulled it open.

Between step and step she passed through into difference. Forest. Change.

Maroussia was in a beautiful, simple place under the trees. Everything rang with a true, clear note, and everything shone out from within itself with its own radiance, fresh and cool. Nothing was anything except what it was. The distances between things were airier and more obvious. The night air – luminous velvet and purple-blue – streamed with perfume. Corn-gold swollen stars spilled flakes of light that brushed her face and settled on her shoulders.

Walking, she left a trail of dark impressions across dew-webbed grass. She came to a wide clump of thorn. Tiny droplets of mist-water, starglittering, hung from every tip and nestled in the crooks and elbows of every twig. The water made her thirsty. She crouched in the long wet grass and licked at the branches, making slow careful movements with her tongue. She took hawthorn twigs into her mouth carefully. The water was cold and good. The wood tasted ... complex. Thorns pricked the inside of her mouth, mingling the iron taste of her blood with the wood and the water.

She looked at her own hands. They were made of leaves.

The world cracked open as if gods were walking through it. It was a breaking of tension, like a shattering downpour of rain. Everything was alive with wildness. Maroussia herself was spilling streams of perfume and darkshine from her mouth and skin and hair: bright stain-clouds on the air, carrying far and broadcasting promises of plenty.

Bez Nichevoi watched the Shaumian woman from his place on the roof of the house. She was walking slowly, barefoot in the snow, bareheaded, straight-backed and thin. Her dark woollen coat hung open, unbuttoned over a white cotton nightdress, spilling the smell of her body still warm from her bed. Between the collar of her coat and the tangle of her short black hair, the nape of her neck showed slender and pale. Bez groaned quietly. Desire was a constriction in his throat, a dark knot in his belly, a rigid knife rising from his groin. He wanted to feed on her slowly, and ... do ... such pleasurable things ...

He followed her for a while. Unhurried. Letting the moment last.

Taking pleasure in anticipation and delay. He worked his way round in front of her and came down into the street.

Her eyes passed over him and did not see. Her gaze was turned inward. He stood and let her come to him. The dark buildings of the raion faded for him too. It was as if he was standing under trees: shadows, the wind among branches, the slip of tiny snowfalls from twigs and needles, the smell of ice and resin and cold earth.

And then she knew he was there.

Her dark eyes widened and stared into his. She opened her mouth: a ragged indrawn breath. He saw the gleam of her teeth. The moistened heat of her tongue.

He immobilised her quickly and slung her across his shoulders. She was surprisingly heavy. He began to run.

47

A thousand miles north and east of Mirgorod, at six in the morning Vayarmalond Eastern Time, Professor Yakov Khyrbysk hurried across the floor of an underground cavern deep inside a mountain. The cavern was as wide as a football field and bright as day: a hundred brilliant fluorescent tubes burned overhead in the ceiling of raw black rock. Their light splashed off the concrete floor, a grey-white dazzle. The cavern was empty except for one flat-roofed building, little more than a large shed, sitting right out in the centre of the echoing space: a crude temporary construction of boards screwed to a steel frame, a cubic carton with sixty-foot edges. Thick rubber-sleeved cables trailed hundreds of feet across the ground towards it. Around the shed the concrete floor was smudged and dirtied with feathered spills of black, as if dark ashes had been scattered there.

Khyrbysk pushed open the door and entered. A dozen men and women were working inside, standing at workbenches. Control panel arrays. Dials and gauges. They all looked up when he came in. They had the pale drawn faces of people who have been working all night. Spotlights on tripods cast harsh shadows.

'Good morning,' said Khyrbysk. 'Please. Carry on.'

Every surface in the room was covered with a layer of fine graphite dust: the technicians' white coats were smeared graphite grey; permanent graphite shadows collected in every crease and fold. Khyrbysk could taste the graphite in the air on his tongue. It made his skin dry and silk-smooth. The interior of the shed was covered with a skin of slate, ceiling, walls and floor. Khyrbysk picked his way with care: graphite dust made the floor treacherously slippery.

Hektor Shulmin was in a huddle in the far corner with Leon Ferenc. Shulmin saw Khyrbysk come in and waved to him cheerily.

'Yakov!' he called. 'Come to see your baby waking up?'

Khyrbysk ignored him.

In the centre of the room, standing on a rubber sheet on a low platform, was another cube – a cube inside the cube – gleaming coal-black under the spotlights. It was a stack of blocks of pure graphite, sixty layers of blocks, rising twenty-five feet high and weighing almost three hundred tons. Half the blocks were solid bricks, but the other half had been carefully and precisely hollowed out. The hollowed graphite blocks formed a three-dimensional cellular lattice within the cube, and each cell in the lattice contained a small, neat gobbet of uranium.

From a rubber-sheeted scaffold over the stack, rods of cadmium plunged down through the black cube. Three men on the scaffold operated the mechanism, withdrawing the cadmium rods one by one with painful slowness. They had barrels of cadmium salt solution ready, to flood the cube if anything went wrong. They called themselves the suicide squad.

Khyrbysk went across to the desk from where Ambroz Teleki was supervising the operation. The neutron counters made their quiet trickling clicking noise.

'One more rod will do it,' said Teleki. 'The reaction will become self-sustaining. It will not level off. We were waiting for you.'

Khyrbysk studied the dials.

'Then do it,' he said. 'Do it, Ambroz. Do it.'

Teleki made a sign to the suicide squad. One of them turned a bakelite knob on a panel one notch forward. Then another.

The noise of the counters went faster and faster, the clicks tumbling over one another, a clattering rattle that turned into a steady hiss, a white waterfall of sound. The needles on the dials swung fully round to the right, hit their limit and stopped. But the pen on the chart recorder continued to rise, higher and higher, tracing a beautiful exponential curve.

A ripple of applause went round the room. The technicians broke into quiet chatter.

Khyrbysk watched the curve on the chart climb higher. Still higher.

'Say the word, Yakov,' said Teleki, 'and we'll drop the Shinn Rod in to close it off.'

Khyrbysk said nothing. His eyes were fixed on the rising graph. His mouth was dry. His hands were trembling. He let the reaction run on, faster and faster, hotter and hotter. The flow of neutrons becoming a roar. A flood.

He was Yakov Khyrbysk, father of stars.

'Yakov?' said Teleki anxiously, touching his arm. 'Yakov. When you are ready, please.'

Khyrbysk paid him no attention. The technicians' chatter fell quiet. Seconds passed. Long seconds.

'Yakov!' said Teleki again.

Then at last Khyrbysk raised his arm.

'OK,' he said. 'Let it stop now.'

He watched the curve drop off and fall away.

Hektor Shulmin hustled over, drawing the ponderous Ferenc in his wake. He clapped Teleki on the shoulder.

'Congratulations, Ambroz! A triumph! She works, man! She works! It's beautiful.' Shulmin produced a bottle of aquavit from his pocket and started handing it round. 'So when are we going to go operational? Why not now? Everything is in place. How many tests do you need, after all? Ready is ready.'

Teleki looked tired.

'Soon, Hektor,' he said. 'Soon.'

Khyrbysk took Shulmin by the elbow and drew him aside.

'A word, please, Hektor,' he said.

'Of course, Yakov. Of course. I hear you were out on the *Chaika* the other night. A fishing trip, eh?'

'You might say so, Hektor.'

'A successful catch, I hope.'

'The best.'

'So friend Blegvad brought another package from our mysterious uncle in Mirgorod? How much? How much this time? Another hundred thousand? Tell me Yakov. I am agog. Our anonymous donor intrigues me. Our mystery philanthropist.'

'A hundred thousand? No. More than that. Much more.'

'How much Yakov? This time, how much?'

'Thirty million.'

'Thirty million? Thirty *million*?' Shulmin looked suddenly serious. 'Fuck, Yakov. We should be careful. We should go cautiously here.

What are we getting into? Dukhonin himself never came up with such a sum, not all in one go. Thirty million! This is not a donation. This is a purchase. Who is this faceless, nameless man with thirty million roubles? What is he after? What did Blegvad say?'

'Blegvad? Blegvad deals only with intermediaries. He has never met the man, never even spoken to him. But I have.'

'Have you, by fuck!'

'He telephoned me. In the middle of the night. And you are right, of course: he has made a request, a most courteous request. Not a purchase, he didn't put it in those terms, not at all. He was most careful not to do that. He is a supporter of our cause, he says. An admirer of our ambition. He shares our common purpose. We are visionaries, doing great work, and he has just a small favour to ask of me.'

'What does he want?'

'Artillery shells. A hundred artillery shells.'

'Is that it? The man's an idiot. He could pick up a hundred shells anywhere.'

'No. He wants the yellow shells.'

'The *yellow*? He knows about them? How can he know about them?'

'He does, Hektor. He was most specific. A hundred yellow shells. They are to be on a train to Mirgorod tonight. Leaving this very night. This can be done, Hektor? There is no problem? I don't want to hear there is a problem. I agreed. Of course I agreed. I gave him an undertaking.'

'Tonight? Yes, it can be done. No problem, Yakov. But—'

'Then arrange it, Hektor. I want you to go with them. Travel with them to Mirgorod yourself and make sure they are delivered safely. There is to be no fuck-up, Hektor. No delay. It is a matter of extreme urgency. Our benefactor was absolutely explicit on that point.'

48

In Mirgorod, in the Raion Lezaryet, Vissarion Lom woke suddenly, heart pounding, the sour taste of sleep in his mouth. The attic was in darkness. He knew instantly by the feel of the room that Maroussia was gone. He fumbled for the matchbox and lit the lamp. Looked at his watch. Just after three.

Shit.

He pulled on his clothes, grabbed the Blok 15, stuffed it into his waistband and went downstairs. The kitchen was in darkness, the banked-up fire in the stove glowing dull brick red. The door at the end of the hall stood open. Maroussia's coat was not on the hook.

There was a small pile of coins on the hall table, a few kopeks and a single rouble. He scooped them into his pocket and stepped out into the dark and icy cold.

49

Bez Nichevoi entered the Lodka by the long tunnels, carrying the unconscious weight of Maroussia Shaumian across his shoulders. He found Chazia in her workshop. Bez noted the changes there: the benches pushed back out of the way, equipment boxed and crated and standing ready in piles beside the old rail track, the stock of angel flesh gone.

The wall of the Pollandore chamber had been smashed and lay in rubble, and the iron construction that held the Pollandore itself had been dismantled and removed. The uncanny, enormous and faintly disgusting sphere hung suspended six feet above the flagstones, apparently without support. It turned slowly on its own axis, milky, planetary, luminescent but shedding no light. Swirls like small storms, oil on water, spiralled across its surface. Bez kept his distance and avoided looking at it, though it tugged at his awareness. The sense of its presence jangled his nerves. Made him feel weak. When he couldn't see it he couldn't tell exactly where it was. As if it circled him. Stalking.

Bez was surprised to realise that he feared it.

He shed the burden of the Shaumian girl with relief, slipping her from his back and letting her fall to the ground. She moaned and stirred. Her face was flushed, her hair matted with sweat. His immobilising scratch had made her feverish.

'Be careful with her!' Chazia snapped. She glared at him with distaste.

'I found her,' said Bez. 'I brought her. I give her to you.'

It had been a hard run from the raion. The smell of the girl on his back, the feel of her belly warm against his shoulders, had nagged at him the whole way.

'Is she all right?' said Chazia, bending over her. 'She is bleeding. You didn't ...?'

Bez noticed how Chazia's fox-red hair was thinning. Patches of angel flesh were visibly growing across her skull.

'A graze,' he said. 'She fell.'

As Chazia straightened up he tossed the stinking knotted ball of twigs and bones and stuff towards her.

'Here,' he said. 'She was carrying this. Only this.'

Chazia caught it neatly and cupped it in her hands. She grinned – a vulpine stretch of thin lips – and laid the thing carefully on the bench.

Bez hated this woman. He'd served her too long. He had *served* for too long altogether. He was *Bez*.

'You are leaving?' he said, indicating the preparations around them.

'The strength of the Vlast lies in the east,' said Chazia. 'We will build a new capital, better, stronger and more pure, at Kholvatogorsk. I intend that Kholvatogorsk will be a *clean* city. Mirgorod is too ... *tainted*. Too near the margins. Old things not properly cleared away.'

She means me, thought Bez. *The bitch. She refers to me.*

'I have not touched the woman yet,' he said. 'You will give her to me when you've finished.'

Chazia looked at him sharply.

'I need her alive,' she said. 'I don't know how long for.'

'I am no lickspittle of the Vlast,' said Bez. 'Service is not its own reward. Service is no reward at all.'

'Your assistance to me, as to my predecessors, has always been appreciated, Bez Nichevoi. If you're leaving by the underground way you'd better go quickly. A train is coming.'

'*A train? Here?*'

'This tunnel connects to the Wieland station. The way was closed after the Pollandore was brought here. I've had the tracks repaired to take it out again.'

'You're taking that thing with you?'

'Mirgorod will fall. I'm not going to leave it here for the Archipelago to find.'

When Bez Nichevoi left the Lodka it was still thick night, but the fierce edge of dawn was burning its way across the face of the Vlast. Already the burning light was less than five hundred miles east of Mirgorod, and the turning of the planet was bringing it closer. He could feel it. He needed to hurry. *Get out of the light.* He knew a place in the cellarage of what had once been a brewery. It would be quiet there. Out of the way, if the bombers returned. Bez never slept in the same nest two days running.

Between him and refuge lay the Black Wisent Quarter. It wasn't wise to pass through the Black Wisent on such a night as this. Old things were near the surface there. But he'd lost too much time already and a detour would cost him more. The sun was coming. He scrambled from roof to roof and ran across open spaces, angry and frustrated. The warmth and smell of the Shaumian woman was still in his clothes.

Chazia's new Vlast in the east was no place for him. Perhaps he would stay in Mirgorod. War was coming and there would be good pickings in the city. Or maybe it was time to go back to the mountains. Some brick-turreted burgh in the Erdyeliu would suit him well. Glaciers and pinewoods. Lynx and chamois. Giants and trolls and rusalkas. His kind had lived off such as them long before the Vlast had come, and still would, long after the Vlast had crumbled and faded.

But he would go back for the Shaumian woman before he left. When night came again he would go back to the Lodka and fetch her and take her with him. Make her last a while. If Chazia didn't like it, he would kill Chazia. That would be good.

Bez was well into the Black Wisent Quarter now. The snow had fallen more thickly here. It lay feet-thick in the squares and mounded in high drifts against walls. He skittered lightly across the surface, his feet scarcely leaving traces.

Something on the wind alarmed him.

Wolf was following. Coming fast.

Dawn was too near. It was better to avoid a fight.

Bez picked up speed. A bitter pre-dawn wind whipped his face. Hard pellets of snow stung his cheeks. Snow. Thick, sudden snow. Snow-thorns scraping at his eyes. Something was wrong. Snow. Too much snow. He ran faster, his sunken chest burning.

He should not have entered the Black Wisent Quarter.

The snow under his feet slipped suddenly sideways, like a rug pulled out from under him. Unbalanced, he fell. Hard. Onto icy cobbles.

Bez picked himself up. The snow was watching him. Waiting to see what he did. He was in an empty space between buildings. Snow-dogs circled in the shadows of the mouths of the streets and observed him from under the low branches of snow-heavy trees. He stood his ground, turning slowly, looking for a way out or a place to make a stand.

Wolf walked out to meet him. A man in a long coat and an astrakhan hat.

'Where is the girl?' said wolf. 'Did you find the girl? Did you?'

'*Fuck you, turd puppy!*'

'Did you find her?' said wolf. 'What have you done?'

'*Too late, teat licker. The bitch fox has her now.*'

Bez hissed and went for wolf, fast. At the last moment he jumped high to come down from above and take his eyes. A quick decisive kill.

But wolf was faster. Faster and stronger.

Wolf ducked sideways and reached up and gripped Bez by the ankle. Caught him out of the air and whiplashed his light body down. Smashed him against the ground, crashing the back of his head against the cobbles. Before Bez could recover wolf was on him and ripped his head clean away from his neck. Foul-smelling black watery ichor sprayed from the mess between his shoulders and dripped from the root of his skull.

Antoninu Florian began to walk, holding the head of Bez in one hand, out to the side, away from his body, like a dark lantern. The head shrieked and cursed and screamed and tried to bite the hand that held it by the hair, but its teeth tore nothing but its own lips and tongue. With his other hand Florian dragged the thrashing, spasming living corpse behind him by the leg. The corpse tried to kick itself free but could not. Arched its back and slashed at the air with needle fingers.

'*Fucker! Fucker!*' the head was screeching. '*You stinking bag of shit! I will lay your eyeballs on your shoulders so you can watch me eat your brain.*'

It was curious, Florian thought, how much noise the mouth could make when disconnected from its lungs. He wondered what the biology of that was.

Somebody pulled aside an upstairs curtain and looked out from a house as they were passing. A pale face pressed against a window. The face disappeared and the curtain fell back.

Florian dragged the body to a place he had prepared in the shell of a bombed-out building. A pyre of roof timbers and furniture waited there, supplemented by a kindling of mattresses and curtains and books. He flung the lightweight, disgusting head onto the pile and threw the body after it. Weighted the thrashing body down with heavy beams and doused the whole heap with kerosene from a jerrycan he'd stashed nearby. Lit a cloth-wrapped chair leg with a match and laid it carefully at the base.

The pyre went up in a sudden explosive flowering. Flags and sheets of flame billowed in their own twisting wind. Dry wood chattered and spat. One more bomb-fire in a city pitted with smouldering buildings.

Florian stayed to watch the body burn, feeling the heat on his face. He had to make sure. The smell of the body burning was very bad. The corpse writhed and thrashed as the fire took it. The head continued to scream and curse as its hair and flesh charred and crisped and peeled away.

One by one, Bez Nichevoi gave up all the deaths by which he had lived. Hundreds, thousands of deaths, human and otherwise, absorbed and accumulated during the long centuries of his existence. Antoninu Florian felt every one. The victims swirled around him in bitter smoke-clouds of sadness, surprise and pain, and their features flickered across his face like fire-shadow. Remembrance. Each death was as raw as the first.

Florian felt each one die. One by one, he reflected their dying faces back into the fire. He worked the subcutaneous muscles of his own humaniform face – zygmatic, corrugator, depressor, levator, buccinator, orbicularis, risorus – until it was agony. Until the skin stretched tight across the shifting bones of his skull was reddened and swollen and burned as if stung by bees. Tears spilled down his cheeks and soaked his shirt. From time to time he turned away to vomit, until he was hollowed out and sour.

On and on they came, the many many dead, and Florian Antoninu wept.

Only when the blaze had collapsed in on itself and slumped to charred stumps and ash and the corpse of Bez Nichevoi was empty and quiet, only then did he turn and walk away, weakened, trembling.

50

Lom had been walking for six hours, looking for Maroussia. All night an uneasy windstream had bundled high dark cloud mass eastwards across the sky. Ragged clearings opened across patches of fathomless star-speckled darkshine. Moon-glimpses dilated and closed. Sometimes Lom knew where he was and sometimes he was lost. The steep intricate streets, courtyards and passageways of the Raion Lezaryet defeated system and pattern. As he walked he tried to make sense of Maroussia's disappearance, but he could not. She had woken in the night. She had not dressed – her clothes were still in the attic – but she had taken the solm and a coat, and gone out into the dark and disappeared.

He climbed the Ship Bastion to see if she was there. He went down to the Purfas Gate, which was closed and barred and unattended. Taking a different route back, he passed the blank darkened windows of a watch repairer, a tailor, a bookseller showing lonely yellow lamplight in an upstairs room. A night reader. The streets of the raion smelled wild and ancient – old woodsmoke, damp stone cellars, pig yards and open drains. The snow, the river mist and the sky. A pony grunted and shifted uneasily on the other side of a fence. A bat flickered close past his face, an indistinct smudge of fur. Lom flinched as if it had touched him, but it had not.

He let the winding narrow streets take him where they would. There was a shape and rhythm to them that was not human. He saw openings and followed them. Narrow corners at acute angles he had to squeeze through sideways. Gateways too low for adults to pass through without bending. Gaps and gratings whose purpose he could not grasp. Rounding the bends of wandering alleyways he felt himself entering localities of awareness: attentive, watchful presences shadowing his, though he could see nothing. Frustrated, he felt himself walking along the edge of something. On the borderline of some discovery he could not make. Nightside. The only sounds were small ones: a latch rattling in the wind, the slump of snow disturbed in a gutter, and once the shriek of a street-scavenging fox. Crossing a wider cobbled square in a splash of moonshadow, he caught a trace of something different. A taint on the air. An intrusion. His stomach tightened. His neck prickled. Something sharp, cruel and disgusting had passed that way. An edge of panic began to scratch away at the edge of his mind and did not stop.

Three times during the night he returned to the house to see if Maroussia had come back. He roused Elena Cornelius and the Count and together they combed the building from cellars to attics. It had obviously occurred to both of them, though they did not say it, that Maroussia had gone. Slipped away. Abandoned him. Left the city. It was in their faces as they helped him search the house. Elena at least thought it would have been a good move. But Lom didn't believe it. He went to Kamilova's house and banged on the door, but no one came.

When dawn came and the Purfas Gate opened, he took the first tram of the day into the city, to the Lodka, on the possibility that Maroussia, unable to sleep, had decided to go there alone, to check it out, to be nearer the Pollandore, perhaps even to look for a way inside. It seemed unlikely, but he had no other ideas. None at all.

51

The wide open space in front of the Lodka, the immense Square of the Piteous Angel, was full of people, the atmosphere muted, determined, grim. Long lines had formed at temporary recruiting booths. Clerks took names under crude and blocky rust-coloured posters of comrades-in-arms charging with out-thrust bayonets, the men square-jawed, the women full-breasted, their hair like sheaves of corn. Those too old and infirm to sign up waited patiently to hand over their kopeks, their cutlery, their watches and chains and little pieces of jewellery at collection kiosks. The wind threw bitter scraps of snow in their faces.

A man came and stood next to him. Together they watched the slow-moving queues in silence for a while. The stranger glanced sideways at Lom.

'Look at them,' he said. 'In other cities they lined the streets when the Archipelago came. But not us. Not here. Not Mirgorod. You understand that?'

Lom looked at the man sharply. Middle-aged, with faded thinning hair, the lenses of his glasses smeared, a day's worth of dark red stubble on his chin and sagging neck. He wondered if he was a *provokator*. But there was a puzzled sadness in his face. He looked lost. He was just talking.

'It's their city,' said Lom. 'Their homes. Their families. They're frightened.'

The man shook his head, as if he was trying to clear his mind. Bring things into focus. 'Of course this isn't everyone,' he said. 'This is the ones who came, not the ones who didn't. There's more will have stayed at home. And people are leaving. Lots are leaving. Did you hear that?'

'It makes sense,' said Lom. 'If they've got somewhere to go.'

'You?' the man said.

'What?'

'You joining up?'

'I'm looking for someone,' said Lom. 'I thought she might have come here. I didn't know it was going to be like this.'

The man nodded. He understood that.

'My wife's gone somewhere,' he said. 'She took the girls. Our house is gone. When I got back there was just this hole, and the back wall sticking up out of a pile of bricks. You can see our wallpaper. The kitchen up in the air. It looks small. Seemed bigger when we were in it.' He rubbed his hand down across his face as if he was wiping something away. 'You haven't seen her, have you? Her hair's grey. Cut short. Like this.' He touched the back of his neck above the collar. 'She's not so old, only forty-three, but grey. Not white, grey. A nice iron-grey. She would have had the girls with her.'

'No,' said Lom. 'I haven't seen them. Sorry.'

'I waited the night but they didn't come. We always said we'd move to the country. You know, if the war came here. They must have gone ahead, but I don't know where. They'll send word. When they're settled.'

Lom didn't have anything to say. After a while the man drifted away. 'You take care now,' he said as he went.

A murmur moved across the square, a turning of heads like wind across a lake. Lom smelled smoke. Somewhere fires were burning. From the direction of the Lodka a thick pall was rising and spilling across the crowd. Scraps of burned paper in the wind. He joined the drift of people moving towards the place. Worked his way to the front.

There was a huge open space in front of the Lodka filled with bonfires. There must have been fifty or sixty at least, set out in neatly spaced ranks. Some were already burning, spilling fierce licks of flame thirty or forty feet high, but most were still being built. Endless lines of soldiers and uniformed officials were filing out of the Lodka's main entrance and down the steps, pushing trolleys and carrying document crates for the growing stacks. To one side a fleet of drays and olive-green trucks was drawn up. Some crates were being diverted towards them and loaded up, but those they did not plan to take, which was most of them, they were burning. The space around the fires was kept clear by lines of conscripts, pale-faced in their ill-fitting greatcoats, steel helmets strapped to their backpacks. Bayonets fitted, they avoided the gaze of the watching crowd.

Behind the fires, the Lodka itself was closed up like a fortress. There was no way in. All the raisable bridges were raised, and the Yekaterinsky Bridge and the Streltski Gate had checkpoints watched by mounted dragoons and sandbagged mitrailleuse positions. The thousand-windowed frontage, rising high above the smoke, was hung with banners, the roofscape forested with flags. Emblems of the Vlast in its pride, red, black and gold, raised in wind-tugged defiance under the low leaden sky.

But the Lodka was evacuating. The scale of what was happening was dumbfounding. The files and documents of a dozen ministries of government and police. The correspondence of diplomats and provincial land captains. Four hundred years of intelligence reports and observation records. The shrill denunciations and sly whispered secrets of informers. Confessions signed on blood-smeared paper. The transcripts of secret trials. The arraignments and sentences of every exile and prisoner in the Dominions. Hundreds and hundreds of miles of shelving. All the vast archives of the Registry, presided over by the towering Gaukh Engine. It would take weeks to burn it all. Months. An immense, tireless beacon to guide the bombers of the Archipelago to their target by night and day. The Vlast was spectacularly killing itself, and would surely take Mirgorod down with it. The watching crowd was beginning to mutter and grumble.

Engines were started. A convoy was moving out. There were angry shouts as the conscripts cleared a path for the trucks and horse-drawn wagons loaded high with crates. They trundled and lumbered through at walking pace. Where were they going? Somewhere far away and safe from the war. South? Unlikely: too near the incursions of the Archipelago. North? They couldn't get far enough, not with winter closing in. It must be east, then, somewhere east, somewhere in the thousands of miles between Mirgorod and the edge of the endless forest.

A thought struck Lom. Hard. *The Pollandore.* They wouldn't leave it to be found by the Archipelago if the city fell. *They would take it with them. Shit.*

If he could think of that, so could Maroussia. She would have. If she had come here, if she had seen the evacuation beginning, she would have asked the question. *Hours* ago. She would have tried to find the answer. She would have followed.

He needed to know where the convoys were heading.

He paced along beside one of the trucks at the back of the convoy edging its way through the crowd. There was only the driver in the cab. He reached up and opened the passenger-side door. Swung himself up and into the seat. Pulled the door shut behind him.

'Hey!' said the driver. 'What the fuck—'

Lom jammed the muzzle of the Blok 15 hard against his thigh.

'Just drive,' he said. 'Like you were, everything normal.'

'You must be fucking—' the driver began.

'There is a gun against your leg. It won't make a hole, it will blow your leg away. Maybe both of them. Shatter the bones. Sever the main arteries. You'll bleed empty in minutes. So just keep looking ahead and driving normally. Don't mind me, I'm only along for the ride.'

The driver, hands gripped tight on the wheel, knuckles white, kept his eyes fixed on the horse-drawn wagon in front. He tried to swallow but his throat was dry and he coughed. The truck stayed in the long line, nosing slowly through the city.

'Where are you going?' said Lom.

'The railway. The marshalling yards by the Wieland station.'

'And after? Where are they taking all this stuff?'

The driver shook his head.

'I don't know. I just turn around and come back for another load. Look. I don't want any trouble. You need to get out now. When we get there, there'll be—'

'Just shut up and drive.'

The convoy turned into Founder's Prospect. There were crowds there too. The shops were being cleared out. People hauling bags and even handcarts piled high with bread and meat and oil. Anything. Some establishments were trying to operate some kind of rationing system. *Two loaves per family, fifty kopeks.* Eye-watering prices. There were long queues outside post offices and pawn shops,. A bank near the Ter-Uspenskovo Bridge was trying to close its doors. There was shouting. Things getting ugly.

At the corner near the Great Vlast Museum they got snarled in traffic. Another convoy was drawn up at the foot of the museum's wide marble steps. Museum staff were carrying out rolled carpets and tapestries, bronze heads, tundra carvings, crates and boxes stuffed with straw, paintings still in their frames. Nothing properly packed. Treasures beyond price being dumped in the back of waiting vehicles.

The truck lurched ahead a few feet and stopped again. The driver was staring at a group of militia watching from the top of the steps. He shifted in his seat, trying to move his leg away from the Blok's muzzle.

'Don't,' said Lom. 'Sit still. Keep looking ahead.'

It would have been quicker to walk, but as soon as he left the cab the driver would be shouting his head off. Lom slumped lower in his seat and tried to look bored.

At last the convoy cleared the museum and picked up to a steady walking pace again. When they slowed at a crowded interchange Lom opened the door and slid out.

'I'd keep quiet about what just happened,' he said, 'if I were you.'

'Fuck you, arsehole,' the driver muttered and gunned the throttle. The truck lurched a few feet forward.

Lom's back itched as he walked away, adrenaline pumping, waiting for shouts, ready to run. But nothing happened. Twenty seconds later he slipped down an alleyway and out of sight.

52

The Wieland marshalling yards were raucous chaos. Locomotives in full steam, whistles shrieking. Shunting engines stalled among crowds of citizens. Families picking their way across the tracks, dragging their luggage, desperate to find places on trains that were already spilling people out of the doors. Railway officials pushing, shoving, yelling and screaming. Crackling tannoy announcements. *Citizen passengers must use station platforms! Access here is forbidden!* No one was listening. There was no way through the heaving mass. No hope of finding Maroussia here, and no sign of the convoys from the Lodka.

Lom skirted the crowds and came to a chain-link fence. Beyond it was another expanse of railway tracks, water towers, mobile cranes and what looked like freight cars raised on iron stilts. He climbed the fence painfully, gripping the wire with fingers numbed with cold, scrabbling for footholds against the stanchions. He rolled over the top and dropped awkwardly on the other side, picked himself up and ran.

He sprinted across the open ground and ducked between two trains. There were more trains beyond: wooden wagons as long as barns and high as houses with six-foot-diameter wheels; the twelve-foot-gauge behemoths of the intercontinental freight lines. He went further in, following the lines of high-sided wagons that stretched away into the distance in both directions. From time to time he clambered through the space between two cars, only to find himself in another identical corridor between identical trains. It was a labyrinth and there was nothing to see. A narrow ladder at the end of each wagon climbed up to the roof. Lom chose one and went up the rungs until his head was clear and he could see across, but there were only the roofs of more wagons. No end to the rows of trains. Hundreds and hundreds, possibly thousands, of identical wagons all lined up ready to go.

He dropped to the ground and took a closer look at the car he'd climbed. There was a tall sliding door along one side. Padlocks looped through iron latches, but they weren't locked. The bottom of the door was at head height, but there was a handle. He hauled at it and the door trundled back, running on small wheels in iron grooves. Greased, nice and easy. He opened up a four-foot gap, jumped and pulled himself up over the edge. Crawled on hands and knees in rough dusty straw. Inside was airy dimness and an overpowering smell of tar, disinfectant and straw. Cattle wagons. Empty. Only there were shadowy structures inside that didn't look like cattle stalls.

As his eyes adjusted to the dimness, he stood up and looked around. There were no windows but narrow slatted gaps ran along near the roof, letting in thin strips of dusty light. The whole of the carriage was lined with slatted wooden racks, like bunks but wider, three tiers high, the top tier four feet under the tarred wooden roof. Each tier was packed with a layer of straw. Lidded barrels lined the narrow aisle that ran between them the length of the wagon. Lom opened barrels at random. Most of them held only water, but from every third one came acrid disinfectant fumes. In the far corner he found a couple of mops and shovels and a stack of galvanised buckets.

They were cattle trucks, but for people. As Lom got used to the air inside the wagon, he picked out other smells under the overpowering reek of disinfectant. Urine. Excrement. Sweat. The trains had been used before, and they'd been cleaned up ready to be used again.

Lom dropped to the ground and eased the door closed. All around him the high blank walls of identical railway trucks blocked out the sky, and each one could carry hundreds of people, jammed in side by side in acrid, excremental shadow. He kept on cutting sideways between them, ducking under or climbing across the heavy couplings. After four or five more he chose another ladder and took another look across the roofs.

He was almost at the edge. A couple more lines of wagons, and then a stretch of dead ground, and beyond that, set apart within its own high perimeter fence, was a long military train. He was pretty much level with its two massive locomotives coupled in series, crudely plated with thick blue steel. Behind them was an anti-aircraft gun on a flatbed truck and a couple of slope-sided armoured wagons with firing slits for windows and roof-mounted gun turrets. The muzzles of twin twenty-pounders at rest, tilted skywards. The rest of the train as far as he could see was mostly made up of freight cars interspersed with passenger carriages, incongruously neat and fresh in their purple livery. The only exception was one flat truck about four or five hundred yards from Lom's position, at the point where the train curved out of sight. It was wider than the rest of the train, and it had been fitted with what looked like wide iron trestles and a high canopy. Soldiers were draping it with grey camouflage netting. Somewhat apart from them, waiting patiently, arms at its side, observing, stood a crudely human-shaped figure. It was broad and squat but taller than the wagons. A mudjhik, formed from a solid block of dull reddish-purple angel flesh.

Lom felt the touch of the mudjhik's awareness brush lightly across the surface of his mind, pass on for a second and flick sharply back. Its sightless head turned in his direction. The full force of its attention gripped him hard like a fist. He tried to close his mind against it and push it away, but the dazzling floodlight crash of its glare pinned him. He was naked and exposed, alone in a wide empty space, his shadow stretching out behind him, inky black and infinitely long. The mudjhik took a step in his direction, then another, gathering pace, opening its legs wider, relaxing into a steady loping jog.

Lom slid down the ladder, crashing his shin painfully against the train coupling, and turned and ran. The long passage between the trains was a tunnel, a trap. He turned and scrambled between the carriages, crossed the narrow space and scrambled through again, and again, heart pounding, fighting panic, desperate to put as many trains as possible between himself and the approaching mudjhik. Repeatedly he slipped and stumbled, crashed bruisingly into couplings and the iron edges of the freight cars.

The mudjhik knew where he was. Never for a moment did the grip of its awareness shift or falter. Lom felt the hunger of its desire to seize him, to pinch the cage of his ribs between its thumbs and squeeze. Somewhere at the margins of that fierce desire Lom sensed the mudjhik's handler fighting to keep some measure of control. It was like trying to dig fingers into polished granite.

The mudjhik could not pass between the railway wagons, it was too large, so it crashed through them, one after another, splintering the wooden superstructures and stepping over the iron chassis.

Run. Lom heard the mudjhik's mind in his. *Run, little man, run. I am coming.*

The wagons could not stop the mudjhik, but they slowed it. When Lom broke through into open space on the other side, it was still a couple of hundred yards behind him. Ahead of him lay the waste ground he'd crossed before, the wire fence, and then the crowds hustling for places on the passenger trains out of Mirgorod. People there were looking his way. There were shouts and screams. They'd seen the out-of-control mudjhik smashing its way towards them through the cattle wagons. Lom sensed their rising fear. He launched himself towards them in a desperate sprint.

He hit the fence at a run and scrabbled up and over, dropping recklessly on the other side. The crowds were backing away and scattering, terrified. There was a sound like a low despairing collective moan. The mudjhik was through the trains and out in the open ground, but it had slowed. Lom felt its riveted focus on him begin to slip and disintegrate. It was the crowd. The background noise of so many panicking minds confused it. It was sifting through them, trying to find him again. It hooked him and lurched forward but he pushed its gaze aside.

The mass of people was a single collective entity, a herd mind with a simple overwhelming purpose, moving on instinct, getting through from second to second, shoving, shouting, pushing, desperate to escape before the mudjhik crashed into them. Lom charged into the middle of it and joined them. For the first time in his life he surrendered himself up to the tidal mind of a mob, obliterating independent thought and sinking without question below the surface into dark, exhilarating waters. The energy that flowed through him was tremendous. The people around him were shadows, rivals, part of him, indistinguishable. Somewhere at the outer edges of his mind he felt the grazing trail of the mudjhik, superficial and negligible. The mudjhik itself was being pulled into the dark vortex and absorbed. Lom ducked away from it and let himself be carried away.

53

Lavrentina Chazia sat alone in the projection room in the deserted offices of Project Winter Skies, running the film of the test explosion at Novaya Zima over and over again. The evacuation of Mirgorod was under way. Her instructions were being carried out. Her train was ready: the Pollandore installed, her angel skin crated and stored, the Shaumian girl under lock and key in a barred freight car. There was nothing that required her attention until the train left at noon. She ran the film again. And again. She must have watched it twenty, fifty times. She could close her eyes and watch it all unfolding inside her head: the technicians busying themselves with the final preparations; their stupid, excited grins; the caption, UNCLE VANYA; the wind across silent level tundra, dwarfing the gantry; and then the cataclysm. The blinding gush of absolute, total, irresistible destructive power. As soon as the film had finished she went back to the projector, rewound it and played it again.

It was almost impressive that Dukhonin had achieved so much alone. She had underestimated him. But whatever he had done, it was hers now. In Mirgorod, Dukhonin had kept the circle tight and she had killed them all. Their families would be rounded up and shipped off east. That they would end up as conscript labour in Novaya Zima itself was an elegance that pleased her.

The Vlast had made a terrible mistake. She realised that now. All of them, and she along with them, had made a terrible mistake. They had been so focused on the fallen angels and what they meant, and what could be done with the flesh of their carcases, they had all failed to realise what human ingenuity could do by itself. They had taken their eye off those obscure laboratories.

But Kantor had not. Kantor had found them. And Kantor had found Dukhonin and made him his puppet. When he needed to tap into the resources of the Vlast he had chosen Dukhonin as his point of entry. Vain, industrious, narrow-minded Dukhonin. It had been a good choice.

Kantor's continuing existence pained her. Him she could not touch, not yet, but his time would come, and soon. He thought he pulled her strings. He thought he could keep things from her. But she would tip him over. She would see him swing from his own lungs. When the time came. Not yet but soon.

On the screen Uncle Vanya erupted once more. Chazia shifted in her chair and grunted at the punch of excitement in her belly and groin.

It was all coming together for her now. Power. Power. Power. The living angel. The Pollandore. And *this*: Novaya Zima. *This* was a strength that would wipe the Archipelago from the face of the planet and build her Vlast for a thousand, a hundred thousand years! The Founder himself would be nothing more than a footnote in the story of the rise of Lavrentina Chazia and the Vlast she would build. With this, the living angel would listen to her. With this, could she not erase the angel itself from the face of the planet? Yes, and burn the forest too. All of it. The whole of the planet would be hers.

54

Lom took a tram as far as the northern edge of Big Side and walked the rest of the way back to the Raion Lezaryet. It was almost midday. The Purfas Gate was open but the VKBD were watching the bridge. They let him cross without question – they weren't interested in who went in – but no one was coming out. A small knot of men stood in sullen silence just inside the wall.

As Lom climbed the steep narrow streets towards the house a distorted loudspeaker voice, high-pitched and hectoring, echoed instructions off the crowding gables. He couldn't make out the words or the direction it was coming from. Shops and offices were closed, the streets almost deserted. Ahead of him two men in frock coats and wide-brimmed hats crossed the road, heads down and walking quickly. They entered the Clothiers Meeting Hall and shut the door behind them. The tannoy was getting louder. Following the direction of the noise, Lom reached the edge of a small cobbled square, defined on one side by the raion's only hotel, the Purse of Crowns, and on the opposite corner by the Lezarye Courts of Commercial Jurisdiction.

A trestle table had been set up in the middle of the square. On it was a contraption like a radio, connected to a hefty separate battery, and next to it stood a sturdy tripod holding the loudspeaker horn. A small man in a dark suit and polished ankle boots was shouting into a microphone, reading from a sheet of paper. Hatless, he looked cold. His cheeks, his nose, the tips of his small ears were pink. Thin black hair slicked across his skull. Sweat-flattened strands across his forehead. He kept stopping to wipe his face and polish the lenses of little wire spectacles with a handkerchief from his jacket pocket. Half a dozen armed VKBD kept watch from the steps of the court. The tannoy and the echoes in the square distorted his voice. Lom had to listen the message through three times to piece it together.

'Attention! Attention! Residents of Raion Lezaryet! The defence commissar and city captain of Mirgorod announces that this quarter is designated for immediate evacuation. There is no reason for alarm. Prepare yourselves for resettlement or work duty in other provinces. Women and children will leave first. Small hand luggage only is to be taken. You must gather at the Stratskovny Voksal at 6 p.m. sharp. Women with babies are to provide themselves with paraffin stoves. You must understand that any resistance to this order will result in police countermeasures. Attempts to avoid resettlement will lead to forced evacuation. It is expected that all demands will be met with punctuality and calmness. I repeat ...'

Apart from Lom and the VKBD, there was nobody in the square to hear him. He was shouting at blank shuttered windows. Drawn curtains. Closed doors. There was a neat stack of paper on the table. Copies of the declaration for handing out. Nobody was taking one.

When Lom reached Elena Cornelius's apartment it was deserted. Maroussia wasn't there, and there was no sign that she'd been back. Their attic room was as he'd left it. Down in the kitchen everything was neatly stacked. The stove was banked up and smouldering quietly, no indication of a hurried departure, but Elena wasn't there and nor were the girls.

Lom found the Count and Ilinca in their salon. They were sitting side by side on a threadbare chaise longue. Dressed for a journey. A pair of old scuffed suitcases and a faded dusty carpet bag in the middle of the floor. The door standing open, ready.

'We knew the day would come,' said the Count. 'We are prepared.'

'Maroussia?' said Lom. 'Did she come back?'

Ilinca shook her head.

'She won't come here again,' said the Count. 'You should go too, Vissarion Yppolitovich. They're coming to collect us soon.'

'What happened to Elena?' said Lom. 'And the girls?'

'Elena went to the Apraksin,' said Ilinca. 'She took Yeva and Galina to school on the way. They would have gone before the announcement came. Elena is sensible. She'll know what to do.'

'You can't wait here like this,' said Lom. 'You have to run. You have to get away now. By yourselves. Don't let them take you. The raion is being cleared. There are trains at the station.' The excrement and straw in the darkness. The reek of disinfectant barrels. 'You don't know—'

'No,' said Palffy. 'We are safe.'

'You have to get away.'

Palffy looked out of the window.

'Away?' said Ilinca. 'Where would we go? How could we travel alone? Will you take us?'

The Count put his hand on Ilinca's arm.

'You'll be all right,' he said, not looking at Lom. 'I told you. They won't hurt us. They know us. They have our names. We are citizens; we're on the list; we did the right thing.'

'What?' said Lom. 'What did you do?'

The Count looked up at him blankly.

'You should leave now,' he said. 'Do not wait here.'

'What have you *done*?' said Lom.

The Count looked away and shook his head. The truth punched Lom in the belly. He felt dizzy. Sick with despair.

'Maroussia,' he said quietly. 'You betrayed her. You told them and they came for her.'

The Count took his wife's hand and gripped it tight in his.

'You did. Didn't you?' said Lom. He took a step towards them. 'You fucker. What have you *done*?'

'No,' said Ilinca quietly. 'Please. Don't.'

'So hit me,' said the Count, staring up into Lom's face. 'You are a violent man, I know this. Here.' He fumbled in his pocket and brought out an antique revolver. Holding it by the barrel, he offered the handle to Lom. 'There. Shoot me. You have a gun. Shoot me. I am ashamed of nothing. I did nothing you would not do. Nothing I would not do again a hundred times over for Ilinca's sake.'

Lom sank into a chair. He was weighed down with bleak despair. There was no strength, not even in his voice.

'Should I protect the Shaumian girl,' the Count was saying, 'at the price of my own wife's life? What was the Shaumian girl to us? There was a chance! She could have taken her place! She could have done her *duty*! For her family and her people. She could have *led* ... but she did not. She made her choice, and I made mine. For Ilinca's sake.'

'You saved your own skin,' said Lom.

'You think you can judge me, Vissarion Yppolitovich? Do you have a wife? No. You are a man alone. Judgement comes cheap for you.'

'They took her, didn't they?' said Lom. 'Last night. Hours ago. And you didn't tell me. You let me go out and search. All this time I wasted. You could have ... When did they come? Where did they take her?'

'No one was here,' said Ilinca. 'What you are saying, it did not happen. Sandu is not to blame.'

Lom stared at the Count.

'The girl is not here,' said Palffy. 'And you should please go too. You should get out of my house now.'

Lom stepped out into the street and started back down the hill towards the Purfas Gate. He would find Maroussia and get her back. He would do that. But he had no idea what to do or where to go. None at all. He needed to get out of the raion, that was his only clear thought.

He didn't hear the staff car until it pulled up at the kerb alongside him, engine running. A long-wheelbase black ZorKi Zavod limousine, six doors, twenty feet long, with high backswept fenders and a spare wheel mounted on the back. A small red and black pennant was flying on the bonnet. The driver wound down the window. A long faintly sad intelligent face. Antoninu Florian in the uniform of a captain of police. On the front passenger seat Lom could see a pair of leather driving gloves laid neatly on top of a road atlas. Beside them a peaked cap with a crisp wide circular crown. Staff officer issue. Lom couldn't see the badge.

Florian nodded to him. Gave him a faint weary smile, almost shy.

'I suggest you get in the back,' he said.

Lom peered in through the back windows. Two benches upholstered in comfortable burgundy leather. Carpet on the floor. Apart from Florian the car was empty.

'Hurry please,' said Florian. 'We have to make a start.'

'Maroussia is gone,' said Lom. 'They've taken her. I don't know where. I have to find her.'

'She is with Chazia,' said Florian. 'Get in the car.'

Lom barely heard what Florian said.

'I have to get her back,' said Lom again.

'Then will you for fuck's sake get in the back of the car like a good fellow and we can be on our way.'

Part Two

55

At four in the afternoon Antoninu Florian's stolen ZorKi Zavod limousine nosed down the hill and out of the raion through the Purfas Gate. Lom held the Blok 15 in his lap, hidden under the flap of his coat. Safety catch off. Florian showed a warrant card. The VKBD corporal leaned over to look into the back of the car. Lom faced front, eyes down, and tried to look bored.

'Stand aside, soldier,' said Florian. 'No questions. Nothing to see.'

The corporal waved them through.

Florian drove the ZorKi with practised smoothness through residential streets and garden squares. Railings and snow. Money houses, finial-ridged with gables and balconies and porches and garaging for cars, set back behind lawns and laurel hedges. The kind of places where bankers and high Vlast officials made their homes. It was a part of the city Lom hadn't seen before. Apart from a few horse-drawn droshkis and private karetas they had the roads to themselves. A gendarme in a kiosk on a street corner saluted them as they passed. Saluted the pennant. Florian nodded in acknowledgement, expressionless.

'I have to find Maroussia,' said Lom.

'I know,' said Florian. 'You said.'

'You know what happened to her? You know where she is?'

'Chazia sent an upyr last night,' said Florian. 'Its name was Bez. Bez Nichevoi. Bez found Maroussia and took her to the Lodka.'

'I should have been with her.'

'It's fortunate you were not.'

'I could have stopped it,' said Lom. 'I could have protected her.'

'No. You would be dead.'

Lom shrugged. 'Possibly.'

'Not possibly. Certainly.'

'You said its name was Bez.'

'Yes.'

'You said *was*.'

'It was a bad thing. It carried many deaths. I burned it.'

The car rolled past tall stuccoed houses. Cherry trees in gardens, leafless now. The snow had been swept from the pavements and piled along the kerb. Twisting on the polished leather bench, Lom could see behind them on the skyline a column of distant smoke drifting up and disappearing into low misty cloud.

'This isn't the way to the Lodka,' he said.

'No.'

Lom leaned forward. Jabbed the muzzle of the Blok 15 into Florian's neck.

'Then turn the fucking car around.'

Florian sighed and pulled in, ploughing the ZorKi's passenger-side fender deep into a heaped-up ridge of snow on the side of the road.

'Don't look back,' said Lom. 'Keep your hands where I can see them. On the wheel.'

Florian did as he was told.

'Where are we going?' said Lom. 'Where are you taking me? We have to get to the Lodka. That's where Maroussia is.'

'No,' said Florian quietly. 'Maroussia was in the Lodka, but now she is not. The Vlast is abandoning Mirgorod to the Archipelago. The government is relocating eastwards to Kholvatogorsk, but Chazia is going further, to Novaya Zima with the Pollandore, and she is taking Maroussia with her. Their train will have left by now. The journey will not be straightforward: it will take them many days, perhaps a week, perhaps more. We also, as you may have observed, are travelling east and we will be quicker. Much quicker. We will reach Novaya Zima before Chazia's train and we will have time to prepare before they arrive. So unless you have a better plan, please be so good as to stop waving your dick around in the back of my car.'

'How do you know all this?' said Lom.

'I was in the Lodka last night.'

'You were in the *Lodka*?'

'She is alive,' said Florian. 'Beyond that, I cannot say, but she is alive, depend on it. Chazia will preserve her. The upyr took her. It did not kill her.'

'Then we have to find that train.'

Florian shook his head.

'The train they are travelling on is also carrying an extraordinary cargo. It will go by a special route prepared in advance under conditions of extreme secrecy. We have no chance of catching up with it before it reaches its destination. But even if we could … It is a military train. An armoured train. Soldiers. A mudjhik. A well guarded mobile prison. No. My plan is better. Come with me.'

'Come with you?' said Lom. 'Who the fuck *are* you? Why would I trust a single thing you've said?'

Florian twisted in his seat and pushed Lom's gun aside.

'There is no time for this,' he said, locking eyes with Lom. His irises were green, flecked with amber. 'Come with me to Novaya Zima, Vissarion. Together we will do what needs to be done. Or get out of the car now, if you think you can do better alone.'

Lom stared into Florian's face. He wished he could read something more in those deep, wise, dangerous eyes, but he could not. He had to make a choice, but it was no choice, not really. He sank back into the wide leather bench and slipped the Blok 15 into the pocket of his coat.

'OK,' he said. 'OK. Drive.'

56

Florian picked up the main route east. The outskirts of Mirgorod diminished to a tideline of subsistence enterprise – one-shed factories, workshops and junkyards, semi-collapsed smallholdings – but the road was getting more crowded, not less, and all the traffic was going in one direction. Away from the city. There were a few trucks and one or two private saloons, but mostly it was horse-drawn wagons and carts and nameless antiquated things hauled by donkeys and bullocks. There were whole families just walking, pushing prams and handcarts, lugging duffel bags, dragging suitcases along the ground, wearing layers upon layers of clothing to keep warm and leave room in the bags for more. The polished black staff car with its Vlast pennant drew hostile glares. From time to time somebody thumped the coachwork or spat on a window. Florian drove in silence, drumming his fingers on the wheel.

It took them hours to get clear. At last the traffic thinned out and Florian gunned the throttle. They were on the open road east of Mirgorod, skirting the southern shore of Lake Dorogha. It was just after six but twilight was already closing in.

'Tell me about Novaya Zima,' said Lom.

Florian tossed the road atlas onto the back seat.

'Follow the Zelenny mountains north,' he said. 'You'll find it.'

Lom found Mirgorod and started turning pages. Page after page eastward from where they were, the country was a flat expanse of pale green, spattered with small blue lakes and the hairline threads of rivers. The atlas was a Solon and Dutke *Standard & Comprehensive*: the best you could buy, which wasn't saying much. Only the largest towns and cities were shown, their names in florid black-letter script.

There were a few highways picked out in pink, but citizens of the Vlast didn't make long journeys by road. They used the slow looping sweeps of the waterways or, if they could afford it, the transcontinental trains. Most roads weren't even shown, and those that were mapped weren't necessarily there, or still maintained, or even passable. The same went for the railways.

Even the map-green of the empty landscape was optimistic. It belied featureless horizons of sandy soil and scrubby grassland, or the silent monotony of birch and moss. If green on a map meant anything, it meant *flat*. For thousands of miles east from Mirgorod nothing rose more than a few hundred feet above sea level. Not until you reached the Zelenny Mountains, a third of the way between the city and the edge of the endless forest. On the map the Zelenny range was a north–south spine of taupe-shaded contours, but in reality they were scarcely mountains at all, just a spine of uplands slightly too elevated, distinctive and topographically important to be called merely hills. The spine of the Zelenny ran north all the way to the coast and continued out across the water, becoming two long thin islands hooked into the belly of the Yarmskoye Sea like a crooked skeletal finger. The south island was contoured taupe, the north island was the blank and featureless white of year-round ice, and adrift in the sea near the islands was a name in the smallest and faintest typeface that Solon and Dutke ran to: NOVAYA ZIMA.

'That's it?' said Lom. 'That's where Chazia is going?'

'Yes,' said Florian.

'It's nowhere. Why the hell would Chazia go to a place like that?'

'That's what I want to know,' said Florian. 'A couple of years ago the Armaments Minister, Dukhonin, started spending money on his own initiative. He was Vlast Commissar for Industry then, but this was a private venture: secretive appropriations, diverted funds, nothing accounted for. He requisitioned building materials, heavy machinery, oil, coal. And it was all for Novaya Zima. He flooded the place with tens of thousands of conscript workers.

'And then, while the heavy labour was still flowing in, Dukhonin started recruiting persons of a different kind: managers, architects, doctors, teachers. He collected specialists. Engineers. Chemists. Mathematicians. Astronomers. Physical scientists of every conceivable discipline. And always the best. Outstanding in their discipline.

I say *recruiting*, but it's a euphemism of course. Some of the people Dukhonin sent to Novaya Zima were zeks, prisoners he pulled out from other camps. In other cases bespoke arrests were made, and an eminent few were simply invited, though it was always made clear to them that refusal was not an option. And no one he sent north has ever come back. None of them has ever been heard from again. No communication comes out of Novaya Zima. None at all.'

'So what is he doing up there?' said Lom. 'It sounds like he's building a *city*. But why build a city up there? It's thousands of miles from anywhere.'

'I don't know,' said Florian. 'I've been combing the archives for weeks, and I've found out some of what's been sent up there, but as to why ... there is no indication, none at all. And Dukhonin is dead now.'

'I read about that in the paper,' said Lom. 'Josef Kantor killed him.'

'Yes,' said Florian. 'Perhaps it was Kantor. Maybe.'

'What do you mean, maybe?'

'It is something of a coincidence, don't you think?'

Lom felt his irritation rising again. He wished Florian wouldn't play games.

'What?' he said. 'What's a coincidence?'

'Dukhonin dies and the very next day Chazia sets off for Novaya Zima with Maroussia Shaumian in tow.'

'You think Chazia killed him?' said Lom.

'It is not unlikely, certainly. And there is something else.'

Florian hesitated again.

'For fuck's sake,' said Lom. '*What* else?'

'Perhaps you have heard someone speak already of the Pollandore? Perhaps Maroussia Shaumian has mentioned this to you?'

'Yes,' said Lom cautiously. 'I've heard of it.'

'The extraordinary cargo to which I referred a moment ago,' said Florian. 'The cargo on Chazia's train? It is the Pollandore.'

Lom's stomach lurched. He felt his skin prickle. A chill in his spine.

'Shit,' he breathed. 'Shit. What the hell is Chazia up to?'

'I don't know,' said Florian. 'But you see now? You understand why I came for you? Why I think we should join forces?'

An hour later twilight was thickening into night. Florian flicked on the headlamps. They were passing through level country, undrained and undyked, a patchwork of woodland and shallow lakes and reed beds. The beams splashed off scrubby birch trees and alders, vegetable patches and makeshift fences, stands of hogweed. From time to time a weathered wooden cabin rose out of the darkness and disappeared behind them.

Lom had been turning over what Florian had told him. He didn't doubt it, not really, but it didn't make sense: the more he thought about it, the less it fitted together, and a big part of the puzzle was Florian himself. Who was he? What was he? What was he keeping back? He glanced at Florian's shadowy profile.

'You can't drive a car all the way to Novaya Zima,' said Lom, remembering the thousands of miles of empty green on the map. 'It isn't possible. You need to tell me where we're going.'

'Still you do not trust me, Vissarion?' said Florian patiently. 'We are going to Novaya Zima, but not by car. We are making for a small lake called Chudsk, but we will not reach it for some hours yet. Why don't you get some sleep?'

'I don't need to sleep. You could let me drive for while.'

Florian hesitated.

'Sure,' he said. 'Fine.'

Florian brought the car to a stop, killed the engine and dropped his hands off the wheel with a sigh. When he cut the headlamps and wound down the window, an immense silence rolled in around them, and with it the smell of damp earth and cold night air. Tiny night sounds could be heard above the ticking of the cooling engine: the wind moving across grass and snow, the nearby trickle of water, the shriek of a fox. Lom got out and walked round to get in behind the wheel. Florian slid across into the front passenger seat.

'Thank you,' said Florian. 'I am tired. Just keep straight on. There's only the one road: you just need to make sure you don't turn off onto any farm tracks.' He settled back in his seat and closed his eyes.

Lom started the engine and pulled away.

'Florian?' he said.

Florian stirred reluctantly and opened his eyes.

'Yes?' he said.

'You need to tell me how you know what you know. You need to tell me who you are.'

'Who I am? In what sense, exactly? Are we discussing allegiances here? Sides? Motivations?'

'Sure,' said Lom. 'Absolutely. For a start.'

'I am ...' He paused, choosing his words carefully. 'I am ... freelance.'

'*Freelance*?'

'Uh-huh.'

'*Uh-huh?*' said Lom. 'You care to expand on that? Because you need to.'

Florian settled lower in the passenger seat and closed his eyes again. Lom thought he wasn't going to say any more, but after a while he started speaking quietly.

'You think I am playing games with you, Vissarion? OK. Maybe. But *really*. You should *look* at yourself. You are angry, and you ask me what I am? You? You, who have that marvellous, that wonderful, that unique and beautiful opening in your head? You sit there and it's spilling out ... shedding ... you don't know *what*, you're not even *aware* ... and you ask *me* to say what *I* am?'

'What do you mean?' said Lom. 'What are you trying to say?'

Florian half opened his eyes and glanced sideways.

'I think you should stop asking yourself what things are and start asking what they can become. I think you should work at yourself. I think you should, to coin a phrase, get a fucking grip.'

57

Colonel-General Rizhin put aside the name of Josef Kantor and the life he'd lived under that name without a backward glance. He killed Kantor without compunction or regret. *There is no past, there is only the future.* Commissar for Mirgorod city defence.

Rizhin began to *work*.

He had an appetite and capacity for work that were astonishing. Relentless. Prodigious. Terrifying. The more he worked the more energy he drew from it and the more work he did. No detail was trivial, no obstacle immovable. He had a nose for men and women whose capacity for work matched his, or almost, and he gathered them about him. Put them to work. Those that flagged or showed the slightest inclination to cling to a private life of their own (the very phrase an abomination in Rizhin's lexicon) were ruthlessly obliterated.

And Rizhin's work was war, his purpose victory.

Within hours of the departure of Chazia, Fohn and Khazar, the pyre outside the Lodka was extinguished. The number of recruitment booths doubled. That very afternoon, he told the people of Mirgorod what to expect. He broadcast on the radio, on the tannoys and loudspeakers. The film was played in cinemas and converted Kino-trams, over and over again. Incessantly. The text appeared that evening in special editions of all the newspapers. Every paper carried the same photograph of Rizhin's gaunt, smiling, pockmarked face. By the evening it had appeared on posters in every public building, on every tram, on every city wall. Yesterday the people of the city might have been asking, who is this Rizhin? Today they knew.

He called the city to war, a war against two enemies: outside the city were the forces of the Archipelago, and inside the city were the diversionists, the traitors, the looters, the spies. It wasn't two wars, it was one war fought on two fronts, and there was nothing that was not part of it. No bystanders. No noncombatants. No civilians.

'At last,' he told the people of Mirgorod, 'we are coming to grips with our most vicious and perfidious enemy The fiends and cannibals of the Archipelago, the slavers, are bearing down on our city. And they have accomplices among us! Whiners. Cowards. Deserters. Panic mongers. Spies. Saboteurs. Traitors!

'The enemy's soldiers and their secret allies must be rooted out and destroyed at every step. This is no ordinary war. Not a war of soldiers but a war of all the people. Everyone and everything is at war! Total war! Our homes are not our own, our dreams are not our own. Our lives are not our own. There is only one life, the Vlast, and only one outcome is possible. Overwhelming triumph!

'Everything must be mobilised, all that we are. Private lives do not exist. Every man, woman and child is a soldier of the Vlast. We will fall upon our enemies as one body, an irresistible mass, roaring defiance, destruction and death with a single voice. With the angels on our side we will certainly prevail. All the strength of the people must be used to smash the enemy. Onward to victory!'

In the cinemas and in the squares the people of Mirgorod broke into spontaneous cheering. The death of the Novozhd had left them adrift, afraid and grieving, but here was a leader again, come in their desperate hour.

Rizhin.

His face was everywhere, and his words.

Onward to victory!

58

Elena Cornelius was working in the Apraksin when she heard from a customer about the forced evacuation of the Raion Lezaryet. She closed the counter immediately and went as fast as she could to the school, desperate to be with her daughters, to see them safe, but when she got there she found the teachers reluctant to let her take the girls away.

'Our instructions are to keep them all together here,' the headmaster said, 'until the trucks come. They will all be taken to a place of safety, far away from the bombs. The whole school is to go, we teachers also. We don't know yet where we are going, but we are excited about this great adventure and so are the children. It is best for them, don't you think? I would think you would be pleased for them, Elena Cornelius. Your girls will be safer with us.'

'I am their mother and I will keep them safe,' said Elena Cornelius. 'Not you. Me. They are coming with me now.'

'But—'

'I am their *mother* and you will not stop me taking them.'

'On your own responsibility, then,' the headmaster said. 'I wash my hands of them. Don't come crying to me later, and do not expect to bring Yeva and Galina back to this school again when the war is over.'

Elena did not return to Count Palffy's house in the raion – all their possessions, their home, the workshop, it was all lost to them now – but she went instead with her daughters to her aunt Lyudmila Markova, who had a one-room apartment in Big Side. Aunt Lyudmila had never married. She kept a caged parakeet for company and was reluctant to take in her niece and two girls as well.

'But there's only the one bed, Elena! Where would you sleep?'

'On the floor. I'll buy a mattress.'

'I don't know, Elena. That doesn't sound comfortable for the girls, and Bolto doesn't like change. It unsettles him. He doesn't like strangers coming in and out. He has his own little ways.' Bolto was the parakeet.

'We are not *strangers*, Aunt,' said Elena. 'And I've got a hundred roubles at the workshop. You'll be glad of the help when the war comes. Things will get expensive.'

'All this talk of war, I don't like it, Elena. It's nonsense. The Novozhd won't let anything happen to Mirgorod.'

'The Novozhd is dead, Aunt. The enemy is coming. There'll be more bombing. There may be fighting.'

'Oh no, not here. I don't think so. They wouldn't dare. Why don't you just go home and wait till it all blows over? Bolto and I will be fine.'

'I can't go home. Everyone in the raion is being taken away on trains and nobody knows where to.'

'I thought you were doing well at the Apraksin, Elena? I thought they liked you there? You've always said—'

'It's not to do with the Apraksin, Aunt. It's everyone.'

In the end Aunt Lyudmila relented.

'Just for a couple of days, Elena, until you get yourself settled. I must say I'm disappointed in Count Palffy; it's very shoddy behaviour to put you out like this. You don't expect it, not from an aristocrat. The Novozhd always said they were enemies of the people.'

When she heard Rizhin's broadcast on Aunt Lyudmila's radio, Elena Cornelius knew she had to do something. She could not go to the raion again, she could not go back to the Apraksin and she could not simply hide away in her aunt's apartment. Sooner or later she would be found and questions would be asked. The girls had to be safer than that. She had to do what she could to protect them. Immediately. That meant she had to have a role. She had to have a place. She had to have a story.

'This new man, Rizhin,' said Aunt Lyudmila. 'He sounds like a strong man. He'll sort out this nonsense about a war.'

That same evening Elena went to the Labour Deployment Office and filled in a form. Where it said address, she put Aunt Lyudmila's apartment in Big Side. She waited in line for two hours and handed the form to a woman at a desk.

'My name is Elena Schmitt,' she said.

'Would I be in this job if I couldn't read?'

'No,' said Elena. 'Of course not.'

The woman studied the form carefully. She had close-cropped fair hair and colourless eyes in a dry, sunless face, striated with fine lines. She must have been about forty. Her fawn uniform blouse was fresh and spotless. Crisp epaulettes. Sharp creases down the outside edge of her sleeves. Elena thought that, close to, she would smell of laundry. The woman pulled out a file and paged through sheets and sheets of typescript.

'This is your address?'

'Yes. Well, it is my aunt's apartment. I live with her.'

'How long?'

'I'm sorry? I don't understand?'

'How long have you lived there?'

'Two years.'

'You're not listed at that address.'

'I came to Mirgorod two years ago,' said Elena. 'To work at Blue's. Before that I lived with my parents. At Narymsk, and before that Tuga. Look, I want to work, citizen. I want to do something. For the city.'

'So. And what can you do, Elena Schmitt?'

'I am a carpenter. I have my own tools. I have a school certificate in mathematics and a diploma in bookkeeping.'

'Can you dig?'

'What?'

'Can you dig? Can you use a pick and a spade?'

'I make furniture. Cupboards. Wardrobes.'

'When the Archipelago tanks arrive, should we put them away in a cupboard?'

'No. But surely—'

'There is a requirement for more workers on the inner defence line. People who can dig. Can you dig frozen soil with your fingers on a quarter-pound of black bread a day?'

'If that is what the city requires of me then I will try, citizen. I will do my best.'

The woman filled in some details on a pink card, stamped it with an official stamp and gave it to her.

'Report at six o'clock tomorrow morning.'

Aunt Lyudmila had already gone to bed when Elena Cornelius got back to the apartment, and the girls were asleep together on the floor, curled up under an eiderdown on cushions from the couch. Elena found a packet of tea in the cupboard, boiled a kettle on the paraffin stove and made herself a pot. The label on the tea packet had a drawing of ladies in high lacy collars with a samovar on a tablecloth, and underneath was written in curly script:

What follows after taking tea?
The resurrection of the dead.

It was an old saying, some kind of joke or pun. It was traditional. Elena had always wondered what it meant.

She sat in a wicker chair in the window, the curtains drawn back, a blanket wrapped round her shoulders. It was too cold to sleep. The moons bathed the city in a bone-white glare, monochrome and alien. Mirgorod looked like the capital of some other planet. Silent search-light beams swept the skyline and flashed across the soft silver hulls of barrage balloons. A remembered phrase from childhood came into her mind and would not leave. *The beneficence of angels.*

At midnight the Archipelago bombers came. Tiny bright anti-aircraft shells crackled and flowered briefly in the dark. Searchlights slashed at the raiders but didn't hold what they caught. Within an hour huge fires were burning on the horizon. Elena watched flames lick high into the air: arches and caverns, sheets and waterfalls of flame. Whirling flame tornadoes. Hurricanes of fire. It was all happening several miles away. She imagined she could feel the heat of the fires against her face, though she could not.

59

L om had never driven anything like a ZorKi Zavod limousine before. He liked it. Eight cylinders, automatic transmission, the flat empty road at night. He pressed his foot down and watched the needle climb smoothly to fifty. The car must have weighed a couple of tons, but the engine scarcely rose above a quiet purr. The bonnet stretched ahead of him like the boiler of a locomotive, pennant flickering. All he had to do was keep his foot on the throttle and his hand on the wheel and follow the patch of lamplit road that skimmed ahead of him, always just beyond arrival. Except for the interior of the car, smelling of leather and polish, and the splash of lamplight on the road, there was nothing anywhere but blackness under a vast black sky. Forward motion without visible result. He kept the window open an inch to let the wind touch his face. When small snowflakes began to speckle the windscreen he found the switch for the wipers and set them sweeping back and forth: a quiet click at the end of each cycle, clearing twin arcs in the sparse accumulating snow.

Lom put his hand to his forehead and felt for the lozenge-shaped wound socket. It was just the right size to accommodate the tip of his forefinger. He touched the smooth newness of young skin covering the uneven rim of cut skullbone, soft-edged and painless. It was a blind third eye, pulsing faintly with the restful rhythms of his beating heart, a life sign, part of him now, absorbed, healed, no longer conspicuous. A mark of freedom. A badge of honour. A legacy of ancient hurt. When he took his finger away he could feel the coolness of the wind pressing against the place with gentle insistence. A nudge of conscience. A memory just beyond the frontier of recollection.

Hours passed. The road stretched on ahead, drifting slightly to right and left. The ZorKi swept along at a steady fifty miles an hour. Villages rose ahead and fell behind. Mostly they were too small for names: just clusters of buildings glimpsed and gone, straggling settlements barely registering against the emptiness. No lights showed: they might as well have been deserted. The needle on the fuel gauge had been creeping round to the left all night, and now it was ominously close to empty. Lom pulled up and got out to relieve himself. Legs and back stiff from the long drive, he walked self-consciously a few yards off the road to a scrubby stand of brush at the foot of a telegraph pole. When he got back to the car, Florian was awake, easing himself upright and rubbing his face

'Where are we?' he said.

'We came through Zharovsk a while back,' said Lom. He looked at his watch. It was coming up towards three in the morning. 'We're running short of fuel.'

'There's more in the back.'

Florian went round to the boot of the car, opened it and dragged out a couple of jerrycans. He found a funnel and began to fill the tank. When he'd done, he stowed the empty cans. Then he brought out a suitcase and changed his uniform for a neat and sober suit, produced his astrakhan hat and chucked the officer's cap on the back seat.

'I'll drive from here,' he said.

An hour or so later Florian slowed the car at a crossroads and turned off the highway onto a rough track between trees. There was no sign: nothing to mark the turning. The woods closed in around them and the ZorKi was suddenly bouncing and slithering through soft rutted mud. Florian handled the car effortlessly.

Eventually, the track emerged abruptly onto the edge of a lake and turned left to follow it. The road, if you could call it that, was almost too narrow for the car. On the driver's side trees pressed in close and overhanging branches clattered and scraped against the windows. To the right the crazily jolting headlamps showed glimpses of a narrow strip of muddy shore: scraps of low mist and the carbon glitter of black water.

They swung round the end of a narrow headland and climbed a slight rise. As they crested the rise, a low wooden building appeared in front of them. It looked halfway between a cabin and a barn. There was a jetty, and a small seaplane moored on the water.

Florian pulled the car in close to the edge of a low stone wharf and killed the engine. On Lom's side there was a three-foot drop to the water. He could hear the quiet lapping of water against stone, the wind in the trees, the breathy wheezing of disturbed waterfowl.

'Wait here,' said Florian. He left the door open and walked towards the building, taking care to stay clearly visible in the glare of the headlamps. 'Lyuba!' he called into the darkness. 'Lyuba! It's Florian!'

A woman's voice answered from the darkness, 'You're late. You said yesterday.'

The voice didn't come from the building, but from somewhere away to the left under the trees. Lom realised that Florian had been facing that way before she spoke. He'd known where she was, out there in the dark.

'There was some delay leaving Mirgorod,' Florian said. 'But I am here now. Is everything ready?'

'There's someone else in the car.'

'A friend. He's travelling with me.'

'You didn't say anything about passengers.'

'Is there a problem?'

'Passengers are extra. The deal didn't include passengers.'

'Of course. Can we discuss this inside? We've come a long way.'

The woman stepped out into the headlamps' glare. She was short and solidly built: not fat, but heavy, and wearing a bulky dark knitted sweater, the kind seamen favoured. Thick curly hair spilled out from under a peaked seaman's cap.

She was carrying a shotgun loosely in the crook of her arm.

Lom got out of the car.

'This is Vissarion,' said Florian. 'Vissarion Lom. Lyuba Gretskaya.'

Gretskaya looked him up and down.

'OK,' she said. 'If you say so.'

Florian took a satchel from the boot of the ZorKi.

'Anything of yours in the car?' he said to Lom.

Lom leaned into the back, picked up his woollen cap and crammed it down on his head.

'No,' he said. 'Nothing.'

Florian reached in and released the handbrake, leaned his right shoulder against the car and, with his hand on the steering wheel, turned it slowly to the right and pushed it off the edge of the wharf.

When the front wheels went over, the fenders crashed and scraped on the stonework. The headlamps dipped below the surface and spilled murky subaqueous yellow-green light. Florian flicked them off and gave a heave with his shoulder that levered the whole massive car, all two tons of it, up and forward. The limousine plunged off the edge of the wharf into the lake, leaving oily swirls of disturbance.

60

Lyuba Gretskaya lived in a single room that did her as a workshop and a kitchen. It smelled of pine and tobacco and engine oil. There was a single bed along one wall. A metal cot piled with blankets. Maps and charts. Racks of hand tools. A lathe.

'Breakfast, gentlemen?'

Lom realised he hadn't eaten for almost twenty-four hours.

'Yes,' he said. 'Please. That would be great.'

He watched Gretskaya cut thick slices off a piece of bacon and fry them on an oil stove in the corner. Her face, lit by a single lamp hung above the stove, was broad and round and weathered to a dark polished brown, with a small stub of a nose. Her bright small eyes were a pale, pale grey, almost lost in the creases of her face.

'Is that your own plane?' he said for something to say.

'Yup,' said Gretskaya, not looking round.

'Where did you learn to fly?'

'Where did you learn to ask questions?'

Lom caught Florian's eye. He was trying not to smile.

'OK,' said Lom. 'Sorry. Just making conversation.'

The bacon was nearly done. Gretskaya threw some chunks of black bread into the pan to fry in the bacon fat and made a pot of coffee. They ate in silence, rapidly, and when they'd finished she cleared the plates, spread out a chart out on the yellow deal table and lit a cigarette. Her fingers were stubby and brown and stained with oil.

'The Kotik will do eight hundred miles on a single tank,' she said. 'We cover more ground if the wind's with us, less if it's not. Maximum speed is one three five, but for efficient cruising I don't go much over a hundred. With a safety margin, that gives us, say, five or six hours airtime before we need to refuel.' She jabbed at the chart with her cigarette, spilling ash. Brushed it away. 'The first leg is straightforward. North-east to Slensk. Refill at the pier head. From Slensk, we have a choice.' She sketched out the options on the chart. 'We can follow the coast to Garshal – see that island there? There's a whaling station, I've used it before – or we follow the river inland' – she traced the course of the Northern Kholomora with her finger – 'and stop at the portage head at Terrimarkh. We'll decide which course to take when we get to Slensk. It'll depend on the weather, mainly: maybe we'll be able to get a forecast at Slensk. Either way, from Garshal or Terrimarkh it's a five-hundred-mile hop to Novaya Zima. I'll have you there tomorrow afternoon.'

Florian lifted the satchel onto the table, undid the buckles and pulled out thumbed and grubby bundles of ten-rouble notes.

'A thousand,' he said. 'I think that's what we agreed.'

'Plus a passenger.'

'So? How much?'

Gretskaya glanced at Lom. 'Has he got travel papers?'

'No—' Lom began.

'Sure,' said Florian. He threw a passport across the table towards him. 'Here. Name of Vexhav. Stanil Vexhav, age thirty-three. You're a former policeman interested in setting up as a timber merchant. But only if anyone asks. Don't volunteer information about yourself. People with nothing to hide don't do that.'

Lom picked up the passport and turned the pages. It looked convincing. The green cover was creased and stained with use, and its pages were spattered with the internal visas and crossing marks of a man who'd been travelling the rivers and ports of the north for the last couple of years. His own face looked out at him, the version of two or three years ago, stern and monochrome, eyes hooded with fatigue. Hair flopped across his forehead to obscure the angel seal.

'You got a photograph of me?'

'It's not you. It's me.'

Lom glanced across at Gretskaya.

'Don't mind me,' she said. 'He pays. I fly. Another two fifty for the passenger,' she said to Florian. 'And you pay to fill the tanks. Also other expenses.'

'Expenses?'

'We'll need to eat. Maybe sleep. Maybe bribe a harbour clerk here and there.'

Florian made a sour face but nodded and counted out the money without protest.

'When do we start?' said Lom.

Gretskaya ignored him. She gathered up the roubles, disappeared with them into a back room and came back with an armful of leather jackets, sheepskin gloves, fur hats, scarves.

'Put these on,' she said. 'It's going to be cold.'

Gretskaya went ahead and turned on the cockpit lamp and the navigation lights. Lom recognised the aircraft: he'd seen one like it moored at the Yannis boatyard in Podchornok. It was a Beriolev Kotik biplane, the clumsy reliable workhorse of the northern lakes. The boat-shaped hull, dented and water-stained, wasn't much bigger than the ZorKi limousine. Beneath the centre of the upper wing was a single stumpy engine nacelle, its two-bladed wooden propeller facing backwards. The lower wings stuck out from behind the cockpit, a canoe-shaped stabilising float slung beneath each one. The wings looked feeble, like arms raised in surrender or despair, like they'd snap off under the weight of the fuselage. Lom remembered the immense sleek bombers of the Archipelago roaring low across Mirgorod. Machines from a different world.

Florian clambered up into the cockpit and ducked down into the cabin behind.

'He always travels below deck,' said Gretskaya. 'Straps himself in and keeps his eyes screwed shut. You take the co-pilot seat.'

She swarmed neatly up the side of the hull and over the windscreen. Lom followed awkwardly and squeezed himself into the tight space beside her. The cockpit was crude and industrial: lime-green steel with canvas bucket seats. No concessions. In front of the pilot's seat was a flat black panel of gauges, dials, knobs and switches, and a small three-quarter wheel on a green steel column thick as an arm. Gretskaya taped several layers of red cellophane across the cockpit lamp, dimming the interior to near darkness, made a few adjustments to her instruments, then stood up in her seat so she could reach behind to start the engine. It burst into life with a reek of oil and smoke. The whole airframe began to vibrate.

Gretskaya slid the cockpit canopy forward and closed them in.

'You flown before?' she said, pulling on her gloves.

'No.'

'Don't touch anything. If you feel like you're going to puke, well, don't.'

'I'll be fine,' said Lom.

Gretskaya opened the throttle and eased the plane away from the jetty, swinging its nose to point across dark open water. Lom looked at his watch. It was half past five. Still three hours to dawn.

The engine bellowed and the machine surged forward, bumped two or three times as it hit the swell, and then ... nothing. It took Lom a moment to realise they were airborne. Gretskaya pulled back sharply on the column. Lom's weight pressed him back into his seat as the Kotik, trembling with the surge of its engines, its airframe creaking alarmingly, climbed steeply into darkness. While they were still pushing upwards at a steep angle, Gretskaya took her hands off the stick and gripped it between her knees. She tested the lamps and added another layer of red cellophane. She saw Lom watching her and grinned.

'Night vision,' she said. 'Don't want to be dazzled by the interior lights. Don't worry, there's nothing up here to crash into.'

Lom grunted and stared out of the side window. The ground below was a broadening, sliding patchwork of barely legible darkness: the foggy glimmer of the lake and the spreading inky absolute blackness of trees, threaded by a dim paler line that must have been the road they came in by. A sudden flash of light outside the starboard window at his shoulder startled him. It was followed by another longer flash, a flicker, and then a trail of intermittent, vaporous brightness was streaming backwards from the wingtip lamp, which until then had been invisible under the wing. The temperature dropped precipitously and the landscape below them disappeared. Lom realised they were flying into cloud. The plane lurched sideways, caught in turbulence. Gretskaya steadied her and kept on climbing. As they reached the upper fringes of the cloud the wingtip lights seemed to flash on and off again, more and more rapidly, and suddenly vanished.

They emerged into clear dark space. Above them, drifts and scarves of stars glittered in blackness. The moons on the horizon illuminated the oceanic cloud below and pinned the tiny aeroplane to it with a bitter mineral glare.

Gretskaya levelled off, balancing the Kotik by gyroscope. Wrapped in the cockpit's companionable little pocket of blood-red dimness, Lom watched the thin radium line of the artificial horizon rise and settle. The dials on the instrument panel breathed slowly. The engine quietened and the aircraft droned onwards, chasing its own mist-haloed shadow on the cloud below. The sky above the clouds was a beautiful, desolate, endless, frontierless world.

Lom had felt the beautiful ache of immensity before – a silent afternoon in a train crawling across continental moss, a night walk among birch trees in the Dominions of the Vlast. Simplification. Purification. Humbling. The mortification of the self. But never anything like this. Never anything to compare with these dangerous, darkly shining, planetary, abyssal eternities. *Up with the moons the angels swam.* Words he hadn't heard since childhood rose up out of the accumulated silt in the bottom of his mind and tugged at him like rusalkas pawing a tiring swimmer. Trying to grab his attention. Trying to pull him under.

What you must do, said Baba Roga, is climb down inside the hollow tree until you come to a cave. Inside the cave there are three doors. If you open the first door, you will find a dog with eyes the size of dinner plates, guarding a treasure of copper. If you open the second door, you will find a dog with eyes the size of millstones, guarding a treasure of gold. And if you open the third door, you will find a dog with eyes the size of moons, guarding a treasure of blood and earth. What do you think of that, my beautiful boy?

I think the eyes of the dogs are moons, Provost. And the dogs are angels. All angels are terrible.

And all the rusalkas had Maroussia's face.

Images of Maroussia crowded his mind. Maroussia's dark serious eyes. Maroussia walking straight-backed away from him down the street. Maroussia's cold work-reddened hands. Maroussia asleep, breathing in the dark. The scent of her hair. The brush of her face against his cheek. Maroussia tied to an iron chair and Chazia leaning over her, running her tongue across her lower lip in concentration. Chazia with a knife in her hand.

61

Lavrentina Chazia watched the Shaumian girl return slowly to consciousness. She stirred. Groaned. Opened her eyes. Vomited. Tried to sit up and vomited again. Her eyes were confused. Unfocused. Whatever Bez Nichevoi had done to subdue her, it had left her feeble, trembling and feverish. No matter. There was time now. Plenty of time.

Chazia had propped her up against the wall of the otherwise empty freight car. Her wrists were cuffed with leather bands, connected by chains to a bar bolted to the floor. The chains, no more than dog leashes really, were long enough for her to move but not to stand. In her present condition she could not have stood unaided anyway. Chazia squatted beside her and held out a cup of water.

'Here,' she said. 'Drink.'

The girl shook her head.

Chazia smiled. 'You think I want to poison you?' she said. 'Of course I don't.' She drank the cup herself. 'Look, it's fine.' She poured another. 'Please. Drink. You need it. I don't know what Bez did to you, but I apologise for it. I'm sure it was both unnecessary and unpleasant.'

This time the girl took the cup and swallowed the water in one gulp. Choked and coughed half of it back out, soaking her chest. She leaned back against the rough plank wall. The freight car swayed as it rounded a curve.

'Where am I?' she said. 'This is a train.'

Chazia poured another cup.

'Take your time,' she said. 'There's plenty more. And food, when you're ready.' She took a handkerchief from her pocket and held it out to her. 'Here. Clean yourself.'

The girl shook her head.

'I am Commander Chazia, but you should call me Lavrentina. We are going to be friends.'

'I know who you are. And we are not friends.'

'No,' said Chazia. 'Perhaps not exactly friends. Associates, then. Colleagues. We have something in common.'

'No. We don't.'

'Of course we do. Together we are going to open the Pollandore.'

Maroussia Shaumian sank back against the wall and closed her eyes.

62

The stars spilled across the sky like salt on the blade of an axe. The broken moons sank away, subsiding into the horizon, leaving the cloud floor dark. Erasing it. The Kotik hung suspended over nothing at all. Only the vibration of the hull suggested, despite appearances, forward motion. Silent and freezing in their dimmed red cockpit, Lom and Gretskaya might as well have been crossing interplanetary space.

And then the world began to separate. Muted discriminations of darkness and lesser darkness. A new sedimentary horizon silting out. A dark line dividing the clouds below from the sky above. The line seemed to be getting further away, as if the aircraft was going backwards. Or shrinking. The last stars swam and trembled, dissolving.

The sky grew grey like the clouds but cleaner, deeper and more still. The banks of vapour beneath the plane thickened and the sky thinned and dilated into purple then green then white then pale immensities of blue. A fingernail of misty brilliance just starboard of the Kotik's nose became an arc of fire, burning steadily at the clouds' rim, pulsing incandescent blazing bars of pink and gold. And then the world was blue and clean and empty and went on for ever, oceans of air above dazzling oceans of cloud. Air that was filled to the brim with an astonishing purity of bright and perfect light. Simplified, wordless, unmappable. Lom felt the coldness of it burn his face. He looked across at Gretskaya.

'How high are we?'

She tapped the altimeter with a stubby gloved finger. The needle rested steadily at 10,000 feet. Lom did the maths.

'That's almost two *miles*,' he said.

Gretskaya grinned.

'You want to go higher?' she said. 'We'll go higher.'

She pulled back on the stick. Lom felt the pressure again in the small of his back. Up and up the tiny aircraft climbed – 12,000 – 14,000 – 16,000 – 18,000 – into a rarefied indigo world. Lom was aware of the air growing thinner. Sparser. It was more difficult to fill his lungs. His pulse rate quickened. He felt it fluttering in the centre of his forehead.

The air grew thinner but the light did not. Every detail of the cockpit and the wings at his shoulder burned itself on Lom's retinas with crystal clarity. Every fold and scuff on the sleeve of his leather jacket was magnified, brilliant and intense. The jacket was translucent. Inside the sleeves, every fine hair on his arms glistened. His skin itself was translucent. The light shone through him like the sun seen through leaves. The organs of his body were sunlit pink and clear. His veins, his bones, his lungs sang with light. He wasn't breathing air, he was breathing illumination.

More slowly now, but still the machine bored upwards. At last the altimeter registered 20,000 feet, and the nose of the machine sank a little until it was on an even keel. Gretskaya gave him the thumbs up and settled back in her seat. Urging on three tons of vibrating metal with her shoulders. Her eyes, creased almost shut against the over-brimming of the light, had seemed grey in the lamplight of her cabin but now they were the same clear clean watery blue as the sky.

Lom searched on the instrument panel for the compass and found it. The needle was pointing steadily north-east. Four miles below, at the bottom of a crevasse in the clouds, he glimpsed the glitter of creased dark water. A lake, or perhaps by now the sea of the Gulf of Burmahnsk.

63

Maroussia struggled into consciousness. There was a foul taste in her mouth. She felt dizzy and sick. Chazia was looking down at her, smiling, her hair backlit with the glare of the single caged bulb in the wooden ceiling. Her skin was blotched with patches of smooth darkness.

'Good,' said Chazia. 'You're awake.'

Chazia was holding the solm. She held it up for Maroussia to see. The ball of twigs and wax and stuff looked tawdry and dead in her skewbald palm.

'I know the paluba was looking for you,' said Chazia, 'and it found you. It brought you the key to the Pollandore. I think this is it. This is the key. It is, isn't it?'

Maroussia shook her head. The movement made her dizzy. Acidic bile rose up in the back of her throat. She turned her head aside to vomit.

'I'm not going to help you,' she said when she'd finished. 'Not ever. Not with anything.'

'You need to understand your position, Maroussia darling,' said Chazia. 'You really do. You are in my world now. There is no hope and no protection for you here; there is only me. I can turn you inside out. It's not a metaphor, sweetness. I can dig around in you. I can pull the guts from your belly and hold them up for you to see. I can do anything I want. And afterwards I can give you to Bez Nichevoi.' Chazia knelt in front of her and took her hand. Her gaze was warm and bright, compassionate and mad. 'I can do this to you, Maroussia,' she said. 'You do believe me, darling, don't you?'

Maroussia stared at Chazia dumbly. Her head hurt. She could find nothing to say. Whatever the foul creature that abducted her had done to her, it was still in her veins. All the energy had been flushed out of her. She felt as if she was watching herself from a distance, listening to voices at the far end of an echoing corridor. The floor beneath her was tipping sickeningly sideways.

'You've imagined people doing cruel things to you, darling, haven't you?' said Chazia. 'Everyone has. In dark moments. But the reality is much more terrible, and lasts much longer. It continues. Not just for hours or days but for weeks. Months. It gets messy. It's not good to see parts of yourself being removed. It's not good to have someone else rummaging about inside your body. Will I be brave? we ask ourselves, but of course nobody is brave, not in the end. Courage only takes you so far.'

Chazia shifted her position. Sat down beside her on the wooden floor, making herself comfortable. Shoulder to shoulder, intimate and companionable.

'But I don't want that to happen to you,' she said.

'You tried to kill me,' said Maroussia, 'You killed my mother.'

'Oh. That.' Chazia waved the memory away with a dismissive gesture. 'That was just a favour for a friend. Before I knew you. I didn't know then how important you were. And you escaped anyway, didn't you. That was resourceful of you, though I think you had help. From Investigator Lom, I think. I've been underestimating him too. I saw the mess he made in the gendarme station at Levrovskaya Square. Who would have thought that of him?'

'It wasn't—' Maroussia began, but Chazia cut her off.

'What became of Major Safran by the way?' she said. 'I've been wondering. Just curious. Did Lom—'

'I cut his head off. With a spade.'

Chazia giggled like a girl. Her eyes shone.

'Did you?' she said. 'Well done you.'

Maroussia became aware of a prickling edginess in the air around her. A smell of ozone, like the sea. She realised that Chazia was still talking.

'Ever since the Vlast confiscated the Pollandore from Lezarye,' she was saying, 'people in the Lodka have been trying to find out its secrets and use its power, but they never could. Only now there's me, and now there's you. *The Shaumian woman.* That's what the paluba called you. You have the key and you are the key. Those are the words, or something like them. So. I know, you see. I know it all. And now you can show me how to use the Pollandore. You can give me these secrets.'

Chazia's face was so close to hers, Maroussia could feel her breath. It was cool, and smelled like damp moss and stone, like the mouth of a deep well, with a taint of meat. Her hair was darkly reddish, cropped short and sparse. The rims of her pale blue eyes were pink, her teeth were small and even and pretty. There was a patch of slate-coloured angel flesh stretching from her left cheekbone almost to her ear.

No! Maroussia was screaming inside. *No!* She closed her eyes and turned her head away.

'I'm the one to have the power of the Pollandore,' said Chazia. 'It is my destiny. I have a great purpose.'

Maroussia pulled her knees up to her chest and hugged them defensively. Her naked feet were cold against the rough plank floor of the freight car. She felt the vibration of its wheels on the rails below.

'The Pollandore isn't a *power*,' she said.

'Of course it's power, darling,' said Chazia. She rested her hand on Maroussia's bare knee, and stroked her comfortingly. Their shoulders were touching. 'And you're going to show me how to use it.'

Chazia slipped her arm round Maroussia's shoulder and leaned her head against Maroussia's head. Maroussia could smell her hair. Clean, with a faint trace of scented soap. The hand on Maroussia's shoulder gripped gently but firmly. Maroussia felt a numbness there, as if her flesh was disappearing, as if the shoulder were merging with the hand that touched it.

Chazia's body was starting to join with hers. Melt into her. Maroussia wanted to shake it off. Push her away. But she could not. The feeling was relaxing. Reassuring. There was something *intimate* about it. She felt they had known each other for ever. Chazia's presence was so completely familiar. Solid and trustworthy. Two thoughts, one thought. Like oldest friends. Like sisters.

'After all,' said Chazia quietly, gently in her ear, 'what were you going to do with it yourself?'

'Destroy the angel in the forest.'

'There you *are*, you see, sweetness,' whispered Chazia triumphantly. 'And you said it wasn't power.' Chazia nuzzled her nose against Maroussia's neck. 'Have a little sleep now, darling. You need to build your strength. There's no hurry at all. We'll have plenty more time to talk before we reach Novaya Zima.'

64

The engine note slowed and deepened. Lom became aware that the Kotik was descending, its nose dipping slightly, the line of the artificial horizon creeping up the face of the dial. He looked at the clock on the instrument panel. It was coming up to eleven. He glanced across at Gretskaya.

'Going down to have a look,' she said. 'See where we are.'

The endless shining oceans of cloud rose to meet them and resolved into detail: rolling vaporous hillscapes, valleys and canyons. Lom braced himself, though he knew it was pointless. The floats under the wings ploughed into the thickening mist, tearing it up like cotton wool. Then fog closed round the machine, so thick the wing tips were lost in it. The Kotik did not appear to be moving forward. Nor did it seem to get any lower, although the altimeter needle was swinging leftwards all the time and the light was fading into subaqueous gloom.

The muffled roar of the engine died as Gretskaya throttled right back. The nose sank lower and the seaplane began to glide. The only sound was the hum of air passing through the slowly turning propeller and over the surface of the machine. The cockpit became suddenly fragile, cosy and close. A den to hide in. Heavy droplets of rain splashed against the windscreen and spread in trembling threads and trails. From north to south, straight across their path, lay a dark uniform green and purple wall. Not a wall. A mouth. Lom noticed that the wing at his shoulder was flexing and bouncing. Agitated water beads danced back across the lacquered surface towards the trailing edge and disappeared into grey fog.

Gretskaya sat quite still, her eyes glued to the altimeter. Lom watched the pointer creep backwards: 4,000 – 3,000 – 2,000. The machine plunged on through a mist of drenching, driving rain. 1,000 – 500. Lom sensed beneath them, blotted out by the foggy gloom, the heaving, queasy belly of the sea.

The engine abruptly roared into life. Gretskaya pulled the stick back, climbed to a thousand feet, and began to circle.

'Trouble?' said Lom.

Gretskaya shook her head, but she looked grim.

'No,' she said. 'Not immediately. There's forty-five minutes left in the tank, and we're not that far off Slensk. But I need to see where we are and the cloud's too low. We can't stay circling up here.'

'So what do we do?'

'Go down and wait for the weather to clear,' she said. 'Only I don't know what's down there, and I daren't go any lower to find out. Could be sea. Could be land. Trees. Hills. Hills would be bad.'

'It's water,' said Lom. 'Open sea.'

Gretskaya looked at him sceptically.

'How do you know?' she said. 'There was nothing to see.'

'I know,' he said. 'Absolutely. I know.'

Gretskaya went quiet, thinking. Minutes passed.

'You can't know,' she said at last. 'But the odds are on your side, and if we stay up here we start to run out of options.' She took a deep breath. 'We'll go a little further west, just to be sure, then drop down and take a closer look.' She opened the throttle, pushing the airspeed indicator up till it was nudging a hundred, and let it run. Ten minutes later she cut it again. Gliding into a shallow descent, she pulled on her goggles and hauled open the cockpit lid. The icy rain in their faces. The noise of the wind.

The altimeter counted down: 500 – 400 – 300. Lom wiped the rain out of his eyes and held his breath. Still there was nothing to see but rain and fog. Gretskaya was leaning out of the cockpit, staring down.

A dark indistinct mass loomed up beneath them. The engine roared and Gretskaya snatched the stick and held it level. The aircraft flattened out and the dark mass disappeared in mist. Then it was back, ink-black and flecked with straggles of foam. Gretskaya hauled the stick right back into her stomach and the Kotik lurched and fell out of the sky. It smacked heavily into the sea, bounced and came down again, throwing up walls of spray. It seemed impossible to Lom that it wouldn't tear itself apart or tip tail over nose into the wall of water.

For thirty seconds the machine forged on, then it slowed and came to rest. Gretskaya flicked off the ignition switch and pulled the cabin cover shut against the rain. The propeller stopped its rhythmic ticking and silence fell.

'Fuck,' she said. 'Fuck.'

The plane had become a boat, rising and falling on the long, queasy swell. They were in a circle of mist. Rain pitted and rebounded from the dark green striated skin of the sea.

'OK,' said Gretskaya. 'So now we wait.'

Lom twisted in his seat as Florian clambered up from the cabin and stuck his head into the cockpit. He looked tired, haggard and slightly green. He contemplated the scene beyond the windscreen for a moment – the rain, the mist, the narrow circle of purple-green sea – and grunted.

'Not Slensk then,' he said.

'Letting the weather clear,' said Gretskaya.

'So where are we?'

Gretskaya shrugged.

'The Gulf of Burmahnsk. At a guess, somewhere between twenty and fifty miles offshore. At a guess.'

Florian grunted again in disgust and disappeared back into the cabin. Lom wondered what he was doing in there. Most likely strapped in a cot trying to sleep. Travelling evidently wasn't his thing. Gretskaya settled back into her seat and closed her eyes and Lom stared out of the window, watching the sea. The Kotik lifted and fell with the swell, dipping one float then the other in the water. In the cockpit it was bitterly cold. Lom's heart sank. Fifty miles of deep dark fogbound icy ocean.

65

Elena Cornelius, crouching knee-deep in an anti-tank ditch, hacked at the solid black earth with a gardening trowel. The wooden handle had split and fallen away, but she gripped the tang in her blistered palm. She was lucky: many women of the conscript artel scrabbled at the ground with their fingers, numbed and bleeding, tearing their fingernails and the skin off their hands. Fresh snow had fallen in the night and the churned mud bottom of the tank trap was frozen iron-hard, sharp-ridged and treacherous, but her cotton gabardine kept out the worst of the wind and the digging was warm work.

Black earth rolled away from her in all directions, level to the distant horizon, skimmed with a thin scraping of snow. In front of her the rim of grey sky was broken only by sparse hedges and clumps of hazel, a line of telegraph poles, the chimneys of the brickworks where they slept. Between her and the sky rolled a wide slow river, crossed by a bridge: steel girders laid across pillars of brick, a surface of gravel and tar. The bridge was why they were there. The retreating defenders would cross it and then it would be blown. But for a while the bridge would have to be held.

At her back the sound of distant explosions rumbled. Every so often she straightened and turned to watch the flickering detonations and the thick columns of oily smoke rolling into the air. The bombers were over Mirgorod again.

The ground they were working was potato fields, harvested months before, but from time to time the diggers turned up an overlooked potato. Most were soft and black with rot, but some were good. Elena stuffed what she found into her pockets and underclothes for later, for

Yeva and Galina and Aunt Lyudmila. She ate handfuls of snow against the thirst. It was OK. Survivable.

'Here they come again!' Valeriya shouted.

Elena looked up. Three aircraft rose out of the horizon in a line and swept towards her, engine-clatter echoing. They were fat-nosed, like flying brown thumbs suspended between short, stubby wings.

Bullets spattered the earth and snow in front of her, and three yards to her left the top of a woman's head came off. Elena had known her slightly. She had been a teacher of music at the Marinsky Girls Academy.

While the planes circled low to make another pass, Elena and the others ran for the river. Breaking the thin ice at the water's edge they waded waist-high into the current, feet slipping and sinking in the silt, and waited, bent forward under the low bridge, for the planes to drift away elsewhere. Oilskin-wrapped packages of explosives clustered under the bridge, strung together on twisted cables that wrapped and hung like bindweed.

Elena saw something in the water out near the middle of the river: a sudden smooth coil of movement against the direction of the current. It came again, and again, slicker and more sure than the wavelets chopping and jostling. She glimpsed a solid steely-grey oil-sleeked gun barrel of flesh. Blackish flukes broke the surface without a splash. A face rose out of the water and looked at her A human face. Almost human. A soft chalky white, the white of flesh too long in the water, with hollow eye sockets and deep dark eyes. The nose was set higher and sharper than a human nose, the mouth a straight lipless gash. The creature raised its torso higher and higher out of the water. An underbelly the same subaqueous white as the face. Heavy white breasts, nipples large and bruise-coloured, bluish black. Below the torso, a dark tube of fluke-tailed muscle was working away.

While she rested upright on her tail, the rusalka was using her arms to scoop water up onto her body. She rubbed herself down constantly, smoothing her sides and front and breasts as if she were washing them, except it was more like lubrication. She smoothed her hair also, though it wasn't hair but flat wet ribbons of green-black stuff hanging from the top of her head across her back and shoulders. While she washed herself, the creature's face watched Elena continuously. There was no expression on her face at all. None whatsoever. Elena gripped the arm of the woman next to her.

'Valeriya!' she whispered urgently. 'Do you see it? Out there! A rusalka!' But when she looked again there was nothing but a swirl on the surface of the water.

After the planes had gone the women waded out from under the bridge and slipped and scrabbled up the bank. A thin bitter wind was coming up from the south. They stood shivering and shedding greenish river water from their skirts. There was a flash on the horizon, the dull thump of an explosion, and one of the brickworks chimneys collapsed in a cloud of dust. Two more explosions followed and the whole building crumpled.

Seven heavy tanks were rolling towards them across the potato fields.

'Our boys,' said Valeriya. 'Running home to mother.'

More muzzle flashes, rapid fire. The chatter of machine guns sounded dry and quiet, like twigs crunching. In the distance behind the tanks long lines of men were coming towards them, making slow progress across the levels of frozen mud.

'No,' said Elena. 'Those aren't us. The enemy is here. We have to run.'

When she got back to Aunt Lyudmila's apartment it wasn't there. The building wasn't there. The whole of the street was gone. Sticking out from the rubble among the smouldering beams and spars was a leg, pointing its heel at the sky. Small enough to be a child's. A girl's. It was black like burned meat. A charred flap of shoe hung from the foot.

66

The rain in the Gulf of Burmahnsk was definitely beginning to ease. Slowly the area of visible sea around the aircraft widened until it was possible to see a mile or more in every direction. Lyuba Gretskaya stirred and opened her eyes. Lom wasn't sure she had ever really been asleep. She slid back the canopy, letting in a blast of freezing spray and the smell of the ocean, stood up precariously in her seat and reached up to jolt the engine into life.

She took off and climbed steeply to a thousand feet, swung round and headed east. After about fifteen minutes they crossed the coastline: a wide shallow lagoon behind a long sandspit. Drab dunes and brown scrub grass dusted with snow. The Kotik swung north to follow the shore. Bays and lagoons. Small scattered settlements tucked a mile or so back from the sea. The fuel gauge lapsing closer and closer to empty.

They came up on Slensk from the south where it hid from the weather in the lee of a low headland. As Gretskaya swung a loop to port, Lom found himself looking down on a tumble of bleached grey rooftops divided by a broad river. Wharfs and piers edged the river, fronting an extensive patchwork of timber yards. Beyond the docks the river frayed, splitting into a threadwork of rivers and streams across a widening triangle of tawny brown mud streaked with veins of livid orange. The Northern Kholomora reaching the sea.

The Kotik swung out over the delta, descending gently, and turned back to touch down neatly in the middle of the river. Gretskaya taxied across to the nearest jetty and found a berth between a rusting hulk and two big pitch-caulked barges roped together side by side. She eased the plane nose first against a solid wall of pine trunks blackened and streaked with lichenous green, and cut the engine.

A giant was sitting on the edge of the wharf, studying the aircraft with frank curiosity. He caught the line Gretskaya threw up to him and looped it neatly round a stump. Lom, stiff and awkward after nine hours cramped into the tiny cockpit, hauled himself up the rusting iron ladder and stood a little unsteadily, relishing the stability of the heavy weathered planking under his feet. He breathed deeply. The cold prickled the back of his nose. It was much colder here than Mirgorod, and the sky was bigger. The air smelled of grasslands and smoke and river mud and the resinous tang of cut timber. It flushed the staleness and engine fumes from his lungs.

He glanced across at the giant and nodded.

'Where do you come from in that?' the giant said. His accent was thick. Consonants roughened and elided. Vowels formed deeper in the back of his throat than a human larynx allowed.

'Mirgorod,' said Lom.

The giant considered him for a while. Though he was sitting with his legs over the edge of the jetty, his massive head was level with Lom's. His thick hair was tied back in a pony tail and the dark glossy skin of his face was covered with an intricate pattern of tattoos. A lacy knotted profusion of thorns and leaves and berries, stained brown and purple like bramble juice, spread up into the roots of his hair and wound down his neck, disappearing inside his shirt. His eyes were large as damsons, bright damson-black, and showed no whites at all.

'I heard Mirgorod is burning,' he said.

'The people are getting out,' said Lom, 'those that can. Like us. The government is moving. There is to be a renewal in the east. The Vlast reborn in Kholvatogorsk.'

The giant shrugged and spat into the sea.

'And where do you go?' he said. 'East also?'

'North,' said Lom.

The giant stiffened, suddenly alert and wary. His nostrils flared. He was looking past Lom at something behind him. Lom glanced back. Florian had appeared at the top of the ladder, wearing his astrakhan hat.

'You keep wild company,' the giant muttered, 'for a Mirgorod man.'

Lom and Florian left Gretskaya to secure the cockpit and sort out the refuelling of the Kotik.

'We must restore our spirits,' said Florian, setting off towards the town. 'Coffee, I think. Cherry schnapps. Pastries. Honey.'

Lom looked sceptically at the subsiding weather-bleached frontages. *Cherry schnapps and pastries?*

Slensk was a timber town. Timber was the only trade, and all the buildings were made of wood – old, warped, much repaired and weatherproofed with tar. Boardwalks were laid across mud, woodsmoke leaked from tin chimneys. There were as many giants as humans in the streets of Slensk. Giants *were* the timber trade. They came out of the forest hauling barges with their shoulders or riding herd on thunderous rafts of red pine logs: down the Yannis, across Lake Vitimsk, then the Northern Kholomora to the sea. The logs were boughs and branches only, never entire trunks, though they were thicker, stronger and heavier than whole trees of beech or oak. When the giants had delivered their charges, some stayed in Slensk and laboured in the sawmills, where they hefted timbers five men couldn't shift, and some travelled onward with the seagoing barges or drifted south and west, itinerant labourers, but most walked back to the forest. Giants tended to observe human life from a height, detached and unconcerned, indifferent to detail. They went their own way and rarely got involved. City people treated them with a mixture of fear and contempt, which bothered the giants, if they noticed it at all, about as much as the scorn of cats. But the giants were noticing Florian. They watched him warily. They bristled.

On a bleak corner a door stood open in a lopsided old house. A tin sign read PUBLIC ROOM. You ducked under a low beam to get in, and stepped down into a room of long benches and sticky tables, wet muddy floorboards, a log stove and a fug of strong tobacco. No coffee, no cherry schnapps. Florian ordered for both of them: big wooden bowls of cabbage soup with blobs of sour cream dissolving in the middle, a couple of hard-boiled eggs, a bottle of birch liquor and two glasses. The bottle was brown and dusty. *LIGAS DARK BALZAM.* The thick black liquor burned Lom's throat. It left a thick oily film down the inside of the tumbler. At the next table a group of seamen were playing cards.

Florian took one of the boiled eggs from the plate and crushed it gently between finger and thumb until the shell cracked. He began to remove the broken pieces one by one.

'The giants are bothered by you,' said Lom.

'Are they?' said Florian.

He finished peeling the egg, and held it up to examine it in the light. It was shiny white and elliptically perfect.

'Yes,' said Lom. 'You make them nervous.'

Florian tossed the peeled egg into the air, and with an impossibly fast movement seemed to lean forward and snap it out of the air with his jaws. He swallowed the egg whole. It was over in a fraction of a second, almost too fast to see. It was the most inhuman gesture that Lom had ever seen a human make. Only Florian was not human of course.

Florian wiped his mouth with the back of his hand.

'And what about you, Vissarion?' he said. 'Do I bother you?'

'Yes,' said Lom. 'Absolutely.'

'I see,' said Florian. 'Well. OK.' He took a sip of birch liquor, made a sour face and sat back as if he'd made an incontrovertible point.

67

Gretskaya turned up at the bar half an hour later, her sheepskin rain-soaked, her thick curly hair heavy with water.

'You tracked us down,' said Florian.

'Where else would you be? There is nowhere else. Give me some of that.' She picked up Florian's balzam glass and emptied it, then slid in alongside Lom on the bench. 'There's heavy weather coming in from the north. It reached Garshal this morning, bad enough that they telephoned a warning to the pier head here. That's not normal. We'll stay here tonight and let it blow through, and start again in the morning.'

'We could go east,' said Lom. 'Follow the river to Terrimarkh, like you said. Keep south of the weather.'

Gretskaya shook her head.

'I will not risk the Kotik over that country,' she said. 'It is a wilderness. Bad weather in daylight over the ocean is one thing. Bad weather at night over 250,000 square miles of moss and rocks and scrub is something else again. But ...' She paused and frowned and looked across the room. A corporal of gendarmes had ducked in under the low doorway. He was standing at the edge of the room, letting his eyes adjust to the light.

When he saw them he came across. He was young, not more than nineteen or twenty, narrow-shouldered and wide-hipped. A velvet moustache, a full moist lower lip, a roll of softness swelling over his belt. The holster on his hip looked big and awkward on him.

'You are the aviators?' he said. 'That is your seaplane at the jetty? The Beriolev Mark II Kotik?'

'It is,' said Gretskaya.

'And you are the pilot?'

'Yes.'

'You are required to register a flight plan with the harbour authorities. This is your responsibility, yet no such plan is registered.'

'I don't have a plan. Not yet. We were just discussing that. There is a problem with the weather.'

The boy was staring at Lom and Florian.

'And these are your passengers?' he said. 'Two men?'

'As you see.'

'Cargo?'

'None.'

'This can be checked. The aircraft will be searched.'

'There is no cargo. It is a passenger flight.'

'For what purpose?'

'I am exploring possibilities in the timber business,' said Lom. 'Naturally, we came to Slensk.'

'But you are not remaining here. You come from Mirgorod, and only the weather detains you. Correct? So your destination is where?'

'We are going north along the coast,' said Gretskaya. 'Garshal. We leave tomorrow, or perhaps the next day. There is no hurry. Not until the storm blows through.'

The gendarme held out his hand.

'Papers,' he said.

'The logs and registration documents are in the plane. If you want to—' Gretskaya began, but the gendarme cut her off impatiently.

'My concern is with persons only. Personal identification. Documents of travel.'

Gretskaya handed over her passport. Florian and Lom followed suit. The gendarme looked through them slowly and carefully, page by page. Then he put all three in the back pocket of his trousers.

'Hey!' said Gretskaya.

'I have certain enquiries to make concerning these documents,' said the gendarme. 'Confirmations I intend to seek. You may collect them from the gendarmerie tomorrow, in the afternoon, and until then you will remain in Slensk. This will be convenient for you, no doubt,' he said to Lom. 'You will have more time to pursue your commercial interests.'

*

'That decides it,' said Florian. 'We have to leave now, straight away, and not for Garshal but east.'

'No,' said Gretskaya. 'It's not a flight to try at night, even without bad weather. Not without a navigator. The only sure way is to follow the river. If we lost the river – it's a wilderness: no features, no landmarks – we'd circle till the fuel ran out, and if we had to go down, no one would come to look for us. No one would know where we went. It would take us weeks to walk out of there.'

'If it's a matter of additional payment …'

'No,' said Gretskaya. 'Not that. Anyway, why the hurry? We've got till tomorrow afternoon.'

Florian shook his head. 'He could send a wire tonight,' he said. 'He could be on the telephone now.'

'Who's he going to call to check out a passport?' said Lom. 'The Lodka's not open for business, not any more. Anyway, he's not waiting for ID confirmation.'

'What do you mean?' said Gretskaya.

'How many gendarmes are there in a place like Slensk? Two or three at the most. My guess is he's on his own. And he's worried about us. He didn't buy our story and he didn't like the odds, so he's calling for help. Reinforcements. Only he knows nobody can get here before tomorrow. Fuck, he's almost begging us to run.'

'So what do we do?' said Gretskaya.

Florian looked at Lom. 'Let him decide,' he said.

Lom emptied his balzam glass. The liquid seared his throat and left his mouth dry and rough. He didn't need to think. Somewhere Chazia's train was rolling north towards Novaya Zima with Maroussia and the Pollandore. It was a race, and nothing else mattered, and the train was moving, and they were not. At the thought of Chazia, Lom felt a tight surge of anger and purposeful violence. The iron aftertaste of angel stuff mixed with the balzam. There would be a reckoning there.

'We leave,' said Lom. 'We leave now.'

Gretskaya poured another tumbler of Ligas Balzam, drank it down, and tucked the bottle inside her sheepskin jacket.

'Then let's go,' she said.

68

In the war against his own people Colonel-General Rizhin's weapons were of necessity crude. When Chazia evacuated the Lodka and removed or destroyed the intelligence files it contained, she decapitated, at least so far as Mirgorod was concerned, the system of informers and secret police that had held the Vlast solid for four hundred years. Rizhin took a more direct approach. It suited him better. He declared martial law. A curfew. Looters and stockpilers were to be summarily shot. Citizens were conscripted to worker battalions and assigned their tasks, and shirkers were shot. If there were no shirkers, some people were to be shot anyway, the weakest and least capable. What mattered was that people were shot.

Spies and saboteurs were captured and their confessions led to further arrests. In quarters where dissent was strongest, collective measures were taken. Reprisals. The citizens of Mirgorod, the newspapers reported, were shocked at the extent of the enemy's penetration of their city and glad that Rizhin was there, relentless and vigilant, to protect them.

Against the enemy without, he ordered concentric circles of defence to be thrown together. Twenty miles out from the centre of the Mirgorod, Rizhin's labour armies of women and children raised earthworks with their bare hands, excavating trenches and tank ditches, building breastworks and redoubts, laying barbed wire and mines even as the Archipelago air force strafed and bombed them. They carried away their own dead, and buried them when and where they could.

The outer ring of defence was expected to delay but not stop the advance. Rizhin's main focus was on preparing the streets of the city itself for the fighting to come. He ordered that all the bridges should be wired with explosives. Machine-gun nests were to be built on high roofs and towers, the blocks around them demolished to provide clear fields of fire. Artillery and anti-aircraft batteries appeared in the parks and squares of the city. Air raid shelters were to be dug and public buildings camouflaged. The Armoury spire was painted grey.

Residents came out to barricade every street with anything to hand: tramcars and overturned carts were pushed across the roads and filled with earth, building rubble, gravestones uprooted from the necropolis gardens. Street nameplates and road signs were removed. All maps, street plans and guidebooks to the city were confiscated, and anyone found with one after that was arrested. Summary execution. Every house and apartment was prepared to be its own fortress. Its own last stand. Strips of paper were stuck across windows to prevent shattering and splinters. Attics were filled with sand. In every office barrels filled with water stood ready, along with spades and beaters and boxes of sand.

Barrage balloons drifted low and pale and fat, their cables invisible against the sky. And every day the beleaguered citizens of Mirgorod waited for the Vlast's own air force to appear overhead. They looked up, expecting and then hoping to see Hammerheads and Murnauviks scattered across the sky, twisting, buzzing, deadly; stinging the lumbering, triple-bellied Archipelago craft out of the air. But the air force of the Vlast did not come. It was delayed elsewhere. After the first attacks on the city, the Archipelago's bombers arrived alone: their fighter escorts no longer bothered to waste fuel by coming along for the ride.

All night and all day Rizhin worked. He planned, he terrorised, he cajoled. He did what he could, but he knew it would not be enough. He needed soldiers. Armies. Guns and tanks and aircraft and ships. And these he did not have. Not enough.

The armour of the Archipelago rolled through the unfinished outer defensive line in a dozen, twenty places, moving fast, and behind the heavy tanks came massed motorised infantry in half-tracked carriers and on motorbikes. Radio operators. Artillery tractors. Rocket trucks. Engineers to rebuild roads and bridges and lay out airfields and telephone cables. And following along behind them, more slowly but in unstoppable numbers, came columns of horse hauling supply wagons, field guns and four-ton mitrailleuses. Cavalry regiments. Division after division of foot soldiers marching.

At certain points, randomly, the armies of the Vlast attempted to make a stand. Men and women in their thousands advanced on the enemy at walking pace. Rifles and bayonets against tanks, artillery and machine guns. Wave after wave the men and women of the Vlast came on, the later waves slowing to pick their way across shell craters and over the mounded corpses of the dead. The attacks faltered, faded, resumed, hour after hour until the machine guns of the Archipelago were too hot to handle and their operators were depressed and sickened by the tedious, grinding slaughter. The awful noise of it dulled their hearing and frayed their nerves. The freezing air was clotted with the stink of hot metal and oil, mud and piss and the leakage of ripped-up and burst-open human bodies. Some of the Vlast infantry reached the enemy: they fought with bayonets and knives when their pocketful of bullets was gone.

The Archipelago covered the last twenty miles to the outer suburbs of Mirgorod so quickly that whole Vlast divisions were simply by-passed and cut off from retreat. Crouched in woodland scrub and shallow swampy depressions, they hid in desperate silence while the enemy marched past. More often than not, Archipelago skirmishers found them by the smell of uniforms stale with tobacco and sweat, the tang of disinfectant and the sickly sweetness of Sauermann's Lice-Off.

When the Archipelago columns reached the Ouspensky Marshes on the eastern outskirts of Mirgorod they halted. They were within sight of the dull red hillock of the Ouspenskaya Torso, the remains of the first angel that fell dead from the sky: the place to which the Founder had travelled, four hundred years before, and where he had ordered the building of the city. The place where the Reasonable Empire had first become the Vlast. And, from her temporary headquarters in the Ouspensky Marshes, General Alyson Carnelian, Archipelago commander of the Mirgorod Front, sent a message into the city. It was an invitation to discuss surrender terms.

Against the advice of his officers, Rizhin didn't send a representative but went to meet General Carnelian himself. The meeting was held in a single railway carriage that had been rolled out to the middle of the Bivorg viaduct and left there, suspended a hundred feet above the scrappy gardens and straggling suburban streets of Vonyetskovo Strel. It looked isolated. Marooned.

The carriage was a plush observation car appropriated from the

Edelfeld-Sparre Line, thickly carpeted and furnished with red leather sofas, its vintage luxury somewhat faded by time. The walls were panelled in dark varnished wood, and the soft yellow light of electric chandeliers made the sky beyond the windows look wintry and bleak. Photographs on the walls showed sunlit southern landscapes: a slope of olive groves, a sun-bleached corniche above a strip of glittering sea. Places where Rizhin had never been. A small diesel generator was humming quietly somewhere.

General Carnelian was a tall heavyset woman of about fifty, uniformed in crisp olive green, greying blond hair cut short under a peaked red cap heavy with braid. Her face and hands were deeply tanned.

'Some coffee?' she said. 'A cake perhaps?' There was a plate of fancy patisseries. The kind you couldn't get in Mirgorod, not any more.

'No,' said Rizhin. 'Let's get on with it. Say your piece.'

She fixed him with small hard green eyes. *She is a soldier*, thought Rizhin. *Of course she is. The flannel with the coffee and the crude trick with the little sugar cakies is misdirection, only that.*

'We can take your city, General Rizhin,' said Carnelian quietly. 'Be in no doubt of that. Our bombers will flatten it. All of it. Every house and apartment, every school, every hospital, every bridge. I have six hundred Bison tanks. Each one weighs ninety tons. They will not bother to use the streets, they will drive straight through the buildings and grind the rubble to dust under the steel treads of their tracks. We will fill your rivers and canals and sewers with coal oil and ignite it. We will fill the cellars and underground shelters with heavy green gas that shreds the lungs of anyone who inhales it. Explosive gas. Once released, it lingers and drifts in ground-level clouds for days. Mirgorod will burn, and all the millions of people who live here will burn. All of you. There will be such death as you cannot possibly imagine.'

She paused to let Rizhin absorb the force of what she had said. The inevitable truth of it.

'However,' she continued, 'I would prefer not to do this. I am a humane person, and I will avoid this cataclysm if I can. The city is already ours, in every sense that matters, but there is a choice, General Rizhin, and the choice is yours.'

Rizhin looked at her, smiling faintly, but said nothing.

'Will you hear my terms?' she said.

Rizhin sat back in his chair and gestured for her to carry on. 'It would be interesting,' he said.

'If you capitulate,' said Carnelian, 'The city will be spared. It will not be destroyed. And I will go further. I am authorised to offer Mirgorod the status of an open city. Renounce all ties of allegiance to the Vlast and Mirgorod may establish its own civilian government and become a neutral bystander in the war. We offer diplomatic recognition of the city as an independent state. We offer advice and supply. We offer Mirgorod a seat in the Governing Parliament of Archipelagal States, with a status equal to any of the smaller Out Islands.'

'And for me?' said Rizhin. 'What would there be for me? I mean me personally, of course.'

'An honourable retirement, General. A small estate somewhere. Froualt, perhaps? And a reasonable pension. We might say two thousand roubles a year, something in that region. There would be limits on your future travel and communication, naturally, but for all practical purposes you would be free to live out a quiet and prosperous end to an illustrious career.'

'These are reasonable terms,' said Rizhin. 'Very attractive.'

'I expect you'll want time to consider,' she said. 'You'll need to discuss your answer with your colleagues, I understand that, and we would of course need to be assured that yours was a collective answer. A reliable agreement. But ...' She paused. 'I would advise you against consulting with your masters who have fled. It's easy to spend other people's lives from a distance. I urge Mirgorod to make its own mind up. I can give you twenty-four hours. No more.'

'There is no need for time,' said Rizhin. 'I speak for Mirgorod. That's why I'm here.'

'Good. Excellent. So, what do you say, General?'

'I say you're full of shit.'

'I assure you—' Carnelian began, but Rizhin held up his hand for silence.

'You and I,' he said, 'what we're fighting for here is a city. A *capital* city. If Mirgorod is not the capital of the Vlast it is nothing, it is meaningless, it no longer exists. You won't burn it. What use to you is a million stinking corpses? What use to you is five hundred square miles of ash and rubble in a marsh on the edge of a northern ocean? This threat of burning is nothing. It's shit. I could burn it myself, more easily than you could. Fuck, I *would* burn it myself, to stop you having it. But to destroy it is to lose it. You burn Mirgorod and you obliterate the idea of it, and it's the idea of Mirgorod we're fighting over here, not some piss and vinegar diplomatic compromise.'

Rizhin stood up to go.

'So,' he said. 'You want my city, you come and get it. You fight for every inch, or you fuck off somewhere else and let the Archipelago find themselves a general who can.'

'You can't save the people of Mirgorod, General.'

'You haven't been listening,' said Rizhin. 'You should pay attention. I don't want to save the people of Mirgorod, they are of no interest to me. What I want is a victory. And I'm going to have one. You're going to give me one.'

69

For three hours out of Slensk, Lyuba Gretskaya followed the Northern Kholomora upstream, flying low through steady drizzle. The river slid beneath them, wide and slow and dark. Carpets of leafless birch and moss gave way to plains of tawny scrub grass and miles-long streaks of bare yellow earth. Twilight was thickening into night when the storm clouds rose from the north, clotting the horizon. Rags of wind buffeted the Kotik, sending it scrabbling and skittering across the surface of the air.

'We'll have to lie up overnight,' said Gretskaya. 'I'm going down while there's still light to land by.'

'Go a few miles north,' said Lom. 'Out of sight of the river. Just in case.'

Gretskaya nodded and swung the Kotik to port. After a couple of minutes she eased off the throttle and began to descend in a wide flat spiral. She pulled a handle and Lom felt the thunk as the landing wheels dropped into position. Almost imperceptibly the nose came up as the aircraft flattened out, engine silenced, gliding. The wind whistling through the struts, the creak of the airframe, the rain against the windscreen, the tick and sweep of the wipers. Even in the dusk and rain the grass was visible underneath them now, not flat and smooth as it had appeared from height, but rough and tussocky and dotted with low clumps of shrub and thorn. Gretskaya flew on, thirty feet above the ground.

And then a wall of scree rose out of the ground in front of them.

Gretskaya hauled back on the stick, dragging the nose up steeply, and raced the throttle till it screamed. They must have cleared the top by a matter of feet. Inches. They were flying over a stretch of gravel and small stones. Patches of illumination from the wing-tip lamps raced alongside them. The ground was so close, Lom felt he could have reached over the side and brushed it with his hand.

The tail dropped, the wheels touched and bounced and touched again, and they were down and trundling, wheels crunching and jolting across the stony surface. The whole aircraft strained as Gretskaya applied the brakes. It skidded and slewed to the right. Suddenly they ran out of gravel and bounced into long grass. A shadowy clump of thorns loomed out of the darkness and smacked into the wing almost at Lom's shoulder. With a screech of protesting metal they lurched to a sudden halt.

Gretskaya cut the engine instantly.

'Shit,' she said quietly. 'That didn't sound good.'

Gretskaya opened the cockpit and climbed down to have a look at the damage. Lom followed. A thin bitter wind tugged at his trousers. Rain flattened his hair and streamed down his face. The right undercarriage wheel was tangled in a mess of thorny branches. The struts, to Lom's inexpert eye, looked bent and twisted awry. Despite the wind and the rain, he could smell an acrid industrial taint on the air. Something was leaking. Gretskaya bent down and dabbed at the mechanism, then sniffed her fingers.

'Brake fluid,' she said. 'Nothing too bad, if that's the only damage. I can fix it up in the morning.'

Florian appeared beside them. His eyes were shining happily.

'I'm going to take a walk,' he said. 'Don't wait up.'

Lom looked at him in surprise but Gretskaya only grunted indifferently.

'Come,' she said and clapped Lom on the shoulder. 'Let's get inside and finish this balzam and get some sleep.'

Antoninu Florian slid down the scree and found a place where he could tuck away his clothes. He pulled them off hastily, shivering happily as the rain drenched the bare skin of his body. He wrapped them in his jacket and stashed the bundle under a thorn tree. He marked the place with his scent so he could find it again.

All around him for hundreds of miles there was spaciousness and weather and, apart from the two left behind inside their stale metal box, no humans. None at all. And no cramped enclosing constructions of stone and brick. No stench of coal and iron. No thundering of engines and petrol fumes. No noise at all but the wind in the grass and the rain. How long? How long since such a moment, a true wolfnight? Too long. Too many years. But now. Now. The joy of it made him want to howl and shout.

Florian ran, and as he ran he stretched out his body, re-articulating bone and cartilage inside their hot tendon sheaths, feeling his muscles bunch and reach and work themselves warm and free, pushing out his ribcage and filling his unfolding lungs deeply, deeply, with the night-freighted air: the smell of crushed herbs, broken twigs and wet earth. At full pelt he tipped himself sideways into the brush and rolled over and over, growling, yelping, laughing. He came to a stop and thrust his face into the ground, just to breath it, just to rub his muzzle against the fragrant wet grass.

Then he picked himself up and stood for a moment, still, the fur on his back raised thickly, mouth open, panting hot breath that steamed on the air, simply listening to the hot blood of his own veins.

He was wolf and he was strong and hungry and he ran. He ran a long way, covering mile after mile, darkly, silently and very fast.

70

Lom woke in the grey light of dawn and climbed stiffly down from the cockpit. The Kotik was canted slightly sideways. Gretskaya's legs were visible, sticking out from under the hull. A toolbox open beside her.

'OK?' said Lom.

'Couple of hours. No problem.'

'Need a hand?'

'No.'

Some yards away Florian was crouching over a small fire, feeding it with brittle clumps of scrub. The herb flared into spitting heat and burned away instantly with an acrid fragrance and almost no smoke. He had a couple of cat-sized creatures impaled on sticks and propped over the fire. They were elongated, sinewy, unrecognisable: narrow fragile heads burned to black, eyes closed slits, carbonised lips stretched back from small sharp chisel-teeth. Threads of fat dripped from the burning meat and spattered into the fire with little explosions of bitter vaporous soot. Lom almost trod on their torn pelts, dropped on the gravel a couple of feet away. Grey bloody rags.

Florian looked up and grinned.

'What the hell are those?' said Lom.

Florian shrugged happily.

'Surok,' he said. 'Ground squirrel.' He held up a chunk of half-cooked meat. 'Breakfast. Want some?'

'No,' said Lom quickly. 'No. Thanks.'

He drifted off by himself, heading away from the aircraft. His footsteps crunched echoless in the silence. It was bitterly cold. Away from the reek of Florian's fire the air smelled faintly of dry cinders and some kind of crushed herb he thought he recognised but couldn't name. Something like sage. Or rue. Scraps of freezing mist hung low on the ground. His face was chilled to the bone: stiffened and numb, skin stretched too tight over his jaw and his skull. The yellow-grey steppe stretched beyond the flat horizon, hundreds of miles in every direction of nothing at all.

The plane had landed on some kind of raised plateau, uplifted some yards above the surrounding grassland. Last night's rain had already evaporated in the thin wind. Lom found he could scuff away the sparse dry gravelly soil with his shoe, scraping down to virgin rock. The herby scrub had virtually no roots at all. When he had been walking for fifteen minutes or so, he began to notice that the ground was scattered at wide intervals with curious slivers, shards and fist-sized stones, ranging in colour from pale pink and rusted blood to bruise-dark purple, some rough and sharp, some rounded and polished to a glassy shine. He picked up a couple at random and cupped them in the palm of his hand, hefting their surprising weight. He knew exactly what they were. Raw fragments of the flesh of a fallen angel. They tingled in his hand, their almost-aliveness calling to him, and the stain of the old angel implant still lingering in his own blood stirred in response. It was like fine wires in his veins tightening and humming faintly. *Follow*, they urged, whispering. *Follow*.

It took Lom more than an hour to find the carcase of the angel itself: a small one, a minor malakh, nothing compared to the red grandeur of, say, the Ouspenskaya Torso. Keeping fifty yards distance, he walked all round it in five or ten minutes: a surprising, impossible crag of deep reds and purples. The angel had not been quite dead when it fell: three starfish pseudo-limbs extruded from one flank and flowed across the shallow crater floor, spreading fringes that trickled away and dissolved into the surface rock. Angels often survived their fall by hours, sometimes days, seeping liquefaction, scrabbling in sad confusion at the ground as the last intelligence drained out of them. But this one was certainly dead now, and had been dead for centuries: long enough for dusty wind-blown soil to gather deeply in the folds and depressions of its body. Even from such a mass as this, Lom sensed nothing but the vague, vestigial after-trace of dissipated sentience.

He was surely the first human to see this thing since it had fallen. The Vlast Observatories paid wealthy bounties for such a find, and failure to report one was a serious crime, but if it had been reported, the angel-miners of the Vlast would have come, hacked and sliced away its substance and hauled it away in slabs. They would have swept up every scattered pebble and strand and web for miles around. But this one had lain unseen and undisturbed since it had fallen, untouched by anything except the abrading weather. It called to him. He wanted to go closer. To touch it. Sheer curiosity. Never before had he been close to more than a mudjhik-sized lump of angel substance, though he had carried a sliver of it embedded in his skull for most of his life.

As Lom slipped down into the shallow crater and walked towards it, the small dead angel loomed over him like the hull of a battleship. The atmosphere sang and prickled against his skin. An ozone reek. He went right up against the flank. Close to, the angel's flesh was dull and pitted, but marbled with streaks of dark translucence, seamed within by dim threads and striations of blood and midnight blue. Lom pulled off his glove and pressed his hand to it. Probing. Deeper and deeper into the dizzying mass. The answering wires in his veins snapped taut, leaving him dizzy, breathless, heart pounding.

An echo of proud intellectual hunger reached out and gripped him, tugging him further down and deeper in. The angel wasn't a solid bulk, it was an open mouth. A fathomless well. He was standing on the fragile edge of terrifying, vertiginous, depths and staring, rapt and self-surrendered, into infinite emptiness: the space between galaxies and stars, not dark and cold and filled with death, but alive, a beautiful shining limitless windfall home. He wanted to fall into it. Fall and fly. The way up and the way down the same. It was his birthright, his just entitlement, his more than human destiny: the everlasting, ever-expanding future to which his history, all human history, was prologue. Just one step more. The flesh of the dead angel opened, a warm inviting gate, parting comfortably to fold around him and take him in.

No! Not this! Not ever this again!

Lom fought it.

Repel! Repel!

But he could not pull away. He screamed and yelled. Choking. Desperate. He hit out and pushed and kicked and bit and screamed. He coughed and vomited. Sour spittle spilled down his chin in gluey strands. Pulling away was appalling and impossible, like drowning himself, like holding his own breath till he died. He was murdering the thing he loved completely, loved more than himself: he was wilfully choosing his own bereavement. The dead angel suffused him and clung to his mind with needle-hooked claws. It was pulling the brain and spinal cord out of his body through the top of his skull. For Lom to withdraw was sickening death and extinction.

No! Not after all that's happened, not this! Was it his own voice or the angel's that screamed this horrified determination, this defiance of despair? It was both. There was only one voice.

And then Lom was out of the dead angel's grasp and stumbling back across the ground, sobbing and vomiting, his lungs heaving desperately for clean cold breath.

Florian found Lom wandering, exhausted and confused, miles from the Kotik. Florian wiped the dried vomit and spittle from his face and made him sit on a rock and gave him water and meat. Lom ate a little but he could not speak. He leaned forward, hands on his knees, and swung his head from side to side, trying to shake it clear.

'Take your time,' said Florian. 'No rush. None at all. Gretskaya is waiting. The aircraft is repaired. She is anxious to make Terrimarkh before dark.'

'Before *dark*?' said Lom. 'What … what time is it, then?'

'It is almost three in the afternoon. You were gone for eight hours.'

'An angel …' Lom groaned and turned aside and vomited again. 'It was dead … It …'

'I have seen it,' said Florian. 'When you didn't come back I followed your trail. I found what you found but I didn't go close, not like you did. I could not have. What made you …?'

He paused but Lom said nothing. He could not.

'I picked up your path again,' said Florian, 'on the other side of it. You were wandering.'

There was a hammering pain behind Lom's eyes. He tried to focus on Florian but flashes of coloured brightness sparked and drifted across his vision.

'How close?' said Florian. 'How close did you go?' His voice reached Lom from far away. Lom jammed the heels of his hands into his eyes. It only made things worse.

'Sorry,' he said. 'Think I'm going to—'

He jerked his head aside and vomited once more. He felt himself toppling slowly, endlessly forward. The world slid sideways into easy and comfortable darkness.

ARE THAN FEAR

He kicked his head back and stamped once, where He felt himself sinking slowly endlessly in with the purple and sideways into easy and comfortable darkness.

71

M aroussia Shaumian sat alone in a compartment on Chazia's train. Her own private travelling cell. The door was locked, the windows barred. The bars were painted dark purple to match the Edelfeld-Sparre coachwork: slender steel uprights, but solid. Immovable. She had tried them, as she had tried the door, a dozen times.

Her clothes had been taken from her on the first night while she slept, when they moved her from the freight car. She had woken to find herself in a simple dress of heavy grey linen. Her hair had been washed and she was barefoot, her left ankle chained to a strut beneath the seat. The cuff was padded leather, and gave her no discomfort. A silent woman came three times a day to bring her food – always a wrapped packet of heavy bread, with sausage or cheese, never both – and to take her to the washroom at the end of the corridor. On washroom trips Maroussia saw no one. The other compartments in the carriage had their blinds drawn or were empty. The linoleum was cool under her feet, the water in the bathroom hot, the towel fresh and rough. The bathroom window was barred. All the windows of the carriage were barred. It seemed she had the entire carriage to herself. The woman who came, the provodnitsa, would answer no questions.

The first time, after the washroom, Maroussia had refused to let her leg be shackled again. 'No,' she said. 'No. Not that.' She kicked viciously at the provodnitsa's hand.

The woman shrugged and left her. Later, Maroussia slept, and when she woke she was chained again. Next time the provodnitsa came, she brought with her an enamel pot and put it on the floor in the corner behind the door.

'You are to let me put the chain back on afterwards,' she said, 'or stay in here always.'

Maroussia stared at her for a long time, considering the hot water, the towels, the feel of the linoleum cool underfoot, then nodded and held out her leg for the chain to be removed. Apart from that one time, the provodnitsa was neither unkind nor kind, and never spoke at all.

Maroussia slept long and often, during the days as well as at night, and woke feeling sluggish and dull. She wondered if her food was drugged, or more likely the tin cups of sickly fruit juice out of a can, which had a metallic taint. But probably she was simply exhausted. A floor vent fed engine-warmed air into the compartment and she could not open the window. There was a large mirror above the opposite bench. Whenever she looked at it her own face gazed back at her, dark-eyed and alone. As much as she could, she avoided it. Avoided catching her own eye.

She wondered what Vissarion was doing, what had become of him, if he was even alive. She remembered lying next to him, freezing cold and wet in the bottom of the skiff, folding his unconscious and desperately injured body in her arms as they were carried down the swollen surging Mir. Trying with her own warmth to not let him die when he had been tortured for her sake. She remembered the smooth cold feel of his skin. The smell of the river water and blood in his hair. He was a good man. He met the world with an open face, not closed up hard like a fist as so many did. She felt obscurely guilty, as if she had abandoned him. And in a way she had.

When the track made long sweeping curves Maroussia could see the rest of the train. There were two armoured engines at the front and two huge guns, each on its own heavy truck, one behind the engines and one at the very back. Long barrels canted to the sky. Four more wagons with thick steel plating lined with firing slits carried gun turrets. The bulk of the train was unmarked freight wagons and a dozen passenger cars, looking tiny and incongruous in the Edelfeld-Sparre purple. Between the turreted fighting cars and the freight wagons was a specially widened truck which carried a shapeless bulk, high and wide as a house, shrouded in pale grey camouflage sheeting.

She knew what it was. She could feel its presence. The Pollandore. She tried to reach out towards it with her mind. There was nothing. No response. On a ledge at the front of the Pollandore's truck a mudjhik stood, motionless and sentinel.

The train seemed to be going east, as far as Maroussia could tell, and perhaps a little north. Sometimes they roared along at speed, sometimes they slowed to a crawl, little more than walking pace. Occasionally the train would halt, never in a station but always in a deserted siding or marshalling yard, some with a surrounding cape of township. Maroussia drank in the names when she could see them, and pinned them to her memory, though they meant nothing to her. Ortelsvod. Thabiau. Sarmlovsk. Novimark. Bolland. Malovatisk. Ansk. She tried to see who came and went from the train. Figures passed in and out of view in early mist or evening darkness. People must have seen her face at the lit carriage window but nobody came near.

On the second day out of Mirgorod, shortly after dawn, the train came to a long shuddering stop with a screaming of brakes and the guns began to fire. The turret muzzles rattled viciously and the big ordnance boomed salvoes. The whole train shifted in the tracks with the recoils. Her face pressed tight against the window bars, Maroussia could see muzzle flashes and drifts of black smoke, but what they were firing at she had no idea. After fifteen minutes or so the firing ceased, but it was several hours before the train moved on.

Time divided itself between periods of trees and periods of lakes. The trees were needle-leaved spars of spruce and pine rising from a carpet of moss. The lakes were leaden grey interludes in a featureless plain of sandy scrub and grass. Flat horizons deadened all sense of forward motion. Days and nights merged one into another.

And then one morning Chazia came to Maroussia's compartment. She looked drained. Exhausted. She filled the compartment with sour staleness and sweat. She sat on the opposite bench under the mirror, swung her legs up onto the seat, and stared at Maroussia. Her pale reddened eyes were unnaturally wide and bright, the skin of her face pallid, grey and dry. She curled up her legs on the seat, cosy and intimate.

'Are you comfortable, darling?' she said. 'Are you sleeping? It must be tedious for you to be so much alone. I will send you books.'

Chazia shifted restlessly in the seat, scratching at the dark patches on her arms and hands, tugging at the skin of her cheek. She was holding the solm of twigs and wax and stuff gently, like something delicate and precious, but in her hand it looked drab and stupid. A bunch of litter. Dead.

'This little thing,' said Chazia. 'It's so fragile. See? You could stick in your thumb and break it apart. It's ephemeral. We need to be quick.'

She winced and scratched vigorously at the skin on the inside of her elbow. There were scabs and wound tracks there. A little fresh blood was oozing. She saw Maroussia looking and smeared the blood away.

'See what it's doing to me?' she said. 'It's making the ants worse. Tiny awful ants. You can't see them, they're too small, but they're there under my skin and I can't get them out. The forest put them there. I went too near the trees at Vig. They're in my arms now, but the face is worse. I can't sleep then. Not at all.' She stopped scratching and looked at Maroussia. Her blue eyes were hot and sore. 'You can't destroy the angel, Maroussia. It isn't destructible. It's too strong. It's beautiful. It spoke to me once, at Vig, and it will speak to me again.'

'Where's this train going?' said Maroussia.

'Novaya Zima,' said Chazia. 'I told you.'

'I don't know where that is.'

Chazia gestured vaguely. 'North.'

'We're not going north.'

'Not yet. We'll turn north when we can.'

'There was shooting yesterday,' said Maroussia. 'Was that the Archipelago? Are you losing the war?'

'Losing it?' said Chazia. 'Of course we can't lose it. The war is good. It is history in action. The old Vlast was stale and tired. Silted up with careerists. They had no energy. No purpose. No imagination. The Archipelago will clear all that away for us. They want Mirgorod? So? Let them have it. Mirgorod is not the Vlast. Mirgorod is one city, yesterday's city. Let them have it. The Archipelago will consume our corruption like maggots in a wound, and for now we let them do their work, and when they have finished we'll brush them away.'

'What if their armies follow you east?' said Maroussia.

'At the time of my choosing I will destroy them,' said Chazia. 'All their armies will count for nothing. They will burn, they will all burn, and the winds of their burning will blow the ashes of the Archipelago from the face of the planet.'

As she talked she was turning the solm over and over in her hands, looking at it from every direction. Cupping it protectively. Holding it up to her face.

'It doesn't do anything,' said Chazia. 'Nothing at all.'

Maroussia felt something moving inside her head. A surreptitious, intrusive touch, like careful fingers probing gently, cool and sly. A secretive violation. It made her feel dizzy and sick.

'What are you doing to me?' she said.

Chazia looked up from the solm.

'You were going to use this,' said Chazia, 'against the Vlast. Against the angel. Against me. You thought you were going to change the world. You thought you could free the planet of angels by the deed of your own hand. You thought you'd got some kind of hero's task.'

'No—'

'It is an interesting form of individualistic delusion. One person does not change the world. History is huge, colossal, unturnable. Look at me. I am building a new, better, cleaner Vlast. By my own efforts I will do this. But I don't think I'm a hero. I know I am not. I reject the concept. I am a conduit, a facilitator. I ride the wave of history but the wave has its own momentum and I go this way because it is inevitable. If I turn aside and try to find my own independent path I will certainly be destroyed. The world is as it is and will be as it will be.'

'Everyone makes their own world,' said Maroussia. 'I will do what I have chosen to do. Because I have chosen. Even if what I do makes no difference to anyone but myself, I'll still have done something that *matters*.'

Again Maroussia felt faint sickening touches inside her mind. Needle probes and clumsy fingers grubbing around. She tried to focus on what was happening but could not.

'But that is such rubbish, sweetness. Can't you hear yourself? Absolute shit. Did you choose the Pollandore, or did it choose you? You don't know anything about what you're dealing with, except what the people in the forest have told you. You're a move in a game, that's all. Someone else's game.'

'No!'

'So what is the Pollandore? What does it do? What is it for? Can you tell me?'

'Take this chain off my leg,' said Maroussia.

Chazia laughed.

'You're stubborn,' she said. 'Determined. I understand what Lom sees in you.'

'You opened his head with a knife.'

'It was a chisel. A fine chisel.'

'You hurt him. You tried to kill him, but it didn't work: it made him better and stronger.'

'He desires you, did you know that?' Maroussia looked away. 'Ah,' said Chazia. 'I see you do. And you desire him? You are lovers perhaps? Are you lovers? Tell me, darling, are you?'

'I want to get off this train,' said Maroussia.

Chazia ignored her.

'There will be time for personal life,' she said. 'One day. We might even live to see it. But not yet, not now, and perhaps for you and me not ever. It cannot be indulged. Now there is work to do, and what is required is clear-sightedness, hardness and resolve in the doing of what is necessary. That will be our gift to the future. Our sacrifice.' Chazia leaned forward and took Maroussia's hand in hers. Stroked it. 'Help me here, darling. Work with me. Help me to use the Pollandore. I don't want to hurt you. I like you.'

'I'm never going to help you. You know that.'

'You will know me better, Maroussia darling, by and by.'

Later that same afternoon the train halted on the shore of an immense and nameless lake. Maroussia watched damson-coloured, damson-heavy cloud heads rise out of the distance and roll towards them, bruising more and more of the sky and darkening the surface of the water, erasing all reflection. Slowly the storm advanced, bringing the closing horizon with it as it came, until the train was enfolded in ominous dim purple-green light. Maroussia stood up in excitement and gripped the window bars. At last fat raindrops splatted on her window, singly at first, but faster and faster, harder and harder. Machine-gun bullets of rain. Water sluiced down the glass in a continuous rippling flood. There might have been arcs of lightning and shattering thunder crashes, or it might have been the glitter and roar of the rain.

Maroussia's shouts of joy were lost in the noise.

And then a crack opened in the world, the rain and the storm split down the middle, and a different sun was shining through the carriage window: splashes of warmth and spaciousness and the quietness of an afternoon in early summer. The sourness in her mouth was gone, and her heart was big and calm with the possibility of happiness.

The Pollandore reached out and touched her face, and for the first time Maroussia felt how close it was, how near in time as well as distance. There had been bad things – bad things that happened and bad things she had done – but she and the Pollandore were travelling together now, and their paths were slowly converging, and the moment would come: the moment of meeting, when good things would be possible again. She could not have said exactly what the good things coming were, but that didn't matter. It made no difference at all.

72

*T*he Pollandore's massive detonation of possibility and different
sunlight sweeps outwards across the continent from its epi-
centre on Chazia's train. It roars like an exploding shock wave
through the certainty of things, gathering momentum as it goes, and the
world of history unfolding stumbles, brought up suddenly smack against
the truth of human dream and desire. In the trenches of the war and the
bitterness of drab town streets the air is suddenly, briefly, rich with the
smell of rain on broken earth; another voice is heard, not in the ears but
in the blood, and for the brief unsustainable duration of the moment of
the Pollandore's passing, nothing, nothing anywhere dies at all.

The surge of change and otherness rolls across the continent and into
the endless forest, where it passes from root to root and from leaf-head
to leaf-head. It is leafburst. It is earth-rooted rain-sifting burning green
thunder. It crashes against the steep high flanks of Archangel like an
ocean storm against the cliffs of the shore.

And Archangel is appalled, because in his delight at his own movement
he realises that he has made a terrible mistake.

He has forgotten to be afraid.

For a moment his painful grinding progress across the floor of the forest
pauses, and for miles around him there is nothing but silence and a second
of waiting.

He gathers. He centres. He focuses.

He remembers this thing.

How is it that he had forgotten? That never happens, but it has happened. This thing has been hiding from him! It has woven a forgetting
around itself, but now it has made itself known.

This is a powerful and dangerous threat.

Archangel traces the path of the passing of the Pollandore moment back to its source. Examines. Analyzes. Knows what he must do.

73

Mirgorod, war city.

Elena Cornelius survived alone. Elena's Mirgorod was zero city, thrown back a thousand years, order and meaning and all the small daily habits of use and illusion scorched and blasted away, the concepts themselves eradicated. Money wasn't money any more when it had no value and there was nothing to buy. Food was what you found or stole. Clothing against the cold and the night lay around free for the taking on the unburied corpses of the dead. Homes weren't security, shelter and belonging: they were broken buildings, burned and burst open to the elements, the intimate objects of interior domestic life scattered on the streets. Apartments were boxes to shut yourself in and wait for the bomb blasts, the fires, the starvation.

She kept moving, ate scraps scavenged from bombed buildings, drank water from rooftop pools and melted snow. She risked being shot for a looter, which she was, and she hid from the conscripters. She existed day by day in the timeless zero city, alien, unrooted, a sentience apart, belonging to nothing. Herself alone. She felt ancient. Places to hide and sleep were plentiful among the cellars and empty streets. When she slept, she dreamed of the rusalka in the potato-field river. She dreamed of her girls. Yeva and Galina. Mornings she woke early into fresh disorientation, the appalling daily shock: always she felt like she had survived a train crash in the night, a bridge that had crumbled beneath her, a house that had fallen down. Life had broken open, and everything was raw and clear. Every day she looked for her girls. Perhaps they had survived. Perhaps they were existing also somewhere, looking for her.

What follows after taking tea?
The resurrection of the dead.

There were no longer newspapers, but the *MIRINFORM* bulletin was posted on walls and telephone poles daily. 'No sooner had Volyana fallen under our fire than the Archipelago soldiers jumped out of the windows with their underwear down and took to their heels. With cries of hurrah the battalion fell upon the slavers. Grenades, bayonets, rifle butts and flaming bottles came into play. The effect was tremendous.' Increases in rations were reported. The city held stockpiles of grain and dried fish in reserve, ready to be distributed if the need arose. *Courage, citizens. One more push, and victory will be ours.* Nobody believed, but everybody gathered to read when a new edition was posted. It did not say that the cemeteries were full and there was no fuel for the mortuary trucks.

Elena walked out to the edge of the city until the way was barred by fighting. Three times she probed the outskirts in different directions, but always it was the same. Cleared firing zones. Shell holes filled with corpses and refuse. Charred skeletal buildings. The clatter of tank tracks and the rattle of gunfire. On her third attempt a sniper's bullet skittered through the broken bricks at her feet like a steel lizard.

Elena knew she was tiring. The effort of keeping moving all day was almost beyond her. She should choose a place to be her permanent home, but she had to keep moving, walking twenty or thirty miles in a day. Looking for her girls.

On the third night the snow came again, a silent softness of feathers thickening the air. She had collected nothing. Her food bag was empty. She broke open the door of an empty house on the edge of the firing zone, drank the last of her water bottle, lit a fire in the grate, laid herself out on the floor and slept.

She was woken by someone kicking her leg. The dazzle of a flashlight in her eyes.

'Stand up! I said stand up!'

Two young men were looking down at her. Well fed bare-headed boys. Waist-length pea coats. Black trousers and heavy black boots. Elena knew what they were. They were the Boots, and they were the worst. She had always known that one day she would be too tired, too hungry, not careful enough, and it would be finished. But she stood up to face them.

'Yes?' she said. 'What?'

Rizhin had co-opted the semi-organised, semi-militarised thugs of the Mirgorod Youth and Student Brigade to support the militia in the war against defeatists, hoarders, looters, racketeers, saboteurs and spies. They were kept fed and left to do as they would. Autonomy without discipline. And what they did was rob and torture and rape and kill. People said that even the VKBD found the Boots excessive. Repellent. Elena had heard the Boots roamed the places near the fighting, but she had been too tired to remember.

The Boots were holding rifles. Bayonets fixed to the muzzles. The one with the flashlight turned it off and put it on the floor. The light from the fire was enough.

'Take off your scarf,' he said. 'Let's see your face.' His friend was grinning.

Elena let the scarf drop to the floor.

'Now the coat.'

She unbuttoned the heavy greatcoat and let it fall.

'And the sweater.'

The two boys were both staring at her now. Not grinning any more. Focused. Eager. Elena saw one of them swallow hard.

'Take off the shirt,' he said.

'And the trousers. Turn around.'

'Go on. Don't stop. Show us. Let's see what you've got. Let's see it all.'

The Boots had laid down their rifles and were opening their own clothing. Fumbling with their belts and flies.

'No,' said Elena. She stopped, her right hand behind her back. She was trembling. Her hands were shaking. 'No.'

'Bitch.'

One of the Boots lunged forward to push her down, his trousers open and falling round his thighs. Elena pulled out the kitchen knife she kept tucked in the back of her trousers and shoved it into his belly. The boy gasped and stopped in surprise, looking down at his stomach. Disbelieving. Elena took a step back, pulled out the knife, swept it upwards and sliced the blade laterally under his chin. Blood spilled out and splashed to the floor. The boy stared at her. He made a small gurgle in his opened throat.

The other one was scrabbling for his rifle.

'Drop it. Now.'

The Boot swung round. A VKBD officer was standing in the doorway, a pistol in his hand.

'Piss off, Brosz,' said the Boot and raised the rifle muzzle, pointing the bayonet towards him. The officer shot him in the knee and he fell, screaming.

'I've had enough of this,' said the officer. 'You're such a fucking pair of pigs.'

He walked over to the screaming boy and shot him again. In the face.

The other boy, the one Elena had cut, was still standing in the middle of the room. He was cupping his throat with one hand, trying to catch the blood. The other hand was pressed against the wound in his belly. He was weeping.

The officer raised his pistol at arm's length and fired. An execution shot.

'This your place?' he said to Elena. She was standing half-undressed in the firelight, the kitchen knife in her hand, held low at her side.

'No.'

'Then you're looting.'

'Yes.'

'That's a hanging crime.'

'Yes.'

The VKBD officer studied her for a moment.

'How long have you been scavenging?'

'Always.'

He nodded.

'And you're still alive. More than that, you're still strong. And a good fighter.'

'If you're not going to shoot me,' said Elena Cornelius, 'I'm going to put my coat back on.'

'Ever used a rifle?' he said.

'No.'

'Come with me. We'll teach you. You'll be more use than a roomful of these pigs.'

'I'm better off on my own.'

'It isn't a choice. It's that, or I string you up in the morning.'

Conscripts to the Forward Defence Units got a day's firearm training and, if they were fortunate, a weapon. Elena Cornelius turned out to have an aptitude for marksmanship. The sergeant took her aside.

'You. You will be a sniper,' he said. 'A woman is good for sniping. You are small. You are flexible. You stand the cold better than a man.'

She was issued with felt overboots, a thick tunic, a fur shapka, the kind with flaps for the ears. A printed booklet with tables that set out how to adjust the aiming point to take account of the ballistic effects of freezing air. And a bolt-action 7.62mm Sergei-Leon rifle with a side-mounted 3.5x Gaussler scope, the one with two turrets, one for elevation and one for windage: effective range 1,000 yards with optics. The modified Sergei-Leon was exclusive to the VKBD; the regular army never had the funds for such precision firearms.

'You learn by doing,' the sergeant said. 'We send you out with someone who knows what they're doing.'

Elena was paired with a woman called Rosa, a student of history until the Archipelago came.

'I volunteered,' said Rosa. 'I was a good shot already. I used to hunt with my father on Lake Lazhka. Wildfowl are harder to hit than soldiers.' Rosa already had seventeen confirmed kills. 'We'll go in the afternoon,' she said. 'Firing into the east, you don't want to shoot in the morning.'

Rosa led to the way a place near a machine-gun post on the roof of a factory. The enemy were only three hundred yards away.

'Shoot when the machine gun is shooting,' she said. 'They won't even know we're here, never mind spot us.'

They were up there for nine hours. When they had finished and returned to the barracks, Elena Cornelius packed her things into a kitbag, slung her rifle over her shoulder and walked away, back into the city to look for her girls.

74

A lone in her private carriage in the dark hours after midnight, Lavrentina Chazia lay, fully clothed and sleepless on her bunk, listening to the rumble of the train wheels on the track. She was exhausted, but she knew she would not sleep: she rarely slept any more, the ants under her skin made it impossible, with their creeping and crawling and the sting of their tiny bites. The patches of angel stuff on her arms and face itched and burned.

After a fruitless day attempting to break through the shell of the Pollandore using various mechanisms of her own devising, she had spent the evening with the Shaumian woman, and even for Chazia, who was hardened to such things, the experience had not been pleasant. Frustrated by the lack of progress, she had concluded it was time to abandon the subtle approach in favour of more direct methods. Maroussia Shaumian was stubborn to the point of stupidity, and after their last talk she had become even more recalcitrant, almost confident. Chazia sensed that something had changed, but she didn't know what and she didn't care: it was a matter of breaking the girl's will, and she knew how to do that. She had decided against using the worm, for fear of doing some damage to the girl's mind that would prevent her doing whatever needed to be done with the Pollandore, so the work had been noisy and messy.

The process was still not complete, but Chazia had grown tired and faintly disgusted, so she'd left the girl to the professional interrogators and withdrawn to her compartment. She needed to find rest: her mind lacked edge and speed, and her spirits were low. She was bored, restless and above all frustrated. The power of the Vlast was within reach, but she had not yet quite grasped it: still there was Fohn, and the feeble

Khazar. The power of the Pollandore was within reach but she could not get there, she didn't know how to use it and the Shaumian woman was giving her nothing. Chazia was coming to doubt she had anything to give. And the living angel, the greatest power of all, had never come to her again. All she heard was silence.

In her sleepless solitude Chazia began to wonder if perhaps, after all her efforts, she was going to fail. Maybe she was simply not good enough to do what she had set out to do. She felt the need for power, any power, in her belly like a hunger. She was incomplete without it. She was *made* for power, she was *capable* of it, she *deserved* it. She had worked so hard for so long. She had made sacrifices. She had given her life to the Vlast unstintingly. She had *served*. When she held her hands stretched out before her in the darkness, palms open, they felt empty, with an emptiness ready to be filled. And yet …

Chazia sat up abruptly and turned on the lamp. She swung her legs off the bunk and stood up. Her self-pity disgusted her. Such moods came upon her when she was alone with nothing to do but think. That was why she must always be working. Never be inactive. Never. Keep moving, keep trying, keep going forward. Always choose the *difficult* thing. Always choose to *dare*.

She went through to the next compartment, where she kept the suit of angel flesh that she had made. The uncanny watchfulness of the thing made her uneasy. She realised for the first time that she was frightened of it, in the way you're frightened to get back on a horse that's thrown you several times. But the reluctance, the fear in her stomach, that was the reason to do it. She took the headpiece from its shelf and put it on. She felt it reach out and clamp onto her, plunging invasive tendrils deep into her mind. It was eager, it was ready, and now so was she. Fresh excitement stirred in her belly. Her mind began to turn faster. It was better already. This was what she needed.

Awakening angel senses trickled information into her mind. She felt with prickling clarity the many lives on the train, the energy of the engine working, the miles and miles of passing trees and snow. The Pollandore. She felt the Pollandore by its absence. Its impossibility. It was a strange blankness. It told her nothing.

She called out to the living angel in the forest.

Where are you? Speak to me. I am here.

Again and again she called into the emptiness, as she had done a hundred times before.

And this time the angel answered.

At last it answered!

When the angel had spoken to Chazia at Vig, it had almost destroyed her. It had come roaring into her mind, a crude appalling destroying storm of sheer inhuman force, as infinite and absolute and cold as the space between the stars, pounding and pouring into her, stronger and more powerful than she could bear, until her head burst open and her lungs heaved for breath but could find none. But this time it was different. Perhaps it was because of the casket of angel flesh enclosing her head, or perhaps it was because she was stronger now, and better prepared, more equal to the encounter. It did not occur to her that the angel had learned subtlety and control.

I see what you're doing, darling, the angel whispered, and its voice in her head was Chazia's own voice, Chazia speaking to Chazia, intimately, the lover speaking to the one it loves. *I see that thing you're bringing, and I see what you want to do with it. You're so brave, my beautiful, so brilliant and so brave. It really is remarkable. But you will not do this. It will not be done.*

'No,' said Chazia. 'No. I want it.'

I am so sorry, Lavrentina. I left you alone for so long. Too much time has passed. It was wrong of me, I made a mistake, I see that now, and I've come back. Can you forgive me, Lavrentina?

Her name! It was using her name. It knew her, it had always known her! Chazia had been right: it had been there watching all along, but silent, so cruelly silent.

I understand you so much better now, darling. You felt abandoned and alone and you turned to this other thing to comfort you. I understand that. But I'm back now. You don't need the other thing, not any more.

The angel went everywhere inside her, turning everything over, Chazia's angel-enhanced senses flared incandescently. It was overwhelming. She felt the strength of her body and the force of her will magnified a hundred, a thousand times. Nothing was impossible.

Is this not what you want, Lavrentina? Am I not enough and more than enough? Am I not all that you would ever need?

'Yes.'

We just need to destroy that thing you're bringing. You don't understand it, Lavrentina. It has deceived you. It's a terrible, repellent thing. We have to get rid of it and then, together, just you and me, we can do ... anything!

'I don't want to destroy it. We can use it. Once I have learned—'

I know what you want, darling, and I will give it to you. I will give you everything. The whole world will see what you are. Just do this for me. The thing must be destroyed. Destroy the disgusting repellent thing. Let it burn.

'I don't want to do that,' whispered Chazia.

But we need to destroy it, my love.

75

L om woke to grey daylight and Antoninu Florian looking down
on him, his hand on his shoulder.

'Vissarion?' Florian was saying. He looked concerned.

'What?' said Lom, warm and reluctant. He was comfortable. There
was a pillow. Sheets. Florian's head was framed in a wide square of
leaden sky.

It was a window. There were thin lemon-yellow curtains, pulled
open.

Lom hauled himself upright in the narrow steel cot. Springs pro-
tested under his weight. The walls of the room were corrugated tin on
a timber frame. There was a table under the window. A desk. Empty.

'Where are we?' said Lom. He had been dreaming of water and
trees. The encounter with the dead angel was a distant and receding
darkness, a stain of metallic fear on the horizon. He didn't want to
think about that.

'The aerodrome at Terrimarkh,' said Florian. 'How do you feel?'

Lom thought about it.

'Good,' he said. 'Hungry. And I could do with coffee. A lot of coffee.
And a piss.'

'OK,' said Florian. 'Good. And then we leave.' He hesitated. 'Can
you do that? Are you well?'

'Of course. Why?'

Florian handed him a razor.

'You might want to shave while you're in the bathroom.'

Lom ran his hand across his chin and felt a thick rough growth of
beard.

'Shit. How long—'

'We have lost much time. You were delirious, confused, and then you slept very deeply. We couldn't wake you at all. Gretskaya is fretting to be away.'

'How long has it been?'

'We have lost three days.'

'*Three days!*'

Lom pushed back the covers, hauled himself out of the bed and walked unsteadily across to the window. Standing was a shock. The bare linoleum chilled his feet. His legs felt feeble. Shaky under his weight. He looked out on bleak expanses of concrete and asphalt under a threadbare dusting of snow. Hangars and huts, low and widely separated. Fuel tanks. A water tower. And beyond the aerodrome, nothing: no house, no hill, no road, no fence, no tree, only the weight of the sky, draining the world of colour. The single runway, swept clear of snow, stretched black into the distance. The Kotik stood ready. There were no other aircraft visible. No sign of life at all.

Three days! Maroussia! Shit!

'How soon can we leave?' he said.

'Get dressed. I'll find you something to eat. Then we'll go.'

Two hours later they were airborne and on their way north to Novaya Zima. Gretskaya stayed below the cloud bank. The altimeter showed a steady 2,000 feet. She found the railway and followed it north. The track cut straight across monochrome tundra, mile after mile, hour after hour, parallel with the low hills on the starboard horizon, misted grey with distance. Drifts of leafless birch trees rolled away behind them, and white expanses of snow pitted with circular lakes. The lakes, not yet entirely frozen, were fringed grey with ice at the shore. The dilated coal-black waters stared sightlessly back at the sky.

At last the coast fell suddenly away behind them and they were over the sea, but the railway plunged on, carried on concrete piers. The track stretched ahead of them, cutting low and arrow-straight across the dark waters to the distant vanishing point. Squadrons of seabirds swept low over the waves, floated in speckled rafts, and lined the concrete parapets of the endless viaduct, roosting.

'That is the Dead Bridge,' said Gretskaya. 'It was built by penal labour. Men, women, even children worked on it. There are hundreds of bodies under the water, thousands maybe, all drowned, frozen, starved, dead of exhaustion. The eels and the fishes get fat on the bodies and the birds get fat on the fish.'

Ahead of them there was no horizon. The sea merged with the sky, diffuse and indeterminate and in the deep distance the Dead Bridge narrowed and faded as if into the air. The Kotik roared on.

After half an hour or so, above the place where the railway viaduct still disappeared into the distance, a paler colourless wash came slowly forward, separated itself from the sky and resolved into a distant mountain, its peak buried in cloud, its base lost in mist.

'That's it,' said Gretskaya. 'That's where we're going. Novaya Zima.' She swung the Kotik away to the north-east, climbing until the railway was out of sight, then turned round, dropped down to a hundred feet and cut the throttle.

And then they were gliding, the wind hissing through the struts, the rotor blades turning slowly. Lom could see small scattered rafts of ice floating on the water below them, rising and falling with the swell.

'I'll come in low and quiet,' Gretskaya said. 'No one will know we're there.'

The island of Novaya Zima was a spine of dark hills ridged with snow, rising higher to the north, towards the still-distant mountain. The lower slopes were covered with trees: a dark monotonous woodland that rolled away from the hills until it met the shore. The seaplane skimmed onwards. The black wall of trees widened and rose to meet them. Gretskaya dropped the tail and they came down, bouncing a couple of times off the swell and settling in a long subsiding skid across the water. She opened the throttle slightly and motored towards the narrow shoreline, a ten-yard strip between the water and the edge of the woods. The seaplane's nose beached gently a couple of yards out.

Gretskaya slid the cockpit open. She kept the engine running.

'Go,' she said. 'Quickly. Go.'

Lom climbed out, dropped to his waist in freezing pine-green water and waded ashore. It was a steep climb, soft mud sucking at his feet. He almost lost his shoes. The beach was an unstable mass of twigs and mouldering needles and leaves, thickly matted with rotting seaweed. His feet broke the surface with every step, dislodging an appalling stench and clouds of tiny black flies that buzzed angrily at his face and neck. He stumbled and fell forward, plunging his hands elbow-deep into the high tideline.

'Fuck,' he muttered to himself. 'Fuck. Fuck.' It was bitterly cold.

He turned when he reached the trees. Florian was coming up the beach behind him, a small canvas knapsack slung from one shoulder by a narrow leather strap. Gretskaya had already pulled the Kotik back and was swinging it round to face out to sea. The roar of the engine rolled along the shore as she raced away, leaving a widening wake, and lifted into the sky.

76

The woodland was a dim, perspectiveless, muted labyrinth of widely spaced birch and pine. Resinous. Twilit. Snow-carpeted. Directionless. Florian seemed to know where he was going: he set off quickly, moving in as straight a line as was possible, away from the sea.

Lom followed.

'We must get clear of the landing place,' said Florian. The moss and the snow and the trees drained all echo, making his voice sound drab and flat. 'We cannot light a fire until it is dark.' He fished a twist of paper out of his pocket. It was filled with solid dark pieces of sugar. 'Here,' he said, holding one out. 'Eat this. We go west until we strike the railway. Then we follow it north wherever it goes. OK?'

'How far?' said Lom.

'To the railway? Ten or twenty miles. Not more. After that, who knows? We follow the track to its end, wherever that is. The south island is a hundred and twenty miles long and fifty wide at the waist, but I doubt we will have to go so far.'

'What we're looking for is on the south island? Why not the north?'

'I think not the north. This island sits across a current of warmer water that flows from the west; the north island does not. It is under permanent ice, glaciers come down from the mountains.'

Florian, in his sombre suit, dark overcoat and astrakhan hat, the knapsack on his back, moved with fast and sure-footed noiseless grace. Lom jogged and stumbled behind him. The Blok 15 was a solid weight in his pocket. He carried nothing else. Shallow streams crossed their path, ice-fringed water running fast over mud and gravel, turning aside and deepening into moss- and root-edged pools. They drank and washed the stinking smears of the shoreline from their clothes. Lom plunged his face into the freezing water and sluiced his matted hair, then sat on a fallen trunk to wipe his eyes with his sleeve. When he looked up he saw the wolves. They were moving under the tree-shadow, silent and indistinct as moths. One turned its face towards him. Wolf eyes. Unhurried, considering.

'Wolf,' he called to Florian in a low voice.

He would fight, if he had to. Wolf mouth on his face, his arm in a wolf mouth, fingers in a wolf throat, digging. Dragging his revolver from his pocket, firing it into wolf belly. Firing again. Blood and blood. Without hope, he would turn and fight.

'I see them,' said Florian. 'There are others behind us. They are following.'

Lom jerked round but there was nothing to see.

'Why didn't you say before?'

'They will not trouble us while I am here,' said Florian. 'They are not hunting, they are curious, that's all. But do not go far alone. Not without me.'

All afternoon and into the evening they pushed on through the trees, Florian moving fast and confidently, Lom struggling to keep up. From time to time he looked for wolves but did not see them again.

They broke out onto the edge of the railway track suddenly, without warning. It stretched away to right and left, twin parallel rails. The massive sleepers and ten-foot gauge of a major freight line. On either side of the track the trees had been cut down and cleared five yards back from the line. It was freshly done work, the toppled trees stacked neatly, the ground scattered with raw yellow axe chippings, the scent of fresh-cut timber in the air. An inch-deep covering of snow. It made the going easier. They turned right and began to jog along beside the rails.

They had been going steadily for about an hour when Florian stopped suddenly.

'Train,' he said. 'Do you hear? A train is coming.'

'I can't hear anything,' said Lom. He was breathing hard. Heart pounding in his chest.

'Get out of sight,' said Florian urgently.

Lom followed him into the dimness under the trees and they

hunched down low to wait. Eventually he heard the rumbling in the rails, rising in pitch to a squeal as the train got closer. It was approaching from behind them. He could hear it now, a locomotive under full steam. The train roared into view and thundered past, close enough to see the moustache glistening on the engineer's face in the firebox glow and catch the smell of hot iron and burning coal. Iron wheels high as a man is tall. Truck after truck followed the engine, ten, twenty, thirty of them, wooden-sided, windowless, each as long as a barn. Lom recognised them. The long trains. He had seen such trains, hundreds of them, waiting in rows in the Wieland marshalling yards. They looked like cattle trucks but they weren't for carrying cattle.

They walked on, following the railway track. There were no landmarks. No horizon except the vanishing point of the track. Walking brought them no nearer to anything and no further away. Motion without movement. The birch trees receded in all directions, endlessly repeating mirrors of trees, misting into brown and grey, dimness and snow. Numberless, featureless and utterly bleak.

'We'll camp here,' said Florian when the light began to fail. They had reached nowhere in particular.

They left the railway and pushed three or four hundred yards in under the trees, to a place where a heavy spruce had fallen, tearing its root mass from the earth, making a small clearing where scrub and thorn had taken root. Florian fished a small bag from his pocket and gave it to Lom. It held a fire steel and a clump of dry tinder: moss and leaves and small twigs, all dry and sweet.

'Here,' he said. 'Keep the fire small. We should be far enough from the track, but we should take no risks.'

Lom gathered a bundle of branches and set them by. He scraped a patch of earth clear with his foot and checked the ground for shallow-buried roots that could catch and smoulder underground. There were no stones to make a hearth. He took a handful of tinder from the pouch and laid it ready: a tight clump in the middle, outside pieces pulled looser to let the air in. When the tinder was set he held the fire steel close above it and struck a shower of sparks. He got it first time, sweet, like he always did, and bent low to breathe on the faint smoulder. Gentle. Gentle. Encouraging the little flicks of flame to come alive. Breathing in the faint smell of woodsmoke.

The wood he had gathered was all damp. He chose a few of the smallest, driest pieces and set them round the smouldering tinder one by one, carefully, to shelter the frail young flame, to barely touch it and take it into themselves. He fed it with a little extra tinder when it started to fail and felt the first brush of heat against his face. A little cup of life in the gathering dark. When he was sure of the small fire, he picked out some of the larger branches from the pile and set them in a careful pyramid around the tiny fire, closing it in like a tent frame. The heat and smoke would dry them out.

Lom sat back for a moment and watched. A bitter breeze had risen as the light faded. The legs of his trousers were still soaked, and now he had stopped moving the cold of it chilled him. But the fire had steadied. It was breathing. He watched the lick of small quick colours, the sparks in the smoke, the heart of it growing stronger.

While Lom made the fire, Florian took a small hand axe from his knapsack and hacked an armful of larger branches from the fallen spruce. He propped them against the side of the tree and wove thinner stem-lengths through them to bind a strong, shallow-sloping wall, on which he piled deep armfuls of brush and damp earth, until he had made a low, dark tunnel closed at one end, with a mouth at the other. He took some branches still heavy with needles and cut them to size, to make a door for the entrance which could be pulled shut once you were inside.

When he had finished, he came across to the fire. Considered it with approval.

'It's good,' he said.

He pulled a little pan from his knapsack and set it on the fire. Used the axe to cut a fist-sized chunk of pork into slices and dropped them in. 'I raided the kitchen at Terrimarkh,' he said. 'The shelter is for you. You should spread more leaves inside on the floor.'

'What about you?'

'I have no need. I will not sleep.'

When they had eaten, Florian set some water to boil in the pan and scattered it with coffee grounds. Dropped in a small pebble of sugar. He set the pan aside to cool and then they drank from it in silence, alternating sips. The drink was dark and bitter and sweet and good. Night thickened between the darkness and the trees.

Lom sat quietly and stared out into the darkness, taut as wire.

77

Hundreds of miles to the south Eligiya Kamilova lay on her back on a narrow shelf in a crowded stinking cattle wagon. The train had been stopped for hours. There was the noise of other trains outside, shunting and moving slowly past. Shouted orders. Men talking. Narrow shafts of bright arc light beamed in through the gap near the top of the wall and splashed across her face. She did not know where they were. She was no longer hungry or thirsty. That had passed. She was not waiting. The time would come when it was ready to come. There was nothing to wait for.

The freight car door rolled open with a crash and light spilled in. Electric light and cold night air which smelled of bitumen and naphtha and trees. More people were being shoved inside, though there was no room. VKBD men swore at them as they hesitated. A woman started to shout and scream. Eligiya Kamilova couldn't understand what she was saying. A young boy in uniform smashed her in the face with the butt of his rifle. That quieted her. Kamilova turned away, staring at the pitch-soaked wooden ceiling close above her face. It would be bad if she were seen looking.

When the door was rolled shut and locked again, she took another look at the new arrivals. They brought with them nothing. No bags. No coats. No food or water. They stood or crouched in the shadows. Some of the men on the lower shelves were jostled. They swore at the newcomers in low vicious voices and pushed them away.

There were two young girls in school clothes standing together near her, close and side by side, their faces drawn and scared in the harsh shadowy light. They were looking for somewhere to go, somewhere to be out of the way. Kamilova recognised them. It took her a few seconds to recollect their names.

'Hey,' she called across to them quietly. 'Galina. Yeva.'

The girls looked round, trying to find where the voice was coming from.

'Over here,' said Kamilova. 'Up here.' The girls stared at her. They didn't move. They had learned not to trust the friendly voice. The invitation. 'You are Elena Cornelius's girls aren't you. Do you remember me?'

'No,' said Yeva.

'Yes,' said Galina.

'It is Eligiya,' said Kamilova. 'I know you. I know your mother. From the raion. I am her friend.' She swung herself awkwardly down from the high shelf and squeezed her way towards them, stepping over the tightly packed people sitting on the floor.

'Is your mother with you?'

'No,' said Galina.

'Do you know where she is?'

'No. She was left behind.'

Hours later, Kamilova lay on her shelf listening for the sound of movement outside the train. There was none. For half an hour, as well as she could judge, there had been none. The arc lights still burned. It must have been nearly dawn. She climbed slowly, carefully down and went to find the girls. They were sitting together on the floor, backs against the door. Yeva was asleep. Galina was watching her with wide blank eyes.

Kamilova knelt down and nudged Yeva gently awake.

'Get ready,' she whispered. 'I am going now and you're coming with me.'

'Where are we going?' said Galina.

'Do you want to stay on the train?'

'No.'

'Then it's time to get off.'

Kamilova stood up and pulled the girls to their feet. They looked uncertain and confused but they did it.

'When I say,' said Kamilova, 'run. Stay together and stay with me and run as fast as you can. Whatever happens don't stop. Don't listen to anything else but me. Don't look back and don't stop running unless I say.'

She turned to face the doors, closed her eyes and took a breath.

Calm. Calm. Think only of the night and the air.

The timbers of the massive heavy door screamed. The wood fibres ripped as it bowed and bellied outwards and split and burst and sprang from its rails and crashed to the ground below.

Kamilova jumped down and turned to catch Yeva and Galina.

'Now!' she screamed at them. 'Run! Now! Run with me! Run!'

78

Every night at midnight General Rizhin gathered his city defence commanders together to hear their reports, review the day just finished and make plans for the next. In the early days of the siege, when they first understood that Rizhin intended to make a stand, the commanders he appointed had attacked their tasks with a fierce commitment and determination. Few among them thought they could actually succeed in driving back the overwhelming force of the enemy, but there was honour, and for some a fierce joy, in fighting not running. A week of bloody resistance was worth more than a lifetime of capitulation, and every day that Mirgorod did not fall was a day stolen from inevitability by their own determination and will. Rizhin had chosen them because that was how they felt, and he'd chosen well.

But now, as Rizhin's gaze moved round the table, examining first one face and then another, he saw tiredness, lack of confidence, reluctance, even despair. One by one they gave their reports, and none of the news was good. Every day the enemy's forces made some small advance, and the best that Mirgorod ever achieved was not to lose more. Defeat was only a matter of time, and the longer it took, the more grindingly desperate, even humiliating the resistance became. Rizhin knew that his commanders were beginning to feel this, and some were even willing quietly and privately to say so. A shared collective opinion was forming among them, in the way that such opinions do, without any one person leading it, that to continue the battle further was to impose pointless suffering on the people of the city. And so, this midnight, Rizhin called the city commanders together, grey-faced and dusty with the struggles of the day, in a different room, one end of which was separated off by a wide, heavy curtain.

When they were assembled, Rizhin took his place at the head of the table, relaxed and smiling, and spoke to them in a quiet voice.

'Colleagues,' he said, 'friends, I know how tired you all are. You are fighting bravely, you do wonders every day, but I see in your faces that some of you don't trust the struggle any more. Perhaps some of you think I should have accepted the enemy's terms of surrender—'

'No!' shouted Latsis, loyal Major Latsis, and some round the table joined in the murmurs of denial, but others kept silent, and Rizhin noted for later who they were.

'I know that some of you are thinking this,' Rizhin continued. 'Where are we going with this bitter, grinding resistance? That is what you ask each other. What is the purpose? What is the strategy?' He leaned forward and skewered them one by one with his stare. None of them would meet his eye. 'Do you think I don't know how you whisper among yourselves?' he continued. 'Do you think I don't hear it all? Do you think it does not reach my ears, this cowardice and doubt? This backsliding? This revisionism?'

Rizhin let the uncomfortable silence grow and spread round the table.

'I don't need to hear it,' he added. 'I can smell it in the room.'

'General Rizhin—' began Fritjhov, commander of the Bermskaya Tank Division.

'Let me finish,' said Rizhin, his voice quiet, reasonable.

'No!' said Fritjhov. 'I will have my say! You call us cowards? *Cowards!* Our soldiers fight for the city, and they will fight to the bitter end, they will fight and die for Mirgorod. But they cannot fight and *win*. We cannot fight without munitions, and munitions do not come. We cannot advance without air cover, and our air force does not come. The Vlast has abandoned Mirgorod to the enemy! The enemy knows this, and do you think our soldiers don't?'

Rizhin poured himself a glass of water. The clink of the jug against the tumbler was the only sound in the room.

'Munitions?' he said. 'Air cover? There's only one weapon that wins wars, Fritjhov, and that is fear. Terror. If the enemy think they are winning, it's because they smell the stench of your fear.'

Fritjhov bridled.

'I am a soldier,' he growled. 'I am not afraid to die.'

Rizhin shrugged.

'Then you will die, Fritjhov,' he said. 'What I need are commanders who are not afraid to *win*.' He fixed the room with his burning, fiery glare. Holding them with all the relentless force of his will and the strength of his imagination. It was Rizhin the poet, Rizhin the artist of history, speaking to them now. 'There are new forms in the future, my friends,' he said, 'and they need to be filled in with blood. A new type of humankind is needed now: individuals whose moral daring makes them vibrate at a speed that makes motion invisible. We here in this room are the first of mankind, and this city is our point of departure. There is no past, there is only the future, and the future is ours to make. Our imminent victory in Mirgorod will be just the beginning.'

'There isn't going to be any fucking victory here, man,' said Fritjhov. 'As senior commander it is my duty—'

Rizhin smiled.

'Victory is coming, Fritjhov my friend. Victory is nearly here.'

'What—'

'A train is coming from the north-east, bringing a consignment of artillery shells.'

'One shipment of shells?' said Fritjhov in derision, looking round the table for support.

'Shells of a new type,' said Rizhin. 'You will need to prepare your guns. I will give you instructions.'

Fritjhov jumped to his feet, sending his chair clattering.

'No more instructions, Rizhin, not from you.'

Rizhin was a restful centre of patience and forbearance.

'Just sit down a moment, would you, Fritjhov,' he said, 'and I will show you what is coming.'

Rizhin stood and walked across the room. He drew back the heavy curtain to reveal a projector and a cinema screen. He started the projector whirring and turned off the lights.

WINTER SKIES

FIELD TEST #5

NORTH ZIMA EXPANSE

VAYARMALOND OBLAST

79

Lom woke in the quiet before dawn and lay still in the cocoon of branches and leaf mould, knees pulled up tight against his belly, head pillowed on the warm knot of his own folded arms. He didn't want to move.

He breathed with his mouth, shallow slow breaths. Breathing the warmth of his own breath, inhaling pine and earth and moss, the smell of damp woodsmoke in his clothes and his hair. He listened for sounds from outside the shelter, but there was nothing: the thickness of the shelter absorbed sound as it absorbed light. Yet the shelter itself had its own faint whispering, a barely audible movement of shifting and settling, the outer layer flicking and feathering in the breeze, and sometimes the rustle and tick of small things – woodlice? spiders? mice? – in the canopy. The shelter was a living thing that had settled over him, absorbing him, nurturing. Deep beneath him in the cold earth the roots of trees, the fine tangled roots, sifted and slid and touched one another. They whispered. They were connected. All the trees together made one tree, night-waking and watchful. It knew he was there.

Twice in the night Lom had heard the long trains passing.

He had done a terrible thing and the guilt of it weighed him down. He had lost Maroussia. He had not been there. He could hear the sound of her voice in his head, but not the words.

Reluctantly he sat up and pushed the entrance branches aside and let in the dim grey dawn and the cold of the day. Harsh frost had come in the night, and now mist reduced the surrounding forest to a quiet clearing edged by indeterminacy. When he crawled out of the shelter the mist brushed cold against his face and filled his nose and lungs, and when he walked his shoes crunched on brittle, snow-dusted iron earth.

Florian was sitting nearby, almost invisible in shadow until he moved. He had left a hare skinned and ready by the remains of the previous night's hearth, and next to it was a small heap of mushrooms and a handful of clouded purple berries.

'I think we could risk a fire,' he said. 'Before the mist clears.'

Lom started on the fire. The intense cold made his fingers clumsy: he fumbled the tinder, dropped it. He couldn't make his stiffened blue-pale hands work properly. He found that the water had frozen in the pan. He went for fresh.

Dawn greyed into morning, sifting darkness out of the mist-dripping branches, condensing detail. Pine needle, twig and thorn. When they had eaten, they went back to the railway track and started to walk north again. Through gaps in the trees they could see the mountain ahead of them, rising pale grey and snow-streaked into the cloud. At one point Florian paused to reach up and pulled a snag from the side of a birch trunk. He studied it, then held it out to Lom.

'Look,' he said. 'It is not right.'

Lom studied the sprig. The leaves were grown too large, and some were misshapen. Sickle-edged. Distorted.

'And here,' said Florian. 'I found this also.' A small branch of pine, the needles long but floppy and fringed with edges of lace. 'They are not all like this, but some. And more near here than when we landed.'

After an hour they found the body of the wolf. Or most of it. Its belly was ripped open and empty and one of its hind legs was gone, torn out at the hip. The wolf carcase was impaled on a broken branch at head height, the sharp-splintered stump of wood pushed through the ribcage and coming out, blood-sticky, from the base of the throat. Its head hung to one side, eyes open. Gibbeted. A warning? Or a larder?

'Was that you?' said Lom.

'No,' said Florian. 'Of course not.'

'I had to ask,' said Lom.

At mid-morning the rain came in pulses, wind-driven, hard, grey and cold, washing away the covering of snow and turning the path to a thick clag of mud. The noise of the rain in the trees was loud like a river. The galloping of rain horses.

Lom's clothes were soaked. They smelled sourly of wet wool and woodsmoke and the warmth of his body. Rain numbed his face and trickled down his neck and chin. Rain spattered across the brown surface of rain-puddles. He kept his head down and walked against it, mud-heavy feet slipping and awkward. Everything distant was lost in the rain.

A wisent stepped out of the trees into the clear way ahead of them. When it saw them it stopped, head bowed, nostrils flaring, watching them with its dark eyes. Lom saw the massive rain-slicked wall of its shoulders, the rufous shaggy fall of hair, thick from neck to chest and down its muzzle from the crown of its head, the fine stocky inward-curving crescent horns. Lom and the wisent faced each other, watching. The wisent tested the give of the mud with a fore hoof and flicked the rain with its ears. Then it turned and walked on across the rails and faded between the trees.

The rain passed, and they came to a place where a stream was running in a ditch alongside the railway track. Lom knelt to drink but Florian put a hand on his shoulder and held him back.

'Don't,' said Florian. 'Look. Over there.'

Half-buried in the bank of the ditch, where a birch tree had canted over, roots unearthed, was a human head. It was blackened, damp and rotting, and wrapped in a length of mud-brown hair. The face stared blackly sideways without eyes, and brown-stained teeth showed in its lopsided sagging mouth. And near the head a human arm reached out from the mud sleeved in sticky green. At first glance the arm had looked like the root of a tree. Too far from the head to be attached to the same skeleton, it trailed mushroom-white and mushroom-soft fingers in the flowing water.

Walking between the railway and the stream, Lom and Florian saw more like that. Pieces of human body. When the stream turned aside from the ditch and retreated under the trees it was a relief.

And then something happened that shook the world.

A silent snap of blue-white light reflected off the clouds and left after-images of skeleton trees drifting across Lom's eyes. Many seconds later he felt the sound of it in the ground through his feet, a roll of noise too deep to hear. Ahead of him Florian stumbled, and would have fallen had he not steadied himself against a stump. A tremble of movement disturbed the underside of the cloud bank like wind across a pool. The trees prickled with fear: the nap of the woodland rising, uneasy, anxious. They stood, listening. Nothing more came. Nothing changed. The clouds settled into a new shape.

'What was it?' said Lom.

'I don't know.'

'It came from the north.'

'I don't know,' said Florian. 'I think it was everywhere.'

The railway track began to sink into cuttings and rise to cross embankments and small bridges. Every few hours one of the long trains came through, heading for the mountain or coming away. Away from the cleared trackside, the going was harder. The trees were sparser now, and they had to push through scrub and thorn and accumulations of snow. They were climbing slowly, the mountain to the north growing clearer and more definite against the sky. Rock and scree. Ice and snow.

They disturbed a parcel of dog-crows gathered on a ragged dark bundle. The birds were a heavy drab and loose-winged black, with unwieldy bone-coloured beaks too heavy for their heads. They carried on picking at the thing on the ground and watched them come. Lom picked up a stick and threw it among them.

'Go on! Get away!'

The crows glared, but moved off a few feet with slow ungainly two-footed jumps. A couple hauled themselves up on flaggy wings to squat low in the trees and stare.

The body on the ground was small and had no head. The crows had picked at its neck and shoulders, spilling red pieces of stuff, and parted the clothes between trousers and shirt to open the belly.

'It's a child,' said Lom. 'Just a boy.'

Florian had walked some way off. Lom thought he was looking away, so as not to see. But he had found something else.

'Not a boy,' said Florian. 'A girl.'

The head was hanging from a branch by the tangle of her hair.

Something was passing near them. Lom felt the woods stir and bristle. The alien watchfulness of what was passing brushed over him, rippling across his mind like rain across a lake. He felt the bigness of it, its steady earth-shaking tread. The top of a distant tree trembled faintly, though there was no wind.

'Mudjhik patrol,' he hissed. 'Coming this way.'

'We separate,' whispered Florian. 'Hide yourself.' He crouched and slipped away. Lom caught a glimpse of him disappearing into the trees, loping from bush to bush, bounding low across the ground.

Lom flattened himself against the ground under a thorn bush and lay quiet, breathing shallow slow breaths. Covered his mind with woodland. Focused his thoughts into a pointy vixen snout, thought vixen thoughts, calm and tired and waiting, warm and cold in the daylight, in a waking sleep. Keeping low. *Pass by. Pass by.* The mudjhik's awareness skimmed across him and moved away, but Lom lay on, vixen-still and thoughtless, faintly stomach-sick, dulled and aching and hungry behind her eyes as if she had not slept at all.

The mudjhik's awareness jerked back, swung round and pinned him. A blank hunter's glare.

I see you. I have sniffed you out. I am coming.

There was a sudden crashing through the trees. Branches breaking, heavy limbs thumping the ground. The mudjhik was rushing towards him. It was still several hundred yards off, but running was not an option and he could not hide.

In panic, reflexively, Lom slammed up a wall against the mudjhik. It was like holding up his hand. *Stop!*

The mudjhik stumbled and fell to its knees.

Lom was stronger now, much stronger. He felt the current flowing between him and the charging alien weight, the mudjhik's alien substance connecting with something tense and fizzing in his own bones and flesh. Lom felt wired and burning. The link between the mudjhik and its handler was a feeble shadowy thing by comparison, a tenuous thread. Lom knew what to do. He broke the handler's cord. Squeezed it closed and ripped it out at its root. Felt for a second the handler's surprise as he lost connection.

The mudjhik was on its feet again, confused and clumsy, rumbling and roaring silently, lashing out at tree trunks with its fists. It was at a loss. Lom pushed himself deeper inside it, feeling for the animal part of it, the inserted mammalian brain. He found it and crushed its awful half-existence out. The mudjhik's mind clouded. Sensation without motion. Without desire. A lump of sentient rock.

*

TRUTH AND FEAR

Late in the afternoon Lom and Florian crested a rise and found themselves on a low hilltop looking out across a wide shallow valley. The railway plunged out across a viaduct above the grey-brown leafless canopy of trees. Five or ten miles away, on the far side of the valley, the mountain was a wall across the sky. And in the plain of the valley floor between them and the foot of the mountain lay the closed township of Novaya Zima.

80

From a distance Novaya Zima looked like a complex device with its back removed – a radio, a telekrypt machine – laid bare amid birch trees and snow. The township hummed and rumbled quietly. No smoke. No chimneys. It was a rectangular grid about three miles square, a compound in the wilderness surrounded by a double fence and a perimeter road. The streets formed blocks, and the blocks were buildings, orderly and rectangular, mostly concrete, ten or fifteen storeys high. Every part of the town was wired to every other part by a network of cables slung between roofs and from tall wooden poles. In the centre of the town, wider streets – avenues, prospects – converged on a spectacular cluster of taller buildings, slender constructions of steel and glass, reflecting the lead-grey sky. Motor vehicles moved with orderly precision along arterial boulevards. Pedestrians, rendered tiny by distance, anonymous and without characteristics, moved along pavements and crossed open expanses of concrete. Raised above the streets on piers of iron, an overhead railway carried snub-nosed carriages. And on the far side, beyond the town and a couple of miles of scrubby trees, the mountain climbed sheer and almost vertical into low cloud. Dark grey rock and scree and streaks of snow. It was like a wall across the world, diminishing east and west into misted distance and further mountains.

Lom and Florian watched from the cover of the trees. It was a town for thousands of people, tens of thousands, freighted in piece by piece across the continent, secretly, and assembled by dying slaves.

'And the labour is still coming,' said Lom. 'There were half a dozen trains yesterday, at least. So where are they? The town's not for them. That's not housing for penal labour. I don't see camps. I don't see factories. I don't see cranes and holes in the ground. So where do they go?'

The rail track crossed the valley floor on viaducts and embankments, bisected the township, cut though an expanse of marshalling yards to the north, and plunged on into a low dark mouth in the mountainside.

'The mountain,' said Florian. 'They go into the mountain.'

There was a gate where the railway entered the township. An asphalt road came out and looped away into the trees to circle the town. The gate stood open, the guard post deserted. It was the middle of the afternoon.

'No security,' said Lom. 'Lazy.'

'Isolation,' said Florian. 'Who could find their way here? And who could leave? Where would they go?'

'We got here,' said Lom.

There was a sign at the gate. A huge billboard meant to be read from incoming trains.

NOVAYA ZIMA

VLAST FOUNDATION FOR PHYSICO-TECHNICAL MACHINES

REFORGING HUMANKIND.

YESTERDAY ENVIES US. TODAY IS OUR DOORWAY. THE FUTURE BEGINS.

THE VLAST SPREADING OUT ACROSS THE STARS.

They walked into the town unchallenged. It seemed colder in the streets than it had been under the trees. Colder than Mirgorod, but not the same cold. Mirgorod cold had an edge of ocean dampness, but the air in Novaya Zima was dry. Lom felt its bitterness desiccating his face, as if his lips would crack. His breath wisped drably away. The snow on the pavement crunched underfoot. Dusty snow, like crystallised ash.

For the first ten blocks or so the streets were given over to huge communal barracks for collective living. *Kommunalki.* Lom had read about such new-style buildings – embodiments of a new, less individualistic mode of life, the basis for modern developments in the industrial belt to the south – but he hadn't seen any, not till now. The buildings were new but already stained and shabby: hastily thrown up to a uniform pattern, the concrete blistered and bled rust where the steel reinforcing rods were too near the surface. Street-level heating vents breathed steam clouds across the pavements. On the ground floors there were public dining halls, public laundries, public baths. They walked past a school with street-level windows. NOVAYA ZIMA JUNIOR LYCEUM FOR THE SONS AND DAUGHTERS OF WORKERS.

Workers? Lom studied the people in the streets. They had neat sombre clothes and smooth white hands. They were clerks, administrators, secretaries, teachers, junior white-collar engineers: more than half were young women. They looked efficient. Nobody was poor and nobody was old and everybody was moving along, eyes down, unspeaking, each in their own small sphere of inwardness and temporary privacy. The rail transit rumbled overhead on its single track.

Nearer the centre of town the buildings were taller and better built. Polygons of steel and glass, each set back in its own apron of concrete and paving. Benches. Kiosks. Cafés. Parks behind railings, leafless and wintry. A deserted outdoor skating rink. An open-air swimming pool with a green and white tiled façade under a low curved roof. Scarves of steam drifted across the surface of the water. Swimmers in bathing caps ploughed steadily up and down the lanes. RESTORE YOURSELVES, CITIZENS! LEISURE REBUILDS! HEALTH IS A PLEASURABLE DUTY!

Florian stopped outside a restaurant with a wide glossy vitrine. the magnetic bakery. Shining tables of polished yellow deal on legs of tubular chrome. It was almost empty.

'We should split up,' he said. 'We need to know when Chazia is coming. It'll be easier if I go alone.'

'Why?' said Lom.

'Because one person is better,' said Florian.

'So why you not me?'

'Because they will tell me what we need to know.'

'You're just going to walk into a VKBD station and ask them?'

'No,' said Florian. 'Captain Vorush Iliodor will ask them. Captain Iliodor is Commander Chazia's aide-de-camp. I carry his identification and warrant cards.'

'Out of uniform and without Chazia? They'll want to know what you're doing here. They'll want to know why you don't already know her plans better than they do.'

'They may wonder,' said Florian. 'In my experience they will not ask.'

'Do you even look like this Iliodor? What if somebody there knows him?'

Florian raised an eyebrow quizzically.

'Oh,' said Lom. 'Of course. Sorry.'

'We'll meet back here,' said Florian. 'Give me a couple of hours. Three at most.' He gave Lom his knapsack. 'You'd better keep this. It's out of character for Iliodor. There's money in the side pocket.'

81

L om wandered the streets aimlessly, angry and frustrated. For days he had been a passenger, a tagger-along, abandoned now to his own devices. He saw the force of Florian's logic but he didn't like it. He'd left Mirgorod thousands of miles to the south and west, burning on the edge of war, and he felt Maroussia's loss as an emptiness next to him. *I've just been pissing about*, he thought. *And I'm still just pissing about.*

He found himself in a shopping street. *Modistes* sold suits and gowns and patent shoes at impossible prices. Bright-lit displays offered cameras, radios, gramophones, perfumes, chocolate, southern sparkling wines, but it was all garish, ersatz and shoddy, and nobody was buying. He walked on up Dukhonin Prospect – six lanes wide, almost empty of traffic – and into the blustery immenseness of Dukhonin Square. The square was lined with gleaming new buildings. The Polytechnical College. The Institute of Metallurgy. The Faculty of Mathematical Design. The Engineers' Euharmonia was giving a concert that night at the House of Culture: a poster next to the entrance promised Zoffany's PSYCHO-INDUSTRIAL SYMPHONY FOR VOICE AND NEW-STYLE ORCHESTRA, WITH THEATRE OF PUPPETS.

Absences worried at Lom. Absences frayed his patience. They made him edgy. The absence of Maroussia. The absence of Chazia. The absence of trainload after trainload of conscript workers. Stolen persons. Thousands of them. They went on north, through the town and into the mountain and disappeared.

Lom wanted a closer look at the mountain.

There was a station on Dukhonin Square. The ticket hall was a brightly lit lofty palace. Stainless-steel arches. Walls of marble and malachite. Chrome fittings. Electric chandeliers. The size and solidity of the place dwarfed the few travellers passing through. Bronze bas reliefs on the walls represented the achievements of science and industry: dynamos and hydroelectric dams; Magnitograd; the Novozhd Factory; mining engineers drilling and excavating the torso of a huge fallen angel. Slogans carved in marble shouted: THOUGHT IS LABOUR! PRIVILEGE IS SACRIFICE! CONTRIBUTION IS FULFILMENT! CADRES DECIDE EVERYTHING! CITIZEN, YOU ARE THE CONDUIT TO THE FUTURE!

With money from Florian's bag, Lom bought the most expensive ticket. Two roubles for all day and all stops. There was a sign that said FOUNDATION LINE NORTH. He bought a coffee in a paper cup and took it up the granite staircase to the platform overhead. A transit car was waiting. It was like a tramcar, but low and round-shouldered, and there was no overhead electric cable. Power came from the single steel rail itself.

KEEP OFF THE RAIL, CITIZEN! DANGER OF DEATH!

Lom took a corner seat. The coffee was good, not so good as Count Palffy's, but sweet and bitter and hot. He took slow sips, making it last, as the train carried him slowly north. Beyond the carriage window the office blocks, parks and squares of the town centre gave way first to a few streets of elite housing – individual homes with yards and gardens – and then more communal blocks. Through the lighted and uncurtained upper-floor windows Lom could see cramped apartments separated by paper-thin partitions, shared bathrooms and shared kitchens. A new world had begun here, a world yet unseen in Mirgorod or Podchornok. Collective endeavour in a place without a past.

Novaya Zima, deposited ready-made in the middle of a wintry wilderness, drained the past. It soaked the life of memory away. There was only now, and an avid, echoing, hungry future. Lom found it drab and ugly and brutal.

The overheated car carried on trundling slowly northwards, stopping every minute or so. The route zigzagged across the town, making the most of its unnecessary existence. The overhead transit was a superfluous municipal showpiece – you could have walked the breadth of Novaya Zima in an hour – but people seemed to use it. Passengers came and went. Without exception they wore thin coats and carried briefcases. The men had knitted ties, the women wore blouses buttoned to the neck.

Lom finished his coffee and propped the empty paper cup on the seat next to him. A young woman, hair tied severely back, was watching him from across the aisle, her face a mixture of disapproval and curiosity. Lom realised how out of place he looked. He grinned at the woman cheerfully and she looked away. She had a pale thin face.

Lom got up and went across to sit beside her. She glanced at him in surprise and looked away. Shifted herself as far as she could along the bench away from him.

'Does this train go all the way to the mountain?' he said.

'*Foundation* Mountain?'

'Is there another one?'

'No,' she said, 'of course not.' She was staring straight ahead. 'This train doesn't go there,' she added.

'So, if I wanted to get to the mountain, how would I do that?'

'Why? Why would you want to?'

Lom shrugged.

'To have a look. Curiosity.'

'Are you assigned to work in the mountain? This is the wrong train. You should have been told ... Why are you asking me this? What is your work?'

'I'm new,' said Lom. 'I don't have any work. Not yet.'

'Nobody comes here without an assignment. How could you even get here?'

'I flew,' said Lom. 'And I walked.'

The woman's cheeks burned. She glanced around the carriage, looking for help, but no one was sitting near. She didn't want to make a scene. She turned and glared into Lom's face.

'Are you drunk or something? If this is some crude attempt at seduction, citizen, then I should tell you—'

The car pulled into a station. The woman stood up. She was trembling.

'This is my stop,' she said. 'Get out of my way, please.'

Lom twisted round to make room for her. She pushed past, holding her briefcase tight against her chest, not looking at him. Her legs brushed against his awkwardly.

'I only want—' he began.

'Piss off,' she hissed over her shoulder. 'Don't follow me. I'll call the police.'

82

When the train reached the end of the line, Lom stayed aboard and came all the way back, continuing on south past Dukhonin Square till he was near the place where he was to meet Florian. Back on the emptying streets the freezing air smelled of engine fumes. Lighted windows shone with a bleak electrical brilliance. From everywhere Foundation Mountain was visible, a darkened wall against the northern sky. Lom thought he could hear a long freight train rumbling through the town, making the pavement tremble. But he wasn't sure.

The Magnetic Bakery was still open but there was no sign of Florian. Office workers were drinking tea and reading newspapers. The radio played band music. Lom ordered an aquavit and grabbed an abandoned paper from the next table. The *Vlast True Reporter*. It was yesterday's edition. He started to read it, just to pass the time till Florian came.

The man called Fohn, whose name he'd seen on various announcements in Mirgorod and who was now apparently the president of the Vlast, had made a speech in the new capital, Kholvatogorsk. So Mirgorod wasn't the capital any more? *And where the fuck is Kholvatogorsk?* Lom had a dizzy feeling that the whole world had changed and shifted while he'd been flying across the landscape in Gretskaya's Kotik.

Fohn's speech was full of dull good news: industrial targets would be exceeded in the coming quarter, despite the recent upheaval of relocation, and steel production was heading for an all-time high. Shock workers had risen to the challenge. Lom skimmed the rest of the paper. Working hours were to be increased again. About the war there was almost nothing: inconclusive skirmishes on the southern front; Seva recaptured from the Archipelago yet again. There was a small inside paragraph about the stalwart resistance of encircled Mirgorod, with extracts from a fierce speech of defiance from a General Rizhin, who was Commissar for City Defence. Reading between the lines, it seemed that Mirgorod was doomed and the Vlast had decided it didn't care. The piece was accompanied by a smudgy photograph of Rizhin. Lom almost ignored it, but something about the long narrow face caught his attention. His heart missed a beat.

It was Kantor. General Rizhin, Commissar for Mirgorod City Defence, was Josef Kantor.

When Florian came, Lom was nursing his untouched aquavit and watching his own reflection in the darkened window. Florian sat opposite Lom and put his astrakhan hat on the table between them. He looked worried. A waitress bustled over but he waved her away.

'Chazia is here already,' he said. 'The train arrived last night. Late. We must have heard it pass. It didn't stop in the town. They went straight through and into the mountain. Travelling at speed.'

For the second time in an hour Lom felt the bottom drop out of his world.

'Maroussia?' he said. 'What about Maroussia?'

'I don't know. Somebody said there was a woman travelling with Chazia. It could be her.'

'We have to get into the mountain,' said Lom. 'We have to do that now. *Tonight.*'

'Yes. Of course.'

'We haven't got time to figure this out for ourselves,' Lom continued. 'We need some assistance here.'

'Yes,' said Florian.

'Someone who can get us past whatever security they have out there. Someone who can take us right to Chazia.'

'The name of such a person,' said Florian, 'is Yakov Khyrbysk. Professor Yakov Khyrbysk, director of the Foundation for Physico-Technical Machines. Professor Khyrbysk spends his days working inside Foundation Mountain but he has an apartment in the Sharashka district, in a building called the Foundation Hall. It's not more than a mile from here. By this time of the evening he will be at home. He is not married and lives alone. I have his address. He is not expecting us. I do not suggest we telephone ahead.'

83

The Foundation Hall where Khyrbysk had his apartment was the tallest building in Novaya Zima: a tall slender blade of steel and glass, a triangular sliver of black ice speckled with bright-burning windows. In the snow-crusted square in front of the Hall stood a floodlit construction of crimson-painted steel: a single swooshing curve reaching hundreds of feet high, a steeply climbing arc of power and ambition and freedom and speed, hurtling up. It looked like nothing so much as the track of a rocket launching into the dark sky, and at the point of the curve, where the rocket might have been, was a squat, massive snub-nosed bullet-shape. It was speeding away from the planet. Escaping the gravity well. Lom remembered the hoarding at the gate into the town: THE VLAST SPREADING OUT ACROSS THE STARS.

Lom and Florian took the wide shallow apron of concrete steps two at a time and pushed open the wooden double door. Inside was a spacious entrance hall panelled with rich dark wood and thickly carpeted in plush brick red. A woman of about fifty in a crisp dark blue uniform tunic was watching them from behind a reception counter. She had short iron-grey hair and her face was powdered. She sat in a cloud of lavender eau de toilette and watched them suspiciously. Behind her on the wall was a noticeboard, a painting of the mountain in sunshine, the tubes of a pneumatic mail system and a large plate-glass mirror without a frame.

'No visitors without an appointment,' the woman said. 'Do you have an appointment?

Florian went up to the counter, confident, purposeful. He was Captain Vorush Iliodor. He held out his warrant card for inspection.

'We are here for Professor Khyrbysk,' he said. 'Commander Chazia requires his presence urgently. You will call him down for us.'

The woman frowned.

'It is late,' she said. 'The professor does not receive visitors at home. He starts early in the morning. You may leave a message with me.'

'We are not visitors,' said Florian. 'He is required. Now.'

The woman glared at him, pale grey eyes blazing, points of pink flushing her cheekbones. In the mirror behind her Lom could see the electric switch under the counter.

'The professor is unavailable,' she said, reaching for the telephone. 'Someone else will assist you. I will call Dr Ferenc. He will—'

Lom pushed past Florian, lifted the counter lid and stepped quickly through. Put his left hand down to cover the emergency call switch before she could get to it.

'We have no time for this,' he said. 'I am an investigator of the Political Police. My colleague is Captain Iliodor of Commander Chazia's personal staff. You will take us to Professor Khyrbysk's apartment. You will do this yourself. You will do this now. You will call nobody. You will trigger no alarms.'

'You cannot order me! Where are your uniforms? Where is your police warrant? There are procedures. You have no authority here. The professor—'

'The authority of the Vlast is everywhere,' said Lom. 'The Vlast *is* authority. There is no other. What is your name, citizen?'

The woman hesitated.

'Tyrkhovna,' she said. 'Zsara Tyrkhovna.'

'You will take us to the professor immediately, Zsara Tyrkhovna. *Instantly.*'

Still she hesitated.

'You would prefer to join one of the long trains, perhaps?' said Lom. 'Would you like to take a journey into the mountain, Zsara Tyrkhovna? That can be arranged. We could give you that choice perhaps. Choose now.'

Tears were coming to Zsara Tyrkhovna's eyes, though they weren't there yet. She didn't know what to do.

'Loyalty is creditable,' said Lom. 'Defiance and stupidity is not.'

Her shoulders slumped. She looked ten years older.

'Come with me,' she breathed.

*

They took the mirrored and chrome-plated lift to the top floor. The twentieth. More thick carpet in the hall, recessed lighting, pot plants and paintings on the walls: abstract constructions of circles and cones in primary colours, slashed across by thin black straight lines. *This is the future!* they said. *The total universal truth of form and speed! No people and no skies!*

There was only one door. It opened almost instantly at Zsara Tyrkhovna's tentative knock. The man who appeared in the doorway was wide and bulky. He had a broad creased face with a heavy stub of a nose, an imposing brow and a mat of wiry black curly hair cut short. Small pale blue eyes appraised Lom and Florian with sharp, watchful intelligence. He was wearing a dark blue dressing gown over a white shirt open at the collar. The gown looked like it was made of silk: real silk, not some petroleum-derivative substitute.

'I'm so sorry, Yakov Arkadyevich,' said Zsara Tyrkhovna. 'These men ... they say they are the police. They insisted. They *threatened* me ... I didn't know what to do. I shouldn't have—'

Florian produced his identification.

'Commander Chazia requires Professor Khyrbysk to come with us now,' he said. 'It is a matter of urgency. She cannot wait.'

Khyrbysk took Florian's card and studied it carefully for a moment. Considered it and came to a conclusion. He nodded almost imperceptibly, as if to himself, as if some hypothesis of his own had been confirmed.

'Don't upset yourself, Zsara,' he said. His voice was deep and complex. 'Everything is in order. You've done all that you should, and more. I am grateful. You can leave us now.'

'Should I telephone someone?' she said. 'I should tell Shulmin what is happening. No, Shulmin is not here. Ferenc then. I will call Ferenc. He will come.'

'There's no need to trouble Leon, Zsara. Really no need. Everything is fine here. Go back to your work.' He stood back from the door. 'Please, gentlemen, come in.'

They followed Khyrbysk into his apartment. It was over-warm and brightly lit, and the white walls were hung with certificates of academic distinction and more paintings. The floor was covered with a thick light blue carpet. There were a few pieces of expensive-looking furniture and rugs in the modern geometric style. The curtains were drawn shut across wide windows.

Khyrbysk indicated a low sofa in the middle of the room. There was a polished oval coffee table in front of it, empty except for a bowl of dried fruits.

'Sit down,' he said. 'Please. You are my guests. Perhaps you would like some wine?'

'There is no time,' said Lom.

Khyrbysk ignored him.

'Captain Iliodor,' he said to Florian. 'We have corresponded, have we not? And spoken on the telephone, I think. A pleasure to meet you in person at last. Also something of a surprise. I was expecting to meet you yesterday with Lavrentina when she arrived, but you were not with her. Indeed, she mentioned that you had disappeared during a bombing raid on Mirgorod. She was concerned for you. There was some suggestion that you might have been injured. Or dead.'

Florian gave him a quick untroubled smile.

'As you see,' he said, 'I am not dead; I was merely delayed. I arrived in Novaya Zima some hours ago.'

'We can talk as we go,' said Lom. 'Get your coat, Professor. Let's be on our way.'

Khyrbysk turned towards him, small eyes narrow in the slab of his face.

'And who are you, please?' he said. 'I know who your associate says he is, but you have not yet accounted for your presence here.'

'My colleague—' Florian began.

'I am an Investigator of the Vlast Political Police.'

Khyrbysk sighed.

'Oh, really, must we continue this charade?' he said. 'I know you are not what you say you are. Whatever you might have told poor Zsara, you are evidently nothing to do with Lavrentina, and you are certainly not from the police, so let us waste no more time on tedious diversions. Spare me that. I am not surprised you have come. I have been expecting you, or someone like you, for a long time.'

'Who do you think we are?' said Lom.

Khyrbysk shrugged.

'Precisely?' he said. 'Precisely, I have no idea at all. Spies? Agents of the Archipelago? The specifics hardly matter. You are outsiders.

People from elsewhere, come to find out what is happening here in Novaya Zima. As I said, I have been expecting that someone like you would come eventually. Our achievements were bound to attract such attention, though frankly I thought there would be a more subtle approach. A less frontal assault, shall I say? Well, no matter. You are here, and I have nothing to hide, so let us be civilised. Share my wine and tell me what you want from me.'

Khyrbysk's manner was smooth and urbane but there was hard calculation in his eyes. *He's playing with us*, thought Lom. *Playing for time. But there is no time.*

'You met Chazia when she arrived?' he said.

'Of course,' said Khyrbysk.

'There was a woman with her. Early twenties. Five foot nine. Black hair cut short at the neck.'

For the first time, Khyrbysk looked surprised. Genuinely surprised.

'I couldn't say. I don't recall seeing such a woman. Lavrentina's entourage was large. I did not meet them all. Of course not.'

Lom's patience had reached its limit. He pulled the Blok 15 from his pocket and pointed it at Khyrbysk's belly.

'Where is Chazia now?' he said.

Khyrbysk glanced briefly at the gun and looked away. Dismissed it from his attention.

'When I left Lavrentina earlier this evening she was in the mountain. She had work to do. She is a woman of remarkable energy.'

'You're going to take us to her,' said Lom. 'You're going to take us into the mountain and vouch for us with your security. Tell them we are your guests. Take us to where Chazia is.'

'Of course,' said Khyrbysk. 'If that's what you want.' He glanced at the gun. 'Your argument is persuasive.'

'Don't over-focus on the gun,' said Lom. 'You should worry more about my friend there. I certainly would.'

84

They went out of the Foundation Hall and across the floodlit square. The sky-aspiring sculpture cast three long black gnomon-shadows. Lom walked on one side of Khyrbysk, Florian on the other. The square was deserted. It was almost nine.

'No transport?' said Khyrbysk, looking around.

'No,' said Lom.

'You don't have much of a plan then.'

'The plan's simple,' said Lom. 'If there's any trouble from you we kill you and think of something else.'

'I see. You have no transport. Well, I'm afraid my driver has gone home for the night, but if we go back inside I could get Zsara to telephone for a car.'

'We'll walk,' said Lom.

'Five miles in the night?' said Khyrbysk. 'Partly across open country? Better to take the train.'

There was a transit station at the corner of the square. The system was still running. They didn't have to wait long for a northbound service. There were a couple of solitary passengers – night workers going on shift – but Khyrbysk led them to seats at the other end of the car.

'The city is beautiful at night,' he said, looking out of the window, 'but you should see it in the long summer days. It is the northern jewel of the Vlast.'

'You call this place a city?' said Lom.

'Yes, certainly Novaya Zima is a city. A city is defined by importance rather than size. By centrality to the culture of the coming times. Novaya Zima is not an agglomeration of buildings, it is a machine for living. A machine for making the future. And it is a metaphor. A work of art.'

He sat back in his seat and unbuttoned the fawn camel-hair coat he had put on over his shirt. It was hot in the carriage. He seemed inclined to talk. Perhaps it was nerves, but Lom didn't think so. Khyrbysk didn't seem too bothered about his predicament at all.

'Take the building where I live, for instance,' Khyrbysk was saying. 'The Foundation Hall. It is made from steel and glass. Above all, glass. What better metaphor than glass for the future we are building? Millions of separate grains of sand, weak and uncohesive when separate, fused together under a fierce transmuting heat to form a new substance. And the new substance is perfect. Unblemished, transparent and strong. This is how we shall reforge humanity. The progress of history is inevitable. It is happening already. The individual is losing his significance – his private destiny no longer interests us – many particles must become one consistent force ...'

Khyrbysk paused.

'You smile,' he said. 'But I assure you, what I am saying is a clearsighted expression of fact. Novaya Zima *signifies*. Everything you see in Novaya Zima, the fine architecture, this mass transit system of which we are so proud, it all *signifies*.'

Florian grunted. 'You have a fine apartment,' he said.

'You sound censorious,' said Khyrbysk, 'You want to make me ashamed of my privileges while others labour hungry and the Vlast is at war?'

'The thought occurred to me,' said Florian.

'But I am not ashamed,' said Khyrbysk. 'The fact that others forgo essentials so we can live like this, that is what drives us on. It shows our strength of purpose. The Vlast may suffer hardships, Novaya Zima says to the world, but we can still do this.'

'This place tells the world nothing,' said Florian, 'because the world doesn't know it exists.'

'Not yet perhaps,' said Khyrbysk, 'but when we are ready it will.'

Lom remembered the smell of the empty trains at the Wieland marshalling yard. The ranks of empty trains. He was surprised by the heat of his own anger

'You've built a comfortable utopia for you and your friends on the bones of slaves.'

'You're trying to provoke me,' said Khyrbysk blandly, 'but I will not rise to it. I am merely a worker in my own field, as are we all. There is no egotism here, only *I* becoming *We*: the clear and perfect simplicity of glass.'

'And the workers under the mountain? Do they see it like that? I've seen the trains.'

'Certainly they do. Most of them. Physical labour is redemptive. Many request to stay on when their terms are complete. They ask for their families to join them. '

Lom turned away in disgust. He caught his own reflection in the window looking back at him. And through his own face he saw the lighted windows of kommunalki buildings moving past. For a moment it was as if he was stationary and the buildings were sliding away, leaving him behind.

'The quality of our city,' said Khyrbysk, oblivious to Lom's reaction, or ignoring it, 'expresses the supreme importance of the work we do.'

Florian leaned forward intently.

'What work?' he said. 'What is happening here? What is all this for?'

'The Foundation for Physico-Technical Machines,' said Khyrbysk, 'is the greatest concentration of human intelligence the world has ever seen. The whole city exists to support our work. There is more brilliance lodged in Foundation Hall, in that one single building, than ... There is no comparator. No precedent. It is our academy. We have sacrificed our careers to be here, all of us. We do not publish, at least not under our own names. We get no fame for what we do, none of the mundane rewards. But the future will know us by our work.'

They stopped at a station and the last passengers left them alone. Shortly after the train restarted, the buildings outside the window disappeared, leaving nothing but blank darkness. Lom realised they had crossed the northern boundary of the township and were heading across open country towards the mountain.

'What work?' said Florian again. 'What is the work?'

'Our work?' said Khyrbysk. 'We look up at night and see a universe of stars and planets teeming with life, and angels swimming the cosmic emptiness like fish. Only the emptiness between the stars is *not* empty; it teems with life and vigour just as the planets do. It merely does not shine so brightly.' There was a light in Khyrbysk's eye that was not entirely sane. For all his craggy bulk, his thick grizzled curls and cliff-like face, he was a prophet burning with the incandescence of a vision. 'That is where history is leading us,' he continued. 'Humankind spreading out across the galaxies in the endless pursuit of radiant light. Only there will we find space enough to live as we are meant to live. It is inevitable. It is the will of the universe.'

Lom could see nothing but blackness outside the carriage window. The reflection of the bright interior obliterated everything. He could see himself, and opposite him a mirror-Khyrbysk and a mirror-Florian. There was less of Iliodor in Florian's face, he thought: more angularity, more darkness. An effect of mirror and harsh shadow, perhaps.

'There are practical problems to be solved, of course, if humankind is to escape from this one cramped planet,' Khyrbysk was saying. 'That's what we are doing here. New means of propulsion, new techniques for navigation, new technologies for sustaining life outside the atmosphere and beyond the light of the sun. And new designs for humankind itself. Crossing the immensities of space will take immensities of time. Our present bodies are too short-lived. They decay and fail. But even this problem will be solved. We know that angel flesh can absorb and carry human consciousness: all that's needed is refinement of technique.'

'There are thousands of workers here,' said Lom. 'They aren't engaged in cosmological hypothesising.'

'Not hypothesising!' said Khyrbysk. 'Practicalities! There are a hundred real and specific problems to be solved. Problems of science, engineering and design.'

'That is not enough,' Florian's voice was a snarl. 'There is something more. Something else is happening here.'

'Not enough! I've shared more truth and vision with you in the last ten minutes than you can possibly have heard in the whole of your life up to this moment.'

Khyrbysk's pale blue eyes were narrow and predatory.

'You think I'm afraid of you?' he said. 'You think I'm your prisoner? I am no such thing. You will not kill me, but I will take you to Lavrentina, and she will surely kill you.'

85

There was a burst of noise as the transit car hurtled straight into the side of the Foundation Mountain and entered an unlit concrete tube barely wide enough to accommodate it. The light from the car's lamps flickered along the uneven wall, illuminating snaking power cables and gaping black side shafts. Ten minutes later they emerged into dazzling fluorescent brilliance and came to a sudden stop. Khyrbysk opened the door and they stepped out onto an iron platform.

They were in the middle of an immense cloister carved out of solid rock, hundreds of feet long and fifty feet high, supported by a field of wide columns: trunks of raw rough stone, left in place when the solidity of the mountain was cut away, sleeved in squared-off concrete for the first twenty feet of their height. Thousands of lighting tubes threw daylight-blue shadowless brightness across gleaming asphalt. The air was body-warm, dry to the point of desiccation and smelled faintly of naphtha. Not air at all but breathable suffocation, it moved in a steady current across Lom's face. Glancing up, he saw rows of ventilation shafts in the rock ceiling and wide rotor fans behind grilles, turning slowly. He felt the terrible weight of the dark mountain overhead, inert, world-heavy, impending.

'Follow me,' said Khyrbysk and set off at a smart pace. His shoulders were broad and bulky. Grizzled wiry curls came down over his collar. He seemed to have forgotten he was being marched along at gunpoint.

'Slow down,' growled Florian. 'Be aware.'

Khyrbysk ignored him and hurried on. Lom and Florian followed him down a wide clattering staircase onto the cavern floor. A complex of temporary huts serving as offices clustered around the base of the nearest column. There was a canteen, open but deserted, a telephone exchange and an operator hub for the pneumatic mail system. Further away, on a low concrete platform, a powerhouse of whirring massive dynamos hummed and buzzed. There were few people about: the night shift, quietly efficient at their business. Men dwarfed by the dynamos stood before expanses of winking signal lights, dials and gleaming bakelite controls. Walkways between the columns were marked by coloured lines painted on the asphalt. They led off in every direction towards square tunnel mouths.

Khyrbysk stopped and waited for them to catch up.

'This is a side entrance,' he said. 'A vestibule, you might say. There are two hundred miles of tunnels under the mountain, and hundreds of chambers, many larger than this one. There are lift shafts, conveyor belts, railways, winches and hauling engines, underground water-courses. All of it permanently lit, ventilated, heated and dehumidified. Workshops. Factories. Laboratories. Storage and stockpiling facilities. We construct most of the machine tools and technical instruments we require right here, ourselves. The city under the mountain is larger than the city outside. It operates in twenty-four-hour daylight, wholly unaffected by winter and summer. It is the most efficient industrial complex the world has ever seen. This part may look deserted but there are tens of thousands of workers here. Most of them are in the mines, of course. The mines are why we are here, not elsewhere. The mountain is full of uranium. Riddled with it. It's all around us, like raisins in a cake. Nowhere else has it been discovered in such abundance.'

It was as if he was giving them a guided tour. As if they were digni-taries on their way to a lunch. Lom had to admire him. He had a will of iron.

Khyrbysk set off again.

'Follow, please,' he said.

Lom and Florian fell in behind him. They had reached an unspoken agreement to let the man have his head and see where he took them. He would surely lead them to Chazia, one way or another.

Khyrbysk bounded up another iron staircase. Another rail car waited there, a rounded oblong box with windows, painted in the same colours as the transit carriages but much smaller, designed to carry up to six passengers with a small luggage bay behind. It hung sus-pended from an overhead rail and swayed slightly when they climbed in. Khyrbysk went to the front and switched on the power. Interior lamps flickered into life and floor-level vents began to breathe heated air into the cabin. The floor was covered with stippled rubber, the steel walls and ceiling were painted cream, the seats upholstered in green leather. A chrome handrail ran the length of the wall on both sides. The interior smelled strongly of rubber and hot engine oil.

A lectern-like brown bakelite panel was set at an angle under the forward window, marked out with a complex map of radial and intersecting lines. There was a tiny switch and light bulb at each labelled node. Some of the nodes bore names – RAILHEAD, POLISHING, REFECTORY IV, CENTRIFUGE, NORTH GATE EXIT – but most were designated by short, impenetrable alphanumeric sequences.

'This is a plan of the entire complex?' said Lom.

'Correct,' said Khyrbysk.

He set the panel with practised speed and the car lurched into life. The last node he activated was labelled EDB/CENTRAL.

'What's EDB?' said Lom.

'You'll see.'

The car rattled through narrow tunnels and swept out high above underground chambers. They saw women in overalls and headscarves worked at assembly lines, operating lathes and welding machines. They passed the slopes of sour-smelling slag dumps. Furnace doors clanged open beneath them, belching blasts of heat and disgorging planks of glowing molten metal onto conveyor belts. A gently descending tunnel took them past honeycomb stacks of artillery shells painted a garish yellow. Notices on the racks warned, with perfect superfluity, DANGER! HIGH EXPLOSIVE!

'Armaments?' said Lom.

'Certainly,' said Khyrbysk. 'We must satisfy our benefactors. The iron law of economics. The Foundation must wash its own face.'

They swung out across a dim shoreless lake of milky-green water reeking of naphtha, its surface wreathed with scraps and scarves of steam. Hard-hat gangers clambered across half-built scaffolding and tramped in silent groups on perilous unrailed walkways. Then, after ten more minutes of featureless tunnel, the rail car lurched to a stop alongside two identical carriages.

EXPERIMENTAL DESIGN BUREAU.

EDB.

TRUTH AND FEAR

Khyrbysk led them through double swing doors into another world. The oppressive scale of the underground complex was gone, replaced by green corridors. Fire extinguishers. Noticeboards. Wall-mounted telephones. The muted clatter of distant typewriters. Linoleum floors squeaked underfoot. Half-glazed doors opened into offices and meeting rooms. SURVIVABLES. LENSING. CENTRIFUGE. DEPLETION. STAGING. NOÖSPHERE. PROJECT WINTER SKIES.

A few people were working late. Men in shirtsleeves and sleeveless pullovers. They sat alone or gathered in small huddles, rumpled, smoking, arguing earnestly in quiet voices. Many of them nodded to Khyrbysk as he passed and he greeted each one by name.

Lom noticed that Khyrbysk's creased heavy face was damp with perspiration. For the first time he looked tense. But there was something about the way he was walking that wasn't nervous, but the opposite: a kind of bravado in the way he carried himself.

'Nearly there,' he said.

Now we are coming to it, thought Lom. He tightened his grip on the gun in his pocket. Beside him he sensed Florian ready himself for action. *Clever Khyrbysk has fooled us all. So he thinks.*

Khyrbysk veered suddenly to the right, pushed open a door and entered a large hexagonal room overlooked by two mezzanine tiers. The central floor was occupied by a circular plotting table twenty feet in diameter, the green baize surface laid out with maps and charts. In the corner a telekrypt whirred and blinked. Up on the mezzanines women in uniform whispered intently into telephones. Half a dozen VKBD officers in pale red uniforms looked up when they entered.

Khyrbysk stepped sharply away from Lom and Florian.

'Draw your weapons!' he barked. 'Lieutenant Gerasimov! Arrest these men! They are spies. They are terrorists. They are assassins. Lock them away somewhere and inform Secretary Chazia immediately. I put them in her hands.'

The VKBD men snapped to their feet, a dozen revolver muzzles covering Lom and Florian.

'The Secretary is not here, Director Khyrbysk,' said Gerasimov. 'She took the observation car to the testing zone. She wanted to witness it herself.'

Khyrbysk frowned.

641

'Gone already? But the test is not till dawn. I was to travel with her. That was the plan.'

'We could telephone, but … She will not welcome a trivial interruption. She took the woman with her.'

'The matter is of no relevance to me. But she must deal with this, Lieutenant. I want to hear no more of these men. And Gerasimov, I have made representations before about the lax security in the city. I will be doing so again, depend on it.'

As he turned to go Khyrbysk threw a contemptuous glance at Lom and Florian.

'Idiots,' he muttered.

86

When Khyrbysk had gone, Lieutenant Gerasimov detached two of the VKBD – heavy grey-faced men with broad dull faces, early forties, running to fat – to take Lom and Florian to the detention area.

'Wait with them there till Chazia comes.'

The VKBD men looked bored and resentful. They didn't like being dragged away from bothering the women working the telephones. Vagant revolvers in hand, they shoved and hustled their captives along the corridors. People glanced at them curiously and quickly looked away, avoiding the eye of the VKBD. Lom shuffled along passively, eyes to the floor, looking defeated. Florian walked with as much dignity as he could muster, bareheaded, holding his astrakhan hat in his hand.

When they reached the transit car, Lom watched carefully as one of the guards set the control panel. The man worked slowly, concentrating on each move. The operation was simple: there was a button under the counter to turn on the power, then you selected your route and flicked the switches of the points you wanted to pass through. If you made a mistake, you flicked the switch the other way to cancel the instruction. The guard made several mistakes. Lom guessed the VKBD had arrived with Chazia the previous day.

The car rocked and settled and lurched into life.

No point in waiting. There won't be a better time.

Lom glanced at Florian, who was watching him with glittering, rapacious amusement. Florian raised an eyebrow. It was a question. An invitation.

'Leave it to me,' said Lom. 'No need to rip their heads off.' He regretted the loss of his Blok 15, which the VKBD had taken. But it didn't matter. It made no difference.

The guard nearest to him frowned.

'Keep your fucking mouth shut—'

Lom stepped in close, inside the gun hand, and crunched his right elbow into the man's face. Felt his nose burst and his head jerk back. In the same movement with his left hand he gripped the Vagant and the fist that held it and twisted. Hard. Felt the trigger finger snap. The gun fired, deafening in the enclosed space. The bullet punched a hole in the wall.

If the other guard had been watching properly, and if he'd been trained, and if he'd practised so much that he didn't need to think, he might have realised what was happening and responded effectively in, what, two seconds? Maybe less. But he wasn't trained, and he hadn't practised, and he didn't have two seconds. He was still standing in the same position with a puzzled look on his face when Lom's right fist, holding the Vagant, powered by the momentum of his charge and with the full two hundred pounds of his weight behind it, crashed into the side of his head. The guard staggered sideways. His gun slipped from his fingers and skittered across the floor. Lom recovered his balance and aimed a vicious kick at the man's kneecap. He screamed and fell. Lom kicked his head again just to be sure. It felt good. The angel taste was in his mouth again.

Both VKBD men were down and not moving. Lom stepped over them to the control panel. The schematic showed the NORTHERN GATE and a single straight line leading away from it, out of the mountain: the furthest terminal was labelled FIELD TEST OBSERVER STATION. He flicked switches, programming the most direct route avoiding major intersections. The car halted, hesitated, and started back the way it had come.

87

For an hour they passed through tunnels and shafts and caverns, climbing steadily. There was less activity in the northern area of the mountain. At first they half-expected the car to seize up and stop, the power cut. Security procedures kicking in to isolate and capture them. But it didn't happen. Florian spread himself out on a passenger bench and closed his eyes but Lom stayed on his feet at the panel, leaning forward to stare through the front window, following their progress. Tiny lamps winked out as they left the nodes behind. The unconscious guards, propped at the back of the car where Florian had dragged them, were breathing noisily.

Lom brought the car to a stop at an empty platform. He and Florian bundled the inert guards out: deadweights smelling of sweat and sour breath and blood. They kept the guns.

The last twenty minutes underground were a long haul down a shallow incline, an unlit featureless tunnel bored through raw rock. They seemed to be speeding up. Then, without warning, they burst out into the night on the far side of the mountain. The rattling echoes of the tunnel ceased. The car travelled on in near-silence. There was only the electric hum of its motor and the wind splitting against the overhead rail. It was coming up to four in the morning.

Lom stood at the front of the railcar. Leaning forward, feet slightly apart. Hands gripping the chrome bar so hard it hurt. The rail ran on ahead into the darkness. It was carrying them towards Maroussia. Ahead of them, somewhere, she was there. He was sure of that. Other possibilities were not admitted. Not considered. She was there and he would find her. He would get her back. But the car wasn't moving fast enough. He leaned into the bar as if he would push it onward faster with his own force of will.

Behind him he heard Florian shift in his seat.

'What time is dawn this far north?' said Lom, not looking round.

'Late,' said Florian. 'Nine? Ten? We have time.'

'We need a plan,' said Lom.

'We should get there first.'

They cruised on through total darkness. Only the light spilling from their own windows showed the unbroken carpet of trees. The snow was thicker to the north of the mountain.

Hours passed. Nothing changed. Lom tried to calculate their speed by his wristwatch, counting the trees passing beneath them and the regularly spaced pylons that carried the overhead rail. He repeated the measurement again and again. Somewhere between thirty and fifty miles an hour. Perhaps. It was something to do.

The trees grew sparser, pine and spruce replacing birch, and the snow was getting thicker all the time, mounding the tree-heads and piling in drifts. The small capsule raced on over frozen lakes, snow-crusted and black. The hour hand on Lom's watched crept round the dial. Five o'clock. Six. Always the single rail stretched ahead of them, pylon after pylon.

They flashed through an unlit platform stop. Rows of vague regular shapes were passing underneath them. Humped shadows. They were aeroplanes. Hundreds of large aircraft parked in neat rows under tarpaulins. Mothballed. Snow-covered runways. A control tower in darkness. Then came two minutes of trees and another wide clearing. A mile-wide expanse of nothing surrounded by a perimeter fence. And then there was a splash of bright light ahead of them. A brilliant pool of arc light bright enough to reflect off the underside of the cloud. The car rose and swept past what seemed like a domed mound, too regular and polished and perfect to be natural. It glimmered dark brick red and was surrounded by a circular blackness. Lom had time to realize he was looking at the top of something rising from a pit several hundred yards across, surrounded by shadowy gantries and lumps of broken concrete. Then it was gone.

As they left the oasis of brilliant light behind, they passed through another empty platform. Lom read the sign as it flashed past the window.

COSMODROME: WINTER SKIES.

There was an emblem: a simplified version of the soaring steel sculpture in front of the Foundation Hall. The rising discus. THE VLAST SPREADING OUT ACROSS THE STARS.

Antoninu Florian sat in silence, flexing taut aching muscle, sinew, flesh. Working his bones with infinitesimal shifts of size and shape. He had been holding this human shape in place too long, and every part of his body was sore: a dull rheumatic ache from his face to his feet, cramped inside their tightly laced boots. He shifted in his seat, though it brought him no comfort, and watched Lom leaning on the handrail and staring out through the forward window at the empty landscape that rolled up to meet them. The intensity of Lom's focus on Maroussia was a tangible tension in the air. It hummed like taut wire in the wind.

For the hundredth time, the thousandth time, Florian studied him. Lom was a vessel of the beautiful forest, all unaware, but he was also saturated through and through with dark angel stuff. The wound Chazia had made in his head had become an opening, a shining perfumed breach, but the angel mark had left its indelible stain. Florian had observed Lom's growing violence in the last few days. The angel stuff was part of what made Lom what he was: an unexpected possibility, an open, borderless, compendious man, the joining together of what could not be joined. In the unsolvable equation of forest and angel and Vlast and Pollandore, the complex impossible strength that just might resolve it was Vissarion Lom.

Unless the Shaumian woman was lost.

Florian was certain that Maroussia was alive and somewhere ahead of them. He could not sense her, but he could sense the Pollandore. It was close and they were closing with it, and so was the Shaumian woman. Florian felt the Pollandore calling her. And he still didn't know what he would do when he caught up with her. The indecision hurt worse than the tension in his distorted bones. Futures contended. All outcomes could be ruinous. When the time of crisis came, then he would know what to do. Then he would decide.

The frozen lakes became larger and more numerous. They were crossing more ice than trees. And then they were suddenly travelling low above the sea. Ten feet below them thick black water rose and fell, viscid and streaked with foam. It was as if the ocean was breathing gently. Rafts of ice, almost perfectly circular, gleamed in the yellow cabin light that raced across them. The floor-level heating vents hummed loudly, struggling to warm the inflow of freezing air. And failing. The cold pinched Lom's face. He felt his hands and feet growing stiff and numb.

Seven o'clock.

They crossed the shore of the north island at 7.45 a.m. The sea fell away behind them and they were riding low over level tundra. Flat expanses of snow and ice. The first hint of daylight was touching the eastern sky. A faint diminishing of darkness. Condensation was frosting on the inside of the window, forming spidery crystal webs. Lom rubbed it away. Metronome pylons ticked past.

At ten past eight they saw the lights ahead of them. A cluster of low buildings in the pre-dawn greyness, dark against the snow. Lom cut the power, plunging the cabin interior into silence and gloom. The car rattled on, slowing. It took several minutes to come to a complete halt, swinging and creaking in the wind.

Florian pushed the door open and let in a blast of freezing air. They were fifteen feet above the ground. The snow looked thick and soft beneath them. He leaped out and landed neatly in a crouch, knee deep.

Lom took a breath and followed. He landed hard and rolled. Ended up on his back in the snow, winded, staring up at the sky. It hurt. He stood up slowly. Stiffly. Testing.

He was OK.

He looked round for Florian and saw him racing silently away across the snow. Within fifty yards he had disappeared. Faded into grey and dropped behind a ridge.

'Fuck,' said Lom quietly to himself. 'Fuck.'

Slowly and painfully he began to follow.

88

In darkness and snow and windswept ice at the centre of the North Zima Expanse, the Pollandore rests in its own uninterpretable space, touching nothing, a slowly turning globe. Worlds do not stand on the framework of flatbed trucks. Worlds do not hang by hooks and cables from a makeshift gantry. Worlds fall. They are always and only falling. Endless ellipses of fall, from no sky towards no frozen ground, turning and tumbling as they go. And everything else falls with them, unaware.

Towering over the Pollandore on its own framework of girders, the swollen samovar – the uranium gobbet in its bulging belly, the uranium seed sleeved in its high-explosive kernel – awaits its moment in the sun. Uncle Vanya's big fat beautiful cousin. Cables snake away across the ice.

Several miles from the Pollandore's crude gantry, in a concrete bunker with walls three feet deep and one thick panoramic window, Ambroz Teleki was handing out tubs of sunscreen and aviator glasses with dark-tinted lenses. Lavrentina Chazia waved him away.

'I'm not staying cooped up inside this hutch,' she said. 'I'm going out to feel the hot wind on my face.'

Teleki was horrified.

'But that's impossible! Secretary Chazia, you do not appreciate the danger … the strength of the blast … Even at this distance—'

Chazia silenced him with a look.

'At dawn,' she said, 'there will be a new sun. Am I not to bask in its warmth?'

She turned to the corner where the Shaumian girl sat watching her with dark resentful eyes.

'And you, Maroussia darling,' said Chazia, 'you will see the flash on the horizon and know the moment for what it is. The destruction of the Pollandore. I'm glad you're here to see it, it's only right you should. That thing has been a source of delusion for us both, in our different ways. To be released from it will be a great step forward. You'll see things in their true relations then.'

Chazia had been reluctant to destroy the Pollandore after investing so much in it for so long. She had wanted to carry out the angel's instruction, but the thought of doing it was deeply painful. She had continued to put up inward resistance until rigorous self-examination and the guidance of the angel had gradually opened her eyes to the truth. It had taken time, but at last, freed from false consciousness by a better teaching, she'd come to realise what a beguiling cipher the Pollandore was: a meaningless emptiness, a zero mirage into which she'd been led to pour her desires, against her true interests and the reality of things as they were. The Pollandore had woven subtle nets of illusion to protect itself while it exploited her, just as it had ensnared Maroussia.

'Make sure she watches,' Chazia said to the SV lieutenant standing guard at Maroussia's side. 'Make her stand there and see.'

Maroussia glared at her but said nothing.

'The pain will pass,' said Chazia kindly. 'Truth hurts but better understanding sets us free.' Then she turned away and went through to the other room, the office. She opened the crate that held her suit of angel flesh and began to put it on.

The excitement of anticipation made her tremble.

Wolf-Florian galloped low across the surface of the snow, stretching his limbs in the relief of being wolf again, bounding over raised drifts. He could sense the Pollandore ahead of him. It was below the horizon but its call burned behind his eyes like he had never felt it before, and the calling pulsed with a desperate joy. He was running through the shadows of invisible trees. The flat disc of ice across which he ran was forested with the ghosts of ancient trees.

Ahead of him was the Pollandore and behind him was Lom, a perfumed beacon spilling his beautiful headstuff into the freezing air, all unaware of what he was and what he could become. And between them – Florian was closing on her now and could sense her presence – was the Shaumian woman.

Florian still did not know what to do.

The woman was change and the woman was desperate threat. A door in the world stood slightly open, which she might fling wide or slam shut. And he did not know which.

He would kill her before she could reach the Pollandore.

With his last dying breath he would carry her safely to it, so she could do what she would do.

When the time came he would know what to do.

But for now, still, even as he ran towards her, he did not know, and the not-knowing hurt. It hurt more than the desperate working of his heart as he pushed himself on at the extremity of his body's capacity across the hardened crunching snow.

A flake of Archangel watchfulness settles upon the gantry of Uncle Vanya's big fat cousin and flexes its fragment-wings of sentience like a bird. Archangel bird is come to taste the joy of destruction.

He observes with pin-sharp joy the diminished, fragile, vulnerable sphere beneath him. Here is the Once Great Threat. Here is the Pollandore. How pathetic Archangel finds it now, so feeble and tiny amid the wastes of ice, and bound with chains to a barrel of death!

To think that in his hurt and wounded beginning on this confining world he – he! Archangel! – once had feared this useless thing! Feared this excremetal node of weaknesses! He does not fear it now.

Destruction time coming.

Pleasurable anticipation thrills.

He lets the time of its coming run slowly. Tasting it.

He will crush this disgusting thing under the heel of his triumph. He will abort it. Soon this trivial gap will be closed, and a new roaring radiant gate will be thrown open.

Archangel-fragment throws back his bird head and crows at the approaching dawn. It is a mighty banner-shout unfurling across the glittering immensities of what will come to be.

When Chazia had gone, Maroussia got up from her chair by the window and went over to the SV lieutenant.

'Please,' she said. 'I would like to visit the bathroom.'

The lieutenant looked at her with relaxed contempt. Memories in the back of his eyes. Memories of what he'd seen Chazia do to her, and what he himself had done. Maroussia pushed the thought away. She wouldn't think of that. Not now and not ever.

'Sit down,' said the lieutenant. 'Wait.'

'Please,' said Maroussia. 'Please. It is urgent. I have to go now.'

The lieutenant swore.

'Come then,' he said. 'But for fuck's sake be quick.'

Lom ploughed on alone through the snow, following the line of the overhead rail. The cluster of huts was at least half a mile away. It was slow going. He hunched his face into his collar against the bitter cold. Stuffed his hands into his pockets, flexing his fingers to keep them mobile. His breath plumed steam clouds. What had seemed flat terrain from the rail car was undulating ridges and dips, crests and berms. The circle of the half-visible around him grew inexorably wider, the twilight before dawn inching towards grey. But there was nothing to see: only the levels of rolling tundra, indistinct under thin drifting mist.

He was holding tight to the idea – the unsurrendered certainty – that Maroussia was there in that cluster of huts half a mile ahead. He had no plan. That didn't matter: plans never lasted thirty seconds when the action started. Here in subarctic near-darkness, alone and driving himself forward, chest heaving, heart pounding, across the sharp crusted snow, he knew what he had to do, the only thing he could possibly do, and he was doing it.

There was nothing else in the world but him and the half-mile of ice between him and Maroussia. It all came down to that. He had chosen this. He had made his decisions and chosen the path that brought him here. He was absolutely responsible and absolutely free and he would not fail; he would not be too late and he would not die, because to fail was to fail Maroussia, and that he would not do.

And he was, in that moment, completely and absolutely alive.

Inside the tiny bathroom Maroussia locked the door. She looked at her face in the mirror hung on a hook above the sink. She looked tired and sick. Bruise-blue shadows under her eyes. A pink graze across her face. There were angry raised welts on her wrists and arms where Chazia's straps had rubbed and cut. She felt sick. She would not think of that. Not now. Not ever. She would not remember.

She wrapped a towel around her hand. Then she lifted the mirror off the wall and smashed it against the sink.

'Hey!' called the lieutenant. 'What are you doing in there?' He tried the door. 'Fuck,' he said, but quietly so that Chazia would not hear. He didn't want her to know. He began to bump his weight against the door, but hesitantly. He would make no more noise than he had to.

Maroussia picked up the biggest shard of broken mirror. Gripped it tight in her towel-wrapped palm. Settled the edge of it firmly in her hand. A vicious, pointed shard of glass about five inches long.

The thumping against the door fell into a predictable rhythmic pattern. The bolt was beginning to give. With her free hand Maroussia slid it quietly back.

At the next crash of the lieutenant's weight, the door burst open and he stumbled in, surprised. Unbalanced, he took a couple of stuttering steps forward. Maroussia stepped in behind him, put the dagger of glass against the side of his throat and pushed. She had to push hard. Two, three times she sawed the jagged edge back and forth. There was a lot of blood. When she let the lieutenant drop to the floor he was not dead. He was trying to shout and scream. He had two mouths now, both of them gaping open and spilling blood, but neither had a voice. Only a desperate bubbling wheeze.

She dropped the towel and knelt beside him, the warm pool of his blood soaking into the skirt of her dress. She went through the pockets of his jacket, searching, hoping what she was looking for was still there, where she had watched him carelessly shove it the night before. It was. Her fingers touched the broken pieces. She pulled out the fragments of the solm her mother had been bringing when she died, gripped them tight in her palm and stood up, careful not to slip on the blood on the floor.

Maroussia left the lieutenant still moving weakly in the growing pool of his own mess. She went out the back of the blockhouse into the dark and the snow.

89

L om was still several hundred yards from the cluster of huts, moving slowly and cautiously, crouching to keep off the brightening skyline, when Florian appeared suddenly beside him as if he had risen up out of the snow.

'Maroussia?' said Lom. 'Did you find her?'

Florian looked at him strangely for a moment and said nothing.

'For fuck's sake,' said Lom. 'Is she *there*?'

'She is there,' said Florian. 'She has been hurt but she is alive. She is very strong.'

Lom felt a desperate knot of tension suddenly dissolve. He hadn't realised how dark his world had grown since he'd lost her. He wanted to throw his arms round Florian and hug him but did not. Florian looked grave.

'What?' said Lom. 'What is it?'

'Nothing,' said Florian. 'Nothing.'

'Then let's go.'

'Yes. But cautiously. There are two huts. One with soldiers. VKBD. Seven. Maroussia is in the other. Chazia is also there, and one soldier, and men who are not soldiers. Scientists. Technicians. Nine.'

Lom pushed his elation aside. *Focus on now.* They needed to get Maroussia out and away. He considered the position. They had two Vagants between them. Full chambers but no spare ammunition. Eight soldiers, plus Chazia herself, who would not be negligible if it came to a fight. And if they could get Maroussia safely away, what then? They were in a snowfield a hundred miles or more on the wrong side of the mountain, on an island in a freezing sea. But then they had Florian. Lom had seen what he could do.

'OK,' he said. 'Could be worse.'

'It is,' said Florian. 'They have a mudjhik.'

'No,' said Lom. He looked towards the distant huts. 'Surely not. I'd feel it by now.'

'It is there. Not a large one. Ten feet tall perhaps. It seems inactive. I was not aware of it until I got close. Its presence startled me.'

'OK,' said Lom again. 'Anything else?'

'Outbuildings for storage. A diesel generator. An overhead rail car like the one we came in on. And there's a single railway track, away to the left over there. It runs on into the north. Towards the Pollandore.'

Lom felt a tightening in his stomach. His mouth was dry.

'Let's get on with it,' he said.

90

Lom was less than a hundred yards from the blockhouses. Florian had slipped away and disappeared, circling round to the left. Lom scrambled forward across the snow until he could see the mudjhik. It was standing upright, motionless, a squat statue of solid brick-red taller than the concrete blockhouses, arms at its side, its head, an eyeless faceless mass, turned towards the north. Lom let his mind drift towards it cautiously, reaching out for a contact, probing delicately, looking for a way in. And found it.

The mudjhik was not dormant. It was absorbed in studying the snow. With angel senses, not sight but precise acute awareness, it was examining individual crystals of snow. Sifting from one to the next with absolute patience, it traced their intricate hexagonal symmetry. The ramification of columns and blades of ice. The uncountable variety. It found the broken ones and tested the edges of their fractures. It teased the nested clumps, the accidental fusions. It followed the prismatic re-fractions of muted light down beneath the mute mirror-glitter surface as the greyness broke into spectrum fragments, growing green then blue then dark. To the mudjhik's patient watchfulness the snow was as deep and mysterious as oceans.

Long slow inches below the surface the mudjhik touched solid compacted ice and sank its attention in. Ran its mind along faults and pressure lines and the million captured imperfections of grit and dust. The mudjhik found it all infinitely, endlessly satisfying. The ice and snow was beautiful and it was happy.

Lom traced the faint cord of connection from the mudjhik to its handler. The line was almost not there at all: the handler's focus was elsewhere, on something inside the building. It had been the same for hours, the mudjhik almost forgotten. Gently, gently, Lom squeezed the connection closed, cut it off entirely, and slid in behind it. The mudjhik was his.

Lom made himself known.

The mudjhik sprang to life. It was like an inward eye opening. Glaring and hot. It opened its thoughtless sentient mind like a dark hot mouth, gaping and hungry. Tried to grasp at Lom and swallow him and haul him fully inside. But Lom was strong. He knew what he was doing. The angel stain in his own blood answered the mudjhik's assault with a fierce roaring.

No, said Lom-in-mudjhik, *I am not yours. You are mine. You are mine. You are mine.*

Lom forced himself through every part of the mudjhik's body, occupying it entirely. Taking possession. He found the animal brain and spinal column of nerves buried deep inside, felt the sparking of dark red electricity along lifeless-alive synapses and alienated neurones, understood and mastered them. Lom-in-mudjhik felt the strength and blazing awareness of the mudjhik. His strength. His awareness.

Go! he screamed. *Go! Go!*

His own human body was nothing to him now: a squatting shell leaning against a wall of snow, slumped, head down, sightless and breathing shallow and rough. Lom-in-mudjhik was moving fast towards the blockhouse where the soldiers were.

Lom-in-mudjhik lashed his fist against the concrete wall. Smashed the wall again and again. Men were in there. Men to hunt and kill.

Lom-in-mudjhik remembered how satisfying it was to burst a human skull between his hands. The sudden splash of warmth as the life went out. The blockhouse was filled with the reverberations in the air that humans made with lungs and mouths. Steel implements made their familiar small explosions. Lom-in-mudjhik traced the path of the small projectiles: some of them struck his body, their kinetic energy becoming gobbets of heat to feed his core. A couple that were going to miss him he slapped out of the air for fun. Lom-in-mudjhik killed the men with methodical deliberation, one by one.

When there was only one left he let it scrabble out through the door and start to run. Waited a moment for the pleasure of the chase. He knew what this one was: his former handler. He began to lope after him slowly, following along as the man raced and skidded and fell, making reverberations with his mouth. Lom-in-mudjhik knew that man's dreams and nightmares, how he had imagined and feared just such an unwinnable race as this.

Slowly, gradually, patiently, Lom-in-mudjhik came up alongside the running man and fulfilled his dreams.

The Pollandore watches Maroussia coming north across the ice. She is wearing nothing but a dress and thin shoes and the front of the dress is soaked in blood which is not hers. The blood is freezing on her dress. Bright crimson crystals stiffen the cotton. The crystals are thin and brittle and sometimes they crack and fall.

Maroussia is so cold that she will die if she does not get warm.

Ahead of her in the dark Uncle Vanya's cousin is waiting.

She will be warm enough soon.

Wolf-Florian sniffed at Maroussia's trail in the snow. Picked up pace and followed it for a while, then slowed and hung back. He circled, a grey prowling shadow in an agony of uncertainty. He paused. Testing whether the time had come.

It had not come.

Wolf-Florian turned away and ran back towards the perfumed breathing beacon that was Vissarion Lom.

Archangel sees him.

Archangel-fragment-bird is alert. Even as his moment of triumph approaches he is monitoring the peripheries. He does not overlook the danger. Archangel has outgrown mistakes.

Archangel sees the wolf. And, following the threads, scanning the environs, he finds the abandoned, dormant body of Vissarion Lom. Archangel perceives the tiny possibility of threat, the hairline crack at the margin of his domain.

Archangel acts.

He tears a hole in the preposterous angel-suit and crashes screaming into the mind of Lavrentina Chazia, who is waiting on the ice for the moment of ignition, when Uncle Vanya's big cousin kindles into cataclysm.

DESTROY THE TRAVELLERS! THEY ARE COMING! CRUSH THEM! BREAK THEM! DESTROY THEM NOW!

TRUTH AND FEAR

*

Lavrentina Chazia burned with ecstatic joy at the coming of the Archangel voice. Her belly exploded with detonations of pleasure. Hot with the obedience-thrill of Archangelic power and purpose, encased in angel substance and gravid with Archangel harvest, she turned and began to run.

91

Lom-in-mudjhik felt a sharp blow across his face. It stung. But it was not Lom-in-mudjhik's face that hurt: it was the face of his old useless abandoned human body. Some creature was leaning over it. Shaking it. Making the air reverberate with quiet urgency. The creature was like a human but not. A hunting beast. A new thing.

A thing to kill, then.

Lom-in-mudjhik began to run.

The creature's reverberations had some faint meaning that percolated down through Lom-in-mudjhik's understanding. To part of him they meant something, to part not. Because Lom-in-mudjhik was two parts now, not one.

Vissarion! Vissarion!

Florian was hissing his name in his ear.

Lom opened his eyes and coughed. Retched sour liquid down his chest.

'Vissarion!'

Florian put his hand under his chin and lifted his head. Lom opened his eyes and brought Florian's face into focus. A pain in the front of his head pounded mercilessly. He puked again.

'You killed them,' said Florian. 'All of them.'

'I thought...' Lom shook his head to clear the pain a little. Wiped his mouth on his sleeve. 'Not me. Not me that killed them. It. I thought I could control it...' He snapped his head up abruptly, looking around. 'Maroussia? Where is *Maroussia*? Where *is* she?'

'She wasn't in the building. She slipped away. Escaped. But she's gone north. Towards the Pollandore. Towards the bomb.'

'Bomb? What bomb?'

'Khyrbysk's bomb. The one that sets the world on fire.'

'*What?*'

'The bomb is the other thing,' said Florian. 'Fucker Khyrbysk's other thing. I knew … He was hiding it. I should have pressed him harder. I should have … I have made mistakes, I have done everything wrong.'

Lom struggled to think. The aftertaste of the mudjhik's mind was still in his, dark red and confusing.

'Why?' he said. 'Maroussia. Why has she gone there?'

'Because the Pollandore is there. Chazia is going to destroy it with the bomb. Maroussia … she has gone there for the Pollandore.'

Lom struggled to his feet. He felt dizzy and weak.

'How do you know?'

'About the Pollandore?'

'About the bomb!'

'The technicians were only too happy—'

'We have to follow,' said Lom.

Florian grabbed his arm.

'You can't help her, Vissarion. The bomb will detonate in …' He grabbed Lom's wrist and looked at his watch: 8.33. 'We have twenty-seven minutes. Not enough. Even here we are not safe outside the bunker. The bomb is the largest they've made. The technicians are not happy about being even this close. They are leaving.'

As Florian was speaking they heard the sound of an overhead rail car starting into life. It trundled away to the south as they watched.

'The detonation cannot be halted from here,' said Florian. 'The operations control room is elsewhere.'

'I'm going after her,' said Lom.

'You can't. It will destroy you.'

'I'm going after her. You get away while you can. There's no need for you—' He stopped suddenly. '*Chazia,*' he said. 'Where *is* she? Did you—'

'Somewhere out on the ice. I could not find her. She has a protective suit. She thinks it will keep her safe against the effects of the blast, but the technicians—'

Florian broke off. His head jerked round suddenly and he leaped aside, landing ten feet away in a crouch. His body longer, thinner, whiplash strong.

The mudjhik was lumbering fast towards them over the ice.

No! Stop!

Lom slammed up a wall in front of the mudjhik. It was like a word spoken. A sheer instinctive act of will. The mudjhik crashed into it and fell to its knees. Dazed. Lost.

There, said Lom-in-mudjhik gently, letting his mind run smooth and quiet across his own anger. *Calm. Patience. Look at the snow. Look. Look at the snow. Together we are better. Together we are calm. Together we are still.*

Vissarion Lom was a separate watchfulness, inside Lom-in-mudjhik but not lost there.

I'm getting better at this. I can do this now.

Lom-in-mudjhik let his awareness run wider, yard by yard, out across the ice. The sky was a widening bowl of grey cloud, filling now with iron day. Blades of wind sifted the surface crystals, moving them into new patterns. Florian was there, tense and watching, crouched ready to run or fight. Florian his ally. Florian his friend.

And there was someone else coming up behind him, moving fast. It was Chazia.

Lom-in-mudjhik knew the taste of Chazia's mind well enough. All too well. He remembered … But this was Chazia different. Chazia something else. Chazia, like a mudjhik but not, with a size and energy not her own. She stank of angel mind and angel flesh. She was coming across the ice with more than human strength, bearing down on Lom's abandoned and defenceless human body and his Florian-friend.

Chazia on fire with angels and coming to kill.

Florian sensed her racing towards him, swung round and leaped at her, rising high and coming down on her shoulders, scrabbling at the crude covering that masked her face. She shook him off. He fell to the ground and twisted and jumped to his feet, snarling, changing, more wolf than man, but hampered by his human clothes and struggling to get a purchase on the snow. Chazia picked him up by the scruff of his neck with one hand and punched his body with the other. Florian felt his body snap and jerk. He kicked at her desperately with both feet. The collar and back of his coat tore in her grip. He twisted free and collapsed to the ground again, panting with pain, moving awkwardly, smearing blood across the snow. His ribs were badly smashed. He needed to get clear and repair the damage.

*

Lom-in-mudjhik watched the strange half-human, half-angel contraption that Lavrentina Chazia had become as she turned towards Lom's inert abandoned human body. Felt the surge of anticipation as Chazia prepared to destroy him.

I am not there, said Lom-in-mudjhik, forcing the thought with ease into Chazia's angel-cased head. *I am behind you. Look at me. I am here.*

Chazia jerked round and stared at the mudjhik.

Lom?

I have been coming for you. I told you that I would.

So you came, said Chazia. *I'm glad you are here. I will enjoy your death. And then the Pollandore will die. Maroussia will be released from illusion and taste the bitterness of truth and then she will die. And the living angel will see it all and know that I am strong and deserving of acceptance.*

A part of Lom that was only Lom, not Lom-in-mudjhik, lurched in pain when it heard Maroussia's name, and Chazia felt the hurt. It was an advantage and she drove it home.

I have spent much time with Maroussia, Lom, she said. *We got to know each other very thoroughly. You should have been there. You should have come sooner.*

I am here now.

Chazia was edging away towards a space of flat open snow where she would have room to move. *She thinks there is going to be a fight. She thinks she is going to fight a mudjhik.*

It was time to kill her.

Lom-in-mudjhik drove swiftly forward, sure-footed across the ice. He swept his fist forward and crashed it into the side of Chazia's head inside the angel carapace. *Always the head is best. Heads are fragile. Heads are weak.*

Lom-in-mudjhik felt Chazia's sharp, sickening explosion of pain and confusion. Her world skidding sideways. Lom-in-mudjhik felt triumph and joy. He knew that this human was weak inside her angel shell. She did not know how to wear it: she was in it but she was not *it*. She was Chazia and Suit, not Chazia-in-suit, and it protected her no more than a skin of tin. Lom-in-mudjhik could kill her inside it. No problem. *Don't damage the suit. I need the suit. She doesn't know how to use it. But I do.*

Lom-in-mudjhik stepped round in front of Chazia. She was on her hands and knees, crawling away. He could feel her pain and fear. She had realised the truth of what was going to happen to her. Commander of killers, torturer, trespasser-invader of lives and minds, Lavrentina Chazia knew she was going to die, and Lom-in-mudjhik was glad she knew. He stepped forward and leaned over her scrabbling form. With precise and delicate fingers – fingers that could separate a snowflake unbroken from the rest and pluck its star points one by one – Lom-in-mudjhik unbuckled the headpiece and removed it from Chazia's head. Then he took hold of her body with one hand under her arm and lifted her up until she was level with him. Bloodshot, panicking and helpless. she stared into his rough-shaped blank and eyeless face.

Lom-in-mudjhik brought Chazia closer and closer to him. His free hand was behind her head, cupping it in his palm. He tangled his mudjhik fingers in her hair and brought her face close against his face, touching her brow against his face of angel rock, touching her mouth to where his mouth should have been if a mudjhik had a mouth.

It was like a kiss.

Sweet kiss.

She was the torturer, the killer, the Vlast, and this was revenge.

With his hand that was behind her head, Lom-in-mudjhik pressed Chazia's face into his. And pressed. And pressed.

Until her head broke against his like a warm, spilling egg.

Lom withdrew himself from the mudjhik more easily than before and left it contemplating snow. Back in his own human form – none too soon, he had begun to feel it slipping away and beginning to die – he crouched beside Chazia's body and began to remove the angel skin. It was heavy, awkward work. He felt empty and sick. He wanted to think the mudjhik had done the thing like that, not him. But he knew differently.

Florian limped up beside him, pale and drawing shallow rasping breaths, wincing as he worked at his chest with his fingers. He looked and said nothing. There was no need.

Lom had no time to think about what he had done. Something else to do.

'Help me,' said Lom. 'Help me get this on. Quickly, for fuck's sake. It can take me nearer the bomb. Chazia knew that; I felt her think it.'

Piece by piece they removed the angel casing from Chazia and wiped it clean in the snow, leaving churned-up places smeared with blood and brain and fragments of bone. Lom was afraid it would be too small for him, but he felt each element adjust itself to him. It was as if the suit wanted him to put it on. He felt it sliding along his skin, stretching and folding itself around him, becoming warm. It felt natural, like sliding into water at body heat. He knew how to do it. *What am I doing? What's happening to me? What is this thing I am becoming?* He pushed the thought aside. *Later.*

92

Maroussia was so cold she no longer felt cold. She had no feeling at all. She wanted to lie down in the warm soft welcoming snow and sleep. She wanted to swim in the comforting snow and float in its amniotic warmth. Wash away the marks and stains and stickiness of what Chazia and the lieutenant had done to her. She wanted to still her memory for ever.

Soon she would do this. Soon, but not yet.

Inside its carapace of angel flesh, Vissarion Lom's human body ran, and the strength of angels carried him over snow and ice. Racing lightly across the surface, scarcely breaking the crust, he moved faster than he had ever moved before. His senses were angel senses and human senses too. The wind was in his face and every crystal of snow on North Zima Island was sharp and crisp and distinct.

Lom ran.

Somewhere ahead of him in the distance, beyond the horizon, he was aware of something waiting. A point of impossibility. Present in the world but not of it. The Pollandore. It pulsed like a heart beating. It knew he was there and called him on. It had location but no shape and no certain size. Sometimes it was a tiny particle, one more grain of snow. Sometimes it swelled to absorb the sky. It was alive and changing. But he could not find Maroussia. He could not do that.

Alongside him Florian ran, easily keeping pace. He was a grey wolf running, and he was Florian, who could have run the other way and might have saved himself, but did not.

*

Wolf-Florian ran in heart-bursting despair, his still-tender ribs sending bright jabs of pain shooting through his chest. The Shaumian woman was too near the Pollandore. He would not reach her now. He would not prevent her. She would get there.

He might have stopped her when he had the chance. But he had not decided, and that had become in the end his decision.

He would live with the consequences.

If only for a short while.

The Pollandore is in front of Maroussia. Neither close nor far away. It hangs in no time and no space. Waiting for her. Inviting her to go on. The gap that separates her from the Pollandore is not a gap in this world. It is the gap between worlds. Unbridgeable. Unmeasurable by any planetary metrication. Worlds apart and not apart at all. Uncrossable.

Maroussia crossed.

Miles away a technician flicked a switch on a control panel. A jolt of electrical current surged along the long rubber-sheathed cables that snaked for miles across the snow. The current reached Uncle Vanya's big fat cousin and gave him a nudge.

Detonation.

A star ignited and the world broke open into light.

The angel suit that carried Vissarion Lom knew what this was. This was home. The angel flesh surged. It flowered. It was itself a skin of woven light. Against the storm of starlight it stood, made itself of light, not moving but moving, pace against pace, light into light, going nowhere. For one moment of eternity time itself slowed and paused. Lom, held safe within the cohesive web of light, was everywhere and nowhere, now and for ever.

The snow was gone and the whole country was lit with an intensity brighter than any midday sun. Gold and purple and blue. Sheets of rock lit with more than planetary clarity. There were mountain ranges in the distance, low on the horizon, he had not seen before. Every fold and gully and snow-covered peak was clear and vivid and scarcely beyond the reach of his hand.

Then the light passed.

Lom was running again, running against the burning wind towards an enormous ball of fire that churned and rolled towards him, and churned and rolled up into the burning sky. Climbing for miles. Lemon. Crimson. Green. The cloud of fire rolled over him like a wave and gathered Lom in.

The wind of light from the new star brushed grey-wolf-Florian-running out of the world in a stream of particles too small for soot.

Archangel screams in the consummation of his joy.

Lom ran. The ground itself was boiling. A roaring column of heat and dust and burning earth lifted the huge flower of fire from his shoulders and carried it up. High overhead the explosion cloud boiled and swelled and spread, blocking out the sky, shedding its own darkening light: a hard rain falling.

The Pollandore was ahead of him, turning gently on its own orbit, following its own parabolas of fall, there but not there, a sphere of greenish milky brightness the size of a small house. It was a survivor. He ran towards it.

Lom stopped in front of the Pollandore and stood there, braced against the howling winds of desolation. He reached out to touch it. It moved with gentle resistance at the pressure of the Lom-in-angel hand and swung back into position.

He was trembling.

Maroussia was not there.

Maroussia had gone into the dark.

Lom felt a hand on his shoulder.

'Vissarion?'

Her voice. He didn't want to turn and look. It wouldn't be her.

He turned.

'Yes?' he said.

Maroussia was standing there, hesitant, smiling. Her eyes were different. She wasn't the same. Standing in sunlight under a different sky.

'It isn't you,' he said.

'Yes. It is.'

She was in sunshine and he was under dry burning rain, encased in angel light. But none of it was there. He put his arms around her and smelled woodsmoke and summer warmth in her hair. He kissed her mouth and felt her hand pressing against his back.

Then she drew away from him. The distance between them was widening rapidly though neither of them had moved. The Pollandore was changing now, the interior pulsing with milky light to the rhythm of a slow inaudible heart. It was shrinking, condensing, diminishing, falling into itself, and the fall was a very long way and no distance at all.

Maroussia's expression changed. Darkened. Her gaze turned inward.

'Oh,' she said quietly. 'Oh ... I see... I see what I have done ... I didn't know.'

'What is it? Tell me.'

She shook her head. Her eyes were wide and dark.

'I have to go now,' she said.

'Wherever you go,' said Lom 'whatever comes next, I will find you.'

'No ... I'm sorry, no ... you can't follow, not where I'm going, nobody can, not any more. The way is shut now and must be held shut. I didn't think it would be like this ... but there's no choice ... I'm so sorry ...'

Smaller and smaller and further away the Pollandore went. It had not moved, but it was separated from Lom by a great and growing distance. It was a mark of misty brightness on a far horizon, small as a fruit. He could have reached out and held it in his hand.

And Maroussia was not there at all.

The Pollandore folded in upon itself until it was nowhere, until it occupied no space and no time, until it was a concentrated singular point of unsustainable possibility balanced on the imperceptible edge between now and not.

And then it exploded, and the explosion passed through him like it was nothing at all.

The shockwave flashed outwards from the unsustainable zero point – not light, not heat, not sound, not energy of any kind, but a cataclysm-detonation of consequence and change – and nothing was like it had been before, and everything was the same, except that Lom was there, in the star-burned wastes of Novaya Zima at the foot of Uncle Vanya's twisted gantry, a frozen cooling torsion-structure under the desultory falling-to-earth of radioactive rain, and Maroussia was not there at all.

Archangel screams again. He sees the implication of what has been done. This time his scream is not for joy.

Lom stood in the cooling ground zero of the exploded Pollandore and the future spread out round him, a carpet unrolled in all directions at the speed of light. Whether Maroussia had done it, or whether it had been done to Maroussia, for good or for ill, it was done, and what came afterwards would all be consequence of that.

'I will come looking for you,' he said aloud to the echoless aftermath world.

93

The world was changed, changed utterly, and the world still felt the same, because it was the same, except that time was all clockwork and inevitable now. History roared on like a building wave across the open ocean, like an express on a straight and single track roaring ahead into an obvious future. Like the train rolling at full speed from Novaya Zima towards Mirgorod, hauling its cargo of a hundred yellow 180mm calibre atomic artillery shells and Hektor Shulmin in the solitary passenger car.

There was a second telephone on the desk in Rizhin's office in the Armoury. He'd had it installed the day he arrived, with instructions that it should be given a certain number, which he provided. The number was of the utmost importance. Nobody was to know that number and nobody was to call it, not ever: Rizhin was quite clear on that point. He left precise instructions with his staff on what to do if it rang when he was not there.

'That telephone must always be watched,' he said, '*always*, twenty-four hours a day, *never* left unattended, and if it rings the call must be taken. Nothing is more important than this. The caller will not ask for me, he will ask for the Singer. Check this. Be precise. If the caller does not ask for the Singer, say nothing and hang up immediately. But if he does ask for the Singer, you must ask him what the arrangements are and note everything he says, everything, note every detail precisely. And I must be told immediately, wherever I am, without delay.'

Every day Rizhin watched that telephone and every day it did not ring. Nevertheless, the top of the raion hill was cleared. All the buildings surrounding the Ship Bastion were razed to the ground. The cobbled square was dug up and replaced with a new concrete foundation, a wide straight way was driven up to the peak and three huge guns were hauled up and set in place there: three two-hundred-pounders from the battleship *Admiral Irtysh* which was currently blockaded in the naval yard. The long muzzles of grey steel pointed silently out across the city. Rizhin had the Ship Bastion scattered with rubble, the guns covered with grey camouflage netting and a circle of anti-aircraft guns emplaced in bunkers to surround and protect them.

The enemy drew its noose tighter round the city as winter closed in. Two weeks passed. The guns on the Ship Bastion did not fire.

One morning when Rizhin was in his office alone the long-silent telephone rang.

'Yes?' said Rizhin.

My name is Shulmin. Is this the Singer please? Are you the Singer? Get him for me please. I must speak to him, only to him.

'I am the Singer. Do you have what I need?'

Yes, but there is a problem. The voice on the end of the line sounded exhausted. Frightened and full of stress.

'Problem?' said Rizhin.

The city is surrounded by the enemy. There is no way through.

'Of course. Where are you now? Where is the consignment? Is it with you?'

It is with me. It is safe. I'm at a railhead on the north shore of Lake Dorogha but the train can go no further, they're talking of turning back, the enemy is close. We can hear shooting.

'Do not turn back,' said Rizhin. 'Do not allow that. Shoot the driver if necessary.'

I don't have a gun.

'Improvise. The train must not turn back.'

There was a long silence on the end of the line.

What should I do? said Shulmin at last.

'Do nothing,' said Rizhin. 'Wait. Wait there. Someone will come.'

The enemy was taken by surprise by the sudden breakout through the siege lines to the north of Mirgorod, a concerted night attack against a weak point in the salient. In the confusion of battle there were reports that three heavy trucks had raced through at speed and disappeared into the darkness. Some said battle-tanks had cleared the way and gone ahead, but this was dismissed as fanciful: the Vlast had no battle-tanks in Mirgorod. Some said a giant man of red stone had come out of the night and wrought appalling damage. They said the giant knew where the snipers were and pulled down the buildings they were in, stove in their chests and crushed their skulls. Whatever the truth of what happened, it came quickly and it was over before anyone in the enemy command was sure exactly what had occurred. After the first flurry of discussion the Archipelago officers paid the event little attention: it was a small breakout and of no consequence.

Three days later it happened again but in reverse: another sudden, confusing and ferocious night attack on a different part of the line. And this time the muddled reports spoke of trucks racing *into* the city.

The following morning Rizhin gathered his commanders and the city administrators around him on the Ship Bastion. Shulmin was there to oversee the firing. It was ten in the morning, Mirgorod time.

'One shot will be enough,' said Shulmin. 'One will send the message. They will see.'

'Ten,' said Rizhin. 'Send them ten.'

The two hundred pound guns of the *Admiral Irtysh* spoke and spoke again. One by one, ten seeds of blinding light were sown along the horizon to the south of Mirgorod, illuminating the underbelly of low grey cloud. A flicker of distant summer warmth on the air. A grove of mushroom clouds cracked and burst and reformed on the skyline and dry thunder rolled back across the city, re-echoing the dying roar of the guns behind them.

'Send a runner to Carnelian,' said Rizhin. 'I will accept her unconditional surrender this evening at six.'

He turned to the dumbfounded watchers at the parapet blinking away their retinal burn. Their faces were reddened and sullen with shock.

'And so I give you back your city, my friends.' he said, 'the first prize of many yet to come. Stay with me now and watch me clear the mess away and set the Vlast in order. We will build a New Vlast, stronger than before. We have a long way to go. Further than you imagine.'

All the rest of that day Rizhin listened out for the voice of Archangel thundering in his head but it did not come. For more than two weeks now it had not come. *I am free of it then,* he said to himself. *Free of it and alone. I am the voice of history. I am the mile high man.*

RADIANT
STATE

Ice cliffs melt
under truth's solar burn.

OSIP MANDELSTAM (1891–1938)

Part One

Chapter One

We will leave our planet by a radiant new path.

We will lay out the stars in rows
and ride the moon like a horse.

Vladimir Kirillov (1889–1943)

On the canals of Mars we will build the palace of world freedom.

Mikhail Gerasimov (1889–1939)

1

She sees with eyes too wide, her ears are deafened with too much hearing, she feels with her skin. She is the first bold pioneer of a new generation: Engineer-Technician 2nd Class Mikkala Avril. Age twenty-three? Age zero! Fresh-born raw today, in the zero day of the unencompassable zero season of the world, she descends the gangway of the small plane sent personally for her, the only passenger, under conditions of supreme urgency. *Priority Override.* (The plane is still in its shabby olive livery of war: no time is wasted on primping and beautifying in the New Vlast of Papa Rizhin.) Reaching the foot of the wobbling steel stair, she steps out onto the tarmac of the Chaiganur cosmodrome, Semei-Pavlodar Province, and into the heat of the epochal threshold hour.

To be part of it. To do her task.

The almost-bursting heart in her ribs is the heart of her generation, the heart of the New Vlast, a clever strong young heart pounding at the farthest limit of endurability, equal parts dizzying excitement and appalling terrible fear.

Today will be a day like no other.

It is not yet quite six years since the armies of the enemy surrounding Mirgorod were swept from the face of the planet in a cleansing, burning wind by Rizhin's new weapon, a barrage of atomic artillery shells. Not quite six years – the vertebrae of six long winters articulated by the connective tissue of five roaring summers – but for the New Vlast the time elapsed has delivered far more and felt far longer. General Osip Rizhin, President-Commander of the New Vlast and Hero of the Peace of a Thousand Years, has taken time by the scruff of the neck. He has stretched the weeks tight like wire and made each day work – *work!* – like days never worked before.

Some may express doubt that all this can been achieved so quickly, Rizhin said on First Peace Day, outlining his Five Year Plan, his Great Step into the Future. *But the doubters have not grasped the true nature of time. Time is not a dimension, it is a means of production. Time is too important to be trusted to calendars and clocks. Time is at our disposal and will march at our speed, if we are determined. It is a matter of the imposition of human will.*

Rizhin had seen the Goal and envisaged the completion of Task Number One. It would be delivered at the speed that he set.

And so it was. In two thousand hammer-blow days, each day a detonation like an atomic bomb, he made the whole planet beat with a crashing unstoppable rhythm perceptible from a hundred million miles away. The New Vlast was a pounding anvil the sun itself could feel: it shook the drum-taut solar photosphere, the 6,000-degree plasma skin.

But no day will ever beat more strongly or echo more enduringly down the corridors of the coming millennia than this one day, and Engineer-Technician Mikkala Avril will play her vital part.

She pauses on the airfield apron, savouring the moment, fixing it in memory. The furnace weight of the sun's heat beats on her face and shoulders and back. Hydrogen fusing into helium at a steady burn. She feels the remnants of the solar wind scouring her cheeks and screws her eyes against the bleach and glare. The air tastes of bitter herb and dusty cinder, of hot steel and of the sticky dust-streaked asphalt that peels noisily away from the soles of her shoes at every step. Breathing is hard labour.

Chaiganur is a scrub of desert steppe, baked dry under the rainless shimmering sky, parched to the far horizon. Flatness is its only feature. The dome of the sky is of no colour, the sun swollen and smeared across it, and the steppe is a whitened consuming lake bed of silent fierce unwatchable brightness. Nothing rises more than a few inches above the crumbling orange-yellow earth and the low clumps of coarse grey grass, nothing except pylons and gantries and hangars and scattered blockhouses: only they cast hot blue shadows. Miles to the south lies the shore of an ancient sea, and when the hot breeze blows it brings to Chaiganur a new covering of salty corrosive grit: ochre dust, clogging nozzles and caking surfaces.

The workers at Chaiganur put scorpions in bottles and watch them fight.

Throughout the two-hour flight from the Kurchatovgrad Barracks, Mikkala Avril had studied the technical manual, memorising layouts and procedures she already knows by heart. The night-duty clerk woke her in the early hours of the morning, agog with news, his part in her drama. A telephone call had come: instructions to go instantly to Chaiganur, transport already waiting. Her principal, Leading Engineer-Technician Filipov, had been taken suddenly and seriously ill and she – she, Mikkala Avril, there was no mistake, there was no one else, none qualified – was required immediately to take Filipov's place. Not an exercise. The thing itself.

As she put on her uniform she spared a thought for Filipov. He and his family would not be heard from again. Their names would no longer be spoken. It was a pity. Filipov had trained her well. Her success this day would be his final and most lasting contribution.

The plane bringing her to Chaiganur flew low. She watched through the window as they crossed the testing grounds and saw scars: the wide grey splash-craters of five years' worth of atomic detonations, the fallen pieces of failed and exploded engineering, the twisted wreckage of spent platforms cannibalised from war-surplus bridges and pontoons. Half-buried chunks of stained concrete resembled the dry bones and broken tusks of dead giants.

Didn't mammoths once walk this land? She might have heard that somewhere. Hadn't someone – but *who*? – taken her once, a girl, to rock outcrops polished smooth by long-dead beasts (by the scraping of scurf and ticks from their rufous hairy sides). That might have happened to her, she wasn't sure. Whatever. Nothing thrives now in all that flatness of stony rubbish but scorpions and rats and foxes and the sparse nomadic tribes with their ripe-smelling beards and scrawny horses.

The plane that brought her leaves again immediately, engines dwindling into sun-bleached silence. She heads for the control block, picking her way across pipes and thick cables that snake along the ground. She might be only one small component in the machine, one switch in the circuit, but she will execute her task smoothly, and that will matter. That will make a binary difference; that will allow the perfection of the most profound accomplishment of humankind. She will make no mistake. She will do it right.

2

Exactly one hour after the arrival of Mikkala Avril, a convoy sweeps at speed past the security perimeter of the Chaiganur cosmodrome trailing a half-mile cloud of dust. Three-and-a-half-ton armoured sedans – chrome fenders, white-walled tyres – doing a steady sixty. Motorcycle outriders and chase cars. They are heading straight for Test Site 61.

The sun-baked sedans carry the entire membership of the Central Committee of the New Vlast Presidium, and in one of the cars – no one is sure which, the bullet-proof windows are tinted – rides the President-Commander himself, General Osip Rizhin. Papa Rizhin, the great dictator, first servant of the New Vlast, coming to witness this greatest of triumphs and certify its momentousness with his presence.

Two jolting trucks bring up the rear. A sweating corps of journalists is tucked in among their movie cameras and their tape recorders. The men in the open backs of the trucks crook their arms in permanent angular shirt-sleeved salute, cramming homburgs, pork-pies, fedoras down tight on their heads against the hot wind of their passage. None but Rizhin knows what they are coming to see.

The party might have flown in to the cosmodrome in comfort but Rizhin refused to allow it, citing the presence among them of ambassadors from the new buffer states. *We must never permit a foreigner to fly across the Vlast*, he said. *All foreigners are spies.* That was the reason he gave, but his purpose was showmanship. He didn't want his audience seeing the testing zones or getting any other clues. None among them, not even the most senior Presidium member, had any idea how far and how fast the project had progressed. And so they all rode for three days in a sweltering sealed train with perforated zinc shutters on the outside of the windows, and then in cars from the railhead, five hours across baking scrubland, to arrive red-faced and dishevelled at Test Site 61, where a cluster of temporary tin huts has been erected for the purpose of receiving them.

The temporary huts crouch in the shade of a two-hundred-foot tall, eighty-foot diameter, snub-nosed upright bullet of thick steel. The bullet is painted crimson with small fins near the base. The fins serve no functional purpose but Rizhin demands them for the look of the thing, to make it more like a rocket, which it is not.

The Vlast Universal Vessel *Proof of Concept* stands against its gantry, an ugly truncated stub, a blood-coloured thumb cocked at the sky, a splash of hot red glimmering in the glare of the sun.

3

Three time zones west of Chaiganur and eight hundred miles to the north, in the eastern outskirts of Mirgorod, a short train ride from the shore of Lake Dorogha, a woman in a shabby grey dress picks her way across a war-damaged wasteland.

Five years of reconstruction across the city have passed this place by, and the expanse of bomb craters and ruined buildings is much as she last saw it: tumbled brick-heaps, charred beams, twisted girders, tattered strips of wallpaper exposed to the sun. There are brambles now, nettles and fireweed and glossy grass clumps on slopes of mud, but otherwise nothing has changed. It is still recognisable.

The place she is looking for isn't hard to find. She chose it well back then. It is a warehouse of solid blue brick, a bullet-scarred construction of blind walled arches and small glassless windows: roofless, but so it had been back then. During the siege this place had been contested territory: again and again the tanks of the Archipelago passed through and were driven back, and each time the warehouse survived. An artillery shell had taken a gouge from one corner, but the walls had stood. She'd used the upper windows herself for a week. It made a good place to shoot from when she was waging her private war, alongside the defenders of Mirgorod but not of them.

She crosses the open ground to the warehouse carefully, taking her time, moving expertly from cover to cover, using the protection of shell holes and bits of broken wall. There are no shooters to worry about now, only wasps and rats, nettles and thorns. Almost certainly there is no one here to see her at all, no faces in the overlooking windows, but it's as well to take precautions. She mustn't be noticed. Mustn't be seen. The sound of the city is a distant hum. She is getting her dress dusty and mud-stained, but she has anticipated that. She carries a change of clothes in the canvas bag slung on her back. She is nearly forty years old, but she remembers how to do this. She was good at it then and she is good at it still.

Inside the warehouse the stairs to the cellars are as she remembers them. She has brought matches and a taper, but she doesn't need them. She finds her way through the darkness, familiar as yesterday, by feel. Nothing has changed. It is possible that no one has been here at all since she left it for the last time on the day the war's tide turned and the enemy withdrew.

She crouches at the far wall and runs clenched, ruined fingers along the low niche, touching brick dust and stone fragments and what feels like a couple of iron nails. For a moment she cannot find what she is looking for and her heart sinks. Then she touches it, further back than she remembered but still there. Her fingertips brush against an edge of dusty oilcloth.

Carefully she hooks the bundle out from the niche. It's narrow and four feet long, bound with three buckled straps cut from an Archipelago officer's backpack. The touch and heft of it – about twelve pounds weight in total, she estimates without thinking – brings memories. Erases the years between. She notices that her hands are trembling, and she pauses, takes a breath, centres herself and clears her mind. The trembling stops. She hasn't forgotten the trick of that, then. Good.

In the blackness of the warehouse cellar, working by feel, she brushes the grit and dust from the oilcloth bundle and wraps it in the towel she stole before dawn that morning from a communal washroom. (The towel is a child's, faded pink with a pattern of lemon-yellow tractors, the most innocuous and suspicion-disarming thing she could find. If she's stopped and searched on the way back, it might just work. Camouflage and misdirection. Though she doesn't expect to be searched: she'll be just one more thin drab widow lugging a heavy bag. Such women are almost invisible in Mirgorod.)

She stows the towel-wrapped bundle in the canvas bag, hooks the bag on her shoulder and climbs back up towards the narrow slant of dust-filled sunlight and the morning city.

4

In a temporary hut at Chaiganur Test Site 61 the ministers of the Central Committee of the Presidium and the other dignitaries assemble to hear a briefing from Programme Director Professor Yakov Khyrbysk. The room is unbearably hot. Dry steppe air drifts in through propped-open windows. Khyrbysk's team has mustered tinned peach juice and some rank perspiring slices of cheese.

President-Commander of the New Vlast General Osip Rizhin fidgets restlessly in the front row while Khyrbysk talks. He has heard before all that Khyrbysk has to say, so he is working through a pile of papers in his lap, scrawling comments across submissions with a fountain pen. *Time moves on, time must be used.* Big fat ticks and emphatic double side-linings. *Approved. Not approved. Yes, but faster! Why so long? Do it now!* Rizhin likes to draw wolves in the margins. *I am watching you.*

He listens with only half an ear as the Director runs through his spiel: how the experimental craft will drop atomic bombs behind itself at the rate of one a second and ride the shock waves upwards and out of the planetary gravity well. How the ship is not small, as space capsules are imagined to be, but built large and heavy to withstand the explosive forces and suppress acceleration to survivable levels.

'Vlast Universal Vessel *Proof of Concept* weighs four thousand tons,' he tells them, 'and carries a fifteen-hundred-ton payload. She was designed and built by the engineers of the Bagadahn Submarine Yard.'

He tells them how the explosions generate temperatures hotter than the surface of the sun, but of such brief duration they do not harm the pusher plate. How *Proof of Concept* is equipped with two thousand bombs of varying power, and the mechanism for selecting the required unit and delivering it to the ejector is based on machinery from an aquavit-bottling factory. That gets a chuckle from the back of the room.

The ministers of the Presidium play it cautiously. They keep their expressions carefully impassive, neutral and unimpressed, but inwardly they are making feverish calculations. *Who does well out of this, and who not? How should I react? Whose eye should I catch? What does this mean for* me?

Rizhin listens with bored derision to their sceptical questioning and Khyrbysk's patient answers. *So that thing outside is a bomb?* No, it is a vessel. It carries a crew of six. *How can explosions produce sustained momentum not destruction?* It is no different in principle to the operation of the internal combustion engine of the car that brought you here. *Is the craft not destroyed in the blast? Will the crew not be killed? I hear there is no air to breathe in space and it is very cold.*

Fucking doubters, thinks Rizhin. *Do they think I'd have wasted time on a thing that doesn't fucking work?*

But he listens more carefully as Khyrbysk explains how each bomb is like a fruit, the hard seed of atomic explosive packed in a soft enclosing pericarp of angel flesh. The angel flesh, instantly transformed to superheated plasma in the detonation, becomes the propellant that drives against the pusher plate.

'We call the bombs apricots,' says Khyrbysk, which gets another laugh and a flurry of scribbling.

Rizhin is deeply gratified by this exploitation of angel flesh. Since Chazia died at Novaya Zima and the cursed Pollandore was destroyed, he's heard no more from the living angel in the forest. No falling fits. No disgusting invasions of his skull. All the angel flesh across the Vlast has fallen permanently inert, and the bodies of the dead angels are nothing now but gross carcasses, splats on his windshield, and he is moving fast. Even the mudjhiks have died. Nothing more than slumped and ill-formed statuary, Rizhin had them ground to a fine powder and shipped off to Khyrbysk's secret factories. Yes, even the four that stood perpetual guard at the corners of the old Novozhd's catafalque.

'And now,' Khyrbysk is saying, 'we will retire to the cosmodrome and watch the launch from a safe distance.'

But there is a brief delay before they can leave. Rizhin must honour the cosmonauts. A string quartet has been rustled up from somewhere, and sits under the shade of a tarpaulin playing jaunty martial music: 'The Lemon Grove March'.

The cosmonauts, three men and three women, march up onto the makeshift podium and stand in a row, fine and tall and straight in full-dress naval uniform in the roaring blare of the sun. Brisk apple-shining faces. Scrubbed, clear-eyed, military confidence. Rizhin says a few words, and shutters click and movie cameras whirr as he presents each cosmonaut in turn with a promotion and a decoration. *Hero of the Vlast First Class* with triple ash leaves. The highest military honour there is. The cosmonauts shake Rizhin's hand firmly. Only one of them, he notices, looks uneasy and doesn't meet his eye.

'Nervous, my friend?' he says.

'No, my General. The sun is hot, that's all. I don't like formal occasions. They make me uncomfortable'

'Call me brother,' says Rizhin. 'Call me friend. You are not afraid, then?'

'Certainly not. This is our glory and our life's purpose.'

'Good fellow. Your names will be remembered. That is why the cameras and all these stuffed shirts have turned out for you.'

On the way back to their cars the dignitaries stare at the stubby red behemoth glowing in the sun: the Vlast Universal Vessel *Proof of Concept* with its magazine of two thousand apricots, rack upon rack of potent solar fruits.

Rizhin is walking fast, oblivious to the heat, eager to be on the move. Secretary for Agriculture Vladi Broch breaks into a waddling jog to catch up with him. Broch's face is wet with perspiration. Rizhin flinches with distaste.

'Triple ash leaves?' says Broch. 'If you give them that now, what will you do for them when they come back?'

'When they come back?' says Rizhin. 'No, my friend, there is no provision for coming back. That is not part of the plan.'

'Ah,' says Broch. ' Oh. I see. Of course. But … so, how long will they last?'

Rizhin shrugs. 'Who knows?' He claps Broch on the shoulder. 'We'll find that out, won't we, Vladi Denisovich? That is the method of science. You should get friend Khyrbysk to explain it to you some time.'

5

In the control room at Chaiganur the tannoy broadcasts radio exchanges with the cosmonauts. From the edges of the room the whirring movie cameras follow every move with long probing lenses, hunting for the action, searching for the telling expression.

'T minus 2000, *Proof of Concept*. How are you doing?'

All is good, Launch. Very comfortable.

The cosmonaut's voice grates, over-amplified and crackling.

'I remind you that after the one-minute readiness is sounded, there will be six minutes before you actually begin to ascend.'

Understood, Launch. Thank you.

The cosmonauts have nothing to do. No function. No control over their vessel unless and until the launch controller flicks the transfer switches. Their windows are blind with heavy steel shutters, which they will take down once they reach orbit.

If they reach orbit.

The last of the ground crew is already three miles away, racing for the safety perimeter in trucks.

And so the cosmonauts wait, trussed on their benches, separated by the thickness of two heavy bulkheads and a storage cavity from a warehouse of atomic bombs. They are sealed for ever inside the nose of *Proof of Concept*, locked in by many heavy bolts that will never be withdrawn, and the ship beneath them is alive with rumble and vibration, the whine of pumps, the whisper of gas nozzles, the thunk and clank of unseen mechanisms whose operations the cosmonauts barely understand.

The technicians who actually control *Proof of Concept* are ten miles away inside a low concrete caisson, a half-buried blockhouse built with thick and shallow-sloping outer walls to deflect blast and heat up and over the top of the building. Not quite twenty in number, the technicians occupy a semicircle of steel desks facing inwards towards the launch controller at his lectern. They lean forward into the greenish screens of their cathode readout displays, flicking switches, twisting dials, turning the pages of their typescript manuals. They wear headphones and mutter into their desk microphones. Quiet purposeful conversations. For them this is no different from a hundred test firings: everything is the same except that nothing is the same.

Behind the controller a wide panoramic window of sloping glass gives a view across the flatness of the steppe. The assembled dignitaries and journalists sit in meek rows between the controller and this window on folding chairs, the sun on their backs, not wanting to cause a distraction. In something over thirty minutes they will turn to watch *Proof of Concept* climbing skyward to begin her journey. They have been issued with black-lensed spectacles for the purpose. For now they clutch them in their laps and observe the technicians, alert for any hint of anxiety in the muted voices. They watch for the flicker of red lamps on consoles, the blare of an alarm, a first indication of disaster. More than one of them wants to see failure today: a grievous humiliation for Director Khyrbysk and his protectors could mean great advantage for them. Others are cold-sweating terrified of the same outcome: if Khyrbysk's star wanes, theirs will tumble and crash all the way to a hard exile camp or a basement execution cell.

Guests and technicians alike smoke relentlessly.

President-Commander Osip Rizhin has not yet arrived in the control room. An empty chair waits for him between Khyrbysk and the chief engineer, whose name is never mentioned for he is a most secret and protected national resource.

*

'T minus eighteen hundred, *Proof of Concept.*'

Thank you, Launch.

'You are all well?'

There is an implication in the question. The captain of cosmonauts carries a pistol in case of … arising human problems. The psychology of each cosmonaut has been thoroughly and expertly examined, but the effects on emotional stability of massive acceleration, prolonged weightlessness and extreme separation from the planetary home are unknown. Every member of the crew is equipped with a personal poison capsule. The foresighted bureaucratic kindness of the Vlast.

We're all good, Launch. We could do with some music to pass the time.

'We'll look into that, *Proof of Concept.*'

The launch controller's gaze sweeps across the technicians at their workstations and settles on Engineer-Technician 2nd Class Mikkala Avril. He raises an eyebrow and she stands up.

Five minutes later, hurrying back down the passageway from the recreation room with an armful of gramophone records, hot with anxiety to return to her console, Mikkala Avril runs slap into men in dark suits armed with sub-machine guns. Rizhin's personal bodyguard, walking twenty-five steps ahead of the President-Commander himself. Papa Rizhin – Papa Rizhin! In person! – is bearing down on her.

Terrified, the young woman in whom beats the heart of the New Vlast presses herself flat against the wall and shows her empty hands, the stack of records tucked hastily under her left arm. She has been taught what to do in such an extremity. *Always look him in the eye, but not too much. Stay calm at all times, be respectful, answer all enquires with humour and firmness, above all conceal nothing.*

Mikkala Avril stands against the wall, back straight, eyes forward. The gramophone records are slipping slowly from the awkward sweaty grip of her elbow. Any moment now they will fall to the floor and there is nothing she can do about it. Desperately she squeezes them tighter between arm and ribs, but it only seems to make the situation worse.

Papa Rizhin glances at her as he passes and notices her confusion. Stops.

'Are you working on the launch?'

His voice is recognisable from his broadcasts but it is not the same. It is surprisingly expressive, with the tenor richness of a good singer.

Up close his cheeks are scattered with pockmarks like open pores, something which is not shown in portraits: the legacy of a childhood illness, perhaps.

'Yes, General,' she says.

'What is your task?'

'To monitor the telemetry of the in-atmosphere flight guidance systems, General. The vessel carries small rockets to correct random walk—'

'Yes,' says Rizhin, interrupting her. 'Good. You are young for this responsibility. And is all in order? Is there any concern?'

'No, General. None. All is in perfect order.'

Inevitably the sweat-slicked gramophone records choose this moment to fall slap in a heap at Rizhin's feet.

Mikkala Avril stares blankly at the wreckage: the titles of the musical pieces in curling script on the glossy sleeves; the monochrome photographs of mountains and lakeside trees. She feels her face turning purple.

Rizhin shows no reaction and does not look down.

'What is your name?' he says.

'Avril, General. Engineer-Technician 2nd Class.'

'That is good then. *Avril*. I will remember the name. The New Vlast needs young engineers; it is the noblest of professions. You are the brightest and the best.'

He glances at last at the fallen records and smiles with this eyes.

'Youth must not fear General Rizhin,' he says. 'He is its friend.'

When he's out of sight she crouches down to scrabble for the records. *Shit*, she mutters under her breath over and over again. *Shit. Shit. Shit.*

'T minus twelve hundred, *Proof of Concept*. We have some music for you.'

A syrupy dance tune begins to play over the tannoy: 'The Garment Workers of Sevralo'.

Yakov Khyrbysk groans inwardly and glares at the launch controller. *Must we?* He glances at his watch and wonders where Rizhin has got to. Wandered off, sniffing out buried corpses. It makes Khyrbysk uneasy, and he is edgy enough already.

On the other side of Rizhin's empty seat, the chief engineer is leaning forward, long dark-suited limbs gathered in tight about him. He steeples his long slender fingers. The fingernails are ruined: blackened sterile roots that will not grow again. The chief engineer (whose name on Rizhin's order is never spoken now, not even by himself) survived five years in prison camps before Khyrbysk found him and managed to fish him out. He hunches now like a bird on a steep-gabled rooftop, watching in silence. He has the pallid complexion of a man who lives his life underground and takes no exercise, but he is hot with energy. It stares from his eyes. Fierce, stark intelligence. Such energy would have burned through a weaker person long ago, but the chief engineer's constitution is a gift of nature. It is hard to tell how old he is, a young forty or a harrowed twenty-five. His hair is cut short at the back and the sides like a boy's.

The convoy of sedans waits outside, lined up, engines running, ready to race Rizhin and the dignitaries to safety in case of disaster. Khyrbysk wonders if someone has thought to issue the drivers with dark glasses. He is considering checking on this when Rizhin arrives and takes his seat. Kicks back, legs stretched out, reclining.

'Today we start the engine of history, Yakov,' says Rizhin. 'Today we blow open the door on our destiny.' He fishes for a paper packet of cheap cardboard cigarettes and lights one, drawing the rough smoke deep into his lungs. 'Those are good phrases. They have a smack to them. I'll use them in my speech.' He exhales twin streams through his nose. 'No problems, eh, Yakov? No fuck-up?'

'We've made test firings every week for the last three months.'

So many tests that the Chaiganur desert is scorched and glassed and pitted for hundreds of miles in every direction, the landscape pocked with scar-pits that show the corpse-grey rock beneath the orange earth. So many tests. Yellow plumes and dust streaks still linger in the upper atmosphere like nicotine stains.

The first test launches carried automatic radio transmitters. Later they sent up dogs and pigs and apes. One of the first monkeys to fly slipped free of its muzzle and screamed for three days until they had to cut the radio off. After that they equipped the beasts with remote-controlled execution collars. A bullet in the back of the neck. Nine grams of lead. Now there is a small menagerie of mummifying corpses orbiting overhead in thousand-ton steel tombs. The success rate was improving all the time, but nothing is certain. Khyrbysk knows that.

Nothing is certain except his own fate if *Proof of Concept* pops its clogs and goes *phutt!* in front of the entire Presidium and the assembled press corps of the Vlast. Nine grams of lead for dear old Yakov Khyrbysk then.

If he were a weaker man, he would think it unfair. He would think Rizhin ungrateful. Was it not Yakov Khyrbysk who sent the shipment of atomic shells to Mirgorod so Rizhin single-handed could break the siege? It was. And was it not Khyrbysk who expanded the town of Novaya Zima into a huge, sprawling secret city where penal labourers built the armoury of manoeuvrable atomic field-weapons that tipped the balance of the war? It was. But Khyrbysk is a canny operator: he has never made the mistake of reminding Rizhin of all that he owes him.

Six months after the victory at Mirgorod, when the war against the Archipelago was still in the balance, Rizhin had ousted the feeble government of Fohn and Khazar and made himself President-Commander of the New Vlast. After that, the first thing he did was fly north to Novaya Zima to see Yakov Khyrbysk.

'You must forget these bombs, Yakov,' Rizhin had said. 'I've got ten men who could run this show better than you. Talk to me about the other thing. Task Number One. Tell me about the ships that will carry us to the stars.'

Khyrbysk's stomach lurched. It was sheer brutal astonishment. *How did he* know?

'And bring me Farelov,' Rizhin added.

'Farelov?'

'Are you the *brain* here, Khyrbysk? Does all this come from *your* head? I do not think so.'

Khyrbysk had blustered. He cringed to think of it now.

'Well,' he said,' of course the theoretical foundations were laid by Sergei Farelov. Sergei is a brilliant mathematician and a visionary engineer, truly visionary, but he is not the sort of fellow to be the leader of an undertaking like this. I *made* Novaya Zima. I am the organiser, I am the efficient man. I am the will that drives it on.'

'Bring me Farelov,' said Rizhin. 'And Yakov ...'

Rizhin paused, and Khyrbysk, caught off guard, found himself looking unprepared into the gaze of a potentate. The neutral brown eyes of a man who knows for certain and unremarkable fact that he can do to you anything that he wants, anything at all – cause you any pain, destroy you and those around you in any way he chooses – and there is no protection for you, not anywhere, none at all. It was not a fully human gaze.

'Do not keep secrets from me, Yakov,' said Rizhin. 'Never try that again. I don't like it.'

Farelov arrived, tall and slender as a birch tree with wide nocturnal eyes.

'You are the great engineer, then,' said Rizhin, raking him with his gaze. 'You are a vital national resource. You belong to the Vlast. Your very existence is a state secret now. Your name will not be spoken again.'

Farelov returned his gaze without speaking. He nodded slowly.

'How long will it take?' said Rizhin. 'How long to build this thing so it works?'

'I will answer,' said Khyrbysk hastily. A promise not kept was a death warrant. He hesitated, mind racing. 'Fifteen years,' he said. 'At the outside, twenty.'

'Five,' said Rizhin. 'Make it five.'

'*Five!* No. Five is impossible.'

'Why impossible, Yakov?' said Rizhin. 'This, nothing else but this, is Task Number One. Tell me what you need and you shall have it. Without limit. The resources of the continent will be at your disposal. A hundred thousand workers. A million. Twenty million. You just tell me. Never hide your needs. How does a mother know her baby is hungry if the baby does not cry?'

Khyrbysk looked at Farelov.

'It can be done,' said the chief engineer quietly. 'In theory it can be done.'

'So,' said Khyrbysk. 'OK. Five years then.'

And in five years, though it was impossible, he had done it. He'd brought Task Number One this far, to this point of crisis: *Proof of Concept* baking quietly on her launch pad in the country of the hot panoptic undefeated sun.

6

In Mirgorod the new clocks are striking noon as the woman with the heavy canvas bag on her shoulder crosses towards her apartment building. The block where she lives is harsh and slabby: a cliff of blinding colourlessness under harsh blue sky in the middle of a blank square laid out with dimpled concrete sheets that are already cracked and slumped and prinked with grass tufts and dusty dandelions. Scraps of torn paper lift and turn in the warm breeze.

She climbs the wide shallow steps and pushes through the door into the dimness of the entrance hall. The sun never reaches in here and the lamps are off. There is no electricity supply during the day. No lift. She nods to the woman at the desk and crosses to the stairwell.

Her room is five flights up. The stairs smell of boiling potatoes and old rubber-backed carpet. On the landing of her floor an oversized picture of Papa Rizhin is taped to the wall. He is smiling.

She opens the door of her apartment into a blast of hot stale brilliance. The brassy early-afternoon sun is glaring in through a wide window. There is no one there. The women she shares with – young girls, sisters from Ostrakhovgrad – are out at work, but the room is heavy with their scent and full of things. The three beds, a table and chairs of orange wood, and shelf upon shelf of purposeless gewgaws and tat: make-up and toiletries, small china ornaments, magazines in faint typeface on thick brittle paper filled with advertisements and optimistic stories. The one big flimsy yellow cupboard stands open, overflowing with nylons and cheap summer clothes. Both girls are conducting affairs with high-ups in the Ministry of Supply. There is a can of raspberries tucked in the underwear drawer.

One of the sisters brought with her to Mirgorod a poster from the wall of the Ostrakhovgrad Public Library and tacked it inside the cupboard door: a photograph of strong women with the sun on their faces, shoulders back, heads up, the wind in their hair. DAUGHTERS OF THE VLAST, COME TO THE CITY! CITIZEN WOMEN! REBUILD OUR LAND! So many men were killed in the war, there was free accommodation on offer in Mirgorod to women of working age with no children.

The woman unwinds the pink towel with the lemon-yellow tractors and lays the long oilskin-covered bundle on her bed. Kneels on the floor to unbuckle the straps. Forcing clumsy hands to do what once went smooth as breathing.

She'd done a good job almost six years before. She'd left the rifle cleaned and wrapped in strips of cotton damp with lubricant, and it had kept well. No damp or grit had reached it. Awkwardly she strips it and cleans and oils each part. The touch and smell of the rifle is as familiar to her as her own body. The wood of the stock is still smooth and dark honey-brown. The magazine and firing mechanism, the telescopic sight rails, the pierced noise-suppressing muzzle and flash guard, all still blue-black steel, are a little scuffed and scratched – she remembers every mark – but there is no sign of corrosion. Only her own broken hands, finger bones snapped and carelessly re-fused, have to relearn their work. Figure it out all over again.

The Zhodarev STV-04 – gas-operated, a short-stroke spring-loaded piston above the barrel, a tilting bolt – weighs eight and a half pounds unloaded and is exactly forty-eight inches long, of which the barrel is twenty-four. Muzzle velocity is two thousand seven hundred feet per second. Effective range with a telescopic sight, one thousand yards. The Zhodarev is not a perfect weapon: it is complex to maintain, a little too heavy, the muzzle flash too bright even with a flash guard; it tends to lift, and the magazine can come loose and fall out. The woman had always wished she had a Vagant. But she knows the Zhodarev intimately. She fitted the muzzle brake herself to counteract the lifting. It is her weapon.

She reassembles the rifle, lays it aside and checks the rest of the kit. Wrapped in a separate bundle of oiled cotton is the olive-green 4-12 x 40 VP Akilina telescopic sight, rarer and more precious by far than the weapon itself, its graticule adjustable both vertically for range and horizontally for windage. And there are paper packages, still sealed, containing five-round stripper clips of 7.62 x 54mm Vonn & Belloc rimmed cartridges. One hundred and twenty rounds. One combat load. Not really enough for what she needs but it will have to do.

7

'T minus six hundred, *Proof of Concept.*'

Ten minutes to go.

Engineer-Technician 2nd Class Mikkala Avril settles herself at the familiar console and tries to calm the churning of her mind. She runs again through the routines. The launch controller is making his final tour of workstation checks before launch. Calling on each desk in turn for confirmation of go. Her turn soon. A matter of seconds. She scans the columns of figures again. All displays are showing within normal parameters. Dead on the line.

She has never actually done this task herself before, not at a real launch, not once, not even under supervision; except for practice exercises, she has always sat at Filipov's left hand and watched while her principal made the necessary settings and corrections. Even so, she's ready. She understands the procedures. It's not that complex. Ever since she joined the Task Number One programme, fresh from graduating top of her year (the first graduating year of the New University of Mathematical Engineering at Berm), she has spent every spare moment in the technical libraries at Kurchatovgrad and Chaiganur studying the classified reports.

It was Khyrbysk's policy to encourage technicians on the programme to learn as much and as widely as they could about the project as a whole and not limit themselves to their own area of work. His attitude to access to papers was liberal, and she took maximum advantage, beginning with the chief engineer's own seminal paper, *Feasibility of an Atomic Bomb-Propelled Space Vessel*, and working her way along the shelves: *A Survey of Shock Absorption Options*; *Trajectory Walk Caused By Occasional Bomb Misfire*; *The Capture of Radiation by Angelic Materials*; *Radiation Spill Around An Impervious Disc*; *Preliminary Sketch of Life Support For A Crewed Vessel*. There weren't many people at Chaiganur who knew more about the history, physics and engineering of Task Number One than Mikkala Avril.

She checks the central readout once more. The eight-inch-square display is connected to a von Altmann machine beneath the floor, which will, when called upon, analyse the telemetry from the vessel in flight and calculate any necessary corrective thrust from the banks of small rockets set in the midriff of *Proof of Contact*. It is her job to send the instructions for those corrections to the rockets themselves. It requires concentration, rapid reflexes, a steady hand. But all she has to do now is confirm readiness.

Launch is looking at her.

'Guidance Telemetry?' says Launch, relaxed and neutral.

And Mikkala Avril freezes.

Her screen has gone dark.

After half a second a short phrase blinks into life: *Fail code 393*.

Everything else, all the rows and columns of figures, have disappeared. She has no contact with the ship.

Fail code 393? It means nothing to her. Heart pumping, hands trembling, she riffles through the code handbook in mounting panic. *349 ... 382 ... 397 ... 402 ... What the hell is 393?*

There is no 393. Not in the book.

Launch asks again, impatient now.

'Guidance Telemetry, are we go?'

Think. Think.

Faces are turning towards Mikkala Avril. She feels the gaze of Director Khyrbysk on her back. The chief engineer is watching her. Papa Rizhin himself is watching her. She can *feel* it.

'Guidance Telemetry?' says the launch controller a third time. 'What's happening, Avril?'

'I've got a 393, Launch.'

'What is that?'

'I'm working on it, Launch.'

Ignore them. Focus only on the immediate need.

She has no idea what Fail code 393 means. It isn't in the book, which suggests it's a core manufacturer's code, not set up by Task Number One. It might be trivial, only a glitch in the machine. But it could equally be a fundamental system failure that would send *Proof of Concept* pitching and yawing, tumbling out of the sky to crash and burn.

It is either/or, and the only way to find out is to switch the machine off and start it up again. And that will take ten minutes.

'Last call, Avril,' says the launch controller. There is tension in his voice now. The beginning of fear.

She hesitates.

It is the epochal moment of the world, and it turns on her.

If she says go and the guidance systems misfire … No, she will not even think about the consequences of that … But if she calls an abort, Papa Rizhin's flagship launch will collapse in ignominy in front of the entire Presidium, the ambassadors, the assembled press of the Vlast. It will be days – possibly weeks – before they can try again. And if the abort turns out to be unnecessary, only a twenty-three-year-old inexperienced woman's cry of panic at an unfamiliar display code …

She hears her own voice speaking. It sounds too loud. Hoarse and unfamiliar.

'Guidance Telemetry is go, Launch. Go.'

'Thank you, Avril.'

Launch moves on to the next station.

With trembling hands, Mikkala Avril powers off her console, counts to ten, and switches it back on. The cathode tubes begin cycling through their ponderous loading routine.

'T minus three hundred, *Proof of Concept*.'

Thank you Launch.

Five minutes. The sugary music cuts out at last. There is a swell of voices and a scraping of chairs as the dignitaries turn to the window and put on their dark glasses.

'Can't see a bloody thing from here,' mutters Foreign Minister Sarsin. (The Vlast needs a foreign minister now. So the world turns.) 'It's below the fucking horizon.'

'You will see, Minister,' says Khyrbysk. 'You will certainly see.'

An argument breaks out as camera operators try to set up in front of the dignitaries.

'You don't have to do this. There's another team on the roof.'

'Something could go wrong up there. We should have back-up footage.'

Khyrbysk makes angry signs to the press liaison officer to close the disturbance down. He hadn't wanted the press there at all, or the ambassadors for that matter, but Rizhin insisted. Rizhin is a showman; he wants to astonish the world.

'The risk,' Khyrbysk had said to him on the telephone. 'What if it flops?'

'You make it *not* flop, Yakov. That's your job.'

Rizhin *needs* risk, Khyrbysk realises. He burns risk for fuel. Everything races hot and fast, the engine too powerful for the machine. Parts that burn out are replaced on the move, without stopping. The whole of the New Vlast is Rizhin's *Proof of Concept*, his bomb-powered vessel heading for unexplored territories and goals only Rizhin understands.

The cosmonauts feel the colossal engineering beneath them sliding into life, the coolant pumping round the shock-absorbing pillars, the bomb pickers rattling through the magazines in search of the first charge. *Proof of Concept* is a behemoth of industrial construction, but it is also very simple.

Mikkala Avril's screens come back up with ten seconds to go. Everything is fine: readouts dead on the line. She is so relieved she wants to cry, but she does not allow herself; she is stronger than that and holds it in. She is the heart of the youth of the New Vlast and she is good at her job and she will not fail.

Two seconds to go, she remembers to put her dark glasses on. She turns up the brightness on her screen, closes her eyes, presses a black cloth against her face and begins her own interior count. For the first ten bombs it will be too bright to see, and *Proof of Concept* will be on her own: then Mikkala must open her eyes and be not too dazzled to work.

Before the chief engineer discovered the properties of angel flesh propellant, what Mikkala was about to do would have been impossible: the bombs' electromagnetic pulses would have broken all contact between ship and ground. But now the ship's instruments will sing and chatter as she rises, and be heard.

The cosmonauts' cabin shivers with the clang of the first apricot locking into the expulsion chute.

Launch control is whited out in a flash of illumination that erases the sun.

Bomp – bomp – bomp. Bigger explosions each time. Brilliant blinding flashes. Slowly at first then faster and faster *Proof of Concept* rises, riding a crumb trail of detonations, climbing a tower of mushroom clouds.

The cosmonauts groan as each detonation slams their backs with a brute fist of acceleration. The whole ship judders and creaks and moans like a bathyscaphe under many thousand atmospheres of pressure.

For the observers in the launch control blockhouse at Chaiganur Test Site 61, the ship itself is lost, the explosion trail hard to watch. The repeated retinal burn forms blue-purple-green jumbling images. Brilliant drifting spectral bruises in the eye. President-Commander Rizhin stands at the window, the hot glare pulsing on his face, an atomic heartbeat.

I am the fist of history. I am the mile-high man.
A long time after the light the sound waves come.

Chapter Two

... in the deep country
Where an endless silence reigns.

Nikolai Nekrasov (1821–78)

1

In Papa Rizhin's world the clocks race forward to the pounding iron-foundry beat, the brakes are off and the New Vlast tears into the wind, riding the rolling wave of continental cataclysm-shock, flung into the future on the impulse-rip of centrifugal snap, taking a piston-blur express ride – six years now and counting and there's no slowing it yet. But pieces break off and get left behind. Because the past is sticky. Adhesive. Reluctant to let go. The continent is littered with broken shards. Arrested fragments of slower time. Unhealed unforgotten memories and the dead who do not die.

A house and a village and a lake.

On a day in the eleventh year of her dislocated life Yeva Cornelius comes gently awake in the first grey light of morning. There is some time yet to go before the rising of the cooler, circumspect, conciliatory sun. Yeva stays quite still on the couch, breathing slowly, watching the curtain stir. Lilac and vines crowd against the house. The room is leaf-scented, leaf-shaded, cool.

Her hair has been braided again in the night with loving gentleness: she feels the tightness of the intricate knotted plaits against her skull and smells the clean sweet fragrance the domovoi anoints her with while she sleeps. The prickle of tiny decorative twigs. Trinkets of seed and bird shell.

Take the domovoi's attention as a mark of favour, Eligiya Kamilova had said. *It's glad there are people again in the house. Leave a little salt and bread by the stove and it won't trouble us.*

The domovoi laid trails of crumbling earth across the floorboards, long sweeps and spirals along corridors from room to room. Eligiya Kamilova was right: it didn't want to hurt, not like those in the rye and oat fields – they were bad. Watchful and furtive, they came at you out of the white of noon and raised welts and sore rashes on your skin. Sly thorn scratches that stung and drew beads of blood. But the ones to be really afraid of were the ones that moved around outside in the night. Darkness magnifies. Darkness changes everything.

Daylight gathers and hardens in the room. Moment by moment the curtain is more visible, rising and collapsing. It's as if Yeva is moving it with her breath. Experimentally, she holds back the air in her lungs and eyes the curtain to see if it pauses too. Half-convinces herself that it does.

The atmosphere of a complicated dream is ebbing slowly away. Her mother was in the dream. Her mother was looking for her.

Her mother looks for her always, every day. She will have come back to the apartment and found it not there because of the bomb. But somebody will have told her the soldiers took them away, her and her sister, and put them on the train, and she will look for them. Only she won't know that Eligiya Kamilova took them off the train again, that Eligiya did something with her hands and broke the door of the train and took them into the night and the snow, and they ran away. Her mother won't know that.

Everywhere they go, Eligiya Kamilova leaves behind messages and notes so her mother can know they have been there and where they are going next. But her mother might not get the messages. She might not know who to ask. Eligiya posted letters to their old address but her mother can't go back to that house, not ever, because the soldiers sent everyone away. Some stranger will have read those letters. Or they'll be in a pile in a big post office room in Mirgorod. Or burned.

They walked south through the winter, Yeva and her sister Galina and Eligiya Kamilova, keeping off the roads and out of the villages, staying in the trees and the snow. The cold was like a dark glittering blade, but Eligiya was a hunter in the woods: she didn't talk much but she knew how to trap, how to make a warm place, how to build a fire in the night that didn't show light and a barricade of thorns against the wolves. Sometimes she slipped away to a village and came back with something they needed. Sometimes she found a hut or a farm where the people would let them sleep, maybe in a barn.

Yeva remembered every night. Every single night.

Her sister Galina was sick for a long time but she didn't die, and in the first days of spring the three of them came out of the trees, following a black stream flecked with brown foam, and found the house in the middle of a wide field of waist-high grass: a big square house of yellow weatherboards under a low grey roof, the glass in the many windows mostly broken. They waded over to it, leaving a trodden wake in the grass that buzzed and clattered with insects. Eligiya Kamilova went up under the porch and broke open the door, just like she had opened the door of the train. A wide staircase climbed up into shadow, and on the bare boards of the entrance hall was a pile of leaves and moss. Twigs laid out around it in patterns like the letters of a strange alphabet. Eligiya stepped round it carefully.

'Don't disturb it,' she said. 'Be careful not to touch that at all.'

There were pieces of furniture in some of the rooms. Mostly they'd had their upholstery ripped open, the stuffing pulled out and carried off for nests. There were chalky splashes of bird mess in the corners and streaks of it down the curtains. In the kitchen there were lamps, and oilcloth spread on the table.

'Are we going to stay here?' said Galina. 'For a while?'

'Perhaps,' said Eligiya Kamilova.

Yeva knew that Galina needed to rest, to stop moving for a long while, to be strong again.

Eligiya Kamilova hadn't give them any choice when she opened the door of the train and took them away into the trees and made them walk. It all happened too quickly to even think about until after it was done. But if they'd stayed on the train and gone where it was taking them, their mother would have known where they were and she could have come there to get them. Eligiya said the train was going to a bad place, a cruel terrible place, and no one ever came home from there, but she didn't even know what the terrible place was called, and Yeva wasn't scared of being in terrible places.

Every day she remembered the bomb. It always jumped her when she was thinking of something else. It wasn't like a memory. Memories change until you don't remember the actual thing any more; you remember the remembering. But of the time when the bomb fell nothing was forgotten and nothing was changed. When it jumped her it was like opening the same page of a book again and again, and the words were always all there, and always the same: Yeva's life hammered open like a bomb-broken building, the insides scattered and left exposed to ruinous elemental fire and rain.

Part of her stopped moving forward when the bomb came. Part of her got stuck in that piece of time for ever, always back there, always smelling the dust and burning, always looking down at Aunt Lyudmila squashed flat, always going down the stairs that used to be inside but were outside now, with nothing to hold on to. Part of her stayed back there, and only part of her was left to carry on. *Now* was a shadow remnant life of numbed and lesser feeling. Now was only aftermath. Aftermath.

That day when they first found the yellow house in the grass they didn't stay there but after looking it over they walked on down the stony dry track into the village. Long before they reached the village fields, Yeva could taste the tang of raw damp earth and animal dung in the air. Rooks chattered, squabbled and wheeled across the wide flatness of black soil just turned, thick and heavy and gleaming blue like metal. In the distance women were stooping and crouching at their work. They wore long red or green skirts, and their hair was wrapped in lengths of white cloth.

The village was a collection of ramshackle dwellings under heavy mounds of thatch, and beyond it was the lake and a line of tall pale trees on the shore, blue and dusty and far away. They walked in among skinny chickens and wary, resentful dogs, grey wood barns, grey corrugated-iron roofs. Scrawny cattle browsed in the dust behind a low fence of woven branches. A tractor leaned, abandoned, its axle propped on a rock.

'What's the name of this place?' said Eligiya Kamilova to the knot of men who gathered to meet them.

'Yamelei,' they said. 'This is Yamelei.'

Women from the nearest field came to join them, treading heavily over the upturned mud in rag-made shoes. Eligiya showed them the intricate brown patterns on her dark sinewed arms, and their eyes opened wider at that. A big old fellow with a ragged beard scoured the skyline behind them.

'There are no men with you?' he said.

'No.'

'A mother and daughters, then.'

'I am not their mother.'

'Grandmother?'

'No,' said Eligiya. 'Who lives in the big yellow house?'

'They left,' a woman said.

'How long ago?'

The woman pursed her lips. It was a question without an answer. Seasons rolled, and once in a while a new thing happened.

'And no one lives there now?' said Eligiya.

While Eligiya was talking to them Yeva watched the people of the village, their broad flattened faces, flattened noses, narrow dark curious eyes in crinkled skin. The men wore linen shirts and sleeveless jackets of animal hide, the pattern of the cows' backs on them yet, and shoes of woven bark that looked like slippers. They had knotted hands and swollen knuckles and their teeth were bad. They were looking at her, and she was looking at them, but the space between her and them was like thousands of miles and hundreds of years. She couldn't feel what they were thinking. They talked the same words but it was a different language.

Eligiya Kamilova told the people of Yamelei she would fix the tractor and make their boats stronger and steadier for the lake, and it was agreed that she and the two girls could stay at the yellow house for a while.

*

'Whose house is it?' said Galina as they walked back. 'It must be somebody's.'

'Small house,' said Eligiya Kamilova. 'Small aristocracy, long gone now.'

'Why doesn't someone from the village go and live there?'

'If someone did that,' said Eligiya, 'the others would have to resent them, and it would lead to trouble.'

They took water from the stream to drink and cook and wash in. Eligiya Kamilova trapped things in the woods. Pigeons and hares. Yeva didn't mind the plucking and the skinning and pulling the inside parts out. Galina wouldn't do it, but it gave Yeva no bad feelings at all.

There was a place behind the house closed in by a high wall of horizontal weathered planking between tall solid uprights. Inside the wall was a mass of ragged foliage, a general green flood: shoulder-high umbellifers and banks of trailing thorn. Week by week Eligiya and the girls cleared it away and found useful things still growing there: cabbage and onion and currant canes and lichenous old fruit trees. On a high shelf in a tool shed Eligiya found a rust-seized shotgun and a half-carton of shells. She fixed the gun up with tractor oil and it seemed like it would work, but she didn't want to try it out because the noise would reach the village and the men would come.

When summer came the walled yard was gravid with acrid ripeness. Lizards sunned themselves on the planking and wasps crawled on sun-warmed fruit. Eligiya Kamilova and the girls went into the garden and ate berries hurriedly, greedily, three at a time, bursting the sharp sweet purple taste with their tongues against the roofs of their mouths, staining their fingers with the blue-black juice.

Every day Eligiya Kamilova went down to Yamelei to work. Yeva was glad when she was gone and the sisters were on their own together without her. Then there were long afternoons of slow lazy time when few words were said or remembered, only the smells and colours and the day-flying moths in the house and the feeling of the long grass against their skin. Yeva would lie on her back by the overgrown stream and shut her eyes and look through closed lids at the bright oranges and soft, swirling, pulsing reds and browns. There were rhythms there, like the rhythms of her breathing. A plenitude of time. Galina got stronger, and in the evenings the sisters swam together in the big deep pond where the stream was dammed, until the air streamed with night-borne scents and the first stars rained tiny flakes of light that brushed their faces and settled on their arms. Then the night fears started to come out of the trees and across the grass, and Galina said it was time to get dressed and go into the house. Galina was getting better, but she still went silent sometimes and far away as if she was looking up at Yeva from under water.

In the evenings, before she went to sleep, Yeva would empty her pockets onto the shelves in the bookless emptied library and pick through the collection of the day. Feathers, empty dappled eggshells, twigs and leaves and moss, stones and fragments of knotty root. The best of them she put out by the stove for the domovoi.

Morning is fully come now. Yeva can see every thread in the thin curtain, and the dust smears on the broken windowpanes. Soon she will get up and put some wood in the stove and get water and wash her hair and brush the tight braids out. Then she will go down by herself into the woods by the lake. But for now she lies without moving and watches the curtain, and her sister is warm and heavy beside her under the blanket, eyes still closed fiercely in sleep. Galina will stay like that for another hour or so yet. Although there are rooms enough in the house to sleep in a different bed every night for a week, the sisters share the couch in the library. Eligiya Kamilova sleeps out on the veranda with the loaded gun.

2

*I*n the coolness under the trees down by the lake at Yamelei the dead artilleryman brushes aside his coverlet of damp memorious earth. Conscript Gunner K-1 Category Leonid Tarasenko. The grave mound is sweet and crumbly, layered with rotting leaves and matted fungal threads. Parts of his body are wrapped in warm, wet, skin-like, papery stuff.

The dead man's mushroom face feels the gentle touch of the conciliatory *morning sun in patterns of leaf shadow. The head turns from side to side, moving its dirt-stuffed mouth. Eyes large and dark as berries stare without blinking. As yet they see nothing.*

There is a faint perfume on the air.

Soldier Tarasenko, throat unzipped and bled out long slow years ago – a whizz of hot shell casing, a shiv wouldn't do it neater – rises slowly from the shallow accidental grave where he was planted like a seed.

Yeva Cornelius, night braids brushed out from her hair, leaves the house and her sister and Eligiya Kamilova still sleeping. The early fields are filled with air and light to overbrimming like a cup.

The path down to the lake passes between sea-green rye and scented hummocks of dried manure. In the bottom land the sorrel bloom is over, the crop coming on heavy and dark. Thick green heady vegetable blood. Yeva comes out onto the yellow grass of the lake margin. Old Benyamin Zoff is there already, on his hands and knees, crawling in his best grey suit along the edge of the water. He moves slowly, intently, with sacramental concentration, murmuring words that are quiet and musical but not a song. He will crawl like that all morning. There is a sunken city under the mirror-calm lake. An underwater world. In the village they keep water from the lake in their houses, in bottles and basins, and in the winter people go sliding face down on their bellies across the frozen surface, staring down, trying to see what is there.

The soul of the people is forever striving to behold the sunken city of Litvozh.

Eligiya Kamilova said that soon after they came to Yamelei. It was a quotation from a book. *They long not for something that will be but for the return of something that was. They have not forgotten and they never will.* The window frames of the village houses are carved with pictures of streets and towers under watery waves.

There are brown wooded islands in the lake and low hills on the horizon beyond the further shore. Yeva waves to Benyamin Zoff, who ignores her, and turns away from the water's edge to climb up into the woods. There is a dead man standing among the trees. She passes quite close to him, but he is not watching her, and Yeva pays him no regard. Yeva isn't bothered by the dead: they are preoccupied with their own thoughts and take no notice of her.

*

War, like storm and famine, has come around the shore of the lake and passed from time to time through Yamelei. The woods near the village are scarred by tank tracks, shallow shell holes and random trenches sinking under bramble, ivy and thorn. The trees are ripped and tattered by gunfire. Here, in these woods, colliding companies of the lost, rolling along on random surges of retreat and advance, attack and counter-attack, stumbled over one another, panicked and rattled bullets into each others' bodies. Field guns set up among the oats and rye in the upper ground rained desultory shellfire on unofficered and bootless conscripts crawling for shelter under thorn bush and bramble mound. One time a whole truckful of people from somewhere else was driven in under the trees, shot and shovelled into three-foot ditches.

In the woods around the lake the killed have not died right. Uneasily half-sentient, not rotting well, they can be disturbed, upset, awakened. Their uncommitted bodies rise through the earth. They will not sink. They float. From time to time they get up from their beds and wander a while under the trees and lie down somewhere else. When the villagers come across a shallow-buried corpse in the woods they cut its head off, sever the tendons in its legs and drive a wooden peg through the ribcage to pin it firmly down. But they will never find them all.

You put new plaster on the walls but the old stains still seep through. That's what they say in Yamelei.

Conscript Gunner K-1 Category Leonid Tarasenko, dead, stands with his forehead pressed against a tree trunk and traces the fissures in the bark with his hands. Pushes his fingers into the cracks and tries to pull pieces of the bark away, to see what is underneath. The pieces of bark won't come free. They slip through the tips of fingers that are sticky from the gash in his throat. His second, silent mouth.

The dead man has probed the inside of the tear in his throat to feel what is in there. He has found soft things and hard things. The hard things are sometimes slippery smooth, and there are some pieces in there that are sharp. There is a hole deeper inside that he can slip fingers into, but the hole is deeper than his fingers are long.

The interiors of things interest him. The inspection of the tree absorbs his attention. He touches the tree with his tongue. Feels roughness, tastes taste.

It occurs to him that the tree is not part of him.

Where is the end of me? the dead man wonders, looking up into the top of the tree. Where is my limit? I am up there. I go past those branches and those branches and up into the bright place up there that looks wet but has no smell of wet. I go past those trees over there, and those trees, and those trees behind me, and that is not the end of it and that is not the end of me. But though I am over there and up there, I am here and not there. It is strange. Fingers and tongue don't go up there to the top of the tree. They stop short.

The dead man apprehends that the tree doesn't stand on the earth but continues down into it. The tree reaches into the ground and fastens there, but it isn't the same with him. Unlike the tree, the dead man seems to be free to go to a different place.

That is interesting.

When he thinks about himself and what he knows and feels, the dead man finds pieces of knowing and pieces of feeling but the pieces are not connected. One of the pieces is angry and one of the pieces is sad because something important has been lost. One of the pieces feels sick, unfathomable horror and despair.

The pieces look at each other as if they have eyes, but they don't have eyes, not really. Eyes are on the outside, in the sticky-soft raggedy face thing, here, where you can touch with hands. When fingers touch eyes, eyes cannot see trees any more and fingers come away sticky. If you press eyes with fingers you see flakes of light, strange muted flakes of different light, but you only see the light and not the other things, not the trees you could see before. The light you make with fingers in the eyes, that light is inside the head.

Yet inside the dead man mostly there is darkness. He can touch the darkness in his throat with fingers, but the darkness is always there and doesn't come out. He cannot press that into light. That too is interesting. The dead have a lot to think about. But the piece in him that is sad and the piece in him that is angry want something. They are saying to go down the path.

What is path? says the piece of him that has all the questions. There isn't any piece with an answer to that, but the feet are walking now, and that seems to be good. That seems to be the answer to the path question.

He notices that if the feet stopped walking then all the other things – all that is not him but other stuff, trees and not trees – stop moving also, and wait, and watch the dead man watching them, waiting.

I am the centre then.
I see that.
That I understand.

Yeva Cornelius passes the dead man by. As she moves away, he catches the sense of her crossing a splash of sunlight between trees, and his heart is surprised by a deep dim anguish, a recognition of kinship.

Leonid Tarasenko does what the dead don't do. He starts to follow.

3

In Mirgorod the woman with the heavy canvas bag on her shoulder takes the tram all the way out to Cold Harbour Strand. She starts out along the spit and, when there is no one to see, leaves the path and disappears into the White Marsh. An hour and a half of hard walking brings her to the edge of a wide muddy expanse of marshland. She unpacks her bundle, spreads the oilskin out on the ground like a mat, sheltered from the breeze in the lee of a fallen tree trunk, and lays the Zhodarev on it. She crouches next to it to push the telescopic sight into the rails and set the graticule. Prises ten rounds from two stiff stripper clips into the toploader. Four hundred yards away across the mud another tree leans sideways in front of a mossy stone wall. She cuts a branch into three short lengths with a knife and binds them with twine to form a makeshift tripod barrel mount. Then she sets the graticule and settles herself into position, kneeling then lying alongside the fallen trunk. Remembers how it feels to be tucked away. Hidden from view. Safe.

She settles the stock of the rifle against her shoulder. Closes her left eye and fits her right eye against the back of the sight. Lets herself relax and sprawl on the ground. Becoming part of it. Settled. Rooted. She has to cock her wrist awkwardly to bring her clawed trigger finger to bear. It feels wrong but she will get used to it.

She fixes the tree in the cross wires. Centres on the place where a particular branch separates from the main bough. Squeezes the slack out of the trigger. The graticule is shivering and taking tiny random jumps. Her heart is busy in her chest. She breathes out, emptying her lungs – calm, calm – and pulls the trigger. The muzzle kicks and deafens her. A puff of dust rises from the wall five feet to the left of the target tree. Waterfowl lift from the mud and circle, puzzled.

Not good.

The woman resettles herself and takes another shot. Forcing her clawed finger to squeeze smoothly.

Two feet to the right of the target. Still not good. But better.

She has put ten rounds aside in a safe place ready for the task itself, which leaves her a hundred and ten to practise with. At ten shots a day that's eleven practice days. Eleven days in which to remember. Eleven days in which to learn again how to put an entire magazine into a spread she could cover with one hand. She used to be able to do that, six years ago.

Eleven days to get it back. That will be enough.

She has eight cartridges left for this morning's work. She adjusts the graticule again and prepares herself for another shot.

4

Galina Cornelius wakes to the empty house. Her sister Yeva is wandering in the woods by the lake and Eligiya Kamilova has gone down to the village to work. Galina is glad to be alone. She has a secret place to go.

She crosses the black stream by a wooden plank and pushes her way along the overgrown margin of the pond, following the rim of still, deep water. The grass, in shadow and still morning-damp, soaks the edge of her skirt. Thorns snag at her clothes and roots try to trip her, but she presses forward. Old statues watch her from the undergrowth with pebble-blank eyes: naked women holding amphorae to their breasts; burly, bearded naked men, long hair curling to their shoulders; a laughing boy riding a big fish. The dark green foliage has almost absorbed them, and some have already lost limbs and faces to winter frost and summer heat. There is a rowing boat beached among the reeds on the lake shore. The oars are still shipped in the bottom but the sky-blue paint on the hull is peeling away. Every time she sees it Galina pictures a mother and her girls, a lilac parasol, a shawl against the cool of the shade, in that boat on the water in the afternoons of summer. She tried to pull it onto the water once, but the wood was soft as cake and came away in pieces.

Galina pushes on towards her destination.

The little concrete building is still there, grey and weather-stained, half ivied-over under the shade of trees. Figurines look down at her from the corners: fat naked children smiling, crumbling, patched with moss. Galina pushes the door open. Inside, in the semi-darkness, there is a dark mouth in the ground, the start of a spiral stone staircase. The air in the stairwell smells cool and earth-scented with a taint of rust. She descends. At the bottom is a narrow tunnel with tiled walls that bow out and then lean in to meet low overhead. The tunnel leads away into gloom, heading out underwater across the floor of the lake, and at the far end is a dim green light. Galina feels her way in near-darkness towards her secret underwater room.

Who knows what kink of imagination caused the people who once lived in the house in the grass to build such a place, a hemispherical glazed dome of white steel ribwork, an upturned glass bowl twenty feet high on the bed of the lake? The water that presses against the glass walls is a deep moss colour at floor level, fading to the palest, faintest green at the top. The steel framework is streaked and patched with rust, and on the other side of the glass is the dim movement of water vegetation and shadowy water creatures. Obscure larvae and gastropods. Muffled fishes. Over the course of the years the lake has rained a gentle silt upon the outside of the chamber, staining the glass yellow and flecking it with patches of muck. The underwater room is filled with dim subaqueous forest light, but when Galina arches her neck to look up she can see light and the undersides of ripples lapping in the breeze, and sometimes the underneath of a waterfowl disturbing the circle of visible surface.

Down here in the underwater room the temperature is constant and cool. The room is furnished. Rugs, a sofa, an empty bookcase, a cupboard, a chair, a desk. A pot of earth stands in the centre of the circular floor, the remains of some long-dead, long-dried plant slumped across it. As Galina moves around, circling, touching, she surprises traces of cigar smoke. The smell of brandy and laudanum lingers in pockets of air.

She has told no one about this place and brought no one here, not Eligiya Kamilova, not even Yeva. It is her own place, where she can come and be herself and think about what she should do. Eligiya Kamilova is not their mother. She has never been a mother to anyone at all. She stays with them and takes care of things, but she would travel further and faster without them; she would go even as far as the endless forest in the east. Eligiya has been in that forest, has travelled there, and it stains the air around her. Part of her is in the forest always and has never come away.

Their mother is in Mirgorod.

I have been too ill to do anything but follow where Eligiya Kamilova went, but that time is coming to an end. I must take Yeva back to Mirgorod. I am the older one, and it is my job to do that. Soon I will be as well and strong as I will ever be, and then I must do that.

But I am not ready, not quite yet.

The rusalka presses its chalky face, expressionless and pale, against the silt-flecked glass and stares in at Galina, watching her intently. It moves its hands through the water slowly as if it were waving. But it is not waving. It is only watching. The first time it came Galina mistook it for the reflection of her own face.

The dead soldier Leonid Tarasenko follows Yeva out from under the trees into the emptiness of tall light. There is a tiny anguished hook of memory somewhere inside him, a diamond-hard strange survivor in the heart, a piece of disconnected understanding no larger than a single word, and the word is child.

The dead man follows child. Child fills his heart with happiness and tears and need. In all the world of the dead man there is only child and follow and no other purpose at all, and the existence of even this one irreducible shard of purpose is a mystery more mysterious than the endless ever-faithful burning of the sun.

But child (all unaware of the following) moves faster than the dead man can. The separation between them stretches and stretches.

The dead man would call out after her if he could, but there is not enough wonder and mystery in the world to provide him with concepts like voice and call. He has been given only child and follow, and it is not enough.

Child is gone.

He moves on, following the line she took. Child is gone, but of following there is no end and nothing else to take its place.

The line of his following brings him again to an edge of trees, different trees, but trees. Trees are familiar to him and the smell of earth is familiar beneath them, and that is a soothing ointment for his heart, but also not soothing at all; nothing takes away the happiness and the tears and the need for following child.

Because trees are familiar to him the dead Leonid Taresenko follows his following in under the trees.

Galina Cornelius stays a long while in the underwater room, but eventually it is time to return to the house because Yeva will soon be home from the woods. As Galina is crossing the plank over the black stream, the dead soldier steps out from a tree and comes towards her.

She sees his open earth-filled mouth, the woodlice in the folds of his face and neck.

She screams. It is blank terror.

All the way to the house she runs, heart pounding, fear-blind, and at the veranda she stops and turns. The dead thing is following her, loping unsteadily through the waist-high grass.

Galina screams again.

'Yeva! Yeva!'

The dead soldier is out of the high grass and coming up the path, coming towards her with fixed and needy dead black eyes, hand stretched out for companionship.

Eligiya Kamilova's gun is lying on the couch on the veranda.

It could blow up in your eyes. Eligiya had said. *Only use it if the other thing will be worse.* But she had shown them how.

Galina seizes the gun and swings the barrel up into the face of the dead soldier. His foot is already on the first veranda step when she pulls both triggers together and takes his head apart. The stock kicks back into her shoulder and knocks her down. She can't hear her own screams any more for the appalling ringing of the double gunshot in her own ears.

5

Eligiya Kamilova finds the two girls sitting side by side outside the house, on the couch on the veranda, staring at the corpse of twice-killed Conscript Gunner K-1 Category Leonid Tarasenko, a good and simple man but not a lucky one. When she heard the shot she was already on the track up to the house, work abandoned halfway done, weightless, spun out of orbit by the kick of the newspaper in her hand.

The girls look up at her in silence when she comes. Their faces are strained and pale, their eyes rimmed red and wide with shock. She knows that she should comfort them, but she doesn't know how, she hasn't got it in her; she searches but it isn't there, the right thing to do to take that shock and pain away. She stands stiffly on the veranda, bitterly, emptily aware of the newspaper rolled and clutched by her side. The ineradicable, undeniable truth of it burns in her hand. She hasn't anything to give them for comfort, not even news, not good news, only bad.

There's no good time to tell them what she knows. She is tempted to wait, but waiting will only make things worse, compounding fact with deceiving, and she has never told them less than truth. She cannot give them loving comfort but she can give them that and always does.

She holds the newspaper out to Galina.

'Look,' she says. 'Read it. Read the date.'

Eligiya was down in the village working on the boats when the musicians came out of the east, walking in with their rangy dog: the gusli player with the long straggled hair and thick coal beard resting on his chest, one leg lost in the war, swinging along on crutches, and the tall old man in the long coat, drum like a cartwheel slung on his back. The drummer carried a newspaper stuffed in his pocket that nobody in the village could read. Kamilova bought it from him for a couple of kopeks.

Galina stares at the newspaper blankly.

'What?' she says. 'What about it? What?'

'The date.'

Galina makes an effort to squint at the stained print.

'It's a couple of months old.' She hands it back to Kamilova and wipes her fingers in the lap of her dress already splattered with the soldier's drying mess. 'It's greasy. It smells bad.'

Galina's eyes aren't focused properly. They stray back to the half-rotten corpse on the veranda boards.

'Not the month,' says Kamilova. 'The year.' She holds the paper up again for the girl to see. Galina stares at it for a while. Furrows her brow in confusion.

'It's a mistake,' she says. 'A printing error.'

'No,' said Kamilova. 'I talked to the men who brought it into the village. I asked them questions. It isn't a mistake.'

'What?' said Yeva. 'What are you talking about.'

Kamilova sat down beside them on the end of the couch. She felt suddenly exhausted. Not able to manage. Not able to lead the way, not at the moment, not any more. The strength in her legs, the straightness in her back, was gone. Yeva squeezed up to make room.

'What is it?' she said.

'I'm sorry,' said Eligiya Kamilova. 'I'm so sorry.'

'*What?*'

'We've been walking in the trees,' said Kamilova, 'and we've been living here in the village by the lake, and it's been seven months, nearly eight – a long time but not quite eight months – that's all.' She takes the paper from where it lies in Galina's lap. 'Look at the date.'

Yeva reads the small print at the top of the page.

'But that's wrong.'

'No.'

'But it is wrong. It's five years wrong.'

'Five and a half. Five and half years gone.'

Kamilova has had longer than the girls to think it through.

The three of them roll the corpse of the twice-killed soldier onto a sheet, wrap it and drag it through the grass far away from the house. They dig a hole up near the woods. It takes all day and they are dumb with exhaustion and heat and stink, and the sun has gone and the fear is coming out of the woods. They go inside and light candles and put wood in the stove, and when the water is hot they wash in the kitchen in silence, the whole of their bodies from head to toe. It takes a long time to get the dirtiness off and they don't quite manage it even then.

Rank warm cheese and a stump of hard bread on the shelf. Oilcloth on the table. Candles burning. The house and the village and the lake. Some people cannot look at their memories, and some people cannot ever look away.

'Our mother thinks I'm sixteen,' says Yeva. 'Sixteen. Or dead. Either way she didn't find us. She never came.'

'I didn't know,' says Kamilova. 'There wasn't a way to know.'

'She couldn't have come,' says Galina. She looks at Eligiya Kamilova. 'But tomorrow we'll go home,'

'Home?' says Kamilova. 'What do you mean "home"?'

'You don't have to come with us, Eligiya. You've done enough; you've done more than you needed to for us. You can have your life back; you can go where you want; you can go into the forest again, or stay here and live for ever.'

Galina's words lacerate Eligiya like the blades of knives.

'I ...' she begins. The pain she feels is shame and guilt and love, inextricable trinity, hands held open to receive the price you had to pay. 'Everything will have changed,' she says. 'You have to think about that. She ... Your mother might not even—'

'You don't have to come, Eligiya.'

'I will come,' says Eligiya Kamilova. 'Of course I will come.'

Chapter Three

If you're afraid of wolves, stay out of the forest.

Josef Stalin (1878–1953)

1

The rain came in long pulses, hard, warm and grey, and the noise of it in the trees was loud like a river. The galloping of rain-horses. Rain-bison. Rain-elk. Maroussia Shaumian followed the trail through rain and trees, splashing through mud-thick rain-churned puddles, the bindings on her legs sodden and clagged to the knee, pushing herself, back straight and face held high, into the future. Her clothes smelled of wet wool and woodsmoke and the warmth of her own body. Rain numbed her face and trickled down her chin and neck. It tasted of earth and nettles. Rain slicked and beaded on the ferns: tall fern canopies trembling under the rain, unfurling ferns, red fern spore. A boar snuffled and crashed in the fern thickets. His hot breath. The smell of it in the rain. There were side paths leading in under the thorns; mud ways trodden clear that passed under low branches. The larger beasts were further off and elsewhere, under taller trees. Cave bear and wisent and the dagger-mouth smilodon.

The land rose and then fell away: not hills but a drifting swell that wasn't flatness. Coming down, the trail took her among broad shallow pools. Maroussia cut a staff and kept her head down and walked against the rain, churning knee-high through water, mud-heavy feet slipping and awkward. Most of the ground here was water. Roots and stumps and carcasses of fallen trees reached up through the rain-disturbed surface, paused in arrested motion, waiting, balanced between worlds, and everything distant was lost in the rain.

Maroussia crouched to dip her hands in the water, letting the rain beat on her back. Rolling up her sleeves she reached right down to the bottom and ran her fingers through the grass there. It looked like hair and moved to her touch, dark green and beautiful. It was just grass. Her arms in the water looked pale and strange, not hers but arms in the shadow world as real as the one she was in. She cupped her hands and brought some water up into her world to drink, feeling the spill of it through her fingers and down her arms. The water tasted of cold earth and leaves and moss. She tasted the roots of all the trees that stood in it and the bark and wood of the fallen ones. She swallowed it, cool and sweet in her throat, and took more, still drinking long after she wasn't thirsty any more.

The forest is larger than the world, though those who live outside it think the opposite.

She was Maroussia Shaumian still. Nothing of that time was forgotten, nothing was lost, though she was more now, more and less and different and changed and far from home. Like the water in the rain she was fresh and new, and as old as the planet, both at once.

You don't know where home is until you're not there any more.

She waded out deeper into a wide pool loud under the rain to where a beech tree lay on its side, its rain-darkened bark smooth and wet to the touch. The beech had fallen but it wasn't dead; it was earth-rooted still, and its leaves under the water were green. She let her hands rest on it and felt the tree's life. She wished she could speak to it but she didn't have the words, and what would she say? *Help me*, perhaps. *Help me to get home.* But that wasn't right. It wasn't what you should ask, and no help would come.

Wolves plashed under tree-shadow, distant and silent and indistinct as moths. One turned his face towards her, wolf eyes in the rain, unhurried, considering. She returned his gaze and he looked away.

*

Some while later she came on the wolf kill. It was an aurochs, huge and bull-like, lying on his side in a shallow pool of bloodied water, his rough fox-coloured hair matted with mud and rain-sodden. From a distance he looked drowned, but when she got close half of him was gone, a rain-washed hole of raw meat. Rain-glistening flies sipped at his eyes and crawled on the grey flopped rain-wet slab of his tongue. The noise of the rain beat in her ears like the rhythm of her own blood, too close and too ceaseless to attend to.

Sudden and uncalled, the killing moment closed its grip on her and she was in it. It was still there, still happening, and she was the happening of it, not outside and watching, not remembering, but being there. She was aurochs not hearing the splashing charge of wolf above the rain, not seeing wolf behind him, not smelling wolf through rain and water and the rich scent of rain on leaf. She felt the appalling shock of the boulder-heavy collision and the clamp of the tearing mouth at her throat. Heard with the aurochs' own strange clarity the small snap deep inside her neck. Felt the wordless sad dismay of ruminant beast, the surge of fear and panicked stumble, the attempted burly sweep of a neck that didn't respond – delivered nothing, moved nothing, connected with nothing. The loneliness of that.

She saw with hopeless aurochs eye the wolf that made the first charge turn and come splashing back through mud-swirled blood-swirled water. Then other wolves were on her back and she fell. Pain and the acceptance of pain. Aurochs could not rise and could not stand. Her leg wouldn't go where she wanted it to go, her beautiful leg was lost. Aurochs grieved for it. Maroussia lived the last long moments when wolves ripped aurochs belly open and pulled the stuff there out and tore and swallowed bits from her beautiful twitching leg and slowly and softly minute after minute aurochs grew tired and far away and died.

And that wasn't all.

She was the death of aurochs but she was also the hunting of the wolves. She was salt on the wolf's tongue and the dark hot taste of blood. She was the sour breath of the aurochs' dying and the glad teeth in the neck of it. She was the crunch of the killing bite and the thirsty suck and tearing swallow of warm sweet flesh.

And that wasn't all.

She was the life and growth and connected watchfulness of every tree and every leaf and every small creature and every water drop in the pool and the rain, its history and the possibilities of what was to come.

And that wasn't all.

Nothing was *all*, because there was no end to the fullness of what she could perceive. Because this was what she had become, this overwhelming surprise of plenitude.

She was Maroussia Shaumian still – Maroussia Shaumian, who had made her choice in Mirgorod and followed her path to its end in Novaya Zima – but she had been inside the Pollandore when the temporary star ignited around it. The Pollandore had imploded and exploded and changed and brought her here, and now it was gone. It was inside her now, if it was anywhere: inside her, new and strong, volatile and unaccommodated. The Pollandore and what she could be ran ahead of her and overwhelmed her until she hardly knew what was her and what was not, because sometimes she was everything.

Time wasn't a river; time was the sea, layered and fluid and malleable, what was past and what was possibly to come all intricately infolded and vividly present inside the rippling horizons of now. Nothing of Maroussia was lost, but she was more. She was changed and become *this*. All *this*.

The seeing faded. (She called it seeing though it wasn't that, but there was no word.) Seeing always came uncalled and surprised her. She suspected she could learn to call it up at will, but she was afraid of learning that. Once she went through that door, there would be no coming back, and she hadn't chosen that and did not want it. She hadn't chosen anything of this, not *this*, but here it was.

She was as lonely in the rain as the dying aurochs and as far from home.

Time to move on.

The meeting place was not far, and they would be waiting.

2

There were three of them at the place on the White Slope, Fraiethe and the father and the Seer Witch of Bones, and Maroussia Shaumian was the fourth.

The father spoke, as he always did, the phrases of beginning.

'And so we are met again under wind and rain and trees and the rise and set of sun. We are the forest; the forest is everywhere and everything, and the forest is us.'

'No,' said Maroussia. 'We are something but not everything.'

The father made a barely perceptible movement of his head, acknowledging the justice of that, but frowned and said nothing. *An antagonist then*, Maroussia thought. *Well, there it is then. So it is.*

The father was not actually present at the meeting on the White Slope. After the first time he had not come in bones and blood and flesh but as a fetch, a spirit skin, while he kept himself apart and somewhere else. The fetch had come as a man with woodcutter's hands and forearms, hair falling glossy-thick across his brow and shoulders. A rank aroma, and burning green eyes that watched her openly. Maroussia thought the fetch crude and suspected a deliberate slight aimed at her. *This is the form*, it said, *that seduced your mother and made her sweat and cry in a timberman's hut in the woods. This the form that fathered you. Like some too?*

But Maroussia didn't believe it. Whatever artifice seduced her mother at Vig would have been more subtle than that, more complex and thoughtful and elegant and patient and kind, to console her for the wasteland of her marriage to Josef Kantor and draw her out of it into the shadow under the trees. It was imagination that seduced her mother, not this unwashed goat. The goat was provocation only.

Then she realised that the father knew this, and knew that she knew it, and in fact the burly woodcutter was not a provocation but a complicitous tease. A wink. A father–daughter joke to be shared.

She didn't resent the father for fathering her. Not any more. When she was growing up in Mirgorod she'd lived with the pain of the consequences of that, but now and here she understood. For the father there was a pattern to be woven, things to be done, opportunities to be taken and prices paid. What he had done to her mother and her wasn't personal. It wasn't even human.

She turned away from him to the other two.

Fraiethe had come in the body. She was really there. Though Fraiethe had guided the paluba that reached Maroussia in Mirgorod, that spoke to her and half-lied and half-bewitched and set her on the course that brought her here; though Fraiethe was part of the deception – if deception was what it had been (which it was not, not a deception but an opening-up) – Fraiethe did not like spirit skins. She stood now under the trees, shadow-dappled like a deer, rain-wet and naked except for the reddish-brown fur, water-sleek and water-beaded, that covered her head and neck and shoulders and the place between her breasts. Fur traced the muscular valley of her spine, and a perfume of musk and warmth was in the air around her. Her skin was flushed because of the rain and cold, and her eyes were wide and brown and there were no whites in them.

The third, the Seer Witch of Bones, was neither body nor fetch, but something else, a shadow presence, a sour darkness, the eater of death, the mouth that opened with a smile of dark leaves and thorns, rooted in neither animal nor tree but of the crossing places, muddy and terrible.

And Maroussia Shaumian, who had sewn uniforms at Vanko's factory and pulled Vissarion Lom out of the River Mir and lain beside him in the bottom of a boat to bring him back with the warmth of her body; Maroussia Shaumian, who had sliced a man's head off with a flensing blade and crossed the snow of Novaya Zima to the Pollandore; Maroussia Shaumian, who forgot none of that but remembered everything: Maroussia Shaumian was the fourth at the White Slope, and she claimed an equal place.

The three of them had drawn her to the Pollandore in the moment of its destruction. Because of them she had been there at that moment and absorbed it – been absorbed into it – and become what she was. Because of them the Pollandore was gone from the world beyond the forest and she was here. It was their stratagem against the living angel in the forest. The forest borders were sealed and she, Maroussia, by her presence here, was what held them so. But the three had no sense of the consequences of what they'd done, none at all; only Maroussia had that, and even to her it came only in broken glimpses, fragments that were dark and bleak and hopeless.

She didn't know if there was a better thing they could have done than what they did, but if there was, they hadn't done it.

The fetch of the father spoke again, the man with green eyes: 'The forest is safe. The living angel is contained and we will deal with him. Already he is growing weak and slow. He subsides and grows mute. His ways out of the forest are closed and he no longer draws strength from the places beyond us. The trees are growing back. He has no influence beyond the forest, and here we are stronger than he is.'

The human woman, dark-eyed Maroussia, answered him, and the voice she spoke with was her voice but not only hers but the Pollandore's also, and sounded strange to her ears.

'Yet the angel *lives*!' she said. 'Whatever you say, it is not yet destroyed, and it is not clear that we alone have the strength to do it. And we must look to the world beyond the forest. The years there are moving hard and fast, the Vlast is resurgent, the last slow places are closing, the giants and rusalkas are driven out.'

'What happens beyond the edge of the trees doesn't concern us,' the fetch of the father said. 'It is outside. That's what outside means.'

'The world beyond the forest is growing steel fists,' said Maroussia. 'There's no balance there, no breathing of other air. They will not rest content with what they have; they want it all. They will come here, they'll cut and burn. There are winds the forest cannot stand against. I've seen—'

'They've come here before,' said the fetch of the father, the green-eyed man of muscle, the rich deep voice. 'And always we have always driven them out. It's not even hard.'

'But nothing is the same now, because of what you did. The Pollandore is gone from that world. There is no balance there, and the Vlast will come in numbers, they will drive and burn and burn and drive. There is a man that leads them. Josef Kantor, called Rizhin now. I know something of him and so do you. You know how far he's gone already and how fast he moves.' The human woman, dark-eyed Maroussia, paused and looked at all of them, not just the father. 'And we all know what he is throwing into the sky. We have all heard the hot dry thundercrash and smelled the burning stink of dead angel flesh cutting open the sky. We know the force and speed of what is passing overhead and looking down on us. It makes the forest small. And that's just the beginning of his ambition. How can you say this doesn't concern us?'

The fetch of the father moved to speak, but Maroussia dark-eyed paradigm shifter, the unexpected outcome and maker of change, held up her hand to stop him.

'You must listen to me,' she said, 'or why did you do this? Why make me as I am and bring me here – which I did not ask for, which I did not choose – why do this and not listen now to what I say?'

The fetch fell into silence. Maroussia realised that the father, wherever he was, had finished his testing of her.

The Seer Witch of Bones said nothing. It didn't matter to her. Whatever came there would be a fullness of death at the house of bleached skulls.

But Maroussia felt the pressure of Fraiethe's attentive examination. Fraiethe knew everything: the heaviness and smell of her wet muddy clothes, the hot sweat of her palms and the beating of her heart, her anger at the trickiness of the father, that she was lonely and didn't like the forest and wanted to go home. It was Maroussia not Fraiethe who was naked on the White Slope.

'What would you have us do?' said Fraiethe.

The human woman dark-eyed Maroussia Shaumian opened her mouth to answer Fraiethe. She felt again the dark earth roots and the watchful sentience of rain. A wind stirred the leaves and moved across her face.

'Nothing,' she said. 'I would have you do nothing. There is another way. '

3

Mailboat Number 437 chugged down the mighty mile-broad River Yannis. Vissarion Lom sat in the stern and watched the low wooded hills roll by. The river was slow and quiet here, taking a wide turn to the south, its green waters a highway for tugs, ferries, excursion boats and barges riding low under the weight of ore and grain and oil. Mailboat Number 437 was a dogged striver. The vibration of her engine defined Lom's world: the gentle rhythmic shocks, the slap of small waves against her iron skin. It was a world that smelled of diesel engine and pine planking and rust. Wet rope and mailbags.

Sora Shenkov, master and sole crew of Mailboat Number 437, was a big man with hard brown hands and eyes the colour of ice and sky. He wasn't a talker. Every day Lom sat in the stern and watched him work, unless it rained: then he would go below and watch the river through the specks and smears of his little cabin window. And every day Shenkov's boat made slow headway: her engine churned the screw, and her forward speed through the water exceeded the south-west slide of the Yannis by a certain number of miles, and the marginal gain accumulated. Not that Lom was keeping count. He'd earned some money and taken passage with Shenkov. He'd paid his way. This boat-world time belonged to him. Lom had never owned a time before, but he owned this one and did not wish for it to hurry to an end.

The last six years had changed him. He had travelled far, keeping himself to himself, taking rough work where he could find it, never staying in one place long. His wanderings had taken him into the forest margins, and he had found the endless forest simply that: an endlessness of trees. There were sounds in the night and pathways that went nowhere. Above all, he had not found Maroussia. Of her no trace at all. When he came out of the forest again, months had passed by, seasons come and gone, and he had imagined much but found nothing. He was heavily bearded now, muscular, wiry and weather-darkened, with shaggy wheat-coloured hair. The hole in the front of his skull was nothing but a faint thumbprint visible in certain slanting lights, sun-browned and almost healed. And slowly, slowly, day by day, he was being carried down the river in Shenkov's boat. He enjoyed these days, which required no decisions, required nothing from him at all. He wasn't going anywhere in particular. His adventure was over and time had moved on. Once giants rode the timber rafts west on the Yannis, but now it was women without husbands or sons, and it seemed on the wide quiet river that it had always been so.

Swinging round a headland, the boat came up on two huge timber rafts sliding side by side downstream on the current. Rather than waste time and fuel going out into the middle passage, Shenkov, in the little wheelhouse, gunned the engine and nosed skilfully though the channel between them. Lom reached instinctively for the boathook, not that it would help if the rafts chose to drift together and crush the boat between them. Each raft was as big as an island and carried a cluster of plank huts with smoking chimneys and fenced paddocks for goats and chickens. The logs were red pine, and though they were boughs and branches only, never the trunks, they were thicker and heavier by far than whole trunks of beech or oak. As the boat eased through the gap, a woman was milking a cow and speaking in a soft easy voice to her neighbour on the next raft, who was hanging out clothes to dry. Shenkov gave the women a courteous nod. The air was thick with the resinous red pine scent.

It was early evening when Mailboat Number 437 came to the timber station at Loess. Shenkov grunted in surprise. The wharves were crowded with military vessels: cruisers in brown river camouflage, crane-mounted barges loaded with stacked pontoons, a requisitioned paddle-wheel ferry painted stem to stern and smokestack in dull sky grey.

Shenkov managed to find a berth in front of the excise house, tucked in under the looming steel hull of a cruiser, and began to unload mail-bags onto the steps. Lom left him to his work and wandered off to have a look at what the troops were doing. Sitting on a bollard at the railhead, he watched a captain of engineers supervising the unloading of vehicles from an armoured train. The engine noise was deafening. The stink of diesel fumes. Heavy grinding tracks churned the mud, splintered the boardwalks and cracked the paving. There were half-tracks and troop carriers, but also tractors and cherry pickers and things Lom hadn't seen before that looked like immense hooks and chainsaws mounted on caterpillar tracks. The sapper platoon was marshalling them off the train and onto waiting barges whose decks were already stacked high with oil drums. The sappers struggled with three Dankov D-9 battle tanks, each towing what looked like a hefty spare fuel tank. Instead of a gun, the tank turrets were equipped with a short and vicious-looking nozzle. Lom knew what they were. He'd seen flame-thrower tanks in newsreels. Seen spouts of burning kerosene ignite buildings and flush trenches. Seen the enemy run. Screaming. Burning.

The captain of engineers saw him watching and came across. Took in Lom's weathered face and thick untidy crop of beard, his mud-coloured clothes and boots.

'You came down the river with the mailboat,' he said. 'Were you ever in the forest?' He was a decent-looking man, efficient and practical, more engineer than soldier. It was a question not a challenge.

Lom nodded. 'Off and on,' he said. 'A little.'

'What's it like there?' said the captain of engineers.

Lom gave a slight shrug. 'Trees,' he said. 'Trees and rivers and lakes. Valleys and hills. Miles and miles of nothing much.' He gestured towards the fleet of machinery, the barges and the armed boats. 'You going in there? With that?'

'That's right. No secret about that.'

'It's been done before. Always got nowhere.'

Once a generation the Vlast mounted incursions against the forest. It was one of the futile repeating rhythmic spasms of the Vlast's history. Patrols wandered, ineffectual and lost, doing a bit of damage till they got bogged down in mud and thorn and disease. Lom's own parents had lived in the forest edge. Soldiers came and killed them and razed their village to the ground. The soldiers had carried him out, an orphaned infant, and left him at the Institute in Podchornok. Lom remembered nothing of that forest time and nothing of his parents: presumably they were buried in there somewhere. Bones under the leaf mulch.

So it was to happen again.

'It'll be different this time,' the captain said. 'This time we're going to do it right. We're going in in numbers, whole divisions on a broad front, with heavy machinery and air support. Three salients along the three big rivers. What you see here is just the tip of the iceberg. We're going to cut and burn all the way through to the other side. We're going to break the myth of the forest once and for all.'

'Guess you people need something to do,' said Lom, 'now the war's over.'

'I was hoping you might give me some advice. The benefit of experience? On-the-ground knowledge? Let me buy you dinner and pick your brains.'

'Not a chance,' said Lom. 'Not a chance in a million fucking years.'

4

Lom went back to the mailboat moored at the jetty but Shenkov wasn't there; he'd gone into Loess for supplies. Lom settled himself on the bench in the stern to wait. There was twilight and silence on the air, and a faint smell of woodsmoke. The lapping of the river's edge against the side of the boat. Tiny white moths coming to the newly lit lamp. Not many, not yet, just a few: there was still some life in the western sky. Time was quiet and hardly moving: like the broad deserted river in gathering darkness, all islands and further shores hidden, it seemed to rest and breathe. Huge. Secretive. Watchful.

Maroussia came to him then in the cool of the evening.

Lom knew she was there before she spoke. Before he turned to see her, he felt her as a presence emerging. Resolving out of the periphery of things. She was watching him from out of the silence and the twilight and the shoals of time.

He turned his head to look at her full on, thinking as he did so that she might not be there if he did that. But she was still there, except it was impossible to say exactly where she was. She was on the jetty and on the deck of the boat and on the river shore and on the water. She was very precisely *somewhere*, but the frame of reference that located her was not the same as his. She was solid and real but she was made from air and shadow, woven out of the river twilight. Not flimsy, but he could not have reached out and touched her; the space between them wasn't crossable. He didn't try. For a long time he looked at her. Studying. She was different: older, wiser, changed and strange. She saw things now that he didn't see.

Lom found he was waiting for her to speak first, but she didn't. He wasn't sure if it was possible to speak, anyway, if sounds and words could cross the space that separated them. If language itself could survive that crossing.

'I went into the forest,' he said at last. 'I was looking for you.'

There was a moment when he thought she hadn't heard. He wasn't even sure he'd actually said anything aloud. And then she spoke. It was her voice, the shock of her real voice speaking. He thought he'd kept the memory of it but he had not. The appalling uselessness of memory, how drab and inadequate it was. The sudden raw and open pain of six lost silent years

'I know,' she said.

Lom felt an overwhelming sudden surge of anger and despair. It ambushed him from within. He thought he'd moved beyond all that, he thought he'd acclimatised to loss and living on, but it was all there, unchanged since the day he'd lost her. Since she'd gone where he couldn't follow.

'You knew?' he said. 'But you didn't ...'

'I couldn't,' she said. 'I'm sorry.'

He pushed the anger aside. That hurting was old business, to be dealt with another time, not now.

'Still,' he said, 'you're here. You came back.'

'No,' she said. 'I can't stay here. I can't come back. It isn't possible. Not yet. Perhaps not ever.'

'But—'

'Listen to me,' she said. 'I need you to listen. I need you to understand. What I'm doing now, somewhere else, not here, is I'm holding the forest closed. The angel is shut in and the intermixing of the worlds is separating out. Time runs at different speeds. My time will become, in your world, small fragments of stillness, areas where there is no time at all. I can't come back; I can't come home.' She stared at him, dark eyes wide and urgent in the twilight. They were made of the twilight and the air of the river breathing. 'Can you understand that? Can you?'

'How long?' he said. 'How long have we got?'

'I don't know,' she said. 'There's no measure. How can I say—'

'I mean today. Now. How much time have we got now?'

'Oh,' she said. 'Today? I don't know. I shouldn't have come here at all. Even being here makes a hollowing, a gap for the angel to come through. If that starts to happen, I must go.'

'I could come to where you are,' said Lom. 'You could show me how.'

'No.'

'I would come gladly. I would want that. There's nothing here for me now.'

She looked away sadly in the gathering river darkness.

'It's not possible. The barrier mustn't be broken.' She paused. 'I don't have a choice. I didn't choose this. But if I had a choice, I would choose it. You have to understand that. If I could choose this, I would.'

'Then why come at all?' he said. 'Why are you here?'

'You did something for me once, and I've come to ask you again. I'm sorry. You should be left in peace, but I'm not doing that.'

'What do you need?' said Lom. 'I will do it if I can. Of course I will.'

'This world is going too fast and too hard. The future here is ... I see it, I see glimpses sometimes, and it's too ... The fracture is deeper and wider and harder ... It was unexpected ... It could bring everything down—'

Sealed inside endless forest, Archangel grinds slowly on. Look away from him now; he is nothing. He feels the desolation of despair and self-disgust. Cut off from history, his futures slow and fade. Time is failing him. He cannot breathe. He is weak. He is dying. Once he was Archangel, strongest of the strong, quickest of the quick, most powerful of soldiers, quintessence of generalissimos, Archangel nonpareil, but those memories burn and torture him. So does the encroaching of the slow grass.

Archangel probes the boundaries of his enclosure, but they are blank to him, utterly without information and closing in. Archangel hurls himself against the borders ceaselessly, searching for a chink, a crevice, the faintest possible thinning in the imperceptible wall, but all the time the roots of forest trees dig deeper, the grass grows back, and every tiny root-hair is a burning agony to him. He is succumbing to frost and the erosion of rain and wind. They will wear him away to insensate dust.

But then something happens.

It is only a beat of quietness in the roar of the storm, only the fall of a twig on the river. None but an archangel could hear it. None but an archangel could sense the flicker of a shadow in the face of the sun. The quick thinning of ice. The opening of a moment's gap in the wall of his cage.

With a scream of desperate hope Archangel launches his mind towards the hollowing.

Maroussia flinched and looked over her shoulder as if she had heard a loud noise.

'Not yet!' she groaned. 'Not so soon!' She looked at Lom in alarm. 'There's no more time. I have to go now.'

'Wait! Tell me what you need me to do.'

'Stop Kantor,' she said. '*Stop* him.'

'You mean kill him?'

'No! Not kill. Not that. If you only kill him, the idea of him will live, and others will come and it will be the same and worse. Don't kill him; bring him down, destroy the idea of him. Ruin him in this world, using the tricks of this world. Ruin this world he has created.'

'But ... how? I'm just one person.'

'You have to find a way. Who else can I ask, if not you? Who will listen to me if you don't listen? There is no one else.'

'And if I can do this,' he said, 'then afterwards ... '

'No,' she said, 'there's no *then*. No *afterwards*. No consequence. No reward. I can't see *then*. I can only see what will happen if this doesn't. Do you understand?'

'No,' said Lom. 'I don't understand. But it doesn't matter.'

She was looking at him across a widening distance, and he knew that she was leaving him.

'I have to go now,' she said. 'I've already stayed too long. I wanted ... Oh no ...'

There was a ripple, a shadow-glimmer, and Maroussia was gone.

In the forest it takes Archangel time to react and time to move, and time in the forest is recalcitrant. Slow. Even as he gets close to the gap, it is closing. By the time he reaches it, the tear in the wall has snapped shut. He is too late.

This time.

But now for him there is hope.

And on the quiet River Yannis it was moonless dark and long after midnight and the stars were uncountably many, scattered like salt across darkness, bitter and eternal. She was gone, and Lom felt they hadn't said anything at all, not really – nothing *adequate*, nothing *enough*. She'd come to him and spoken to him, but he didn't know anything, he didn't understand more; in fact he understood less than ever, and all the terrible loss and solitude of the last six years was open and fresh and raw once more: the bleak ruination, the need and the grief and the necessity of acting, of doing something, of finding her again. Perhaps that was the point of her coming. Perhaps that was what she had done.

Lom packed his bag and left the mailboat without waiting for Shenkov to return.

5

The Vlast Universal Vessel *Proof of Concept* circles the planet at tremendous speed, outpacing the planetary spin, passing by turn into clean sunlight and star-crisp shadow. The cabin's interior days and nights come faster and last for less time even than the rapacious advancing days of Papa Rizhin's New Vlast, but aboard the *Proof of Concept* there is no perceptible sense of forward motion.

Cosmonaut-Commodore Vera Mornova, tethered by long cables to her bench, drifting without weight and having nothing much to do, presses her face against the cabin window. The air she breathes smells of hot rubber, charcoal and sweat. The spectacle of the stars unsettles her: they burn clean and cold but seem no nearer now, and all she sees is the infinities of emptiness that lie between. It is her lost, unreachable home that captures her loving attention: the continent, striated yellow and grey by day, the glitter of rivers and lakes, the sparse scattered lamps in inky blackness that are cities by night, the dazzling reflection of the sun in the ocean, the green chain of the Archipelago, the huge ice fields spilling from the poles towards the equator and the edgeless forest glimpsed under cloud.

Misha Fissich drifts up alongside her, accidentally nudging her so she has to grab the edge of the window to stop herself spinning slowly away. He offers her a piece of cold chicken.

'Hungry?' he says. 'The clock says lunchtime. You should eat.'

She shakes her head.

'No, not now, Misha. I'm not hungry. Thanks.'

'You should eat,' he says again. 'The others are watching you, Vera. If you don't bother, neither will they.'

'OK,' she says. 'Thanks.' She smiles at him and takes the chicken and chews it slowly.

When she's finished, it's time for the radio interview: a journalist from the Telegraph Agency of the New Vlast, her voice on the loudspeaker sounding indistinct and far away.

Commodore Mornova, she says, *the thoughts of all our citizens are with you. You and your crew are the foremost heroes of our time. Parents are naming their newborns after you. Will you tell us please what it's like to leave the planet? What do you see? How does it feel? How do you and your comrades spend your time?*

'We feel proud and humble, both at once,' says Vera Mornova. 'It is humankind's first step across the threshold: a small first step perhaps, but we are the pioneers of a great new beginning. History is watching us, and we are conscious of the honour. Space is very beautiful and welcoming. We test our equipment and make many observations.'

Such as? Please share your thoughts with us.

'Well, from orbit one can clearly discern the spherical shape of the planet. The sight is quite unique. Between the sunlit surface of the planet and the deep black sky of stars the dividing line is thin, a narrow belt of delicate blue. While crossing the Vlast we see big squares below – our great collective farms! Ploughed land and grazing may be clearly distinguished. During the state of weightlessness we eat and drink. It is curious that handwriting does not change though the hand is weightless.'

And do you have a message for your loved ones left behind?

'Tell them,' says Vera Mornova, 'tell them we love them and remember them in our hearts.'

Part Two

Chapter Four

We have raised the sky-blue sky-flag –
the flag of dawn winds and sunrises,
slashed by red lightning. Over this planet
our banners fly! We present ...
ourselves! The Presidents of the Terrestrial Globe!

Velemir Khlebnikov (1885–1922)

1

The sky above Mirgorod was a bowl of luminous powdery eggshell blue, cloudless and heroic. Enamel-bright coloured aircraft buzzed and twisted high in the air, leaving trails of brilliant vapour-white. The loudspeakers were broadcasting speeches and news and orchestral music at full distorted volume. The production of steel across the New Vlast exceeded pre-war output by 39 per cent. The cosmonaut-heroes continued to orbit through space.

Citizens! Today is Victory Day! Congratulate yourselves!

From all across the city hundreds of thousands of people were making their way towards Victory Square on buses and trams and trains for the celebration parade. Hundreds of thousands more were coming on foot. Already an inexhaustible river of people was moving up the wide avenue of Noviy Prospect (newly paved and freshly washed before dawn that morning). Half the population of Mirgorod must have been there, going in a slow tide between the towering raw new buildings of the city centre. Vissarion Lom, less than twenty-four hours back in Mirgorod, sat at a café table under a canopy on a terrace raised above the sidewalk, nursing a cooling birch-bark tea, and watched them pass: more people in one place than all the people he'd seen in the last six years put together. Sunlight glared off steel and glass and concrete fresh out of scaffolding; glared off the flags and banners that lined Noviy Prospect; glared off the huge portraits of Papa Rizhin and the lesser portraits of other faces Lom could not name.

Lom disliked crowds. Even sitting somewhat apart and watching them made him uneasy. Edgy. Even anxious. The noise. The faces. He couldn't understand how it was that most people could merge into a throng so readily, so gladly even. To him it felt like submersion. Surrender. Drowning. He couldn't have done it even if he'd wanted to. But he saw the woman with the heavy canvas bag on her shoulder.

He almost missed her. She was moving with the crowd, one small figure in the uncountable mass, going in the same direction as everyone else. Someone else might not have noticed her or, if they had seen her, wouldn't have understood what it meant. It would have been a coincidence, nothing more. But because he was Lom, not someone else, he saw her, and recognised her, and knew what she was doing.

She was just another slight ageing woman in shabby sombre clothes: there were dozens like her, hundreds, shuffling along among the uniformed service personnel, the families, the classes shepherded by harassed teachers, the young women workers in blue overalls and sneakers, the salaried fellows in shirtsleeves and fedoras, the limping veterans, the veterans in wheelchairs and the tight little groups of short-haired and pony-tailed Young Explorers in their blue shorts, grey shirts, red neckerchiefs, knee-length woollen socks and canvas shoes. The women in dark clothes walked alone or in twos and threes. They had their special place that day: they were the widows, the childless mothers, come to watch and remember on bittersweet Victory Day. Lom's gaze passed across the one with the canvas bag on her shoulder and moved on. But something about her caught his attention and he looked again.

People in a large slow crowd surrender themselves to it. They all have the same purpose, all heading for the same destination. Simply being part of the crowd is itself the occasion and the only reason for being there. There's no rush. They have no need to do anything except move along at the crowd's speed and take their cues from the crowd. So they look around and take in the sights and talk, or absorb themselves in their own thoughts. Some bring drink and food and eat as they go. They won't miss anything. They're already where they need to be.

But this one woman was different. There was a tension and separateness about her. Something about the way she held her head and looked around: an obsessive, exclusive watchfulness that snagged his attention, raw and jangled as his nerves were by the numbers of people everywhere. She was making her way through the crowd, not moving with it, and she was alert to her surroundings as those around her were not. She knew where the security cordons and the crowd watchers were, and kept away from them. She tracked her way forward, intent on some private purpose.

And then there was the bag. A drab and scruffy canvas bag, nothing remarkable except Lom could tell by the way she carried it that it was heavy, and the object inside was long and protruded from the top. The thing in the bag was wrapped in a bright childish fabric, which was clever because it attracted attention but also disarmed suspicion. It looked like something that belonged to a child, or used to. The kind of thing an older woman might carry for her grandchild. Or keep with her for ever and never lay down, to remember the dead by. Only this woman seemed a little too young and a little too strong, and it wasn't easy to guess what sort of childish thing this long heavy object was. It scratched at Lom's crowd-raw nerves.

As she passed near where Lom was sitting, the woman with the bag glanced sideways at something, and as she turned Lom glimpsed her face in profile. And recognised her. Six years had changed her. She was leaner, harsher, a stripped-back and sanded-down version of the woman who'd once given Maroussia and him shelter in the Raion Lezaryet, but still he knew instantly that this was Elena Cornelius: Elena, who used to have two girls and live in an apartment in Count Palffy's house and make furniture to sell in the Apraksin Bazaar.

He watched her move on through the crowd. She was good but not that good. Intent on her work, she was just a little too interesting. Too noticeable. Too vivid. She made use of sightlines and available cover for protection. She made small changes of pace. She was moving instinctively as a hunter did. Or a sniper. But snipers move through empty streets, not crowds. In a crowd she was conspicuous. If he could spot her, so could others. Like for instance the security operatives, who were no doubt even now scanning Noviy Prospect from upper windows, though he could not see them.

Lom got up from the café table and followed. He moved up through the crowd to get closer to her, working slowly, cautiously, so as not to be noticed himself and above all not draw the attention of other watchers to her. He felt her vulnerability and her determination. He wanted to protect her, and he owed her his help, but he couldn't let her do what she was going to do. She had to be stopped.

She made a sudden move to the right, picking up speed and making for the ragged edge of the moving crowd. Lom tried to follow, but his way was suddenly blocked by a knot of loud-voiced broad-backed men. They had just spilled out from a bar and stood swaying unsteadily and squinting in the glare of the sun. They smelled of aquavit. By the time Lom got past them, Elena Cornelius had disappeared from view.

2

The meeting room of the Central Committee of the New Vlast Presidium was painted green. The conference table was simple varnished ash wood. There were no insignia in the room, no banners, no portraits: only the smell of furniture polish and new carpet. *There is no past; there is only the future.* Each place at the table had a fresh notepad, a water jug, an ashtray and an inexpensive fountain pen. A single heavy lamp hung low above the table, a flat box of muted grey metal shedding from its under-surface a muted opalescent glow. The margins of the room where officials and stenographers sat were left in shadow.

On the morning of the Victory Day Parade the Committee gathered informally, no officials present, to congratulate their leader and President-Commander General Osip Rizhin, whose birthday by happy chance it also was that day. At least, according to the official biography it was his birthday, though of course the official biography was a tissue of fabrication from beginning to end.

All twenty-one committee members were present: twelve men and eight women, plus Rizhin. Sixteen were makeweights: bootlickers, honest toilers, useful idiots, take your pick – placeholders just passing through. Apart from Rizhin there were only four who really mattered, and they were Gribov, Secretary for War; Yashina, Finance; Ekel, Security and Justice; and Lukasz Kistler. Above all, Lukasz Kistler.

Kistler was a shaven-headed barrel of a man, boulder-shouldered, hard not fat, his torso straining at the seams of his shiny jacket. Kistler liked money, drank with workers and didn't care about spilling his gravy. His shirt cuffs jutted six inches beyond his jacket sleeves. But the intelligence in his small creased eyes was sharp and dangerous as spikes. Kistler was never, ever tired and never, ever got sick and never, ever stopped working. His energy burned like a furnace. He had made huge amounts of money before he was thirty out of iron and oil and coal, anything big and dirty that came out of rock and was hard to get. He was a digger and a burrower and a hammerer. When Rizhin found Kistler he was turning out battle tanks from a factory that had no roof. It had been bombed so often Kistler had stopped rebuilding and left it a ruin in the hope the enemy would piss off and bomb something else. Within half an hour of their first meeting Rizhin put him in charge of producing battle tanks for the whole of the Vlast. Since the war ended, Kistler had expanded into oilfields, gasfields, hydro turbines, petroleum refineries, atomic power. Energy. Energy. Energy. Lukasz 'Dynamo' Kistler made Papa Rizhin's Vlast burn brighter and run louder and faster every day.

And Lukasz Kistler was a clever, subtle, observant and far-sighted man. He saw that Rizhin knew how to spend money and people but had no idea where such resources actually came from. Rizhin didn't know how to turn dirt into cash or people into workers. Rizhin grabbed and stole to spend, and spent what he could not make, and in the end he would spend the whole of the world until he had nothing left. Kistler suspected that one day he and Papa Rizhin would come to blows.

Kistler was watching Rizhin now. Rizhin was on his feet and prowling behind the seated committee members in his soft leather shoes. He liked to walk behind them. It made them uncomfortable. And today Rizhin was wielding a sword. He gripped it in his swollen fist and made experimental swipes at the air as he prowled. (Rizhin's hands fascinated Kistler: hard, thickened, stub-fingered hands, butcher's hands, raw-pink hands that looked like they'd been stung by bees. Long rough work on stone in ice and cold could make such hands. Many years in labour camps. That was something not in Papa Rizhin's official biography.)

The sword was ridiculous. *The Severe Sword*. The Southern Congress of Regions had presented it to him that morning as a birthday gift. Its blade was inscribed on one side SLASH THE RIGHT DEVIATION! and on the other SLASH THE LEFT DEVIATION! and on the hilt it said PUMMEL THE CONCILIATOR!

'They give me a *sword*?' Rizhin was saying. 'And what are we to make of *that*? I give them jet engines and atomic space vessels and they give me a sword. What am I to do with a sword? What does a sword say? You see how riddled we are with aristocrats and peasants still? Fantasists. Nostalgists. Am I to ride out on a fucking horse like a khan? Do they mean me to butcher my own people? Well, if there is butchery to be done, let us start with the Southern Congress of Regions.'

'The sword is an emblem, Osip,' said Yashina. 'That's all.'

'Everything is an emblem,' said Rizhin. 'A generator is an emblem. A sky rise is an emblem. Those fuckers need to get better emblems.'

Rizhin laid the sword on the table and sat down, slumping back in his chair. He picked up a pen and began to scrawl doodles on his notepad.

'The people call me Papa and sing hymns about me,' he said. '"Thank you Papa Rizhin. Glory to our great commander." It's laughable. I'm not Papa Rizhin; I'm a simple man. I am Osip, a worker and a soldier just like them.'

He paused and looked around the table, fixing them one by one with his smiling burning eyes.

'Even you, my friends,' he said, 'even you do this to me. You want me to walk out there today on that platform and let you make me Generalissimus. Do I need this? No. Does Osip the simple industrious man need such empty titles? No, he does not. I do not. I will not accept it. I give it back to you. Take it back, I beg you, and make someone else your Generalissimus, not me.'

There was silence in the room. Everyone froze. Everyone looked down. Secretary for Agriculture Vladi Broch stared glassy-eyed at the sword on the table in front of him as if it would leap up and stab him in the neck. Rizhin doodled on his pad and waited.

For one horrifying moment Lukasz Kistler thought the idiots were going to accept. *It's a test!* he screamed inwardly. *A loyalty test!* If someone didn't speak soon he would have to do it himself, and that would be no good. He wasn't on trial – everyone knew he was Rizhin's dynamo – but if he had to step in and repair the situation it would be the end for some of them.

It was Yashina who rescued them in the end. Smooth, calm, cultured Yulia Yashina.

'We're nothing without you, Osip,' she said quietly. 'No one else could step into your shoes. It is unthinkable.'

They all swung in behind her then. General acclamation, a clattering of fists on the table. Rizhin sighed and straightened himself up in his chair.

'Very well, then,' he said. 'If you insist … I do not like it, you hear me. I protest. Let the record show that. Well … let's get this over with, and get back to our real work.'

Lukasz Kistler glanced down at Rizhin's notepad as they filed out of the room. There was a jagged black scribble in the corner of the top sheet: the scrawled angular face of a wolf glaring out at him from a wall of dark trees. The wolf's jaw was open, showing its teeth.

3

Elena Cornelius climbed the concrete stairwell in near-darkness, counting floors as she went. Five. Ten. Fifteen. Twenty. The light filtering through fluted glass panes in the landing doors was enough to climb by, but too dim to read the floor numbers. It didn't matter. She could count. She knew how many storeys up she needed to go. The key to the service entrance of the New Mirgorod Hotel was in her pocket. Vesna Mayskova, a floor attendant at the New Mirgorod, had got it for her, and she'd left a bucket of dirty water and a mop in the alley outside, the signal that the area was clear of militia patrols.

On the twenty-second floor of the New Mirgorod Hotel, Elena

Cornelius stopped climbing and shoved open the door onto the second-tier roof. The sudden daylight was blinding: the shock of air and sky and the noise of the city after the dim stairwell. Elena held the door open with her foot, swung the canvas bag off her shoulder and rummaged in it for a small sliver of wood. Panic rose for a moment when she couldn't find it, but there it was. Putting the bag on the ground, she let the door almost close and slipped the wooden sliver between the edge of it and the jamb. From the stairwell it would look shut, but there was just enough edge left proud of the surround to wrench it open again from outside with the tips of clawed fingers.

She turned and looked out across the roof. Taking stock. Considering. Checking. She had been here before – a rehearsal run – but nothing must be taken for granted. Check and check again. That's what had kept her alive in the siege.

She was trembling from the effort of the long climb, but that was OK: she knew that it would pass and her hand would steady. There was plenty of time. The impersonal oceanic murmur of the crowd in Victory Square twenty-two floors below was oddly restful. It didn't sound human but like the power of waterfalls or the wind in forest trees.

There was no chance of being seen from below as long as she kept back from the edge. Only the newly built Rizhin Tower on the other side of Victory Square was tall enough to overlook her, and that was still unoccupied. If she were in charge of security, she'd have posted an observer with binoculars in one of the deserted rooms high in the Rizhin Tower. Maybe somebody had, but the architect who designed the three-tiered edifice of the New Mirgorod Hotel had set thirty-foot bronze allegorical figures at the roof corners of every stage. He hadn't worried that he was giving cover for shooters.

The final tier of the New Mirgorod Hotel rose dizzyingly high behind her, casting a deep shadow all the way to the parapet. There was a risk of being seen from one of those upper windows, but she'd checked the angles when she scouted the location. The danger was only when she crossed the roof. Once she was in firing position the hut-like lift mechanism housing would hide her, as long as she kept low.

The roof crossing was only half a dozen paces. Crossings were always a risk, and there was no point in waiting. Elena Cornelius picked up her bag and went. In the cover of the lift housing she crouched low.

Knelt. Lay flat, stomach to the ground, face inches from the mix of rough gravel and tar that coated the roof. The waist-high parapet was five yards in front of her.

During the siege she had crawled on her belly every day. Now she crawled again, hauling herself, knees and elbows and belly across the rough surface, dragging the canvas bag, until she was in the shelter of the parapet. Then she moved right until she was tucked in under the plinth of the bronze statue in the corner.

The statue was a woman in military uniform facing out across the city, a rifle held at an angle across her breast. Above her huge bronze military boots her calves swelled, shapely and muscular. Elena scrabbled into a sitting position and pressed her back against the parapet wall. She was in a safe high place, a vantage point to hide and watch from and not be seen. She knew how to do this. It was familiar. It was a kind of home. She didn't think about why she was there, what had led her to this point. All the decisions were already taken. When you were at work, you worked. That was how you survived.

She unwrapped the Zhodarev rifle, checked the magazine and banged it into position with the heel of her hand. Found the telescopic sight at the bottom of the bag, polished the optics with her sleeve and pushed it onto the rail, easing it forward until it clicked solidly. Then she folded the faded pink towel with the lemon-yellow tractors into a thick sausage, reached up and laid it on the parapet for a barrel rest. Raising herself into a kneeling position, she propped her left elbow on her left knee and raised the rifle, made sure the barrel sat good and solid on its towel rest, settled the stock into her shoulder, pressed her eye to the scope and adjusted the focus.

The VIP viewing platform jumped into view, crisp and clear, down and to the left of her firing position. Tiers of empty seats. They hadn't started to arrive yet.

It was a long shot. She could have done with a more powerful scope, but she didn't have one. She checked the adjustment of the graticule. It was unchanged from how she'd set it that morning before she left home. The range was six hundred and fifty yards – she'd paced it out a week ago plus some simple geometry to allow for height.

The warm morning air rested gently against her cheek. Windage, zero.

Nothing to do but wait and watch.

4

Lom had lost sight of Elena Cornelius at the top of Noviy Prospect just before it opened into Victory Square. He tried to find her again, but it was hopeless: there were any number of alleys and doorways she might have taken, or she could have switched direction and ducked past him back down the avenue against the flow of people without him seeing. He hesitated. Considered abandoning looking for her. After all, it was possible he was wrong about what she was doing. Maybe she'd just come to see the parade.

But he didn't believe that.

He made his way out onto the fringe of Victory Square. The open space, laid out on what had once been the much smaller Square of the Piteous Angel, was staggeringly vast. Block after block of streets and buildings (Lom remembered them) had been demolished to make room for it. Rivers and canals had been covered over, the city completely reoriented. And now it was completely filled with people come for the Victory Parade. It was impossible to estimate how many were there: half a million? A million? There were high terraces for seating, and crowds of people standing shoulder to shoulder in the gaps between. He could see across to the raised platform where Rizhin would take his place. The VIP seats were beginning to fill up.

Not far from the platform the Lodka still stood, the dark and many-roofed headquarters of the old Vlast, no longer on an island between river and canal, occupying one small corner of the square. The Lodka had survived siege bombardment and aerial bombing raids, but now – eviscerated when Chazia removed the great archives and burned most of the contents, overtopped by the surrounding sky rises of concrete and granite and glass with their wedding-cake encrustations and monumental bas-reliefs – the huge cliff of a building looked isolated and diminished. Smartened-up but mothballed. A museum piece.

And next to the Lodka, dwarfing it, climbing higher – far higher – than any other building in the city, rising tier upon tier of stark grey stone, fluted, slender and almost weightless against the sky, was the Rizhin Tower, which was to be formally declared open that day. The top of the tower, constituting one tenth of the total height of the building, was an immense and gunmetal-grey statue of Papa Rizhin. He was in civilian clothes, standing bare-headed, his long coat lifting behind him slightly in a suggestion of wind. He was stepping forward towards the city, his back to the sea, his right arm raised and outstretched to greet and possess. The statue's civilian clothing puzzled Lom. Not the military tunic and shoulder boards of the standard Rizhin portrait, it struck an odd note.

Then the truth struck him. This dizzying and mighty behemoth was not a statue of Rizhin at all; it was a statue of Josef Kantor. Kantor the agitator, the plotter, the revolutionary orator, the killer, the master terrorist.

Josef Kantor had transformed himself into Papa Rizhin at the siege of Mirgorod. He kept his origins secret, hidden, suppressed. All hints of his former self were ruthlessly obliterated. But here in Victory Square in the heart of Mirgorod – in plain sight, in the most visible, most spectacular place of all, full in the face of the whole of the Vlast – Rizhin thrust the truth of himself at them all, and nobody could see it, or if they did they dared not say. The Rizhin Tower was an act of the most astonishing hubris: a challenge, a yell, a dare, a spit in the eye of the world.

At that moment a strange noise started to swell and grow in Victory Square. Lom had heard nothing like it before. It began as a low clatter and hum and grew to a great roaring, deafening buzz. It was the sound of the crowd rising to greet the arrival of Papa Rizhin, who had stepped out onto the raised platform. It wasn't cheering. It was a vibration of excitement like the agitation of a billion bees. The extraordinary noise reverberated around the square and echoed, magnified, off the surrounding buildings.

Lom turned his back on it. He shoved and threaded his way back into Noviy Prospect, which was almost deserted now, its flags and banners and portraits of Rizhin stirring in a gentle rising breeze. Everyone who was going to Victory Square had found their place; the parades and speeches were about to begin. But where was Elena Cornelius?

5

Eligiya Kamilova walks once more the five level miles, the long straight stony road south out of Belatinsk and back to Nikolai Forshin's dacha. The dacha of the Philosophy League. Keeping her eyes down, no longer even consciously hungry, she walks with slow and fierce determination. One step. One step. One step. All her attention is fixed on her dust-yellowed boots and the pale stalks that are her shins.

To either side of her, electricity pylons march away across bare earth and dried yellow grass, level to the encircling blued horizon. Grey wooden sheds and grey corrugated-iron roofs. Dust and bone sunlight. The pylons carry no cables. The pylons are built, but the gangs that bring the cables have not yet come.

Kamilova notices none of this. Not any more. Every day the same. Nothing changes.

One step. One step.

She has done this walk every day for a week. Five miles out and five miles back. She wonders how much longer she can.

Her legs are so thin it frightens her. These fleshless wasted sticks are not hers; they are the legs of one who died long ago. How do they carry her without the shifting contour of muscle? Dried knots and tendons only, visibly working. Her knees are crude obtrusions, like the stones in the unmade road. Her own hands startle her: demonstration pieces of skeletal articulation for the instruction of anatomists.

My face is gone. I have transparent skin. I have forgotten how to be hungry.

All day Eligiya Kamilova has stood in line in Belatinsk, Galina's ration card in her pocket. (Galina has found a job running messages at Lorschner's. The wage is pitiful but the ration card is more valuable than platinum and silks.) She didn't know what she was queuing for. People in line in Belatinsk hold tight to the belt of the one in front to keep their place. Too weak to stand alone, they lean against strangers and do not speak.

All day Kamilova's line waited and did not move. In the afternoon the shopkeeper closed up.

'Fuck off now,' he screamed at them. 'Fuck off. Fuck off. There's nothing here.'

So Kamilova turned away and walked back out through the town.

Belatinsk was everywhere silent, subsided under dugouts, shacks and shanties of rusty iron, planks, cardboard, wire, glass and earth. There was no water, no electricity, no sewerage. Paved streets were dug up for scraggy allotments where nothing properly grew. Everything wood – benches, hoardings, fences, boardwalks – had been ripped up and burned. Vermin everywhere and no repairs to anything.

She passed a scrap of municipal garden behind iron railings. Sign on the gate: DIG NO GRAVES HERE.

No cars or trucks on the road out of Belatinsk to Forshin's dacha. On the verge a mare had died, her body swollen hard. Black lips stretched off yellow teeth in a snarl. Black jewel flies were sipping at her eyes and crawling over the blue fatness of her tongue. Kamilova wanted to sit in the dust and lean against her like a couch, just for a while.

One step. One step. One step.

She docs not know how many more days she can do this. Hunger is not the absence of food. It is a big black rock you carry that fills the sky. It crushes you while you sleep.

Yet things are better now at Forshin's dacha than they were on the road.

The evening after they buried the twice-killed soldier, Kamilova stole a boat from the village at Yamelei. She still felt bad about the boat, but the village would survive and the girls could not walk. Not so far, not all the way. The equations of necessity.

So Kamilova had taken the boat, and in her they crossed the lake above the sunken city. Still purple waters at twilight and the sound of a distant bell.

The soul of the people is forever striving to behold the sunken city of Litvozh.

Kamilova knew boats. All night she let the chill wind take them west, and in the dawn they followed the shore to where the westward river flowed out.

'What river is this?' said Yeva.

'I don't know,' said Kamilova, 'but it's going the right way.'

Low wooded hills and scraps of cool dawn mist. The girls slept under dewy blankets in the shelter of the gunwales, and the river took them into strange country. Unfamiliar hunting beasts called to one another across the water. Dark oily coils surged and rippled, and the backs of great silent fish broke the surface of the river. Kamilova sat in the stern with the gun across her knees and steered a course clear of the black bears that swam slow and strong and purposefully from shore to shore. They passed through a city ruined in the war. Nobody was there. Not anybody at all.

The end of day brought them across the sudden frontier out of slow memorious places into the hungerland.

In the deep past and in remoter places even now families and villages might fall into hunger and all of them die. That was one thing. In the towns and cities of the Vlast a wretched person sick and alone without a kopek might starve in a gutter. That was another thing. A ragged inconvenience. But when entire regions, millions of people, conurbations and suburbs and the penumbra of organised rural production, plunged into sudden and total desperate famine, that was something else. That was something never seen before.

That was the hungerland.

The boat came to a weir. A tremendous white-water fall. Nothing for it but to sleep and in the morning leave the boat and walk.

Kamilova, thinking the house on the edge of the nameless town empty, broke in the door. The family was gathered in darkness, curtains drawn against the day. The smell was bad. There were puddles of water on the floor.

Two chairs were pushed together, and across them lay the corpse of the boy. He might have been fourteen but starvation aged you. You couldn't tell. The baby was propped in a pram, head to one side on the pillow, dead. The mother on the bed was dead. The daughter sat beside her on the stained counterpane, rubbing at the mother's chest with a linen towel.

'Where is your father?' said Kamilova. 'Did he go for help? For food?'

The girl glanced up at her without expression and carried on rubbing the dead woman's chest. The smell of embrocation.

Kamilova took from her bag a piece of hard dry bread and a handful of potatoes brought from Yamelei and laid them on the bed. The girl didn't look. The food just lay there on the counterpane.

When Kamilova reached the door she stopped and turned back, picked the food up again and put it back in her bag. The equations of necessity.

The girl didn't glance up when Kamilova left the room.

Days rose dark in colourless sunshine and set in bleakness. The hungerland walk was one long unrelenting road. Aftermath, aftermath. Deadened days after the end of the world.

Slowly they realised how late they were. The distortions of slow time in the memorious zone. Here in the hungerland six years had passed, the war was over and this was Rizhin country now.

'Mother will think we forgot her,' Galina said. 'She must think we are dead.'

'She is waiting,' said Yeva. 'She would never stop waiting.'

'I will take you home,' said Kamilova. 'I promise. We're going there as quick as I can.'

The girls wrote letters and posted them when they came to towns. *We are OK, Mother. We are alive and fine. Not long now. We'll be with you soon.*

Silence, horrible silence, settled across the hungerland. Livestock, cats and dogs, all dead. Birds and wild things all hunted or driven away. The only sound in the early morning was the soft breath of the dying. The footfalls of carrion eaters on patrol.

A woman in a garden held up her baby as they walked by.

'Please. Take him, take him. I beg you take him. I cannot feed him. They will eat him when he dies.'

The child had an enormous wobbling head. A swollen pointed belly. He was already dead.

They studied starvation and became connoisseurs of hunger. Darkened faces and swollen legs were the symptomology of famishment. Corpse faces with wide and lifeless eyes, skin drawn skull-tight and glossy and covered with sores.

First your limbs grew weak, then you lost all physical sensation. The body became a numb and burdensome sack. The circulation of the blood grew sluggish until the unnourished muscles of the heart, unable to shift their own weight any more, simply failed to beat. By then you no longer had the energy to care.

People died working at their desks. They died as they walked the streets.

There was a shape to it, a pattern of progression. The speed of it surprised them. A few weeks was all it took before the people started dying. Those died who refused to steal or trade their bodies for food. Those died who shared their food with others. Parents who made sacrifices for their children died before them, and then their children died. Those died who refused to countenance the consumption of the most forbidden flesh. In the end it made no difference because everyone who didn't escape the hungerland died.

The hungerland was spreading westward, and Kamilova and the girls walked in the same direction. Sometimes they took a lift in a truck and sometimes they got ahead of the hungerland wave. Behind them the cannibal bands were coming. Mobile platoons of mechanised anthropophagi grinding their butchering knives.

Kamilova shot two men with her gun to save the girls. The equations of necessity. Five shells left.

All three of them were growing weak. Kamilova knew the signs.

A cart brought them to Belatinsk one morning, and there they were stuck. Yeva and Galina could walk no more.

'How far to go to Mirgorod?' Kamilova enquired.

'Twelve hundred miles,' said the post office clerk. 'Fifteen maybe.'

The only way out was the railway.

'Sixty-five roubles,' said another clerk at another window. 'Third Class. One way. Each.'

Kamilova had money, scavenged from the bodies of the roadside dead. Money didn't help in the deep hungerland, not unless you ate the paper. She had a sheaf of roubles in her pack. It was not enough.

She sat on a bench by the station in Belatinsk with Yeva and Galina. She had simply reached the end. She didn't know what to do.

And then she saw the gleaming domed brow and wild flowing hair of Nikolai Forshin, six foot three and swinging an opera cane, come to the station to enquire about the arrival of a parcel of journals expected from the printers at Kornstadtlein.

'Eligiya? Eligiya Kamilova?' he called across the road. "Is that you?'

Not all the members of Forshin's Philosophy League were happy at the arrival of three extra mouths. Some of the wives were the worst. But Forshin decided, boom-voiced disputatious Nikolai Forshin of the purple bow tie and the hard bright visionary eye. Forshin led. Forshin prevailed. It was Forshin's dacha and Forshin's crazy hopeless League.

At the dacha there was a clear stream for water, a few scrawny chickens that didn't lay and a meagre vegetable patch. Potatoes were coming on. It was something but not enough. Not nearly enough. Kamilova gave her share to Galina and Yeva, though the girls didn't know it.

Forshin's League was growing fearful. They looked to their defences. There were rumours of gangs in Belatinsk and a trade in human flesh. Starveling packs had already approached the dacha more than once. Stick-people stood in the road and looked. The hungerland was coming, and the walls of Forshin's dacha were not strong enough to hold it back.

Eligiya Kamilova reaches the end of the road and turns into the track to the dacha.

This is the last return. I cannot do that fruitless walk again. It will kill me.

Forshin himself is standing on the veranda smoking his pipe and watching her come. He is excited. He steps out to meet her, waving a piece of paper in his hand.

'A letter, Eligiya! A letter from Mirgorod is come! The winds are changing. Rizhin himself has made a wonderful speech. "Times of Enlightenment", that's what he calls for. We are invited back! The League is to go home, I'm sure of it. We are to have a meeting this evening to resolve the matter. Come with us, Eligiya Kamilova, and bring your bright wonderful girls. Come! It will be a treat for them. Would they not *adore* to see the streets of Mirgorod again?'

6

Elena Cornelius couldn't get a clean shot. The head of the woman sitting next to Rizhin – Secretary for Finance Yulia Yashina, long neck, aquiline nose, grey hair pulled tight back off a long pale face – floated in the centre of the scope's optic, and behind her Rizhin's nose and shoulder.

That was OK. Eventually he would stand and come forward to the microphoned lectern to speak. Elena Cornelius could wait.

Marching formations and rumbling military vehicles were passing interminably under the viewing platform. A huge cheer – the kind that used to greet the earth-shaking trudge of the old Novozhd's platoon of forty-foot war mudjhiks – rose at the sight of atomic bombs on wide flatbed trucks. To Elena they looked ridiculous, like elephantine boiler-plated pieces of plumbing equipment.

The fresh-painted weaponry of the Vlast – battle tanks, mobile artillery and radar vehicles, rocket launchers – was followed by a display of captured enemy war machines looking battered and drab. Then came the March of the Heroes of Labour. Smiling blond men in overalls. Women in skirts and white ankle socks, waving. To pass the time, Elena let her telescope sight climb the endless rising walls of the Rizhin Tower. Since she could not see Rizhin himself, except one shoulder, she scanned the statue instead. It wasn't stone or bronze but steel, constructed by armaments engineers from the melted-down ships and guns and shell casings of the enemy. In her scope she could see the polished, shaped sections riveted together. The welding scars like patchwork.

She got the eye of the statue in her cross hairs.

Lom had lost time and found nothing. It was hopeless. He couldn't find her by wandering and randomly looking, not if he had a week. He wondered if he was wasting his time and taking an unnecessary risk by lingering here. He was beginning to feel visible, and if something was going to happen he was probably already too late to prevent it. Elena Cornelius had most likely just joined the crowd to see the parade. But that's not what he'd sensed when he watched her, and he'd learned to trust feelings like that.

If I was a sniper, he thought, *where would I choose? Where would I go?*

The only way to find her was to think like she thought. Work it out from first principles. Narrow down the options and make a throw of the dice. It was fifty-fifty: choose right or choose wrong. Except it wasn't fifty-fifty. How many high buildings looked across Victory Square? How many rooftops? How many windows? There were a thousand options, and all of them wrong except one.

Think it out. Narrow the odds. You're a lucky man. Things work out for you. Yeah, right.

The criteria were: a clear shot, access to the shooting position, inconspicuousness, an escape route.

The first was useless. It didn't narrow the field. Any building on three sides of the square would give a clear shot from the fourth floor up. The last was useless too: he had no information. And maybe she didn't intend to escape. That was possible. So he was left with access and inconspicuousness. Access. That was the key. That had to come first. She'd choose a building she could get into, then look for a shooting position, and she'd only abandon it and move on to the next one if there wasn't a place to fire from.

But that was no good either. Access to anywhere in the vicinity today was a nightmare. Places were either locked down tight and shuttered, or they had people crowding every window to get a view of the parade. There were police and militia everywhere. Regular sweeps and patrols. There *must* be a way in somewhere – he knew that because he knew she'd found it – but there was no possibility that he could spot it or guess. Not today.

Not today.

Of course not today. But it wasn't today that mattered. Today she'd have come already knowing where she was making for. She must have scouted the place out beforehand, on another day. She must have poked into corners, looked for vantage points, worked out lines of sight and ways in and out. Preparation. Planning. That meant that, wherever she was now, she'd have had to go there at least once before with plenty of time to look around. The access that mattered wasn't today but any other day. Any normal day.

He was getting somewhere. Maybe. He could rule out offices and residential buildings. You couldn't wander around places like that without attracting attention – not unless you worked or lived there. Well maybe she did. But if so he was defeated: he had no chance. So rule all those buildings out anyway. Which left public places: shops, hotels, museums. And say the place she'd chosen wasn't too far from where he'd lost her. There was no reason to think that, except that when he'd noticed her she was in the open, visible and vulnerable, and he could assume she'd expose herself as little as possible. It was likely he'd lost sight of her because she'd ducked in somewhere. Not certain, but the odds were in his favour. And this was all about odds.

He looked around, scanning the buildings. There were three good possibilities: two hotels and the Great Vlast Museum. The museum was closed. She might be in there, but if so he couldn't follow. Not quickly. Perhaps not at all. That left the two hotels. He was back to fifty-fifty.

He chose the bigger, which was also nearer to where he'd last seen her. It was a thirty-storey three-tier granite cake. The entrance was guarded by two militia men and cast iron bas-reliefs of steelworkers with bulging forearms and collective farmers brandishing ten-foot scythes.

Lom took stock of himself. When he arrived yesterday he'd had a shave and a haircut and bought himself a suit. In his pocket he had a thickish wad of rouble notes and ID papers in the name of Foma Drogashvili, which he'd been using on and off for several years. So how did you get to look around inside the New Mirgorod Hotel? You went up to the desk and asked for a room.

Elena Cornelius watched the aircraft fly past low in the brilliant early-afternoon sky. The bass rumble of slow ten-engined bombers. The screaming of new-made jets trailing coloured vapour. Parachutists spilled from a lumbering transport plane and drifted down under brilliant blossoming canopies of red and yellow, alighting with perfect precision in the space in front of the viewing platform.

Twisting, ducking fighters enacted dogfights against the warplanes of the Archipelago. One enemy bomber spouted oily smoke and flame and sank lower and lower as it limped from view. When it was out of sight behind the Rizhin Tower there was a loud flash and a white pall rose into the sky as if it had crashed. Perhaps it had. Elena remembered no such dogfights during the siege of Mirgorod. Then, the bombers had come day and night unopposed.

Gendarmes had thrown a cordon across Karolov Street. On the other side of it a battered old delivery truck was propped up on a jack at the kerb, one wheel off. Two bearded young men lay on the ground, spreadeagled, rifles pointed at their heads. The back of the truck was open, being searched. And beyond the truck was the side entrance to the New Mirgorod Hotel. Lom had a choice: wait, or retrace his steps and try the front entrance on Victory Square.

He didn't want to keep going over the same piece of ground. If there were watchers – and there surely were – he would be noticed. He made a quick calculation. Something would be found in the truck or it would not. Either way, within five minutes the situation here would change. But for ten long edgy minutes he waited and nothing was different. He turned back the way he had come.

The dark-panelled lobby of the hotel, when he finally reached it, was almost deserted. Ornate gilt-framed mirrors. Empty leather sofas under glowing chandeliers. The doorman was settled at a low marble table, cap off, drinking tea. Lom rang the bell at the desk. Waited. Rang it again. He could feel the eyes of the doorman on his back. From the room at the back came a radio commentary on the parade unfolding outside. He wished the doorman would just step outside and take a look.

Finally the reluctant clerk appeared.

'A room?' he said, raising his eyebrows sceptically. It was as if no one had ever asked him for such a thing before. 'Regrettably, that is not possible. Naturally for Victory Day all our rooms are taken.'

'All of them?' Lom laid a stack of roubles on the table. The clerk scowled at him.

'Of course all of them. Tomorrow you can have a room. Today, not.'

'Then perhaps someone could just bring me coffee.'

'Now?'

'Now. Yes, now. Thank you. And a newspaper.' Lom indicated a low sofa against a pillar near the entrance to the lifts. 'I'll be over there.' He went across and sat down to wait. The clerk, scowling, spoke into the telephone on the counter then returned to his back room.

Minutes passed and Lom's coffee did not come. He knew he should get out of there. He'd drawn attention to himself. If the clerk hadn't been calling for tea, who had he been talking to on the phone? And Elena had already had plenty of time: if anything was going to happen it would have happened by now. But he stayed and waited. Eventually the doorman stood up with a sigh from his table by the window, set his cap on his head and went out through the plate-glass doors to take up his position outside on the steps.

Lom moved.

Elena Cornelius heard a roar from the crowd twenty-two floors below. An amplified voice was crashing out across the city, carried not only by the loudspeakers in Victory Square but also by every tannoy and radio in Mirgorod. Rizhin had come to the lectern and was speaking.

The vast crowd hushed, but the hush had its own noise, like waves over shingle. Rizhin's amplified speech bounced off the wall behind her. The echo confused sense. She could only make out fragments.

'... *life has become better, friends, life is happier now... remember yesterday's sacrifices, yes, but look to tomorrow ... a greater victory to come ...*'

She re-settled the rifle. Pulled back the bolt with the outside of her hand to drive the first cartridge into the breech. One should be enough, but there were nine more in the magazine. She let the cross hairs move along the line of faces on the platform. You. You. You. The graticule came to rest clear and steady in the middle of Papa Rizhin's head.

'... *our vessels explore the cosmos, but we must master our own planet also ... inevitably the Archipelago will crumble and fade ... the force of history will do our work ... the forest ... no more dark areas of super-stition and myth ... this time we will not be prevented, we will take a strong grip ...*'

In the siege she had shot without thought or conscience. The whole city then was filled with a loud dinning noise that made everyone always deaf. Sleepwalkers. The invaders wore blank masks. This, today, was different: the face in the cross hairs the focus of all the world and more familiar than her own. A killing imagined a thousand times. Long sleepless years. Her heart beat faster. Perspiration on her forehead. In the roots of her hair.

She breathed in and breathed out slowly, emptying her lungs.

Calling up calm. She reached back to wipe her hand dry on her skirt. Cocked her wrist into the firing hold she had practised till it came easy and smooth. Began to squeeze her obtuse finger gently. Taking up the slack. A breath of wind kissed her sweat-damp cheek.

Lom pushed open the door onto the hotel roof and stepped out into dazzling glare. The rooftop was empty. There was nobody there and nothing to see but parapet and sky.

He heard the sound of a single rifle shot. It was unmistakable. And it had come from somewhere above him.

Not the first-stage roof, the second.

Shit.

He spun round, went back inside and ran up the darkened staircase, taking the steps three at a time.

Elena Cornelius saw the bullet strike the cushioned seat of the chair behind Rizhin. It must have passed his skull by inches, but he didn't react. Didn't pause. Didn't flap a hand at the zip and crack by his ear, like she'd seen people do. He'd heard nothing above the amplified echoes of his own speech.

Lukasz Kistler was staring, puzzled, at the hole that had been punched in the seat beside him. In a second it would dawn on him what it meant.

She lined up the cross hairs on Rizhin again, took a deep slow breath, exhaled and fired again. Rizhin's face disappeared in a puff of soft pink. The energy of the bullet snapped his whole body backwards. He went down as if someone had smashed him full force in the temple with a baseball bat.

Even in the dim stairwell Lom heard the horrified moan of the crowd. It was like the lowing of a stricken herd. He pounded on up the stairs, floor after floor.

He almost ran smack into Elena Cornelius coming down, the rifle held delicately in splayed fingers, pointing at the floor.

'It's me, Elena. You know me. Vissarion. Vissarion Lom.'

Her eyes were wide and unblinking, glassy bright in the shadows.

'I've killed him,' she said.

It was like a punch in Lom's stomach. All the air went out of him.

Less than a day in Mirgorod and he had failed. Mission over.

He took the rifle from her awkward grasp and propped it against the wall.

'You have to lose this,' he said. 'Leave it. The bag too. Lose it. We need to get out of here.'

She didn't resist. She didn't move. He took her by the arm and led her down the stairs.

7

On a broad front the divisions of the New Vlast army entered the endless forest. Fleets of barges up the wide slow rivers and under the trees.

The forest is woods within woods, further in and further back. It has an edge but no central point and there is no end to going on. Deeper and deeper for ever. Strange persons live there. It is not safe.

As long as the divisions kept to their barges on the rivers they made progress, but five yards back from the bank all was impassable: layers of dead wood, luxuriant undergrowth, lake, bog and hill. Oak, ash, elm, maple and linden tree. Thorn and fir. A trackless catalogue of all the forests of northernness and east. Disoriented compass needles swung. Radios sucked in static. Green noise.

The forest removed irony. It was the place itself. Woodland and shadow and the lair of wild beasts. Every divisional commander was on his or her own. One by one each hauled up on some bend of their nameless river and disembarked and began to burn. Petrol-driven chainsaws ripped resinous raw avenues. The noise echoed down the river valleys. Trundling battle tanks pissed arcs of singeing ignition, the soldiers' smut-grimed sweat-shone faces gleamed dull and lurid orange, and every day the churned and stinking ash-carpeted swathes extended deeper into the interior of the forest. Fingernails scraping at the heart of green silence. A war against the world.

The rivers became supply lines for the beachheads. Barge trains shuttled fuel day and night from New Vlast base camps at the forest edge.

In a week the black smoke had darkened the midday sky.

Divisions encountered waterlands that would not burn, marshes that sucked at the tracks of wallowing tanks. Engineers sank to the waist in bog and floundered. Horses drowned. Methane pockets burst and burned behind them. Divisions came to sudden rising cliffs and turned aside. Divisions reached the brink of mile-wide bottomless mist-rimmed holes in the ground. Trolls blundered out of the thickets, roaring, hair on fire and blackened blistering skin.

The advancing swathes of engine-driven desolation drifted left and right, circling round to rejoin themselves, beginning to lose direction, tracing mazy aimless scribbles on the margins of elsewhere under the trees.

Chapter Five

Skulking along behind the revolution's back
the petty functionaries stuck out their heads ...

From the motherland's farthest corners they assembled,
hurriedly changing their clothes and settling in
at all the institutions,
their chair-hardened buttocks
solid as washbasins.

Vladimir Mayakovsky (1893–1930)

1

Dead shock pulsed out across Mirgorod from the head of Papa Rizhin obliterated in a pink flower. His poleaxed fall punched the city in the face.

There was a spontaneous attempt to put a roadblock across Noviy Prospect, but the tide of dazed and weeping spectators rolled down out of Victory Square and swept on through, and nobody seriously tried to stop them. Militia patrols gathered in stricken leaderless huddles. Officers with panic in their eyes jogged between them barking orders no one seemed to hear.

Elena Cornelius pulled herself together quickly. She dropped her dark coat in an alleyway. In a white short-sleeved blouse she was taller and ten years younger, narrow shoulders and pale muscular arms, almost unrecognisable as the woman of the morning crowd. From six years back Lom remembered a rounder, fuller face, but she was all bone structure now. Nose pushed askew and night-blue eyes. The lines of a mouth long kept pressed tight shut to keep words back. Lom noticed her damaged hands. Fingernails not grown properly back.

'What are you *doing?*' she said.

'Helping you,' said Lom. 'Two are less visible than one.'

They walked among the stricken, the shocked, the wandering. Not fast, not slow, catching no one's eye. Gendarmes were hauling people from the crowd. Pushing them against the wall. Spilling the contents of pockets and bags onto the pavement.

'I don't need you,' said Elena. 'I'm better alone.'

'I'm good at this kind of thing.'

Bright banners fluttered in the strengthening wind. Rizhin's huge smiling face watched over them. Rizhin's face – Josef Kantor's face – the man Lom had known, become a monstrous bullying avuncular god. The death of him left the world strangely deflated and pointless. *Not the world*, thought Lom. *Only me.*

'Were you following me?' said Elena. 'Were you looking for me?'

'Later,' said Lom. 'We'll talk later, when we're clear.'

'What were you *doing* there? How could you *know?*'

'I didn't know. I saw you in the street. You were pretty obvious. But I lost sight of you, and by the time I found you again it was too late.'

'Too late? For what?'

'Too late to stop what you did.'

She left him then. Turned on her heel into a side alley, a narrow chasm between high windows and steep blank walls. Lom thought of hurrying after her. Catching up. *What happened to you? How are you become this?* But he let her go and watched her until she reached the far end of the alley and turned to the right. She didn't look back.

Then he followed.

2

Elena Cornelius was going east. The streets were almost empty. She took a low underpass beneath the thundering Rizhin Highway: a urinous pillared human culvert.

She was easy to follow. Lom trailed her across waste and cratered rubble-lands and through pockets of still-standing bullet-pitted soot-grimed war damage. She led him into a wilderness of elephantine newness: concrete apartment buildings hastily thrown up among the ruins, already stained and dispirited and bleached colourless in the watery afternoon desolated sun. Lom logged the meaningless street names and recognised nothing at all, but he always knew where he was: wherever you went in Mirgorod you could tell your position by the Rizhin Tower. The skied statue of dead Josef Kantor was a beacon. A steering star.

He remembered the old city, the shifting rain-soft city, layered with glimpses, haunted with strange perceptiveness, turnings and doorways alive with contending futures, but now the triumphant future was here, and if the city was littered with shards and broken images, they were dry bone fragments of the past. Angels and giants were gone, rusalkas also: the waters had closed over them and people behaved as if they had never existed.

The blank blinding sky on concrete and asphalt made him squint. He was thirsty, and heavy with obscure guilt. He had made a mistake somewhere, taken a wrong turning, this future now and in Mirgorod his fault. His intentions were good, but history judged only results, and all his choices so far had been bad. The world around him had come out wrong. One day back in Mirgorod and here he was, trailing across wasted ground after a damaged and solitary woman who had killed a monster and made things worse. He didn't know why he was here, except there was nothing better to do.

He kept following Elena Cornelius. She entered an apartment block indistinguishable from the others except by a name. KOMMUNALKA SUBBOTIN NO. 19.

Lom waited in a doorway across the square to see if she would come out again, but three hours later she had not. He turned away then, back towards the clustered sky rises under the reaching steel arm of the Rizhin statue.

3

General-Commander Osip Rizhin held himself rigidly upright in the chair while the doctor leaned in close and did his work. Papa Rizhin stared at the desk in front of him and focused his mind on the pain. He held himself open to it and felt it to the full.

His right eye was swollen shut but his left eye was good. Water streamed from it, not tears but cleansing salt burn, and when the doctor offered him morphine Rizhin cursed him. He had borne worse, in other chairs in other rooms, chairs with straps in rooms with barred high windows. Pain was a good harsh friend. An honest friend. Pain was strength and focus. Everyone who had ever leaned over him in a chair and caused him pain was dead now, and he was still here, the survivor, the indestructible.

The whole of the right side of his face was a swollen, shifting, stiffening map of numbness and pain. Every fresh insertion of the needle, every tug of thread, every application of the burning antiseptic pad, brought its own unique and individual new agony. Rizhin paid attention to the particularity of them all, the thing that made each pain different from every other pain he had ever felt. Pain magnified the right hemisphere of his head until it was bigger than the whole of the rest of the world, but Rizhin knew all the intimate topography of it. Carefully, attentively, he traced across it every new event in the intricate history of hurting.

The collar and back of his dress-uniform tunic were drenched with cold sticky blood. Fragments of human meat and bone. Most of the blood and all of the fleshy mess was not his but Vladi Broch's. The sniper's bullet had deeply furrowed Rizhin's cheek as it passed on by and entered the seated Broch on a downward trajectory, finding the soft gap between left shoulder and neck. A trajectory that took the top of Broch's spine out through a hole in his back.

The doctor straightened up and dabbed at his handiwork on Rizhin's cheek with an iodine cloth. He washed his hands in a bowl of soap and then took a clean handkerchief from his pocket to polish his round-rimmed spectacles. The doctor had soft subtle hands. He wore his thinning hair combed back.

Trust no doctor, that was Rizhin's iron rule. Doctors were the cunning eunuch viziers of the modern world. Mountebank snake-oil alchemists. Obfuscating cabalists of a secretive knowledge. Master superciliists. All surgeons and physicians played you false. In comfortably upholstered rooms they wove their mockery and plots.

Doctor, respected doctor, fear your patient.

'There will be a scar, I'm afraid,' the doctor said. 'There's nothing I can do about that. I've been as neat as I can.'

He began to prepare a dressing pad.

'A battle scar is a source of pride,' Rizhin growled at him through lopsided tongue and uncooperative mouth. 'A million of our veterans bear far worse than this, and they're the lucky ones.'

4

Nikolai Forshin convenes a conference of the Philosophy League at eight in the evening to consider the letter from Mirgorod.

'Of course you must come to our meeting, Eligiya Kamilova,' he says. 'You are one of us, and I may need your support.'

They gather in the principal room of the dacha, part salon, part library: a room of divans and cretonne and canework chairs, threadbare rugs on a parquet floor. Forshin has left the doors to the veranda open, admitting sullen lilac evening. The birch avenue flimsy and skeletal.

Everyone is there: Forshin himself, standing tall and wild-haired at the fireplace, brimming with enthusiasm; the economist Pitrim Brutskoi; Karsin the lexicographer; Olga-Marya Rapp, novelist of the woman's condition; the historians Sitzenvaldt and Polon; Likht the architect and tiny birdlike Yudifa Yudifovna, one-time editor of the short-lived *New Tomorrows Review*. Wives and husbands and lovers are crammed into the room too, squeezing onto sofas, propping cushions on the floor. Here are all the members of Forshin's odd ad-hoc league of the self-exiled and self-appointed intelligentsia, withdrawn into obscurity when the air of the Writers and Artists Union began to chill against them. One by one they got out before the cycle of denunciation, ostracism and arrest got an unbreakable grip. Forshin recruited them. Encouraged them. Gathered them in. Told them they were awaiting better times. At Forshin's dacha they could work and write and plan. There were schemes and journals to be prepared for publication when the wheel turned.

All are thin now, gaunt, their clothes worn thin and polished with age and overuse.

We are the last of the last of the cultured generation, Forshin had said to each of them tête-à-tête over tea and petit-beurre biscuits in a quiet corner of the Union. *Confronted by horrors on such a scale, such a massiveness and totality of alien attitude, our cultured souls can have no response. There is no place for us here. We are numbed. We are enfeebled. We are without resources. We are exiled from the world itself. Our own country no longer exists, so we must learn to breathe in a vacuum and float three feet above the earth. We must withdraw from the world and wait for other times, until the call comes – as one day it will – for us to return.*

But now – this very day – that call has come. So Forshin believes. Pacing in front of the mantelpiece he reads to them once more extracts from Pinocharsky's momentous letter.

'*Come back to the capital, Nikolai! The times are changing, and much for the better. Now is the moment for the Philosophy League to step into the light.*'

Pinocharsky told in his letter how Rizhin himself had commissioned him to found a great new institution, the House of Enlightened Arts!

'*We are to have our own new building,*' Pinocharsky wrote. '*A splendid and beautiful place. A true monument of modernity! The plans are already drawn. I have seen them, Nikolai! Rizhin himself had a model before him on his desk when he spoke to me. Oh, you should have heard him speak, Nikolai. He is a surprisingly cultured man. Not crude at all. He speaks our language. I did not expect this at all. I remember his exact words. "Get me writers, Pinocharsky!" That's what Rizhin said to me. "Get me musicians. Artists. Intellectuals. Build me a palace of culture. What we need now is people who will look at life clearly and show us its truth. Intellectuals will produce the goods we require most of all. Even more than power plants and airplanes and factories, we must forge strong new human souls."*

'I must confess I was reserved at first. I played my cards close to my chest, as you can imagine. Factories are important too, I said wisely. But Rizhin leaned towards me and touched my arm. "I myself," he said, "I myself wrote verse in my youth. You doubt me but I did. I respect poetry. I respect art. I am myself a creative man. I am your brother and your friend."

'I declare, Nikolai, that Papa Rizhin had tears in his eyes! "Do you mean this?" I said to him. (I wanted him to see I was a canny operator. A fellow with something about me.) "Let there be an amnesty," that's what Rizhin said then. "A great homecoming welcome for our finest minds, and past disagreements forgotten: that was then, this is now; we had to be tough, but now it is time to be kind."'

Forshin finishes reading the great letter aloud, stuffs it in the pocket of his jacket with a flourish and pauses to light his pipe.

'And there you have it, friends,' he says, effortless powerful voice booming. 'We have no choice; our duty is clear. Our country and our people need us now and so we must return to Mirgorod. And the call has come none too soon, for frankly the conditions here are worsening. Belatinsk is no longer safe for us.'

'I agree,' says Brutskoi. 'We can do more for Belatinsk in Mirgorod than here. We can speak up for the provinces in the capital. We can protest against the inefficiency of this neglect.'

'Indeed,' says Forshin. 'If Pinocharsky is right, we will have the ear of Rizhin himself.'

'Colleagues,' says the miniature, frail Yudifa Yudifovna quietly, 'I cannot believe you are falling for this transparent shit. Do you not know a trap when you see one?'

'No, no, Yudifa!' Forshin protests. 'This is no trap. What about that speech of Gzowski's that Pinocharsky enclosed?' He quotes a part of Gzowski's speech from memory. *'We are in danger of destroying the spiritual capital of our people. We risk breeding a new crop of brutal and corrupt bureaucrats and a terrible new generation of cruel and lumpen youth. The New Vlast needs poetry and culture and art fit for our great aspirations. The people themselves call for it.* Such words could never have been printed without sanction from the very top. It's is as if

Rizhin himself had spoken directly in public to us. This is no trap. This is enlightenment.'

'Well I'm too old to fall for that crap again,' says Yudifovna. 'I'd rather take my chances here with a temporary shortage of beans than risk ending up in a VKBD cell. I've been there already. I'll wait here and see how you get on.'

'I think Yudifa is right,' says Sitzenvaldt. 'Pinocharsky is overexcited and misled. What he describes will never be permitted. We should stick together. If you leave us here we are too few to defend ourselves, and I for one know nothing of chickens.'

'But how much longer do you think we can hold out here?' says Polon. 'One day the mob from Belatinsk will come for us, and what can people like us do then? We cannot fight.'

'These shortages are a natural corrective mechanism,' says Pitrim Brutskoi. 'There will be a rebalancing before too long, you'll see. The human soul is basically sound, and economic society is naturally efficient. I'm sure our fellows in Belatinsk will sort themselves out soon enough: all they need is systematic collective organisation.'

'Well I've had enough of hiding in the country!' cries Olga-Marya Rapp. 'Personal safety is secondary. We must see what is happening and write about it. My duty as an artist requires me to share whatever faces the women of the capital and report on it fearlessly!'

'Are there no women in Belatinsk?' mutters Yudifovna. 'Is what's happening here not worth writing of?' But only Kamilova hears her.

And so, to Forshin's dismay, the League divides. Some are for Mirgorod, and some are for staying at the dacha and waiting out the famine.

'And what about you, Eligiya Kamilova?' says Forshin at the end. 'Will you and the girls come with us to Mirgorod? Surely you will? You'd be safe with us. You'd be travelling under the protection of the League.'

Kamilova hesitates.

'All we want to do is go home to Mirgorod, Nikolai,' she says, 'only we cannot afford the tickets.'

Yudifa Yudifovna leans across and puts a hand on Kamilova's arm.

'How much do you need, Eligiya?' she says.

'Ninety roubles. But—'

'I will give you all of that,' says Yudifovna. 'I'll give you a hundred if you will sell me your gun.'

5

Lom spent a broken night between unclean sheets in his room in the Pension Forbat overlooking the Wieland Station and rose late and ill slept to the news that Papa Rizhin had survived the attempt on his life. He stared at the newspaper headline blankly, too stupid-tired and slow to take it in. His mind was still stuck with the noise of night trains shunting. The clank of points and signals. The echo of klaxons. Porters calling. An arc light splashing bone-sharp shadow across his wall. The empty wardrobe with the door that wouldn't close.

Unshaven and only half awake he went out into the morning and bought black coffee and cigarettes in a railway workers' café-bar on the corner by the pension. Laid the paper out on the table in front of him. Lit a cigarette with a cardboard match from a match book on the bar marked LOCOMOTIVE STAR. The unaccustomed smoke tasted bad and caught in his throat. His chest clenched. He ground the unfinished cigarette into the ashtray and lit another. Scooped sticky sugar into his coffee and swallowed the whole cup to take the taste away. Got another. That was breakfast.

The paper still said the same thing, which wasn't much. Some minister for agriculture was dead and Rizhin was not. There was a photograph of Rizhin at his desk and in command, a wad of cotton stuck on where the bullet had grazed his face. Rizhin glared straight into the camera, purposeful, confident. Burning with determination undimmed. No day's work lost for the man they couldn't kill. Lom felt that the picture was meant for him personally: the dark energy of Rizhin's gaze locked eyes with him. It was a challenge. *See what I am? See what I can do? Did you think I could be stopped? Then think again. What's it like to be alone?*

Lom got a third coffee.

In the sleepless watches of the night he'd lit the dim bedside lamp and read again the official biography of Osip Rizhin. There was a copy in every guest house, pension and hotel room across the whole of the New Vlast. It went with the head-and-shoulders portrait on the wall. In the night the book had been an obituary, the shadowed Rizhin face above the dresser a funerary mask, but in the morning the man had climbed out of his grave, fresh and ready for the day.

You couldn't kill a man who wasn't there.

When Lom read the biography of Rizhin, what he saw was nothing. Gaps. Elisions. Lacunae. Imprecision covering emptiness. The testimony of witnesses who were not there. It was a life that had not happened. All the hardness and roaring industrious speed of Mirgorod and the New Vlast were a tissue of words laid across nothing at all.

And two other simple words, one name spoken out loud, a double trochee on a single breath of air – *JO-sef KAN-tor* – would scatter the whole construction and blow it all away.

Don't kill him, Maroussia had said. *Bring him down. Destroy the idea of him. Ruin him in this world, using the tricks of this world, and ruin this world he has created.*

For centuries the Vlast had wiped histories away. The stroke of a bureaucrat's pen created unpersons out of lives and made ruined former people the unseen, unheard haunters of their own streets.

So there it was.

Turn the weapon on the wielder of it. One name spoken would turn Osip Rizhin into another empty unperson.

JO-sef KAN-tor.

Lom's heart was beating faster. He shifted in his seat with excitement. He wanted to be moving again. He had seen the way. He could do that, and he would.

What was needed was proof.

6

President-Commander Osip Rizhin had at his disposal the entire security machinery of the New Vlast. Two million police and militia men and women, their agents and informers and surveillance systems. Interrogators, analysts, collectors and sifters of intelligence. Torturers, assassins and spies. Rizhin had all of that, but trusted none of them because he of all people knew what kind of thing they were, and knew they must themselves be watched and kept in fear.

And so Rizhin had created the Parallel Sector. The Black Guard. The Streltski.

The Director of the Parallel Sector was Hunder Rond, and Rond was Rizhin's man. Narrow-shouldered and diminutive, Rond had the cropped grey hair and brisk featureless competence of a senior bank official. In the brief civil war against Fohn and his crew, Rond – then a colonel of militia – had shown himself assiduously and unflamboyantly effective as an eliminator of the less-than-committed within Rizhin's own camp. As an interrogator he was imaginatively destructive. He had certain private desires (which he gratified) that Rizhin disliked and documented, but in Rond he overlooked them. He needed someone, and Hunder Rond met the requirement as no one else. When Rond entered a room he brought darkness with him.

'Keep that doctor locked up for now,' Rizhin told Rond. 'I want no blabbing from him.'

(Did Rizhin trust Hunder Rond? He did not. But he was sure Rond had no involvement in yesterday's sniper attack. Rond had no friends, no allies because Rond hurt everyone – Rizhin made sure of that. Rond had no independent means of support and wouldn't survive a week with Rizhin gone. Rond would not have tried to cut off the branch he sat on.)

'Grigor Ekel's outside,' said Rond. 'He's been sitting there for two hours in a pool of his own piss and sweat. As secretary for security he is *most distraught* at this failure on the part of others outside his control. He wishes to abase himself and name the negligent.'

'Have the fucker sent away,' said Rizhin. 'Tell him he's lucky he's not already under arrest. And tell him he's got better things to do than lick my arse. Like find the fucker who shot me.'

Rond nodded. If he noticed that Rizhin spoke more slowly and emphatically than normal, through swollen lips that barely moved – if he observed Rizhin's tunic soaked with blood, Rizhin's face half-hidden under bandages, the slight tremor in Rizhin's right hand – then Rond gave no sign. He was reassuring efficiency, only there to serve.

'And there has been nothing?' Rizhin was saying. 'No further moves? No claims of responsibility?'

'Nothing,' said Rond. 'Nobody seems to have been prepared for this. Everybody is watching everybody else and waiting to see what happens. The situation is drifting. Perhaps we should make a public statement? You could make an appearance. Reassert control. Vacuum is the greater risk now. Nerves are shot. We need to worry about the whole continent, not just Mirgorod.'

'Not yet,' said Rizhin. 'Keep it vague a few more hours. And watch. Someone may still make a move.'

Rond made a face.

'I think the time for that's gone,' he said. 'We'd have seen something by now. The more time passes, the more likely it is that this was a lone wolf.'

Rizhin looked at him sharply.

'A *wolf*? You say a *wolf*?'

'Someone working alone,' said Rond. 'A grudge. A fanatic. A private venture. It was always a possibility. It's the hardest threat to see coming and protect against.'

'Nothing comes from nowhere,' said Rizhin. 'I want to know who did this, Rond. Find the shooter. Find them all. I want them disembowelled. I want them swinging in the wind and screaming to be let die.'

7

Lom passed the morning in a ProVlastKult reading room among stacks of newspapers six years old. The whole of the story was there if you knew how to read it.

There was the assault on Secetary Dukhonin's residence in Pir-Anghelsky Park: Dukhonin and all his household butchered by a terrorist gang who then themselves all died at the hands of the militia, including their leader the notorious agitator Josef Kantor. The papers gave a surprisingly full account of Kantor's history: his involvement with the Birzel plot; his twenty-year confinement in the labour camp at Vig; his death in a hail of bullets as he tried to escape the Pir-Anghelsky charnel house. There was no photograph of Kantor though, not even a prison mug shot. Of course there wasn't.

And then the very next day after Dukhonin's death, the Archipelago bombers had come for the first time and Mirgorod began to burn. The government withdrew and it seemed the city would quickly fall. But there was Colonel-General Osip Rizhin, suddenly come from nowhere, an unknown name (there were no prior references in the index, none at all) to lead the city's defence. To stem the enemy advance and hold the siege. To conjure out of nowhere atomic artillery shells, a whole new way of killing, and turn the tide. Step forward Papa Rizhin, father and begetter of a new and better Vlast. *Times are better now, citizens.*

What Rizhin stood for was never made clear. If there were principles they were not spoken of. It was all about racing ahead. Dynamism. Taking the future in hand. A fresh beginning. Victory and peace and a bright widening tomorrow. *Papa Rizhin works on the people*, an editorial read, *as a chemist works in his laboratory. He builds with us, as an engineer builds a great bridge.*

In the early weeks and months after Rizhin's first appearance in the world the papers had carried vague and inconsistent accounts of who he was and where he'd come from. Stories came and went, made little sense and did not stick until the publication of the little pamphlet *An Account of the Life of Osip Rizhin, Hero of Mirgorod, Father of the New Vlast.* Ten million copies of a little book of lies.

But who knew the truth? Hundreds must have known. Thousands. People who would have seen the portraits of Osip Rizhin and recognised Josef Kantor. For a start there would be those who knew him from his childhood among the families of Lezarye. Lom turned cold. He went back to the newspapers from the first days of the siege and read again a passage he had seen there. The whole of the Raion Lezaryet had been cleared and every last person of Lezarye 'relocated in the east'. There was no reference to Lezarye in the journal index after that. No account of the place or its people ever again. He felt dizzy. Sick.

Of course there would have been others who could identify Kantor as Rizhin. Fellow inmates in the camp at Vig, for a start. But how easy it would be to reach out from Mirgorod and silence them if you had already removed an entire city quarter.

Josef Kantor knew who knew him, and Osip Rizhin could kill them all.

Lom went through the list in his mind. Under-Secretary Krogh (who knew because Lom had told him) was dead: his obituary was there in the paper, a eulogy to a lifetime's service cut short by heart failure in his office a week before war came to Mirgorod. Raku Vishnik was dead. Lavrentina Chazia was dead (not killed by Kantor because Lom had saved him that trouble). Kantor's wife, Maroussia's mother, was dead: Lom had seen her shot down in the street in front of him. They had come to kill Maroussia herself more than once. And they had tried to kill him, Lom, as well.

Who else? Who else? Was there anyone left at all, apart from Maroussia and himself, who had been so comprehensively lost to view that Rizhin could not find them?

Lom racked his brain. There was one more face he remembered, a wild-eyed prophet of the new arts, standing green shirt half unbuttoned in the rain in the alley outside the Crimson Marmot. The painter Lakoba Petrov. He knew Josef Kantor. He was one of Kantor's gang. *Kantor the crab*, Petrov had called him. *Josef Krebs. Josef Cancer. Nothing but shell, shell, and lidless eyes on little stalks staring out of it, like a crab.* Lom remembered Petrov swaying drunk in the red glow of the Marmot's sign, oblivious of the rain in his face. *And shall I tell you something else about him?* Petrov had said, speaking very slowly and clearly. *He has some other purpose which is not apparent.*

Lom went back to the index and searched for Lakoba Petrov, painter.

For the second time he turned cold. Sick and dizzy with disbelief. Following a couple of references to reviews of Petrov's paintings, there was one last entry: 'Petrov, Lakoba: assassination of the Novozhd; death of.' Petrov had blown himself up and taken the Novozhd with him. The papers presented it as some mad kind of anarchist artwork, the ultimate product of a degenerate corrupted mind. But Petrov's act had paved the way for Chazia, and ultimately Kantor, to seize the Vlast, and Petrov was Kantor's man.

Lom ripped the page from the newspaper, stuffed it in his pocket and walked out of the library in a daze. Sat on the steps in the early-afternoon sunshine and lit a cigarette. There were still a couple left in the packet.

The story was there in the archive to be read if you knew what to look for, but everyone who could have known even part of it … Papa Rizhin had raked the Vlast with a lice comb and killed them all, every one, as he would kill anyone who came forward with a rumour or began to ask around. There was no proof. And what would proof look like anyway? What were the chances of finding a police file with Josef

Kantor's photograph and fingerprints neatly tagged and docketed?

But there had once been such a file. Lom had held it in his own hands. He'd stolen it from Chazia's personal archive in the Lodka: the file that contained Chazia's account of her recruitment of Kantor as an informant and conspirator, and of her contact with the living angel in the forest. That file was proof enough to bring Rizhin down. But it was gone. Lom remembered how he'd left it hidden in the cistern in the bathroom of Vishnik's apartment, but he knew the militia had searched the building when they killed Vishnik. *They looked all over*, the dvornik had told him. *The halls. The stairwell. The bathroom. They pulled the cistern off the wall.*

That surely meant they had found it, and the file was gone. But it had gone *somewhere*. Where? Back to Chazia presumably. The efficient paper handling of the old regime.

It came back to him now. There had in fact been two files in the folder he hid in the cistern: Chazia's folder on Josef Kantor, and Lom's own personnel record, which he'd also lifted from Chazia's archive and brought away to read. Lom remembered the manuscript note on the second file from Krogh's traitorous private secretary, who'd extracted it from Krogh's office and passed it to Chazia.

Lom felt a sudden waking of excitement and hope. The private secretary. He was Chazia's man, and he'd known something, perhaps a lot. He'd certainly known all about Lom's mission to track down Kantor. But Kantor almost certainly would not have known about him.

Lom could still see the private secretary's face.

His name? What was his name?

It was there somewhere, neatly lodged away in his long-unused policeman's brain.

Find it. Find it.

Pavel!

Pavel. First name only, but it might be enough.

Lom raced back up the steps and into the library again. In the reference section next to the newspaper index he'd seen the long rows of annual volumes of the *Administrative Gazette Yearbook*, which among much other turgid information listed the ministers and senior officials of the Vlast. Including details of their private offices. Heart pounding, Lom pulled down the volume of the *Gazette* he needed and flipped through the pages until he found the one he needed. And there it was, in small italic typeface under the name of Krogh himself: '*Private Secretary: Antimos, Pavel Ilich*'.

It was a lot to hope that Pavel Antimos had survived: survived the siege, survived the war, survived Rizhin's lice comb; survived it all and continued to work for the government of the New Vlast. A lot to hope for but perhaps not too much. Men like Pavel did survive. They even kept their jobs. He might still be there.

The long unbroken run of the *Administrative Gazette Yearbook* had gold lettering on blue spines fading to grey as the years receded to the left. Tucked in at the right-hand end of the last shelf were five volumes with the same gold lettering, but the spines were green and shining new. *Administrative Gazette Yearbook, New Series*. Lom took the last one, the most recent volume. Antimos, Pavel Ilich had not only survived but his career had flourished. He was an under-secretary now, in the Office for Progressive Cultural Enlightenment, with a private secretary of his own.

Lom didn't want to approach him in his office. Better to do it in the evening, at home. Pushing his winning streak for one last throw, he scouted around for a Mirgorod residential telephone directory. He found it. And Pavel Antimos was in it. Lom memorised the address. It was a tenuous lead but the only one he had.

Pull on a thread. See where it takes me.

Just like the old days.

8

Maroussia Shaumian feels small beyond insignificance. The trees spread around her in all directions, numberless, featureless and utterly bleak. A still, engulfing, unending tide of blankness. The skin between her and the forest is permeable: she wants to spill out into it, a scent cloud dispersing under the branch-head canopy. The forest tugs and nags at the edges of her. Pieces of her snag on the trees and pull free.

She is walking again. Walking.

When it rains the rain clags the mud and makes the forest hiss and whisper. Mud clumps and drags and weighs on her boots. Every time it rains the rain gets colder and there are fewer leaves on the trees. Winter seems coming too soon, but she has boots and blankets and she will be OK.

Towards the end of the day she finds a dry rise of ground and a heavy oak tree, half fallen, its root mass torn from the earth. With her axe she hacks off some branches, props them against the fallen tree's side and weaves thinner stem-lengths through to make strong, shallow, sloping walls. When the walls are solid she heaps leaves on top, pile on pile, until it swells, a natural earthy rising of the ground, skinned with leaves an arm's length deep, at one end a low dark mouth. She rests another layer of branches across the outside, for the weight of them, to hold the leaves in place, and crawls inside, dragging more leaves after her, the driest she has found. Spreads them deep across the ground and packs the far end until she has a narrow earth-smelling tunnel scarcely wide enough to lie in. With more leaf-heavy branches she makes a door to pull in place behind her.

She works quickly but the light is failing.

The forest is too dark to see beyond the fire circle but she feels its presence. Trees rolling without end or limit, their roots under the earth all touching and knotting together, root whispering to root as branch brushes against branch. Connected, watchful, they merge and make one thing, the largest animal in the world. Night-waking. Watchful. It knows she is there.

There are stars in the gaps between branches, and a deeper purple-green shining blackness.

Maroussia crawls into the enclosing darkness of her leaf-and-branch cocoon. Her hiding, her little burial, her dream time, her forgetting. Deep beneath her in the earth the fine tangled roots sift and slide and touch each other. They whisper.

The shelter has its own quiet whispering too, a barely audible shifting and settling, the outer layer flickering and feathering in the night breeze. She hears the rustle and tick of small things – woodlice, spiders, mice – burrowing in the canopy. The shelter absorbs her, mothering, nurturing. Hiding her away.

The blanket is wrapped tight around her, rough against her face. Knees pulled up tight against her belly, feet pressed against the solid weight of her pack, head pillowed on her arms, she breathes with her mouth, shallow, slow breaths. Breathing the warmth of her own breath. The smell of leaves and earth and moss. Woodsmoke in the blanket and in her clothes and hair.

This isn't right. This isn't what I meant at all.

She is a rim of troubled consciousness encircling immensities without and immensities within. Sustaining it hurts. Her fragility and capacity for fracture terrify her.

A hand of fear in the darkness covers her face so it is hard to breathe. Fear grasps her heart inside her chest and squeezes out breath. Everything inside her is tight. Tight like wires. The trees she cannot see in the night prickle with the same fear. She wants to dig herself into the ground and be buried.

One break and I could lose myself for ever.

The Pollandore speaks its presence softly all the time, a voice inside her that sounds like it is outside, whispering dangerous promises. It swells and grows. The spaces inside her are as measureless as the forest and less human. Maroussia-Pollandore holds the green wall shut: the forest is withdrawn from its borders and does not leak. It holds no traffic with the human world, not any more. She feels the human world grow hard and quick and dying, and she is the engine of that. She is the separation and the holding back. She is the border patrol.

I wanted the opposite of this. I chose to open the world not close it. This is not me. My name is Maroussia Shaumian. When the angel in the forest is gone, then I can go home.

All she has to do is keep on walking. Keep it clear and simple, that is all she has to do. Be hard and strong and clever, and somehow she will keep the darkness from her. Somehow she will do that.

Trees in the forest walk, but slowly, year by year. Inching.

She will outrun them yet.

9

Lom had never heard birdsong in Mirgorod before. Never smelled new-cut lawn.

The lindens on the street where Pavel Ilich Antimos lived must have been planted fully grown. The fragrant asphalt, the raked gravel, the clipped laurels, they were all fresh out of the box, but those late-afternoon-sun-kindled shade-breathing linden trees would have taken fifty years to reach the height they were. They cast a kind of quiet privacy over Voronetsin Heights that made you feel like an intruder, just being in the road.

Atom House, the residence of Pavel Ilich Antimos, was a low-rise apartment building in walled grounds. A pleasant low-key fortress. The gate in the wall was wrought iron, painted to a gleam like broken coal. Lom watched the block for fifteen minutes. He saw domestic staff and deliveries checking in and out; wives coming back from shopping; children being driven home from school. The gate opened for them and closed behind them, and no way was the woman in the kiosk going to open that gate, not unless she knew you or you had an appointment and you were in her book.

Thus lived the List – the managers, the lawyers, the officials, the financiers and architects and engineers of Rizhin Land – spending different currency in different stores.

Lom went round the corner out of sight of the kiosk, jumped to hook his fingers on the coping ridge, hauled himself up till he could scrabble over the wall and dropped on the other side. The soft earth of a rose bed. A quiet formal garden in the slanting sun.

Pavel's apartment was at the end of a short corridor, top floor back. It felt like an afterthought in the building. Single occupancy, one of the less expensive units, not a family home. Lom hoped so. He didn't want to find Pavel's wife at home. Or children. That would complicate things. The only other door in the passage was a cleaner's storeroom. Lom checked it. Empty. Smelling of bleach and musty mops.

He knocked on Pavel's door, brisk and businesslike. The door felt solid. His knocking sounded dull and didn't carry. There was no bell push.

He knocked again.

'Hi!' he called. 'Residence Antimos! Is someone at home? Open please!'

Nobody came. No matter how long he stared at it, the door stayed shut. It had a solid Levitan deadbolt lock, heavier than was normal for domestic use and fitted upside down to make it more awkward to pick.

Lom had spent his time productively since leaving the ProVlastKult library that morning. From a dusty shop by the Wieland Station (broken clocks and watches on velvet pads in the window) he'd bought a basic lock-picking kit: a C-rake, a tension wrench and short hook, all wrapped in a convenient canvas roll. He'd also acquired a neat small black rubber cosh in a silk sheath, with a plaited cord lanyard. The cosh was expensive but the proprietor sewed an extra pocket for him in his jacket sleeve. No extra cost. You had to know how to ask.

He popped the Levitan deadbolt without too much trouble. The door was solid hardwood a couple of inches thick. It took weight to open it.

'Hi,' he called again quietly. 'Pavel, old friend? Are you there?'

The place was cool and dim and still and obviously empty. Lom stepped inside, pulled the door shut behind him and relocked it. On the inside it was fitted with two heavy bolts and a chain. Lom looked around. It was a single man's apartment: kitchen, bathroom, sitting room with one armchair and a desk, a bedroom with a single bed. Pavel didn't get many visitors obviously. Didn't seem to spend much time at home at all.

Lom moved from room to room. Everything was neat. Possessions carefully put away. There was a phonogram cabinet in the sitting room, the lid closed. A shelf of recordings arranged in alphabetical order of composer. On a low glass-topped table with splayed tapering legs Pavel had stacked some literary magazines – *New Cosmos*, *The Forward View* – and three days' worth of newspapers, crisply folded. In the bedroom there were books, also carefully arranged, the spines unbroken, on a low shelf under the window. The food in the kitchen was brightly coloured packages and tins – fruit juice, condensed milk, rye bread, caviar – all high quality List Shop brands.

There was something about Pavel's apartment that was odd. It took

Lom a moment to realise what it was. Nothing in the whole place was personal: nothing was old or well used or could possibly have had sentimental value. The pressed dark suits, the careful ties, the white shirts folded in drawers, the carpets, the curtains, the coverlet on the bed, the gramophone recordings of new composers singled out for favour by the Academy of Transformational Artistic Production (chairman, Osip Rizhin). Pavel had kept nothing that was made before the inception of the New Vlast. Nothing that deviated from post-war cultural norms. Pavel had accepted Rizhin's world utterly, immersed himself in it, acquired with the obsessiveness of a connoisseur the top-rank artefacts of its material culture and surrounded himself with them. This was the apartment of an exemplary fellow, New Vlast Man to the core, from whose life all vestiges of the past had been removed with surgical thoroughness. Pavel was a chameleon, a caddis fly. He raised the art of blending in to new pinnacles of ruthless ostentation.

In a drawer of Pavel's desk Lom found a travel agent's confirmation of a booking for one – two weeks at the Tyaroga Resort Hotel on the Chernomorskoy Sea, single-berth rail sleeper included. He also found a carton of small-calibre shells and a diminutive pistol. A Deineka 5-shot Personal Defender. It looked like it had never been fired.

Lom loaded the gun, slipped a round into the chamber and put it in his pocket. Then he went into the kitchen, opened a packet of Pavel's Oksetian Sunrise coffee, filled Pavel's coffee pot and put it on Pavel's stove. When the pot hissed and bubbled he poured himself a cup, picked up a book from the kitchen counter and went back into the other room to wait for Pavel to come home. The window was slightly open, letting in a stir of warm early-evening air. The quiet sound of distant traffic. Liquid blackbird song.

The book from Pavel's kitchen was the Mikoyan Institute's *Home Course of Delicious and Healthy Food*. Lom flicked through the pages to pass the time. Monochrome photographic plates displayed smiling family faces and crowded tables: meat loaf canapés filled with piped mayonnaise; bottles of sparkling Vlastskoye Sekt wine and shining crystal goblets; a platter of pike in aspic decorated with radish rosettes. There were recipes for crab and cucumber salad; vinaigrette of beetroot, cabbage and red potato; crunchy pork cutlets; mutton aubergine claypot. Papa Rizhin himself had provided a foreword. 'The special character of our New Vlast,' it began, 'is the joyousness of our prosperous and cultured style of life.' There were no grease spots on the herb-green cloth binding. No spills. No stuck-together pages. Pavel didn't have any favourite recipes then. Pavel Ilich Antimos would eat them all with equal relish. *Anything that Papa Rizhin recommends.* Lom looked at his watch. It was well past six o'clock. He hoped Pavel wasn't working late or dining out.

Lom got another coffee and occupied himself with the pictures on Pavel's walls. The pictures people put on their walls told you as much about them as their books – more, because they were meant to be seen. *This is what I like. This is my mind. This is who you should think I am.* Pavel's visual world was framed prints advertising exhibitions of art promoted by the Office for Progressive Cultural Enlightenment. He'd probably picked them up free at work. There was a jewel-bright painting of a Mirgorod Airways Skyliner over snow-capped mountains. Dancers in a town square. The storm-beset factory ship VV *Karamazov* riding glass-green churning foam-flecked waters under a purple thunder-riven sky (*Recall Our Heroic Sailors of the Merchant Marine!*). Pride of place went to a large colourised photograph of the Vlast Universal Vessel *Proof of Concept* climbing on a column of fire into a cloud-wisped sky.

Three hours later it was getting dark outside when Pavel Antimos let himself into his own apartment with his own key. Lom heard him lock the door behind him, drive the bolts home top and bottom, safe and sound, and hook the chain in place for the night. He let Pavel find him in the sitting room. In his armchair. Reading his books. Drinking his coffee. From his mug.

'Pavel,' he said, 'it's been too long, old friend. How're you doing? Working late tonight? You're looking well. You haven't changed.'

And Pavel hadn't changed, hardly at all. Some thickening at the neck and shoulders, maybe. A suggestion of jowl under the chin. A darkening around the eyes, the pallor of long office days.

He blinked. But only once.

'You,' he said. 'You're Lom.'

'You remembered.'

'I'm efficient. What do you want?'

Lom saw his eyes flick to the desk. To the drawer left open where the gun had been. A small loss of hope. You had to know it was there to see it.

'I want a talk,' said Lom. 'About Josef Kantor.'

Pavel's eyes widened. Not so missable this time.

'Who?'

'Please don't spoil it,' said Lom, 'the memory thing. Let's talk Papa and Joe. The Rizhin–Kantor nexus. Identities.'

'You're insane.'

'He never knew about you, did he?' said Lom. 'You were never on his list. You've been lucky. It's been a long time now, and you're in the clear unless somebody mentions you to him. An anonymous note would be enough; a phone call would be better. He might even remember your name then, and if he didn't he might check it out, but probably he wouldn't bother. It wouldn't make any difference. He'd err on the safe side. That would be bad for you. And I can make that happen, Pavel. Maybe I will.'

Pavel didn't flinch. No bluster. No threats. No visible emotion of any kind. He absorbed the position and adapted to it. Instantly. It was a masterclass in how to survive.

'This is wasting time,' he said. 'I understand you perfectly. You have information dangerous to me, and you come to my home to threaten me because you want something in return for your silence. I do not like this but I accept the inevitability of it. Well, I am listening. So what do you want?'

'I want proof,' said Lom. 'I know that Rizhin is Kantor, but I want evidence. Photographs. Police files. Intelligence reports. Identification.'

'Like I said, you're insane,' said Pavel. 'You really are. Fortunately for both of us, what you're asking for is impossible. The Lodka archive is long gone. Most of it was burned when the Archipelago came, before the siege.'

'Only most of it?' said Lom.

'Some papers were sent to Kholvatogorsk, but Rizhin has been there. He's been everywhere. You won't find any files on Josef Kantor; they're all gone, and everybody who might have dealt with such information is dead or disappeared into a labour camp.'

'Has he been to Vig too?' said Lom. 'The courts? Provincial stations?

There must have been a lot of paper on Kantor. A lot of people who would recognise his face.'

'All of it,' said Pavel. 'He's been everywhere, you can be sure of that. He's a thorough man.'

'Even Chazia's personal archive?' said Lom.

Pavel missed a beat. 'What?'

'Chazia had her own private papers,' said Lom. 'She kept them in a room in the Central Registry. I saw them. And they wouldn't have been burned or shipped off to Kholvatogorsk. No way. Chazia would have made arrangements to keep them separate and safe.'

'I know nothing about this,' said Pavel.

'Don't you?' said Lom. 'Well you should. Chazia had papers there with your name on, Pavel. Papers that you passed to her from Krogh's office, including papers about me and how Krogh wanted me to find Kantor. I saw them, Pavel, and you don't want Rizhin finding them, do you?'

Pavel sat down. He looked suddenly diminished.

'What do you want from me?' he said.

'I want the same thing you want for yourself. I want you to retrieve those papers.'

'For fuck's sake!'

'I'll tell you what you're going to do, Pavel. You're going to find out what happened to Chazia's archive, then you're going to find it and you're going to get the file on Kantor from it and bring it to me. It's there. I've read it. What you do with the rest is up to you.'

'What if I can't do this?' said Pavel. 'The archive could have been lost or destroyed by now. And even if it still exists, who will know where it is? I can hardly ask.'

Lom shrugged.

'I don't care how you do it. These are your problems, not mine. They're administrative problems, the kind you're good at solving. If you bring me the Kantor file, you won't hear from me again. If not, well ... I don't like you, Pavel. I don't like the kind of person you are, and I remember how you pissed me about when I was working for Krogh. I'm not your friend.'

'Look,' said Pavel, 'OK. I'll try to find it, but it may not—'

'I'm not interested in intentions,' said Lom. 'Only outcomes. I'll come back for it this time tomorrow. Have it ready.'

'No,' said Pavel. 'One day isn't enough. And you are not to come to my home again. Not ever again.'

'Two days then,' said Lom. 'But no more.'

Pavel nodded. He looked sick.

'There's a konditorei on the lake in Kerensky Gardens,' he said. 'If I can get what you want, I'll be there. I will arrive at 10 p.m. and I will wait till eleven.'

10

Night in the city, and Mirgorod celebrates the survival of Papa Rizhin the unkillable man. Lamps project the immense face of Rizhin all ruby-red against the underbelly of broken scudding cloud. Moon-gapped, star-gapped, streaming, he fills a quarter of the sky and floods the city with dim reflected redness.

In the rebuilt Dreksler-Kino, Ziabin's greatest work, *The Glorification of Time Racing*, makes its triumphant premiere before an audience of twenty thousand. Oh, the ambition of Ziabin! Two thousand performers fusing music, dance and oratory! He will unify the arts! He will raise humankind to the radiant level! New instruments constructed for the occasion emit perfumes and effusions of vaporous colour in accordance with Ziabin's score, and the auditorium reverberates to wonderful sounds previously unheard. Towers and mountains rise from the floor and cosmonauts descend thunderous from the sky, waving and smiling as they join the chorus in polyphonic harmony. Across the enormous cinema screen roll images of Rizhin country against a backdrop of galaxies. And all in glorious colour! The roars of wonder of twenty thousand watchers echo across the city, new gasps of rapture in perfect time with the long under-rhythms of Ziabin's scheme. A synchronised crescendo every seventh wave.

Rizhin himself is there at the Dreksler-Kino, seated in a raised box. The wound on his face is agony but his chair is gilt, the walls of his box padded and buttoned velvet. *Like a brooch in a jeweller's box*, he says to Ziabin. It is not a remark intended to put the great artist at his ease. *Haven't we shot you yet?*

11

The Vlast Universal Vessel *Proof of Concept* tumbles slowly, describing twenty-thousand-mile-per-hour corkscrew ellipses of orbiting perpetual fall. The cosmonauts ride in silence, having nothing to do. Sweeps of shadow and light. Cabin windows crossing the sun. Nightside passages of broken moon. The internal lighting has failed.

The frost of their breath furs the ceiling thickly.

Hourly they flick the radio switch.

'Chaiganur? Hello, Chaiganur? Here is *Proof of Concept* calling.'

Universes of silence stare back from the loudspeaker grille.

In Mirgorod the twenty-foot likenesses of cosmonauts in bronze relief carry their space helms at the hip. In bright mosaic above the Wieland Station concourse they look skyward with chiselled confidence, grinning into star-swept purple. *Our Starfaring Heroes. Mankind Advances Towards the Radiant Sun.*

On the giant screen in the Dreksler-Kino wobbling smoky rockets descend among rocks and oceans out of strange skies. Bubble-cabin tractors till the extraplanetary soil, building barracks for pioneers. The audience roars and stamps its forty thousand feet. All children know their names from the illustrated magazines.

Our Future Among the Galaxies.

The Vlast Universal Vessel *Proof of Concept,* two-thousand-ton extraplanetary submarine, makes a shining white mote against the nightly backdrop of the stars. It slides on smooth invisible rails across the sky. You can set your clock by it. It is clean and beautiful and very sad.

Silent the cosmonauts, eyes wide and dark-adapted, having nothing to do.

The turning of the cabin windows pans slowly across vectors of the lost planet, blue-rimmed, beclouded, oceanic. Shadow-side campfire towns and cities glitter. Ant jewels. The shrouded green-river-veined darkness of forest. Lakes are yellow. Lakes are brown. The continent is a midriff between ice and ice. Glimpses of the offshore archipelago.

Complex geometries of turn bring the snub nose of the *Proof of Concept* round to face the world. It's a matter of timing. Her fingers stiff with cold and lack of use, Cosmonaut-Commodore Vera Mornova engages console mechanisms. The distant tinny echo of whirr and clunk. The magazine selects a charge.

Her companions observe unspeaking with heavy-lidded eyes and do not move.

'I'm going home now,' she says and pushes her thumb into the rubber of the detonation button.

The response is a distant bolt sliding home.

A half-second delay.

The tiny silent star-explosion of angel plasma smashes them in the small of the back. They do not blink.

Vera Mornova jabs her finger into the rubber button again and again.

Her aim is true. *Proof of Concept* surges forward into burning fall. The world in the window judders and bellies and swells.

The melting frost of their breath on the ceiling begins to fall on them like rain.

12

After leaving Pavel's apartment, Lom took a night walk on the Mir Embankment. The Mir still rolled on through the city, carrying silt and air and the remembering of lakes and trees, but it was silent now and just a river. Everything was hot and open under the Rizhin-stained sky. He didn't want to go home, not if home was a room in the Pension Forbat.

He was looking for something. Shadows and trails of what used to be. Old wild places where the forest still was. Giants and rusalkas and the dry ghosts of rain beasts in a wide cobbled square. There must be something left, something he could work with. But he was the only haunter of the new ruined city, caught between memory and forgetting, listening to the silence of dried waters. The city had turned its back on the Mir, and he was on the wrong side of the river.

In the very shadow of the Rizhin Tower, almost under the walls of the Lodka, he crossed into a small field of rubble. Mirgorod was aftermath city yet, and the heal-less residuum of war still came through. Stains under fresh plaster.

Lom stepped in among roofless blackened walls propped with baulks of timber. Night scents of wild herb and bramble. The smell of ash and rust and old wood slowly rotting. A grating in the gutter and running water down below – moss and mushroom and soft mud – the Yekaterina Canal paved over and gone underground.

Follow. Follow.

Gaps and small openings into blackness everywhere. Subterranea.

He kicks aside a fallen shop sign. CLOVER. BOOKS AND PERIODICALS.

Down he goes into old quiet tunnels and long-abandoned burrowings. There is no light down there, no lurid Rizhin glow, but he is Lom and needs no light to find his way.

Chapter Six

The sisters all had silent eyes
and all of them were beautiful.

Velimir Khlebnikov (1885–1922)

1

The Lodka, sealed up and abandoned by Papa Rizhin – New Vlast, new offices! Sky rise and modern! Concrete and steel and glass! – stands, a black stranded hulk on Victory Square, doors locked, lower windows barred and boarded, the silent and disregarded River Mir at its back. Papa Rizhin refuses to use it at all. *It is a mausoleum*, he says. *A stale reliquary. It stinks of typewriter ribbons and old secrets and the accrual of pensions. Four hundred years of conferences and paper shuffling and the dust of yesterday's police. Will you make me breathe the second-hand breath of unremembered under-secretaries? Titular counsellors who died long ago and took their polished trouser seats with them to the grave? Fuck you. I will not do it.*

And so the panels of angel flesh were removed from the Lodka's outer walls to be ground up for Khyrbysk Propellant, and the vast building itself – its innumerable rooms and unmappable corridors, its unaccountable geometry of lost staircases and entranceless atria open to the sky, its basement cells and killing rooms – was hastily cleared out and simply closed up and left.

Inside the Lodka now an autumnal atmosphere pervades, whatever the external season. Time is disrupted here, unforgetting and passing slow. Many windows are broken – shattered bomb-blast glass scattered on floors and desks – and weather comes in through opened oriels and domes. Paint is flaking off leadlights. In the reading room the great wheel of the Gaukh Engine stands motionless, canted two degrees off centre in its cradle by an Archipelago bomb that fell outside. Animals have taken up residence – acrid streaks and accumulations of bird shit – bats and cats and rats – but they do not penetrate more than the outermost layers, leaving undisturbed the interior depths of this hollowed-out measureless mountain. Only shadows and paper dust settle there, little moved by slow deep tides of scarcely shifting air.

In the inner core of the Lodka, unreached by traffic noise and the coming and going of days, the silence of disconnected telephones drifts along corridors and through open doorways, across linoleum, tile and carpet. Nowhere here is ever completely dark: bone moonlight sifts and trickles eventually through the smallest gaps. Dim noiselessness brushes against walls painted ivory and green and the panels of frosted glass in doors. Quietness drifts along empty shelving and settles like ocean sediment inside deed boxes, cubbyholes, lockers and filing cabinets, the drawers of desks. Chairs still stand where they were left, pushed back. Abandoned pens rest on half-finished notes and memoranda. Jackets hang on coat stands in corners. Spare shoes are stowed under cupboards. Muteness insinuates itself into the inner mechanisms of typewriters, decryption machines, opaline desk lamps and heating boilers. Tiny fragments of angel flesh, inert now, lie where they fell on workroom floors. Obscurity preserves in grey amber the strangely intimate and homely office world of government. The Lodka is an ungraspable archaeology of administration. Surveillance. Bureaucracy. Interrogation. Death. Suspended and timeless. An unfathomable edifice. A sanctuary. An abysm.

Vissarion Lom found his way into the abandoned Lodka by subterranean ways. Following passages till recently used by only the most secretive of confidential agents of the secret surveillance police, he crossed the barely tangible time-slow frontier into memorious residuum, and long hours he wandered there, a warm attentive ghost. There was endless freedom in the Lodka now. It was the one free place in Rizhin's new city. Free of everything but memories and a strange nostalgia for faded old oppression. It suited Lom better than the Pension Forbat.

But about one thing he was wrong.

The abandoned Lodka is not empty.

The vyrdalak sisters are light and fragile, almost weightless. They dress in brittle patchwork fabrics of subtle colour unlike anything in Rizhin world, and they have wide nocturnal lovely eyes. Inside them is very little body left at all. They are not of the forest but older and stranger than that.

Lom, entering the Lodka, spilling bright perfumed pheromone clouds of forestness all unawares, drew the hungry vyrdalak sisters to him like a warm candle flame.

'He's beautiful,' said Moth. 'I'd almost forgotten the good smell of trees.'

'But he stinks of angel also,' said Paper. 'Violence is coming back.'

'We should go to him,' said Pigeon. 'One of us must go.'

'Let it be me then,' said Moth. 'Let me. I will go.'

2

Under-Secretary Pavel Ilich Antimos had a natural talent for dealing with complex administration, matured by years of experience. He was subtle, clever, far-sighted, cautious and patient, and he grasped the elegant beauty inherent in meticulous precision and detail. He had been around a long time in large institutions and knew instinctively how to make his way.

Lom's appearance in his apartment had put Pavel in an uncomfortable place, caught between risk and risk. Through a long evening and sleepless night he weighed up options, measured the balance of danger and reward, and by the time he rose in the morning he had decided to do as Lom suggested. He would find the private Chazia archive. It was a dangerous project, but who could tackle it better than he could, and do it without attracting notice? He knew the ways of government offices: the harmless word in the corridor, the enquiry hidden inside the request, the flicker of reaction, the silent tell. The oblique and traceless passage through a filing list.

By the first afternoon Pavel was beginning to feel he was getting somewhere. There was a book of cancelled requisition slips in a box under a counter at the former address of the Ministry of Railways, a building located out towards the old Oxen Quarter and now occupied by an outpost of the Catering Procurement Branch. If certain papers were not there, if a certain circuit of communication had not been closed, he would be several steps nearer the missing archive, which he was increasingly certain did actually exist.

He made a good job of it, a brilliant job actually – Pavel Antimos was a genius at that kind of thing. But Hunder Rond was better, and Rond had had years to prepare, so Pavel had no way of knowing that, when he put in a chit for a particular registry number, a tag on the file triggered a clerk to marry a pink perforated slip with its other half and slide them both into a manila envelope addressed only to a box number. The arrival of the same envelope some hours later in a post room halfway across the city led to a telephone call, which led to another call, to the Parallel Sector, to the office of Hunder Rond.

'It could be nothing,' the caller said. 'A random coincidence.'

'We have anything on this Antimos?' said Rond.

'No. Nothing at all. He has an exemplary record.'

Rond took a decision.

'Let's pick him up,' he said. 'Collect him now.'

'Shall I talk to him?'

Rond looked at his watch.

'No,' he said. 'Leave him to me.'

And so, at the end of the day, when Pavel called in at the Catering Procurement Branch on his way home from work, two women in the black uniform of the Parallel Sector emerged from a side room and took him into custody with little fuss. Pavel showed no rage. He was not distraught. It was a moment he had prepared himself for, many years before, and when it happened he went along with them, numb and automatic. The only thing that really surprised him was how little his arrest actually mattered to him, now that it had finally come. He hated his life. He hated his apartment. He wouldn't miss anything at all.

'You don't need to hurt me,' Pavel said to Rond in the interrogation room. 'I will tell you anything you want. I will say whatever you ask me to say. Let me be useful to you. I help you, and you keep me alive. Yes?'

He was half right anyway. One out of two.

3

L om encountered the vyrdalak Moth in the reading room of the Central Registry. She came down silently, weightlessly, out of the moon-dim lattice, the glass-broken rust-scabbed ceiling dome, the strut and gondola shadows of the Gaukh Engine. (The Gaukh Wheel! Stationary and permanently benighted sun wheel, ministering idol of information now burned, ash-flake-scattered, released to rain.) Out of the wheel Moth came to him, face first, noiseless and beautiful. Her presence brushed across his face like settling night-pollen. Quiet vortices of neck-prickling wakefulness. She was young with the freshness of ageless moonlight. Youngness is the oldest thing there is.

Close she came and tipped at the air near his face with a quick dry tongue.

'You smell sweet,' she said, wide dark eyes shining. 'Foresty. Earth and trees.' Her sunless skin was warm, her wide mouth purple-dark. 'I'm Moth,' she said. 'Who are you?'

'My name's Vissarion.'

She sniffed.

'No, it isn't,' she said. 'What do you want?'

'I thought no one was here,' said Lom. 'The giants and rusalkas have left, the river's gone silent, but you're still here?'

'The forest is closed, but we're not of the forest. We've always been here.'

'We?'

'Three sisters, all nice girls. I'm the one that wanted to come. My sister Paper thinks you're dangerous, name's-not-Vissarion. She says you stink of angel like Lavrentina. I say you stink of angel like nothing else does now, but not like Lavrentina; you're also sweet. I say you're liminal compendious duplicitous. I say you're beautiful but violent and you've hurt and killed much in your time but you're not dangerous. Which is right, name's-not-Vissarion? Say whether Moth or Paper.'

'Lavrentina?' said Lom when finally she took a breath.

'Changing the subject?' said Moth. 'That's an answer of a kind. Do you know Lavrentina? She said she was coming back but she hasn't come back yet. Do you know where she is?'

'What do you have to do with her?'

'Oh, she knew us! There were more of us then and some of us she *used* for purposes and missions and death. Some liked it. It was purpose. Bez liked it a lot but he hasn't come back either. The word that Lavrentina liked was coterie but we didn't like all that my sisters and me. We kept from Lavrentina far away. Keep to the rafters when Lavrentina's about! Come down when she's gone! The rest of us have gone away but not the three sisters we like it here. Is Lavrentina ever coming back?'

'I don't think so,' said Lom.

'So answer the question then name's-not-Vissarion are you a danger thing?'

'Are you?'

'Not to you.'

'Then Moth,' said Lom. 'The answer is Moth.'

She laughed.

'I like you name's-not-Vissarion even if I don't believe you even if you bring us fire and death.'

'No,' said Lom. 'I don't.'

She frowned.

'We're not stupid,' she said. 'Listen this is how it is. The days pass slowly here it's quiet and cool there's shade and moonlight and the sun doesn't reach in here. There are other places like this across the city. But no giants, no rusalkas. No wind walkers. They've all left the city and gone far to the east under the trees. The Pollandore drew things to itself while it was here including us but all those ways are closed now. We consider ourselves abandoned the new city has no time for us they would hate us if they knew. This red man Kantor has no time for us Kantor you know Kantor? Has a new name but still the same we know we're memory. Ask us what we do here all the time I'll tell you what we do here all the time we read a lot. They took much but they didn't take it all away there's lots still here to read.'

She leaned in confidentially to whisper something in his ear, as if it was a secret.

'The libraries,' she said, 'have libraries in them.'

She paused.

'Do you understand anything I'm talking about?' she said. 'Anything? Anything at all?'

'Yes,' said Lom. 'I do. I understand it all.'

'I think you do,' said Moth. 'There's noise and fire in the city anxiousness hunger bombs it has not stopped yet it goes away but it doesn't it never stops. We go out sometimes to the city to forage. That's better now. More for us. No! Not killers idiot! The bins at the back of the market. You can stay here with us if you want. You'll find plenty to read. Stay out of the basements though the corpses in the mortuary make a lot of noise they thrash about but they can't get out and anyway there's nowhere else for them to go.' She paused again and gazed deeply into his eyes. Hers were warm dark waters. 'I'd like to kiss you, name's-not-Vissarion, you smell good.'

'What?'

'Weren't you listening? I thought you were listening. I want to kiss you. Can I do that? Only once to see what it is like. You're very fierce and warm.'

'If you want,' said Lom. 'If you want to, yes.'

Moth's mouth on his was dry and cool and dark as a well and tasted faintly of fruit. Something inside her was buzzing lazily like a wasp in a sunlit afternoon window.

'What time is it now?' she said.

'I don't know,' said Lom.

'No you don't because the clocks don't work any more. Clocks tell you something, but it's not the time.'

Lom stayed in the Lodka, walking and thinking, long after Moth had left him alone. There was water in the basins and when he tired he went back to the reading room and slept. Better than in the Pension Forbat. Morning sun flooding the broken dome woke him. He didn't want to go back out into the city, but he went.

4

There were three of them in Rizhin's office: Rizhin himself, Hunder Rond, Director of the Parallel Sector, and Secretary for Security and Justice Grigor Ekel.

'We are making good progress, Osip,' Ekel began. He opened a folder and consulted his notes. 'All my best people are working on this. Nothing is more—'

Rizhin held up his hand. 'Rond,' he said. 'Rond first.'

'The rifle that was used to shoot you,' said Rond, 'was a Zhodarev STV-04. Military sniper issue. It was found in the stairwell of the Mirgorod Hotel.'

Ekel jerked forward in his chair. 'You *have* it?' he said. 'You have the weapon? Why wasn't I told of this?'

Rond ignored him. 'Two sets of fingerprints,' he continued, speaking without notes. 'The majority belong to a woman. Name, Cornelius. Trained as a sniper by the VKBD but deserted. Operated as a lone shooter during the siege. History of involvement with dissident elements. Arrested. Deep interrogation. Two years in the Chesma Detention Centre.' He glanced at Ekel. 'Released. Disappeared. Presumed to have left Mirgorod. Evidently did not. This is your shooter, Generalissimus.'

'We must find this woman!' said Ekel. 'Why have the militia not been informed?'

'They have the name, Grigor,' said Rond. 'Didn't they tell you?'

'Two,' said Rizhin quietly. 'You said two sets of prints,'

'Yes. The other gave us a little trouble, but we tracked them down. They belong to a former senior investigator of the Political Police. A career in the eastern provinces. Effective but insubordinate, made no friends, under investigation for antisocial attitudes when he came to Mirgorod six years ago and immediately got into trouble with Chazia. There's been no trace of him since. The assumption was, he was killed on Chazia's orders. His name—'

'Lom,' said Rizhin. 'Vissarion Yppolitovich Lom. From Podchornok.'

Rond looked at Rizhin in surprise. 'You know of him?'

Rizhin was sitting upright and leaning forward intently. 'Is he back, Rond?' he said. 'Is it him?'

'He was in the Hotel Mirgorod at the time you were shot. A clerk and a doorman identified his photograph. The same man took a room at the Pension Forbat the night before Victory Day under the name of Foma Drogashvili. He took the room for a week, stayed there two nights but has not returned since.'

Ekel's face was chalk. Neck flushed pink. The sheaf of papers in his hands trembled. A leaf in the breeze. He glared at Rond.

'None of this was shared—'

'There is more,' Rond said to Rizhin, taking no notice of Ekel. 'I had a conversation recently with an under-secretary in the Office for Progressive Cultural Enlightenment. Antimos. A man with a hitherto blame-free record who suddenly upped and started to search for some old files. Highly sensitive old files. During my conversation with Antimos he mentioned this same Lom. There was a history between them.' Rond glanced at Ekel meaningfully. He was about to enter into topics which Ekel must guess nothing of. 'It concerns a certain six-year-old mission that Lom has apparently reactivated. A certain former intelligence target.'

Rizhin nodded. Expressionless. 'I understand,' he said. 'Please go on.'

'Lom was blackmailing my friend Under-Secretary Antimos,' said Rond. 'He wanted Antimos to find and bring him files that were closed long ago.'

'Thank you, Rond,' said Rizhin. 'That's enough for the moment. I congratulate the Parallel Sector again.' He turned to Ekel. 'And now, Grigor, what do you have for me? Your report please? Tell me, what have the VKBD, the gendarmes, the militia and the secret police done to clear up after the attempt on my life you failed to prevent?'

Ekel was quivering with frustration and rage. Also fear. Primarily fear. He addressed Rizhin but he could not tear his eyes from Hunder Rond.

'This is a stitch-up! My people have done their best, Osip!' Ekel's voice was becoming more high-pitched and nasal. 'I have done my best! But you see what I am up against? Obstruction ... hiding evidence ... deliberate betrayal! Fuck!' He turned to face Rond. 'I will not let you do this to me! I will not be hung out to dry!'

'Someone must be,' said Rond quietly. 'In circumstances like this, it's an inevitable necessity. You know that, Ekel.'

'But not me, you fucker! Not *me*! You see, Osip, see how he's trying to protect himself, that's all! But I know you see through him, like I do.'

'No, Grigor,' said Rizhin. 'It is you. I smell conspiracy on you. It's on your breath. You stink of it.' He put his right hand – five fat fingers – on his heart. 'You hurt me, Grigor, here. Just here. I gave you all you have. I gave you my trust, and you repay me how? You are complicit in this attempt on my life. There is no other explanation.'

'No! Osip, please! I have been more than just loyal. I *like* you, Osip. I'm not like the others. I *love* you. As a man I am your *friend*.'

'We will have the names of your gang out of you, Grigor. Then we will see.'

'The thing is,' Rond said to Rizhin after Grigor Ekel had been taken away, 'we think the archive Lom is looking for may actually exist. But we don't yet know where it is.'

'Archive?'

'Lavrentina Chazia kept her own personal files, and it seems they have not been destroyed. They are still out there somewhere. Antimos was on their trail but he hadn't found them yet. They're likely to contain compromising material.'

'Of course they'd be *compromising*. That mad old vixen Lavrentina Chazia was a cunning poisonous bitch. Find what she kept, Rond, and bring it all to me.'

'Of course,' said Hunder Rond. 'We'll find the Cornelius woman too.'

Rizhin shrugged. 'Naturally, but she won't be anything much. Find Lom. He's the one that matters. Him I want alive. Him I want to talk to.'

5

The railway station at Belatinsk is crowded for the departure of the Mirgorod train. Forshin's Philosophy League has booked an entire carriage. They struggle with chests and suitcases full of books and papers. The atmosphere is grim determination under a bleak grey sky. Dusty wind whips at their clothes.

'I put on a mask of good cheer for the others,' says Forshin to Kamilova, 'and perhaps above all for myself, but I do not underestimate the task ahead.'

There are forms to be filled out in triplicate. Municipal officials search their luggage for what they can confiscate. Brutskoi's wife weeps and protests at the loss of all her roubles and silver. A gendarme ruffles Yeva and Galina's hair in search of hidden jewels.

'Let us exult in leaving this place, comrades,' says Forshin, waving his cane at the lowering sky. 'We carry with us the flame of our people's future. No customs officer can confiscate that!'

Kamilova and the girls climb aboard at last. They have no baggage. Yeva and Galina huddle together, looking out of the window. The locomotive trembles. Steam is up.

'Don't worry, Galina,' says Yeva. 'You know we'll see our mother soon.'

6

Lom reached Kommunalka Subbotin No. 19 early and ran up the steps two at a time in fresh midsummer Rizhin-morning sunshine. There was a fresh efficient woman in the glassy walled lobby cubicle: patterned cardigan, horn-rim spectacles, blond hair tied back, young and cheerful, not unsmiling, ready for the day.

'What is the number of the apartment of Elena Cornelius, please?' he asked her.

'I'm sorry,' she said. 'There is nobody of that name. Not here.'

'Perhaps she left recently?'

'I've worked here ever since the building opened. Eleven months. I know all the residents. There is no Cornelius here and there never has been. I'm afraid you have the wrong address.'

It was not yet eight o'clock. Lom waited on a bench with a view of the exit. Perhaps she was using another name. Perhaps she had married again. It was possible.

Forty minutes later he saw her come out alone, in her dark clothes again, intense and purposeful, not looking around. She was coming his way. When she got near he rose to meet her.

'Can we talk?' he said. 'Not here. Is there a place?'

'I have to be at work.'

'Say you were sick.'

'I'm never sick.'

'Then they'll believe you.'

She hesitated.

'Please,' he said.

'All right then. OK.'

She took him to a workers' dining hall. Long wooden benches and sticky chrome-legged tables. Yellow-flecked laminate tabletops. The floor was sticky too. The place was crowded with people taking breakfast – young women mostly, girls in sneakers and overalls with tied-back hair. Sweet smells of make-up and scent at war with the black bread and apricot conserve, tea and coffee and steam. The din of cutlery and crockery, the chatter of women with the workday ahead.

Lom and Elena found a space at the end of a bench, near a wide window which looked across an empty paved square to an identical dining hall on the other side.

'Where's Maroussia?' said Elena. She held her cup awkwardly in clawed, broken hands.

'I lost her.'

Elena nodded. In the aftermath of war, when half the world, it seemed, was lost, you didn't ask. People told you or they did not. The stories were always more or less the same.

'I lost my children,' Elena said. 'Galina and Yeva. You remember them?'

'Of course,' said Lom.

'The building they were in is gone, built over now, but I go there every day, and when they come back they'll find me waiting. They're not dead, I know that at least. Of course I'd know if they were killed. A mother would feel that, wouldn't she? In her bones? They were taken away but nobody would tell me who took them or where. They all denied knowing anything about it – *Taken away? Nobody was taken away* – but some of them were lying, I could see. There's a post office box in my name, so when Galina or Yeva writes me a letter it should go there. The system is very reliable and good, everyone says that.'

'Is that why you want to kill Rizhin?' said Lom quietly. 'Because of what happened to Galina and Yeva?'

'Not his fault,' said Elena. 'Before him, that. That was others. Rizhin came later.'

'What happened to your hands, Elena?' said Lom.

'These?' She shrugged.

'Did they do that in the camps? Did they interrogate you?'

'These are nothing, not compared to what they did to others ... not compared to ...' She stopped. Looked out of the window.

'They hurt someone you knew?' said Lom.

'What good is this doing? Talking never does any good. None at all.'

'Who was he?'

'He was trying to make a new start,' she said, still looking out across the sunlit concrete square. 'New ideas. A better world after the war. Some of us believed in that. We tried ... We wanted to ... Why would I tell *you* this? You wanted to stop me killing Rizhin. You were trying to save him. Weren't you?'

'Yes,' said Lom. 'And now I'm trying to stop you trying again.'

'But ... why?'

'Because simply killing Rizhin is no use at all. It's worse than useless: it would be disastrous. It's the idea of him that needs to be destroyed. Killing the man will only make the idea of him stronger. Things will only be worse if you kill him. Much, much worse. '

'No,' said Elena. 'You're wrong. Why do you think that?'

'I don't think it,' he said. 'I know it.'

'What do you want from me? Why are you here?'

'I want your help. I want to bring Rizhin down. Not kill him, but worse than kill him. Destroy him. Ruin him. Ruin his memory. Make it so people will hate all his plans and all he wants to do, and never do any of it simply because it was what he wanted.'

'How? How would you do this?'

'With information. With proof of what he really is.'

'And you have this?'

'Not yet. I should have it tomorrow. But I'll need help to use it properly. That's why I came to see you. I thought you might know people. You could put me in contact—'

'What kind of people?'

'Like you said. People with new ideas. Do you know people like that? People I could talk to?'

'Maybe. Perhaps they would talk to you. You could show them what you have.'

'I'd need to meet them first, before I brought them anything.'

Elena looked hard at Lom. Her thin dark face. Her broken nose. Eyes burning just this side of crazy.

'I don't know,' she said. 'But Maroussia trusted you.'

'And this is Maroussia's work I'm doing. Unfinished business.'

Elena moved her head slightly. That connected with her.

'Is it?' she said.

'Yes, it is.'

She took a deep breath. 'OK. Come with me. I'll take you there now.'

7

Maroussia Shaumian walks in the forest and as she walks she picks things up. Small things, the litter of forest life that snags her gaze and answers her in some instinctive wordless way. Smooth small greenish stones from the bed of a stream. Twigs of rowan. Pine cones. Galls and cankers. Pellets and feathers of owl. A trail of dark ivy stem, rough with root hairs. A piece of root like a brown mossy face. The body of a shrew, dead at the path-side, a tiny packet of fur and frail bone, the bright black drupelet of an open eye. She stops and gathers them and tucks them in her satchel.

When she rests she tips the satchel out and sorts through them. Holds them one by one, interrogates them, listens, and shapes them. Knots them together with grass, threads them on bramble lengths, fixes them with dabs of sticky mud and resin smears. She is making strange objects.

Each one as she makes it becomes a tiny part of her, but separated off. Each one is an expression, a distillation, a vessel and an awakening: not the whole of her, but some small and very specific part, some particular and exact feeling, one certain memory that she separates from herself and makes a thing apart. Some don't work. The investing doesn't take, but slips through the gaps and fades. Those, the emptied ones, the ones that die, she buries under earth and moss and leaves. But many do take, and she knows each one and gives it a name. Lumb. Hope. Wythe. Frith. Scough. Carse. Arker. Haugh. Lade. Clun. Mistall. Brack. Lund. In the evenings she hangs them at intervals around her camp. They dangle and twist and open themselves to the night, to watch and listen while she sleeps.

No one showed her how to do this, not Fraiethe or the father or the Seer Witch of Bones. She found her own way to it.

She comes to where a wide shallow beck crosses the path, running fast and cold, spilling across mounded rocks. Trees on either side lean across it, leaf-heads merged, darkening the water. She drinks a little from the stream and sits a while on the bank. Makes a leaf boat, pinned in shape with thorns, weighted with pebble ballast.

When the leaf boat is ready she reaches for one of the figures she's made. Brings it close to her eye and studies the tiny striations on the twig bark, the exact complexity of grass-stem knots, the russets of moss, the lichen maps like moth wings. She tries to feel her way into it, curious to find what part of herself it is that the object holds. But it is opaque now and keeps its own counsel. She puts it in the boat.

Holding the boat in one hand, carefully, raising it high, she makes her way out into the beck to a dark wet flat of rock. Downstream of the rock the stream has dug a pool, dark brown, slower turning. She crouches and leans out to set the leaf boat on the water and let it go. It turns a while, uncertain, listing, testing the way, then settles and rights itself. The water carries it clear of the matted litter on the bank. It wobbles and turns, tiny under the trees, until it goes beyond where she can see.

It is not a message, not even a messenger, but an explorer: a voyager sent ahead where she can't yet go.

All morning the ground climbs under her feet and the trees grow sparser, lower, more widely spaced, until in the middle of the day she crests a rise and finds herself on a scrubby hilltop among hazel and thorn, looking across a wide shallow valley. The grey-brown canopy of leaf-falling woodland spreads out at her feet. Solitary hunting birds circle below her on loose-stretched flaggy wings. A range of low hills on the further side rises into distance and mist. Without trees above her she can see the sky.

Smirrs of mist hang over thorn and bramble scrub, pale and cold, motionless and patient, like breath-clouds: the trees' breathing. The finger-touch of damp air chill is on her face. Her hands are bunched in her pockets for warmth. She is walking on a thick mat of fallen leaves and wind-broken tips and twigs, bleached of colour. It crunches underfoot. There is winter coming in this part of the forest. Every edge and rib of leaf has a fine sawtooth edge of frost.

The body of the lynx lies on its side in a shallow pool as if it has drowned. Maroussia crouches beside it to look. The pool is dark and skinned with ice: forest litter is caught in it, and tiny bubble trails. The lynx is big like a large dog: sharp ears, a flattened cat-snout, ice-matted fur. She puts out her hand to touch its side. It feels cold and hard. She closes her eyes and reaches out with her mind, groping her way, and touches a faint distant hint of warmth. A last failing ember. A trace. Life, determined, hanging on.

She isn't dead. She isn't gone. Not yet.

Maroussia feels her way cautiously into the cold-damaged body. The sour smell of death is there: an obstacle, an uneasy darkness she has to push through. She feels the death seeping into her and pushes it back, trembling with revulsion.

'Get out,' she whispers aloud. *Get away from me.*

She is feeling her way inside the lynx, looking for the core of life, reaching out to it. *Here*, she is saying. *I am here. Where are you?*

The lynx barely flickers in response, so faintly that Maroussia doubts at first that it is there at all. But it stirs. She catches a weak sense of lynx life.

Who are you? she says to the lynx life. *Who are you?*

Leave me. I am death.

No. Not yet. Not quite.

I am tired and death. I am the stinker. The rotting one.

Not yet. Take something from me. I want to share.

It is too much and I am death.

I have life. Share some.

I am lynx and do not share.

The lynx is faint and far away. Drifting. Maroussia pushes some of her self into it, shoving, forcing like she did with the objects she made, but stronger. Harsher. Until it hurts to do it.

Who are you? she says again to the lynx.

Leave me alone.

Who are you? Remember who you are.

Maroussia pushes more of herself into the lynx, feeling the weakening of herself, the draining of certainty, the forest around her grow fainter. The sound of death is like a river, near. She will have to be careful. But the lynx is stronger now. Maroussia can see her, as if the lynx is at the back of a low dark cave. There is something behind her that she cannot quite see. A shadow moving fast across the floor.

Who are you? says Maroussia again.

Plastered fur and soaking hair.

More than that, says Maroussia.

Weakness and all-cold all-hungry and wet and full of dying cub. All strength gone.

More than that!

I am shadow-muzzle, dark-tooth, wind-dark and rough. Faintness and lick and dapple, and pushing, and bloody hair. I am mewler and swallower and want, the shrivelled one, the suckler. I do not need to share.

Take it then. Because you can. Maroussia pushes again. *Who are you?*

Meat-scent on the air at dusk. Salt on the tongue and the dark sweet taste of blood. I am the eater of meat. I do not share. I do not need to share.

No, you don't.

I am shit in the wet grass. Milk on the cub's breath and the cold smell of a dead thing. I am the bitch's lust for the dog I do not need. I am the abdomen swollen full as an egg, the pink bud suckler in the dark of the earth den.

Yes.

I am the runner hot among the trees. Noiseless climber. Sour breath in the tunnel's darkness and teeth in the badger's neck. The crunch of carrion and the thirsty suck and the flow of warm sweet blood-or-is-it-milk. Shrew flesh is distasteful, and so is the flesh of bears. I am shit and blood and milk and salty tears. I do not share!

No. But you can take.

I am the lynx in the rain with the weight of cubs in my belly. Cub-warm

*sleep under the snow, ice-bearded. I am life and I am called death. I am
the answer to my own question, and if you look for me, I am the finding.
Leave me alone now. I am not dying but I want to sleep.*

Eat something first. Then I will carry you and you can sleep.

My teeth are sharp. My claws are sharp.

Don't bite me.

I do not share.

OK.

Maroussia sits on the ground and lifts the animal into her lap. Holds
a piece of pigeon to its mouth. Lynx glares at her but takes it and chews
at it warily. Resentfully. Maroussia sees the needle-sharp whiteness of
teeth.

The Pollandore inside her gives an alien grin. The growing human
child in her belly stirs and kicks. She is alone and very far from home.

8

The place Elena Cornelius took Lom to was a wide field of
broken concrete and brick heaps and hummocks of dark
weed-growth. It rolled to a distant skyline of ragged scorched
facades.

Such landscapes were everywhere in Mirgorod. Lom had seen other
war-broken towns and cities that were all burned-out building shells
and ruined streets – grids of empty windows showing gaps of sky
behind – but during the siege of Mirgorod the defenders had pulled
the ruins down and levelled the wreckage, creating mile after mile of
impassable rubble mazy with pits and craters, foxholes and rat runs
and sniper cover, all sown with landmines, tripwire grenades, vicious
nooses, shrapnel-bomb snares and caltrops. Trucks and half-tracks
were useless. Battle tanks beached themselves. The enemy had to
clamber across every square yard on foot, clearing cellar by cellar with
flame-throwers and gas. Artillery and airborne bombardment could
not destroy what was already blasted flat.

Elena led him through pathless acres of brick and plaster and dust.
A girl emerged from one of the larger rubble piles and passed them

with a smile, neat and clean and combing her hair. Two men in business suits came up a gaping stairwell. A woman in a head cloth with a market basket. Patches of ground had been cleared for cabbage and potato. There was woodsmoke and the smell of food cooking. Soapy water. The foulness of latrines.

'People *live* here?' said Lom.

'They must live somewhere,' said Elena. 'There aren't enough apartments, not yet, and what there is is far away, and there are so few buses … For many people, this is better.'

She pulled aside a sheet of corrugated iron and went down broken concrete steps. Knocked at a door.

'Konnie? Konnie? It's Elena.'

The door opened. A woman in her early twenties, vivid red hair straight and thin to her shoulders, green eyes in a pale freckled face. A clever face. Bookish. Intense. Interesting. She looked like a student. When she saw Elena her eyes widened.

'Elena! Shit!' She grabbed her by the arm and pulled her forward. 'Come in quickly. Maksim is here. We can help. Maksim!' she called over her shoulder. 'It's Elena! Elena is here!' Then she saw Lom and frowned. 'Who's this?'

'A friend,' said Elena. 'It's OK, Konnie. He's a friend.'

'Oh.'

'I trust him,' said Elena. 'I want you to help him.'

Konnie hesitated.

'OK,' she said 'Then you'd better come in.'

Lom followed the women through the entrance into a low basement space. Bare plaster walls lit by a grating in the ceiling with a pane of dirty glass laid across it. The room was divided in two by a tacked-up orange curtain. It smelled of damp brick. The part this side of the curtain had planks on trestles for a table. There were two chairs, a sagging couch, a single-ring gas stove on a bench in the corner.

'You have to get away, Elena,' Konnie was saying. 'The militia have your name. They know it was you that shot Rizhin. They're searching for you. You have to leave the city.'

'No,' said Elena. 'I'm not leaving. Never. My girls—'

'Maksim!' Konnie called again.

There was a stack of books on the table. Lom glanced at them. Drab covers with ragged pages and blurry print. Wrinkled typescripts pinned with rusting staples. Dangerous thinking, circulated hand to hand. He scanned the titles. *The Ice Axe Manifesto. Bulletin of the Present Times. Listen, We Are Breathing.* Someone – Konnie presumably, it was a woman's handwriting – had been making pencil notes in a yellow exercise book. Lom picked it up. *'ALL GOVERNMENT,'* she had written, *'rests on possibility of violence against own citizens. Cf Jaspersen! – Principles of Interiority Chap 4. Apeirophobia.'*

'Hey!' said Konnie. 'Put that down.'

'Sorry.'

Maksim came out, buttoning his shirt, from behind the orange curtain, where presumably there was a bed. His hair was long and tangled. He was tall, taller than Lom. He looked as if he'd just woken up.

'Elena?' he said. 'What's happening?' He saw Lom and Konnie glaring at him. 'Who is this?'

'It's OK, Maksim,' said Elena. 'He's a friend.'

'What's he doing here?'

'I'm looking for advice,' said Lom. 'Maybe some information. Elena said you might—'

'What's your name?' said Maksim. He was trying to get the situation under control. An officer, used to command.

'Lom.'

Konnie frowned.

'I know that name. They're looking for you too.'

Lom looked at her sharply. 'Who is?'

'The militia. They have two names for the shooting of Rizhin: Cornelius and Lom.'

'No!' said Elena. 'Not him. He wasn't there.'

'How do you know this?' Lom said to Konnie.

Konnie shook her head. 'We know.'

'I was on my own,' Elena was saying. 'He only came later.'

'I let them see me in the hotel. I put my prints on the gun.'

'You did that deliberately?' said Elena.

'Yes.'

'Why?'

'To make things happen. To get their attention. To get involved.' *Pull a thread. See where it leads.* 'They've done well. I thought it would take them longer.'

'That's insane,' said Maksim.

'It was quick,' said Lom. 'I can't do what I do from the outside look-ing in.'

'And what exactly is it you do?' said Maksim.

Lom looked him in the eye. 'I'm here to bring Rizhin down.'

Maksim pulled the outside door shut.

'You've put us in danger coming here,' he said.

'I'm sorry,' said Elena. 'I didn't know. About the militia. The names. I'd never have come here if I'd known.'

'You have to get out of the city quickly,' said Maksim. 'Both of you. We have a car. Konnie, you will drive—'

'No,' said Elena. 'I'm staying. I'm not going anywhere. I can't leave Mirgorod. It's impossible. I must be here when Galina and Yeva come home.'

'Elena, it's not safe,' said Konnie.

'They won't find me at the Subbotin. I am Ostrakhova there.'

'They'll come for you. They always find you in the end.'

'The VKBD will hunt you down,' said Maksim. 'You cannot imag-ine. You cannot begin to imagine how they will hunt you now.'

'You have no children, Maksim. I will not abandon my girls.'

'Six years, Elena, it's been six years. I hope they survived the bomb-ing, but even if they did … They're not coming back. You must know that.'

'My girls are not dead. They were taken but they will find their way back.'

'You must disappear now,' said Maksim. 'If they capture you, if they question you … you will endanger us all, Elena.'

Konnie put a hand on Maksim's arm. 'Please. Enough.'

'You don't need to leave the city,' Lom said to Elena. 'You can come with me. I know a place. They won't find you there, and you can stay as long as you want. You'll be safe.'

'With you?' said Maksim. 'Who the fuck are you anyway? Where did you come from? We don't know you.'

'I trust him, Maksim,' said Elena. 'I want you to help him. That's why we're here.' She turned to Lom. 'Maksim is an old friend,' she said. 'A comrade. He was in the army, an officer, a good fighter. After the war he was one of the ones who wouldn't go back to the old ways.'

'You're right to be cautious,' Lom said to Maksim. 'I would do the same. But I just need some advice, that's all. We're on the same side.'

'Side?' said Maksim. 'What side is that?'

'The side that Rizhin's not on.'

Maksim studied him. Weighing him up. 'Were you in the army?'

'No,' said Lom. 'I was with the Political Police.'

'The *police*?'

'It was a long time ago.'

'Maksim,' said Elena, 'I'm only asking you to listen to what he's got to say.'

'But ...' Maksim let out a long slow breath. 'Oh shit. OK. You're here now. So what do you want?'

'If you had proof of something that could bring Rizhin down,' said Lom, 'if you had documentation which, if it was used properly, would expose him and empty him out and turn the world against him, would you know what to do with it?'

'What kind of proof?' said Maksim. 'Proof of what?'

'Later,' said Lom. 'Say there was such proof, what would you do with it? How could it be used? Do you have the means? Are you prepared for this?'

Maksim thought for a moment.

'It's good, is it?' he said. 'This proof? It's something dangerous? Something big?'

'Yes. It would be explosive. It would make Rizhin's position impossible. Everyone would turn against him. Everyone. He'd be finished. He would fall.'

Maksim's eyes gleamed.

'That would be a great thing indeed,' he said. Then he frowned. 'But no. We couldn't use it. We wouldn't have a chance. We haven't the means. We are too few.'

'We know journalists,' said Konnie. 'The newspapers—'

'The papers wouldn't print it,' said Maksim. 'Never.'

'The Archipelago then. We have friends at the embassy.'

'If it came from the Archipelago, who would believe it? It would be dismissed as propaganda and lies.'

'Then wouldn't you need ...?' Konnie began and trailed off.

'Yes?' said Lom.

'Someone in the government. Someone big, with power and influence, who isn't afraid of Rizhin. Someone who could step in and push him out.'

'They're all Rizhin's creatures,' said Maksim. 'They're all terrified of him, and anyway whoever ousted Rizhin would be just as bad, or worse.'

'All of them?' said Lom. 'Is there no one?'

'Well.' Konnie paused. 'There's Kistler. You hear things about him. There are rumours. He has connections ... Kistler could be worth a try. Maksim?'

'Maybe,' said Maksim. 'Maybe Kistler. Possibly. He's stronger than the others. He has an independent view – sometimes, apparently.'

'Do you have a link to this Kistler?' said Lom. 'Are you in communication with him?'

'No,' said Konnie. 'Nothing that firm, but there is talk about him. Like I said, you hear things.'

'How would I reach him?'

'I'm not sure about this,' said Maksim. 'I wouldn't trust Kistler more than any of the others. But ... we have the address of his house. We have all of them. We know where they live.'

'Give it to me, please,' said Lom. 'I'll go and see what this Kistler has to say.'

He was flying blind. Throwing stones at random, hoping to hit something. But he didn't know another way.

'Like I said, it's just a rumour,' said Konnie. 'A feeling. You shouldn't place any weight on what I say.'

'It's the best lead I've got,' said Lom. 'The only one.'

'Do you have this proof, then?' said Maksim as Lom and Elena were leaving. 'Really?'

'No,' said Lom. 'Not yet. But tomorrow, I hope so. I should have it on Wednesday.'

Maksim looked puzzled. 'But today is Wednesday,' he said.

'Is it?' said Lom. 'Is it?'

The clocks tell you something, but not the time.

9

Rizhin had not yet appointed a successor at the Agriculture Ministry for the unfortunate Vladi Broch, killed by the assassin's bullet meant for another, so Broch's deputy, an assiduous man named Varagan, was summoned in his place to the weekly meeting of the Central Committee.

For Varagan this was a once-in-a-lifetime opportunity. His chance to step out from the shadows and demonstrate his quality. Poor Varagan. A man of prodigious administrative capacity and earnest zeal, he had profoundly mistaken his purpose, having got it firmly (and regrettably) fixed in his head that it was his job as Under-Secretary for Food Production to identify and address the causes of growing starvation in the eastern oblasts of the New Vlast.

When Rizhin called on him to speak, he rose and hooked his wire spectacles behind his ears, cleared his throat nervously and began to introduce his report. He was a freshly washed sheep among wolves.

'Everywhere the population shows the demographic impact of war,' he began. 'Six hundred men for every thousand women, and worse among those of working age. The rebuilding of our factories proceeds far too slowly. Water, electricity and sewerage everywhere are in an abysmal condition. Above all the prices for agricultural producers are ruinously low, though the prices in shops still rise—'

Rizhin raised a hand to interrupt. 'Is it not your own ministry, Varagan, that fixes these prices?'

'Precisely, sir. I have recommendations which I will come to. I am sketching the background first. The rural populace has fled to the cities. They eat dogs and horses and the bark of trees. In many of our towns we see black-marketeering. Gangsterism. Bribery. The rule of this committee in such places is nominal at best.'

Rizhin sat back in his chair, doodling wolf heads as he listened with half-closed eyes.

'Steady, Varagan,' said Kistler quietly. 'Remember where you are.'

But Rizhin waved Varagan on. 'Let the man speak,' he said. 'Let us hear what he has to say.'

The committee looked on in silence as Varagan methodically ploughed his furrow.

'Grain is exported to the Archipelago even as our own people starve,' he said. 'Our errors are compounded by poor harvests. Famine is widespread and growing. Deaths are to be counted in hundreds of thousands, perhaps millions, and—'

'But surely,' said Rizhin, raising his eyelids and looking round the table, fixing them one by one with a stony gaze, 'this is not right? Did not our old friend Broch tell us just the other week that this talk of famine was a fairy tale? Am I not right, colleagues? He said so often. And you are telling us now, Varagan, that Vladi Broch's reports were false?'

Varagan looked suddenly sick, as if he had been punched in the stomach.

'I ...' he began. 'I ...'

'Who drafted Vladi's reports for him?' said Rizhin. 'Who produced those false statistics?' He made a show of riffling back through old papers in his folder. 'Come, Varagan, I want the name.'

Poor Varagan was shaking visibly now. He was beginning to understand what he had done. The pit he had dug for himself with his own honest shovel. His face was blood-red. His mouth opened and shut soundlessly. Kistler wondered if he might collapse.

Varagan snatched at a glass of water and drank it down.

'But people are *dying*,' he said, struggling to speak. Mouth dry, voice catching. 'I have ideas for saving them. I have drawn up a programme ...'

'And yet,' said Rizhin, 'week after week we have had reports to the precise contrary. Tables of figures. I have them here.' He lifted a file from his pile. 'Figures from the Secretariat of Food Production. Signed by your own hand, Secretary Varagan. How do you account for this? How do you explain?'

'I ...' said Varagan again, eyes wide in panic, and snapped his mouth shut.

Rizhin threw the file down on the table.

'There is no famine in the New Vlast,' he said. 'It is impossible. What there is, is pilfering and theft. Corrupt individualism! Starvation is the ploy of reactionary and deviationist elements. Our enemies hate our work so much they let their families die. The distended belly of a child is a sign of resistance. It is good news. It confirms we are on the right track that our opponents grow so desperate.'

'Yes,' whispered Varagan, casting desperately around the table for support, but no one caught his eye. 'Of course. I see clearly now. I have misinterpreted the data. I have made a mistake. An honest mistake.'

Rizhin was suddenly trembling with anger.

'Mistake?' he said. 'Oh no, I think not. This is a power play, Varagan. Transparent viciousness. You wriggle now, oh yes, you squirm. That is always the way of it with men like you. First you come here and throw accusations at your own dead boss, yes, and at others around this table, honest hard-working fellows, and now you row backwards. I know your type, my friend. You are ambitious! You would rise! You ache for preferment, and you cover your tracks. You are at fault and blame everyone but yourself. Well I see now that there is someone to blame, and it is you.'

'No,' whispered Varagan. 'I wished only—'

Kistler leaned across to him. 'Leave the room, man,' he said quietly. 'This agenda item is closed.'

Varagan nodded. Wordless and methodical, shaking like a leaf, he collected his papers. Unhooked his wire spectacles from his ears and popped them into the top pocket of his jacket. Rose, turned, pushed back his chair and went out slowly into the lonely cold.

10

After sundown in the balmy nights of summer the well dinnered families of the List, Rizhin's plush elite, take to the paths of the Trezzini Pleasure Gardens in the Pir-Anghelsky Park. Entering the blazing gateway of crystal glass – lit from within by a thousand tiny flickering golden lights – they move among pagodas and boating lakes. Arched bridges, tulips and water lilies. Straight-haired girls walk there with mothers sleekly plump. Awkward boys with arrogant blank eyes wince as father calls to father with penetrating voice. There is music here. Sugared chestnuts and roasting pig and candyfloss. Take a pedalo among enamel-bright and floodlit waterfowl! Visit the

Aquarium and the Pantomime Theatre! Ride the Dragon Swing! The Spinner! See the pierrot and the dancing bear!

The List regarded their pleasures coolly, with the assurance of natural entitlement. They were the experts. The competent ones. You would not know that a handful of years ago none of them was here. No old money in Papa Rizhin country! But the polished faces of the List reflect the coloured lamps strung among wax-leaved dark exotic trees. Their soaps and perfumes mingle with evening-heavy blossom.

Lom stayed in the darkness under the trees. Pavel had chosen this meeting place to make a point – *This is the coming world. Here it is. I'm at home and familiar among these people. I belong here, and you, Lom, you ghost, you do not* – but also because the konditorei was on an island in the shallow lake reached by a causeway. Light blazed from the filigreed iron glasshouse and blazed reflections off dark waters. Within, the List at white-linen-covered tables ate pastries from tiered plates and drank chocolate from gleaming china jugs. The gilt-framed mirror behind the central counter showed the backs of master patissiers and konditiers: their crisp white tunics, shaved necks, pomaded hair.

The narrow causeway was the one way in and the one way out.

Pavel Ilich Antimos was achingly visible, sitting alone at a table in the window. Lom had watched him for half an hour and he had not moved. He might as well have been under a spotlight. *Here I am. See me. Come to me.* He stared at the untouched chocolate in front of him, twisting a knotted napkin, his injured right shoulder hunched up against his neck. He never looked up. Never looked around.

The konditorei was crowded but the tables near Pavel were empty. Perhaps the customers had been warned away; more likely they shunned him through instinct: the unerring sense of the List for avoiding the tainted. The untouchable. The fallen. Even from across the lake Lom could detect the sour grey stink and sadness of the already dead.

Ten feet from Lom, in the dark of the lakeside trees, a corporal of the VKBD was also observing Pavel Antimos. From time to time he scanned the brightly lit approach to the causeway through binoculars. There were three other VKBD at intervals in the shadow near Lom, and no doubt there were more on the other side of the lake. Probably they had a team in the konditorei as well. Lom couldn't see them but they would be there.

Poor Pavel. He wouldn't have gone to the VKBD with his story

– he'd have known that was suicidal – so they must have caught him with his fingers in the drawer. And they'd taken the trouble to keep him alive and use him as bait. So they wanted Lom too. That told Lom something. That was information.

He could have simply slipped away, back in under the rhododendron trees, and left the VKBD to their watching, but the corporal ten feet from him had a pistol on his hip and Lom wanted that. He needed to broaden his options.

He waited till the brass orchestra in the bandstand reached the finale of 'We Fine Dragoons'. They made a lot of noise. The corporal didn't hear him coming.

11

An hour later, with no secret Rizhin file from Pavel Antimos but a VKBD pistol in his pocket, Lom re-entered the Lodka by underground ways. He came up past empty cells and interrogation rooms into the tile-floored central atrium. There was no moonlight. He felt the corridors, the stairwells, the doorways, the ramifications of office and conference room as spaciousness and slow currents in the air. Opened up, arboreal and dark-adapted, Lom scented out his way. Forest percipience. He knew the difference between solid dark and airy dark. He felt the invitation of certain thresholds, the threat beyond others; he heard the echo of entranceless passageways on the far side of walls, and the restless shuffling of the basement mortuary dead.

This forest-opened world was not like *seeing*; it was *knowing* and *feeling*. Everything – absolutely everything – was alive, and Lom shared the life of it. Raw participation. The boundaries of himself were uncertain and permeable. Shifting frontier crossings. He felt history, watchfulness, weight and presence.

And there was something else. Another spectrum altogether. Liminal angel senses came into play, the residuum of the coin-size lozenge of angel flesh fitted into his skull in childhood and gouged out by Chazia; the residuum also of Chazia's angel suit, its substance seared into him and joined with his by Uncle Vanya's atomic starburst at Novaya Zima. Angel particles and angel energies had soaked through him to the blood-warm matter at the heart of bone. Synapses sparkled with alien angel speed and grace. By the faint afterglow of the Lodka's radiating warmth, Lom saw with a crisp and prickling non-human clarity that needed no more light.

Always at some level he was these two things: the heart of the forest and the heartless gaze of the spaciousness inside atoms, the spaciousness separating stars. He saw further and better in the dark. Darkness simplified.

In the Lodka's cool central atrium (a huge airy space lined by abandoned reception desks, a plaza of echoing linoleum, a node for wide staircases heavily balustered and swing-door exits, surfaces dust-skinned and speckled with the faeces of small animals) Moth was waiting for him. She had sensed his perfumed brightness coming, and he knew she was there: from several floors below he had felt her agitation.

'Men are here!' she hissed. 'They have lamps and guns. We know the black uniforms they wear, my sisters and I. They are *Streltski!*' She spat the word. Anger and hatred. 'They have your friend. Some threaten her; others look for papers.'

Lom had brought Elena Cornelius to the Lodka before he went to look for Pavel in Pir-Anghelsky Park. *She is my friend*, he'd said to Moth. *She's here under my protection*. He'd thought she would be safer here than at her apartment.

'It's bad the black Streltski are here,' Moth was saying. 'We remember them from long ago, but Josef Kantor who is Papa Rizhin brought them back. Streltski burn us! If they find us they burn! Two of us they roasted in the Apraksin. My sisters blame you for bringing them here and for bringing this woman here, and they blame me for this because of you. There will be a bad end of things now.'

'How many men and where?' said Lom.

'Two with the woman in the reading room under the wheel and two in the locked corridor nearby where they look for Lavrentina's private archive. I heard them say that.' She grinned, a wide dark gaping slash of mouth. 'But they will not find what they want it is not where they look.'

'Lavrentina's archive?' said Lom. 'I want that too. I need that very much.'

Was it possible the papers he needed were still in the Lodka? That Chazia hadn't moved them before she left for Novaya Zima with the Pollandore? In the chaos of the withdrawal and burning of that day, it could have happened.

'My sisters are right,' said Moth. 'It's because of you the Streltski are come here where we were forgotten and safe.'

'Moth?' said Lom 'Do you know where Lavrentina's papers are?'

Her wide nocturnal eyes flashed in the darkness.

'The black uniforms will not find them,' she said. 'However long they search. We took them to be safe. Lavrentina will want them when she comes back.'

'Lavrentina isn't coming back,' said Lom. 'She's dead. It's Rizhin who wants her archive now. He must know I'm looking for it, and that's a danger to him. He wants to find it first. ' *Poor Pavel. And Chazia's papers here all the time.* 'That's why he sent the Parallel Sector here – I mean the Streltski.'

'Oh?' said Moth. 'Lavrentina is dead?' She reacted to that with the incurious indifference of the non-human who measure their lives in centuries. Then he felt her gaze in the darkness harden and grow colder. Dangerous. 'And now you want to take Lavrentina's papers away from us? You didn't say.'

'One file, Moth. Only one file. Lavrentina had papers about Josef Kantor that I need to find. I didn't tell you before because I didn't think the papers were still here.'

'Kantor papers? Papers that endanger *Kantor*? Kantor whose Streltski drive us out and burn us '

'Yes.'

Lom felt Moth smile. A malevolent smile. A playful smile with rows of pin-sharp blade-edge venomous teeth.

'I could take you there,' she said. 'My sisters, though ...'

'Elena first,' said Lom. 'The men with the guns.'

12

H under Rond swept his torch across empty shelves.

'Well?' he said.

'This is the correct room,' said Lieutenant Vrebel. 'There's no mistake.'

'So where are the fucking papers?'

'According to the register they should still be here. Permission to remove them was issued to a Captain Iliodor but the completion slip was never matched. He did not come for them. They were never released.'

'This Iliodor,' said Rond. 'Who is he?'

'He was Commander Chazia's aide,' said Vrebel. 'He went missing the first day of the withdrawal, and he was presumed killed in the first bombing raids though no body was found. The paperwork is clear. Chazia commissioned him to remove her archive to some other place but he never did. That's what Pavel Antimos was on to when we took him.'

Rond played his torch over the emptied shelving again. 'So where are Chazia's files now?'

'I cannot say, Director Rond. I do not know.'

'Do you understand,' said Rond, 'how dangerous those papers could be? Who knows what poison that woman stored away for her own use and protection. If such an archive falls in the hands of antisocial elements, or rivals for the Presidium ... This archive must be found, Vrebel. It has to be destroyed. Our lives depend on this now. Rizhin knows of its existence, and if we can't bring it home—'

He broke off suddenly and spun round, his torch skipping wildly. 'What the fuck!'

From somewhere down the corridor behind them came the sound of gunshots. A man screaming and screaming in terror. Pain. Screams without hope.

Lieutenant Vrebel pulled out his gun and ran.

'Vrebel! Wait!' called Rond.

Too late. Vrebel was disappearing down the corridor towards the reading room.

'Idiot,' said Rond quietly. Hunder Rond was no kind of coward but he understood caution. Circumspection. Explore and comprehend your position, test your enemy, discover your advantage, then exploit it with surprise and overwhelming deadly force. Survival is the first criterion of victory, and in the end the only one. He switched off his torch, drew his pistol and began to follow Vrebel's jerky flashing beam.

Lom watched the attack of the vyrdalaks on the Parallel Sector men from an upper gallery of the Lodka reading room.

Moth had led him there. Together they had crept out onto a balcony from where, by the starlight spilling through the broken panes of the dome, he could look down on the rows of reader's desks that radiated out from the insectile bulk of the motionless great wheel. He'd seen Elena Cornelius sitting at one of the desks, upright and fierce. Men in black uniforms were sitting on desks either side of her, swinging their legs. Relaxed. Waiting for the others to return.

'Let me take them,' he had whispered to Moth. 'I'll do it quietly. No fuss.'

'Too late,' she'd hissed. 'See! My sisters are vengeful. Blood for the burnings at the Apraksin!'

Two dark uncertain shapes were swarming head-first at silent impossible speed down the gantry of the great wheel. White mouths in the moonlight. Lom felt the fluttering shadow-memory of vestigial papery wings brush against his face. Liminal whisperings. He remembered Count Palffy's collection in the raion. The glass cases mounted on the wall, the pinned-out specimens, some drab, some gaudy. *My specialism is winter moths. Ice moths. Strategies for surviving the deep winter cold.*

The Parallel Sector men had also felt movement above them and looked up, swinging their torch beams. They saw what was coming.

'Elena!' Lom had yelled. 'Run! They don't want you. Get clear! Run!'

He'd started to run himself then, racing for the iron spiral stairway down to the reading room. But before he reached the head of the stairs there were shots and then the screaming began.

When the vyrdalak sisters attacked her guards, Elena Cornelius had backed away, retreating to the edge of the room. Lom made his way across to her between the desks.

'Keep back out of the way,' he said. 'This isn't for us.'

There was a flash of light in the frosted pane of the doorway behind her. Lom sensed someone was coming fast. Another one of the Streltski. He felt the man's fear. He was coming for a fight.

Lom pulled from his pocket the VKBD pistol he'd acquired in Pir-Anghelsky Park. There was no time to think. Just react. The door crashed open and Lom fired.

The shot probably hit the man in the chest, but Lom never knew for certain because Moth swept past him noiselessly, knocking him aside, and took the man's head off with a slash of a pale-bladed hand. The detached head thudded against the wall as the body collapsed. Moth leaped over it and flew on into the darkened corridor beyond.

In the reading room the vyrdalak sisters were making thin papery screams of triumph and delight.

Hunder Rond got only a vague impression of what had destroyed Vrebel before the lieutenant's head flew off and his torch fell to the floor, but it was enough. He knew what it was. He knew it was coming for him next.

He emptied his entire magazine in the direction of the approaching vyrdalak. Seven blinding muzzle flashes in the dark. Seven deafening explosions. Somewhere among the noise he heard a high-pitched shriek and a stumble. Then he turned and ran back into the corridors of the private archives.

13

Moth, struck by seven bullets from the pistol of Hunder Rond, collapsed in a heap on the corridor floor. Lom crouched over her. Moved her hair aside to clear her face. She hissed and pushed his hand away.

'Hole in my chest,' she said. 'Harmless. Piece gone from my leg. I'll be a limper for a while.'

'Is there pain?' Elena was there. 'Let me see. You must be bleeding. I can try to stop it.'

Moth began to haul herself upright. Lom put a hand under her arm to help her. There was almost no weight at all.

'No bleeding,' she said, leaning her back against the wall. 'No blood to bleed. As for pain, there is pain sometimes. Existence hurts. This will pass.'

'Can I leave her with you?' Lom said to Elena. 'I need to go after the one that escaped.'

'Leave the Streltski for my sisters,' said Moth. 'When they have finished with the others they will hunt him. Pigeon and Paper will bring him down. You come with me and look at Lavrentina's papers.'

It was ten minutes before Moth was ready to move. The vyrdalak sisters had gone into the shadows, leaving the torn and ruined bodies of the dead Parallel Sector men where they lay. Lom collected their torches and switched them off to save the batteries, all but one for Elena's benefit.

'This way,' said Moth when she was ready, and set off limping towards the lobby. She was halting and slow. 'We will have to go by corridors and stairs.'

For twenty minutes at least they climbed, slowly and circuitously. Lom recognised the backwater corridor where his brief office had been, buried among cleaning cupboards and boiler rooms, when he was Krogh's man. His typescript card was still tucked into the slot on the door, yellowing and faded now. INVESTIGATOR V Y LOM. PODCHORNOK OBLAST. PROVINCIAL LIAISON REVIEW SEC-RETARIAT. He stuck his head inside. The same desk and coat rack were still there but the placard on the wall had gone.

Citizens! Let us all march faster
Through what remains of our days!
You might forget the fruitful summers
When the wombs of the mothers swelled
But you'll never forget the Vlast you hungered and bled for
When enemies gathered and winter came.

Someone had remembered the old Vlast well enough to take that away. Lom wondered if it had been Pavel.

*

In the mazy unlit corridors behind the reading room there was no panic for Hunder Rond, though he knew he was vyrdalak-hunted. There was fear – there was horror in the dark – but he knew that panic would kill him. The vyrdalaks would come fast; they would not lose him in the passageways; they would not give up. They would come and come, quick and silent and relentless in the darkness. Out of shadows and ceilings and lift shafts they would come. He had seen the remains of vyrdalak kill. He had heard the screams.

He had also seen vyrdalaks burn. He knew how that sounded. How it smelled. How it felt.

Hunder Rond moved on at a slow even pace and put aside terror for later. Stored it up for a better time and place. This was his forte, his talent, advantage and pleasure: clinical self-restraint – ice and iron – primitive emotions under unbreakable control to be retrieved for private release *when he chose*. The trembling hot sweat, delirium, anger and screaming could be brought to the surface then, and satisfied *in his way*. Not now. Later. There was energy and pleasure to be had from it then. A heightening.

He smiled grimly in the dark as he cleared and focused his mind and considered his situation from every angle with dispassionate accuracy. He had one spare magazine for his pistol, which was now empty. That was not sufficient, but then no number would have been. Bullets rarely killed a vyrdalak, though a lucky shot might give it pause. Seven cartridges were better than none. He ejected the empty magazine, inserted the spare and loaded the first round into the breech.

And he had a map.

That was foresight. That was efficiency. Cool administrative imagination.

There was no point blundering around in the dark and getting lost. He switched on his torch and unfolded the floor plan of the Lodka.

Century by century the interior of the Lodka had evolved to meet the needs of the day. Corridors and stairways were closed off and new ones opened. Cables and heating were installed. Angel-fall observatories, and radio antennae in attics. Rooms knocked together and repartitioned and requisitioned for new purposes. Subterranean railway access opened and abandoned. A vacuum-pipe internal postal system. Every few years the superintendent of works sent expeditions into the building to update the master survey, but the results were obsolete before the work was complete, and the edges and margins, the heights and depths, remained ragged and obscure. For the core areas and the zones in regular use, however, the map was reliable enough. The Gaukh reading room and the layout of the main archives hadn't changed much. They were near the public door that used to open onto the Square of the Piteous Angel, now Victory Square.

Rond studied the map and chose his way out. It wasn't far. Ten minutes in the passageways and across two wide hallways should do it. He refolded the map and jogged forward at a steady sustainable pace, vyrdalak-horror and primal prey-animal fear tucked away in a closed interior filing system of his own.

Moth led Lom and Elena higher, up narrower stairwells. There was more light up here: more windows, and the yellow moons were shining, nearly full, low and sinking towards the western skyline. Lom switched off the dimming torch. There was no need for it now. They were passing along some kind of high covered gangway. Narrow windows to their right looked across the Lodka's tumbled inner roofscape – slopes of lead and slate, dormers and gables and oriels, downpipes and guttering, naked abandoned flagpoles – and through to their left Mirgorod spread out towards the sea. Dawn was breaking pink and green. Traffic was moving slowly along the eight-lane Rizhin Highway. The sun-flushed thousand-windowed sky-rise towers – the Rudnev-Possochin University, the Pavilion of the New Vlast, the Monument to National Work – heaved up from the plain. Warm-glow termite nests.

'Here,' said Moth at last. She stopped and pushed open a door. The sudden wave of cloying enclosed air that escaped from the room made Lom take a step back. Elena Cornelius put her hand across her mouth.

'Oh god,' she muttered under her breath. 'Oh god, what have they been doing?'

Hunder Rond was within sight of the threshold, the door he'd left open, when the two vyrdalaks rose at him from the shadows of a downward stair.

The light of early morning spilled through the doorway, and the sound of the waking city. *Day already?* Rond had thought. It was barely an hour since he'd come this way the evening before with Lieutenant Vrebel and the others now dead.

The vyrdalaks closed on him with impossible speed. He heard a gasp of pleasure and smelled the age and mustiness of rags. The sickly sweetness of unhuman breath.

Rond's panic box broke wide open then. He felt the shriek from his own throat, the hurt of it; it wasn't his voice but it was him. He turned into the attack and pulled the trigger of his gun, and as he spun he slipped on dusty polished marble and fell. The charge of the day-blinded vyrdalaks missed him. He felt a slicing tear across his upraised forearm and that was all. The crash of his shot echoed impossibly loud in the airy space as the bundle of screeching vyrdalaks skittered across the floor. Rond scrabbled to his knees and jabbed at the trigger again and again until the mechanism clicked empty, and then he hurled the gun at them and threw himself headlong scrambling towards the door into air and sunshine, and he was outside and he was safe and free.

Rond's car was where he'd left it the previous evening (scarcely an hour ago). He was trembling. *Focus. Focus.* His left arm was numb, the jacket sleeve ripped open and wet with blood, his forearm opened above the wrist, an oozing superficial tear. *Drive one-handed then. How hard is that?* He needed to clean himself up. Get the wound dressed quickly. Vyrdalak strikes fester.

But then, when he'd done that, he would come back and he would burn them. Burn the vyrdalaks. Burn the foulness. Burn their nests. Burn whatever archives were still inside that should have been burned years ago. Burn the whole fucking Lodka to the ground.

14

Moth led Lom and Elena into the broad interior of some kind of tower. For five or six floors it rose above them, but wide jagged holes were broken through all the floorboards and plaster ceilings so they could see all the way to the roof. Dust-ridden daylight splashed in through pointed-arch windows. The tower was some kind of library. It was also a beautiful attic nest.

The vyrdalak sisters lived among chambers of sweetness. The whole of the inside of the tower was hung with great webs and pockets and caverns of chewed paper and fruit. Rotting-fruit-and-paper extrusions. Files and books and sea charts, centuries of memoranda and reports – diplomatic letters, records of surveillance, interrogation and betrayal – they ate them all. Masticated and regurgitated them to make hundreds of comfortable translucent compartments the colour of ivory and bone. The floor was uneven papier mâché, matted and lumpy with stalagmites of eaten newsprint and maps and confessions under torture, and all crusted with a yellow-brown craquelure of age.

The whole construction had a perfect, proportioned elegance. It was like standing inside dried egg casings. The sea-worn honeycombed interiors of bone. Wasps' nests like lanterns under eaves. It was the work of centuries and it was beautiful.

'We read and read,' said Moth with quiet pride, 'and as we read we chew.'

Half-eaten fruits – long ago dried to leathery sweetness – and rotting foraged stores were tucked away in cavities and corners.

Hunder Rond returned to the Lodka with men in trucks. They threw a safety cordon around the building and Rond sent in six two-man burning teams, one for each of the half-dozen main public entrances. Pressurised fuel tanks strapped to their backs, they penetrated as far as they dared, leaving themselves escape runs, and began to spray arcs of fire.

The Lodka burned. Oh yes, it burned. The desks, the chairs, the conference tables, the books and files and carpets, the pictures on the walls, the beams, the floor boards, the staircases, all tinder-dry and hungry for combustion.

At the first licks of flame up the walls, the firestarters turned and ran. They took up fallback positions outside the doors, flame-throwers ready for anything that tried to escape.

Moth led Lom and Elena into side rooms off the main tower. There were libraries within libraries, collections and cabinets of curiosities, some small as cupboards with cramped connecting ways, some large as salons. Dormers and airy roof constructions. Moth swept ahead, motley fabric train swishing bare floorboards and fading patterned rugs. Lom and Elena followed more slowly, lingering by items shelved, ranged and museumed with their own mysterious logic.

The sisters had picked up and hauled back home things they had found in tunnels and the city and the Lodka itself: detached fragments of the old Vlast and its predecessors. Flotsam from the wreckage of forgotten worlds. They had gathered furniture and papers, pieces of porcelain and pottery, broken and not, astronomical instruments, components electrical and mechanical. There was a whole wing for works rescued from Vlast storerooms of confiscated art.

Lom paused over aquatints and engravings and photographs of vanished cities. He glanced through the correspondence of margraves, landgraves, electors and county palatines. Accounts of coats of arms, lineages and uniforms. Canvas bags still bearing the brittle broken seals of the *corps diplomatique*. Orders of battle for campaigns of which he'd never heard. The Yannis River Advance. Battles on frozen lakes. Cavalry charges against artillery. The repulsion of the northern dukes. *A Model Village Prospectus on the New Rational Principle. Schools Not Guns Will Feed Our People.* Displayed under glass were ancient un-dated maps of the continent. Small countries Lom had never heard of remained like ghosts, a stained patchwork of counties and princedoms. All maps ended in the east with forest.

The sisters had hung their collection with tiny pieces of other people's privacy: combs and portrait lockets; the headcloths and bast shoes and tin cups of the nameless. The more Lom lingered there, the more aware he became of beginnings that had had no continuation, lines cut off and possibilities unrealised. Ways and places these begin-nings might have gone but never did. It was a museum that told no story except absence.

A circular window gave a view across the sky-rise city: Rizhin Highway, Rizhin Tower. It was perpetual zero hour – null o'clock – in the real world outside. *All the things that might have happened (some of them good, some bad, some beautiful) did not happen. They did not happen because this happened instead.*

Moth came bustling worrisome back for him.

'This way,' she said. 'This way. Hurry.'

The sisters had lovingly recreated Lavrentina Chazia's private archive in every detail. The green-painted walls. The empty desk. Floor tiles lifted from downstairs and relaid. Rows of steel-framed racks holding files and boxes of papers. Every shelf brought up, placed and labelled as it had been; every file and box exactly where it should be according to the former commander of the secret police's own scheme.

'We took them away and hid them,' said Moth. 'We kept them safe for when Lavrentina came back.'

Lom found what he wanted, exactly where he had found it once before. The lavender folder for Josef Kantor was in its place on the *K* shelf. It was fat and full. He took it and pushed it inside his jacket.

At that moment the echo of shrill distant screeching reached them. It found them even here, even in this quiet archive of an archive.

'What's that?' said Elena.

Moth stiffened and screamed. Her sisters crashed in through upper windows, flew down and scuttled, rattling, in circles around them.

'Fire! Fire! They are burning us! Fire!'

Throughout the Lodka the fires were roaring now, blinding vortices of flame and heat. Flames crawled along the walls and floors of corridors, meticulous and thorough, spilling into every room. Floor by floor, shaft by shaft and stair by stair, ignition spread. Rooms unopened for centuries popped into sudden combustion. Thick worms and blankets of smoke flowed across ceilings. Whirlwinds of burning paper. Billowing flakes of fire. Caves of red heat. Explosions and backdrafts sucked whole floors in. Fire smouldered against locked doorways and burst through, searing irruptions, sucking whole annexes into the hot mouth.

Paint blistered. Pigments boiled off canvases and the canvases burned with their frames. Countless linoleum acres bubbled and stank to sticky residual ash. Inkwells boiled dry in burning lecterns. Typewriters buckled and twisted, their ribbons burned, the enamel licked away. The immolation of code books and cipher machines. A fire-clean forgetting of four hundred years of lost secrets.

A column of fire surrounded the leaning skeleton of the Gaukh Engine, heat and smoke pouring with the hurtling updraft through the broken dome and into the outside air.

In the basement mortuary the restless corpses thrashed and subsided. Fire tongues licked the cell-floor bloodstains clean.

Rats and bats and cats and mice and birds escaped or died. Shelves of forgotten files burned unread. Fire touched the hem of the vyrdalak sisters' beautiful galleried nest and it exploded. Libraries within libraries, their long careful centuries' archives and collections, the last secret memories of absence and what did not happen, burned.

Moth and her sisters took Lom and Elena across rooftop gangways and down through the most central heart-stone stairwells and unopened passageways of the Lodka where the fire had not yet reached.

The burning was a distant roar, a smell of searing, heat on the face and the thickening of smoke clogging the chest. The vyrdalaks skittered and jumped and flew short distances on vestigial fabric wings. At lift shafts they carried them down: Moth scooping up Lom in her weight-less bone-strong arms, one of her siblings with Elena. They jumped into space and leaped from stanchion to bolt, barely touching, barely slowing their plunge. Dull orange glowed far below and a cushion of heat rose from it.

Somebody screamed. Lom wondered if it might have been him, but he doubted it. He kept the lavender folder grasped tight to his chest: the truth he saved from the burning building.

Down and down they went into the closing heat, racing against it.

The outer walls of the Lodka were a crumbling sooty crust enclosing cubic miles of roaring roasting heat. Quiet crowds gathered at the cordon to watch the ancient building burn.

The Lodka's thousand exterior windows glowed baleful red. Panes burst and shattered and rained glass on the margin of Victory Square. Fragments splashed into the River Mir. Smoke cliffs, orange-bellied and flecked with whirling spark constellations, billowed above the collapsing roofscape and darkened the eggshell sky. Smuts and ash scraps drifted and fell far across Mirgorod. The whole city smelled of burning.

The Lodka – for four hundred years the dark cruel heart and flagship memory ark of the Vlast, the crouching, looming survivor of bombs and siege – the Lodka was ceasing to be, and that was a good thing happening.

Part Three

Part Three

Chapter Seven

Man will make it his purpose to master his own feelings, to raise his instincts to the heights of consciousness, to make them transparent, to extend the wires of his will into hidden recesses, and thereby to raise himself to a new plane, to create a higher social biologic type, or, if you please, a superman ... Man will become immeasurably stronger, wiser and subtler; his body will become more harmonised, his movements more rhythmic, his voice more musical. The forms of life will become dynamically dramatic. The average human type will rise to the heights of an Aristotle, a Goethe or a Marx. And above this ridge new peaks will rise.

Leon Trotsky (1879–1940)

There is no substance which cannot take the form of a living being, and the simplest being of all is the single atom. Thus the whole universe is alive and there is nothing in it but radiant life.

Konstantin Tsiolkovsky (1857–1935)

1

Engineer-Technician 2nd Class Mikkala Avril receives the letter that will change her life. It is waiting for her in the morning. Breakfast at the Kurchatovgrad Barracks.

Today is her twenty-fourth birthday, but she isn't counting years;

what matters is the accumulation of knowledge, the contribution she can make, not the piling-up of finished days you don't get back again. Only achievement is notable. Next week she takes examinations that will lead to her promotion, and she has a report to finish: her paper on the dynamics of volatile angel plasma under intense shearing pressures. There are efficiencies to be gained by scoring microscopic fresnel grooves in the face of the pusher plate. So she believes. The equations are beautiful: they click into place inevitably, like good engineering.

Mikkala Avril dreams of making universal vessels that are less crude and primitive and brutal. More *evolved*. She has had her hair cut short to save time in the mornings.

Citizen women! Race ahead of the lumbering carthorse years! Consecrate yourselves to speed!

Every day she devotes forty-five minutes to the gymnasium. A good worker is healthy and strong.

The envelope waiting for Mikkala Avril on the morning of her twenty-fourth birthday is flimsy and brown and bears no official crest. A crinkly cellophane window shows the typed address within. She has smoothed it and read the address three times. It is for her. On the gummed back flap there is a purple ink-stamp, slightly off centre – PERSONAL & CONFIDENTIAL – and a manuscript addendum neatly capitalised: *RECIPIENT ONLY. POST ROOM DO NOT OPEN.* She notices that the flap has not been slit. The envelope is unopened, its peremptory instruction to the surveillance office (remarkably) obeyed. They must have known where it was from. But who communicates confidentially with an engineer-technician 2nd class at the Kurchatovgrad Barracks and has the weight to give the censors pause?

Mikkala's heart runs faster: wild momentary anxieties show themselves, and crazy hopes she didn't know she had. It's probably nothing. Some error over her pay. A rebuke for some omission in the weekly returns. She leaves the envelope unopened on the tray and finishes her coffee.

Mikkala Avril is eking out the last empty moments of her old life. She is hesitating. She is wasting time. The letter stares back at her from the brink.

She rips it open and hooks out the single sheet.

RADIANT STATE

FROM THE DIRECTOR, PROJECT PERPETUAL SUNRISE
PROFESSOR YAKOV KHYRBYSK

Technician Avril!

Please be informed, you have been selected for participation in Project PERPETUAL SUNRISE. You are to present yourself for duty at the Yarkoye Nebo Number 3 Institute immediately on receipt of this communication. Personal effects are not required and none should be brought. All necessary items will be provided. Onward travel will be arranged.

This is a secret appointment which you should discuss with no one. Conversation with your current colleagues and officers must be avoided. You are now under my command, and all other instructions are herewith superseded and void. The nature of your new duties will be explained to you at the institute.

I congratulate you, Technician Avril. You will be contributing to special and challenging tasks of tremendous significance for the future of the New Vlast.

You should know that your name was brought to my attention as a candidate for this task by President-Commander Rizhin himself, acting personally. Your courageous determination and clarity of thought at the launch of *Proof of Concept* has been recognised by the award of Hero of the New Vlast . This is of necessity a secret decoration, of course. No medal can be given. Your promotion is confirmed without examination. I look forward to knowing you better.

Yakov Khyrbysk, Director

2

L om sat at the desk in the guardhouse at the entrance to the drive that led to Lukasz Kistler's house. The guard was slumped in the corner, unconscious. He'd have a headache but he would recover: nothing a few days' rest wouldn't put right. Lom was wearing the guard's cap. The interior light was dim: his profile would pass muster. Casual inspection from a distance, anyway. There was always risk.

There were two telephones on the desk: one an outside line, the other connected to the house's own internal system. A typed list of extension numbers was pinned next to it. LOBBY. GARAGE. HOUSE-KEEPER. SWITCHBOARD. SECURITY. STUDY. BEDROOM. Lom took a guess and chose the bedroom. It was almost midnight. He dialled the three-digit number.

And seven miles away in a windowless basement in the headquarters of the Parallel Sector a lamp on a switchboard console winks into life. The night duty operator stubs out her cigarette, puts on her head-phones, flicks a switch and begins to type.

Kistler Residential – Internal
23.47 Transcription begins

Kistler: Yes?
Unknown caller: I wish to speak with Lukasz Kistler.
Kistler: This is Kistler. Who the fuck are you?
Caller: You don't know me.
Kistler: Where are you calling from? How the hell did you get this number?
Caller: I have information for you and I am told you are someone who might make use of it. I am told you are a person of courage and independence. Was I told right?
Kistler: Who is this? What are you talking about? What kind of information?
Caller: Information of consequence. Documentary proofs.
Kistler: Proofs? Proofs of what?
Caller: Proofs that a certain person is not who he says. Proofs of conspiracy. Deception. Assassination. The seizure of power by a revolutionary terrorist operating under a false name with the collusion of certain very senior elements within the official security services.
Kistler: When would this happen?
Caller: It has happened. It has already happened. I am talking about the greatest power there is, and I am talking about incontrovertible documentary proofs.

Kistler: [*Pause*] Why are you telling me this?

Caller: I want to give these proofs to you. I want you to use them.
I am told you are a person who could do this. You have strength
of will. You have influence and you are independent of mind.
You are also perhaps a decent man. I offer you these proofs,
which in the right hands are dangerous – I would say deadly – to
the utmost power.

Kistler: Who are you working for?

Caller: Nobody.

Kistler: This is a trap. A loyalty test. Or you are a crank. Either way,
I cannot speak to you. Fuck off and leave me alone.

Call disconnected

23.50 Transcription begins

Kistler: Hello?

Unknown caller: I am not a liar. I am not a crank. This is not a
trap.

Kistler: Then you are a most dangerous kind of man. You should
not have this number.

Caller: I'm offering you a chance to act. To make a change. Perhaps
to take power yourself if that's what you want. The utmost
power in the land is a deception. A plot. A man who is not what
he seems. See my proofs, Kistler. Let me bring them to you. I
will come to your house. See what I have, Kistler. Listen to me,
then decide.

Kistler: [*Pause*] When?

Caller: Now. I am at your gate. All you need do is tell your door
security to let me in. [*Pause*] I'm coming now, Kistler. Five
minutes. Tell them to let me in.

Kistler: They will search you.

Caller: That is reasonable. I expected that. I am unarmed. I'm
coming now.

Kistler: Wait. Who are you? What is your name?

Call disconnected

23:51 – Transcription ends

The transcription operative pulls the sheet from the platen, slides it into an envelope, adds it to the pile in her tray and lights another cigarette. She gives no thought to what she has heard. No reaction at all. Nothing she ever hears leaves any trace: she listens and types and then she forgets. She is a component in a transmission mechanism only, an instrument with no more capacity for retention than the headphones and the typewriter she uses. That's the safe way, the survivor's way, and she has been in her job for many years. If she happens to see the consequences of her transcripts later in the rise and fall of magnates and the newspaper reports of arrests and trials, she takes no notice and never says anything. Even to herself she makes no remark.

It's for others to read the transcripts in the morning and make of them what they will.

3

L om walked the length of Kistler's gravel drive in darkness, waiting for the sudden flood of light, the harsh call of a challenge, a bullet in the back. But there was nothing, only the restless animal calls from Kistler's menagerie in the summer night: the grunting of monkeys, the growl of a big cat. The air was heavy with the scent of orchids and roses. A peacock, startled, disgruntled, stalked away across the starlit lawn.

What am I doing here? Blundering on. Butting my head in the dark against trees to see what fruit falls, and every moment could be my last.

Kistler received him in his study, a dressing gown over his pyjamas. He sat on the couch, chain-smoking, and listened in silence as Lom outlined the facts against Rizhin. Told him the story of the rise of Josef Kantor, the list of his terrorist acts, Lavrentina Chazia's connection with him, their involvement in the assassination of the Novozhd by Lakoba Petrov. Lom made no mention of the living angel in the forest, Maroussia or the Pollandore.

'But you haven't brought me these papers from Chazia's archive?' said Kistler when Lom had finished. 'They're not with you now?'

'No.'

'Then you misled me.'

'I have them,' said Lom. 'They're nearby but safe, where you will not find them. If I don't emerge from here in another hour, they will be destroyed.'

'Perhaps that would be for the best.'

'They are as I have said.'

'But who are you? You ask me to take your word on trust, yet I don't even have a name. You attack my guard and force yourself into my house, and tell me this wild story, which if it's true—'

'It is true,' said Lom. 'I told you: I have authentic documentary proofs.'

'If it's true, for me to even hear it is lethal. Even if it's not true, look at the position you put me in by coming here. How am I to react? I should make a report immediately, but if I do that Rizhin will feed me to Hunder Rond anyway. You tell me others have died to keep this rumour silent, and I don't doubt that, even if all the rest of this is horse shit. The only thing I can safely do is have you shot myself, here and now. Get rid of your carcass quietly and forget you ever came. There are a half a dozen VKBD men in the house. It would be straightforward enough to arrange.'

'You'd have done it long before now, if you were going to,' said Lom. 'You wouldn't have let me reach the door. Though I'm not so easily killed.'

'Maybe I was curious,' said Kistler. 'Maybe I'm not afraid of a little risk. You're an impressive fellow. You intrigue me. But I need to know who I'm dealing with.'

'My name is Lom. I used to be a senior investigator in the Political Police. Six years ago I was commissioned by Under-Secretary Krogh to pursue the terrorist Josef Kantor. This is what I have found out.'

'Used to be?' said Kistler. 'And what are you now?'

'My official career came to an end. I'm freelance now.'

'You work for no one? Really?'

'I work alone,' said Lom

'You're one of Savinkov's experiments, I think?' said Kistler. 'That I can see for myself.'

Lom's hand went to his forehead, reaching for the indentation in his skull where the angel piece had been before Chazia gouged it out.

It was an involuntary movement. He caught himself and pulled his hand away. Too late. It was a weakness shown, but there was nothing to be done.

'That's gone now too,' he said.

'I see,' said Kistler. 'OK. Let's say I accept all this. Let's say I take you for what you say you are. Let's say you're a good fellow and your heart's in the right place. My advice to you is to destroy these proofs of yours. Burn them. Forget it. Get on with your life and find something else to do.'

'You're not interested then. You will do nothing. You will not take my proofs.'

'Nobody will take them, man! What you have is useless. Worthless. Rubbish. It is no good, no good at all. Oh it's good police work, surely, but police work will not bring Rizhin down.'

'But—'

'Listen. I'll tell you something about Rizhin—'

'Kantor. Josef Kantor.'

Kistler shrugged.

'Rizhin or Kantor,' he said. 'It makes no difference. It's just a name.'

'No!'

'Listen to me. I sympathise with you, Lom. I should not say so, but I do. Osip Rizhin is a terrible man. He bullies, he intimidates, he kills. He diverts resources to the military and to idiotic pet projects like the fucking space programme. He sells our grain to our enemies while our people starve by the million. The ordinary economy is collapsing and he has no idea at all. Industrially the Archipelago walks all over us. We have no chance. You can't run a modern nation on the labour of convicts and slaves, for fuck's sake. It's not sustainable. In ten years this Vlast of Rizhin's will be history's forgotten dust. I see this and it pains me. I do what I can—'

'You do nothing,' said Lom.

'I do what I can. Here's the truth about Rizhin. Not the story, the truth. The public fiction is maintained that Papa Rizhin runs his New Vlast alone. He sits in his plain office and smiles, bluff and avuncular, and through the haze of his pipe smoke he sees everything that happens. He intervenes everywhere. Nothing is done without Rizhin's permission and every decision is his. He is the authority on all subjects. Politics. Culture. History. Philosophy. Science. Works in his name are published in their millions and studied by millions. That is the fiction for the people. Recognise it?'

Lom said nothing.

'It's shit,' Kistler continued. 'Of course it's shit. The New Vlast is huge, complex and technical. One man couldn't possibly direct the government, the armed forces, the security services and the economy. Rizhin needs support. He needs lieutenants. People with the expertise and competence to make decisions of their own. Yes?'

'Go on,' said Lom.

'Have you never wondered,' said Kistler, 'what kind of person works for Rizhin? Does it not astonish you that people will do this, knowing what they do? They tolerate the bullying and the humiliation and worse; they accept terror and purges; they know the fate of their predecessors and still they step forward, still they accept appointment to the Central Committee, still they do Rizhin's work, assiduously and as well as they can. Don't you wonder why?'

'You should know. You're one of them.'

'Not really. You do not know me yet. Rizhin's lieutenants are a special sort of person. Iron discipline and faithful adherence to the norms of thought. They continuously adapt their morality, their very consciousness, to the requirements of the New Vlast. Without reservation, Lom. Absolutely without reservation. But above all – you must understand this, it is the key – they are *ambitious*. For *themselves*. They don't support Rizhin because they believe in him, but because they believe in *themselves*. They want the power and prestige he gives them, and the gratification of their nasty little needs. Half of them will be imprisoned or dead within the year, but everyone thinks it won't happen to *them*. They all believe, in the face of all the evidence, that they're different from the rest, that they can hang on and survive the purges and arrests. Blind ambition. They support Rizhin because he is their security, their leader and the feeder of their desires. It's a very distinctive cast of mind.

'And Rizhin understands this. Perfectly. He is the greatest ever player of the game. In the early days, when he was still fighting the civil war against Fohn and Khazar, he used to shoot his commanders at a rate of one a week, but he learned he couldn't shoot everyone. The people around the President-Commander must be effective, not paralysed. Terror is still the most powerful tool but he's more subtle now. He purges sparingly. He lets others do the intimidation for him. I've watched him learn. It's been a masterclass.'

Kistler paused to light another cigarette.

'So you see why your plan won't work?' he continued. 'To bring down Rizhin, you must win the Central Committee. There's no other way. But if you tell the Central Committee he's not Rizhin but Josef Kantor, they'll say – like I do – what's in a name? Tell them he killed the Novozhd and owes his position to Lavrentina Chazia, and they'll say – like I do – where are the Novozhd and Chazia now?'

'You see, Lom? You can't shake the Central Committee's faith in Rizhin's integrity of purpose, because they've no thought of it anyway. They simply couldn't give a flying fuck. Everyone has skeletons in the cupboard, and personal ambition is everything. Nobody in Rizhin's New Vlast wants to rake up memories. What's past is nothing here.'

'You're saying, do nothing, then,' said Lom, 'because nothing can be done. This is the counsel of despair. Like I said, you're one of them. You are ambitious too.'

'Perhaps. But my ambitions are of a different quality. I see further. I want more. I want better.'

'It makes no difference.'

'You know,' said Kistler carefully. 'A man like you might dispose of Rizhin if he wanted to. Nothing could be more straightforward. A bomb under his car. Seven grams of lead in the head. No Rizhin, no problem.'

'No good,' said Lom. 'Someone else would take his place. It's not the man that must be destroyed, it's the idea of him. The very possibility has to be erased.'

Kistler's eyes widened. He studied Lom carefully.

'This isn't just squeamishness?' he said. 'It's not that you're afraid.'

'I've killed,' said Lom, 'and I don't want to kill again, not unless I have to. But it's not squeamishness. Call it historical necessity if you like. It doesn't matter what you think.'

'I see. You really are more than a disgruntled policeman with a grudge.'

Lom stood to go. 'I made a mistake,' he said. 'I shouldn't have come. You're not the man I was told you might be. I'll find another way.'

'Wait,' said Kistler. 'Please. Sit down. I have a proposition for you. Perhaps I could use a fellow like you.'

'I'm not interested in being used.'

'Sorry,' said Kistler. 'Bad choice of word. But please hear me out.'

Lom said nothing.

'I share your analysis,' said Kistler. 'To put it crudely, Rizhin's way of running the show is a bad idea. It's effective but not efficient. History is against it. Frankly, I believe I could do better myself, and I want to try, but for this I need a weapon to bring him down. You have the right idea, Lom, but the wrong weapon. To make my colleagues on the Central Committee abandon Rizhin and come across to me, I need something that convinces them that his continued existence is against their personal interests *now*. If you can make them believe it'll go worse for them with him than without him, then he'll fall. But they *all* have to believe it, all of them at once, and they have to strike together; if not, Rizhin will just purge the traitors and his position will be stronger than ever. I need to convince them he's a present danger. A terrible weakness. A desperate threat. That's what I need evidence of, not your tale of forgotten misdemeanours and peccadilloes in the distant past.'

'But—' Lom began.

Kistler held up a hand to silence him.

'There is a way, perhaps,' he said. 'Let me finish. There's something going on that my colleagues and I have sensed but cannot see. It makes us uneasy and afraid. Rizhin has created a state within a state. The Parallel Sector. We are blind to Hunder Rond and his service, but it is vast, its influence everywhere. And Rizhin has secrets. A plan within a plan. Resources are still being diverted, just like in Dukhonin's day. Funds. Materials. Workers. The output of the atomic plants at Novaya Zima is far greater than we see the results of. Whole areas on the map are blank, even to us.

'A man in my position can't ask too many questions. I have my resources but I can't use them: the Parallel Sector's reach is too deep and the penalty for being caught is, well, immediate and total. But for you, Lom, it's different. I think you might just be the man for the job. I'll tell you where to look. I'll give you money. Whatever you need. If you fail, if you're caught, I'll deny all knowledge of you. No, I'll have you killed before you can implicate me at all. But if you find me something I can really use, then we'll be in business. You bring me back the weapon I need, Lom. This will be our common task.'

'I don't work for anyone but myself,' said Lom. 'I'm not a police-man. Not any more.'

'Ego talk,' said Kistler. 'I'm offering you an alliance, not fucking em-ployment. Call it cooperation in the mutual interest. Call it a beautiful friendship. A meeting of minds. Call it whatever soothes your vanity – I don't care. I don't need you. I was going along just fine before you came, but now I see an opportunity that's worth an investment and a risk. That's what you came here for, isn't it? What the fuck else are you going to do?'

4

Lieutenant Arkady Rett of the 28th Division (Engineers) left his division behind and led his men deeper into the forest. The division had become hopelessly bogged down. They were going in circles.

'Take a small party, Rett, and scout ahead,' the colonel had said. 'Three or four can travel more quickly. Find us an eastward path. Find us solid ground and somewhere to go.'

Rett chose two men, Private Soldier Senkov and Corporal Fallun, and walked out of the camp with them. Behind them the sky was black with the smoke of burning trees, and ahead lay woods within woods, always further in and further back, deeper and deeper for ever. There was no end to going on.

Rett had thought that entering the deeper woods would mean disappearing into darkness. He'd imagined a densely packed wall of trees. Impenetrable thorn-thicket walls. Endless columns of tall trunks disappearing up into gloom, and beneath the canopy nothing but silence. But the reality was different: open spaces filled with grass and fern and briars and pools of water; occasional oak and ash and beech, singly or in small groups; hazel poles so slender he could push them with one hand and they would bend and sway like banner staffs. Ivy and moss and sticky mud and fallen branches underfoot. The forest was the opposite of pathless; there were too many paths, and none led somewhere.

'Paths don't make themselves,' said Senkov.

The compass was useless. After the first day he didn't get it out of his pack.

On the second day Rett woke feeling small. The world was inexhaustible and he was one tiny thing alone. There was no human scale: hostile, featureless, relentless, the forest defeated interpretation. Rett was a constructor of bridges, a worker with tools, a rational man: he looked for pattern and structure and edge, and found none here. His mind filled the gaps, the spacious lacuna of unresolvable chaotic plenitude, with monsters. There were faces in the trees. Movement in the corner of the eye. Presences. Watchfulness. The nervous child he no longer was returned and walked alongside him.

Senkov and Fallun fell silent, sour, but the invisible child talked. The child saw the shadow-flanks of predatory beasts between the trees: witches and giants and forgotten terrors returning; the fear of being forever lost and never finding home again; men that were bears, stinking eaters of flesh. Trolls crowded at the edge of consciousness, importuning attention at the marginal twilit times. Dusk and dawn.

The 28th had crossed the edge into the trees at the start of summer, but it was chill and autumnal here. Mushrooms and mist and the damp smell of coming winter. There was always a cold wind blowing in their faces. The wind unsettled them: they didn't sleep well, tempers were short, always there was a feeling something bad was about to happen.

As they penetrated deeper into the trees Rett saw signs of ancient construction: overgrown earthworks; lengths of wall and ditch built of huge boulders, shaped by hand and smooth with moss and age, collapsing unrepaired; broken spans of bridge; tunnel entrances; empty lake villages rotting back into shallow green waters. Shaggy-haired grazing beasts, wisent and rufous bison, faded into further trees at their approach.

On the fourth day they came to the edge of an enormous hole in the earth's crust: not a canyon or a rift but a gouge, dizzyingly immense, approximately circular, about half a mile across. It was like a great throat, a punched hole, a core removed from the skin of the world. It was terrifying to stand at the brink and lean over, staring down into bottomless darkening depths. It seemed to Rett that there were faint distant points of light down there. It was as if they were stars, and he was seeing through to the night on the other side of the world. More than anything else he wanted to jump off and fall for ever. It cost him tremendously to tear himself away.

Rett and his men skirted the edge of the great gouge and pressed on. Deeper into the inexhaustible forest. They hacked white strips in the bark of trees to mark their way back out. On the eighth day Rett woke early, before the others. He woke in confusion out of stupefying dreams, a thick heavy pain in his head, his mouth dry and fouled.

Hard frost had come in the night. Mist – damp, chilling, faint, insidious, still – brushed against his face, filled his nose and lungs, reduced the endlessness of the surrounding trees to a quiet clearing edged by indeterminacy. His boots crunched on brittle, whitened grass and iron earth. The sound was intrusive. Loud and echoless. The trees seemed suddenly bare of leaves, sifting a dull and diminished light through the monochrome canopy of branches.

The intense cold made his fingers clumsy. Breath pluming in small clouds, he fumbled the tinder, dropped it, couldn't make his stiffened blue-pale hands work to get a fire started. The water was frozen in the bottle and the pan felt clumsy, and fell, spilling chunks of ice across the hearth. It took an age to coax a meagre, heatless flame into burning. There were a few dusty grains, the last of the coffee. He scattered them across sullen water. It didn't boil. He built up the fire with thick stumps of log and put a neat pile of others ready. The heat chewed at the wood, smouldering, strengthless, with occasional watery yellow licks of flame the size and colour of fallen hazel leaves. Smoke hung over it, drifting low, thickening the mist. Clinging to his hair.

Rett left Senkov and Fallun to sleep and climbed the shallow rise they'd chosen last night for shelter. The trees were awake. The many trees, watching. The weight of their attention pressed in on him, sucking away the air. It was so cold. His ankle was hurting. His limbs were stiff from too much walking.

Ten minutes later he was on a scrubby hilltop among hazel and thorn, looking across a wide shallow valley. Without trees above him he could see the sky, the grey-brown canopy of leaf-falling woodland spread out at his feet. A range of low hills on the further side climbing into distance and mist.

There was a new hill above the treeline. It hadn't been there the day before. A fingernail clot of dark purple-red, the rim of a second sun rising.

Rett hurried back down the slope to rouse the others.

All that day they walked in the direction of the red hill rising. The sky settled lower with thickening cloud banks and strange copper light. Trees spread around them in all directions, numberless, featureless and utterly bleak, a still, engulfing, unending tide of reddening blankness. Hour followed hour and always they passed between trees, and always the trees were replaced by more trees, and always the trees were the same. They were moving but getting nowhere because the forest was without boundary or finish or variation. Its immenseness was beyond size and without horizon. Walking brought them no nearer and no further away. Motion without movement. Everything unchanging copper and grey except the red hill. That was coming closer. They walked on towards it until it was too dark to move, and then they camped without a fire. Rett felt small beyond insignificance and absolutely without purpose or hope.

In the morning the red hill was nearer. It had moved in the night. Its lower slopes were ash-grey. Rett started towards it. The air prickled, metallic. The trees were looking ill. They had no leaves.

Fallun hung back. 'I don't want to,' he said. 'It's not right.'

The sky was low and copper again. The air tasted of iron, the fine hairs on their skin prickled.

'We must,' said Rett. 'Orders. I think that's what we've come to find.'

Fallun stared at him. 'Orders?'

'"Find a hill that might be moving,"' said Rett. 'It's the primary objective of this whole thing. Burning the forest is secondary. The icing on the cake. The colonel told me before we left.'

'A hill?' said Senkov? 'A moving *hill*? What the fuck's it meant to be?'

'An angel,' said Rett. 'But alive.'

Fallun took a step backwards. Hitched his pack off his shoulder and dropped it. 'No. No way. Not me.'

Rett stared at him. He didn't know what to say. He was an engineer. 'It's an order.'

'Fuck orders.'

'An *order*, Fallun.'

Fallun looked at Senkov. Rett felt sick, like he was going to throw up again. Senkov blushed and looked at his shoes.

'Fuck orders,' said Fallun again, 'and fuck you both. I'm going home.'

Rett hesitated. Then he shrugged. 'Wait here,' he said. 'We'll pick you up on the way back.'

Shreds of low bad-smelling mist drifted across the ground. A sour sickening smell under the copper sky, the light itself dim and smeary. The earth in places a crust over smouldering embers – the roots of trees burning under the ground – but there was no heat.

The wind brought the smell of burning earth and something else, something edgy, prickling and dark. Like iron in the mouth.

'Something bad,' said Senkov. 'Careful.'

'We have to see,' said Rett. 'We have to go there.'

'OK,' said Senkov. 'But be careful.'

The red hill was hundreds of feet high. Rounded, fissured, extending shoulder-slopes towards them. Rett felt the pressure of its gaze.

A mile before they reached it, the earth was a brittle cinder crust that crunched and broke underfoot. Boots went through ankle-deep into smouldering cool blue flames. The ground was on fire without heat and the air sang with electricity. Ahead of them were pools of colourless shimmering. Small lakes but not water. The undergrowth and the trees were white as bone. Ash-white, they snapped at the touch.

A grey elk struggled to get to her feet and run from their approach but couldn't rise. She had no hind legs. She gave up and collapsed to her knees and watched them with dull frightened eyes. Milky blue-grey eyes. Like cataracts.

Rett felt dizzy and almost fell.

'I can't feel my feet,' said Senkov. 'Please. This is far enough.'

'Just a bit further,' said Rett. 'Then we'll turn back.'

Five more minutes and they came upon the bodies of the giants. The giants weren't simply dead; they were destroyed, their bodies eroded and crumbling like soft grey chalk. Parts of the bodies were there and parts were not. Broken pieces were embedded with fragments of hard shining purple-black skin. Flinty bruises.

Objects crunched underfoot.

Senkov picked up an axe from the ground. The iron was covered with a sanding of fine grainy substance, a faintly bluish white, as if the metal had sweated out a crust of mineral salt. When he tried it against a tree the axe head broke, useless.

'What did this?' he said quietly

The copper was draining from the sky, leaving it the colour of hessian. Darker stains seeping up from the east. A hand of fear covered Rett's face so it was hard to breathe. Everything inside him was tight. Tight like wires.

'They're moving,' he said. 'Oh god, they're moving. They're not dead.'

The ruined giants were shifting arms and legs slowly. Scratching torn fingers at the air. Eyes opened. Mouths mouthing. Wordless. The eyes were blank and sightless and the words had no breath: they were parodic jaw motions only. One body was twisting. Jerking. A hand seemed to grasp at Rett's leg. He recoiled and kicked out at it, and the whole arm broke off in a puff of shards and dust. Gobbets of bitter stinking sticky substance splashed onto his face. Into his mouth. Rett made a noise somewhere between a groan and a yell, leaned forward and puked where he stood.

'They're dead,' said Senkov. 'The poor fuckers are dead, they just don't know it.'

'We need to get out of here,' said Rett. 'We need to move. Now.'

Senkov stumbled and fell, twitching, shuddering, struggling to breathe. White saliva bubbles at the corner of his mouth. Thick veins spreading across his temples, the muscles in his neck standing out like ropes. His back arched and spasmed. He fell quiet then but his chest was heaving. His eyes stared at the sky. They were dark and intent, unfocused inward-looking whiteless bright shining black. Senkov's mouth began to speak words but the voice was strange.

'Tell him,' he said monotonously and forceful and very fast, over and over again. 'Tell. Tell. Tell I am here. Tell I am found. Come for me. Come for me. Nearer now. Nearer. Tell him to come.'

5

Engineer-Technician 1st Class Mikkala Avril, secret Hero of the New Vlast, personally selected for a glittering new purpose and destiny by Papa Rizhin himself, freshly uniformed, all medicals passed A1, tip-top perfect condition in body and mind, ready and willing to hurl herself into the shining future, takes a seat across the desk from Director Khyrbysk himself. In his own office. A welcome and induction from the very top. She is conscious of the honour, flushed and more than a little nervous. She must work hard to concentrate on what he is saying, and the effort makes her frown. It gives her an air of seriousness that belies the trembling excitement in her belly. She holds her hands together in her lap to stop them fidgeting.

Here she is, twenty-four years and two days old, a thousand miles north-east of Kurchatovgrad and Chaiganur, in a place not shown on any map, on the very brink of what it's really all about. This is Project Perpetual Sunrise. This is Task Number One.

Khyrbysk is a cliff of a man, a slab, all hands and shoulders and clipped black curly hair, but his voice is fluent and beautiful and his pale eyes glitter with cold and visionary intelligence. They burn right into Mikkala Avril and she likes the feeling of that. Director Khyrbysk sees deep and far, and Mikkala Avril is important to him. He wants her to hear and understand.

'All known problems –' Khyrbysk is saying in that voice, that fine beguiling voice '– all known problems have a single root in the problem of death. The human lifetime is too brief for true achievement: personality falls away into particulate disintegration before the task at hand is finished. But this will not always be so. Humanity is not the end point of evolution, but only the beginning.

'Now is the telluric age, and our human lives are brief and planetary. Next comes the solar age, when we will expand to occupy our neighbour planets within the limits of our present sun. But that is merely an intermediate step on the way to the sidereal age, when the whole of the cosmos, the endless galactic immensities, will be ours. This is inevitable. The course of the future is fixed.'

Director Khyrbysk pauses. Mikkala Avril, brows knotted in concentration, wordless in the zero hour and year, burning with purpose and energy, nods for him to continue.

I understand. I am your woman. Papa Rizhin was not wrong to pick me out.

'You see immediately of course,' says Khyrbysk, 'that the contemporary human body isn't fit for such a destiny. Active evolution, that is the key: the extension of human longevity to an unlimited degree; the creation of synthetic human bodies; the physical resurrection of the dead. These are the prerequisites for the exploration and colonization of distant galaxies. The living are too few to fill the space, but that is nothing. The whole of our past surrounds us. Everybody who ever lived – their residual atomic dust still exists all around us and holds their patterns, remembers them – and one day we'll resurrect our dead on distant planets. We will return our ancestors to life there! The whole history of our species, archived, preserved, will be recalled to live again in bodies that have been re-engineered to survive whatever conditions prevail among the stars. And when that time comes the whole cosmos will burn with the light of radiant humankind.'

Mikkala Avril, astonished, excited, confused and strangely disturbed, feels it incumbent upon her to speak. She opens her mouth but no words come.

'You doubt the practicality of this?' says Khyrbysk. 'Of course you do. These ideas are new to you. But there is no doubt. We have already seen the proof of it. What do you think the angels were, but ourselves returning to greet ourselves. It is a matter of cycles. The endless waves of history. The great wheel of the universe turns and turns again.'

Mikkala Avril is puzzled by this reference to angels. It stirs vague troubled memories. Uncertain images of large dead forms. Dangerous giants walking. She thinks she might have heard talk of such things long ago, but nothing is certain now. She can't remember clearly. Rizhin's New Vlast burns with such brightness, the blinding glare of it whites out the forgotten past.

'Of course,' says Khyrbysk, 'our science is far from being able to do this yet. The success of *Proof of Concept* was a great step forward, but there are technical problems that may take hundreds, even thousands of years to overcome. Yet surely if all humanity is devoted to this one single common purpose then it will be done. And that, Mikkala Avril, is what the New Vlast is for. Rizhin himself appointed me to this task, as he appointed you to yours. "Yakov," he said to me then, "devote all your energies to this. Abandon all other duties. This, my friend, this is Task Number One."'

6

When Mikkala Avril had left him, Yakov Khyrbysk reached for pen and paper. A man of many cares and burdens, he had a letter to write.

Secretary, President-Commander and
Generalissimus Osip Rizhin!

When you entrusted me with the responsibilities of Task Number One, you invited me to come to you if ever I needed your help. 'I am a mother to you,' you said (your generous kindness is unforgettable), 'but how may a mother know her child is hungry, if the child does not cry?' Well now, alas, your child is crying.

Our work progresses better than even I might have hoped. We have had technical successes on many fronts, and our theoretical understanding of the matters under consideration advances in leaps and bounds. I claim no credit for this: our scientists and academicians work with a will. Your trust and vision inspire us all daily. Building on the success of the Proof of Concept (which came to an unfortunate end, but the fault there lay with the human component not the ship herself, and we have stronger human components in preparation now), we are well ahead in production of the greater fleet. Both kinds of vessels required are in assembly. The supply of labour continues to exceed attrition and our mass manufacturing plants outperform expectations (see output data enclosed).

But we have struck an obstacle we cannot ourselves remove. Our reserves of angel matter are exhausted. We simply do not have a supply sufficient to power the launch of the numerous ships envisaged. All known angel carcasses have been salvaged and there is no more.

*Helpless, I throw myself at your feet. Find us more angel matter and
we will deliver you ten thousand worlds!*
Yakov Khyrbysk, Director

Three days later he received a scribbled reply.

*Don't worry about the angel stuff, that's in hand. Forget it, Yakov –
soon you'll have all you can imagine and ten thousand times more.
Drive them on, Yakov, drive your people on. Make the clocks tick faster.*
O. Rizhin.

7

Kistler had given Lom an envelope with a thousand roubles in
it and a place name.
    *I hear whispers, Lom. Phrases. Vitigorsk, in the Pyalo-
Orlanovin oblast. Post Office Box 932. That's all I can give you. Make of
it what you can*

A thousand roubles was more than Lom had ever held at one time
in his life. He bought an overnight bag, some shirts and a 35-millimetre
camera (a Kono like Vishnik had, but the newer model with integral
rangefinder and a second lens, a medium telephoto). He also bought
ten rolls of fast monochrome film and an airline ticket to Orlanograd.
From there he took buses. Four days and several wasted detours
found him set down at a crossroads in a blank space on the map. He
shouldered his bag and began to walk west into the rhythmic glaring
of the late-afternoon sun.

Grasslands and low, bald, rolling hills.

Lom measured his progress by the heavy pylons and the rows of
upright poles that stretched ahead of him: high-tension power cables
and telephone wires. If the wires and cables were heading somewhere,
then so was he.

The road was straight and black and new, a single asphalt strip edged
with gravel. Wind hummed in the wires, slapped his coat at his knees,
scoured his face with fine dry sandy dust. He'd never felt so alone or

so exposed. He was the only moving thing for miles. Whether he was going forwards or backwards he had no idea. There was no plan. He put no trust in Kistler, except that Kistler's demolition of his proofs had the compulsion of truth, and Kistler had shown him a different tree to shake.

One tree's as good as another in that regard.

The world's turned upside down, and I'm the terrorist now and this is Kantor's world. Everything is changed and gone and new, and I am become the surly lone destroyer, opening gaps into different futures by destruction, ripping away the surfaces to show what's underneath.

One target's as good as another when everything is connected to every-thing else.

Maybe I'm just a sore loser, and this is nothing but resentfulness and grudge.

I never saw Maroussia on the river. Trick of memory. Didn't happen.

Six years. I've been alone too long.

A huge truck thundered up the road behind him. He had to step off into the grass to let it pass. Three coupled sixteen-wheeled containers in a cloud of diesel fumes and dust, the wheels high as a man. There were no markings on the raw corrugated-steel container walls, just fixings bleeding streaks of rust. The driver stared down at him from the elevation of his cab, a blurred face behind a grimy window. Lom nodded to him but the driver didn't respond.

Time to get off the road.

The forty-eight-wheel truck dwindled into the horizon and silence, leaving him alone under the weight of the endless grey sky. Lom turned and left the asphalt behind him. The grass was coarse under his feet, tussocky and sparse.

For the first time in far too long he opened himself to the openness around him. There was a hole in his head. A faint flickering drum-pulse under fine silky skin. A tissue of permeable separation.

He let the wind off the hills pass through him. The soil under the grass was thin. A skimming of roots and dust. He ignored it and felt for the rock beneath, the bones of the living planet. Beneath his feet were the sinews of the world, the roots of ancient mountains, knotted in the slow tension of their viscid churn. The low surrounding hills were eroded solid thunderheads.

Lom's heart slowed and his breathing became more quiet and easy.

He kept on reaching out, down into the dark of the ground, till he touched the heart rock of the world: not the sedimentary rocks, silt of seashell and bone, but the true heart rock, extruded from the simmering star stuff at the planetary heart. Layered seams of granite and lava, dolerites, rhyolites, gabbros and tuffs, buckled, faulted, shattered and upheaved under the pressure of their own shifting. Rock that moved too slowly and endured too long to grieve. He felt the currents of awareness moving through it, eddying and swirling, drifting and dispersing: sometimes obscure and indifferent and sometimes watchful; sometimes withdrawing inwards to collect in pools of deep dark heat, and sometimes sharpening into intense, brilliant, crystallised moments of attention.

There was life in the air. The ground wore a faint penumbra of rippling light like an electrostatic charge, the latent consciousness of the stone fields. He let the currents play across his skin. Felt them as a stirring of the fine small hairs of his arms and the turbulence of his blood. He was alive to the invisible touch of the deep planetary rock. It reached into his body to touch the chambers of his heart.

This is who I am. I will not lose sight of this again.

The grasslands were not empty. Everywhere, invisible vivid small animal presences burrowed and hunted. Bright black eyes watched him from cover. The high-tension power lines were black and sheathed in sleeves of smoke. When he opened his mouth to breathe, their quivering tasted metallic on his tongue.

Rizhin's new world was thin and brittle. Translucent. Lom reached up into the sky and made it rain simply because he was thirsty and he could.

Beyond the skyline was the place he was going to. He knew the way.

Walking in the endless forest, Maroussia Shaumian feels the stirring of the trees and the cool damp touch of moving air against her cheek. The faintest ragged edge of a distant storm.

Chapter Eight

See him – rescuer, lord of the planet,
Wielder of gigantic energies –
In the screaming of steel machines,
In the radiance of electric suns.

He brings the planet a new sun,
He destroys palaces and prisons
He calls all people to everlasting brotherhood
And erases the boundaries between us.

Vladimir Kirillov (1880–1943)

1

Vacation season came early for the Central Committee that year. A motion was tabled in plenum in the name of Genrickh Gribov, Secretary for War: 'To grant Osip Rizhin a holiday of twenty days.' It was a formality, preserving the fiction that Papa Rizhin worked for them; naturally the motion was approved by acclamation.

The wound on Rizhin's face was healing more slowly than he'd have liked: the assassin's bullet had reawakened the old problem with his teeth. He wanted southern sunshine, a change of food and good dentistry, so it was with some relief that he settled into his personal train for Dacha Number Nine in the mountains overlooking Zusovo on the Karima coast. Lobster and citrus trees.

VKBD detachments secured the route, six men per kilometre. Sixteen companies guarded the telephone lines and eight armoured trains continually patrolled the track.

And where Rizhin went the Central Committee followed. Holidays were serious business in Rizhin's New Vlast. Gribov and Kistler, Yashina, Ekel and the rest packed hastily and piled into their cars and trains. They all had dachas in the Zusovo heights. Hunder Rond flew on ahead to be there when they came.

2

E ngineer-Technician 1st Class Mikkala Avril works fourteen hours a day in a windowless room in the basement of a nine-floor block in the centre of the Vitigorsk complex, pausing only to bolt food and sleep in her one-room apartment in the House of Residence: bed, bookshelf, desk and chair.

They've given her a bank of von Altmann machines, six of them wired in linear sequence. Each machine has six cathode tubes, and a tube is 12,024 bits of data in 32 x 32 array. Each phosphorescent face is read, written and refreshed a hundred thousand times a second by electron beam. The smell of ozone and burning dust thickens the air. At the end of every shift her skin and clothes and hair stink of it. The odour pervades her dreams.

Her task is calculating pressure, force and trajectory. The vessels under development at Vitigorsk are larger and heavier than *Proof of Concept* by orders of magnitude – crude sledgehammer monsters – and the question presented to her for consideration is, one pressure plate or two? It's a matter of running the models again and again. Mikkala Avril is trusted to work alone, unsupervised, in silence, with her von Altmann array. She works through the models diligently. Progress is ahead of target.

But something is going wrong. Day by day Mikkala Avril's wide-eyed joy at the greatness of her purpose, her privilege, the task she's been selected for, is growing hollow. The sustenance it gives her is getting thin. The song of the New Vlast wearies her heart and jangles her nerves, even as her skin grows chalky-grey and her cropped hair loses its lustre.

The power of the detonations required to haul such behemoths crawling up the gravity well is terrifying: the ground destruction would gouge city-wide craters in the rock, obliteration perimeters measured in tens of miles. Mikkala Avril understands the numbers. She knows what they mean. But that's not the trouble: the continent is wide, the atmosphere is deep and broad.

In her rest periods she has ventured out into the Vitigorsk complex. She's seen the glow on the skyline at night from the forging zone, and she knows convict labour works there. The children sleeping on concrete. She's seen the people trucks come in. Yet that's not the trouble either: the labourers reforge their consciousness as they work; they welcome it and leave gladdened and improved. An efficient system that brings benefit to all.

No, it's the double mission parameter that corrodes her confidence. She doesn't understand it. It has not been explained.

She has not one model to work with, but two. Vessel Design One must hold propellant bombs sufficient to take it out of planetary orbit and speed it on its way across the cosmos into the sidereal age, and it will carry a store of empty casings to be fuelled on the moons of the outer planets. Staging posts. But Vessel Design Two, even more massive and with a payload provision twice that of Design One, needs no more power than to lift it into near orbit. A fleet of several hundred platforms, each dwarfing any ocean-going ship, lifted into orbit two hundred miles above the ground and settled stable there? What is the reason for this? It has not been explained. The variable is unaccounted for, and that's a lacuna of trust, a withholding of confidence that tugs at the edge of her and begins to unravel conviction.

She isn't fully conscious of what's happening. She doesn't have the right words, and if she ever did she's forgotten them now, the vocabulary of doubt eroded by the attrition of continually reset clocks, the accelerating repetition of year zero. What she feels is the uneasy itch of curiosity and upset at a distressing flaw in the machine. She takes it as a shortcoming in her own comprehension and sets about rectifying the fault, but her superiors frown and brush her off with critical remarks and the repetition of familiar platitudes. It never occurs to her that they don't know either.

Unhappy and alone, Mikkala Avril lingers in the refectory over the evening meal. Having no circle of companions (the theoretical mathematicians exclude her, so do the engineers of the von Altmann machines), she attaches herself to other groups and listens. She gets to know the bio-engineers – the humanity-synthesisers, the warriors against death – and picks up fragments of their talk. There are rumours of strange zones where clocks run slow and the dead climb from their graves. Quietly she joins the groups that gather around people returned from expeditions to find such places, which they say are shrinking fast and will soon be gone. She listens to the news of specimens collected. Samples of earth and air. But nobody knows or cares about the parameters of vessel design.

A chemist called Sergei Ivanich Varin, eager to seduce her, invites her to see the resurrectionists' laboratory after hours.

'Come on,' he says. 'I'll show you the freak shop.'

Strip lights flicker blue. The sickly stench of formaldehyde. Shelf after shelf of human babies in jars: misshapen foetuses and dead-born homunculi with bulging eyes, flesh softened and white like they've been too long under the sea. A boneless head, creased, flattened and flopped sideways. A torso collapsed in flaps of slumped waxy skin, diminutive supplicating arms raised like chicken wings. A lump with two heads and no internal organs, its shoulders ending in a ragged chewed-up mess.

Mikkala Avril coughs on choked-back sickness. Varin comes up close behind and nuzzles his face into her neck.

'No need to be frightened of the fishes. Big Sergei's here.'

She feels his hand sliding inside her jacket and blouse to cup her breast.

3

The lurid sleepless glare of the arc lamps and foundries and waste gas burn-off plumes of the Vitigorsk Closed Enclave was visible from two hours' drive away. A billboard on the approach road celebrated the shattering of the Vlast record for speed pouring concrete. TAKE SATISFACTION, LEADING WORKERS OF VITIGORSK! THE ENGINEERING CADRES SALUTE YOU! YOU HAVE RAISED A NEW CITY AT A PACE HITHERTO THOUGHT POSSIBLE ONLY FOR DEMOLITION! The entire ten-mile sprawl was enclosed by barbed wire and observation towers.

Lom brought the truck to a halt at the checkpoint, turned off the engine and swung down from the cab into a wall of noxious chemical fumes, plant noise, the smell of hot metal and the brilliance of floodlights bright as day. A guard in the black uniform of the Parallel Sector came over to check his papers. Two more hung back and covered him with automatic weapons.

The guard frowned.

'You're three hours late.'

Lom shrugged.

'Brake trouble,' he said. 'Fixed now.'

He shoved the sheaf of documents towards the guard. They were creased and marked with oily finger marks. Lom was wearing the truck driver's scuffed boots and shapeless coat. His hands were filthy.

'I could do with a wash,' he said. 'And I haven't eaten since breakfast.'

The guard glared at him.

'The transport workers' kitchen's closed. You're late.' He went through the papers slowly and carefully and took a slow walk around the truck, checking the seals. Comparing serial numbers with his own list. Kicking the tyres for no reason. Making a meal of it. *Bastard.*

Lom's heart was pounding. He smeared a greasy hand across his face, rubbing his eyes and stifling a yawn. There was a tiny sleeping compartment at the back of the cabin. The truck driver was in there, hidden under a blanket, trussed up with a rope, his own sock stuffed into his mouth.

The guard came back and handed Lom the signed-off papers. He looked disappointed.

Lom had wanted to come in late to avoid other drivers and catch the night-shift security: less chance they'd know the regular drivers by sight, that was the calculation. He hadn't reckoned on a guard who was bored and looking for trouble.

'What was the trouble with the brakes?' the guard said, still reluctant to let him go.

'Hydraulics leak,' said Lom. 'I patched it up. It should hold till I get back.'

He knew nothing about trucks and hoped the guard didn't either. *Please don't look in the cab.*

The guard signalled to the kiosk and the first barrier lifted.

'OK,' he said. 'Bay Five. Follow the signs. Check-in won't open till six but you can park there, and if you walk over towards the liquid oxygen generators there's a twenty-four-hour rest room for the duty maintenance. You might be able to get something to eat there. Maybe someone'll look at those hydraulics for you.'

Lom nodded. 'Thanks. Appreciate that.'

The gates of Bay Five were closed. No one was about. Beyond the chain-link fence was a row of dark containerless cabs. Lom checked on the driver. The man glared back at him with hot, frightened angry eyes. He pulled against the ropes and grunted through the sock in his mouth.

Lom hauled him up and propped him in a sitting position.

'Someone will find you,' he said, 'but not before morning. Don't try to call out; you'll make yourself throw up and that'll be very bad for you. You'll choke on it. Sit tight and wait.'

The man grunted again. It sounded like a curse.

Lom left the truck on the unlit apron in front of Bay Five, locked it and dropped the keys through a drainage grating. He reckoned he had seven hours before anyone would investigate. Maybe another half-hour before the alarm was raised.

So what the fuck do I do now?

He shouldered his bag and walked. The gun he'd taken from the VKBD man in Pir-Anghelsky Park was a comforting weight in his pocket.

He wandered among vast hangars and metal sheds. Chemical processing plants. Yards stacked with enormous pieces of shaped steel: curved components for even larger constructions. There was a river running thick and green under lamplight and a poisonous-looking artificial lake: scarfs of mist trailed across the surface and the acrid rising air warmed his face. Klaxons blared and gangs of workers in overalls changed shift. Parallel Sector patrols cruised the main roads in unmarked black saloons. It was easy to see them coming: he stepped into the shadows to let them pass.

For an hour he walked steadily, keeping to one direction as far as he could: east, he thought, though there was no way of telling. Vaporous effluent columns from a thousand vents and chimneys merged overhead in a low dense lid of cloud that shut out the night sky and reflected Vitigorsk's baleful orange glow.

A cluster of signs at an intersection pointed to meaningless numbered sectors but one caught his attention: PROTOTYPE – ASSEMBLY. Cresting a low hill, he found himself looking out across a floodlit concrete plain. From the centre rose a huge citadel of steel capped with a rounded dome. It resembled a massively engorged grain silo with stubby fins at the base. The trucks parked at the foot of it gave some sense of scale: if it had been a building, it would have been twenty or thirty floors high. Lom had seen pictures of the *Proof of Concept* – everyone had – and this thing was the same but much larger: a parent to a child.

From the cover of a low wall he took a couple of photographs just for the sake of it – he couldn't see what use Kistler could make of them, even if the facility was being kept secret from the Central Committee – and slipped away.

He glanced at his watch.

Almost 1 a.m.

He felt like he was playing at espionage.

What he needed was someone to talk to. Human intelligence.

PROJECT CONTROL. INSTITUTE OF RESEARCH. RESIDENTIAL CAMPUS.

It was a labyrinth of office blocks and apartment buildings, all crammed in and pressing against one another cheek by jowl: ramps and bollards and courtyards, walkways and flights of shallow concrete steps. Scrappy shrubs in concrete containers. Unlit ground-floor windows, service roads and areas of broken paving. A yard for refuse bins. Lom could see into uncurtained corridors. A few lights still burned in upper rooms.

Steps led up from a square with benches and flower beds to a revolving door. He heard voices, hushed but urgent. A couple standing in the splash of yellow light at the foot of the steps, arguing.

'No, Sergei. Please. I have to go now. I must go in.'

The woman was young. Slight and not tall, with cropped hair. Neat, sober office clothes. The man was bigger, older. Aggressive. Standing too close.

'Why not, Mikkala? What's wrong with me?'

'Nothing's wrong with you, Sergei. It's just ... It's late. I have to go.'

He grabbed her arm. 'Come on, Mikkala,' he said. 'You'll like it. I'm good. I'm the best.'

She pulled her arm away and stepped back. 'I said no.'

'You fucking bitch. All evening you've been ... What's a man supposed to think? You can't just turn round and say no, you cold fucking...' He reached out and pulled her towards him. Moved his head to hers. She turned her face away.

'Please, Sergei.'

Lom stepped out of the shadows.

'Hey,' he said. 'What's happening? Is this man bothering you?'

Sergei turned. 'Who the fuck are you?' He was swaying on his feet. Squinting. Lom smelled the aquavit thick on his breath.

'You should leave her alone,' said Lom.

'It's nothing to do with you, arsehole. Piss off. I'll break your fucking neck.'

Lom ignored him. 'Is this where you live?' he said to the woman. 'Come with me. I'll take you inside.'

'I said piss off, fuck-pig,' Sergei growled. 'You can't push me around.'

'Sergei,' said the woman. 'Don't.'

Sergei made a shambling lunge and swung a fist at Lom. He was big but soft and clumsy, and there wasn't much speed or power in the punch. Lom could have stepped out of the way. But he didn't. He raised his arm awkwardly as if to ward off the blow but he let it through. Turned his head slightly to take it on the side of the nose.

It hurt. A lot. He rocked back and put his hands to his face. Felt the warm blood flooding from his nostrils.

'You hit me!' he said to Sergei. 'I'm bleeding.'

'You were lucky, pig. Next time I'll break your fucking spine. And yours, bitch. I'll see you again. I'll ruin your fucking career. I'll ruin your *life*. People will listen to me.'

He turned and walked away, swaggering, unsteady. Lom tried to staunch the bleeding with the sleeve of the driver's coat. Smeared it around. It made quite a mess. His whole face felt stiff and sore.

'Are you all right?' said the young woman. She was thin and pale. Narrow shoulders. Her eyes glistened blurrily. She had been drinking too. 'Did Sergei hurt you? 'I'm sorry.'

'Not much,' said Lom. 'Not really. I'll be fine in a moment.' He pressed the back of his hand to his nose and brought it away covered in blood. Red and gleaming in the light from the doorway. 'I could do with a little cold water. And perhaps a towel. Is there somewhere …?'

The young woman hesitated. Made up her mind.

'Come with me,' she said. 'I'll find you something.'

4

Lom sat on the bed in Mikkala Avril's room. She brought a bowl of cold water and a couple of rough grey towels. He dipped the end of one in the bowl and dabbed at his face.

'I'm sorry,' she said. 'I haven't got a mirror. There's one across the way, in the bathroom, but it's women only. Actually we're not meant to have men in this building at all.'

'Don't worry,' said Lom. 'I'll manage. You tell me how I'm doing. Is there much blood?'

She sat down next to him on the bed and studied his face. Her face was very thin, her eyes unnaturally wide.

She hasn't been eating. Pushing herself too hard.

'There's still blood coming from your nose,' she said. 'There's some in your hair, and it's all over your coat.'

He wet the towel again and pressed it against the side of his nose.

'I don't even know your name,' he said. His voice was muffled by the cloth. 'I'm Vissarion.'

'Mikkala. And … thank you. For what you did just now.'

Lom waved it away. 'It was nothing.'

'But I feel awful,' said Mikkala. 'I was so *stupid*; I should never have gone with Sergei and got drunk like that, it's not the kind of thing I do. Ever. I'm not … I wasn't good at it. I didn't handle it. It all went wrong. Everything's gone wrong here. I was so proud when I came, but nothing's going right ... '

She was really quite drunk. Words tumbled out.

'Is Sergei your boyfriend?' said Lom.

'No!' She shook her head fiercely. 'No, no, not at all – nothing like that. I've met him two or three times, that's all. It's just ... I don't know many people here. I work on my own; there's no one I can talk to, and the resurrectionists are more friendly than the others. They drink and talk and they're not so cold and stuck-up. I started spending evenings with them. It was ... a mistake.'

'How long have you been here?' said Lom. 'At Vitigorsk?'

'Not long.'

'Same here,' said Lom. 'It's an odd sort of place. It's hard to know what it's all here for. It's not easy to fit in.'

Mikkala nodded. Her cheeks flushed.

'Yes!' she said. 'Yes! That's it exactly. That's how I feel too. I thought I could be friends with the resurrectionists. I thought they liked me, and it made me feel part of something, not just on my own.'

Lom put down the towel and showed her his face.

'How is it now?' he said.

Mikkala frowned and squinted.

'Your nose has stopped bleeding,' she said. 'It looks a bit sore though, and I think you're going to have a black eye. Oh, there's still blood in your hair. You poor man, I'm so sorry.'

Lom dipped his hands in the water and pushed them through his hair.

'So what went wrong tonight?' he said. 'I mean, if you don't want to talk about it ...'

'Oh it was awful,' said Mikkala. 'Sergei took me to see the resurrectionists' building, where they work. He showed me the freak shop and it was *horrible*. It made me really upset. I was sick on the floor, and afterwards ... Sergei had a bottle of aquavit and we went somewhere and drank it. He said it would make me feel better but it didn't. I drank too much – we both did. I don't normally drink at all. But after what I saw ...'

'At the freak shop?'

'Yes.'

'How's my hair, Mikkala? Do you mind just checking?'

'What? Oh, yes, it's fine now – I think so – but your coat ...'

'That's nothing.' Lom took it off and began to dab at the sleeve. 'What did Sergei show you at the freak shop?'

She shuddered. 'Dead babies. In *jars*. Ruined babies. Deformed foetuses.'

She went quiet.

Keep going, thought Lom. *Don't stop now.*

'Dead *babies*?' he said gently.

'It's not right,' said Mikkala. 'What they're doing. I don't think it's right. Of course they have their duty. It's their part of Task Number One, they're working to solve the common problem and that's a good thing, but ... they're experimenting with the effects of exposure to different isotopes, and it goes wrong all the time. It *feels* wrong. They have old bodies too. From graves.'

'Why are they doing that?'

'It's the resurrection programme, learning to grow artificial bodies and bring people back from death, making it so people can live for ever and not die any more. So we can make the long journey to planets around other stars. The Director told me himself, one day we'll be able to bring someone back to life if you have even just a few atoms left from their bodies, because atoms have memories and they're alive. Sergei said they're thinking now that you don't need living people on the ships at all, only a few crew: you could maybe just send out small pieces of the dead and bring them back to life when you get there.'

Lom remembered Josef Kantor's strange invitation to him, six years before, alone in Chazia's interrogation cell in the Lodka. Looking into Kantor's dark brown eyes was like looking into street fires burning.

Humankind spreading out across the sky, advancing from star to star!

Impossible, Lom had said, and Kantor slammed his hand on the table.

Of course it's possible! It's not even a matter of doubt, only of paying the price! Imagine a Vlast of a thousand suns. Can you see that, Lom? Can you imagine it? Can you share that great ambition?

It had seemed like an invitation. Lom had turned him down without a thought.

'But you must know this already,' said Mikkala. 'Everyone here knows about the resurrectionists.'

'Not me. I'm just a grease monkey. Rivets and bolts. I do what I'm told. I haven't been here long. Still learning the ropes.'

Mikkala got up from the bed and moved to the chair at the desk.

'I shouldn't talk so much,' she said. 'I feel giddy. I've had a lot to drink.'

'It's fine, Mikkala,' said Lom. 'You're fine. That thing with Sergei was a shock, but you'll be OK.'

'I'm sorry,' she said, 'I can't remember your name. I don't know what you do. I've never seen you before.'

'Vissarion. I'm a construction engineer.'

'What are you working on?'

Lom thought fast. 'Prototype assembly.'

'Yes? Really? Then maybe you can tell me about the—'

She stopped.

'I don't think I'm supposed to ask,' she said. 'I ought to know, for my work, but nobody will say. They don't trust me; they keep me in the dark and they expect me to work alone. I don't like it. I don't feel comfortable here; it doesn't feel *right*.'

'I'll tell you what I can, Mikkala. We're all in this together. Working for the common purpose. That's what Vitigorsk is all about. What do you want to know?'

'Oh, nothing.'

'What?'

'It's just … the vessels, the planetary ships … I'm supposed to be working on launch calculations, only there are two kinds, and one kind is meant to leave this planet and make the long voyages, but the other only needs to reach a low orbit, and I think there are going to be more of those. But that makes no sense, does it? It doesn't fit in and I don't know why. Which kind is it you're building? I've never even seen it.'

She was looking at him, hot and staring eyes. He could see the wildness there. She was on the edge.

'I don't know,' said Lom.

'Oh.'

'Like I said, I just build what I'm told.'

'You mean you wouldn't tell me,' she said fiercely, 'even if you knew.'

'Of course I would.'

Her shoulders slumped.

'I don't feel well,' she said. 'I'd like to sleep now.'

'I would tell you if I knew, Mikkala. I tell you what: I'll help you to find out.'

She got up unsteadily from the bed.

'I think you should go,' she said. 'You're not meant to be here, you know.'

'Of course.' Lom stood and started putting on the truck driver's coat. There was blood soaked into the sleeve.

'Who would know?' he said.

'Know what?'

'Who knows about the plans for the different ships? Where could we find out about that?'

'Some people know, but they won't say.'

'So who knows? Who could we ask, if we wanted to?'

'I … Oh, lots of them know. The von Altmann programmers, the supervisor of mathematics, the chief designer. And the Director of course. Khyrbysk knows everything.'

'Khyrbysk? Yakov Khyrbysk?'

'Of course.'

'Khyrbysk is here? Where?'

'What do you mean, where?'

'I mean where's his office?' said Lom.

'Why?'

'We're old acquaintances. I'd like to go and see him. Where's his office?'

Mikkala slumped down again on the bed.

'In the Administration Block,' she said. 'But …' She stared up at him. Her face was drawn and chalky. Dark tears behind her eyes. 'Oh god. I've made another mistake. I thought you were my friend.'

'I am your friend. Of course I am.'

'I don't think so.'

'You're a good person, Mikkala. I don't mean you any harm. I'm glad we met.'

'Please go now.'

'Get some sleep,' said Lom. 'Everything'll be fine.'

5

It was almost 2.30 a.m. when Lom found the Administration Block. Parallel Sector security patrols had slowed him up.

The building was dark and locked. He took a small torch and the roll of lock-picking tools from his bag, let himself in and locked the door behind him. Made his way up the stairs and started from the top. Fifteen minutes later he was in Khyrbysk's office. He extinguished the torch, drew the curtains and switched the desk lamp on.

He should have at least three hours before someone found the driver in the cab of his truck. Unless Mikkala raised the alarm, but he didn't think she would.

He felt bad about Mikkala.

There was a row of steel cabinets along the wall of Khyrbysk's office. Locked, but the locks were flimsy. No obstacle at all. He went through them methodically one by one, taking the most promising files across to the desk to read.

Piece by piece the story came together. Some of it he knew, but the rest … There were plans within plans. The *ambition*. Some of it was flat-out insane. He thought about trying to take photographs of the documents, but the light was poor and he had the wrong kind of lenses. He'd seen too many blurred and badly exposed copies of documents. He started pulling out pages and stuffing them into his bag. Whole files if need be. It wasn't ideal – Khyrbysk would know he'd been burgled – but it couldn't be helped.

By 4.30 a.m. he had the whole picture. It was lethal. All that Kistler needed to work with, and more. Except that nothing tied it for certain to Rizhin, and he was running out of time.

There was a green steel safe behind the door. He hadn't touched it yet because of the combination lock. He didn't know how to open those. But everyone wrote their combination somewhere.

Lom went through the drawers of Khyrbysk's desk. Nothing. Checked the blotter but it was no help. Looked inside the covers of the books on his shelves. There was nothing that looked remotely like a combination to a safe.

Think. Think.

He went out into the corridor. There was a card on the door of the next office, tucked into a holder by the handle: ASSISTANT TO THE DIRECTOR.

Secretaries always knew the combinations to their boss's safe. Lom went into the room. There was an appointments diary next to the telephone. He flicked through the pages rapidly. On the inside back cover was a sequence of numbers. Four groups of four. In pencil.

Why would pencil be more secure than pen?

So you could erase it later.

He took the diary back into Khyrbysk's office and tried the numbers, but they didn't work. The safe didn't open.

Shit.

Then he tried them backwards.

The tumblers fell into place and he heard the lock click open.

On the bottom shelf of the safe was a small stack of brown folders. Not official files. Titles printed carefully in manuscript. Black ink.

Private Correspondence.

Conference – Byelaya Posnya.

There was no time to look inside: grey light was beginning to show behind the curtains in the window. Lom pushed the folders into his overloaded bag and switched off the desk lamp.

When he came out of the Administration Block there was a dull band of light across the eastern sky. Dawn came late and dark to Vitigorsk under the livid permanent cloud. In the plush quiet of Khyrbysk's office Lom had forgotten how the air stank. His bag was bulging. The sleeve and lapels of his coat were stained with his own dried blood. He looked a mess.

There was another truck loading bay a few blocks away. He'd noticed it in the night. He hustled, half-walking, half-running. The alert could come any moment now. He had to get clear of the checkpoints and on the road.

The gate of Bay Nineteen was open. An early driver unlocking his containerless cab. Lom circled round behind it.

The driver was lean, compact, energetic; long nose, flashing white teeth, thick black moustache; glossy black curls under a shiny leather cap. The kind of fellow that carried a knife. Bright black eyes narrowed viciously when he saw Lom's gun.

'Keep your hands out of your pockets,' said Lom. 'I'll be in the back of the cab. All I want is a ride out, no trouble for you at all. But I'll be watching you. I'll have the gun at your head. You say anything at the checkpoint, you make any move, any sign at all, and there'll be shooting. Lots of it. And you'll be caught in the crossfire, I'll make sure of that. You'll be first. I'll splatter your brains on the windscreen.'

The driver spat and stared at him. Said nothing. Didn't move.

'And I've got five hundred roubles in my pocket,' said Lom. 'It's yours when we're fifty miles from here.'

'Show me.'

Lom reached into his inside pocket with his left hand. Showed him the thick sheaf of Kistler's money.

'Pay now,' the driver said.

'Fuck you,' said Lom. 'We're not *negotiating*. It'll be like I say. Nothing different. Move. Quickly.'

The driver spat again and nodded. Stood back to let Lom climb aboard.

'You first,' said Lom

The driver swung up and slid across behind the wheel. Lom followed and squeezed into the sleeping compartment. Crouched down behind the driver's seat.

The engine roared into life.

6

Investigator Gennadi Bezuhov of the Parallel Sector, Vitigorsk Division, arrested Engineer-Technician 1st Class Mikkala Avril at three the next afternoon, less than ten hours after the discovery of the intrusion into Director Khyrbysk's office. Bezuhov presented her with his evidence: the statement of assaulted truck driver Zem Hakkashvili; the accusation of assaulted chemist Sergei Varin; the reports of communications operatives Zoya Markova and Yenna Khalvosiana, who overheard a male voice in Avril's room in the small hours of the night; the damp towel under her desk, stained with blood and engine oil. Suspect descriptions provided by witnesses Hakkashvili and Vrenn were undoubtedly of the same person.

The interrogation was brief. Suspect Avril, in a condition of marked emotional distress, immediately made a full confession and provided a detailed account of her encounter with the terrorist spy, whom she knew as 'Vissarion'. She admitted discussing with him restricted information concerning the work of Project Continual Sunrise. She had provided guidance and assistance in breaking into the Director's office and stealing Most Secret papers.

Engineer-Technician Avril's attitude under interrogation demonstrated poor social adjustment, psychological disturbance and instability, personality disorder, pathologically exaggerated feelings of personal importance, severe criticism of senior personnel and opposition to the purposes of her work and deep-seated internal deviation from the norms, aims and principles of the Vlast. Investigator Bezuhov permitted himself to observe that the subject had been promoted to her current rank without passing though normal processes of assessment, and had been allowed to work unsupervised on tasks for which she lacked the necessary intellectual capacities and technical credentials.

Bezuhov's superiors – Major Fritjhov Gholl, commander, Parallel Sector, Vitigorsk, and Director Yakov Khyrbysk himself – saw the broader perspective. They were acutely aware that Mikkala Avril was a Hero of the New Vlast, recruited and promoted on the instruction of Osip Rizhin himself, and she was in possession of information which must not be permitted to escape the confines of the project. Also they were not blind to the fact that the supervision of Mikkala Avril at Vitigorsk was not above criticism.

In the light of these additional considerations it was clear to Bezuhov's superiors that the Avril case required sensitive and flexible treatment. Embarrassment must be avoided. Their own careers were at stake, and surely Rizhin himself would prefer to know nothing of this. A judicial trial followed by a period in a labour camp was out of the question.

'Special handling, Gholl,' said Khyrbysk. 'In the circumstances? Don't you think?'

Gholl accepted the Director's judgement was sound, as ever.

Special handling. Seven grams of lead in the back of the head and the body dumped in the Cleansing Lake to dissolve.

'But retain a sample of body tissue, Gholl,' said Khyrbysk. 'Mikkala Avril had promising qualities. Death is temporary and she will be recalled, not once but millions of times, to walk for ever in perfected forms under countless distant suns.'

It was a comforting thought. The Director was not a harsh man. He looked to the radiance of humankind to come, and in dark days he lived by that.

'You understand, Director, I will have to report back to Colonel Rond?' said Gholl. 'I must do that.'

'Naturally.'

'You need not be concerned; the colonel is always discreet.'

7

The 28th Division (Engineers), guided by Lieutenant Arkady Rett, arrives at the edge of the living angel's cold-burning anti-life skirt where the trees are dying. They build walkways across the cold smouldering embers, the flimsy crusts of ground. The red hill advances and they retreat before it. Observations suggest it is picking up speed.

The commanding officer wrestles with many practical problems. Prolonged contact with the hill's margin is troublesome. The metal of his machines grows weak and brittle, and his people fall sick. Their limbs and faces and bodies acquire strange patches of smooth darkness. Their extremities grow numb, whiten and begin to crumble. An hour a day is the safe limit, all they can stand. But the commanding officer makes progress. Now he has lines of supply, he puts the sappers on rotation. The excavation gear arrives. They reach the lower slopes and begin to dig.

Corporal Fallun, who refused an order and abandoned his comrades, was never seen again. Rett didn't find him on his way back, and Fallun is assumed to be lost in the woods. The commanding officer classifies him a deserter and thinks of him no more. Fallun's comrade, Private

Soldier Senkov, who returned with Rett but never regained his senses and babbles relentlessly, never sleeping, is sent back out of the forest on a returning barge. He did his duty and the commanding officer recommends a sanatorium cure.

A piece of Archangel rides Senkov's mind down the river and out of the trees. Quiet and surreptitious, all hugger-mugger, he slips the green wall and squeezes a tenuous blurt of himself through the gap into Rizhin world.

It is the merest thread of Archangel. A wisp of sentience. But he is through. He inhales deeply and shouts defiance at the sky.

This – this! – this is what he needs!

The impossible slow forest behind the green wall was killing him. There was no time there. There was no history.

But he finds Rizhin world different now. Hard. Quick. Lonely. There is no place for living angels here: the whole world stinks of barrenness and death.

Desperately he scrabbles for purchase and purpose.

Archangel! Archangel! I am beautiful and I am here!

And a tiny distant voice answers from the west. A shred of shining darkness from the space between the stars.

Chapter Nine

My age, my predatory beast –
who will look you in the eye
and with their own blood mend
the centuries' smashed-up vertebrae?

Osip Mandelstam (1891–1938)

1

Vasilisk the bodyguard, six foot three and deeply tanned and sleek with sun oil, naked but for sky-blue trunks, runs five springing steps on his toes, takes to the air and executes a long perfect dive. Enters the pool with barely a splash, swims twelve easy lengths, hauls out in a single smooth movement and lies stretched out on a towel – blue towel laid on perfect white poolside tiles – in the warmth of the morning sun.

He lies on his back with eyes half closed, arms spread wide to embrace the sun, the beautiful killer at rest, empty of thought, breathing the scent of almonds. His slicked yellow hair glistens, his firm honey-brown stomach is beaded with water jewels. Through damp eyelashes he watches blue shimmer.

The pool is filled with water and sunlight. The surface glitters.

A warm breeze stirs the fine pale hairs on his chest.

A dragonfly, lapis lazuli, fat as his little finger, flashes out of the rose bushes, disturbed by a quiet footfall in the garden. The chink of glass against glass.

A housemaid with a tray of iced tea.

Vasilisk the bodyguard, blond and beautiful, half asleep, listens without intent to the bees among the mulberries, the shriek and laughter from the tennis court, the *pock pock pock* of the ball, the sway of trees on the hillside that sounds like the sea.

The sky overhead is a bowl of blue. Brushstroke cloud-wisps. Vasilisk closes his eyes and watches the drift of warm orange light across translucent skin.

Far away down the mountain a car drops a gear, engine racing to attack a steep climb. The sound is tiny with distance.

2

Lukasz Kistler's sleek ZorKi Zavod limousine took the corniche along the Karima coast, purring effortlessly, a steady sixty-five, glinting under the southern sun. Two and a half tons of engine power, bulging wheel arches, running boards, mirrors and fins.

The road was a dynamited ledge, hairpins and sudden precarious fallings-away. The mountains of the Silion Massif plunged to the edge of the sea: bare cliffs and steep slopes of black cypress; sun-sharpened jagged ridges and crisp high peaks, snow-capped even in summer. And always to the right and hundreds of feet below, the white strip of sand and the sea itself, discovered by glittering light, a tranquil and brilliant horizonless blue.

This was the favoured country: sun-warmed Karima rich in climate and soil, with its own little private ocean. Karima of the islands and the hidden valleys. Karima of the flowering trees, hibiscus, tea plantations, vineyards and orange groves. Karima of the white-columned sanatoriums in the wooded hills and on the curving quiet of the bays. Rest-cure Karima. Union-funded convalescent homes for the paragons of sacrificial labour in olive and lemon and watermelon country: the bed-ridden propped under rugs in their windows to watch the sea, the ambulatory at backgammon and skat under striped awnings.

Secluded private hotels with balcony restaurants (LIST ROUBLES ONLY ACCEPTED). Resort Karima. Twenty-mile coastal ribbons of pastel-blue concrete dormitories for the ten-day family vacations of seven-day-week leading workers. War never touched Karima. The Archipelago never got there, neither bombers nor troops nor cruisers nor submarines. Civil war was fought elsewhere. Karima was never hurt at all.

The municipal authorities of Karima made the most of the annual Dacha Summer of the Central Committee. The road to Rizhin's Krasnaya Polyana, Dacha Number Nine at Zusovo, was remade fresh each year: the velvet shimmer of asphalt, the gleam of undented steel crash barriers.

The limousine tyres hissed quietly. The driver dropped a gear and slowed into a hairpin switchback, and the turn brought Kistler suddenly face to face with the biggest portrait of Papa Rizhin he'd ever seen: two hundred feet high, surely, and the benevolent smiling countenance outlined with scarlet neon tubes, burning bright against the cliff face even in the noonday light.

ALL KARIMA LOYALLY WELCOMES OUR GENERALISSIMUS!

Lukasz Kistler had his own dacha, a white-gabled lodge in the Koromantine style tucked in among black cypresses a mile or so from Krasnaya Polyana. They all did – Gribov, Yashina and the rest – all except Rond, who travelled with his staff and had rooms in Rizhin's place. No vacation for the assiduous Colonel Hunder Rond.

Studded timber gates opened at Kistler's approach. The car entered a rough-walled unlit tunnel cut through solid mountain and ten minutes later emerged into sunlight and the courtyard of Krasnaya Polyana, a sprawling low green mansion on the brink of a sheer cliff.

The sun-roofed verandas of Dacha Number Nine looked out across the sea. Some previous occupant had planted the gardens with mulberry, cherry, almonds and acacia. Tame flightless cranes and ornamental ducks for the boating lake. Rizhin had added tennis courts, skittles, a shooting range. Papa Rizhin holidayed seriously.

Kistler found Rizhin himself in expansive mood, rigged out in gleaming white belted tunic and knee-length soft boots, Karima-fashion, paunch neat and round, hair brushed back thick and lustrous in the sunshine. He seemed taller. Mountain air suited him. The bullet scar on his cheek, still puckered and raw, gave his long pockmarked face a permanent lopsided grin. A show of white ivory teeth.

'Lukasz! You came!' Rizhin clapped him on the shoulder. 'So we haven't arrested you yet? Still not shot? Good. Come and see Gribov playing tennis in his jacket and boots, it's the most comical thing – everyone is laughing. But he wins, Lukasz! He plays like a firebrand. What a man this Gribov is.'

They linked arms like brothers and walked around the edge of the lake.

'Zorgenfrey came up yesterday from Anaklion,' said Rizhin, 'and completely fixed my teeth. No pain at all. Why can't we have such dentists in Mirgorod? The Karima sanatoriums get the best of everything. Yet he tells me he can't get his daughter into Rudnev-Possochin. He wants her to study medicine but the university puts up no end of obstructions. We must do something there. Talk to them for me, Lukasz. Iron the wrinkles out.'

'Leave it with me, Osip,' said Kistler. 'I'll take care of it.'

There were twenty-four at dinner: the Central Committee, Rizhin's bodyguards Bauker and Vasilisk, uncomfortable and self-conscious ('Come,' said Rizhin. 'We're all family here.') and silent, watchful Hunder Rond. They ate roasted lamb in a thick citrus sauce. Sliced tomatoes, cherries and pears. Red wine and grappa. Rizhin kept the glasses filled, and after dinner there was singing and dancing.

Bauker and Vasilisk pushed the table to the side of the room and rolled back the carpet. Rizhin presided over the gramophone, playing arias from light operas and ribald comic songs. He led the singing with his fine tenor voice. The bodyguards circulated, refilling glasses.

'Dance!' said Rizhin. 'Dance!' He put on 'Waltz of the Southern Lakes' three times in a row, loud as the machine would go. The men danced with other men or jigged on the spot alone. Yashina, tall and gaunt, twirled on her spiky heels, arms upraised, face a mask of serious concentration. Gribov went to take her in his arms, and when she ignored him he pulled out a handkerchief and danced with it the country way, stamping and shouting like the peasant he used to be. He lunged at Kistler, breathing grappa fumes. Kistler ducked out of his way.

'Osip!' shouted Gribov. 'Osip! Put on the one with dogs!'

'What's this about dogs?' said Marina Trakl, the new Secretary for Agriculture, red-faced. She was very drunk. 'Are there dogs? I adore dogs!'

'These are dogs that sing,' said Gribov. He started to dance with her.

'Then let us have singing dogs!' Marina Trakl grinned, snatching Gribov's handkerchief and waving it in the air.

'Of course,' said Rizhin. 'Whatever you say.' He changed the record to Bertil Hofgarten's 'Ball of the Six Merry Dogs'. When the dogs came in on the second chorus Rizhin started hopping and yelping himself, face twisted in a lopsided beatific smile. Kistler hadn't seen Rizhin so full of drink. Normally he left the aquavit and the grappa to the others and watched.

'Come on, you fellows!' called Rizhin, dancing. 'Bark with me! Bark!'

One by one, led by Gribov, the members of the Central Committee pumped their elbows and put back their heads and howled like hounds and bitches at the broken moons.

'Yip! Yip! Yip! A-ruff ruff ruff! Wah-hoo!'

'Come on, Rond!' yelled Rizhin. 'You too!'

Peller, the Secretary for Nationalities, slipped on spilled food and fell flat on his back, legs stuck out, laughing. He wriggled on his back in the mess.

'Yap! Yap! Yap!'

When the music stopped Gribov slumped exhausted and sweaty on a couch next to Kistler, undid his jacket, put back his head and began to snore. Kistler jabbed him when Rizhin, face flushed, eyes suddenly on fire, drained his glass and banged the table. It was time for Rizhin's speech.

'Look at ourselves, my friends,' he began. 'What are we?'

He paused for an answer. Somebody made a muffled joke. A few people laughed.

'What was that? I didn't hear,' said Rizhin, but no one spoke. The atmosphere was suddenly tense.

'I'll tell you what we are,' Rizhin continued. 'Nothing. We are nothing. Look at this planet of ours: a transitory little speck in a universe filled with millions upon millions of far greater bodies.' He gestured towards the ceiling. 'Out there, above us, there are countless suns in countless galaxies, and each sun has its own planets. What is any one of us? What is a man or a woman? We are, in actual and literal truth, nothing. Our bodies are collections of vibrating particles separated by emptiness. The very stuff and substance of our world is nothing but light and energy held in precarious patterns of balance, and mostly it is nothing at all. We are accidental temporary assemblages in the middle of a wider emptiness that is passing through us even now, at this very moment, even as we pass through it. Emptiness passing through emptiness, each utterly unaffected by the other. The energies of the universe pass through us like Kharulin rays, as if we are not here at all. We are our own graves walking. We are handfuls of dust.'

Several faces were staring at Rizhin with open dismay. Gribov leaned over in a fug of grappa to whisper in Kistler's ear, 'What the fuck's the man talking about? What's all this crazy shit?'

Kistler winced. 'You're too loud,' he hissed. 'For fuck's sake, keep it down.'

Every time Kistler glanced at Hunder Rond the man was watching him. Their eyes locked for a second, then Rond turned away.

One day, little prince, thought Kistler. *One day I'll snap your fucking thumbs.*

'But what a gift this nothingness is, my friends!' Rizhin was saying. 'It is the gift of immensity! Once we see that this world, this planet, is *nothing*, we realise what our future truly holds. Not one world, but all the worlds. The universe. The stars like sand on the beach. The stars like water, the oceans we sail. Our present world is trivial: it is merely the first intake of breath at the commencement of the endless sentence of futurity.'

Rizhin poured himself another glass, the clink of bottle against tumbler the only sound in the room. He fixed them with burning eyes. It was Rizhin the poet, Rizhin the artist of history, speaking now.

'I have seen this future! Red rockets, curvaceous, climbing on parabolas of steam and fire. making the sky seem small and wintry-blue. Because the sky *is* small. We can take it in our fists! I have seen these rockets of the future rising into space, carrying a new human type to their chosen grounds. Individuals whose moral daring makes them vibrate at a speed that turns motion invisible. There are new forms in the future, my friends, and they need to be filled with blood. We are the first of a new humankind. Where death is temporary a million deaths mean nothing.'

After the dinner and the dancing, Rizhin led the way to his cinema. Blue armchairs in pairs, a table between each pair: mineral water, more grappa, chocolate and cigarettes. Rugs on the grey carpet. They watched an illicit gangster film, imported from the Archipelago: men in baggy suits with wide lapels fought over a stolen treasure and a dancing girl with silver hair. Then came a Mirgorod Studios production, *Courageous Battleship!* Torpedoed in the Yarmskoye Sea, a hundred shipwrecked sailors line an iceberg to sing a song of sadness, a requiem for their lost ship.

Halfway through the film, Rizhin leaned across and gripped the elbow of Selenacharsky, secretary for culture.

'Why are the movies of the Archipelago better than ours?'

Selenacharsky turned pale in the semi-darkness and scribbled something in his notebook.

Dawn was coming up when they filed out of the cinema into the scented courtyard. Kistler was going to his car when Rizhin appeared at his elbow.

'I shoot in the mornings at the pistol range. Join me, eh, Lukasz? We'll have a chat, just you and me. Man to man.'

Kistler groaned inwardly. His head hurt.

'Of course, Osip.'

'Good. Nine thirty sharp.'

3

Kistler managed a couple of hours' sleep and returned to Rizhin's dacha stale and depressed, unbreakfasted, the dregs of the wine and the grappa still in his blood, a sour taste of coffee on his tongue. The dinner of the night before weighed heavy in his stomach. He felt queasy.

He followed the sound of gunfire to Rizhin's shooting range, a crudely functional concrete block among almond trees. Vasilisk the bodyguard, six foot three, blond and beautiful, was lounging on a chair by the door, white cotton T-shirt tight across his chest. He was wearing white tennis shoes and regarded Kistler with sleepy expressionless sky-blue eyes.

Kistler nodded to him and entered the shooting range.

Vasilisk rose lazily to his feet and padded in behind him. Closed the door, leaned against the wall and folded his arms. Kistler watched the muscles of the bodyguard's shoulders sliding smoothly. His thickened honey-gold forearms.

Rizhin was alone inside the building, bright and fresh in shirtsleeves, firing at twenty-five-yard targets with a pistol. Three rounds then a pause. You could cover the holes in the target with the palm of your hand.

He paused to reload. The gun was fat and heavy in his swollen fists but his fingers on the magazine were lightning-quick. Nimble. Practised.

'Do you know firearms, Lukasz?'

'Not really.'

'You should. Our existence depends on them. The powerful should study and understand the foundations of their power. This, for instance, is a Sepora .44 magnum. Our VKBD officers carry these. Heavy in the hand, but they shoot very powerful shells. Very destructive. They tend to make a mess of the human body. The removal of limbs. The bursting of skulls. Large holes in the stomach or torso. Butchery at a distance. Not a pretty death.' He turned and fired seven shots in rapid succession. The noise was deafening. An unmistakable acrid smell.

Rizhin offered the gun to Kistler.

'Would you like to shoot, Lukasz? It's important to keep one's skills up to scratch'

'No,' said Kistler. 'Later perhaps. I drank too much grappa last night.'

Rizhin shrugged.

'Your hand's trembling,' he said.

Kistler couldn't stop himself looking down at his hands. It was a sign of submission. He cursed himself inwardly.

Careful.

He held his hands out in front of him, palms down.

'I don't think so,' he said.

Rizhin ejected the magazine from the pistol and reloaded, taking a fresh magazine from his pocket.

'You enjoyed our evening then?' he said. 'I hope so.'

'Of course! It's good to know one's colleagues better. The holiday season is valuable. Time well spent.'

'I thought you were bored. You seemed bored. Gribov can be over-powering.'

'Not at all. A little tired perhaps. I'd had a long journey.'

Rizhin raised his arm and squeezed off three rapid shots. 'But you keep a distance – I see you doing it – and that's sound. I admire it in you. Music and feasting are excellent things, Lukasz; they reduce the bestial element in us. Song and dance, food and wine, good company: they calm the soul and make one amiable towards humanity. But we aren't ready for softness yet, you and I. Today is not the time to stroke people's heads. Of course, opposition to all violence is the ultimate ideal for men like us, but you have to build the house before you hang the pictures. Your attitude last night was a criticism of me, which I accept.'

'No. Not at all, Osip. I only—'

'But yes, it was, and I accept it. I've sent the others home, you know. I've packed them all off back to Mirgorod, back to their desks. There is work to be done and they must get to it.'

'What? All of them?' said Kistler.

'I thought you'd be pleased. Our colleagues bore you, Lukasz, isn't that so? Be honest with me. I'll tell you frankly, they bore me too. For now I must use people like them, but they're narrow, they have limited minds. Not like you and me. We see the bigger picture.'

Where is this going?

Vasilisk the bodyguard moved across to a wooden chair. The neat brown leather holster nestled in the small of his back bobbed with the rhythm of his buttocks as he walked. Vasilisk settled into the chair, crossed legs stretched out in front of him, and absorbed himself in studying his fingernails.

Rizhin was turning his pistol over with thick clumsy-looking fingers.

'What I was trying to say last night,' he continued, 'but I was drunk and over-poetical … what I was trying to say is that this – *this*, all around us, our *work* and our *diplomacy* and our *cars* and our *dachas* – this is not the point to which history is leading us. This is only the beginning: the first letter of the first word of the first sentence of the first book in the great library of futurity. You see this as well as I do.'

'There's a lot more to be done,' said Kistler cautiously. 'Of course. Certainly. Our industry ...'

Rizhin fished out three more shells from his pocket, ejected the magazine and pressed them into place one by one. Replaced the magazine in the pistol.

'I'm talking philosophically,' he said. 'The moral compass is not absolute, you see. It has changed and we have a new morality now. A new right. A new good. A new true. Our predecessors were scoundrels; the angels were an obfuscation, the things of the forest bedbugs. Leeches. A distortion of the moral gravity. Whatever serves the New Vlast is moral. That's how it must be, for now. Where all death is temporary then death is nothing. Killing is conscienceless. A million deaths, a billion deaths, are nothing.'

'But we need people,' said Kistler. 'Strong healthy people, educated, burning with energy. We need them to work. And we need steel. We need oil. We need power. We need mathematics and engineering. We need to be clever, Osip, or the Archipelago will—'

Rizhin brushed him off with a gesture. 'The Archipelago will be ground to powder under the wheels of history, Lukasz,' he said. 'You underestimate inevitability.'

He raised the pistol and levelled it at Kistler's head, the ugly blackness of the barrel mouth pointing directly between his eyes.

'History is as inevitable and unstoppable as the path of the bullet from this gun if I pull the trigger. Effects follow causes.'

Kistler made an effort to take his eyes from the pistol. His gaze met Rizhin's soft-brown gentle look.

'Osip ...' he began.

Rizhin turned away and fired a shot at the target. The raw explosion echoed off the concrete walls. Kistler realised his hands were damp. The back of his shirt was cold and sticky against his skin.

'I had hopes for you, Lukasz,' said Rizhin. 'I was going to *involve* you. You're a man of fine qualities. An outstandingly useful fellow. I was going to take you with us. But I find you are also a sentimentalist. Your belly is soft and white and you aren't to be trusted. You've let me down. Badly.'

'I don't understand this,' said Kistler. 'What's happening here, Osip? Where is this going to?'

'Tell me about Investigator Vissarion Lom.'

'Who?'

'Feeble. Feeble. Where is the famous Kistler fire in the guts? Where is the energy?' Rizhin pulled a crumpled typescript from the back pocket of his trousers and pushed it towards him. Kistler read the first few lines.

Kistler Residential – Internal
23.47 Transcription begins

Kistler: Yes?
Unknown caller: I wish to speak with Lukasz Kistler.
Kistler: This is Kistler. Who the fuck are you?

'I know this is Lom,' said Rizhin. 'He's a man I know. He circles me, Lukasz. He buzzes in my ear. I can't shake him off.'

'So shoot me.'

Rizhin shook his head.

'I want you to extend your vacation, Lukasz. Another week or two maybe. I've had enough of this bastard Lom. I want to trace him. I want to tie him down and finish him. And he's not doing this alone; there are conspiracies here, Lukasz, and you're deep in the whole nest of shit, and I'm going to know the extent of it. The whole fucking thing. Names. Dates. Connections. Circles of contact. You'll stay here and spend some time with Rond and his people. We're going to be seeing a lot more of each other. We'll have more talks.'

4

Back in Mirgorod again after the long journey from Vitigorsk, Lom wasted no time. He dialled from a call box at the Wieland Station. The contact number Kistler had given him rang and rang. He hung up and tried again.

Eventually someone answered. A woman's voice. Cautious.

Yes? Who is this?

'I want to speak with Lukasz Kistler.'

Name, please. Your name.

'I will speak to Kistler. Only Kistler. He is expecting me.'

Secretary Kistler is unavailable.

'I'll call back. Give me a time.'

The Secretary will be unavailable for some considerable time, perhaps days, perhaps longer. You may discuss your business with me. What is your name?

Lom cut the connection.

He took a cab across the city and walked the last few blocks to the war-levelled quarter of the rubble dwellers, to the cellar Elena Cornelius had led him to. His link to the Underground Road. Konnie and Maksim were there. So was Elena, looking strained. Hunted.

'I can't reach Kistler,' said Lom. 'I've got something he can use. Devastating material. Dynamite. In Kistler's hands it will bring Rizhin down. Definitely. But Kistler is out of contact. His number's no good. I thought you could—'

'Kistler has been arrested,' said Maksim.

Lom felt the warmth drain from his face.

'No,' he said. 'No. When?'

'He went to Rizhin's dacha. He's being held there under interrogation. Rizhin is there with him, and so is Rond. Nobody else.'

'How do you know this? How can you be sure.'

'We have somebody there,' said Konnie. 'On the dacha staff. There is no doubt.'

'But Kistler is alive?'

'Oh yes,' said Maksim. 'For now he is alive, though what state he's in …'

'Is there anybody else?' said Lom. 'Anyone else who could use the material I have, like Kistler could?'

'In the Presidium? No. Not a chance.'

'Then I have to get Kistler out of there and back to Mirgorod,' said Lom.

'That's impossible,' said Maksim. 'He's being held by the Parallel Sector in Rizhin's own fucking dacha.'

'Nothing's impossible,' said Lom. 'I need Kistler. Tell me about this dacha. Tell me about your contact there.'

'No,' said Maksim. 'It's out of the question.'

'This material,' said Konnie. 'It's as big as you say? It's that dangerous for Rizhin?'

'Absolutely,' said Lom. 'Poisonous. Lethal. In Kistler's hands it will bring him down.'

'What is it?' said Maksim.

'No,' said Lom. 'First you tell me about Rizhin's dacha.'

'But what you've got is really that good?'

'Yes. If we can get Kistler back to Mirgorod, free, and arm him with what I have, he can turn the Central Committee against Rizhin and he will fall.'

Konnie glanced at Maksim.

'We won't tell you where Rizhin's dacha is,' she said. 'You'll need help. We'll take you there. We'll go with you.'

'Konnie ...' said Maksim.

Konnie ignored him.

'You can't get Kistler out of there all by yourself,' she said. 'We have some resources, not much maybe, but better than one man on his own.'

Lom considered. 'Thank you,' he said. 'Yes. That would be good.'

Konnie turned to Elena.

'You're welcome to stay here,' she said. 'You'll be safe. You won't be found. Someone will bring you food. It won't be more than a week.'

Elena Cornelius bridled. 'I'm coming. I'm tired of hiding. I've got a job to finish and none of you can do what I can do. Get me a rifle and I will come.'

5

Every day in the first pale pink and violet flush of another new morning Vasilisk the bodyguard runs in the hills above Dacha Number Nine. Ten easy miles on yellow earth tracks before breakfast, taking the slopes through fragrant thorny shrub with cardiovascular efficiency, the early warmth of the sun on his shoulders. He sees the soft mist in the valleys. Sees the black beetles crossing the paths and the boar pushing through thickets. Watches the big hunting birds, high on stiff wings against the pale dusty blue, circling up on the thermals. Miles of rise and fall unrolling smoothly and effortlessly.

No words. No thoughts.

He knows the routes of the security patrols and the places they watch from and he does not go there; he prefers to drink the mountain solitude in, like cool sweet water. The watcher doesn't like to be watched. Doesn't like the feel of a long lens on his back. Ten miles of nobody in the morning sets him up for the day.

Two hundred push-ups, breathing steady and slow, two sets of fifty per arm, and a downhill sprint between pine trees – jumping tussocks and stony glittering streams – and Vasilisk the bodyguard steps out onto the road, corn-yellow hair slick with sweat. Sweat patches darkening his singlet.

The guards at the gatehouse phone him in through the gate, as they do every morning. He glances at them lazily, indifferent small blue eyes blank and pale behind pale-straw eyelashes. He goes to his room, picks up a towel and heads for the pool.

6

The streets of Anaklion on the Karima coast were wide and shaded by trees. Many of the houses were modern, every fifth building a guest house or hotel. Women at the roadside and in the squares sold figs and watermelons and clouded-purple grapes. Warm air off the sea disturbed the palms and casuarina trees.

Konnie, Lom and Elena took the funicular up to the Park of Culture and Rest. Gravel paths between long plots of enamel-bright flowers. Statues of dogs and soldiers. Wrought-iron benches for the weary and the convalescent. At the Tea-Garden-Restaurant Palmovye Derevya they took a table some way from the other customers, at the edge of the cliff, shaded by waxy dark green leaves against the low morning sun. A hundred feet sheer below them youths swam in the river, and across the gorge balconied houses recuperated: quiet lawns, striped awnings.

A waiter materialised at their table. Tight high-waisted trousers, a pouch at his hip for coin.

'Tea,' said Konnie. 'With lemon. For four. And some pastries.' Her long fine hair was burnished copper in the flickering splashes of sunlight between leaves. Her eyes flashed green at the waiter. A hint of a conspiratorial smile. 'You decide which ones.' A beautiful young woman with friends, on vacation. A husband or boyfriend would join them soon.

They'd arrived the night before. Lom used the last of Kistler's roubles for rooms at the guest house Black Cypress. Maksim hadn't appeared at breakfast.

'He went up the mountain before dawn,' said Konnie. 'He wanted to have a look for himself.'

Lom said nothing. Since they had left Mirgorod, Maksim had changed subtly. His face cleared. No longer pent-up and clouded with frustration, he was self-contained, competent and direct. Back in the military again, he was a man at his best with a mission. A simple purpose. Lom liked him. He'd started to trust him too.

'We can do this,' said Maksim when he arrived. 'It is possible. There is a way. But it's all about timing. Everything has to work precisely right. Absolute discipline.'

'OK,' said Lom. 'Go on.'

Maksim glanced at him. The two men had never quite resolved the unspoken question of who was in charge.

'The dacha is a fortress,' Maksim began. 'A compound surrounded by steep hills. The only way in is a tunnel through the mountain. There's a gate at the entrance from the road: wooden but three inches thick and reinforced with iron. There's a gatehouse – always two guards, with binoculars and a view for miles down the mountain. They'd see any vehicle coming ten minutes before it reached them. The gate is kept closed and barred from within. It's opened at a signal from the gatehouse, when they're expecting company. But nobody comes and nobody goes, except the domestics make a shopping trip once a week. A couple of guards go with them.'

'And inside?' said Lom.

'VKBD security. Plus Rond is there, and he's got Parallel Sector personnel with him. And Rizhin has his own personal security. Two bodyguards. Part of the family. Very dangerous. Say, twenty in all.'

'Not so much,' said Lom.

'There's a militia company in the town, an armoured train five miles away, a cruiser in the bay. They think they're safe enough.'

'Patrols in the hills?'

'No information,' said Maksim. 'But assume so. Yes.'

'So what's the plan?' said Lom.

'We must have the gate open at eleven tomorrow morning. Eleven o'clock exactly, to the second. No sooner and no later. Kistler will be coming out in a car.'

'A car?' said Konnie.

'Rizhin's personal limousine. It's the most powerful and heavily armoured they have. Bullet-proof glass in the windows. Thick steel panels underneath too. Hell, even the tyres are bullet-proof.'

'And all we have to do,' said Lom, 'is open the gate tomorrow?'

'Yes.'

'How?' said Konnie.

Maksim's face clouded. 'It can't be unbarred from outside, so we'll need explosives.'

Konnie looked around at the Park of Culture and Rest, at the teenage boys and girls in the river and stretched out on flat slabs of rock, lazy under the sun.

'Where do you get explosives in a place like this?' she said.

'Every construction project here has to start with blasting rock,' said Maksim. 'There's got to be a supply somewhere. A builder's merchant. An engineering yard.'

'That won't be necessary,' said Lom. 'You can leave the gate to me. I'll take care of it. And the guards in the gatehouse too.'

Maksim looked at him doubtfully.

'How?' he said.

Lom hesitated. Maksim's expression was soldierly. Sceptical. He couldn't begin to explain. Explaining would make it worse.

'It'll be fine,' said Lom. 'Please. I know what I'm doing. Leave it to me. If you can get Kistler to the gate at eleven, it'll be open.'

Maksim bridled.

'I must know what you intend,' he said. 'I will not lead my people blind. Lives depend on me.'

Lom shrugged. 'Stay here then. I'm grateful for what you've done, and from here I will go on alone.'

'Maksim,' said Elena Cornelius quietly, 'I think we should trust Vissarion. He has brought us this far. Without him we would be nowhere. We owe the chance we have to him.'

'Chance!' Maksim began, but thought better of it. 'OK,' he said. 'But I'll be at the gatehouse with you.'

'Good,' said Lom. 'Thank you.'

He took a long draught of hot sweet tea and considered the plan. It was terrible. A really shit plan. But it would be fine.

Just keep blundering on. Plough through the obstacles as they come. Way too late to back off now.

7

Weary after weeks of frustrating travel – delays over paperwork, failed and diverted trains, fuel shortages, their carriage attacked by a hungry mob – the Philosophy League arrived at the Wieland Station. Penniless – all their money spent on unexpected expenses along the way – but back in Mirgorod at last.

They'd hoped for more of a reception. Forshin had wired ahead to Pinocharsky to warn him of their arrival. They'd expected journalists and prepared the lines they would take: Forshin had the text of a speech in his pocket, and Brutskoi had written an article for the *Lamp*, a manifesto of sorts, a call to intellectual arms. But there was no one to meet them. The League stood together in a disgruntled huddle on the platform, surrounded by their suitcases and chests of books, their luggage much battered and repaired. They all looked to Forshin for answers.

'Well?' said Yudifa Yudifovna. 'So what are we to do?'

Eligiya Kamilova stood somewhat apart from the rest with Yeva and Galina Cornelius. The girls were restless and unhappy.

'Do we have to stay with these people any more?' said Yeva. 'Can't we go home now?'

Home? thought Kamilova. *What is home?*

'Ha!' said Forshin, visibly relieved. 'Here's Pinocharsky at last.' He waved. 'Pinocharsky! I say, Pinocharsky! Here!'

Pinocharsky came towards them, arms open in a mime of embrace. He was wreathed in smiles but looked harassed, his wiry red hair wisping.

'Well then!' he said. 'Here you are; you have come at last! But you're late. I was expecting you two hours ago. You have to hurry. Your train is waiting on the next platform.' He gestured for porters. 'What a lot of luggage you have. But no matter, there's no doubt plenty of room.'

The members of the League were looking at one another in dismay. Forshin took Pinocharsky by the arm.

'Train?' he said. 'What train? We've only just arrived, man. We need a hotel. We need a meeting. Editors. Publishers. We need a plan. We have much to say to the people.'

'Ah,' said Pinocharsky. 'Well, no, not exactly. Not yet. There's been a change of plan. Unfortunately I wasn't able to contact you.' He was looking shifty.

'A change of plan?'

Yes. The House of Enlightened Arts … Rizhin decided Mirgorod wasn't the place for it after all. He has a new plan, a better plan. You'll see the advantages when you understand.'

'What?' said Forshin. 'No. This is unacceptable.'

'I'm to take you there directly,' said Pinocharsky. 'The train's waiting—'

'This is outrageous,' said Forshin. 'I protest. On behalf of the League. There must be consultation.'

'These are the instructions of Rizhin himself,' said Pinocharsky stonily.

'At least let us have some time to rest and recover from the journey. The ladies—'

'I'm sorry, that won't be possible.'

'Then tell us where we are going, man,' said Olga-Marya Rapp. 'At least tell us that.'

'A new town in the east,' said Pinocharsky. 'A pioneering place. Leading edge. A city of the future. A place called Vitigorsk. There's a great project under way there. I don't know much about it yet myself.'

The League muttered and grumbled and cursed under their breath but there was no rebellion. They were too weary, too inured to disappointment; they knew in their hearts the limits of their true worth. Porters picked up their baggage and moved along the platform, and they followed in a subdued huddle.

Eligiya Kamilova caught up with Forshin.

'Nikolai …'

Forshin looked at her, puzzled. She and the girls had slipped his mind in all the fuss.

'Oh, Eligiya, of course …'

'I wanted to thank you, Nikolai. You've been very kind to the girls and me. You've done more than we had any right to hope for.'

'Oh. You're not coming with us? No, of course not. But do. Come with us to this Vitigorsk place, Eligiya. See where all this excitement leads. The future is opening for us, I feel sure of it.'

'I can't, Nikolai. I must take Galina and Yeva to look for their mother.'

'Of course you must do that.' He held out his hand and she took it. 'Well, goodbye then.'

'Thank you, Nikolai. And good luck.'

Eligiya Kamilova watched Forshin walk away purposefully, hurrying to catch up with Pinocharsky. She never saw or heard of him, nor any other member of the Philosophy League, ever again.

'Eligiya,' said Yeva, 'can we go now, please? We have to go and find our mother.'

Two hours later they were standing in the street where their aunt's apartment building had stood, the place where the Archipelago bomb had fallen: six years before in Mirgorod time, but for them it was a matter of months.

Everything was different. Everything was changed.

Of their mother Elena Cornelius there was of course no sign at all. They waited a while, pointlessly. It was futile. They were simply causing themselves pain.

Eligiya Kamilova wondered what to do. It was only now she was here that she realised she had no plan for what came next, no plan at all.

'We'll come back again tomorrow,' said Galina to Yeva. 'We'll come every day.'

8

The next morning, early, Lom went up into the mountains with Maksim, Konnie and Elena. Konnie had rented a boxy grey Narodni with a dented near-side wheel arch. The interior smelled strongly of tobacco smoke. There was a heaped ashtray in the driver's door. The streets climbed steeply out of Anaklion into scrub and scree and dark dense trees. No sun yet reached the lower slopes.

They drove in silence. Lom, squeezed onto the scuffed leather bench-seat in the back next to Elena, watched out of the window. The Narodni struggled on the steep inclines and Konnie swore, fishing for the second gear that wasn't there. The back of Maksim's head sank lower and lower between his shoulders.

After forty-five minutes Konnie pulled off the road onto a rough stony track. Out of sight among boulders and black cypress she killed the engine.

'This is it,' she said. 'You walk from here.'

Maksim, Lom and Elena left her with the car and started up a steep narrow hunting trail. Elena carried a rifle slung across her back. When they crested a ridge and clear stony ground fell away to their right, she broke away on her own. Two minutes later Lom couldn't see her at all.

It took him and Maksim another hour to work their way around to the thick woodland above and behind the gatehouse of Dacha Number Nine. Maksim picked his route carefully, stopping to look at his watch. He seemed to know what he was doing. Once he had them crawl on their bellies in under thick green spiky vegetation.

'Patrol,' he hissed.

The sun was higher now, kindling scent from crushed leaves and crumbling earth. Slow pulses of purple and blue rippled across the cloudless sky. A liminal solar breathing.

Lom's every move and step was a startling noise in the thin motionless air.

They crouched in the shadow of a pine trunk. The roof of the gatehouse was fifty feet below them, and beyond it the closed gate itself. Maksim checked his watch again and put his face close to Lom's ear.

'Now we wait,' he whispered. 'I will tell you when.'

9

Lukasz Kistler was lying on a low cot bed in his cell. Every part of him was in pain. He followed the passing of days and nights by the rectangle of sky in the high window, but he didn't count them. Not any more. He divided time between when he was alone and safe and when he was not, that was all.

When the key turned in the lock and the door opened he wanted to open his mouth and scream but he did not. He knotted his fingers tight in his grey blanket and pulled the fabric taut: a little wall of wool, a shield across his chest. A protection that protected nothing at all.

Vasilisk the bodyguard stepped inside and padded across to the bed. Looked down on Kistler impassively with sleepy half-closed eyes.

'Please,' said Kistler. His mouth was dry. 'Not any more. There is no more. It's finished now.'

'You've got friends outside the dacha,' said Vasilisk. 'They're coming to take you away.'

Kistler tried to focus on what he was hearing. He couldn't get past the fact it was the first time he had heard Vasilisk speak. His voice was pitched oddly high.

'They're going to try to blow up the gate,' he said. 'Stand up. You have to come with me.'

'I refuse,' said Kistler. He pressed himself deeper into the thin mattress. The springs dug into his back.

'You refuse?' Vasilisk looked at him with faint surprise, like there was something unexpected on his plate at dinner.

'I refuse,' said Kistler again. 'Absolutely I refuse. No more. I will not come again. Not any more. I'm finishing it. Now.'

Vasilisk bent in and hooked a hand under Kistler's shoulder, iron fingers digging deep into his armpit, hauling him up. Kistler resisted. Pulled away and tried to fall back onto the mattress.

Vasilisk leaned forward and jabbed him in the solar plexus.

Kistler screamed and retched and tried to bring his knees up, curling himself into a protective ball, but the last of his strength had gone. Rizhin's bodyguard yanked him to his feet and held him upright, though his legs failed him and he could not stand.

Kistler heard a strange sound and realised it was himself sobbing.

'Shut up,' said Vasilisk and jabbed him again.

On the slope above the guardhouse Maksim nudged Lom in the ribs and gestured with his chin.

Go! Go!

Vasilisk the bodyguard half-carried, half-dragged the unresisting semiconscious Kistler through the rose garden and past the swimming pool. There was no one there. From half past ten to half past twelve there was tennis.

Iced tea at half past eleven.

Rizhin's car was parked in the courtyard and Vasilisk had the keys in his pocket. He checked the time on his watch: 10.51.

He opened the rear door and bundled Kistler inside. Pushed him down into the footwell. Kistler groaned and retched again, spilling sour vomit down the front of his shirt.

Vasilisk took his place in the driver's seat and settled down to wait.

Lom eased open the door of the gatehouse. Maksim entered first, pistol in his hand. The guards swung round in surprise: one reached for his holster, the other made a grab for the telephone receiver.

Maksim fired twice. Neat and precise.

Lom ripped the phone cable from the wall.

At 10.55 Rizhin himself came round the corner of the veranda into the courtyard. Vasilisk followed him in the rear-view mirror. Saw him glance across at the car and see his bodyguard in the driver's seat. Puzzled, Rizhin started to come over.

Vasilisk turned the key in the ignition and the engine purred into life. He slipped the car into gear and headed for the tunnel entrance. A cool dark mouth in the rock. In his mirror he saw Rizhin standing in the middle of the courtyard watching him go.

Vasilisk increased the weight of his foot on the accelerator pedal.

The car roared forward. The barrier was down but the car weighed nearly three tons.

As the barrier splintered it occurred to Vasilisk in an abstract way that he was probably beginning the final two minutes of his life.

Lom walked up to the massive gate across the tunnel and pressed the flat of his hand against it, feeling the dry solid wood. Its grain and fine flaws. The bars of iron within it. The blackened studs. The wide sunlit air. The scent of cypress and resinous southern pine. Feeling and remembering.

In the dark time, after Maroussia went, Vissarion Lom moved fast across ice fields and raced through the snow-dark birch trees. Part man, part angel, part something else, body and brain saturated with starlight and burn, all the dark months of winter he ran the ridges of high mountains.

He pushed his fists deep into solid rock just to feel it hurt.

Ten days and more he had stood without moving on the thick frozen surface of a benighted lake. Cold dark fishes slid through darkness far below him and bitter black wind scoured his face with particles of ice.

Lom-in-burning-angel counted the needles on pine trees and ignited them one by one with an idle thought. Little bright-flaring match flames.

He had forgotten who he was and he didn't care.

But slowly he had been moving south, and slowly the star-fire faded from the angel skin casing Lavrentina Chazia had made. In the early sunlight of that first spring five years ago Vissarion Lom shed his angel carcass and pushed it off a rock into the river.

He squirrelled the recollection of that dark inhuman time deep in the secret fastnesses of the heart where bitterness festers, and guilt. Kept it there, locked under many locks, along with the memory of all the winter slaughtering Lom-in-burning-angel did, or could have done and thought he might have. The iron smell of blood on ice.

After that long inhuman winter in the north without the sun, Vissarion Lom wanted to be nothing more than simply human again, but secretly he knew he never could be quite that. Possibly he never entirely had been: the earliest roots of himself were buried in oblivion and inexhaustible forest. As everyone's are.

*

'Turn your back and cover your face,' Lom said to Maksim. 'Splinters.'

Lom focused. Tried to drive all other thoughts and memories from his mind. Tried to calm the rising anxiousness and the beating of his heart.

There was only him and the gate.

He probed. Pushed. Nothing happened.

Changing direction, he gathered all the urgency, the growing white panic inside him, squeezed it all into a tight ball and forced it out from him. Hurled it into the timbers, deep into the corpse limbs of forest trees.

Burst open by the pressure of tiny air pockets – the desiccated fibrous capillaries suddenly and violently expanding – the heavy wooden planks of the gate exploded loudly from within, split open and shattered.

The rock tunnel behind the broken gate was dark and silent. It smelled like the mouth of a well.

'What the fuck?' said Maksim. 'What the fuck did you *do*?'

'Later,' said Lom.

Where the hell was Kistler's car?

They stood side by side for thirty long slow seconds.

'Where is he?' said Lom. 'He's not coming.'

Engine roar echoed, and the sound of gunfire.

The long black limousine was racing towards them. Lom glimpsed a face behind the thick windscreen as he scrambled aside. A tanned impassive handsome face. Cropped yellow hair.

The limousine slowed to a crawl. Maksim pulled open the front passenger seat.

'Get in the back!' he yelled at Lom.

Lom slid in alongside the collapsed form of Kistler, who was crouched on the floor. Dirty shirt and soiled trousers. Unshaven face grey. He looked up at Lom with glassy eyes. No recognition. There was a smell of urine and vomit in the car.

The driver didn't look round but gunned the engine and raced off down the mountain.

The heat of the sun, now high in the sky, beat against the side of Elena Cornelius' face. She could feel her skin burning. Insects buzzed and clattered in the grass, crawled across the back of her neck, sunk tiny probes into her arms and her ankles. She fought back the urge to scratch. All movement was dangerous.

She was still. She was nothing but eyes watching. She was part of the rock.

From five hundred yards she saw the gate shatter and the limousine emerge, slow to pick up Maksim and Lom, and hurtle away down the hill, jumping culverts, taking the hairpin too fast, scraping its side along the crash barrier.

The racing of the engine and the squeal of tortured metal echoed off cliffs and scree.

Elena Cornelius waited. Less than a minute later two vehicles came charging out of the tunnel mouth: a black Parallel Sector saloon and an open VKBD jeep with three men cradling sub-machine guns on their knees.

Elena moved the rifle slowly, sliding the graticule smoothly along the road, catching up with the windscreen of the leading pursuit car. The driver's head was a shadow. She moved the scope with the saloon for a moment, matching speed for speed, then shifted her aim three car lengths ahead and lifted it half an inch.

Squeezed the trigger gently.

Half a second after she fired, the glass in the windscreen shattered. From where she was it seemed to collapse and dissolve. The Parallel Sector saloon swung wildly to the left, crashed against the rock face and spun twice.

The jeep, following close behind, had nowhere to go and no time to stop. It crunched sickeningly into the side of the saloon. The men in the back of the jeep were thrown out. They landed badly.

Elena shifted the scope back to the driver. He was folded into the jeep's steering wheel, his head pushed through broken glass in a mess of blood.

She watched a man stagger from the back of the saloon. Limping. He pulled at the driver's door. It wouldn't open. None of the men from the jeep was moving at all. The two crashed vehicles together completely blocked the road.

She shouldered her gun and slid backwards away from the ridge, stood up and began to move, half running, half sliding down through the trees. This route would cut off a mile of road. In seven minutes she would be back at the track where Konnie would be waiting with the boxy grey Narodni.

10

*A*rchangel hurls himself across the continent, Rizhin world. He is a fisted pocket of certainty crashing from mind to mind – land and pause and look and leap again – leaving a crumb trail of sickness and fall. Hunting the only angel trace still left in Rizhin's New Vlast.

Brother, I am racing to you! Brother, call again and I will come!

He has scarcely the strength for it. Mile by mile the connecting cord back to his rock-lump-grinding-carcass in the forest lengthens and thins. The thread grows weak and spider-fine.

In the deep concrete cistern under the Mirgorod Sea Gate, Safran-in-mudjhik pummels the imprisoning wall with shapeless fists. His mind is dark with anger at his fall.

Lom pushed him in there.

He cannot get out.

Six years.

The endless surging weight of water, the whole force of the River Mir, pins him on his back. The noise of it fills his head and deafens him. The lost mind of Safran huddles in a silent corner, curled and foetal, wanting only the sound and the shouting and the hopelessness to cease.

Hairline fractures are opening in the concrete.

Two thousand days ago an aircraft of the Archipelago returning from a raid emptied its bomb bay, dumping its unspent load across the White Marshes. Two bombs fell against the dam. No visible damage done, but in the secret places, in the dark interior of immense solid walls, weakened bonds began to shear and slip.

Predator-Archangel plummets from height, daggering into the mind of Safran-in-mudjhik and taking possession with a shriek of triumph.

Instantly he expands to fill the space. Scoops the remnants of the weaker mudjhik mind from their runnels and crannies with a spoon and eats them all.

Sorry, brother.

Archangel glows with satisfaction and joy. He has a worthy body now in Rizhin world. He flexes. He samples. He trials his goods.

In a dark corner he finds Safran cowering and hauls him out wriggling and retching by the ear.

What use are you? he wonders briefly, rummaging with clumsy fingers through the maddened Safran mind before crushing it for ever out of existence.

Deep in the endless forest the Seer Witch of Bones is the first to discern the gap in the wall. She shrieks in dismay, 'Close it! Close it! The angel is through!'

Maroussia Shaumian walking under the trees, preoccupied with the child in her belly and Vissarion Lom, reluctantly turns her attention to the call. She traces the fine connecting threadway. It is weak and she is strong, invested with the Pollandore. It costs her no more than a tussle with the weakened and attenuated angel mind. She pinches her fingers and the cord is cut.

The forest is secure.

But the archangel fragment in the mudjhik, isolated from the depleted mother hill, clings on to life and purpose. In the mudjhik carcass he is strength and fire and brilliance like nothing has been in a donkey work-horse mudjhik ever before.

Slowly Archangel-mudjhik rises to his feet against the power of the crushing river and puts his shoulder to the wall. Shoves and batters and kicks against the weakening concrete.

Brute force does it. Boulders come tumbling down, the river is unleashed and Archangel-mudjhik is swept out, twisting and floundering in a torrent of broken concrete and white water, out into the deeper colder darkness of the bay.

Chapter Ten

They all believed their happiness had come,
That every ship had reached harbour,
And the exhausted exiles and wanderers
Had come home to bright shining lives.

Aleksander Blok (1880–1921)

1

They changed cars at a small fishing port ten miles east along the coast from Anaklion, ditching the Narodni for a spacious pre-war Tsvetayev with cloth-covered seats, more tractor than automobile, and drove back to Mirgorod. By the direct northeast route it was only nine hundred miles, but it took them five days of doubling back and taking less-used circuitous routes. They assumed they were being searched for. Trains and flights were out of the question, even if they'd had the money for that.

There were five of them in the car: Lom and Elena, Maksim and Konnie and Kistler. They left Vasilisk at the fishing port, where Maksim had arranged a place for him on a boat. He would work his passage south and disappear. As they were leaving, Vasilisk shook hands with Maksim and snapped a military salute.

'He was in my unit,' was all Maksim would say afterwards. 'In the war.'

They drove long hours on ill-made roads, sharing the driving and sleeping in the car, picking up food where they could and stopping as little as possible. North of the Karima mountains they skirted the hungerland. What they saw was bad and the rumours were worse. Ruined and abandoned farmland, the people of the towns gaunt, grey-faced, weak, watching them pass through with sullen hopeless eyes. Villages where there was nobody at all, only crows and pigeons and packs of dogs that circled, heads down, ribcages, dirty lustreless coats.

'I didn't know,' said Konnie. 'None of us knew about this.'

They ran into a roadblock in a birch wood: a tree across the road and five men in rags with staves and a shotgun rising from a ditch. An attempt to steal the car: fuel and food and a way out. Maksim had to shoot two of them. The rear window of the Tsvetayev was broken.

Maksim had been wary of Lom since the incident of the gate. Lom felt himself watched. By Konnie too. Maksim tried to ask him about it once, but Lom didn't answer. Where to begin and what to say? The atmosphere was strained.

Elena Cornelius just wanted to get back to the city. She'd been away too long. She was terrified that her girls had come home and she had missed them.

Kistler recovered slowly. They cleaned him up and fed him, found him fresh clothes and let him sleep most of the day. He had lost weight in Rizhin's interrogation cell. His eyes were dark, blank and anxious, and for long hours he sat in the back of the car next to Elena, pressed up against the door, leaning forward, hands on his knees, staring at nothing. Every few minutes he would open his mouth to speak but say nothing. On the second day tears came, silent tears soaking his face. He didn't wipe them away.

Lom feared he was permanently gone, that they'd lost him for ever in Rizhin's interrogation cell, but slowly with the passing of the days some of Kistler's fire and energy returned, though not like before. When Lom had first seen Kistler he was a master of the world, filled to the brim with confident assurance. The smooth sheen of real power. It had been there in his voice, in his gaze, in the way he moved. Now he was coming back, but darker, more determined, altogether more dangerous. His hurt and his fall, the shock of his humiliation and psychic destruction at the hands of Rizhin and Hunder Rond were raw and near the surface and he was vengeful. His face was thinner and he glared at the world through dark-hooded eyes.

'I should thank you,' Kistler said on the third day. 'All of you. I know what I owe, and I will not forget.'

'We came because we need you,' said Lom. 'I went to Vitigorsk as you suggested. I've got information you can use. If you want it. If you feel you still can.' Lom paused. 'Or my friends can help you get far away, if that's what you want. To the Archipelago, even. That is possible. It can be done.'

'Yes,' said Konnie from the front seat. 'We can arrange that. We've done it before, for others. It's what we do.'

Kistler said nothing. He looked for a long time out of the window: there was dry grass out there, dull grey lakes and low wooded hills in the distance.

'We would understand,' said Lom, 'if you decided to go. No shame in that.'

Kistler didn't look round.

'Liars,' he said. 'You people didn't risk yourselves just to let some sick old fucker go free. Certainly not a bastard and a criminal like me.'

Kistler's eyes followed a young girl leading a horse across a hill, until they left her far behind. Lom thought he wasn't going to say any more. Long minutes passed before Kistler spoke again.

'I'm going to bring the fucker Rizhin to his knees,' he said. 'And I will do whatever it takes, *whatever it takes*, to make that happen. I want to see him *broken*. I want to see him *hurt*. I want to see him *crawling* on the floor in his own *shit* and *piss* and *puke* and *blood*. I would *die* to make that happen and be *glad*. I would *suffer* and *howl* till the end of fucking *time*, as long as it was him and me there *together*. So tell me. What have you got?'

'Pull over,' said Lom to Maksim, who was driving. 'I'll get my bag from the back.'

As they drove on, Lom told Kistler about the vast construction plants at Vitigorsk. The plans for a fleet of atomic-powered vessels to go to the planets. The experiments in resurrection and synthetic human bodies. The aspiration to abolish death.

'Insane,' said Kistler, 'insane, but—'

'That isn't all,' said Lom. 'It's just the beginning.'

He opened his bag and brought out the papers from Khyrbysk's office.

'They are building vessels of two kinds,' he said. 'There was a conference a couple of years ago. A hotel on a lake. Rizhin was there, and Khyrbysk, and the chief engineer. Others too. Some names you know. Papers were circulated and minutes taken. All most efficient, and Khyrbysk kept a copy.'

He spread a folder open on his knee.

'They are constructing two kinds of vessel,' he said again. 'One, a fleet to go to the planets and the stars. Five years, they think, ten at the most before they are ready. Resources are no obstacle. Rizhin promised them whatever they need. They will be arks. Transport ships to carry pioneers and the equipment they will require. It's all planned. They'll select the people carefully. Even two years ago they'd begun to draw up criteria and candidate lists. They are gathering scientists, artists, writers, athletes. The best of the armed forces and the finest workers.'

'Let me see,' said Kistler. 'Show me the names.'

'They need huge amounts of angel matter to power the craft,' said Lom. 'More than all the carcasses can supply. But there is a living angel in the forest and Rizhin says it's huge. Immense. An angel mountain. He's going to find it and excavate its living flesh. Army divisions are already in the forest searching.'

Kistler was still looking at the lists. The people at the conference.

'I don't recognise these names,' he said. 'None of the Central Committee is here. No one from the Presidium or the ministries. Only Rond.'

'They don't know,' said Lom. 'None of them know about it because they're not going. They're not invited to the stars. But the arks are just part of it. There's another kind of vessel design. These are for low planetary orbit only, and there are to be thirty of them. They're also building bombs. Huge atomic bombs. *Emperor Bombs*. The power of these weapons can't be understated, it can't even be imagined: a single one would have the power of sixty million tons of high explosive, big enough to flatten entire cities and destroy half a province on its own. They expect them to set the air itself on fire. The orbital craft, the second design, will be artillery platforms. Flying gunships, each one equipped with twenty Emperor Bombs. That's six hundred of them. The dust will blacken the skies for years. Five years of darkness and winter. Clouds of poisonous elements will cover the continent, raining disease and death. The atmosphere of the world will burn away.'

'Even if they could build such weapons,' said Kistler, 'they could never use them. We know the Archipelago has its own atomic weapons now. We would destroy each other.'

'No need for the Archipelago to do that,' said Lom. 'Rizhin's orbiting gunships are intended to do it all. Burn the Archipelago, burn the Vlast, burn the endless forest too. Burn it all. Scorched earth. Leave the planet a smoking cinder.'

Kistler stared at him. Lom saw growing understanding in his eyes.

'I see,' said Kistler. 'Rizhin and his arks will leave the planet and destroy it behind them so no one can follow, so no such ships are ever built again.'

'That's part of the reason,' said Lom, 'but also so that no one who goes with Rizhin to the stars can ever dream of coming home again.' He took the note of the conference and found the page he needed. 'Rizhin's own words were recorded verbatim.'

He handed the paper to Kistler.

'We must leave nothing behind us. No before-time. No happy memory. No nostalgia for golden age and home. And above all, no one to come after us. We will be the first and the last. There is no past, there is only the future.'

Kistler read it over several times. Shaking his head.

'A single man might think this,' he said, 'but that others should follow, and help him, and do his work …?'

'Khyrbysk for one didn't care,' said Lom. 'Nor did the chief engineer. There are letters between them that Khyrbysk kept.'

Lom quoted a passage. He had it by heart.

'"Where death is temporary, a million deaths, a billion, ten billion, do not matter. When we have mastered the science of retrieving memory from atoms we can come back here for the dust, if we have need of the ancestral dead to fill the planets we find."

'I'm not sure if Rizhin believes the resurrection stuff himself,' he added. 'You can't tell that from these papers.'

'But,' said Kistler, 'can they really do this? Could they actually build these things? Could they truly hope to travel to the stars?'

'For our present purposes,' said Lom, 'that doesn't really matter, does it? It hardly makes any difference at all. Rizhin intends it. He has corresponded with Khyrbysk – I've got letters in his own hand here. The project has begun.'

Kistler stared at him.

'Fuck,' he said. His face flushed. 'Fuck. You're right. Hah!' He reached across and put his hand on Lom's knee. Squeezed it affectionately. 'Of course you're right, you marvellous fucking marvellous man. It doesn't matter at all.'

'So did I get you what you need?' said Lom.

'You did,' said Kistler. 'You bloody well did. Get me back to Mirgorod and I'll tear the bastard down. I'll bury him.'

2

As soon as he was back in Mirgorod, Lukasz Kistler went to work. It took time. There were no phone calls. No letters. No traces. Kistler travelled across the city only by night, with the assistance of Maksim and the Underground Road, and by day he lay up in hiding and slept and prepared himself for the next night. He visited every single member of the Central Committee. In secret he came to them, unannounced and unexpected, when they were alone and at home. Each one was shocked by the thinness of his body, the new lines in his face, the black energy burning in his eye.

But you were dead, Lukasz. We all thought you were dead.

He sat with them, whispering into the early hours of the morning in studies and bedrooms while the households slept, and told them his story. He showed them the documentary proofs that Lom had brought back from Vitigorsk. The notes of meetings. The lists. The letters to Khyrbysk in Rizhin's own scrawl.

And as he spoke, they saw the intact intelligence in his face. They understood the clarity of vision, the urgent determination: this was not Kistler broken and made mad by fear and detention and loss of power; this was Kistler commanding. Kistler on fire. Kistler the leader they had been waiting for.

And one by one in the watches of the night each man and woman of the Central Committee made the same response to what he told them, as Kistler knew they would. He knew his colleagues. He knew the stuff of their hearts.

What shocked and horrified them most was not the plan Rizhin had put into effect; it was that they were not in it. They were not included. *I am not on the list! He was going to leave me behind. I was to burn. My husband, my wife, my children, all were to burn.*

One after another Kistler reeled them in. Stroked their vanity, fed their fear, bolstered their courage and swore them to secrecy. And when he had them, he convened a secret meeting at two in the morning at Yulia Yashina's house, and presented them with his proposal.

'We must all be signed up to this,' he said. 'Absolute and irreversible commitment. Every single one without exception. You must understand – you already know this well, of course you do – that if one of us falters we are all, all of us, doomed. The man or woman who loses courage now, who believes that he or she can gain advantage by moving against the rest of us: that betrayer is the one Rizhin will kill first. You all know this as I do. Concerted collective decisive action, this is the only way. One swift and irresistible blow!'

3

Yeva Cornelius stares up at a tall cliff of concrete and windows. The concrete is grey but the building is somehow brown, and the windows reflect brown and yellow although the sky is blue. The paving of the street is brown and everything is strange.

Eligiya Kamilova has told them that this is Big Side, and this is the street where Aunt Lyudmila's apartment was, before the bomb; she's told them they can't go back to the raion where their proper house was, with the Count and Ilinca and the dog and all the other people who lived there too, because the raion isn't there any more. Yeva is beginning to doubt whether Eligiya is right about that or anything else. This doesn't look like Big Side at all. Maybe there was another city, the one they lived in, and this is a different place, another city with the same name but somewhere else, and everything is a bad mistake.

Eligiya doesn't say much any more, and Galina is thin and tall and her eyes are big and dark and she never says anything at all. They sleep in a dirty room with only one bed and come here very morning, but Yeva's more sure every day that it's the wrong place. The women who live here wear pale blue dresses and coats, and their hair is wavy and doesn't move in the breeze, and they wear small hats, though it's not cold or raining, and the hats are the same colour as the dresses and coats. Always the same colour. That's what you have to do here. The men wear hats too, and thin shoes.

Yeva Cornelius thinks she's eleven years old still, but she hasn't counted the days and the dates here are wrong. She knows what date it is here – the newspaper has that – but when the date of her birthday comes, it won't be her birthday. No one asks how old she is anyway. Birthdays are for children, and this is the wrong place; her mother is somewhere else.

'This is the wrong place,' she says again to Eligiya Kamilova, who's standing next to her with Galina. They come here every day at ten o'clock and wait for half an hour. That's their plan.

'You say that every day, Yeva,' said Eligiya, 'but it's not.'

A woman in black is watching them from the other side of the road. She looks like their mother but she's smaller and she has browner skin and shorter hair and the hair's grey and she's very thin. Even from so far away, Yeva can see her eyes are black and sad.

The woman in black is watching Yeva just like the dead soldiers used to watch her at Yamelei: patient and with nothing to say and watching for ever and never getting bored or wanting to look at something else instead. But the eyes are black and sad and that shows the woman is alive.

It is their mother.

Galina has seen her too but she doesn't move and she doesn't make a sound.

Yeva wants to run across the road but she doesn't because … because her mother is not the same and Yeva is not the same and nothing is the same. The awkwardness of strangers meeting. Yeva watches her mother back, from the opposite side of the road, and says nothing and doesn't move.

Eligiya doesn't know yet. She hasn't seen.

The woman in black makes a small movement, almost a stumble. Yeva thinks she's going to turn round and walk away. But she doesn't.

4

The Sixth Plenum of the New Vlast convened in Victory Hall in central Mirgorod under low ceiling mosaics of aviators and cherry blossom, harvesters and blazing naval guns, all depicted against the same brilliant lucid eggshell-blue cloudless sky. Victory Hall was not large: despite the brutal columns of mottled pink granite and the banners of gold and red, the atmosphere was surprisingly intimate.

The Central Committee took their seats on the platform in a pool of golden light. The floor of the hall before them – the sixty non-voting delegates from the oblasts, the observers from the armed forces in their uniforms, the leading workers in crisp new overalls of blue – murmured anticipation. Order papers were shuffled. An official in a dark suit tested the microphone at the lectern.

This was the day of accounting. Annual reports were to be delivered, production targets exceeded, measures of increasing wealth and prosperity noted, improvements celebrated without complacency. *Your committee can and must do better, colleagues, and in your name we will.* Revisions to the rolling Five Year Plan would be proposed, and adopted by acclamation.

Watching from the tiered side-galleries, the fifteen chosen representatives of the press, snappy in new dresses and suits, were relaxed and slightly bored, their copy already written and filed according to tables of information and officially approved quotations previously supplied. The seven ambassadors and their assistants from the independent border states measured their shifting relative importance and influence by the seating plan. In the rows behind them, squinting at the platform, trying to identify the members of the committee by name and thinking of what they would tell their families and friends later, sat several dozen selected members of the public – outstanding citizens all, decorated heroes of the Vlast. And among them, perched at the end of a row, inconspicuous in shadow, Vissarion Lom waited alongside Lukasz Kistler.

Every person in the Victory Hall was waiting for Rizhin to appear.

At two o'clock precisely he did. The small crowd gave a soft wordless visceral rising moan of delight.

Rizhin, simple white uniform blazing under the lights, paused a moment to acknowledge the reception – a modest deprecatory smile – and took his place with the rest of the committee. His chair was no grander, his place no higher than the rest.

I am the servant of our people. I do what I can.

As soon as Rizhin had settled, the Victory Hall was flooded with warm pink illumination. The chamber orchestra in their cramped pit below the platform began to play. At the sound of the first familiar bars every person except Rizhin rose to their feet, and they all began to sing, falling naturally into the fourfold harmonies of which everyone always knew their part.

Thank you! Thank you! Papa Rizhin!
All our peace is owed to you!
All new truth and all fresh plenty!
A million voices, a thousand years!

Kistler leaned across to whisper in Lom's ear. 'When the time comes they will not do it, Lom. All this, it's too strong. It's too much to go against. They'll lose their nerve.'

'It'll be fine. You've done what you can.'

The members of the Central Committee came to the lectern one by one to deliver their reports and were received with warm applause. The afternoon wore on. Rizhin was to speak last, and as the time approached he began to flick through his script. Shifting in his chair, preparing to stand.

Gribov was in the chair. He cleared his throat nervously and stood. 'Colleagues ...'

Rizhin was already coming to take his place. Gribov held up his hand to stop him. Rizhin paused and looked at him, puzzled.

Gribov motioned him back to his seat.

Rizhin hesitated, shrugged and sat down again.

'Colleagues,' said Gribov again, 'at this point the planned business of the Plenum is suspended. I require the public galleries to be cleared.'

There was a collective murmur of surprise. A burst of muttered protest.

Lom kept his eye fixed on Rizhin, who frowned and looked at Gribov, but Gribov was ignoring him. Then Rizhin glanced at Hunder Rond, but Rond was avoiding his gaze.

'Clear the room!' called Gribov. Plenum officials and officers of the VKBD began to usher the protesting ambassadors and the press corps towards the door. Lom and Kistler moved to one side, half-hidden from the platform. The officials ignored them as Gribov had arranged.

The non-voting delegates were permitted to remain. Gribov called the room to order.

'The Central Committee by collective agreement in accordance with Standing Order Seven has resolved to bring before you an urgent and extraordinary resolution.' Gribov's voice was gravelly. He struggled to make himself heard. Took a sip of water. 'The resolution, in the name of Secretary Yashina is, "To remove Osip Rizhin from all official positions, responsibilities and powers with immediate effect."'

Silence fell in Victory Hall. No delegate moved. None spoke. None made a sound.

Rizhin sat back in his chair. He looked relaxed. Almost amused. A wry scornful smile on his scarred face.

'So it comes to this,' he said, scanning the line of faces, fixing the committee one after another. 'Well done then. Bravo. Of course it's all shit, it's nothing, but let's see what you make of it.'

You mustn't let him react, Kistler had said to Gribov when they made the plan in secret conclave at Yashina's house. *Once you start, the momentum is yours, but you have to keep it. If he speaks, if he fights back, it'll be a battle between competing authorities and you could lose control. It'll turn into a shouting match. Don't get into a battle with him.*

Gribov turned to Rizhin.

'You may leave us now, Osip,' he said, 'or you may remain and hear what is said. But you may not speak. The resolution will be proposed and a vote will be taken. There is to be no right of reply. If you speak you will be ejected from the hall.'

There was a commotion on the floor of the hall.

'Shame!' someone shouted. 'Criminals! Betrayers!'

The cry wasn't taken up. It fell on silence. The shock and bemusement in the chamber was palpable. And fear, above all there was fear. The observer delegates collectively maintained a tense, terrified silence.

Lom guessed some of them were beginning to wonder if they would make it out of the room alive. If they would ever go home again.

He saw Rizhin look towards Hunder Rond again. The two men's eyes locked. Rond kept his face studiously, stonily impassive. Rizhin raised his eyebrows and gave an almost imperceptible nod: *And you, Rond? That's how it is then? Well it's your loss. It means nothing to me.*

Lom wondered what kind of deal Kistler and his cronies had made with Rond. He watched Rizhin's eyes slide from Rond to Yashina and from her to Gribov. Rizhin was obviously wondering the same thing.

Rizhin sat back in his chair and slipped his hands into his tunic pockets carelessly.

'Thank you, Gribov,' he said. 'I will not leave. This is my chamber and I am President-Commander of the New Vlast. I'll go when and where I choose. But this could be interesting. So come on, let's hear what you arseholes have to say.'

Gribov ignored him. He yielded the floor to Yulia Yashina.

'They're doing it,' hissed Kistler in Lom's ear. 'They're fucking *doing* it. I have to go now.' He squeezed Lom's arm as he left. 'Oh I could kiss you, you beautiful man. Look at that fucker wriggle.'

'It's not finished yet,' said Lom as Kistler disappeared.

5

Tall and slender, elegant, Yulia Yashina moved to the microphone and began to speak. Like Gribov, for the first few sentences her voice was dry and weak. She then drank some water and proceeded, more loudly and with growing purpose and confidence, speaking the words that Kistler had drafted for her.

'When we analyze the practice of Osip Rizhin in regard to the direction of the Vlast,' she said, 'when we pause to consider everything which this man has perpetrated, we see that his achievements in leading our country during war have transformed themselves during the years of peace into a grave abuse of power.'

A single gasp broke the silence in the hall. Yashina pressed on. She spoke slowly, with absolute clarity and determination, looking occasionally towards Rizhin as she went. By this moment she would live or she would die.

'As President-Commander, Osip Rizhin has originated a form of rule founded on the most cruel repression. Whoever opposes his viewpoint is doomed to removal from their position and subsequent moral and physical annihilation. He has violated all norms of legality and trampled on the principles of collective leadership.

'Friends, of the original ninety-four members and candidates of this plenum after the war, sixty-seven persons have been arrested and shot. Yet when we examine the accusations against these so-called spies and saboteurs we find that all their cases – all of them, every single one – were fabricated. Confessions of guilt were gained with the help of cruel and inhuman tortures—'

'No!' called a voice.

'Yes!' called another. 'Yes! It's all true!'

'Here we see it, friends,' said Yashina, looking out across pained faces. Shock and disbelief and fear. 'This is the fate that will come to us all if the man Rizhin remains in his position.

'He has elevated himself so high above the Vlast he purports to serve that he thinks he can decide all things alone, and all he needs to implement his decisions are engineers, statisticians, soldiers and police. All others must only listen to him and praise him and obey. He has created about himself a cult of personality of truly monstrous proportions, devoted solely to the glorification of his own person. This is supported by numerous facts.

'His official biography is nothing but an expression of the most dissolute flattery, an example of making a man into a god, an infallible sage, the sublimest strategist of all times and nations. It is a confection of lies from beginning to end, and all edited and approved by Rizhin himself, the most egregious examples added to the text in his own handwriting. I need not give other examples. We all know them.'

Lom noticed that Kistler had slipped onto the platform and taken a seat at the back. Rizhin had seen him too.

'Friends and colleagues,' said Yashina, 'we must draw the proper conclusions. The negative influence of the cult of the individual has to be completely corrected. I urge the Central Committee to declare itself resolutely against such exaltation of a single person. We must abolish it decisively, once and for all, and fight inexorably all attempts to bring back this practice. We must in future adhere in all matters to the principle of collective leadership, characterised by the observation of legal norms and the wide practice of criticism and self-criticism.'

She paused.

'I present the motion stated by Secretary Gribov to the Central Committee for the vote,' she said. 'Long live the victorious banner of our Vlast.'

Yashina returned to her seat, visibly shaken. The observer-delegates sat absolutely still. A woman was sobbing. A naval officer had his head between his knees, being quietly sick.

Rizhin sat looking at his fingernails with the same faint smile.

'I ask my colleagues,' said Gribov at the microphone, 'to indicate assent or dissent.'

For long moments nobody moved. Rizhin looked along the row of them, and none would meet his gaze. He began to smile. Then Kistler raised his hand.

'Yes,' he said. 'Assent. Assent.'

Another hand went up.

'Yes.'

And another, and another, and the dam broke, and all hands went up, every one, and the Victory Hall exploded into tumultuous shouting. In the body of the auditorium the observer-delegates – knowing now which way the wind blew – were on their feet, applauding, roaring, weeping their relief and joy.

Alone, Lom watched from the balcony corner. Rizhin was still sitting in the same attitude, still with the same supercilious smile. He seemed frozen in time. Gribov and Yashina embraced, and Kistler's face was alight with the clear happy grin of a child. The face of a man to whom the future belonged.

Lom listened to the ecstatic cheering and asked himself why he wasn't cheering too. He had won. He had done what he set out to do – Rizhin was fallen, the beast was down, the very idea of him in tatters – but his own first emotion was a flood of tired cynicism. Here he was, watching the rulers applaud themselves. All was decided now: Rizhin was a criminal; no one else was to blame, and the banners of the Vlast still flew. The roaring in the hall was the sound of survival, and of ranks closing.

He pushed that weariness aside: it wasn't right, it did no justice to the courage of Kistler, Yashina and the rest, and it did no justice to himself. The fall of Rizhin might not be an end, but it was a beginning. Things which only that morning could not have happened were once again possible now. Doors were opening. Possible futures multiplying second by second. He had done a good thing, and it had been hard, and he had a right to a moment's satisfaction. And more than that. *Maroussia.* He had a right now to go home.

He looked across at Rizhin once again, but his chair was empty. The man was not there.

Lom took the steps up to the exit from the gallery three at a time, crashed open the door into the deserted corridor and began to run.

Part Four

Part Four

Chapter Eleven

Green shoots swell and burst
and your back is shattered, you broken
once-lithe hunting beast,
my lovely miserable century,
but still you go on, gazing backwards with a mindless smile
at the trail you leave.

Osip Mandelstam (1891–1938)

1

The man who was Osip Rizhin moves alone through the corridors of the Victory Hall. No praetorian troopers precede him, ten paces ahead, sub-machine guns in hand, sweeping the way. None follows ten paces behind. But he wears his white uniform still and he walks with the confidence of absolute power.

If you see him coming, press yourself against the wall, show the palms of your hands, lower your eyes. Do not meet his gaze. Papa Rizhin can break you open and smash your world. The modest gold braid on the white of his shoulder, the ribbons at the white of his breast: these are the crests of the truth of the power of death.

He looks at you with soft brown burning eyes as he passes.

The news of his fall has not yet escaped the plenum chamber.

*

Papa Rizhin, President-Commander and Generalissimus of the New Vlast, walks the passageways of the Victory Hall with measured pace and purposeful intent, but he does not exist. He is ghost. He is after-image. He is lingering, fading retinal burn.

The man who hurries towards the exit is Josef Kantor, wearing Papa Rizhin's clothes.

He pushes his way through heavy bronze doors and finds himself on a high terrace overlooking the River Mir. No one else is there. Above him the sky and before him the city of Mirgorod in the sun of the afternoon. He stands at the parapet and sees the city he saved, the city he rebuilt from the burned ground up: the great sky-rise buildings spearing the belly of cloudless blue, the tower that bears his face but Rizhin's name, the tower at the top of which Josef Kantor's immense and far-seeing statue stands.

Josef Kantor looks out across the city that is still his. Below him is the great slow silent river sliding west towards the sea. Barges call to barges, ploughing the green surface burnished in the afternoon sun, and a warm breeze palms his face. Summer air stirs his thick lustrous hair and gently traces the tight puckered scar on his cheek. Gulls wheel above the city lazily, flashing white in the sunlight. Their whiteness answers the whiteness of his tunic.

Josef Kantor does not move. He is calm. He is waiting. It is nearly time.

The revolutionary has no personal interests. No emotions. No attach-ments. The revolutionary owns nothing and has no name. All laws, moral-ities, customs and conventions – the revolutionary is their merciless and implacable enemy. There is only the revolution. All other bonds are broken.

He slips his hand into his pocket and folds his fat fingers round the tiny warm piece of angel flesh he always carries there. Always. He is never without it and never was.

He lets the last of Osip Rizhin drift away and dissolve on the air.

There is no past, there is only the future.

There is no defeat, there is only victory.

I am Josef Kantor, and what I will to happen, will happen.

There is a movement in the currents of the Mir, a disturbance at the near embankment. A roiling and rising stain of yellow sedimentary mud. An obstruction in the green flow.

The brutal faceless head and shoulders and torso of Archangel-in-mudjhik lifts itself out of the river, a blood- and rust-coloured thing of stone flesh spilling water as it punches holes in the embankment wall and hauls itself higher and higher, climbing towards the terrace of the Victory Hall.

Archangel tears open Josef Kantor's mind and pours himself in, flood after flood of vast glittering black consciousness, the voice of the shining emptiness between galaxies.

You remembered, my son, while I was gone. You remembered me and did well. You have built me ships for the stars.

Archangel! Archangel! Archangel!

I come for you now so that you can come for me! Carry me out from under the poisonous trees and bring me home!

It begins, oh it begins!

The voice of Archangel singing among the suns!

The foundations of the Victory Hall shook as Archangel-in-mudjhik, twelve-foot-high lump of mobile dull red angel flesh, climbed the embankment up towards the terrace, smashing through the skin of brick and gouging hand- and footholds in the concrete beneath. The waters of the Mir sluiced from him. The parapet crumbled and crunched under his weight as he heaved himself over.

Josef Kantor stood and faced him. He could not speak, his throat was stopped, but he did not fall.

The voice of Archangel filled his mind.

Join with me, faithful, beautiful son. Come inside me now and I will carry you.

Josef Kantor felt the mudjhik mind opening like a flower. It was a deep, scented well and he was on the brink. He was in a high and lonely place and desired only to fall.

Josef Kantor felt his body dying. His heart in his chest burst open, a dark gushing fountain of blood. His lungs collapsed. His ribs flexed and his throat gaped but no air entered. He was drowning in sunlight. His own name separated from him and drifted away.

Archangel-in-mudjhik pulled him in.

Vissarion Lom, running through the corridors of the Victory Hall, felt the irruption of Archangel into the world. A shattering rearrangement of the feel of things. A detonation of total and appalling fear.

He ran, and as he ran he felt the piledriver-pounding and -shaking of the floor. He was near and getting closer.

He ran.

There was no time and it was too far to go.

Lom shoved open the heavy bronze doors and burst onto the terrace. The paving stones were cracked and shattered, pieces of parapet broken and scattered across the ground. A corpse in a crumpled white uniform curled on the floor, leaking dark blood from mouth and nose. Lom looked over the wall down into the river. He could see nothing but he knew what was in there, moving eastwards, pushing strong and fast against the stream.

2

The River Mir is strong and green and brown. The last mudjhik in the world walks submerged, shoulder against the flow, up the river towards the forest. The archangel fragment, small and lonely and triumphant, is going home.

The river is a strong brown word, endlessly spoken, driving back towards the sea, but the mudjhik is stronger: every mighty footfall stirs puffs of silt. The dark voice of the river is loud: it is a hand against his chest, pressing. It ropes his feet and erodes the ground from under them. Eddies and water vortices stir and turn behind him, sucking him back, tugging him off balance. Thick mud in water whorls. The water ceiling just above his head glimmers and ripples.

Gravity operates differently here: he has no weight. All the forces shove and shear sideways and backwards, lifting and toppling, pushing back against archangel will.

Slip and fall. Tumble and roll. The strong brown river voice is running heavy. It turns everything over and over, slowly. Carries all away through city and marsh towards the ocean.

The river knows mudjhik is there. The river is a watchful, purposeful water ram. The river, the ever-speaking voice of the inland forest, opposes.

But mudjhik resists. Slow-motion walking like a brass-helmed diver in canvas and rubber, leaning forward into the slow conveyor of the water-wind, he hauls his clumsy mud-booted feet up and over lumps of half-buried concrete, brick and stone. Clambers clumsily over the weed-carpeted black and broken spars of a sunken barge, where worms and shell creatures rout and gouge the softening wood and frond gardens stream with the stream.

The engined hulls of riverboats lumber past his shoulder. He strokes their iron and timber with his palm and edges them gently aside. Eels and lampreys slide and flick, feeding in the silt clouds the mudjhik's feet kick up. Mudjhik pays attention to their slick dark mucus gleam. They flash like muscles of lightning in the paunch of storm clouds. They are bright marks of hungry life. Avid. Their needle teeth are sharp.

Larger fishes watch from shadow and darkness, curious, circumspect, holding themselves effortlessly in position against the force of the stream.

Mudjhik admires fish. Fish brain is cold, intent and unconcerned: the pressure of water currents is the book the fishes read. They trawl the turbid water with cold tongue. With cold and dark-adapted eye. They know what the river is: where it has come from, where it goes; the taste of earth and forest, lake and rain, and the fainter shadow-taste, the dangerous killing taint of oceanic salt. The river is their living god, and they are part of it, and there is nothing else and never was.

Josef Kantor knows that he is underwater in the river, and he knows that he is dead. The will of Archangel, heart and brain and total mudjhik commander, is a hot red fire that burns him. The overwhelming intent of Archangel drives all other thought away. Archangel is inexhaustible and unending dinning shout, all on a single note.

Archangel! Archangel! Archangel!

Archangel is bands of iron and wires of steel. Archangel is thunderous wheels on rails. Archangel is the blinding brilliance of internal suns. Archangel is the only force that drives. Archangel is …

Joseph Kantor is dumb with it.

3

Mudjhik climbs from the river and stands in the evening sun to dry. The city is far behind him, a murmur in the wind, a skyline stain.

Archangel is well satisfied.

You remembered and did well, my son. You were my voice in the silence and prepared for me the way home. Walk with me now, back to the mountain under the trees. Be my voice a while and I will yet show you the light of the stars.

Josef Kantor is fist. All fist. He rises from the quiet floor (which smells of dead dog and stinks of dead Safran still) and fights.

I am nobody's son.

All the long day, all the river walk, Kantor has been watching from the shadows, crouching, growing tired of the taste of defeat and death. He has been gently, silently, testing the boundaries of Archangel, weighing strength against strength, will against will. He knows now that this Archangel is fragment only, stretched thin and small and far from home.

He knows the prize to be won, and that the risk of failure is death, but he is dead already, so what does it matter? And he is strong, stronger now than he was, and stronger than Archangel knows.

Josef Kantor hurls himself at the Archangel root shard. Pushes his fist into Archangel mouth.

I am Josef Kantor, and what I will to happen, will happen. I am nobody's prophet and nobody's labouring hand.

Archangel screams shock and indignation and turns on the sudden enemy within. Crushing. Squeezing. Smashing. He is speed beyond perceiving, strike and strike and strike again: he is the lancing burning blade and the crushing stamping heel. Burst upon burst of hammer-blow force. He is the turner-to-stone and the acid lick of a fire mouth. He is the bitter adversary against whom nothing stands.

Archangel! Archangel!

He is warrior nonpareil; his birthright is all the stars.

Josef Kantor goes down before him like a blade of dried grass under the wheel of a strong wind. Archangel burns him and he flares, weightless and brittle, crumbling to ash and dust. He vanishes into instant vapours of nothing like a scrap of paper in the belly of the white furnace.

The brevity of his destruction cannot be measured in the silence between tick and tick. Josef Kantor is simply instantaneously gone.

But Josef Kantor returns.

Every time Archangel destroys him he returns.

Archangel's force is fabulously, immeasurably, gloriously greater. He extinguishes Josef Kantor instantaneously every single time – blows him into nothing like a candle flame – but this is not a contest of force, it is a contest of will and nothing else. Archangel-fragment fights for pride and dignity and purpose, because he is Archangel and cannot fail; that cannot be conceived. But Josef Kantor fights because he will not die.

Study what you fear. Learn and destroy, then find a stronger thing to fear. Endlessly, endlessly, until the fear you cause is greater than the fear you feel. This is the dialectic of fear and killing.

Even before birth it began for Josef Kantor, the triumphant twinless twin spilling out onto the childbirth bed, accompanied by his shrivelled and half-absorbed dead little brother. Josef Kantor does not let rivals live. He doesn't share space in the womb.

All night long the mudjhik stands without moving on the bank of the river, and when morning comes the archangel-conscious fragment is dead.

Josef Kantor explores his new body, and oh but it is an excellent thing! Senses of angel substance show him the world in all its surge and gleam and detail, alive in a thousand ways he knew nothing of before. Mudjhik strength is power beyond dreaming: with a flick of his arm he splinters trees. This is the eternal body Khyrbysk dreamed of! Tireless, impervious, unfailing, free of death.

I have died once. I will not die again.

And yet this mudjhik body is imperfect. It has no face. No voice. No tongue with which to speak. It is a crude and clumsy roughed-out template of massive earthy red. So Josef Kantor does what no mudjhik dweller ever thought to do before, nor ever had the will: he begins to reshape the mudjhik clay from within. He gives it mouth. He gives it tongue (a fubsy lozenge of angel flesh, awkward now but he will learn). He gives it teeth and lips and palate for the enunciation of sibilants and plosives and fricatives, and all other equipment and accoutrements necessary for the purpose of making voice.

He gives its massive boulder head a face.

Josef Kantor's face.

Josef Kantor made of angel flesh the colour of brick and rust and drying blood and bruises.

Josef Kantor dead and immortal now and twelve feet high.

Josef Kantor in the warmth of the morning walking east towards the forest.

Find the thing you fear and strike it dead.

This is my world and I will not share it.

4

*T*housands *of miles to the east, on the edge of the endless forest, Archangel feels himself in the mudjhik die. He knows that Josef Kantor has killed him, this one little piece of him sent out wandering across the world, and he knows what that means.*

Archangel opens himself out like an unfolding fern and shouts at the oppressing sky of this poisonous world in absolute and ecstatic joy.

For Josef Kantor is strong!

Stronger than Archangel had ever guessed. The will of Kantor is harder than iron; his purpose is stronger than the heart rock of the world; his heat burns hotter than the sun. The strength of his arm grinds the wheels of time faster and faster.

Archangel knows and has always known that without Josef Kantor he is a dumb mouth shouting, a blowhard bully trundling about for ever in the forest, spilling futile anti-life: a liminal and ineffectual pantoufflard grumbling at the margins of history, claiming primacy but in clear-sighted truth merely scratching an itch.

And Josef Kantor without Archangel, one-time emperor of the Vlast though he may be, is brief-lived and tractionless. A powder flash in the pan.

But together!

My champion! My ever-burning sun!

It is Archangel who is the generator of power and endurance, Archangel the ever-spinning dynamo of cruel expansive energy, Archangel the permission and the totaliser. But it is Josef Kantor who is the conduit, the bond, the channel that lets Archangel reach out into the world and seize the bright birthright. Kantor is the face on the poster and the arm that wields the burning sword that turns the skies to ash.

Josef Kantor, freed now of his organic bodily chains, a will and a voice and a mind released into history and driving an angelic body, is coming to the forest with a mind to kill him, but there will be no need for that.

Faster and faster Archangel grinds towards the edge of the forest.

Kantor will come and break down the border.

Kantor will let him loose in the world.

Run my champion Josef Kantor faster and faster, run as I run towards you. Carry to me the banners of victory. The time is short and our enemies are upon us.

Archangel returns to his work with fresh vigour. There is much to do. His champion generalissimo needs a new army.

5

A week after the fall of Osip Rizhin, Vissarion Lom woke hollow and drenched with sweat from a dream of trees and Maroussia, and knew by the feeling in his belly and heart, by the anger and the anxiety and the desperate desolation, by the need to be up and moving, by the impossibility of rest, that it wasn't any kind of dream, no dream at all.

Maroussia was different – older, wiser, changed – she saw things he didn't see, she was distant, she was … august. She was something to be wary of. Something of power and something to fear.

Kantor is making for the forest. The angel is calling him there. Nothing is over yet, nothing is done. Come into the forest, darling, and I will find you there.

Helping. Answering the call. That was Lom. That was what he did.

931

In his dream that was no dream at all he'd seen the living angel in the woods. Seen the trail of poisoned destruction and cold smouldering crusted earth it left in its wake as it dragged itself, an immense hill the colour of blood and rust and bruises, towards the edge of the trees. A cloud of vapours burned off the top of the angel hill, cuprous and shining. Energy nets like pheromone clouds, dream-visible, dream-obvious. The soldiers of the Vlast were crawling about on its lower slopes like ants, digging and dying.

The living angel was recruiting an army of its own, infesting a growing crowd of dark things: bad dark things coming out from under the trees. Men and women like bears and wolves. Giants and trolls from the mountains and moving trees turned to ash and stone and dust. Lom's dream heart beat strangely when he saw the men like bears. The living angel found them in the forest and took their minds and filled them with its own. He gave them hunting and anger and desire and pleasure in death. He gave them bloodlust and greed and berserking. The smell of blood and musk. There were not many yet but more each day, and the nearer it got to the frontier of trees the more it found.

Lom heard faintly, insistently, the voice of the living angel in his own mind. It pulled at him like gravity, seeped through the skin, and polluted the way he tasted to himself.

I will not be silenced. I will not be imprisoned. I will not be harassed and consumed and annoyed and troubled and stung. I am Archangel, the voice of history and the voice of the dark heart of the world. My birthright is among the stars and I am coming yet.

Lom felt the living angel's attentive gaze pass over him and come to rest, returning his regard as if it knew it was watched. As if it knew its enemy and disdained him. It came to him then, dream knowledge, that he was Maroussia watching. He was seeing with Maroussia's eye. Alien Maroussia Pollandore, preparing to kill this thing if she could.

It was still dark when he woke but there was no more sleeping. In the first light of dawn Lom went to see Kistler, and then he went to find Eligiya Kamilova, who was back in her house on the harbour in the shadow of the Ship Bastion. That house was a survivor. Eligiya was there, and so were Elena Cornelius and her girls, Yeva and Galina. Rising for the day. Having breakfast.

I bring your children home to you Elena, Kamilova had said that day in the street. *I have looked after them as well as I could. You can stay in my house until you find your feet.*

What I owe you, Eligiya, said Elena, *it's too much. It can't ever be repaid.*

When he came for Kamilova in the early morning, Lom found Elena's girls just as he remembered them from when he and Maroussia stayed at Dom Palffy six years before. They had not grown. Not aged at all. That was uncanny. It disturbed him oddly. Kamilova was dark-eyed, thin and haunted. She had a faraway look, as if she felt uncomfortable and superfluous, marginal in her own home.

'I want you to come with me into the forest,' Lom said to her. 'Bring your boat and be my guide.'

Kamilova was on her feet immediately. Face burning.

'When?' she said.

'Now. Today. Will you come?'

'Of course. It is all I want.' She turned to Elena Cornelius. 'Keep the house,' she said. 'It is yours. I give it to Galina and Yeva. There is money in a box in the kitchen. I will not be coming back. Not ever.'

For all of the rest of her life Yeva Cornelius carried an agonising guilt that she hadn't loved Eligiya Kamilova and didn't weep and hug her when she left, but felt relieved when Kamilova left her with Galina and her mother. It was a needless burden she made for herself. Kamilova didn't do things out of love or to get love. She did what was needed.

Lom and Kamilova had the rest of the day to make arrangements. Kistler had arranged a truck to come for Kamilova's boat. The *Heron*. It was to be flown by military transport plane, along with Lom and Kamilova and their baggage and supplies, as far east as possible. As near to the edge of the forest as they could get.

Lom spent the time with Kamilova in her boathouse. She knew what she needed for an expedition into the forest and went about putting it all together while he poked about in her collection of things brought back from the woods. He felt excited, like a child, anxious to be on his way. He'd been born in the forest but had no coherent memories of life there. All his life he'd lived with the idea of it, but he'd never been there. And now he was going. And Maroussia was there.

When it was nearly time for the truck to come, Kamilova looked him up and down. His suit. His city shoes.

'You can't go like that,' she said.

She found him heavy trousers of some coarse material, a woollen pullover, a heavy battered leather jacket, but he had to go and buy himself boots, and by the time he got back the truck had come and the boat was in the back and Kamilova was waiting.

Elena and the girls were there to see them off.

'You're going to look for Maroussia, aren't you?' said Elena.

'Yes,' said Lom.

'You're a good man,' she said. 'You will find her.'

She looked across the River Purfas towards the western skyline where the sun was going down. The former Rizhin Tower, now renamed the Mirgorod Tower, rose dark against a bank of reddening pink cloud. It was still the tallest building by far, though the statue of Kantor was gone from the top of it. The new collective government with Kistler in the chair had had it removed and dismantled.

'They should call it Lom Tower for what you've done. People should know.'

'I wouldn't like that,' said Lom. 'I'd hate it. Nothing's done yet. It's just the beginning.'

Kistler had found jobs for Konnie and Maksim, working for the new government, and he'd sent out word to look for Vasilisk the bodyguard – Kistler was a man to repay his debts – but so far he could not be found. There was trouble brewing: many people had done well out of Rizhin's New Vlast, and not everyone was glad to see the statue gone. There were Rizhinists now. Hunder Rond had disappeared.

Kistler had offered to find a job for Elena Cornelius but she had refused.

'What will you do?' said Lom.

Elena smiled. 'I'm going to make cabinets again.' She hugged Lom and kissed him on the cheek. 'When you find Maroussia, bring her back here and see how we have done.'

'Maybe,' said Lom. 'That would be good.'

He swung himself up into the cab of the truck next to Kamilova and the driver.

'OK,' he said. 'Let's go.'

6

The plane carrying Lom and Kamilova and the *Heron* landed at a military airfield at the edge of the forest: three runways, heavy transport planes coming and going every few minutes. Soldiers and engineers and their equipment were everywhere: rows of olive and khaki tents in their thousands; roadways laid out; jetties and pontoons and river barges clogged with traffic; the smell of fuel and the noise of engines. Huge tracked machines churned up the mud and eased themselves onto broad floating platforms. It was an industrial entrepôt, the base camp of a massive engineering project and the beachhead for an invasion, all combined in one chaotic hub and thrown now into reorganisation and dismay. Orders had been changed: the collective government under Lukasz Kistler required the living angel not mined for its substance but destroyed. Eradicated. Killed. The order came as a signal, unambiguous and peremptory.

Destroy it? the commanders of the advance said to one another. *Destroy it? How?*

A few miles east of the airfield low wooded hills closed the horizon: rising slopes of dark grey tree-mass which stretched away north and south, unbroken into the distance, shrouded in scraps of drifting mist. Westward was clear summer blue, the continental Vlast in sunshine, but a leaden autumn cloud bank had slid across the sky above the forest like a lid closing, a permanent weather front coming to rest at the edge of hills.

In hospital tents men and women on low cots stared darkly at the ceiling. Others slumped in wheelchairs, legs tucked under blankets, or hobbled and swung on crutches, aimless and solitary, muttering quietly. Bandaged feet. Arms, hands and faces marked with chalky fungal growths and patches of smooth blackness.

'Have you seen this before?' Lom said to Kamilova.

'No. This is not the forest doing this.'

'The angel then,' said Lom. 'They've found it.'

*

Out of the trees through a gap in the low hills the broad slow river flowed, turbid and muddy green. An unceasing traffic of barges and motor launches and shallow-draught gunships cruised upstream, heavily laden and low in the water, and came back downstream riding higher, empty, bruised and rusting.

'There's another way,' said Kamilova. 'The old waterway joins the river downstream of here.'

The *Heron* and their gear was loaded on a flatbed truck. Early in the morning, before their liaison officer was up and about, Lom and Kamilova drove out of the camp alone. Nobody questioned them at the gate.

A day's sailing downriver and the sinking sun in their eyes was gilding the river a dull red gold when Kamilova swung the boat in towards the left bank under overhanging vegetation. Lom saw nothing but a scrubby spit of land until they were into the canal and nosing up slow shallow waters clogged with weed. Disgruntled waterfowl made way for them, edging in under muddy banks and exposed tree roots, or rose and flapped away slowly to quieter grounds.

'This way is navigable?' said Lom.

'It's a few years since I was here,' said Kamilova.

Ruined stonework lined the water's edge: low embankments, mossy and root-broken and partly collapsed, the stumps of rotted wooden jetties, rusted mooring rings. Back from the canal edge were low mounds and rooted stumps of standing stone. Broken suggestions of fallen ruins lost. Earth and grass and undergrowth spilled in a slow tide across ancient constructions and slumped into torpid water.

'It's an old trader canal,' said Kamilova. 'It connects with another river over there beyond the hill. In the time of the Reasonable Empire, when the Lezarye families were hedge wardens and castellans of the forest margin, you'd have seen a town here. Trading posts. Warehouses. Of course the trade was already ancient when the Lezarye came. There was always trade into the forest and out of it.'

'Timber?' said Lom. 'The canal seems too narrow.'

'Not here, that was always big-river trade. In places like this you'd find charcoal burners and wood turners. Fur traders selling sable, marten, grease beaver, miniver, fox, hart. There were markets for dried mushrooms and lichens and powdered barks. Syrups and liquors.

Scented woods. Wax and honey and dried berries. Antler and bone. Anything you could bring out of the forest and sell. And there'd have been shamans and völvas and priests. Giants of course, and the other forest peoples would come out this far too. Keres and wildings. This was debatable land then. Marginal. Liminal. A crossing place.'

They passed under the long evening shadow of a round-towered and gabled building of high sloping walls: red brick and timber, collapsing, overgrown, roofless and empty-windowed.

'A Lezarye garrison way fort,' said Kamilova. 'The trade leagues paid the Lezarye to keep the peace and the Reasonable Empire paid them to watch the border and make sure the darker things of the forest stayed there.'

The pace of the boat slackened as the evening breeze dropped away. There was thinness and a still, breathless silence in the air. Lom felt he was at the bottom of a deep well filled up with ages of time.

Kamilova shook herself and looked wary.

'Things are slowing here,' she said. 'I know the feel of this from when I was with Elena's girls. We shouldn't linger.'

She unshipped oars and began to row, nosing the *Heron* forward through thickening standing water. Lom watched her muscular arms working. The intricate interlaced patterns on her skin were like winding roots and knots of brambles and young tendrils reaching out across the earth. They seemed fresher and more vivid than he'd noticed before. There was much he wanted to ask her. But not yet. The wooded hills of the forest edge rose higher and denser before them, closer now, catching the last light of the setting sun. A rich and glowing green wall.

After an hour or so the waterway widened and the going was easier, but the last light of the day was failing. Kamilova tied up the *Heron*.

'We'll camp for the night,' she said. 'Tomorrow we'll go in under the trees.'

7

Yakoushiv the embalmer presented himself at the office of Colonel Hunder Rond, commander of the Parallel Sector. Yakoushiv was clammy with sweat. He felt sick. He could hardly speak for nerves. He thought his end had come.

'You did a nice job with the corpse of the old Novozhd,' said Rond. 'Very pretty. I have more work for you, if you're interested.'

Yakoushiv's legs trembled with relief. He almost fell. He felt as if his head had become detached from his neck and was floating a foot above his shoulders. He dabbed at his face with a sweet handkerchief.

'Of course,' he said. His voice came out wrong. Pitched too high. 'The subject? I mean … who is the … ?'

'Come through and I'll show you.'

Rond led him through to the other room. Yakoushiv's eyes widened in surprise. Another wave of sick nervousness and fear. The corpse of the disgraced Papa Rizhin was laid out in Rond's inner office on a makeshift catafalque.

'You will work here,' said Rond. 'You will write me a list of what you need and I will obtain it for you. There is need for great haste. He must be ready tonight. You understand? Is that possible?'

'Of course.'

'Make it your best work ever. And get rid of the scar on his face.'

Yakoushiv worked as rapidly and as neatly as he could. It was impossible to avoid making a mess in the room. There was … spillage. But when he had finished the corpse of Osip Rizhin was glossy and shining and fragranced with a cloying sickly sweetness.

When Rond returned he examined Yakoushiv's work from head to foot.

'You've done well,' he said. 'You should be pleased, Yakoushiv. Your last job was your best. I hope you can take some satisfaction from that. I'm only sorry you can't go home now.'

Yakoushiv turned white. 'No,' he said. 'Please. No.'

'There can be no blabbing, you see. No tales to be told.'

'I won't. Of course. I promise. Please—'

'I'm sorry, Yakoushiv,' said Rond.

8

Next morning Lom woke at the outermost, easternmost edge of the world he knew, he and Kamilova alone in an emptied ancient landscape.

The sun had not yet risen above the edge of the forest. Close now, the hills were dark shoulders and hogs' backs of dense tree canopy draped in mist and cloud. Home of ravens. On the lower slopes he could see the relics of long-abandoned field boundaries under bracken and scrub, and out of the scrub rose great twisted knobs and stumps of rock, shoulders and boulders of raw stone. Stone the colour of rain and slate.

The stone seemed to hum and prickle the air.

The Lezarye used to keep the debatable lands by patrol and force of arms, Kamilova had said, *but the forest maintains its own boundary. It's stronger now than I've ever felt it before.*

I feel it, said Lom. *Yes.*

Kamilova, bright-eyed and alive, raised the *Heron*'s brown sail, and the little wooden boat took them up the river and into the trees.

As they travelled, Kamilova kept up a stream of quiet talk, more talk than Lom had ever known from her before. She talked about the people who went to live among the trees.

'The forest changes you,' she said. 'It brings out who you are. The breath of the trees. Giants grow larger in the woods.' She talked about hollowers, hedge dwellers who dug shelters in the earth. 'They don't hibernate, not exactly, but their body temperature falls and they're dormant for days on end. They sleep out the worst of winter underground like bears do.'

She told him the names of clans. Lyutizhians meant people like wolves, and Kassubians were the shaggy coats.

'I saw things once that someone said were bear-made. They were rough things, strange and wild and inhuman, for paws and muzzles and teeth to use, not dextrous fingers. But it was just a rumour. Humanish forest peoples keep to the outwoods, but there's always further in and further back.

'The forest is a bright and perfumed place,' she said, 'with dark and tangled corners. It is not defined. It includes everything and it is not safe. The forest talks to you, but you have to do the work; you have to bring yourself to the task. Communication is indirect and you must pay attention. You have to dig. Dig!'

Lom hardly listened to her. The river was passing through a gap between steep slopes, almost cliffs, under a low grey sky, and there was the possibility of cold rain in the air. The troubling ache in his head that had been with him all morning, the agitated throbbing of the old wound in his forehead, was fading. His sense of time passing had lurched, dizzying and uncomfortable, but it was settled now. Time present touched the endless eternal forest like sunlight grazing the outer leaves of a huge tangled tree or the surface of a very deep and very dark lake. The forest was all Kamilova's stories and more, but it was also a breathing lung made of real trees and rock and earth and water. He felt the aliveness of it and the way it went on for ever.

Doors in the air were opening. The skin of the water glimmered and thrilled. Promising reflections, it almost delivered. The breath of the forest crackled. It bristled. There were black trees. There were grey and yellow trees. He was watching a single ash tree at the river margin and it was watching him back, being alive.

Lom was opening up and growing stronger. He was entering a place where new kinds of thing were possible, different stories with different outcomes. He was coming home. He reached up into the low roof of cloud and opened a gap to let a spill of warmth through that made the river glitter. A moment of distraction, lost in sunlight: there were many small things among the trees – animals and birds – and they were all alive and he could feel that.

Then he became aware that Kamilova had stopped talking and was watching him. Intently. Curiously. A little bit afraid.

From the slopes of the hills and among the trees they are watched. The small boat edging upriver against the stream; the woman whose arms are painted with fading magic; the man spilling bright beautiful scented trails from the hole in his skull, tainted with dark shades of angel: all this is seen and known by watchers with brown whiteless eyes, and by things with no eyes that also see. Word passes through roots and leaves and air. Word reaches Fraiethe and the Seer Witch of Bones. Word reaches Maroussia Shaumian Pollandore.

He is coming. He is here.

Chapter Twelve

Nothing that lives and dies ever has a beginning, nor does it ever end in death and annihilation. There is only a mixing, followed by the separating-out of what was mixed: and these mixings and unmixings are what people call beginnings and ends.

Empedocles (*c.* 490–430 BCE)

1

Kantor-in-mudjhik runs through the endless forest, tireless, exultant and strong. The continental Vlast is behind him. He has run it, ocean to trees, without a pause.

Under the trees he has heard the voice of Archangel talking and they have sealed the deal.

I will give you body after body, says Archangel, *a chain of human bodies without end, vessels for my champion son. Worthy and valid strength of my strength, bring me out of the forest and for you I will break down the doors and shatter the doorposts. For you I will raise up the dead to consume the living. I will give you armies without end, and you will carry me, speaking my voice, across the stars.*

Josef Kantor in his mudjhik body likes the sound of that.

I am nobody's son, he says, *but I will be a brother.*

It's not enough, but it will do for now.

2

Into the forest old beyond guessing, the first place, primordial, primeval, primal, the unremembered home, fair winds carried them day after day, deeper and deeper, up the river against the stream. Trees stood silently, lining the banks, fading away in every direction into twilight and indistinction.

'How will we find her?' said Kamilova. 'I mean Maroussia?'

'We keep going in,' said Lom, 'and she will come to us.'

Things that find their way into the forest grow and change. They grow taller, shorter, thinner, fatter; they change colour. Each thing grows out into its true shape and becomes more itself. A dog may become more wolf-like. It unfolds like a fern.

In the forest you can't see far or travel fast; detachment and analysis fail; you can't see the wood for the trees. Aurochsen and wisent, woolly rhinoceros, great elk and giant sloth browse among the leaves, and the corpses of those killed in great and terrible massacres are buried under shallow earth. The labyrinth of trees is filled with travelling shadows and all the monsters of the mind. In the forest, things long thought dead may be alive and the hunter become the prey. Green pools glimmer in the shade. More is possible here.

It is hard enough to get in, but leaving, that is the labour, that is the task. The forest is receding, back into its own world. Ancient silences are withdrawing like the tide.

Nights they slept out under blankets on the deck boards of the *Heron*. Kamilova cut thorns to make a brake on the bank against wolves and left a slow fire burning.

'If a big cat comes, set the thorns alight,' she said.

'Lynx is worse than wolf?' said Lom.

'Not lynx,' said Kamilova. 'Bigger than lynx, much bigger. Heavy as a horse, and teeth to snap your spine.'

Lom lay awake and heard the grumbling of predators in the dark, but nothing troubled them.

'I don't think wolves hunt in the night,' he said.

'You want to bet your skin on that?'

'No.'

Kamilova took the pan of stewed rosehips off the fire and set it in the grass. Pulled her knife from her belt and wiped it carefully clean. Unwrapped the axe and did the same, and sharpened the blades of both to a clean fineness with her stone. By the time she'd done, the stewed hips were cool enough. She picked a handful out of the pan and squeezed the juices back in. Lom watched the bright redness dribble between her fingers. She threw the seed-filled pulp away and scooped another handful, working it between her palms to release as much as possible of the blood-warm liquid. By the time she'd picked the last few softened fruits out of the liquid and pressed them between finger and thumb she had the pan half-full of rich rose liquor.

'Here,' she said and passed the pan to Lom.

He took a sip. Without honey it was bitter enough to roughen the roof of his mouth, but it was good.

'I know this place,' she said, 'but there were people here then, and fewer wolves. Everyone's gone, but there's somewhere nearby I'd like to see again. I'll take you there'

'OK,' said Lom. 'Tomorrow.'

Morning came quiet and cold, suppressed under low featureless skies. A drab unsettling breeze stirred brittle leaves. The forest felt shabby and grey. Snares and fish traps laid the evening before held nothing. Lom ate some berries and drank a little of the sour red rose-drink. It left him no less hungry.

The absence of Maroussia nagged at him. Her failure to come. Since they'd passed through the gap in the hills he'd felt nothing of her. Morning succeeded morning, timeless and inconsequential: a perpetual repetition of movement without progress against the narrowing river that always tried to push them back and out. The resinous taste of the air, the hungry excitement of opening up into the possibilities of the forest, was fading. Immensity and endlessness were always and everywhere the same, and he felt small and ordinary and lost. He was growing accustomed to the inexhaustible sameness of trees, and knew that he was somehow failing.

He crouched among fallen leaves, blotched and parchment-yellow and fragile, like dry pages scattered from an ageing and spine-cracked book, disordered out of all meaning. He picked up crumbling hand-fuls and sifted them, dealing them out like faceless cards in a game he couldn't play, returning leaves to the infinite mat of fallen leaves, every one different and all of them the same, abundant beyond all counting, further in and further on forever, abundant to the point of absurdity. Autumn was coming in the interminable forest and there would be no numbering of the trees.

He pushed his hands down, digging through the covering of dry leaves into darkening dampness and rot and the raw deep earth beneath. The cool fungal smell. Mycelium. Earthworm. Shining blackened twig fragment and softening pieces of bark. Truffle-scented leaf rot. Fine tangled clumps of hair-like root.

Lom closed his eyes and breathed.

Trunks of trees rise separately out of the earth and each stands apart from its neighbours. We overvalue sight. In the rich dark earth the roots of all the trees of the forest are intertwined. Knotted filaments and root fibres grow around and through each other, twist each other about, intertangled and nodal, meshed and joined with furtive fungal threads, digging down deeper than the trees grow tall. Slow exchange and interchange of mineral currency. Burrowing capacitors and con-ductors of gentle dark electric flux and spark. You can't say one tree ends and the next begins; it's all one sentient wakeful centreless tree and it lives underground.

Lom listened to the circuitry of the earth. He felt the living angel get-ting stronger. The first weakening of hope. A cruel thing coming closer and the rumourous growth of fear. There was a hurt in the forest and a wound in the world. He missed Maroussia and wished she would come.

3

Josef Kantor embodied in mudjhik reaches the lower slopes of the Archangel hill. The ground he stands on is burning with cool fire, thrilling to the touch, and the immense body of the living angel rises in front of him, higher, far higher, than he had imagined. Hundreds of feet into the sky. Even hurt and weakened, grounded as it is, it is a thing of glowering power. It crackles with life. The mudjhik body loosens and grows light. It feeds. Archangel feeds Kantor and Kantor feeds Archangel, strength mixes with strength, distinctions blur.

Archangel separates several hundred chunks of himself and sends them into the sky to circle his top on flaggy wings. The coming of his prince deserves such glorious celebration.

4

Kamilova took Lom to see the place she knew. She was happy in the forest. This was where she could be who she was.

They approached through old earthworks and turf-covered stone dykes. Redoubts. Salients. Massive boulders that had been tumbled into place and now settled deep into the earth. Rooks chattered and flocked among thorn trees.

The full extent of the stronghold was invisible, immersed in trees, and it felt smaller than it was because the chambers were small. Intimate human scale. Inside was gloomy, rich with earth and stone and leaf and wood, and the river ran through it, in under the hill. The place was burrow, sett and warren. Tunnels extended into darkness, every direction and down.

Kamilova took and lit a tar-soaked torch. The flame burned slow and smoked.

'Come on,' she said. 'This way.'

Distinctions between inside and outside, overground and underground, meant little. There were low halls with intricately carved ceilings and curving wooden walls, like the hulls of underground ships, polished and dark with age and hearth smoke, into which real living trees, their limbs and roots and branches, were interwoven and included. Chambers and passageways were floored with stone flags or compacted earth, leaf-carpeted. Older places were rotting and returning to the earth, moss and mushroom damp.

'I'd thought there might be someone still here,' said Kamilova. 'Stupid, but I hoped it.'

Lom's feeling of unease was growing.

'We shouldn't stay here,' he said. 'There's something not right.'

On the path back to where they had left the *Heron* they heard riders approaching. The footfall of horses. The clanking of bridles and gear. The scuffing of many feet through mud and forest litter. No voices. There was a quiet wind moving among the trees, but Lom could hear them coming.

'Get out of sight,' he said. 'Quickly.'

They crouched behind low thorn and briar. There was movement visible now through the trees.

Kamilova put her face next to his ear. 'Did they see us?'

'I don't know.'

He pulled off his pack and crawled forward on his belly, turning on his side to squeeze between thorn-bush stems. A root in the ground dug into him. He felt the spike of it gouging into his flesh, dragging at him. It hurt. He eased himself slowly forward across it, his face pressed close to the earth. Thorns snagged in his hair and grazed the skin of his scalp. A strand of briar hooked itself across his back. He reached back to pull it away and inched himself forward until he could see the track. He scooped a lump of earth and moss and rubbed himself with it, smearing it on his forehead and round his eyes, working it into the stubble on his face. The scent of it was strong and sour in his nose. He was sweating despite the cold.

Kamilova squeezed up next to him. The sound of her ragged breathing. He didn't look round.

There were three riders at the front, and men walking behind, strung out and silent. Lots of men, dirty and ill dressed. More riders followed, the horses dragging long heavy bundles wrapped in cloth. The bundles were heavy, deadweight, trailing furrow-paths through the leaves on the path. The horses pulled slowly against the weight.

The riders were bulky and hooded, soiled woollen cowls shrouding their faces, their heads heavy and too large. They rode alert, scanning the trees. Lom felt the pressure of their attention pass across him. It made him feel uneasy. Exposed. He inched his way cautiously backwards under the thorn.

'Don't move,' Kamilova hissed in his ear. 'There's one behind us.'

Lom lay on his back, face turned up, looking into the close tangle of the leafless bush. Outriders scouting the trail. Fear made his heart struggle. He wanted to breathe clear air. He forced himself to lie still and wait. Let them pass.

Long after the last sound of their passing had gone, the two of them lay without speaking under the thorns. The touch of the riders' eyeless gaze stayed with them, a taint breath, a foulness in the mind. They listened for any sign of more following or the scout returning, and when that purpose faded they still didn't move.

'What were they?' said Kamilova. She didn't look at him but stayed lying on her back, watching a spider moving slowly among the branches.

'I don't know.'

'Did you feel ...?'

'Yes.'

'That wasn't ... normal. That wasn't right.'

'No.'

Neither of them said anything for a long time.

'We should go,' she said at last. 'We should move on.'

'Yes.'

Stiff and cold, they picked up their packs and began to walk.

'Perhaps we should stay off the track,' she said. 'There might be more coming.'

'We have to get back to the boat,' said Lom. 'We have to keep going.'

It began to rain. Sheets of wind-driven icy water soaking their clothes. The noise of it was like an ocean in the trees. The track led them between shallow green pools, rain-churned and murky.

Lom didn't hear the splashing charge of the bear-man over the noise of the rain. Didn't smell it through the rain and the mud and the drench of the leaves. But he felt the appalling shock of the boulder-heavy collision that drove the air from his lungs, crunched the ribs in his chest and hurled him off the path into the water, crashing his spine against the trunk of a beech tree.

He could not raise his arms. He could not move his legs. The water came up to his waist. Propped against the slope of the tree root, he watched the grey-hooded figure turn and come back, wading towards him through the mud-swirled green pool. Its cowl was pulled back off its head.

Lom smelled the bear-man's hot sour breath on his face, on his wide staring eyes. He saw deep into the dark red mouth as its jaws widened to clamp on his face. The mouth reeked of angel. He observed with detached and distant surprise that half its head was made of stone.

Lom punched the side of the half-stone head with closed-up forest air, boulder heavy and boulder-hard. A swinging fist of rain and air. The bear-weighted bear-muzzled skull jerked sideways, crushed and broken and dead in a sudden mess of blood and bone.

5

*T*he bear-man, the angel rider of horse, opens his mouth to scream out the shock and outrageous surprise of his death, his death out of nowhere. He is instantaneously silenced. Cerebral cortex sprayed on the air like a smashed fruit.

But the screaming instant is heard.

Archangel, O Archangel all-surveying, connected by iron filaments of Archangel mind to all the doers of his will – all the absorbed living syllables through which he gives voice, all the soldiers in the army he is building for his brother in arms Josef Kantor – Archangel hears and feels the killing of the bear and knows it for what it is. It is familiar. Anomaly and threat.

And there is something else.

He has seen it now. Resolved out of endlessness and trees it has locality. The eye of his surveillance has pinned it, and this time it is close and he can reach it.

She shows herself and he has found her.

Everything comes together in the forest, and out in the forest hunting now is his racing engine, his destroyer, his fraternal champion and his pride.

Kill them all. Kill them quickly. Do it now.

Archangel calls and his champion runs them down.

6

'They were riding for the angel,' said Lom. 'I think we're coming closer to where it is.'

There was strain in Kamilova's eyes. She was watching him warily again. There was always a separateness about her: a wordless watchfulness, a lonely, withheld and self-postponing patience, doing what she must and waiting for the dark times to go.

'It was going to kill you,' she said. 'Then it was like its brain exploded.'

They were back at the *Heron*, and the rain had passed leaving watery afternoon sunshine. Lom had wiped the dark bear blood off his face and neck but still he felt unclean. The angel-residue in his own blood was strung out taut like wires in his veins again. He didn't like Kamilova's scrutiny and wanted to be alone.

'I'm going for a swim,' he said.

He followed a game trail up to the crest of a low slope and looked down on dark green water. The trail took him down to the edge of it, a stillness fringed on the far side with dense bramble. A fallen tree dipped a leafless crown and branches like arms into the mystery of the pool. Goosander gave muted echoless mews. Lom took off his rain-damp clothes and waded out. The water, cold against his shins, was moss-coloured, icy, opaque. He felt the thick cool of silt sliding between his toes and up over his feet. It felt like darkness.

After a few steps the lake bottom fell away steeply and he slipped, half-falling and half-choosing, into a sudden clumsy dive. The water closed over his head. How deep it might be he had no idea and didn't care. Bands of iron cold tightened round his skull and bruised ribs, squeezing out breath. He opened his eyes on nothing but pale thickened green light.

Floundering to the surface he swam with cramped clumsy strokes, arms and legs working through the cold. Broken twigs and fallen leaves littered the surface: he nosed his way through.

Once the first shock of the chill subsided, he immersed himself in the wild forgetful freedom of swimming in the forest, washing the sourness of killing and angel from his skin and hair. He took breath and dived for the bottom, reaching his arms down for it, but couldn't touch it, and surfaced, gasping. Floating on his back he watching the canopy of trees turning slowly overhead against the heavy sky.

He swam until the icy bitter cold of the water returned to the attack, then hauled himself up onto the bole of the fallen tree and lay there for a long time, face down, the bark's hard roughness against his skin, the air of the forest resting against his naked back. Lazy and reluctant to move he watched the pool opaque and green below him.

When he was dry he crawled back along the tree and swung himself down onto the bank, and she was there, her eyes brushing across him, bright and dark and happy.

Maroussia.

She put her hand against his chest, tracing the rise and hollow of his ribs. His hands and face were weather-brown, his body pale. The warmth of her fingers was on him. He smelled the sweetness of her breath.

'Is it you?' he said. 'Not a shadow but you?'

'You're cold,' she said. 'Your skin is rough and hard and cool like stone.'

She looked into his face and opened her mouth a little, and he kissed her, his arms around her shoulders awkwardly, uncertain. She tasted like hedge berries, and she leaned in and pressed herself against him. The scent of woodsmoke and forest in her hair. She took his hand and pressed it against her belly gently.

'Do you feel our child moving?'

For him it had been six years and more, but for her hardly any time at all.

7

It was late afternoon when Lom and Maroussia walked together back down the trail to the river where the *Heron* was moored.

Eligiya Kamilova received Maroussia with quiet reserve. She was generous and fine, but Lom could see her withdrawing. She was displaced again: having done her part she was finding herself edged to the margin of other people's reunions and plans. Lom found himself feeling slightly sorry for her. It was guilt that he felt, he knew that – he'd brought her here, he'd used her as his guide – but it was the path she'd chosen. The solitary traveller. She'd wanted to come. The forest was her travelling place, but she'd come back and found it an emptier, harsher place than before.

Kamilova had caught a fish in her trap. A pike. She shared it with them. The smoke of the cooking fire hung about in the still air of evening, clinging and acrid. It stuck to their skin. The flesh of the pike tasted muddy and was full of fine sharp bones. Not pleasant eating. Maroussia said little and ate less.

The sliver of an ominous new hill had appeared above the trees in the west. It glowed a dull rust-red in the last of the westering sun, and above it dark shapes circled like flocks of flying birds.

'I'm sorry, Eligiya,' said Maroussia.

Kamilova frowned.

'Sorry? Why?'

'A bad thing is coming and I am bringing it here. I show myself now to draw it out before it gets any stronger. It may already be too strong.'

Maroussia turned to Lom. She was almost a stranger, fierce and strong. Her hair was black, her eyes were dark and wide. She was carrying his child. He hadn't even begun to absorb the truth of that yet.

'Are you ready?' she said.

'Ready for what?' said Lom, but he knew.

He'd felt it coming for some time: the pulsing rhythm of blood in his head was the rhythm of a heavy, pounding footfall crashing through the trees, growing louder and coming closer. The hairs on the back of his neck prickled as he felt the touch of the avid hunter's tunnel-narrow gaze. He saw that even Kamilova was feeling it now: a faint drumbeat in the ground underfoot.

'Kantor is coming,' said Maroussia. 'I'm sorry. There is no time to prepare. It has to be now. Kantor is here.'

'Oh,' said Lom. 'Oh. Yes. I see.' A sudden sick lurch of fear. 'OK. Well there's no time like now.'

The mudjhik stepped out from the grey twilit birches, dull red and massive, balanced and avid and bulky and strangely beautiful and as tall as the trees it stood among. Its eyes – it had eyes – took them in with a gaze of confident relaxation and intelligence. Its expression was almost elegant and almost amused. It had grace as well as size and power. It was a perfectly realised angel-human giant of stone the colour of rust and blood and bruises, a new thing come into the world, and it had the face of a hundred million posters and portraits and photographs. The face on the statue at the top of the Rizhin Tower. The face of Papa Rizhin. The face of Josef Kantor.

And when it spoke it had the voice of Kantor too, warm and expressive, loud and clear among the trees. You heard it in your head and you heard it in your ear. Tall as the trees, it had a tongue to speak.

'So it is you, my Lom, my investigator, my troublesome provincial mouse, my annoyance still and always,' said the voice and face of Josef Kantor. He looked from Lom to Maroussia. 'And here is the trivial bitch-girl not my daughter too, my betrayer's bastard whelp, the spill of my cuckolding. You stink of the forest like your mother did. Both of you stink of it. Well the mother is dead and I will destroy the daughter also, and the man. You run and you wriggle and you hide, you sting me and skip away, but I have you cornered now.'

Kantor-in-mudjhik took a pace forward and spread its arms wide, arms with a suggestion of muscular flow. Fists opened flexing fingers. It had fingers. Thick stubby fingers. Josef Kantor's hands.

'I'm going to make quite a mess. Dog crows will clean it up.'

While the mudjhik Kantor spoke, Lom felt the dark electric pressure of angel senses passing across him, probing and examining. The touch of it, obscene and invasive, brought a surge of anger and hatred, a knot of iron and stone in his belly like a fist.

The mudjhik stopped mid-stride and gave a bark, a sudden laugh of surprised delight. Its blank pebble eyes glittered with warmth and pleasure.

'And there is a child!' the voice of Kantor said. 'How perfect is that? Good. Let me kill it too. Let it all end now, and then I will take the blustering bastard angel down and be on my way out of these trees and get my world back. This triviality has gone on long enough.'

Lom felt surge after surge of anger and desperation and the wired strength of his own angel taint welling up, overbrimming and bursting walls inside him. The taste of iron, a hot suffusion in the blood. He was the violence. The smasher. The fist. He was defender. He was bear.

That was the secret of his birthing. Fathered by a man-bear in the deeps of the forest, he was the blade-toothed muzzle, the gaping tearing snout, the heavy carnivore with heavy paws to break necks. He felt himself unfurling into bear and killing, and let it come. Let it come! Barriers and frontiers dissolving, he was coming into the myth of himself, he was the man-bear with angel in his blood.

Lom felt the power of the angel substance tugging at his mind, a hungry undertow pulling and hauling him out of his body, dizzying and disorientating. The forest sliding sideways. Peripheral vision darkening. Connection with reality slipping away.

It wasn't Kantor doing that, it was the thing his mudjhik body was made of.

Lom didn't resist. He threw himself into the pulling of the current and went with it into the mudjhik, leaving his soft body fallen behind, taking the war onto Kantor's own ground to kill him there.

All power is done at a price, but the price is not paid by those who wield it. It is paid by the victims. Kantor was human and he was not, and there was an end to it.

Lom in the mudjhik found Kantor there and fell on him, tearing and snarling, a blood-blind frontal killing assault of unwithstandable fierceness. To end it quickly before Kantor could react.

Lom hit a wall.

The wall of Kantor's will. Impregnable will. A hardened vision that could not be changed but only broken, and it would not break. Lom could not break it.

The force of his attack skittered sideways, ineffectual, like cat's claws against marble slab. It wasn't a defeat. The fight didn't even begin.

He felt the gross stubby fingers of Josef Kantor picking over his fallen, winded body. Ripping him open and rummaging among the intimate recesses of memory and desire. Kantor's voice was a continual whisper in his dissolving mind.

I am Josef Kantor, and what I will to happen will happen. I am Josef Kantor, and I am the strongest and the hardest thing. I am the incoming tide of history. I am the thing you hate and fear and I am stronger than you. You fear me. I am Josef Kantor and I am inevitable. I am the smooth and uninterruptible voice. I always return. I am total. I am the force of one single purpose, the voice of the one idea that drives out all others. The uncertain dissolve before and forgive me as they die. I am the taker and I have killed you now.

Vissarion Lom wasn't strong enough. He wasn't strong at all. He was dying. He could not breathe. He was dead.

And then Maroussia was in the mudjhik with him. Her quiet voice. A mist of evening rain.

The Pollandore was with her, inside her and outside her. Clean light and green air. Spilling all the possibilities of everything that could happen if Josef Kantor did not happen and there were no angels at all. The endless openness and extensibility of life without angels.

She followed him into death.

Come back with me. Come back.

8

L om was in a beautiful simple place among northern trees. Pine and birch and spruce. The air was clear and fresh as ice and rain. Resinous dark green needles carpeting the earth. Time fell there in sudden windfall showers, pulses of night and day, evening and morning, always rising, always young, always new. There were broadleaf trees, and laughter was hidden in the leaves, out of sight, being the leaves.

Everything alive with wildness.

He could see trees growing: unfurling their leaves and spreading overhead, reaching towards each other with their branches until they met, a green ceiling of leaves, and all the light was a liquid fall, green as fire, that spilled through the leaves, enriching the widening silence.

*

Josef Kantor slammed together the walls of his will to crush Maroussia between them and extinguish her utterly, and it made no difference to her at all.

Lom saw Maroussia walking towards him, and a figure was walking beside her through the trees. It seemed at first to be walking on four legs like a deer, but it must have been a trick of the shadows, because the dappled figure appeared to rise on its hind legs as it came and he saw that it was like a woman. A perfume of musk and warmth was in the air. Her eyes were wide and brown and there were no whites in them. She was naked except that a nap of short smooth reddish-brown fur covered her head and neck and shoulders and the place between her breasts and spread down across her brown rounded belly.

'Who are you?' said Lom. *Engage in dialogue with your visions.*

She smiled, and a long warm pink tongue flickered between thin white pointed teeth.

'You mean, what am I?'

'Yes.'

'Do you want to know?'

'Yes.'

'You know what I am.'

'Tell me.'

She opened her mouth and spilled a flow of words, green foliage tumbling, heaped up, all at once. A chord of words.

I am the vixen in the rain and the hungry sow-badger suckling in the dark earth. I am salt on your tongue and the dark sweet taste of blood.

I am scent on the air at dusk, sweet as colostrum. I am the belly-warm womb of the she-otter in the river. I am the cub-warm sleep of the she-bear under the snow. I am the noctule, stooping upon moths with the weight of cubs in my belly.

I am the she-elk, ice-bearded, nudging my calf against the wind, and I am the mouse in the barn, suckling the blind pink buds of life. I am the sour breath of the stoat in the tunnel's darkness and I am the vixen's teeth in the neck of the hen.

I am the crunch of carrion and I am the thirsty suck and the flow of warm sweet milk. I am tired and cold and wet and full of cub. I am shit and blood and milk and salty tears. I am plastered fur and soaking hair.

I am the abdomen swollen taut as a drum and full as an egg. I am the ceaseless desperate hunger of the starveling shrew. I am the sow's lust for the boar, the hart's delight in the pride of the hind.

I am the fucker's laughing and the smell of droppings in the wet grass. I am the sweetness of milk on the baby's breath and the cold smell of a dead thing. I am the hot gates opening into light.

I am all of us and I am you. I am the mirror of your coming here to meet yourself.

'I don't understand.'

You understand, said Fraiethe. *Though understanding doesn't matter. You are green forest and dark angel and human world, compendious and strong. Forget what you cannot do and do what you can do.*

Fraiethe opened her mouth to kiss him, as she had kissed Maroussia once, though that he did not yet know.

She bit him, she swallowed him up and he was not killed.

9

Things can change. Borders are not fixed. Permeability. Mutability. Trees can speak. A man may become an animal. A woman may become time like a god. Everything is alive and humans are not separate from that.

There is power which is the exercise of will and there is power which is openness and letting go. It has to do with air and breath and consciousness. A freeing not a binding. A removal of bonds.

Josef Kantor – Papa Rizhin – fraternal angel champion – mudjhik – came lumbering at them out of the trees to silence and kill. Maroussia Shaumian and Vissarion Lom, side by side, the child inside a possibility between them, watched him come.

They saw right round him and through him and he wasn't there.

The mudjhik was an empty column of stuff like stone.

10

The prototype Universal Vessel *Vlast of Stars* stood on the concrete apron at Vitigorsk, a swollen citadel of steel, a snub and gross atomic bullet thirty storeys high. Hunder Rond had personally overseen the stowage on board of the embalmed corpse, the earthly remains of Papa Rizhin. A chosen crew had taken their places, eager and proud, the brightest and the best, prepared to live or die, but in their hearts they knew that they would live. They would reach their destination. There were other, better suns awaiting them.

Rond stood now on the asphalt, uniformed in crisp new black. The hot wind that disturbed his hair was heavy with the industrial chemical stench of Vitigorsk

'There have been no tests,' said Yakov Khyrbysk. 'It is the prototype. You know what that means.'

'You can come or you can stay,' said Rond. 'Your choice.'

Khyrbysk shook his head.

'I'm staying here,' he said.

Rond looked around.

'The backwash will destroy all this,' he said.

'We have evacuated. We will be far away. We will rebuild better somewhere else.'

'Perhaps,' said Rond. 'Perhaps. But we will get there first. You will not find us.'

Khyrbysk shrugged. 'I have to go now.'

Half an hour later and twenty miles away in Tula-Vitisk Launch Control, Yakov Khyrbysk gave the word. He was curious. It was a prototype. Whatever happened he would learn from it and move on.

The horizon disappeared in a flash of blinding light.

When the light cleared, a column of expanding mushroom clouds was climbing into the pale blue sky, puffs of distant smoke and wind illuminated by inward burn. Higher and higher they climbed, a rising stairway of evanescent stellar ignitions, a trajectory curving towards the west and the sinking of the sun.

*

At the sweet spot of the rising curve, several hundred miles high, the entire magazine of the *Vlast of Stars* exploded at once. The brightness of the detonation spread across the whole of the western sky. It overwhelmed the sun. The vaporised residue drifted for months through the upper atmosphere, borne on high fierce winds. Intermixed with the shattered molecular dust of the earthly remains of the corpse of Papa Rizhin it slowly slowly fell to earth, becoming rain.

The dust of Engineer-Technician 1st Class Mikkala Avril was in it too. Yakov Khyrbysk was as good as his word.

11

The great hill of the living angel, blinded, muted and unchampioned, abraded by wind and rain, crawled slowly on, lost among limitless trees. No fliers crowded the air above its sad peak. Already, scrubby vegetation was beginning to claim the crumbling lower slopes. The rain washed from it in slurries of tilth and rolling scree.

Directionless, inch by inch, withdrawing from the borderland, not knowing where it was, the ever-living angel turned inward from the forest margin into inexhaustible trees. There it would crawl on for ever and get nowhere at all. Of the heartwood, the inward forest, there is no end, and so there can be no ending of it.

12

Lom and Maroussia were together on the bank of the river. Fraiethe was there, and the Seer Witch of Bones, and the father also, though his presence was indistinct and Lom felt he had not really come there at all.

Eligiya Kamilova was standing apart. Alone again. A secondary role.

Fraiethe spoke to her.

'You can remain here, Eligiya Kamilova, in the forest with us. Go further in and deeper. If that's what you wish? You've done your part.'

'Yes,' said Kamilova. 'That would be good. I would like that.'

'In that case,' said Lom, 'perhaps we could borrow your boat?'

'You're not staying?' said Kamilova.

'No,' said Maroussia. 'No. We're going home.'

13

The Political Bureau of the interim collective government met in the former Central Committee cabinet room. Lukasz Kistler took the chair. Unrest was continuing. Rizhinites had barricaded themselves in the administrative block of the university and a large crowd had gathered in Victory Square. Already it had been there three days, penned in by a cordon of gendarmes. The crowd was smashing flagstones and levering up cobbles. Bonfires had been lit.

'It's a stand-off,' said Yulia Yashina.

'Negotiations?' said Kistler.

'No,' said Yashina. 'At least not yet. They have no leader; they have no clear demands to make. They want to turn back the clock, that's all.'

'Give them time,' said Kistler. 'We can do that. Are more people joining them?'

'Not for the moment,' said Yashina. She paused. 'We could end it now,' she said. 'The militia is standing by in the Armoury. There are tanks within two hundred yards.'

'The commanders are loyal to us?' said Kistler. 'They would fire on their own people?'

'Of course they would, if you give the word. Government rests on civil order. It's the prerequisite.'

Kistler looked around the table, each face one by one. They all avoided his eye. The decision was to be left to him, then, and they would follow where he led.

'We must not do it,' he said. 'And we will not. Give the order to withdraw the tanks and the militia to their barracks, and make sure the people of the city see them go.'

ABOUT GOLLANCZ

Gollancz is the oldest SF publishing imprint in the world. Since being founded in 1927 Gollancz has continued to publish a focused selection of bestselling and award-winning authors. The front-list includes **Ben Aaronovitch**, **Joe Abercrombie**, **Charlaine Harris**, **Joanne Harris**, **Joe Hill**, **Alastair Reynolds**, **Patrick Rothfuss**, **Nalini Singh** and **Brandon Sanderson**.

As one of the largest Science Fiction and Fantasy imprints in the UK it is no surprise we have one of the most extensive backlists in the world. Find high quality SF on Gateway written by such authors as **Philip K. Dick**, **Ursula Le Guin**, **Connie Willis**, **Sir Arthur C. Clarke**, **Pat Cadigan**, **Michael Moorcock** and **George R.R. Martin**.

We also have a strand of publishing in translation, which includes French, Polish and Russian authors. Gollancz is home to more award-winning authors than any other imprint, with names including **Aliette de Bodard**, **M. John Harrison**, **Paul McAuley**, **Sarah Pinborough**, **Pierre Pevel**, **Justina Robson** and many more.

The SF Gateway
More than 3,000 classic, rare and previously out-of-print SF novels at your fingertips.
www.sfgateway.com

The Gollancz Blog
Bringing you news from our worlds to yours. Stories, interviews, articles and exclusive extracts just for you!
www.gollancz.co.uk

GOLLANCZ
LONDON